M000306574

BANSHEE RIDERS

By P.A. Derringer

PADROWSKI
PUBLICATIONS
Woodstock, IL

Copyright © 2020 By Peter Albert Derringer
ISBN 978-1-63760-342-0
Padowski Publications
Woodstock, IL 60098

All Rights Reserved

No portion of this book may be reproduced in any form or by
any electronic or mechanical means including information
storage and retrieval systems, without express written permission
from the publisher, except for the use of a brief quotations in a
book review.

ACKNOWLEDGEMENTS

The impetus for writing this book came from Tom Hallman Jr, a Pulitzer Prize winning reporter whose extraordinary talent is matched by his humility. His ego remains unscathed by success. I'm fortunate enough to have met Tom at a time when humility had taught me to listen and accept ideas with an open mind. When he suggested I should "Write this stuff down," I had just enough wisdom to accept his suggestion. The following pages are, therefore, dedicated to his ability to recognize a story that some might consider worthy of sharing.

I also want to thank States Attorney Patrick K. who contributed his time and expertise so that scenes involving the police and courtrooms rang with a greater touch of realism. Patrick also read the manuscript and offered his suggestions and encouragement.

I would be amiss if I didn't mention others who read the manuscript for this work at different stages of its development: Tom Sellars, Richard K. Gelscheit, Brad Bellmore, and V.L.Stuart. Thank you all for your friendship and willingness to provide your time and perspectives.

DISCLAIMER

This is a work of fiction. Names, characters, businesses, places, events, locales, and incidents are either the products of the author's imagination or used in a fictitious manner. Any resemblance to actual persons, living or dead, or actual events is purely coincidental.

INTRODUCTION: A NOTE FROM THE AUTHOR

If you're looking for a story of super-hero bikers who grind their rivals randomly under their steel-toed engineer boots, you'll want to look elsewhere. If you want a story that paints motorcycle club members as deviant psychopaths who, in the end, get their just desserts, turn to another book. There are plenty of novels about bikers whose physical prowess borders on the stuff of sci-fi fantasies. There are also stories where the writer, in an act of self-indulgent mental masturbation, delivers up evil bikers for due punishment at the hands of the righteous. This is neither of those. This is a simple book that, through a fictional presentation, wrapped around numerous and essentially true anecdotes, attempts to offer a factual account of what it was like to ride with a smaller motorcycle club in the early 1980s. Based loosely on the author's personal experiences, as well as stories he has heard, he has weaved a story of a fictional club, with fictional members (no one in the book is intended to represent anyone living or dead) who have, at their hearts, desires and ambitions that which members of the club of the author's experience wouldn't find too far out of place.

This is also not another rendition of what is found in recent biker shows, such as 'Sons of Anarchy.' The club is not an organized crime family, though its members certainly play fast and loose with the law. They are not afraid to break the law but always hope to get away with whatever transgressions they commit. The members of this fictional club, as with those who inspired this story, are proud, independent and more than a little bit wild. They don't live by the 9-to-5 rules of society. They are generally pleasantly disposed to others unless they are crossed. When they feel they've been done wrong, they don't waste a lot of time psychoanalyzing the situation. By the nature of their lifestyle, they've done the groundwork for confrontations ahead of time. Most would hesitate while considering the implications of their actions in a potential physical altercation. The brothers in this fictional motorcycle club, as with members of actual clubs, often have the advantage over citizens (non-biker-club folk) because the bikers react instantly while the others are often vacillating, unless the confrontation, of course, is between members within the biker fraternity.

Our story follows the experiences of one particular member of this fictional club, from prospect, to probate, to full-patch brother. He isn't necessarily representative of all the brothers in the club. However, he has one thing that is almost assuredly in common with his brothers: he's an outcast, a social reject and ill-equipped for success in the mainstream of 1980s society. But when joining the club, a strange thing happens to our lead character. He discovers himself in ways that he wouldn't have expected, in ways that equip him for success in life, even if not in the 'more acceptable' corners of society. Through his experience with the club, he develops a personal sense of honor, a sense of belonging and family, and a sense of loyalty. He discovers that there is an entire world outside of his self-indulgent abuse of alcohol, not that the club would expect him to give up drinking or drugging. These are not required but enthusiastically encouraged. Essentially, our main character finds that he has gained a greater level of maturity in the most unlikely of places – with an outlaw motorcycle club.

The experiences in this book, whether complete fabrications from the mind of the author, or based on his experiences, range from good to bad, from humorous to tragic. But to the best of the author's ability, they strive to tell a story that is true to the spirit of riding with an outlaw motorcycle club in a day before cell phones, video-game mania, or the PC culture. Be warned, there is nothing Politically Correct about this book and no effort was made to make it so.

Peter Albert Derringer

TABLE OF CONTENTS

Chapter 1 — Gears (1959)

The rustling of the leaves was the only sound along the country road as the doe gave a determined tug at the branch with no more success than several previous efforts. Persuaded of the twig's resilience, she simply chewed the leaf in place as though the branch was a hand holding it out for her convenience. But then she froze, her ears erect and twisting independently from side to side the way radar dishes search out a threat otherwise hidden from view. Poised and alert, she sensed the vibration of the leaves on the roadside bush. The pulsation seemed to run up the branch, across that one leaf and into her mouth. Then a barely perceptible sound seemed to catch up to the tremor that was increasing until it shook the pebbles along the side of the pavement. As though thunder was rolling down from the hills, the symphony of vibration and sound cascaded out across the clearing where she stood, every muscle taut and ready. Just as she let go of the leaf, her head erect, the crescendo blasted forth and tripped the trigger that sent her running away from the road as leather-clad monsters, mounted on throbbing, glimmering chargers of chrome and assorted pigments swept around the bend. The mix of Harley Davidson and Indian motorcycles pounding the pavement headed east in the direction of the county seat. The mostly crewcut bikers, several with leathered women hanging on behind them, hardly noticed the panicked deer charging into a lone pine tree several yards back from the road, falling and rising again and again before gathering her wits and disappearing across the field and into the woods.

Minutes later, the bikes erupted in a collective growl as their riders rolled off their throttles coming into town. The somber expressions of the riders were mirrored by frowns of pedestrians on the sidewalks, as though everyone knew the purpose of their visit. It wasn't surprising that the pedestrians looked on knowingly since the story had rated front-page coverage two months prior when Lionel Reeves first died, and more recently with the trial and today's sentencing.

The club abided by the attorney's wishes, stayed away during the trial. And they would wait outside the courtroom today. It made sense, but they still didn't like it. Clearly, a group of boisterous bikers cheering for the defendants wouldn't play well with the judge. And it was in the judge's hands that the fate of the club's vice president and warlord resided this morning. So, maintained its distance for the trial. They only felt safe to come today because the judge would surely pass sentence before reading in the papers about the outlaw motorcycle club that congregated in the parking lot waiting for the outcome of the judge's decision; by the time the judge knew they were out there it would be too late for him to change the sentences.

They arrived at the last minute so that there was less risk of the judge seeing them on his way into the courthouse. But this meant that they had to park across the street as the lot by the courthouse was full. The club met on the sidewalk next to where they parked and, leaving a prospect behind to watch the bikes, and with half-a-dozen of their women, they stepped out into traffic together, forcing several cars to brake hard. They walked across the street, as though oblivious to the traffic, to wait at the bottom of the courthouse steps.

No sooner had they arrived, most of them lighting up cigarettes, then a disheveled man in his early 50s came shuffling around the corner of the building wihle hugging a briefcase that bulged with papers sticking out at the seams the way the shirt tail he struggled with stuck out below the back of his wrinkled suitcoat. He paused for a moment when he saw the club, as though contemplating the back door, but a couple of the brothers from the club had already seen him. It was too late, and he forged ahead pushing thin strands of long-grey hair up over his head in a ridiculously futile attempt to hide the barren area between the parietal ridges, the area a little above his ears, on both sides of his head. Stylistically speaking, his unkempt hair and all-day 5-oclock shadow fit well with a brown suit that hung from his bony frame the way a Shar Pei puppy wears its fur. With hunched knees and shoulders, he moved with a duck-footed gate that was short, erratic and seemingly consumed with a constant case of the jitters.

Most of the bikers simply frowned as they watched him ap-approach. But when he was passing through the group, a woman with a patch on her back that read 'Property of Outcast,' said with bitter reproach, "Running a little late today, Mr. Louie?"

"Uhm," they struggled to hear him mumble, "not to worry; no, they won't start without me." The bikers gave each other worried looks, some rolling their eyes. And then he was gone up the steps, stumbling once and catching himself with his freehand as he looked back at the bikers while strands of grey hair fell back across his face.

Matthew McCarthy looked at his watch and then glanced at the bailiff in the blue uniform who shrugged in response. McCarthy was dressed as though ready for a photoshoot for a men's formalwear catalog. The two men at the other table looked as though they were wearing suits and ties for the first time. They shrugged when McCarthy looked their way as one of the men, twisted his head side to side while running two fingers inside a collar that, no doubt, was chafing. McCarthy stepped into the aisle and asked, "Have you called his office."

"Yeah," the one said. "His secretary said he left for court a while ago."

McCarthy was just shaking his head in exasperation when the swinging doors at the back of the courtroom burst open and the attorney for the defense shuffled in still clutching his briefcase and, once again, trying to wipe strands of hair out of his eyes.

Mumbling again, all that any of the others could make out was the word "late" and what was probably some kind of explanation or excuse. The two at the table didn't say anything as the lawyer slouched into the chair beside them while dropping his briefcase on the table.

For the umpteenth time during the trial, his now convicted clients shared looks of doubt. They had accepted Adam Louie as their attorney because he was the attorney closest to what they and the club could afford, and they accepted a plea deal because Louie had told them they faced sure convictions for first-degree murder if they didn't. Now they were waiting for a judge's sentence: one for second-degree murder and the other for accessory to murder. Somehow, from their perspective, it didn't seem right, and they were inclined to believe they got what they paid for with this attorney.

Two months ago, Shotgun, the president of their club, had said good night to his brothers and was riding his bike home from the club's hangout, The Hideout, around midnight. He was in a good mood. It was a beautiful night, and he was in no particular hurry. He coasted along at the 65-mph speed limit.

As he went through one of several wooded stretches, he passed Rusty's Lil' Cabin, the tavern where the president of his rival club was a regular. But he knew Gears' bike and didn't see it in the parking lot. He had no way of knowing that Gears drove his pickup truck that night. He also had no way of knowing that Gears was watching him ride by from the window. Watching Shotgun ride by, Gears saw an opportunity. He slipped out the door as unobtrusively as possible and hurried to his truck.

Entering another wooded area, Shotgun saw the headlights approaching from behind but hardly gave them a second thought. As he was coasting along it didn't surprise him that the driver would want to pass. Shotgun drifted to the right side of the lane so the 4-wheel driver could pass after the turn. But this driver wasn't waiting for the No-Passing Zone to end. Shotgun wondered if he was dealing with a drunk driver as he noticed the truck drifting into his lane. He pulled further to the right and glanced over where he could see the shadow of the driver behind the wheel. He yelled, "Hey!" but knew it was doubtful the driver could hear him over the combined rumble of the motorcycle and the truck, even if the driver had cared. As the truck came closer, Shotgun yelled again and kicked out with his left leg into the passenger door of the truck. As they came into the back end of an 'S' curve to the left, it dawned on Shotgun that he was in trouble. He began hitting the brakes, but it was too late. The driver suddenly turned the wheel hard to his right. As the side of the truck made contact with Shotgun's left handlebar, with both vehicles going onto the rocky shoulder, he glanced back at the driver. For just a moment, a break in the canopy of trees allowed moonlight, like a spotlight on a helicopter, onto a spot in the road as the driver passed through. It was at this moment that Shotgun recognized Gears at the wheel. The next moment, Shotgun's tires left the ground, and the Harley Davidson went airborne as Gears swerved back onto the road.

Without contact with the ground below him, there was nothing Shotgun could do to avoid a stand of elm trees in his path.

Gears had every reason to believe his rival was dead. Shotgun hit the trees while still traveling more than 50 mph. As Gears continued down the highway, he saw a ball of fire flare up in his rearview mirror seeming to confirm his suspicions that his rival couldn't possibly have survived. But Shotgun hadn't died.

Had Shotgun's head hit that particular elm tree full on, the result would have resembled a melon smacking a wall and exploding fatally. And it was a close thing. Instead, Shotgun's head hit a glancing blow off the tree. As it was, the bike hit the trees just above the ground. The bike hit the tree hard and spun to the left, then hit another tree and spun back in the opposite direction going horizontal as it hit the ground. As it spun, the gas cap came off spaying gasoline in a circumference away from the tree. What sparked the fire, Shotgun had no way of knowing as he was knocked unconscious at the moment of impact. Separated from the bike, his left shoulder hit and broke against the tree to the left of the tree trunk where he banged his head. His body whipped back and folded neatly between the trees except where his right leg slapped against the trunk on the right and snapped the tibia midway between the knee and ankle. Otherwise, it was as though his body was designed to fit that way. He landed hard against a rise in the ground on the other side of the trees.

As he was away from the fire, the explosion was almost a good thing alerting a car coming up the highway from behind him. If not for the fire, the driver probably wouldn't have seen anything and how long Shotgun would have laid in the woods is anyone's guess. But the driver saw the fire and, within the hour, Shotgun was conscious again as he was wheeled into the emergency room of the Walter Hopkins Memorial Hospital in Millbrook 20 miles to the northwest. Even before he was wheeled into surgery, the club's vice president and warlord where there to see him.

"What happened?" the warlord asked.

Shotgun was in pain and found it difficult to speak. As two nurses began wheeling his stretcher out of the room, he grabbed the doorway with his good hand stopping their progress. The warlord walked over and leaned his face down close to the president's. Shotgun said one word: "Gears."

A curtain of hatred washed over the warlord's face. It was a frightening appearance the president had seen before. It didn't bode well for Gears.

Lionel Reeves, aka Gears, drove his truck straight home to his cabin by Lake Chinookan. Pulling the truck back by the side of the barn, he jumped out with a flashlight from the glovebox and urgently examined the passenger side where the rival president had kicked the door and where he had made contact with the bike's handlebar. There was a small dent in the door with a rubber smudge Reeves easily rubbed away. There were also some minor scrapes, but he counted himself fortunate that he didn't find any incriminating paint from Shotgun's Harley. Then, just as quickly, Gears pulled his bike, a flat-black 1952 Hydra Glide with wide-low handlebars, out of the barn and headed back to Rusty's Lil' Cabin where he had spied Shotgun 10 minutes earlier. With any luck, no one would have missed him, and he could hold to his argument that he'd been there all night, should the authorities have reason to ask him about the motorcycle accident out of town. It was crucial, of course, to get back unnoticed. He would have returned with the truck but was worried about the scratches and the dent on the side of the vehicle; could the police trace them to Shotgun's bike? He wasn't sure but thought it better to avoid the question. There were other bikes at Rusty's, when he left in his truck; he assumed he could argue that his was among the other bikes there all night. Who would notice? He had no way of knowing he'd be better off with the truck that night.

The vice president and warlord from Shotgun's club were not familiar with Gears' pickup truck, but they knew his bike well. They didn't wait for Shotgun to get out of surgery; they went out hunting for Gears right away, before Gears could muster forces in his defense. They knew he haunted Rusty's, that it was down the road from where Shotgun was found, and that was their first stop. As 4 a.m. was approaching, most of the patrons of Rusty's had drifted back to their homes. The once crowded parking lot had only a few vehicles left. Among these was Lionel Reeves' motorcycle, the only motorcycle in the lot. Immediately recognizing the bike, Shotgun's brothers pulled onto the gravel lot and parked so their bikes boxed the rival biker's motorcycle in. Without a word, they got off their bikes and went inside.

Rusty had opened the tavern after returning from the war. Knotty pine paneling on the walls, a rough-hewn floor and tongue-and-groove paneling on the ceiling made the dark-wood, sculpted bar he purchased from a bar that was closing in the city look out of place. The sculpting framed red-velvet inlays on the front of the bar, with a brass footrail at the floor and another brass rail a few inches out from the inlaid surface of the bar. Out of place or not, Rusty was distinctly proud of his establishment and the bar was the crowing jewel.

As two members of his rival club walked in, Gears eyed them cautiously but was careful not to act alarmed. His primary goal was to avoid the appearance that he had anything to hide. He feigned innocence from the way he casually leaned against the bar to the 'who-me' look on his face. Rather than prepare to defend himself, as the other bikers approached, making a beeline towards him, Gears smiled the way he would greet a friend he hadn't seen in a while.

"So, what brings you boys out to this neck of the woods in the wee hours?" he asked when they were only a few feet away.

"You know why we're here," said the vice president as the warlord quietly glared at the rival biker.

Gears should have prepared to defend himself. Instead, he shrugged his shoulders and began to protest he didn't know what they were talking about. The warlord wasn't one to telegraph an assault.

The punch he landed on Gears' chin would have knocked most men out cold. But Gears was hardly a pushover. While the one ring of the upper brass rail scraped his cheek and ear, Gears hadn't even hit the floor as he came up swinging. The two exchanged a couple blows before Gears launched himself into the warlord's midsection driving him back onto a table that collapsed under their combined weight and impact.

From the floor, the warlord got in the next shot sending Gears falling onto his back. As Gears got to his feet, there was a flash of stainless steel as he extracted his ivory-handled switchblade from his back pocket. Seeing the knife, the warlord grabbed a chair and stabbed at the biker with its legs. Gears mostly sidestepped the assault but, in the process, stumbled back into the bar. The warlord brought the chair down overhead in a fresh attack. Once again, Gears stepped back out of the way and the chair smashed into pieces as it put a dent in the brass rail. Dodging this assault with the chair, Gears was in an awkward position, his right knee on the floor, his left foot inside the foot rail, his left elbow on the bar and the stiletto extending from his right hand now behind his back. But the warlord was also in an awkward position. Expecting to make contact before the chair hit the bar, expecting to make contact with Gears' head, the warlord had fallen forward into the bar. It presented Gears with an opening the other biker didn't plan to waste.

The vice president allowed the two to fight without interference until he saw the knife and the imminent peril his warlord faced at that moment. When Gears came up from that position, swinging the knife around aimed towards the warlord's chest, the vice president caught the biker's arm in the crook of his left arm.

Gears didn't see it coming and was caught off guard. This allowed the warlord an opening. He landed a crushing blow to Gears' gut, on the left side and just below the rib cage. Something critical inside must have broken and the effectiveness of the punch was instantly apparent. Gears collapsed to the floor, dropping his knife and clutching his side as he doubled over on top of the foot rail, agony etched across his face.

In spite of Gears' condition, the warlord stepped forward prepared to deliver the coup de grâce. The vice president, however, stepped forward and caught the warlord with the same arm that had caught Gears' knife hand. As the two stood over Gears, the biker slumped unconscious off the rail and onto the floor. Somehow, the vice president knew the president of the rival club was seriously hurt. He grabbed the warlord by the front of his shirt and said, "We'd better go."

As the warlord stepped back and looked up, he saw the bartender with the phone in his hand no doubt calling the authorities.

"I suppose you're right," said the warlord and, seconds later, their Harleys were heard winding at high rpms as they headed out of town.

Gears never got off the floor on his own power. The bartender conveniently threw his switchblade into the woods behind the bar before the police or ambulance arrived. When they did arrive, he quickly identified the two bikers who had come in to assault the regular customer on the floor.

Later that day, after speaking with an attorney, and after checking to see how Shotgun was doing, the vice president and warlord turned themselves in at the Biesenthal Police Station. They had heard on the radio that "A man was critically injured early this morning in a barroom brawl at Rusty's Lil' Cabin, a tavern outside of Biesenthal." They were unpleasantly surprised, when the police took them into custody, to find out that Gears had died.

The death was front-page news in a small town like Biesenthal, particularly when it turned out that the fight was between "members of rival motorcycle gangs." The locals followed the initial maneuvering of the prosecutor and defense attorney closely and almost seemed disappointed when, instead of a trial, there was a plea-deal settlement.

While the warlord and vice president were both brought up on first-degree murder charges, the state settled for second-degree murder for the warlord and accomplice to murder for the vice president.

"If you don't take the deal," their lawyer mumbled, "the death penalty is a distinct possibility."

It didn't help that no knife was ever found, not that the police made any effort to find one. It also didn't help that the bartender, the only person in the tavern at the time sober enough to make any kind of a 'reliable' statement, described the two as having walked into the bar and attacked Lionel Reeves without a word of warning. "The shorter guy was holding Mr. Reeves when his partner hit him."

Attorney Louie pointed out, "Mr. Reeves was a member of a notorious motorcycle gang and that he had run Shotgun off the road that same morning.

But the prosecutor retorted, "Witnesses at Rusty's Lil' Cabin have testified that Mr. Reeves was at the bar all night. Besides, it really has no bearing on this case. The defendants are both members of an equally notorious gang." And so, the deal was struck and a date for sentencing was set.

When the bailiff saw Adam Louie enter the courtroom, he immediately went through the door to the Judge's Chambers. A moment later, he returned, holding the door open behind him and announcing loudly, "All Rise!"

Judge Vincent Peterman entered the courtroom and took his seat behind the bench. No sooner had his backside hit the chair than the bailiff called out, "Be seated."

Judge Peterman looked up over the tops of his gold-rimmed glasses at the defense table pausing a moment, as though for effect. With a forced smile flashing across his face and as quickly disappearing, said to Louie, "Everything OK, Mr. Louie?"

Louie was looking down at some of the papers he was sifting through in his open briefcase on the table. He looked up suddenly, as though startled by the question, and mumbled, "There's no problem …" and something else, no doubt in explanation for his late arrival, but the words were lost to everyone in the courtroom, including the two defendants at his side.

The judge took in the ruffled defense attorney for a moment while the judge nodded his head in apparent understanding that was probably more familiarity. "Very well," he said, and looked down to open a folder on the bench in front of him.

At last, he looked up, turned to the convicted men in front of him, and, reading the warlord's name, he began, "You have been charged with first-degree murder. However, it is my understanding that, on the advice of your attorney, and in agreement with the prosecution (he turned to look at Mr. McCarthy at this point, as though to give the prosecutor an opportunity to confirm what the judge was saying), you have reached an agreement whereby (looking back at his papers to make sure he got the names correct) you agree to plead guilty to second-degree murder …," and then he looked up at the warlord.

The warlord understood the judge was asking if this was true – if he agreed with what the judge had said, and responded, "Yes, your honor."

Then he turned to the vice president. "… and you have agreed to plead guilty to a charge of accomplice to murder." The judge then gave him the same look.

"That's correct, sir," said the other biker.

The judge put the papers down on the bench and then sat back in his seat where he eyed the defendants while appearing to roll the matter over in his mind. Finally, clasping his hands together as though prepared to pray, the judge said, "I'm not sure that the public is best served by this agreement. It appears to me that the two of you, in a premeditated fashion, went into (he leaned forward to look at the papers again) the Rusty's Lil' Cabin bar and assaulted Mr. Reeves without warning. As the prosecution has pointed out, you are both members of a notorious motorcycle gang that has had frequent additional brushes with the law."

It seemed that the judge was letting them ponder what he was saying a bit before the judge continued. "On the other hand, while you have both had minor prior infractions, these are your first felonies. I'm also aware that you both served honorably during the war. In fact, I understand you received the Silver Star in the South Pacific," he said while looking at the warlord. "That is very commendable, and your country appreciates your service.

"That, however, does not provide you with a free pass to behave in any manner you choose now that you have returned to civilian life. Were you still in the military, it's my understanding that you would likely be facing far more serious penalties for the same charges. But instead of a court-martial, you are in my court. And it is up to me to decide what to do with you. My hope is that you will put the time I give you here today to good use; it's my hope that you will reconsider what you're doing with your lives. There are many veterans of America's recent wars who are living productive lives and contributing to society. You should look to them as examples."

During a long pause, it seemed the judge was trying to look inside their hearts and minds to see if the message was getting through. Both men looked back at the judge with contrite expressions and then, almost simultaneously, looked down at the table.

"Very well," said the judge. "Baliff."

"The defendants will rise," said the baliff.

Speaking to the vice president, the judge said, "Taking into account your service to your country, I remand you to the state penitentiary for six years." And to the warlord, he said, "I sentence you to 10 years, both sentences to begin immediately."

With that, the judge slapped the gavel down on the bench, stood up, and said, "Court adjourned."

Adam Louie shook his clients' hands, mumbled something about 'good luck' and began turning to go outside where he faced the unpleasant duty of giving the bad news to the club. But he noticed that a woman behind them was leaning over the rail and giving his clients hugs with tears in her eyes. "I'll let everyone know."

"Let me know how Shotgun's doing, will you?" the warlord said.

"Of course," she said as two impatient Correctional Guards prompted the bikers to start walking towards a door on the side of the room.

"We'll come out to see you," she said as they walked away looking back over their shoulders.

When they were gone, the lawyer looked at the young lady and said, "So, you'll tell everyone outside what happened?"

She looked annoyed but said, "Yes, I'll tell them."

When she came out of the courthouse, she was surprised to find that the throng of bikers now included a man in jeans and a button-down, short-sleeved, pale-yellow shirt, his left arm in a cast and sling, leaning on a crutch with his right arm, and his right leg in another cast. It was Shotgun's first venture out of the house since he was released from the hospital almost two months earlier as the combination of a broken arm and a broken leg clearly made mobility a problem.

The girl went right up to Shotgun and gave him a gentle hug. After asking how he was doing, she turned to the group as a whole and spilled the bad news.

Several of the brothers swore as there was a collective groan from the group.

It seemed they were looking to her for more details so she added, "The judge lectured them about the club, told them how great they were for serving in the Marines, and then gave them 'time to think about what they're doing with their lives.'"

At first, it was as though the bikers didn't know if they should stay or leave. Finally, the biker who had led the pack into town said to the group, "Why don't we go to The Hideout and have a drink to our brothers."

They began to walk back towards the street when, seeing the pack leader looking at Shotgun, they stopped. "What about you?" the pack leader asked.

Shotgun seemed uncomfortable with the question but finally looked up at the others and said, "I'm headed back to the city.

Gonna stay with the in-laws until I get back on my feet."

"Take care," "Be in touch," "Come back soon as you can," And other such parting words were directed towards the injured biker who responded a little tentatively. "We'll see how it goes," he said. And then the club headed one way while he headed the other. Several of the brothers watched him hobble off to his car, his wife waiting at the wheel. From the looks on their faces, they may have sensed that he wouldn't be back.

Chapter 2 — The Sermon (1981)

"... and these also stagger from wine and reel from beer ... they stagger when seeing visions, they stumble when rendering decisions.' So sayeth Isaiah 28:7-29."

The semi-muffled voice reverberated in his ears. "... Achan replied, 'It is true! I have sinned against the LORD, the God of Israel. This is what I have done,'" the voice blared ever louder.

The weight of shame held Harold's head to the floor. He wanted to lift his head – to return the glare of his accuser but his head felt like a sack of wet cement, it barely budged. There, standing over him, was the portly Pastor he'd seen so many times before ... but where? The pastor's robe-draped arm extended a pudgy, sweaty finger pointing directly at a spot that burned between Harold's eyes as he struggled to get his arms and legs under the sack of cement. Guilt, like a hot-wet cloth slapped across his face, soaked through his skin until his head began to spin sending him collapsing back to the floor as he sensed, more than heard, the sounds of laughter mocking his plight.

Then, as though all the air was sucked from the room, an expectant silence followed as Harold made it to his knees and spun to a precipitous halt before spinning quickly, and involuntarily, back in the opposite direction as he collapsed to the floor again. Mercilessly, the pastor stepped closer until the exposed side of Harold's face burned with embarrassment and shame. And still that finger hung there illuminating Harold's sudden nudity, his guilt and the absurdity of his condition, illuminated in disgrace.

How had he gotten into this predicament? He had a vague memory – more of a sensation – as though an unseen hand had gripped him by the collar and yanked him back off his barstool? Or ... was it something else. Why couldn't he remember? Was it possible that the glistening finger had magically lifted Harold from his seat and tossed him, like a ragdoll, onto the floor. Was this some kind of divine, overdue punishment?

Driven by a desire to run away – to escape, Harold renewed his struggles to rise but, like a new-born calf that has yet to take its first tenuous steps, he collapsed under his own weight. With all his might, Harold made a final and determined effort to rise, his arms and legs shaking from the exertion, but to no avail. Then, panic gave way to resignation as Harold rolled onto his back and found the minister standing over him, much too close, a customary sickening smile replaced by piercing angry eyes that left no place for Harold to hide his shame, that same accusing finger virtually touching that spot on the drunken 24-year-old's face. "But … wait. Dad?" he cried. And the gaze and finger burned ever hotter.

"Wait, that can't be you? You're dead?" Harold shook his head as though that would clear away the fog. But Dad was still standing there – glaring at him. Confusion mixed with guilt leaving him vulnerable - defenseless. He felt like a dog that had rolled onto its back exposing itself in an act of submission. And now anger elbowed its way into this emotional mix.

He couldn't bear it any longer as, once again, the evangelist raged forth in a fresh volley of scripture, in a voice that shook the very joists below the floor, passing eternal judgment on Harold: "…The wrath of God is being revealed from heaven against all the godlessness and wickedness of men who suppress the truth by their wickedness."

Those around him broke into laughter again and his humiliation built to a fresh crescendo, pushing his anger on before it. "Or were they singing? Would they sing to mock his condition and guilt?"

Harold couldn't see the grinning faces but somehow knew they were there, in the shadows, they looked deep into his soul. Stripped naked of all defenses, Harold waited for the blow to fall, as though a bolt of lightning would strike him on the floor and turn him to ashes. And he knew this would all come to the complete satisfaction of those enjoying his plight, particularly the pudgy preacher and … and … *his father*? And still, Harold didn't know the source of his pain; he was confused about the judgment of his tormentor and the joyful condemnation of those gathered around him.

In his embarrassment, he could feel the blood rushing to his face. Was it the blood that made his face feel so flushed and warm? No. It couldn't be … it had to be those burning eyes sunk deep in that round and puffy face of the preacher … or his father. It was those eyes that burned as if they would melt his flesh and destroy his soul.

A fresh flicker of resolve built in Harold as, again, he struggled to rise from the floor. As he groped for control, Harold hollered,

"Leave me alone. Just get ..."

And as he yelled, the sack of cement that had held home down was punctured and exploded into a cloud of ashen powder as Harold sprang to his feet. In his confusion, he surveyed his surroundings through swollen red eyes. Swaying and collecting his thoughts, it dawned on him that the bar had vanished, as had the Pastor and the faceless crowd around him, and his father. Still, Harold could hear the Pastor's voice, though now it seemed to plead. Slowly, as he recognized his bed in front of him, understanding dawned. He realized that, not for the first time, he was the victim of subliminal messages planted by the television evangelist his mother watched every Sunday morning. Glancing around his room, like an investigator at a crime scene, Harold saw his desk chair lying on its side next to one of his shoes and an open beer can with the shadow of a stain on the brown carpet where its contents had spilled and started to dry.

He slumped back onto the bed and took a personal inventory. Except for one shoe, he was fully clothed. His legs ached a bit, and his head throbbed. But he was accustomed to that. No one could drink the way he did the night before and expect to not feel that way. He sensed moisture at one corner of his mouth and saw that he had drooled on his bed cover. His face hurt, and he ran his fingers over his cheek and jaw where he had peeled them off of the messed, yellow-and-white-flowered polyester bedspread. He could feel the pattern of wrinkles transposed from the cloth into his skin as he used the back of his hand to wipe the saliva from the corner of his mouth. It was then that he also felt something crusty. Glancing into the mirror above the dresser, he discovered a swollen and purplish bruise, about the size of a man's fist, extending from his left eye and down the side of his face. He licked at the crustiness and tasted the saltiness of dried blood. Putting his hand to the un-crinkled side of his face, he found it warm and saw that the curtain was open enough that the sun was shining across the spot where his face was recently pressed to the bedspread.

Harold felt at his lip and the bruise as though doing so would provide clues to their origins – clues to unravel the mystery of another lost night. From the facial damage, he guessed that someone had hit him, not that he knew who or why. That he might have done something to cause someone to hit him wasn't unlikely. Still, he wondered while acknowledging the possibility that the issue might not be settled. The mystery also extended to simple questions, such as how he had gotten home or how much money was left. It took a couple minutes of searching the darker corners of his mind before flickers of cognitive light pierced his foggy recollection. He vaguely recalled a fist crashing against his face before he landed on the floor. He had the vaguest recollection of an assailant standing over him. Was it this man's finger that pointed menacingly down at Harold? Rather than preaching, it was a warning, wasn't it? But what warning? As Harold scoured his memory for additional clues, a familiar face came into focus. Slowly, it dawned on Harold – his mistake, a mistake he had made before.

Harold had briefly dated Char. But even for Char, a burgeoning alcoholic in her own right, Harold was too much the lush. The relationship ended in a confusing fog that also challenged Harold's semi-pickled memory. Harold had a vague memory of another incident from another intoxicated episode. He had done something to raise Char's ire. But what? Then again, the scene at Freddie's Place, his stomping grounds they both frequented, the same bar from Harold's strange pastoral vision that morning, was all-too-vivid. Her words were harsh, but only half as harsh as the tone in which they shot, rapid fire, through her clenched teeth. She didn't really say what he did but there was no question about how she felt about it, whatever 'it' was. Did he want to remember how he had made her so mad? What he knew was that this wasn't the 'we're-having-a-boyfriend-girlfriend-fight' kind of mad; it was the kind of mad people reserved for someone they loathed irreversibly. Maybe it was better that he didn't know.

Examining the recollection, Harold had a feeling that his latest predicament might have involved Char, too. Or was it another girl he occasionally saw at Freddie's. Char looked similar to this other girl. It wasn't as though they were twins. They simply had the same build and facial features. Their hair was the same color, and they wore it in roughly the same style. They probably even shopped at the same stores for their wardrobes. It was as though they were both trying to fit the same image in a magazine. As Harold was attracted to Char it was only reasonable that he would also feel an attraction for her quasi-twin.

The pieces began to fall loosely into place. He was definitely at Freddie's, and more than a little drunk. The other girl, not Char, came into the bar – or was it Char, even now Harold wasn't sure. He was too drunk to make the call last night, it was less likely he would figure it out now. He vaguely remembered casting a slurred comment in the girl's direction, though he couldn't recall what he said.

Whatever he said, Char, or the other girl, had taken offense, as had the muscle-bound dude she was with.

With another fleeting glance at the mirror, as though it were painful to look too long, Harold pondered the bruise through glassy eyes and wounded pride, as he had a vague sense of a heavy fist crashing against his face. There was a second crash, this was caused when he hit the floor. He sensed that it was more than his imagination that those around him were amused. There were people at Freddie's that Harold got drunk with but few he would actually call friends, at least not in the true sense of the word. If there was any hope for relief from the embarrassment of the situation that now weighed on his mind, tearing at his long-battered self-esteem, it was that this wasn't the first time Harold had come off looking the fool during one of his binges. And he knew it was unlikely that it was the last. His ability to accept scorn and ridicule based on his drunken antics was increasing as his capacity to care what others thought of him diminished. He told himself he didn't care. It helped to assuage the mental anguish associated with such embarrassing events. He was learning to laugh it off.

A shrill whistle grew from the kitchen, momentarily disrupting the depressing thoughts that were spinning in Harold's head, thoughts more painful than Harold's physical wounds, drowning out even the sound of the television evangelist on his mother's white-plastic, 13-inch Philco television.

Marge had a morning routine that, for years, had hardly deviated from one day to the next. It was a routine she could carry out proficiently blindfolded. With curlers in her reddish-greying hair, she was short and so slender her arms and legs poked out emaciated from the sleeves of her floral nightgown. In spite of her deceivingly spinster-like appearance, she moved about the kitchen like a modern, military tank with the capacity to hold its gun on target as the chassis roared over any terrain. Marge would traverse the kitchen fixing her tea without changing her orientation to the television. She'd walk in her fuzzy pink K-Mart slippers to a big, white stove, purchased as a wedding gift in 1952, and turn the heat off under a tarnished, stainless teapot with a partially blackened copper bottom. Rotating 90 degrees to her left, her head still tracking the television, she would reach, with sightless precision, for the jar of instant coffee at the back of the stainless-steel counter. Unscrewing the lid and setting it on the counter, she would remove a spoon from a drawer under the counter and take a scoop of grounds. These she would drop into the same thick ceramic mug she removed from a hook screwed into the bottom of the dark-stained cabinets that hung from walls pasted with aged and faded wallpaper remarkably similar to the floral pattern on her nightgown. Then, she'd return to the stove for the teapot and, holding one finger over the edge of the cup to feel when it was full, she would fill the cup with hot water, never taking her eyes off the pastor as he delivered his latest Sunday morning sermon with all the splendor possible on the small black-and-white, rabbit-eared television on the counter by the backdoor. She would place the pot on the stove and deliver the mug to the table in the middle of the kitchen. She would give the cup a couple of stirs with the spoon and then, setting the spoon next to the cup, she would turn almost 180 degrees away from the television, with her eyes still glued to the screen, she would move in her crouch to the other side of the kitchen and remove a small plate with a partially used stick of butter from an avocado-green GE refrigerator, and she would carry the butter back to the counter where, just in time, she would catch two slices of toast as they emerged from the old, chrome Etsy toaster. Pulling a knife from the drawer under the counter, she would butter the toast and place them on a piece of paper towel she tore from the roll under the cabinet next to the hooks where she kept her mugs. Then, after she carried the butter back to the refrigerator, she would slip into the padded chair ready to drink her instant coffee and nibble at her buttered toast. The only thing that really changed, from day to day, was the programming – it was only on

Sunday that she could count on the televised sermon. Otherwise, she preferred watching "Good Morning America" with Joan Lunden and David Hartman, the latter for whom she carried quite a crush.

On this particular Sunday, Marge was first aware that her son had returned from his customary drunken debauchery when she woke to find the backdoor wide open. Then, she heard muffled shouts from his room down the hall. She could hear him moving about and wondered why he would wake so early on a Sunday morning – early by his standards but hardly by the standards of someone who didn't drink to excess every Saturday night, as well as most nights. Finally, his door opened, and she caught a glimpse of him stumbling towards the bathroom. By the sound of his urinating, Marge could tell that he had left the bathroom door open, which aggravated her almost as much as finding the back door open.

"Close the damn door while you pee," she growled in a voice grown gruff from years of smoking non-filter Camel cigarettes, a pack of which was on the table next to a dirty ashtray a few inches from her coffee mug. She heard the door close as she continued, "And speaking of doors, you left the backdoor wide open last night."

When her son didn't respond, Marge continued, "Maybe we should just take all the doors off their hinges. The raccoons can come in and raid the refrigerator."

She pondered whether the raccoons could actually open the refrigerator when she heard Harold, retreating to his bedroom again, offering a typically lame excuse: "It must've blown open."

"If you lock the door it can't blow open," Marge barked. "And if you came home at a reasonable hour maybe you wouldn't be so drunk that you wouldn't know the difference."

Having diverted her attention from the television, Marge sensed that Harold was standing by his door, no doubt contemplating whether to engage in the argument she was brewing. But before he could decide, Marge changed the subject. "We have to go downtown tomorrow."

"You mean, you have to go downtown," she heard him growl, half under his breath, where he stood out of sight by his door.

"Fine," Marge said, eagerly enjoying the thought of catching him off guard. "I'll tell the lawyer you want to donate your inheritance to Goodwill, then."

There was another pause and then her son appeared by the entrance from the hallway to the kitchen, "What inheritance?"

At last, Marge looked away from the television. But when she looked over at Harold, she resisted the temptation to answer his question outright. There he stood in a badly wrinkled version of the jeans and flannel shirt she'd seen him in the other day. His red hair, long overdue for a haircut by Marge's standards, was matted to one side and messy. He wore one gym shoe. In spite of his condition, which included another bruise on his face, he had the potential for good looks. A shave would help but, otherwise, he had the chiseled facial features that reminded Marge of her late husband. At a couple inches under 6-foot, he had broad shoulders and strong arms. His body was well proportioned except that the effect of all that beer, compounded by a year or more's unemployment, was spreading across his midsection.

"You look like crap," she said. "If you're trying to drink yourself to death before you're 30 you're off to a good start?"

"You're one to talk," he muttered in her direction trying to get a word in without pushing far enough to start an argument that would delay his return to his bed.

What was it? Did Marge resent the way Harold was throwing his life down a bottle? And if so, what about the bottle her life slipped into day after day? It had to be something else. Somewhere, deep down inside, Marge knew that at least part of the answer was that knocking Harold down somehow, made her feel better about herself - as though, if she could criticize his drinking she could rationalize that she wasn't too bad off herself. Yes, maybe she drank a bit too much but at least she didn't drive drunk. She drank at home where no one else could get hurt. But she didn't want to think that she was building herself up at her son's expense, so she suppressed the thought quickly whenever it reared its ugly head. Besides, contemplating their drinking habits tended to bring up other uncomfortable thoughts, such as guilt that she wasn't a better mother – that she, at the very least, shared blame for his drinking habits.

"You said something about an inheritance?" said Harold, quickly changing the subject.

"Oh, did I get your attention," Marge said mockingly as she made a show of looking back to the television. Addressing her son with the back of her head, she continued, "Maybe you'll inherit enough money that you won't have to find a job after I'm gone."

"Could you drop the bullshit and stick to the question?" Harold asked, a twinge of diminishing patience in his voice.

Marge's husband and Harold's father – Carl Schneider – had died on the job six years earlier after almost 18 years at the factory where he'd risen to the position of foreman. Marge reflected on the image of irresponsibility Harold had already presented to his parents by the time of his father's death. She knew Harold had sufficiently shown his irresponsible nature to the extent that Carl had prudently left everything in his will to Marge. The house was paid for and, between a little savings in the bank and a small pension, Marge had enough to cover her basic expenses, with a little left over for an occasional indulgence, and, or course, her booze. Harold, unemployed for more than a year, except for an occasional odd job, would nag her for some pocket money from time to time. Marge would often succumb, mostly just to get him off her back, though also because she secretly liked to keep him in her debt. Harold was dependent on her and had no reason to expect an inheritance from his father, or anyone else, at this time.

She glanced back at Harold and could almost see the wheels turning as he tried to unravel the mystery. It was as though she could read his foggy, hungover mind: "Who would leave anything to me, the town drunk?"

After watching him standing unsteadily in the doorway a few moments, Marge finally solved the mystery for him: "Your Uncle Harold died. I'm sure he didn't have more than a pot to piss in, so don't go spending your inheritance just yet."

"MY UNCLE HAROLD?" he yelled, a flabbergasted look of surprise on his face. "Since when have I had an Uncle Harold? Or, maybe I should ask, why didn't anyone tell me I had an Uncle Harold?"

Marge took a bite of buttered toast and washed it down with a sip of coffee, savoring the moment and her control of the situation. "Harold – your uncle – was a good for nothing: the black sheep of the family," Marge said without looking up. "Your father told him not to come around a long time ago. That was the only decent thing he ever did – not coming around anymore ..." In a voice Harold barely heard, she added, "that and dying."

Looking back at her son for a moment, Marge said, "Funny thing is, you and Harold were cut from the same cloth – no good, drunken bums." As she looked away again, she added, "You were even named after your uncle."

Harold scowled but didn't bite at her insults. Instead, he shook his head and returned to his bedroom, no doubt to continue sleeping off the one he'd tied on the night before.

She barely heard him mumble, "Great. 'Hey Harold, how would you like to meet your uncle? Oops, sorry, too late, he's dead.'"

"I take it you'll be going with tomorrow, then?" she yelled down the hall as he retreated.

"What time?" he asked.

"We need to leave the house about 8 a.m.," she said. "I want to stop at K-Mart," she added and laughed quietly when she heard his anticipated groan of acknowledgment. She didn't really need anything from the store but liked to stop there, especially when Harold was with her. She relished that it bothered him so much.

As Harold disappeared into his room, Marge hollered, "And you'd better take a shower before we go. You smell like an outhouse." This comment also seemed to strike her as funny and she laughed at his expense as she heard his door close.

Chapter 3 — The Inheritance

"You'll be straight home tonight?" Julie Ruskin asked as she came into the kitchen and predictably found her husband sitting behind the newspaper, a gold-rimmed, bone-colored cup of straight-black coffee and a matching saucer with cream-cheese-and-locks-topped bagel slices within easy arm's reach — one slice exhibiting evidence of a couple of missing bites from perfectly aligned rows of teeth.

Julie's deep-lavender, Chantilly robe, open at the front exposing her light-lavender, silk pajamas, flowed behind her as the speed of her approach to the kitchen carried her across the room to an abrupt stop before the stainless percolator on the counter. Another gold-rimmed cup awaited her, along with the set's sugar bowl, though she had to retrieve the creamer from the black, side-by-side Amana refrigerator. Her long, raven hair gleamed blue in the morning light that reflected off the onyx kitchen table cut and polished from the same material as the counter tops.

When her husband didn't answer, as she sipped her coffee, she asked again: "You will be coming straight home tonight, won't you?"

Stuart Ruskin used his forefingers on both hands to deftly fold down the top half of The New York Times Section 1 that was delivered daily halfway across the country from its high-rise newsroom. Through gold-rimmed glasses, perched precariously near the end of his nose, he studied her for a moment as though to find the answer in the depth of eyes seemingly mined from the same onyx as the table. At last, he responded, "Have I told you how stunning you are in the morning?"

"Is that your way of telling me you aren't coming straight home?"

He smiled, as though bestowing a gift upon her, flipped twice to bring the paper back to its upright position and, from behind its veil, lied, "I have a prospective client coming in late. I'll have to let you know if I can get away."

Julie paused a moment allowing some of the frustration to seep from her voice before responding: "You know the fundraiser's tonight. I told you months ago. I reminded you last week. It's black tie and it's important. This is our last chance to reach our goal for the season." When he didn't answer, she barked, "Stuart! I'm asking you a question."

"Yes, dear. I hear you," he said in a voice less carefully scrubbed of boredom.

"Well …! Stuart! Is it too much to ask that you come out and support the cause once each year."

"I give generously to the orchestra," he said. "I've done so for, what, 15 years now?"

Julie sighed, "If you won't come out for the orchestra, won't you come out for me? I really don't want to go to another of these events alone."

"I go to your events all the time," he complained.

"They're not 'my events' and you've missed the last two. You didn't even come to the Mayor's inaugural ball in January."

"I didn't go to the Windbag's ball because it was absurd. What, does he think this is New York City? We're a small Midwestern town. You don't think that was just a little bit pretentious, not to mention how much it cost taxpayers?"

"You're always talking about rubbing elbows with the right people. Well, they were all there," she complained.

"I know how and where to 'rub elbows' and it's better on the fairway than some marble dance floor."

There was silence, only broken by the sound of Stuart flipping a page, as Julie pondered how the conversation had led her into this dead-end. At last, appealing to his sense of compassion, she asked, "Won't you try to make it for me."

Stuart folded the paper down again and studied his wife as though trying to gauge a jury. "I'll see what I can do. Maybe I can get this prospect to reschedule, although, I doubt they would see a party as equally important as their legal problems."

For Stuart, the silver, 1981, turbocharged, convertible 745i BMW in the garage, was a reflection of who he was. As he climbed in, pulled on the leather driving gloves, and pressed the button for the garage door opener, he hadn't really decided whether to go with Julie to the fundraiser. He knew how much it meant to her. But he also knew that he had stood up Linda, his reception-ist, the previous night. Linda was usually fairly understanding. She would pout a little but, with a little cuddling, teasing and a gift or two, she always came around. Still, he was worried that she was beginning to realize that his promises to leave his wife were made from the same cloth that he used to cover up the affair from his wife. Linda would not have appreciated the romantic occasion he had orchestrated for Julie the night before though, if she did know, he would have argued that it was necessary in order to keep up the pretense until he was ready to ask her for a divorce, a divorce he never intended to seek. If Linda ever really considered how much he had married into his wealth, not that he didn't do well as an attorney, she would have had additional cause to doubt his sincerity.

These thoughts raced through his head as he sped down the expressway to his downtown office. Some mornings, he would turn off an exit early to go straight to the County Building for court, usually to defend some punk who was charged with a DUI or some other minor infraction. Occasionally, he defended someone with a felony though never anything as exciting as armed robbery or murder. And then there were the divorce cases. He liked these the most. They could stretch on for months with the sound of cash registers figuratively ringing in his ears. From time to time, the divorces came with the fringe benefit of a grieving wife who required a little comforting in her hour of need, comforting he was happy to give if she was young enough and/or attractive enough. That comforting often came between the sheets of the Poplar Grove Holiday Inn or, at times, in the front seat of his BMW. By necessity, he was extra careful about these affairs as he had to hide them from his mistress and his wife. This was particularly difficult with Linda as she would see the women in the office, from time to time, and it wasn't hard to recognize the extra appreciation a divorcing wife would show their obliging attorney.

As he rode up the undersized, clunky elevator to the 11th floor, Stuart still hadn't made up his mind about the evening. He knew he'd pay a price if he sent Julie off to the event alone. On the other hand, he'd much prefer a quiet dinner with Linda knowing that it would end in her queen-sized bed. Julie was still an attractive woman, but she had 16 years on Linda. The secretary fell short of his 5-10 wife by about five inches, but she made up for that with a firm, youthful body and double-Ds that were far beyond what Julie had to offer in that department. Besides, Linda was far-less demanding. Julie expected to be pleased. Linda sought to please.

If Stuart was fair about this, he'd admit that marriage probably had a lot to do with this. A wife generally has more expectations than someone who is in a courtship, even if the courtship is a sham.

As the elevator doors opened, he frowned realizing the landlord hadn't done anything about the moldy odor that met Stuart in the lobby. It was an older building and Stuart occupied an office here because it was close to the County Building but also because the rent was uncommonly low for a downtown office.

His frown quickly vanished as he stepped into the office and Linda came into sight. She was seated, reading a romance novel, with her back to the door, a back that was unusually covered by a high-collar blue dress. The absence of exposed flesh was a definite sign, as was her customarily flowing auburn-blonde hair, which, this morning, was up in a bun on the back of her head. He wasn't surprised when, in reply to his greeting of "Good morning," Linda didn't respond at all. He was about to go into the office and drop the briefcase off on his desk but decided this situation couldn't wait.

Setting the briefcase on the floor, he slipped behind the secretary and, starting at her shoulders, slipped his hands down to caress the length of her arms and, feeling a reassuring gentle shudder as his hands covered hers where they held the paperback, he nuzzled his face gently against hers. She pulled away but not before he felt the dampness of a tear from her cheek. He was about to stand back up when he felt her head gently return to rest against his face again.

"You bastard," she said in a voice that trembled.

"I'm so sorry," he said in his most adolescent pouty voice. "You know I wanted to be with you."

Linda shuttered as she fought back the urge to cry. "I missed you so much last night."

"I missed you, too."

She snorted derisively, "Sure, you missed me alright. I slept on the sofa with the cat while you went to bed with … her."

"Oh baby, you know I wanted to be with you. We had to take the kids to her folk's for dinner. I couldn't get out of it. Besides, your cat is better company anyhow," he lied.

Stuart kissed her gently on the cheek and whispered in her ear,

"I'll make it up to you tonight. How 'bout we drive out to that night club up by the lake, where we went to last fall – the place you liked so much?"

"I thought you liked it, too" she said, pulling away again but this time playfully.

"I did," he said. "That's why I thought of it – that and the hotel with the hot-tubs."

"It's not a hotel when they charge by the hour."

"It's not by the hour," he said as he stuck his fingers into her lower ribs on both sides making her jump and giggle as he tickled her. He was just saying, "It's for three hours," when he heard someone cough and realized they weren't alone.

Stuart stood upright and stepped back from Linda as she picked up the book that had fallen to the floor and set it on the desk. There, on the other side of the desk was an older woman and a young man. The prior seemed to have made some effort to dress for the visit, though in a fashion that might be called 'mothballed.' The latter, his hair disheveled, wearing a faded-black ZZ Top concert t-shirt, tattered jeans, sockless sneakers, and with a large bruise on one side of his face, hadn't seemed to make any of that effort. Stuart assumed these were his 9:30 a.m. appointment.

The woman, short and thin, as though undernourished, wore a brown-plaid dress suit, buttoned to the neck, that was probably chic in 1945. Her hair was pulled back in a bun as if drawn tight to ensure a prunish frown as she surveyed Stuart and Linda, eyebrows raised, with obvious disfavor.

"Are we interrupting?" she asked in a voice gone gruff from decades spent pulling on cigarettes.

Where she seemed annoyed, the young man seemed to have a hint of a grin on his face, which almost made Stuart laugh. "Yeah, like you'd ever have a chance with her punk," Stuart thought to himself, sizing the young man up as unemployed and living at home with his mommy – a partier who had never grown up.

"Uhm ... no. No ..." Stuart stumbled. "You, uh, you must be ..." Stuart craned his neck to line up with the words written on the desktop calendar where he saw the name at the top line for that Monday, "... the Schneiders."

The older woman didn't give any indication of an answer. However, Stuart saw the slightest nod from the young man.

"Yes," Stuart said, more to himself than anyone else. "You are a bit early …"

"Apparently," said the older woman as she gave Linda an additional scornful stare.

Stuart saw the look and glanced at Linda to see her reaction. For her part, it seemed Linda was struggling to control the urge to burst into laughter. He smiled at her knowing they'd have a laugh about it later.

Now trying to control the urge to grin himself, he looked back at the two and said, "Well, why don't you come on into my office and we can get this … uhm, we can take care of this right away."

The older woman couldn't help giving Linda another sharp glance as she walked past and into the room as Stuart politely held the door open. The young man was also looking at Linda, but his look was that of a young man checking out an attractive woman. He even smiled flirtatiously, which almost pushed Linda over the edge into laughter.

In the office, Stuart introduced himself and was surprised by a firmer handshake than he expected from the young man. Before moving behind the desk, he asked the Schneiders to have a seat and offered some coffee or water but realized they seemed to be engrossed in their own conversation, or at least the woman was busy speaking while the young man had a tired look on his face as though wishing she would just shut up. She was speaking in a hushed tone as though trying to whisper so the lawyer wouldn't hear their discussion from only a few feet away.

"If you'd got up on time we'd have had time to stop at K-Mart."

This finally brought the young man out of his shell as he barked, "I told you I'm not going to K-Mart. You can drop me off at Freddie's first."

Giving up on his effort to offer them refreshments, Stuart cleared his throat to get their attention.

"I'm sorry," said the woman but in a way that suggested she was apologizing for the young man rather than her own interruption of the purpose of the meeting.

Following some obligatory small talk about the drive in and the weather, he got down to business. "The typical Hollywood version of the 'reading of the will' isn't that common anymore. And the dispositions from this estate are small enough that a formal reading isn't really justified."

"Told you," Mrs. Schneider snorted half under her breath in the direction of her son. Having looked in his direction and recognizing the need for action, she added, "Sit up straight" as though he were a young boy in a church pew.

The young man looked off, as though into the distance, annoyed and, Stuart guessed, slid back in his seat just to shut the woman up.

Seeming to have their attention again, Stuart continued, "As I was saying, we can usually dispense with the reading of the will. However, Mr. Schneider, your uncle," Stuart said as he nodded towards the young man, "expressed concerns to ensure that his estate would be dispensed with in accordance with his wishes, and paid for this occasion prior to his passing."

He scanned their faces a moment to make sure they were understanding what he was saying and was surprised to see that the young man seemed slightly offended as though the lawyer was patronizing them, which he was. The look suggested more intelligence than Stuart had suspected when first meeting the young man.

"We understand," said the woman.

Stuart smiled and continued, "As I was saying, Mr. Schneider had limited assets. But on the other side of the ledger, he had no debts either.

"This is the 'Last Will & Testament of one Harold Louis Schneider'" Stuart said pulling a legal form out of a vanilla folder in the briefcase on the corner of the desk, "who passed away two weeks ago Friday, the 2nd. Included here," Stuart continued as he pulled another document out from under the will, "we have the Coroner's Death Certificate indicating that Mr. Schneider died of natural causes.

"I, Harold Louis Schneider," he began reading, "being of full age and sound mind, do declare this be my Last Will and Testament, hereby revoking and annulling any and all Last Will and Testaments or Codicils at any time heretofore made by me."

In "Item I," Stuart read and explained that, as the Executor, he had resolved the matter of two small debts related to the funeral and explained that, otherwise, there were no known levies against the estate. Then, he came to "Item II.

"The remainder of my property, real and personal ... I bequeath to my Nephew, Harold Matthew Schneider."

When Stuart had completed the reading of the Will, he set the document down on the desk before him and looked across the desk at the Schneiders. The mother still wore the scowl that was on her face when she arrived. The young man, however, had a puzzled look on his face. Stuart looked at him a moment before it registered that the young man didn't know what his uncle's estate amounted to.

"Oh," said Stuart, as he reached back into the briefcase and the vanilla folder again. From the folder he withdrew a plain white envelope. Though the envelope was now flat, it was apparent that it was previously folded twice and, from the battered edges, probably shoved into someone's pocket. There was also an outline of a key in the bottom of the envelope at one corner. Stuart held the envelope by the upper corner above the key and extended his arm across the desk to the young man.

The young man reached out, almost tentatively, and took the envelope, which had been sealed. He looked back at Stuart, as though checking for permission to open the letter. Stuart had loosely folded his hands on the desk in front of him. He made the slightest forward gesture with his index fingers and thumbs to indicate that the young man should go ahead. As he began to cautiously tear the envelope open, Stuart noticed that the woman was watching intently.

Finally, he had opened the top of the envelope. He pulled a sheet of paper, folded twice, out of the envelope and opened the folds. He looked up at the attorney as it was apparent that he realized what he had in his hands.

"I understand that's the Title for a 1957 Harley Davidson," said Stuart. "The key is in ..." but he stopped as the young man had tipped the envelope, so the key fell out into the palm of his hand followed by a small piece of paper.

The woman had a flabbergasted look on her face as she spoke, "I knew it. That damned old fool."

"What are you talking about," the young man asked.

"That," she said, gesturing angrily toward the key and Title in his hands. "Giving you a motorcycle, he might as well just have shot you."

The young man looked back with an angry frown spreading across his face.

"Oh, come on," she continued. "The way you drink, you'll be dead in a week."

"It's not up to you," he barked.

"Fine," she said. "But you're not bringing that piece of junk home. There's no place for it, and the neighbors don't need you waking them up in the middle of the night. So, you might as well just sell it."

"I'm not selling it," he said, though Stuart had the feeling he was speaking more out of resistance than determination. In fact, it occurred to Stuart that, if she had left him alone, he might have decided to sell the bike on his own. But Stuart could tell that he was getting his back up. His jaw was set, and he was examining the small piece of paper, which held nothing but an address and phone number.

Stuart gestured towards the piece of paper and said, "That's where you'll find the motorcycle. It's the home of a friend of your uncle's where your uncle lived. Any other possessions he had you'll find there, as well."

The young man examined the piece of paper a moment longer then looked up at Stuart and said, in a simple and straightforward tone, "Thank you." Then he reached across the table and gave Stuart another firm handshake, the whole time the mother griping beside him.

"We should start planning your funeral right now, too."

The young man ignored her and headed out the door, the woman following behind him. Stuart came out from behind the desk and followed them to his office door where he and Linda watched them leave. The last thing Stuart and Linda heard as the couple stepped out into the lobby was the young man saying, "I told you, I'm not stopping at K-Mart." Stuart and Linda looked at each other and chuckled, all concern about their own problems apparently washed away by the experience of meeting the Schneiders.

Chapter 4 — Riding with the Rubber Elf

Down in the shadows at the far side of Freddie's Place sat a gnome, apparently having escaped a garden somewhere, nursing a martini. Though his diminutive stature was disguised somewhat as he slouched quietly on a barstool, if he had stood, any observer would have discovered the gnome was barely 4-11 and weighed in at a mere110-pounds. On his head, the gnome had red hair combed over a spreading bald spot that extended from his forehead into the back of his head. From protruding ears, a red and bushy beard and mustache extended around the bottom of its broadly smiling face. Its facial hair partially obscured a grizzled, pock-marked complexion that had suffered a losing battle with teenage acne. Forty-two-year-old Miles O'Sullivan was accustomed to the way people often overlooked him, as was, apparently, the case this sunny Monday afternoon. Though this had troubled him deeply in his youth, now, he no longer minded. He had learned to use his relative-physical obscurity to his advantage, moving in and out of establishments hardly noticed. But as his martini was nearing the bottom of the glass, he was hoping the attractive, 20-something blonde bartender would pay him attention long enough to refill his drink before he was forced to clear his throat and yell over the jukebox. He doubted she would.

Just as Miles was used to people overlooking him, this was hardly the first time he was ignored by this particular bartender. In this case, he knew there was more to it than his diminutive size. The bartender was once mildly friendlier when he came into Freddie's Place while making his rounds. But then he had shared a little joke she didn't seem to appreciate – that and she probably thought he was coming on to her, which, if Miles was honest, he was. As Miles told himself, when you're not even 5-feet tall, and your face is scared, you have to assert yourself, from time to time, if you ever hope to get laid.

Unfortunately, he had watched his joke fall flat, unlike the condom that 'magically' rose on the bar from the shot-glass with water and Alka-Seltzer. Men and women, alike, had appreciated his little joke. But not Mindy, the bartender in the torn jeans and tight concert T-shirts. Mindy's reaction to the joke was to give Miles an icy stare before walking away without a word. Since that time, she no longer feigned friendliness when Miles stopped at Freddie's. He still stayed for a couple of martinis, courtesy of Mindy's boss, but Miles had grudgingly accepted that he was persona non-grata in the bartender's eyes.

This Monday afternoon, Mindy was at the other end of the bar, one leg up on a cardboard case of Budweiser bottles, leaning forward on the bar as she conversed with a regular customer – an equally attractive brunette Miles had seen in Freddie's many times before. He recalled trying to strike up a conversation with the brunette once but had the impression Mindy had already poisoned that well. If Miles had to guess, he would have said that the women were friends outside of the bar. He had noticed that Mindy frequently filled the brunette's beer glass from the tapper without collecting for the drink. Maybe she was running a tab, but Miles doubted it.

Just then, Mindy had thrown her head back in laughter at something the brunette had said. From what Miles could hear, it was another of the frequent jokes the brunette seemed to make at her absent husband's expense. No longer nursing any hope of a successful encounter with either woman, in his own mind, Miles had created an image of the brunette's husband as a good man who was putting in a good day's work while his bimbo wife drank up his pay check at Freddie's day after day. Whether this was true or not didn't matter; either way, it served as salve for Miles's bruised ego; it was easier to accept the rejection if he could convince himself that the women weren't really worthy of his attention anyhow. Of course, deep down, Miles knew he'd jump at the opportunity if either girl ever gave the slightest inclination that his advances were accepted. The age difference wouldn't hold him back any more than the fact that both girls were at least six or seven inches taller.

Just then, a bright light shattered the shadows in the dimly lighted tavern as the front door opened. Framed in the doorway by the afternoon sunlight was the outline of a man close to 6-feet tall. But Miles, who had looked back that way when the door opened, couldn't make out anything else about the new arrival until the door closed and Miles's eyes re-acclimated to the shadows again. By that time, he noticed that a young man had walked to the bar about halfway down between Miles and the two women. Miles had seen this man in here before. This time, however, he noticed that Mindy gave this guy the same icy look she usually reserved for Miles.

Without moving from her perch by the case of Budweiser, it was apparent Mindy was taking the young man to task for something. 'You've got some nerve coming back in here.'

Though the young man barely spoke above a whisper, Miles could tell he was claiming innocence.

Finally, and with apparent reluctance, the blonde made a production of walking down the bar and filling a beer from the tap, which she slid across the bar to the young man. As she did so, she added, "Any trouble this time and you're out for good."

The young man pulled fifty cents out of his pocket and slid the two quarters across the bar while mumbling, "Thanks."

The bartender took the two quarters, eyeing them as though there was a chance they were counterfeit and looked up at the young man. "What are you so glum about — piss off someone else's boyfriend?"

The young man slouched down further over his beer as though the words were thrown like a heavy blanket over his shoulders. Miles could tell that Mindy seemed to relish the effect. However, as though to soften the blow, she continued, "No, really, did someone run over your dog or something?"

His tone sounding just a tad bitter, the young man shot back, "I don't have a dog."

Miles, who didn't have a good track record of keeping his nose out of places it didn't belong, and sensing he'd found a kindred spirit, jumped into the conversation. Thinking it would cheer the young guy up a little to divert the conversation, in his Irish brogue, Miles said, "You can't top a dog as a pet, you know? 'Man's best friend' for sure."

The young man seemed startled as though he didn't realize anyone was sitting down at that end of the bar. Or, maybe, he was surprised by Miles's high-pitched Irish accent. Mindy also seemed surprised. Rather than wait for them to recover from the shock of his intrusion, Miles slid off the bar stool, walked over and sat down in the barstool next to the young man.

"You don't mind if I have a seat beside yeah, do you, son?" he said though he was already seated. Before the man could answer, he looked up at Mindy and said, "Another round for the two of us, if you please," though the young man had yet to take the first sip from the glass she had just poured.

Finally finding his voice, though still in the flat tone he had used with the bartender, the young man muttered, "Thanks." Mindy produced another glass of beer for the young man and mixed another martini for Miles. Once she had served the drinks and collected several dollars from Miles, who told her to 'keep the change,' she used the moment as an opportunity to escape back to the other end of the bar with her friend. From the way the young man's eyes followed her back down the bar, Miles had a sense that he wouldn't turn down a roll in the hay with Mindy, either. Rather than a sense of jealousy, this seemed to cement Miles's sense that the two were friends only waiting to meet. They were both victims of Mindy's cold-hearted rejections.

When Mindy was out of earshot, Miles said, "Don't mind the ice queen. I'm sure it's nothing personal."

The young man glanced down the bar at the blonde again for a second then, looking back at his drink, he said, "Screw her," though he didn't quite sound convincing.

"Can't say that I'd mind," Miles said, laughing.

When the young man didn't laugh along with him, Miles paused for a second and then extended a hand and introduced himself – "Miles O'Sullivan, salesman, friend of the workingman and old-world philosopher for the modern age. And you?"

The young man looked at the hand as though contemplating whether to shake it back. Finally, and resigned to the social obligation, he took Miles's hand and said, "Harold Schneider" but neglected to share his profession.

Miles noticed the absence of a one-word resume and pursued the question: "So, what kind of work do you do?"

"This and that," said Harold. "I did a little machining, once."

"Now, that's an honorable profession," said the gnome. "To take a block of metal and sculpt it into something practical, that's saying something."

"You've done some tool and die?" Harold asked.

"Oh no, not me," said Miles, chuckling as though it were funny to suggest. "I've been in sales all my life. Made my first sale when I talked Sarah O'Connor into the storage locker in the 4th Class of Primary. Oh, I drove a cab a bit. But the closest I've come to machining – I did work on an assembly line for a while when I first came over."

"From Ireland?" asked Harold.

"Aye, the Emerald Isle of Eire," said Miles as though it was an opportunity to lay on his brogue at its thickest.

For the first time, Harold seemed to smile. Miles took this as an invitation to call down to Mindy for another round of drinks, though the prior round he'd bought was still untouched.

"Thanks again," said Harold, with a bit more enthusiasm.

"Tá fáilte romhat (taw FAWL-cheh ROH-ut)," said Miles.

"Tall what?" said Harold.

"Ah, that's Irish for you're welcome," Miles said, as he happily shared a little of his Irish culture.

"Well ... here's to yeah," said Harold.

Miles lifted his glass and clinked against Harold's and said, "A bird never flew on one wing."

Harold looked at Miles for a moment, apparently contemplating whether to ask for an explanation, then simply added "Cheers" and downed the rest of that beer before picking up the next.

"So, I hate to agree with icy," said Miles, nodding in the direction of Mindy, "but you did seem a bit glum when you entered this fine establishment."

"It's nothin'," said Harold, as Mindy arrived with the next round. Mindy seemed to be looking at Harold, too, as though waiting for an answer.

Finally, appearing annoyed to do so, Harold said, "I need to get out to Biesenthal to get my bike."

"Your bike," said Mindy, "You mean a bicycle, right?"

"No," said Harold, sounding indignant. "I mean my bike – my Harley."

"You have a Harley?" Mindy laughed, as though the idea was preposterous.

"Never mind her," said Miles, receiving a fresh icy stare from Mindy. "So, what kind of Harley have you?"

The young man paused giving Miles the impression Harold was contemplating what story to tell. At this, Mindy snorted in disdain and collected another $5-bill from the bar and, simply treating the difference as a tip, walked back to her friend at the far end of the bar.

"To tell you the truth, I don't know," said Harold.

"You don't know?" said Miles.

"I just inherited it," he said. "My uncle left it to me."

"I'm sorry of your loss," said Miles.

"It's OK," said Harold. "I actually never met him. I didn't even know about him till the other day when I was told he had died."

"Hmmm," mumbled Miles somberly. Then, with a much cheerier tone, he added, "Well, I'm heading in that direction. I even have a stop in Biesenthal. I'd consider it an honor to drive you out there."

"Really?" said Harold. "Cool."

"Just as long as you don't mind a couple stops along the way?" said Miles. "I have to make a couple of deliveries."

"No problem," said Harold.

"Well, drink up and we'll go," said Miles, lifting his glass in a fresh toast.

Miles led Harold out to a battered, butterscotch-colored 1977 Plymouth Volare Country Squire wagon. Miles unlocked the driver's door and slid behind the wheel before reaching across to unlock the passenger door. As Harold made to sit down, he realized the seat was overflowing with boxes and packs of condoms. Miles began cleaning the condoms, along with empty paper cups and hamburger wrappers, parking tickets and business forms that cluttered the seat and the floor, tossing them indiscriminately into the backseat.

"You must do OK with the ladies," said Harold, as he watched Miles clear room on the seat.

Miles paused, surprised by the statement and looked up at Harold. Noticing that Harold was looking at all the condoms Miles was randomly tossing into the back, Miles laughed and said, "Well, I've had some luck with the girls before, but, these (he held up a fistful of tinfoil-wrapped condoms) ... these are what I sell."

Harold laughed, "You sell rubbers?"

"Well, the rubber machines in the Jacks won't fill themselves, you know?" said Miles.

As Harold was climbing in, Miles put the key in the ignition and gave it a turn. For a moment, the starter whined, and the engine sputtered a moment before rumbling to life with the roar of a cancer-ridden muffler. The engine had only just caught when Miles jammed the steering-column shifter into gear and hit the gas. The car lurched forward as loose gravel on the asphalt pinged off the sides of the cars parked behind. As the tires fought for traction, the car lurched forward, burning rubber from the right rear of the limited-slip rear-end. The car flew recklessly into the street as Miles spun the wheel to the left, forcing a driver in a car from the left to slam on the brakes, thereby adding to the squeal of tires. Whether Miles hadn't noticed the other driver, or chose to ignore him, wasn't clear. As that car screeched to a stop, and the driver honked the horn, Miles rolled down the window and, with his left hand extended, raised his middle finger to the driver just before disappearing down the road to the North. Miles didn't seem to notice the nervous glance Harold gave him either as the car sped up to 65 on the 35-mph roadway.

Miles chattered constantly in a nervous staccato peppering Harold with questions as they went from the local thoroughfare to the interstate and back onto another local street. "How long you been going to Freddie's?" "You ever get anywhere with Mindy?" "Ever been to Ireland?" "What do you think of the constables in these parts?' Even when Harold sought to answer, Miles would interrupt as suddenly with commentary or additional questions. Harold had the feeling that the little man wasn't used to having company in the car and, in his excitement, had forgotten whatever few social skills he possessed.

In what seemed like minutes, the car whipped into a gravel lot, a cloud of dust washing over it as they skidded to a gravely stop.

"One More For The Road," Miles announced in a matter of fact sort of tone that gave Harold the impression the gnome had stopped for another drink. But as Harold looked up, he saw those words on a sign mounted halfway up the roof in yellow letters on a painted length of plywood with a painted fist holding a slopping beer stein on the right end of the billboard.

"Oh," said Harold as recognition caught on.

Miles, who had reached into the backseat for a box of condoms, paused and looked Harold's way when he heard him utter the one-syllable word. Then, Miles shrugged his shoulders, said, "Come on," and headed for the front door.

Harold followed along expecting his eyes would have to adjust indoors again. To his surprise, he found "One More For The Road" was as brightly lighted inside as the sun provided outside. Sitting at the end of the bar, neither in front or behind, was one of the plumpest women Harold had ever seen. Dark-oily hair hung stringy over her shoulders and, Harold suspected, in an equal patter on her back. She wore a thread-bare, plain cotton gown exposing massive cleavage at the front and a straining brassier through the wide-open sleeveless sides.

Hardly had they stepped in the door than Harold heard a deep, yet feminine voice sing out, "Miles, my little leprechaun."

"Maria," Miles responded with a rising tone as he wagged a finger in the fat woman's direction as though admonishing a misbehaving child. At the same time, he walked quickly toward the woman who rose from her stool at his approach. When they met, as Miles dropped the condoms on the bar, they threw their arms around each other. Miles' arms extended like a child's at Maria's sides, and Maria's engulfed Miles to the point where it seemed she would swallow him up into her immense girth. As they hugged, Miles announced affectionately, "Maria, my little Mexicali Rose, you ain't been cheatin' on me, have you?" Then he looked back at Harold, who was still standing by the door, a startled look on his face, and motioned for him to approach while saying, "Come over here and meet my best girl."

"BEST GIRL?!" Maria cried out with faux indignation.

Miles ignored her protest other than to wave Harold over all the faster, his hand rotating rapidly.

Harold had recovered but was reluctant to appear to eager as he strolled across the floor.

As Miles stepped back from the woman, his hair tussled comedically, she acted as though she had noticed Harold for the first time. "So, who's your friend?"

"Ah, this is Harold," my trainee, said Miles.

"Trainee? You showin' him how to install rubbers?" she asked, with a laugh.

"I'll leave that to you," said Miles as he slapped and grabbed a handful of her fat bottom. "So, you got a drink for me and me friend, you beautiful hunk-a woman?"

"You do go on," said Maria. "And don't stop," she added smiling at Harold.

"So, I know what he wants," she said to Harold. "What'll you have?"

"Beer," he said.

"What kind?" she asked.

"Whatever's on tap," he said.

Miles had picked up one of the boxes from the bar and was heading into the woman's bathroom, only knocking after he was halfway inside. "Damn, no one in here," he said, loud enough to ensure that Harold and Maria would hear him.

"You stop trying to catch the girls with their pants down," Maria yelled to Miles but with a smile. "A couple of girls have complained," she said to Harold while shrugging her shoulders to suggest she didn't really care.

After a couple rounds with Maria, they were back on the road to Miles' next stop. The driving pattern was the same as, this time Miles spoke at length derogatorily at Maria's expense to the extent that Harold was surprised at the insincerity of the greeting he'd seen in the bar. Miles glanced at Harold and, apparently worried lest he Harold begin to doubt him, explained, "She's a customer. Gotta keep up appearances."

Just as suddenly as before, they skidded to a stop in the parking lot of their next stop – a bowling alley where they only had one drink. The bartender, the owner's wife, recommended they might not want to stick around. Miles could hear the owner yelling and swearing from the back of the alleys where he was, apparently, working on the ball returns, or pin setters, and not having a lot of luck in the process.

In only minutes after their arrival, they were back on the road and headed towards Miles' last stop and Harold's destination – Biesenthal.

"You come out to Biesenthal often?" Miles asked as the additional martinis appeared to have the car drifting across the center line and, when Miles recovered, drifting back over the shoulder. As the sun fell below the Western skyline, they pulled into Biesenthal and, as if by second nature, Miles pulled into the parking lot of the first tavern they came to – a pub called Cal's Drift Inn.

The car had barely come to a stop when Miles was jumping out, a box of rubbers in his right hand, and was weaving through the full parking lot and past several Harley's by the front door. The sound of country music boomed out of the bar's doors and windows, as though the entire building was an over-sized juke-box. The volume of the music was well beyond the capacity of the speakers to play clearly and they could barely make out the lyrics "Why must you live out the songs that you wrote" over a cacophony of competing voices from inside. Working their way through the crowd of the smoke-filled tavern, Harold followed Miles, squeezing between a couple groups at the bar where Harold pulled out some cash, presuming to pay for a round, or was it to give Miles some cash for gas. But Miles laughed drunkenly, "Your money's no good with me" and scooped a handful of quarters, he'd recovered from the condom vending machines, out of his pocket. He slapped the quarters down on the bar and tried to catch the attention of one of the bartenders, a middle-aged woman with a nice figure wearing a black Harley shirt with frilled lace around the edges.

"Friggin' asshole," Miles slurred as she went by without stopping, though he might have noticed her obvious rush to keep up with orders that were coming from every direction along the bar. Apparently, it didn't matter that it was Monday night; Cal's Drift Inn was packed, and the party was roaring.

Miles might have prudently noticed the look from the biker, a patch on his back of a snake-wrapped arm and handgun pointed out of the patch under bold, red letters that read "Road Rattlers, standing a few feet away. But Miles was beyond noticing and drunkenly turned to Harold to say, "She wasn't ignoring me last time when I had her out in the backseat of the Rubber Monster," an apparent nickname for the Plymouth.

Harold found this doubtful. She didn't look like the kind of woman who would give Miles the time of day other than to politely serve his drink. Additionally, he wondered how Miles could bring any girl into the backseat of the Plymouth when it was filled to overflowing with condoms, boxes of condoms and other debris. But Harold did notice the increasing interest of the bikers.

Harold tugged clandestinely on Miles' shirt trying to get his attention without speaking too loudly. He turned his head so the bikers wouldn't see his lips moving as he said tried to mumble loudly enough, but not too loud, to Miles, "Hey, maybe you don't want to talk about that right now." But Miles was sufficiently ine- briated that he was beyond noticing or caring.

As Harold stepped closer and tugged again at Miles' sleeve, the drunken Irishman obliviously shoved the hand away. When Harold edged closer and, with his mouth close to Miles' ear, said, "There's no hurry, man. She's busy. She'll get to us," instead of seeing reason, an ugly, intoxicated side of Miles' nature ap- peared.

"Bullshit," Miles barked even louder. "She'll get that tight-little ass over here quick or she can forget her tip." Then he laughed as though this was a very funny joke.

"I think you'd better chill out a little," Harold said. Seeing no response, he added, "Hey, I gotta make a call. I'll be right back."

Miles glared at Harold with his new-found wrath, as Harold pulled a piece of paper out of his pocket and walked away. Then, Miles turned and pounded his fist on the bar, while yelling, "Hey, how 'bout some service, Goddam-it?"

As if she hadn't heard any of it, the bartender took Miles' order and turned to bring a martini, a beer and a shot glass of water. But as she turned to walk away, Miles reached out and grabbed her arm. She yanked her arm away and went back to rush of or- ders that hadn't ceased or slowed.

"Bitch," he muttered as she walked away. Then, the gnome looked around for someone else to share his joke with. He found a tall girl with a cutoff leather jacket over another Harley T-shirt. The jacket had the same curved red-on-white-lettered patch on the back, though it didn't have the snake-wrapped hand and gun. It did have another patch – a patch Miles would have done well to notice: "Property of Slash."

If Miles had noticed these details, he might not have slapped her arm with the back of his hand while saying, "Hey, check this out," repeatedly, as though he were a gnat pestering a horse until it got the horse's attention. By the time he had her attention, he had also regained the attention of the bikers who, up until that point, had shown considerable patience.

Miles had a vague sense that he was falling but without hitting the ground. He growled, "What the fuck," as he tried to understand how he had come to be hovering above the floor, dangling as though hung from a coat hook. He then had a sensation of pain as a small-but-solid fist slammed against the side of his head. He also had a vague sense of someone, most likely someone named Slash, yelling, "What'd you say ... my old lady ... you little cockroach?"

A larger fist now took him by the front of the shirt and, as that hand lifted him well off his feet, an equally large fist smashed into Miles' face. With blood running from his nose, he was only vaguely aware that someone was carrying him, feet off the ground, by the front of his shirt through the bar as the crowd parted, some laughing some making the inhaled sound of shock at the sight of Miles' bloody face. Finally, he had a sensation of flight, which ended abruptly as he skidded painfully across the asphalt.

As Miles was gathering himself up and half crawling over to his car: dragging himself up into the driver's seat, his antagonists, and the spectators from the bar had turned their attention back to their prior revelry. Drunk and bleeding, the beating had sobered Miles just enough to decide it was time to leave. He'd had enough of this place and quickly started the car. When he whipped the car onto the road, weaving back to the interstate, Miles mind was on getting away; he had forgotten all about filling the rubber machine just as he had completely forgotten his passenger, who was just then returning from the pay phone where he had discovered that the phone number the lawyer had given him was for a phone that was disconnected. Harold was returning to the bar in time to be confronted by two bikers who wanted to know if he "came in with that little asshole."

"I just met him today," Harold said in a tone that protested innocence. "He volunteered to drive me out here from Poplar Grove."

Miles was turning back on the interstate as Harold decided it was best to follow the bikers' advice, which was more of a subtle warning, and was leaving the bar. As Harold left, he glanced at the bar where he saw a rubber condom collapsed over a shot glass.

Chapter 5 — The Farmer and the Crow

"There they go again, Biesenthal's Laurel and Hardy," folks would say of Grant Bauman and Virgil Mitello. But the comments weren't derogatory. Rather Virgil was lanky and tall and carried a grin with him the way some men can't hide a receding hairline. Grant, on the other hand, was equally tall but stocky. Virgil's face was thin, and Grant's was almost as large and round as a basketball. They looked so much like the famous comedy duo that they had even performed a short diner skit they'd seen on the Dick Van Dyke Show at the VFW's variety show a couple years in a row.

Not as immediately obvious was the deep physical strength of both men, the kind of strength that comes from long years working in the fields with cattle and crops. As farmers, they were usually seen in coveralls and dust-covered boots. They were also, customarily, in bed by this time. Still, there were occasional nights when they were found out beyond their bedtimes and dressed in suits that were once in fashion about the time when Lillie's Café was first opened, in other words, around 1950.

The coats of paint applied to the walls inside the diner had built up until they had that thick appearance the way paint does on a battleship. Otherwise, with a relatively admirable attention to cleaning, Lille's Café had the appearance of having traveled through a time warp, from the yellow-and-speckled ceramic counter to the chrome stools, topped with yellow vinyl. Likewise, the suits looked as though they came off the rack in the morning before arriving at the diner decades later. While the formal attire might have fooled some about the nature of their professions, their tanned, weathered faces and hands, including a missing forefinger on Virgil's right, were giveaways that they were not business executives. Even more so, as though they didn't realize it would foil their disguises, or that the accessories would throw their suit-and-tie wardrobes a bit off kilter, like fence posts that lean in random directions, both men topped their heads with baseball-style hats. Virgil wore a faded-yellow hat with the word "DEKALB" inside of a winged outline of an ear of corn. Grant wore an equally battered green hat with the large word "BRETT-MAN'S" above an irregular box with a jumping yellow deer above the words "John Deere."

"What are you two doing out at this hour?" the waitress had asked when they entered the diner. She was a waitress who looked like a typical waitress at any other diner throughout the Midwest. A wispy, middle-aged woman, her auburn hair crowned by a small yellow hat, wearing a matching yellow, knee-length cotton dress with her name embroidered in brown thread near the left shoulder and a dirty white apron tied around her waist. If it were Friday night, she would have had a good idea of the answer to her question. But a Monday night ... that just wasn't part of the Grant's and Virgil's routines.

As they slid onto stools near the far end of the counter, Virgil said, "Well, we had to run out to Earlsville." But he left it at that and Vivian didn't pry any further.

She knew that they attended AA meetings Friday nights and suspected this had something to do with service work they did for the program. She had known them both long enough to remember how they were years ago when they were young, rambunctious and prone to trouble when they drank, which was often. She suspected they were probably trying to help some drunk get on 'the program,' as they called it when they mentioned it at all, or she overheard them talking among themselves. And she was right.

Grant and Virgil had just returned from dropping off a friend's son at the detox center in Earlsville. The lateness of the hour, and the need to get up before the crack of down the next day, was a small price to pay, from their perspectives. They never beat anyone over the head with the program. In fact, they seldom mentioned it without good cause. But they understood that, as was said in 'the program,' "You have to give it away to keep it." That meant that, if they lost sleep one night, they worked without sleep the next day and were happy for the opportunity. It was what they called "1st Step Work" though it was "12th Step Work" for them: it was a 1st Step for the newbie who might find 'the program.' It was a 12th Step for them as they shared their "experience, strength and hope." But now, the work was done. They should have headed straight back to their homes to catch as much sleep as possible, but both were too awake after the experience to go straight to sleep. And the flickering neon light in front Lillie's Café beckoned subliminally "Pie" in a language they couldn't resist.

They were only at the counter 10 or 15 minutes before the bell hanging above the front door jingled, interrupting one of Grant's jokes and announcing the arrival of another guest. Simultaneously, their heads turned that way with expectation. It wasn't unlike Officer Louis Spenoza to stop by about this hour for a late dinner while making his rounds. But this wasn't Officer Spenoza. Rather, a young man in a faded-black concert T-shirt, had come through the door. His mop of red hair, with matching red eyes, and a slight unsteadiness suggested some state of intoxication had come in the door with him. On the odd occasion, a group from the bar down the street would drift in for something to eat. But with the frequent visits of Officer Spenoza, the word seemed to have gotten around that Lillie's wasn't a receptive environment to carry on the party. Other times, a lost soul from the bar, having too much to drink, would stumble in the door. Grant, Virgil and Vivian would have guessed this was the case with this young man.

The young man stood at the door, wavering slightly, as he surveyed the surroundings as though checking to make sure it was safe. He had yet to move when Virgil hollered, "Well, come on in. We don't bite."

He looked at Virgil with an expression that suggested he wasn't entirely convinced but, as though he also realized he couldn't stand at the door forever, he finally made his way tentatively to the seat at the counter nearest to the door. As he sat, however, he looked back out the large picture window at the front of the store, as though checking for an angry mob that might come down the street with pitchforks and torches looking for him. As almost an afterthought, he slid down a few more seats closer to the others in the diner.

"You alright there, young man?" asked the man with the "DEKALB" hat.

Eyeing the man suspiciously, Harold mumbled, "I'm fine."

While Harold might have hoped his aloofness would dissuade the others from pressing the conversation, it was quickly apparent that these folks were not inclined to pass on a chance to converse with a stranger. After a short pause, the farmer asked, "You're not from around these parts, are you?"

"Don't make a pest of yourself, Virgil," said the heavy-set man, seeming to come to Harold's defense.

The thinner man reflected on it a moment before he apologized: "I'm sorry. Didn't mean to pry."

"It's just kind of our way," said the thicker man. "In a small town, folks are often just friendly that way. Guess it can come off a little nosy to other folks."

"It's OK," said Harold, in the hopes that this short response would short-circuit any further conversation.

As he looked up, however, he found that the waitress had made her way down to where he sat and was standing in front of him with her pencil poised over a pad of paper she'd taken from a pocket in the front of her apron, as though she were ready to take dictation. "So, what can I get you?"

Harold had merely come in from the night, wanting to avoid any threat from the bikers from down the street. He should have but hadn't really considered that someone would ask him to order something. The waitress smiled patiently as Harold looked from right to left as though he would find some clue to help answer the unexpected question. Then, as the waitress reached for a menu pinched behind the napkin holder at the back edge of the counter, Harold said, "Coffee."

She slid the pad back into the pocket of her apron, the pencil back above her ear but still asked, "Are you sure you wouldn't like something to eat."

Rather than sounding as though she were trying to sell something off the menu, her tone was exactly what Harold would expect to hear from a hostess when someone is visiting. It reassured Harold more than the words of comfort the farmer had offered.

Harold looked back at the waitress and, with a slight smile of appreciation, and said, "No, the coffee is fine. Thanks."

The waitress reached below the counter and came up with a thick, ceramic coffee cup on an equally beefy saucer. As she returned from the counter with an orange-handled Pyrex coffee pot, the heavyset man with the 'BRETTMAN'S' hat opined, "You really should try the strawberry pie – best in the county."

Harold looked his way with a bare crease of a smile but didn't respond. The waitress had stopped, coffee pot in hand, watching to see if the young man would take Grant's recommendation to heart. She rightly took his silence as a negative response. But now the man with the DEKALB hat took over.

"Vivian, get that young man a piece of pie. Just put it on my bill."

When Harold began to politely protest, Vivian interceded, "You might as well take the pie. He'll pester you to death until you do."

Harold looked back at her in a way that suggested he was distracted and not entirely paying attention to the conversation – was unsure what to say.

She reassured him, "It's OK. And they're not kidding. It really is about the best pie you'll find in these parts."

As though resigned to his fate, Harold accepted the pie with a thanks to the waitress and a nod to the man in the "DEKALB" hat.

Almost mindlessly, he took the fork and carved at the tip of the pie, brought it up and into his mouth as the others watched expectantly. The explosion of flavor seemed to wake him from a stupor. His mouth puckered, he looked up at the waitress as though for the first time. Though he had swallowed the piece of pie, he was unable to completely erase the pucker as he said, "WOW! That is good."

"One thing we don't kid about is Lillie's pie," said the man with the "DEKALB" hat.

"I see what you mean," said Harold with a grin.

The pie did more than break the ice; it completely melted it. By the time he was done with the second bite, Harold had already explained how he had come up from Poplar Grove and how he thought his ride might have left him stranded.

"City boy," said Virgil, as though benignly identifying Harold. "Watcha doing out here?"

Harold hesitated before answering: "I'm out here to pick up my motorcycle."

If he was expecting a reaction, something to say that they were impressed that he had a motorcycle, Harold was disappointed. Instead, the three of them merely looked his way as though he had left a thought dangling. Harold would have preferred that they considered him a full-blown biker who was simply in town to pick up the bike he had, for some mysterious reason, left in town. But something about these folks seemed to make pretenses feel wasteful, as though he were watering a garden in a rainstorm. It was as though their openness stripped away any illusions he might want to hide behind. Instead, he admitted that his uncle had died and that he had inherited his uncle's Harley.

"Who was your uncle?" asked Virgil.

"VIRGIL!" the waitress barked admonishing the farmer for his prying curiosity.

"That's OK," said Harold. "My uncle was Harold Schneider, but the name didn't seem to register with any of them.

Finally, Harold pulled a piece of paper out of his pocket. "I've got an address and a phone number where the bike's at," he said. "It's at 14327 Willow …"

"… Willow Lane," said Grant.

"You knew him?" Harold asked a glimmer in his eye.

"It's a small town," said Grant. "Folks know just about everyone in town. Your uncle lived out at the old Schultz farm, a bit north of town. Can't say I really knew him as much as I knew who he was." He paused a moment, then added, "I am sorry to hear of your loss."

As Harold said, "Thank you," the others nodded their condolences.

After another short pause, Grant said, "I'm headin' that way after I drop off this tall drink of milk. I can give you a lift, if you'd like?"

Hearing the offer, a fresh glimmer of a smile appeared in Harold's eyes. It seemed to please the farmers and the waitress.

"That would be great," he said trying to restrain his enthusiasm.

"Why don't you finish your coffee, and that pie, and we'll go?" said Grant. "Can't be staying out to the wee hours. Gotta get up in a few hours."

Harold finished the last of the pie in one bite, gave the mug a quick swig and said, "Ready."

Willow Lane was about five miles out of town. After dropping off Virgil at a farm a few miles back, Grant asked Harold if he'd lost his jacket, "I think you'll need one." There was just enough moonlight for Harold to see that both sides of the road were fringed with freshly plowed fields. The farm fields continued after Grant turned his '62 Chevy pickup right onto Willow Lane. About two miles along, however, the cultivated fields gave way to fields of weeds on top of ruffled rows of dirt, as though some-one had the idea to plant crops a few years back but never fully carried through on the thought.

Most of the farmhouses on the way out had lights glowing on poles in the back between the farmhouse and barn. The houses and barns were in relatively good repair. In one barn, the large doors were open out front and Harold could see a light on inside. He had a sense that a farmer was probably in the barn working at this late hour. But amid the untilled fields, Harold spied the dark shadow of an unlighted, gable-peaked structure that faced the road. There was a darker shadow of another building off behind the first. It was into this driveway that the Grant turned the truck and came to a stop. Up close by the moonlight, Harold could see the front screen door hanging by one hinge. Though the night had robbed it of its color, Harold could also see that the paint on the house was faded and peeling. Weeds out front and around the back were knee high and taller. There was one abandoned vehicle in the front yard and two more along the gravel drive as it extended back toward the barn. The latter sat with a slight tilt as though it was dropped in place from a height that had cracked its spine.

"Well, here you are," Grant said.

Hesitating to get out of the truck, Harold asked, "Does anyone live here?"

"Oh yeah," said Grant. He looked at Harold for a moment and then said, "Did you want me to wait a bit while you check to see if he's home?"

It occurred to Harold that might not be a bad idea. But instead, he said, "No, I'll be OK." As he stepped out, and before he closed the door, he shook Grant's hand and thanked him again for the lift.

As Grant's truck ground back from the gravel to the pavement, Harold stood in the headlights and watched him go. Then the headlights turned away and faded into the distance. Harold turned back to the house and waded through the weeds, almost falling over something hidden below, before walking up the steps to the front porch. He shielded his eyes to look in the front win-dow, but the room was so dark that the only thing he noticed was the large crack that ran from top to bottom of the window.

When he went to move the screen door out of the way so he could knock on the front door, the last screw holding it in place pulled out of the frame and the wooden screen door crashed to the porch as he jumped back out of the way. It seemed to Harold that no one could sleep through the sound of the screen door falling; knocking would be unnecessary. But no one came, and Harold knocked anyway. After a few seconds, he knocked again. The house remained as silent as a tomb.

After another minute, Harold took the steps back down from the porch and walked around to the back of the house. Knocking at the backdoor was equally unproductive so Harold waded back into the tall grass to check the barn. In the tall grass and darkness, he failed to notice another boulder, mislaid car part or other solid object waiting to ambush him on his path. This time, when it caught his toe, he fell into the dew-covered grass hurting his right wrist a bit as he broke his fall.

"Son of a bitch," Harold barked from where he had landed in the weeds. When he climbed back to his feet, he found that his shirt and pants were soaked from the dew. With that, and a slight breeze, Grant's comment about needing a jacket became prophetic.

Shivering, Harold felt his way cautiously over to the barn door, which was locked. He banged a few times with his fist before recognizing the futility of the act as the padlock was on the outside. Then he stumbled up one of the tire-worn ruts in the drive back to the front of the house.

"Now what do I do?' he said out loud as though expecting an answer to rise from out of the tall grass. He considered walking back to town or trying to hitch a ride that way. But he hadn't seen another car since Grant had first turned onto Willow Lane. He realized it was unlikely he'd get a ride. Besides, what would he do when he got back to town?

Harold went back to the house and tried both doors again with the same results. He even considered expanding the crack in the front window with a brick but decided that wasn't such a good idea. Then, pondering his situation, and feeling desperately that he wanted to sleep, Harold looked over at the abandoned car in the front yard. A rusty old Checker cab with no doors or windows, it didn't seem much better than stretching out in the weeds. But the rusty old pickup truck across the drive from the side of the house had doors and unbroken windows. He went over where the truck sat on its frame and fought open a creaking passenger door. The seat inside was ripped with springs visible between a ring of yellowed stuffing, but otherwise not in as bad of shape when considered in light of Harold's weary condition. He also noticed a burlap sack in the back of the truck that might serve as a makeshift blanket. Inside the truck, Harold pulled the 'blanket' up to his neck, yawned and leaned his head back against the door.

Against the cold, he fought to fall asleep. Harold shivered under the burlap for close to an hour. He considered trying the doors again or looking for another place where he could force his way into the house. As he pondered his situation and as he asked himself, "What am I doing here?" Harold finally fell into a fitful sleep. It wasn't a good sleep or the kind that would leave him feeling rested and refreshed in the morning. However, by this time, any sleep at all was more than welcome.

Chapter 6 — Chester and Magdelina

As the first rays of sunlight speared through the curtains again, Harold discovered a blackbird standing on the windowsill outside his room tapping a staccato with its beak against the glass. He rolled to his left, struggling to press one ear against the pillow while bending his other arm up over his other ear. But that didn't help. Instead, it seemed as though the bird had come through the window and was drumming the same beat painfully on Harold's head. Harold rolled back blurting out, "Go away" and was stunned when, in a graveled voice, the bird replied, "You go away."

As Harold pondered the absurdity of a talking bird, it pecked him hard, with a blunt thump, against the forehead again and growled, "Wake yer ass up."

Harold jumped with a start to find himself back in the front seat of a battered and rusty pickup truck. The early morning sun stung his eyes as he struggled to see out the passenger window. A shadow crossed before his eyes giving him a moment's relief. He fought to put the pieces together – the gnome and the ride up to Biesenthal, the bar and the bikers, the ride out to the farm – the pieces were there though they were fitting together loosely. These recollections washed away as quickly as they assembled when he also recognized that the blackbird's beak was actually the cold steel of a double-barreled shotgun now resting on the bridge of his nose. His eyes traveled up the barrels, past one gnarly hand clamped on the barrel and another on the stock, two leaden slugs, behind black-rimmed sunglasses, peered at him menacingly as the voice repeated, "What the hell you're doin' here? And you'd better start talking fast."

Harold sat up like a shot, banging his forehead between his eyes against the barrel, as his heartbeat raced to catch up with the urgency of the moment. The sunglasses were perched on the end of a pugilistic nose, the slug-like eyes, deep set and close together in a weathered hide, peering over the rims. The sneer on the tight-stretched lips was nearly hidden by an untrimmed, unkempt mustache and beard, matched by a full-head of equally frazzled long gray hair. This angry apparition was mounted on the broad shoulders of an intimidating wild creature that seemed much taller than its actual 5-5 stature. A tint of red gave a clue to the hair's original color.

"You better start explaining what you're doin' here, son," growled the man through clenched teeth. "This ain't no hotel for punks and drug addicts."

The burlap sack slipped to the floor of the truck, as Harold reached for the truck door to steady himself as he got up. The door creaked from its weight as Harold stepped onto the grass along the driveway while the shotgun and its owner backed away slowly. Harold held his hands out and open as the man leveled the shotgun at Harold's chest.

Seeing that he had Harold's undivided attention, the man said, "You was just 'bout to explain what you're doin' in my truck."

Like a typical farmer, the man with the shotgun wore blue-jean bib overalls, though one strap was unhooked and hanging in front. Unlike a farmer, this man was barefoot and wore a tie-dyed T-shirt. Harold glanced at the house and saw that the backdoor was propped open.

"I'm ..." Harold began, though, like backwash, his first words of the day stuck in his throat. He coughed to clear the obstruction and tried again, "I'm looking for Chester Pearl."

The man cocked his head to one side from behind the gun and drew his eyelids tighter, and, accenting the first word, asked, "Who's lookin' for Chester Pearl?"

Thinking a hand extended in friendship might help, Harold took a step forward. "I'm Harold ..." only to draw a sharp jab in the ribs from the gun.

"Just state your business," the man said.

Pulling his hand back, Harold explained, "I'm Harold Schneider. I was told ..."

The storm clouds instantly broke to reveal a bright, sunny smile that transformed the face from threatening to embracing. The man lowered the barrel of the gun and interrupted, "You Harold's kid nephew?" He paused and glanced at the truck as though contemplating the clues of a mystery and said, "What the hell you sleepin' in the truck for?"

Harold explained how he'd knocked on both doors several times the night before.

"Yeah got yerself a better chance wakin' the dead," said Chester Pearl as he switched the shotgun to his left hand and extended his right. As they shook, Chester looked back at the truck and said, "Don't imagine that was terrible comfortable, was it?"

"Not so bad," said Harold as the thought seemed to awaken a kink in his neck and back. He rotated his head to work it out, which brought a smile of understanding to Chester Pearl's face.

Chester pointed at the backdoor with his head and said, "Why don't we get acquainted inside."

As they reached the backdoor, Chester paused and asked, "Why didn't you call first?"

"I tried but I got a message saying the phone was disconnected."

Chester sighed, "Probably forgot to pay the damn bill again" as though it was nothing for him to forget to pay a bill. "They charge too much anyhow."

As Harold followed Chester in the back door and into the kitchen, he felt as though he had stepped into a sepia-tone photograph. Yellowed wallpaper, probably hung in the '40s or '50s, with a pattern of chickens and roosters, was separating at the seams and pealing. The floor had splotches of reddish dirt matching the soil outside, as well as darkened-oily wood where the occasional asbestos tile was missing. Harold thought the floor might once have been yellow. Large chunks of sun-drenched, pink linoleum were missing from the counter, presenting moisture-softened particleboard. Where the linoleum remained, it was lifting at the edges. This was only evident beyond the mound of dirty dishes that filled the large, single-tub, off-white-ceramic sink and the counter on both its sides. The once-white appliances, with round-bumper corners, appeared of the same vintage as the rest of the kitchen, including a bleached pink linoleum tabletop, held in place by a wide, tarnished chrome frame. Similarly, tarnished-metal-tube-frame chairs had seats covered in slick, pink vinyl, but the vinyl had numerous rips and missing patches where browned padding was receding so that the wood backs and seats were visible.

Chester set the shotgun by the backdoor and gestured toward one of the pink chairs. He poured a cup of coffee from a battered aluminum pot he took from the back burner of the stove, placing the cup in front of Harold giving the younger man the sense that, in this region, coffee was simply expected, and no one bothered to ask. All the same, and though Harold wasn't one who used coffee to start his days, it was rather welcome after sleeping in the truck all night. As the shock of the shotgun-wake-up-call faded, Harold began to notice that he felt as though he'd gone 10 rounds with George Frazier. His legs hurt, his back and neck hurt, his head was pounding. In fact, almost every part of his body was sore and aching to one degree or another.

Chester asked if Harold would like some breakfast. When Harold accepted the invitation, Chester cracked a few eggs into a bowl of yokes and whites that was sitting on the counter where he had, apparently, left it before grabbing his shotgun on the way out the door. As he whipped up the eggs with a fork, Chester apologized for the shotgun.

"I've been having some trouble with some of the kids in the area," Chester explained. "Last year, they planted marijuana out behind my cornfield by the tree line. Wouldn't care so much 'cept I had to explain it wasn't mine when the law knocked on the door one day. The kids broke into the barn a couple times, too. A few months back, your uncle chased one of 'em out of the there with the shotgun. Put some rock salt into his backside. You shoulda seen that kid run," Chester laughed while looking out the back window as though he could see it all happening again.

As he poured the eggs into a blackened, cast-iron skillet on the stove, Chester nodded toward the stairs. Harold looked where Chester had gestured and noticed a round pattern of pellet-sized holes on the wall below the stairs.

"Another kid came in the backdoor as though he owned the place a while back. He was headed for the stairs but hadn't noticed that your uncle was sittin' in the dark," said Chester.

"Why was my uncle sitting in the dark?" Harold asked, though he was really thinking that, as the house looked abandoned, it wasn't surprising that kids might walk in as though no one could possibly live here.

Chester turned back slightly from the stove and looked over at Harold. "The last few months, Harold couldn't sleep much, what with the pain," Chester said, his voice taking a more solemn tone. "He'd open the blinds and sit in the rocker looking at the stars and such."

"He was in a lot of pain?" Harold asked.

Chester shrugged as he dished the eggs onto a semi-clean pair of plates. "He didn't complain much," Chester said. "But I could tell he didn't feel like dancin' or anything."

Chester took a couple forks out of the sink and held them up close to his eyes. Then he ran some water over the forks and wiped them with a filthy towel hanging off the side of the cabinet next to the window.

Harold was still taking in his surroundings, looking at the only picture in the room, a painting of chickens pecking at corn on a cobblestone street somewhere, when Chester noticed his guest's curiosity. "Can't say where I got the picture," Chester said. "For all I know, it might've been here when I bought the place."

Then, as though he'd noticed the mess for the first time, Chester said, "You'll have to excuse the house. I don't exactly entertain much."

As Harold sipped his coffee, he asked, "So, how long did my uncle live here?"

Chester pondered on the question a while. "Well, I've been here the better part of 30 years myself," he said. "Your uncle came and went several times over those years. He was gone about six years once when he got married. Came back when it didn't work out."

Harold looked closely at Chester. "Sounds like you were good friends," Harold said.

"Well, we went back a bit, son," Chester said as he starred off into a distance that extended beyond the walls in front of his eyes. "Served together in the war. That kind of experience tends to make bonds that don't break so easy."

"Which war?" Harold asked.

"Which war?" Chester said as though the question was absurd. "The war. The big war."

Harold shrugged as though to apologize as Chester went on. "Met in boot camp – Camp Lejeune."

There was a long pause as Chester stared out the window giving Harold the impression the man was reminiscing in his mind. Then Chester shook his head snapping himself back to the present. As he carried plates of scrambled eggs to the table, he changed the subject and asked Harold where he was from and what kind of work he did. "Ever worked on a farm?" he asked.

"Not really," said Harold, though the real answer was, 'Not at all.'

When the eggs were about gone, Chester asked Harold if he wanted to take a shower.

"Bathroom is up the stairs at the end of the hall," Chester said. "Don't spend too much time though unless you don't mind cold water. Hot-water heater don't hold out too well anymore."

As Harold stood up to go, he asked, "You wouldn't know why my uncle never came to see me, would you?"

Chester gave Harold a long look and then said. "What makes you so sure he didn't?"

Harold laughed, "You know, a couple days ago, I didn't even know I had an uncle?"

"Things work out kinda funny sometimes, I guess," Chester said with only a slight note of sympathy. "If it helps, as the end got closer, I think he regretted not knowing you better all these years."

Chester looked as though he might say something else on the matter then, having decided otherwise, he turned back to clearing the table. Without looking, he said, "You may have a little trouble finding a clean towel, too. But there should be a dry one up there in the pile on the floor."

Harold nodded, happy to take shower if there were no towels at all and headed up the stairs to the shower.

As he showered, Harold pondered what Chester had said – "What makes you so sure he didn't." Harold tried to imagine some time he might have met his uncle. But it was a fruitless effort as he'd never even seen a picture of the man. The shower didn't completely repair the physical wreckage of the previous day, but it did help.

He dried himself, put his clothes back on and headed down to the kitchen running into Chester at the bottom of the stairs.

"Feel better?" Chester asked.

"Sure do," said Harold. "Thanks."

Chester didn't answer. Instead, he looked inquisitively at Harold for a moment. At last, as though he had made a decision, he said, "Well then, maybe you're ready to meet Magdelina."

"Magdelina," Harold asked wondering if there was a woman sleeping in one of the rooms upstairs.

Chester gestured with his head for Harold to follow and led the way out the backdoor and to the barn. At the doors, Chester dug far into a deep pocket, pulled out a key and unlocked the padlock letting it fall to hang on a rusted chain that was welded to one end of the equally rusty hasp. As he slid one side of the door open, he said, "I try to keep it locked. Shotgun comes in handy keepin' the kids outta the barn, too. Kids are startin' to learn how painful it is to get hit with a blast a salt."

"Doesn't look like salt did that to the wall in the house," Harold said.

Chester shrugged. "I suspect Harold had the shotgun loaded with pellet. I think he was planning to do some duck hunting."

Chester seemed to realize that Harold hadn't bought the explanation, so he added, "It's a different matter when they come into the house."

The inside of the barn was pitch black and, as Chester disappeared inside, Harold only followed a couple steps before stopping to let his eyes adjust.

With a hum, crackle, and flicker, a pair of eight-foot fluorescent fixtures fought their way to life as though woken from a deep sleep. The light swayed in unison with the dancing pull-cord Chester must have yanked a moment before. Under the swaying light, Harold spotted three motorcycles parked on a slab of concrete apparently poured as a parking space for the bikes. One of the bikes was covered with a heavy-green-canvas tarp.

"We got tired of laying in the dirt when we worked on the bikes," Chester said. "So, we poured this concrete floor a few years back.

Behind the bikes was a long workbench. At one end, a red toolbox rested on top of the bench beside a rolling stack of red toolboxes next to the bench. A pegboard wall behind the bench held several tools but, mostly empty pegs. It was as though someone's efforts at organization had fallen short in the end. Instead, the tools were scattered, amongst various motorcycle and tractor parts across the top of the bench (the tractor parts, apparently, came from the tractor parked on the dirt floor to the right of the barn door. More parts, along with boxes of parts, oil, and other items, were on shelves to one side of the pegboard. More parts and cases of oil were on a shelf below the bench. Among the parts on the top of the bench was an entire V-twin motorcycle engine.

The concrete pad extended about 15 feet back from the front wall and out from the side wall towards the center of the barn about 12 feet. The rest of the barn floor was covered with the same reddish dirt found in the drive and by the backdoor of the house. Unused stalls for livestock were along both walls beyond the front area where the motorcycles and tractors were located.

The covered bike was closest to the front wall. The next bike in line was painted flat green and had a large white star painted on each side of the split gas-tank sections. The bike had a large, bicycle-style seat covered in battered black leather. Leather saddlebags hung over each side of the rear fender. Mounted with leather straps to one of the front forks was a leather rifle holster that extended up to the black-painted handlebar.

As Harold looked at the bike, Chester said, "My bother rode one of those for Patton during the war."

Sure enough, Harold noticed a picture resting on a couple metal pegs and leaning back against the pegboard of several soldiers on motorcycles. "Is your brother in the picture?" Harold asked.

"Yeah," said Chester. "He's second from the right." As Harold stepped over to look closer, Chester added, "He didn't make it home."

Harold looked back and said he was sorry to hear that.

"It happens," said Chester before turning to the second bike in line.

The second bike in line was a large Harley with a big, black faring and fiberglass saddlebags. The faring and gas tanks were trimmed with red pinstripe and the tanks had Harley Davidson decals on their sides. A thin coat of dust could not fully disguise the new-bike shine below. Somehow, considering the general disrepair of the house and farm, the bike seemed out of place. Or maybe it simply demonstrated a particular sense of priorities.

"Sweet, ain't she," Chester said. "Bought her last year in Millbrook."

A relieved smile showed that Harold admired the bike but was glad it wasn't his inheritance. "That's a lot of bike," he said thinking to himself that it was a lot more bike than the Hondas and Suzukis he had ridden.

"What did it run, if I could ask," Harold said.

"Well, it hurts a little still to talk about that," Chester said.

"Let's just say it wasn't cheap."

Harold looked at the bike and then looked at Chester, "What do you do if it falls over?"

"Well, I guess you pick it up," Chester said. "Mostly, I try not to fall over much."

Chester then said, "Well, I suppose I should introduce you to Magdelina already."

Walking back around the army bike, Chester gently removed the tarp from the bike closest to the front wall. Even in the dim light, the bike sparkled in red luster as it came into view. It had a bicycle-style seat like the green bike next to it, though smaller. But instead of a battered condition, the brown-leather seat on Magdelina was soft and supple. The frame tapered back in clean lines to the rear axle without the benefit of shock absorbers. The rear fender flared upward above an oval taillight with a translucent blue dot in the middle. The license plate hung below the taillight. A fat tire fit snuggly in the back fender. As he continued around the bike, Harold saw that the exhaust pipes hung low from the heads, ran back along the bottom of the frame and then swept up past the axle to finish in flared fishtails. The handlebar was a nearly straight chrome bar that ran across the top of a chrome front end. Two chrome springs were mounted at the top of the front end and Harold could see there were pivot points built into the mechanism. A thin, red fender was mounted above the thin, front tire. As Harold's eyes moved to the split tanks on top of the frame, instead of Harley decals, which Harold had somehow come to expect, someone had painted a curvaceous Spanish dancer on each side. With a red rose in her jet-black hair, her red dress hung low on her shoulders and exposed ample cleavage. A black garter, with its own red rose, adorned a thin and shapely leg that extended from a slit in the front of the dress. Long, thin arms were held high over her head with castanets in her hands. Though her eyes were looking down, and almost closed, her head was held high with attitude above a thin neck with a black choker that was also adorned with a red rose.

At the heart of the bike was the engine with black wrinkled block and heads and turned out with ample amounts of chrome. The chrome extended back to the transmission, which was also wrinkle black in between the chrome outer covers. Above the transmission was a large, curved-chrome tank that served as the bike's oil reservoir. Harold took all of this in silently. But the glow in his eye betrayed his admiration for the bike. It was richly adorned but, still, simple.

"I see you approve of Magdelina," Chester said with a smile. "Your uncle had her repainted a couple years ago. She's a real sweetheart, ain't she?"

"Why Magdelina?" Harold asked.

"Magdelina was a little Chiquita your uncle knew when he lived in Tijuana after the war. He was nuts about that girl."

"What happened?" Harold asked.

"Not sure. I get the idea her family didn't exactly approve of your uncle," Chester said. "Then your uncle got into some trouble and had to skedaddle back over the border."

Harold nodded as he looked back at the bike. "Can I sit on her," he asked.

"She's yours now," Chester said. "You can do whatever you want with her."

The seat sat low enough that, when Harold cautiously threw a leg over the top and sat down, he found that his knees bent comfortably with his feet flat on the ground. The bike tipped lightly off the kickstand and he rocked back and forth a couple times as though getting the feel of the machine.

"How's she feel?" asked Chester with a grin.

With the smaller bikes he'd rode, they always felt like he was riding up on top. With Magdelina, it was as though he was seated down in the heart of the bike, as though he were part of the machine. The foot controls were out at the front of the frame and, placing one foot, and then the other, onto the pegs so that the bike wouldn't tip over, he realized their placement enhanced the fit of rider to machine. To the right was a pedal that was mechanically linked to the rear brake. The pedal on the left was linked to a chrome rod that ran back by the transmission. Above this pedal was a chrome mechanism with a spring vertically mounted on its face and a cable running up to the left-hand lever.

Chester seemed to anticipate Harold's next question: "That's the mousetrap. It's actually a booster for the clutch but it looks enough like a mousetrap that that's what they call it."

Harold didn't have to say a word. He sat back and looked up at

Chester as a big smile spread across his face – a smile that said it all.

Chester chuckled, "Like I said, 'She's a sweetheart.' Just wait till you get her out on the road and she starts purrin' between your legs."

Harold also asked Chester about the unusual frontend assembly. "That's a springer," Chester explained. "It doesn't ride as smooth as the newer hydraulic forks, but it handles like a dream. It gives you a real solid feel for the road. Most people think it looks nicer, too. Well, I think so. Your uncle thought so, too."

Harold looked at the leather strip that ran between the gas tanks below a raised, chrome dash with the speedometer and the key switch. Stamped into the leather was a picture of a vulture sitting on a branch. Just below the vulture was the word "Gizzard."

"What's this?" Harold asked, pointing at the etching.

"Oh, well, lot of us called your uncle Gizzard," Chester said. "It was kind of a nickname."

"Why Gizzard?" Harold asked.

Chester chuckled again, "Don't get me wrong, when your uncle was a younger man, he was a fine-lookin' specimen. But years of riding with his face in the wind and such, well he got kind of a grizzled look on his face. Name fit his demeanor pretty good, too."

"What do you mean?" Harold asked.

"Well," Chester continued, "you couldn't ask for a better friend. He'd give you the shirt right off his back. But if Gizzard didn't know you, it would take a while for him to warm up to ya. I guess you could say he was a bit ornery at times."

Harold nodded, realizing it sounded a little like the way he remembered his father. He figured that probably had something to do with the duration of whatever feud there was between them. The bad blood had outlasted both of them. Harold knew that, once his father set his mind on something, hurricanes and earthquakes couldn't sway the man.

"Why don't you take her for a ride?" Chester suggested.

Harold's heart was pounding in anticipation. He looked back at Chester and smiled a devilish little grin.

"She's all gassed up and ready to go," Chester said. "I even ran a trickle charge on the battery over the weekend 'xpectin' you'd be out here sometime soon."

Harold pulled the envelope out of his pocket, opened and tipped it so that the key fell into his hand. He was about to put the key in the switch when Chester pointed out that the key merely locked and unlocked the switch. As it was already unlocked, Harold really didn't need the key. He put the key back in his pocket and turned the switch to "On." Chester stopped Harold again.

"It's just a suggestion," Chester said, "But you might want to give it a few slow kicks first, just to prime the carb a little."

Harold turned the switch to "Off" again and flipped out the rubber pedal on the kickstarter sticking up next to the right side of the transmission. When he attempted to kick down on the pedal, however, it barely budged.

"Try stepping off on this side so you can put your weight into it," Chester said.

Harold was beginning to feel a little flustered. With the other bikes he'd ridden, you got on, turned the key, pressed the starter button and off you went. He was discovering there were several nuances he needed to learn in order to ride this custom Harley Davidson.

After pushing the pedal through twice, Harold flipped the switch on again. At that point, Chester reached under the gas tank and showed Harold a lever on the top of the carburetor, which Chester called a tickler. He explained that it adjusted the fuel mixture when starting the bike. He also showed Harold a lever on the other side under the gas tank and smiled, "You'll need to turn the gas on. Oh, and don't forget to shut off the gas when you turn the bike off. If the float hangs up in your carb you could find yourself pouring gas into the cylinders."

Harold nodded slightly. With everything that had gone into it so far, Harold was anticipating that it would take considerable effort to get the bike started: he'd have to kick it several times before the engine would fire up and run. Instead, with the first post-priming kick, the engine roared to life.

Harold sat on the bike for a minute feeling it vibrate between his legs – listening to the low, throaty rumble of the engine. "You ever ride one of these before?" Chester asked almost belatedly.

"I've rode before," Harold said. But then he admitted this was the first time he'd ever ridden anything this big."

"It's pretty much like riding a smaller bike," Chester said, "except you may find it's a bit more powerful. Just don't override it."

Seeing the puzzled look on Harold's face, Chester said, "Get used to her a little before you open her up. I don't think your uncle left her to ya so you could kill yourself the first day out."

Harold winced a little, realizing this wasn't the first person to warn him not to get killed on the bike. But Harold nodded.

Chester pointed at the foot control on the left side. "It's one up for first gear. Three down from there – backward of most bikes," he said, speaking with a raised voice over the sound of the engine. "You also might want to favor the rear brake over the front a little, too."

Harold used his toe to yank the shift lever up into first gear. Then he started to let the clutch out as he turned the grip on the right end of the handlebars. Though he probably didn't need to give it as much gas as he did, it didn't matter. Harold had let the clutch out to fast and the bike jumped forward and died as he awkwardly caught the bike before it fell.

Chester could see that Harold was feeling a bit despondent by this time. He told him not to worry. "It happens," Chester said. "Just give it a little gas and ease the clutch out. You'll get used to it."

Harold put the bike back on the kickstand and reached between the tanks to shut the key switch off again. Chester intervened, "I don't think you need to prime it again."

Harold stopped to think for a minute and realized that, since he hadn't shut anything off, all he had to do was kick the bike again. However, on his first kick, the bike launched forward a little and almost came off the kickstand as it was still in gear. He sat down on the seat again and negotiated the shifter back into neutral, rolling the bike a little to make sure. Then he got off on the right side again and, this time when he kicked it, the pedal was about two-thirds of the way down when the engine popped, and the pedal whipped back up. As it came up, it threw Harold's foot off roughly. Harold felt more than a little pain in his ankle. He looked over to discover Chester was laughing again.

"I should've warned you about that," Chester said. "She usually warms up a little more than this before she bites back."

"Bites back?" Harold asked as though Chester was trying to tell him the bike was actually alive.

"She starts real nice when she's cold. She also starts real nice when she's at running temperature," he said. "She's just a little ornery when she's a little warmer than cold but a little cooler than hot."

"What do you do when she kicks back?" Harold asked feeling as though someone had just told him that his new dog has a tendency to bite its owner.

Chester was laughing again. "About the only thing you can do — get your foot out of the way as quick as you can."

"Thanks a lot," Harold said with just enough sarcasm to make Chester cough another throaty laugh again.

As Harold mounted the kicker again, he brought it down cautiously and was pleased when it didn't kick back. However, it also failed to start the bike. As Chester put it, "You still gotta kick her if you wanna ride."

Harold almost closed his eyes as he got up on the pedal again. Coming down hard as he held his breath, he was rewarded with the throaty rumble of the engine roaring to life again. Harold felt a small bit of satisfaction as though he was beginning to get the hang of it.

He pulled in the clutch and used his toe to shift the lever back into first again. At last, he was about to pull out of the barn when Chester tapped him on the shoulder. Harold looked over to find that Chester was holding out a pair of sunglasses. "You might need these," Chester said. "Cops can pull you over without 'em. Oh, and you can probably turn the tickler off on top of the carb now."

Harold looked like he was about to burst. His face was even beginning to turn a little red. Chester looked at him a minute wondering what would happen. Then, with his face stretching into a big smile, Harold accepted the glasses and said, "Thanks."

Chester stood in the drive watching as Harold pulled the bike out of the barn and down the driveway. He stopped at the end of the drive to contemplate which way to go. Even though it was dark the night before, and Harold had been a bit drunk at the time, he was a little more familiar with the road to the left. He guided the bike out onto the road and was about to cross the centerline to the westbound lane when Harold glanced back to his right. At the sight of a pickup bearing down the road, Harold locked up the brakes before he had a chance to pull in the clutch. He managed to stop before he was run down by the truck, which passed by blasting its horn in anger. But now the bike was sitting in the middle of the road and Harold had to get it started again.

He looked back at the barn and Chester was nowhere in sight. It occurred to Harold that Chester might have seen what happened and ducked away in time to save Harold's pride a little. Whatever the case, Harold felt it was best he got the bike started quickly on the chance another farmer came barreling down the road. Harold was about to kick the bike when he remembered that it was still in gear. This time, after shifting into neutral, Harold was too anxious to start the bike to worry about it kicking back. One kick later, it was running, and Harold was rolling down the road.

Slowly, cautiously, Harold gave the bike more gas. He heard a heavy clunk when he pulled in the clutch and popped the bike into second. By the time he hit third gear, Harold was doing close to 50 mph. The bike shifted smoothly into fourth gear as he continued past 60 mph.

The wind in his face felt good in light of the portion of his hangover that remained and the aftereffects of sleeping in a broken-down 1950s Chevy pickup truck overnight. The shower had helped. The ride was helping even more. Though the temperature was 70 degrees, the air felt cool and crisp as the morning sun burned the dew off the farmers' fields. In fact, the faster Harold rode, the colder the air felt. He began to wish he had a jacket.

"What a damn fool," he said to himself. "Here you are in bum-fuck Biesenthal with $17 in your pocket and you don't even have a coat. What the hell were you thinking?"

But his self-criticism was short lived as the exhilaration of the ride washed all other thoughts from his mind. There was a freedom to this ride that Harold had never felt before. And it was far more apparent with 1200 ccs of iron reverberating between his legs than on the little scooters he'd ridden before. His lungs filled with the fresh air of the countryside as his mind filled with an unfamiliar sense of self-confidence. Suddenly, he was no longer Harold Schneider, town drunk and dependent 27-year-old son. He was in control, commanding the iron below, directing it to go where he wanted it to go. He was part of the bike but, unlike in a car, he was also part of the world.

People climb into a car, close the door and take their private domain with them. They traverse crowded highways as though they're still in their own living rooms. A sweet, middle-aged woman, her face contorted in rage, makes an obscene gesture at a teenager while screaming a string of words that fit well with her one-fingered salute. It never occurs to her that the teenager may be a friend's grandson. And it's as if she thinks no one of consequence will ever see her behavior. She doesn't have to worry about someone seeing her, she's in her car. She doesn't have to worry about how her actions would affect her reputation because she's all alone. Who will notice?

But Harold found that it's not the same with a motorcycle. He realized that, instead of locking yourself away behind the wheel where you can pretend you're alone, with a motorcycle, you're right out there for everyone to see. There's no room for pretense when you act outrageously. People will see you and, if they know you, your reputation will suffer accordingly, not that Harold had much to worry about when it came to his bruised and battered reputation. And in Biesenthal, no one knew him anyhow. But sitting on this bike, purring down the highway, Harold was at one with the world. He and the birds passed through the same oxygen unimpeded by a glass and metal compartment. The experience made Harold feel good about himself in a way he hadn't felt in a long, long time.

Harold let the bike take him out about 5 miles down Willow Lane where he followed a frontage road to an onramp for the interstate. As he continued northwest on the interstate, he noticed the way people looked at him on the bike. A man in a white shirt and a tie cast an envious glance. A mother, with two children in the backseat, looked nervously Harold's way, as though it were a real concern that he might abruptly and randomly attack. A young guy in a souped-up Mustang yelled out the window, "Nice bike." With each encounter, it seemed as though his shirt stretched tighter across his chest.

About 5 miles down the interstate, however, Harold realized it was just too cold to continue without a jacket. A warm day walking on the sidewalk was a cool day on a motorcycle. His fingers were beginning to turn a little blue and his goose bumps had goose bumps. Harold took the next exit ramp and turned the bike back the other direction on the interstate. The cold, however, couldn't wash away the warm sensation washing over him as he rode Magdelina back towards Chester's farm where, with any luck, he could borrow a jacket.

Chapter 7 — Tex, Morticia and Cindy

Harold found Chester in the barn working on the old, red tractor across from the bikes. Chester had heard Harold pull up and, as Harold approached, Chester asked without looking up from what he was doing, "So, what do you think?"

"Sweet," said Harold. "She's really something."

Chester smiled as he asked Harold to pass a 9/16-inch, open-end wrench. "Yeah well, Gizzard sure new motorcycles."

Harold nodded in agreement and then mentioned, "I'd have gone further but it was getting a little chilly."

"I was thinking when you left you might find yourself wishing you had a coat," Chester said. "I think we can take care of that."

"You've got a coat I can borrow?" Harold asked.

"I'll do you better than that," Chester said. "Just give me a minute to finish changing the oil on old Betsy here."

"You call the tractor Betsy," Harold asked as he began to suspect Chester had a name for all the machinery.

"Nah, not really," Chester said. "I call her that sometimes but only when she cooperates. Other times … well, I've got some other names for this old piece of junk."

When he had finished, Chester gathered up the tools and dumped them unceremoniously on the workbench. He asked Harold to bring the Rubbermaid pan of dirty oil along, too, and gestured for Harold to leave it on an open spot on the workbench. Then Chester led Harold back to the house and up the stairs again. Chester opened a door that was against the wall to the left of where the stairs came up from the first floor. Behind the door was another flight of stairs going up. "Your uncle could've taken any one of these other rooms," Chester said, pointing to a couple doors on the opposite wall. "I think he just preferred the solitude of the attic."

Harold followed Chester up the stairs, which came up near the center of the attic with a 2X4 railing around three sides of the opening and an unfinished-plywood floor, mostly in front of the stair opening that extended close to the pitched walls of the roof so that pink insulation was visible around the edges of the room. A small octagon window at that end of the attic let in a stream of sunlight illuminating all the dust and particles in the air. A couple feet past the stairs, where the plywood ended, there was a brick chimney extending up through the roof. Beyond the chimney, like ribs of a whale, Harold could see the rafters supporting the ceiling below, the cavities between them filled with dirty-pink insulation. Several boxes and items were scattered about on top of the ribs.

Beside the chimney, and in front of the floorless area, a length of ¾-inch plumber's pipe was suspended on two ends by heavy wire and bore the weight of what Harold surmised was his uncle's Spartan wardrobe. Not far to the left, a mattress and box spring were sitting on the plywood perpendicular to the sloped roof. A small nightstand rose above the mattress on its left. On top of the nightstand, a yellowed photo of two smiling soldiers leaned back against the frame's center leg. To the right, a weathered oriental rug covered most of the area between the bed and the gable-end wall with the octagon window. Across from the bed was an old dresser with wooden handles. An ornamental mirrored tray was on top of the dresser with some loose change and a photo of a woman who looked a bit like the girl painted on Magdelina's gas tanks. To the right of the tray was another framed photo, this one of Harold's uncle. His uncle was older in this picture than in the military photo, but he was still relatively young. He was kneeling and holding a pump-action shotgun with one hand as it rested back against his shoulder. The other hand was wrapped affectionately around the neck of a Spaniel. On the ground in front of them were the carcasses of several ducks.

"That's my uncle?" Harold asked, pointing to the hunting photo.

"Yep," said Chester. "That's him, too, over by the bed. I'm the other handsome devil."

Harold could see the resemblance between his father and his uncle. He could even see a little of himself in his uncle's face. And next to his uncle, he vaguely recognized a younger, clean-shaven Chester.

Between the dresser and the stairs, four hooks were screwed to the sides of the pitched rafters below the roof. Hanging from one was a battered Confederate hat. Another had a brown-tweed sports coat, with matching pants, on a hanger and covered with plastic as though it had just come back from a dry cleaner, except that the plastic was covered with dust. The next hook was open. On the last hook was a worn and battered leather motorcycle jacket. The

Jacket hung with the sleeves open as though it had long since taken on the shape of Harold's uncle's arms. In places, the soft, black leather had tinges of velvety brown where the surface material was rubbed away by time and wear. In the back, however, rather than time, some incident had left a light-gray scar that faded away about four inches in from the shoulder. Hanging from the front below the zippered opening were a pair of attached-belt halves, one with the rusted buckle and the other more brown than black.

Chester took the coat off the hook and handed it to Harold saying, "This was you're your uncle's. I'm pretty sure he'd want you to have it. Kinda comes with the bike."

Harold took the coat reverently and examined it as though it were a rare archeological treasure. He paused to run a finger over the scar on the back.

"Some jerk ran your uncle off the road a few years back," said Chester.

"Did he get hurt?" asked Harold.

"Broke his leg," said Chester. "Banged him up a little otherwise."

Harold took the coat and slipped it onto one arm, over the shoulder, and plunged the other arm into the sleeve. The coat fit as though it was made for him. With the coat on, Harold felt bigger somehow – bigger and tougher. He liked the way it felt. He even liked the smell of leather. He wished there was a mirror handy so he could see how he looked in the coat.

"I figure you're about the same size as Gizzard," Chester said. Then, gesturing toward the floor below where the coat had hung, he added, "If they fit ya, these boots might come in handy, too. They'd make it a little less painful when Magdelina bites back."

Harold looked over and saw a pair of brown, faded cowboy boots standing open at the top the way the sleeves of the coat had formed to Gizzard's limbs. However, the boots were tipped to each side as the result of heals worn badly on the outsides suggesting his uncle was a bit bowlegged.

Harold took the boots, sat on the end of the bed, and held the bottom of one back to back with the bottom of his left foot. It looked good so he slipped his foot inside. Then he put on the other boot, got up and took a few steps back and forth. "Seems good," he said to Chester.

"Well, maybe you'd like to take Magdelina for another ride without freezin' your ass off," said Chester.

Harold smiled and went to follow him down the stairs. Just then, Chester stopped and said, "Anything this side of the chimney, you can figure it's yours. If it's on the other side of the chimney, do me a favor and ask me first."

The way he said it, Harold had the sense there was an implied invitation to stay, if Harold wanted. Still, he felt he should clear away any ambiguity. But before he could ask, as though Chester could read his mind, Chester said, "Stay as long as you like."

As Harold headed for the backdoor, Chester said, "Oh" and handed Harold a key. "Works on the backdoor only. This way you won't have to sleep in abandoned trucks anymore." Then he handed Harold a smaller key, "For the barn. Just make sure you don't leave it unlocked."

As Harold went out the backdoor, Chester went out the front. Harold walked across the backyard sliding the keys onto his key-ring while listening to Chester cussing as he apparently discovered that the screen door was knocked off the hinge. When Harold began rolling back out the driveway on Magdelina, he spotted Chester sitting on a wicker chair on the front porch. Harold lifted one hand lightly off the right-hand grip to wave. He wasn't sure if Chester nodded in reply or if he was merely rocking in the chair.

Harold was getting used to the bike already and didn't have any of the difficulties of his first ride. Back at the road, he headed west again planning to go into town. However, with the wind in his face, and not really paying attention, he missed his turn. He considered turning back but, instead, continued on and came to a road sign pointing to "Biesenthal" at the next intersection, under a sign that read "Route 46."

He turned left and soon found himself behind a gravel truck driving about 10 mph under the speed limit. Unfortunately, the road turned and twisted serpent-like leaving few opportunities to pass. Finally, there was a short straight-a-way. Harold could see a car coming from the other direction but decided he could make it. He pulled into the opposite lane of traffic and cracked the throttle. Magdelina responded with authority and he jumped from 45 to 75 mph almost instantly. He had reached 85 by the time he pulled back in the East-bound lane just before it went into a turn. It was then that he saw a turn lane to the right marked "Biesenthal" and realized it was his turn.

He hit the ramp with enough speed to challenge a far more experienced rider. A sense of panic gripped him by the throat as a thought flashed through his mind – "You won't last a week on that thing." Isn't that what his mother had said? Of course, she was assuming he'd die on the motorcycle while drunk. Here he was, stone-cold sober, and racing into the jaws of death. Still, a small voice suggested Harold should keep his head. He let off the throttle and tapped the rear brake. Though he didn't think he'd hit it that hard, the rear tire broke loose with a loud squeal.

A more experienced rider would have ridden it out concentrating to keep the bike under control until he had lowered the speed enough. But Harold didn't have that confidence yet. For Harold, the gods were rolling the dice and, for those precious seconds, his future hung in the balance. Suddenly, he was off the pavement and on the gravel. With all his concentration, he fought to keep the bike under control as though it were a wild mustang that was spooked by a snake. Eyeing the gravel, Harold recognized its painful potential. Finally, as his speed dropped enough, he brought the bike under control and came to a stop as a cloud of white-rock dust caught up and washed over him. Under his jacket, Harold felt a cool sensation and realized his shirt was soaked in sweat. He put his feet down and took several deep breaths as he watched the truck he'd passed go by. His face felt flushed and he imagined the driver looking his way and laughing.

Harold closed his eyes and rested his chin on his chest a moment. He took another deep breath as he took inventory of his situation. His jacket was dry and covered with dust; his shirt was wet and, since, in his panic, Harold hadn't pulled in the clutch, he would have to kickstart the bike again.

Harold kicked the bike up to first gear and knocked it down lightly into neutral. He rolled the bike a little to check that it wasn't in gear and prepared to kick the pedal through to start the bike again. Poised over the pedal, it suddenly occurred to him, "What if the bike won't start? Chester had said there was a point between hot and cold when the bike was harder to start; what if this was that point?" For a moment, he pictured himself stranded on the side of the road. Then, holding his breath, he kicked and was immediately rewarded with the low rumble of the bike idling below him. A flicker of a smile crossed his lips and he started pulling forward, preparing to get back on the road. He had moved only a few feet when a horn blasted to his left. Startled, Harold came to an unsteady stop again as a green Grand Prix sped by, a teenage boy hanging out the passenger window and yelling something Harold couldn't make out. At first, Harold felt that hot chill of embarrassment again. Then, it dawned on him he hadn't done anything wrong. "I wasn't pulling out yet. I planned to look … Asshole," he muttered to himself.

Taking a good look over his left shoulder now, and finding the road clear, Harold pulled onto the pavement and continued on his way, though a bit more cautiously. It took him a couple miles before his pulse returned to normal and the adrenaline was burned out of his veins, replaced intravenously with confidence that seemed to come from the steady and powerful throb of Magdelina purring between his legs. Like the sun coming out from behind the clouds, that confidence spread through his body, eventually working its way to his right hand, which steadily rolled up the throttle. He had barely hit 55 when he found that he was entering the village limits and had to back off the throttle again.

Up ahead was a stop light that had just turned red. As Harold rolled to a stop, a rider on a red Kawasaki pulled to a stop beside him in the right side of the lane. Where Harold sat with his knees bent and his feet flat on the ground, the Kawasaki rider's toes were pointed down stretching for the ground. Though the 19 or 20ish rider was crouched over behind a small sport fairing, he was still high enough to look down at Harold's Harley. After glancing from one end of Magdelina to the other, the rider flipped up the tinted visor on his helmet exposing a stubbly beard and mustache. He smiled at Harold enthusiastically and said, "Nice bike."

Harold hadn't known what to expect from the Kawasaki rider. In Harold's mind, they both rode bikes, but they traveled in different universes. It never occurred to him that this 'rice rider' might have a Harley at home in the garage and had merely chosen the sport bike to ride today or that this rider might have many more miles under his belt on motorcycles. It also didn't occur to Harold to return the compliment. After all, Kawasaki's were a dime a dozen. An old-custom Harley, such as Magdelina, was a rarity. But that wasn't why Harold didn't consider complimenting the other rider's bike. Though he had only taken ownership of Magdelina that day, the aura of social superiority in the motorcycle world had firmly taken hold in his mind already. He had jumped to the top of the motorcycle food chain; he should act accordingly. And so, it felt wrong to politely return the gesture and say something nice about the Kawasaki. It was as though doing so would break some unwritten rule. Harold's mind searched for the correct response. He glanced at the other rider with a look suggesting Harold received such compliments 10 times a day and was rather bored by the whole thing. Then, he nodded ever so slightly and mumbled, "Thanks."

The other rider accepted Harold's measured response as though he expected nothing more. Harold turned his gaze to the road ahead, and the red light swaying lightly in the breeze as it hung above the intersection, as if to say that the conversation was over. The two sat side by side mostly looking straight ahead, though the Kawasaki rider occasionally glanced back at Magdelina, possibly trying to think of something else to say or, maybe, just to admire the Harley some more. Apparently sensing there was nothing else to say, and seeing the light turn yellow for cross traffic, the rider began revving the Kawasaki in preparation for a burnout. Socially superior or not, Harold sensed that, while the Harley had the upper hand in terms of class, the Kawasaki was out of his league in a drag race. He glanced toward the other rider who smiled and flipped his visor back down just in time for the light to change and for the Kawasaki to pull the front tire off the ground as the rider burned away from the intersection. Acting cool, Harold pulled away from the light as though there was no urgency, and he were all alone on the road – ignoring the Kawasaki completely.

Harold turned left on Main Street several blocks down and found himself in front of the bar where he'd arrived in town with Miles the night before. There were several cars in the parking lot, as well as a pair of Harleys right outside the front door. Though it occurred to him he might find the bikers from the night before inside, Harold stopped his bike and pedaled his feet to back the bike into a parking space next to the other bikes.

The bikes were choppers like his. One had a long, extended front-end and a picture of a snake intertwined with a naked woman painted on each side of a black split gas tank. The bike was nice though it showed a little more grease and road grime than Magdelina. The other bike was also basically black, but with a less radical front-end. A black peanut tank sat on top of the frame. If there were chrome parts on this bike, they were well hidden by grease and rust. While it was clear that the prior bike was assembled with care and purpose, the latter bike appeared as though it was put together by someone who had never seen a motorcycle before and was only guessing. Parts hung precariously here and there. In some cases, parts were held in place by bailing wire and a prayer. As expected with such a bike, a significant puddle of oil had formed on the ground below the bike. Looking closer, Harold noticed that a bungee cord was holding the battery in place under a torn-leather seat.

Harold put his bike on its kickstand and locked the ignition before proceeding into the tavern. As his eyes adjusted, Harold found a number of patrons sitting at a couple tables and at the bar. Most looked like construction worker's or farmers. At the right end of the bar were the likely owners of the Harleys outside. Like the night before, these bikers wore patches on their backs. However, Harold noticed the patches were different, apparently representing a different motorcycle club.

The top patch curved down over the center patch and was embroidered with the name "Banshee Riders." At the bottom of the vests, the bikers had a small patch with the letters "MC" and, a little higher and to the right, the two capital letters that were obviously the state's initials. In the middle of all the writing, the bikers wore embroidered center patches that were strangely erotic. As though her body was the frame of a motorcycle, a naked woman, with blood-dripping fangs in a screaming mouth, under burning red eyes, had long black hair pulled back tight from her head. Her arms were stretched forward, above bare breasts, to grasp the axle that went through a thin, spoked motorcycle wheel. Her tight waste curved back past naked hips to the point where her thighs hung down and were bent at the knees so that her feet could grip the rear axle of blurred spokes connected to a fat tire spinning between her legs. Sitting with its hips pinching hers was a skeleton wearing heavy biker's boots, cutoff vest and a German-style WWII helmet that had a Swastika on the side. Like a rodeo rider, the biker had his right arm up in the air while his left hand was firmly gripping and pulling back the woman's hair and head.

From their appearance, Harold quickly matched each up with the bikes outside. The one, a shorter biker looked as though he might be oriental, or Mexican, Harold wasn't really sure. This biker wore a clean, black-leather vest over a relatively clean leather jacket. His jeans were fairly new if not relatively clean. His boots were also relatively new. He had a neatly trimmed goatee, dark hair pulled tight in a ponytail and a clean black Harley shirt. On the upper, front-right portion of the vest, he wore a patch that read "Samurai." Harold deduced that he probably owned the bike with the mural.

The other biker's appearance was the antithesis of the first biker. He was put together as haphazardly as the rat bike out front. His Levi vest had light-grey tendrils of thread where the sleeves were torn away. While the club patches were carefully placed on back, the vest was otherwise covered with various patches sewn on only generally right-side up and, sometimes, partially covering other patches. One patch offered "Mustache Rides - $1." Others were company logos, such as a couple of Harley patches, a Pennzoil patch and an "S&S Cycles Performance Carburetors" patch. Other patches offered up various profane suggestions. He had long, scraggly, light-brown hair that worked its way, like thorny vines, down over his shoulders. The beard was parted down the middle, creased by the wind rather than any intentional attempt at grooming. Probably in his mid-30s, he was well over 6 foot and appeared strong but wiry with long legs encased in oil-soaked jeans. The one patch on the front of his vest that appeared to have been placed with purpose was a rectangular name patch that read 'Tex.'

Harold also noticed a tall brunette standing behind the two bikers. She also wore a vest, a small leather garment that accentuated her thin yet shapely figure. The back of her vest also had a top rocker with the name of the club, but, at the bottom, was another patch that read "Property of Tex" in three rows. Her black-leather pants looked as though they were painted on.

She had high, black, pointed-leather boots with spiked heels. Her leather riding jacket was tapered at all the right places. Under the jacket, she wore a black Harley T-shirt that was fringed with black lace. The shirt was small enough to reveal substantial cleavage while allowing her pierced navel to peak out at the bottom. Her round face was attractive but with heavy makeup that failed to fully hide an earlier battle with acne. Her big, brown eyes looked out doe-like on the world. When Harold came in and the girl looked his way, he could see a kind of innocence in those eyes. But he saw something else, too – a hint of instability and unpredictability.

Harold strode to the bar and nodded to the bikers. The taller biker glanced briefly his way, as the girl continued to check him out. It seemed the shorter biker was taking the measure of Harold, too, while still engaged in a conversation with the taller biker. At the bar, Harold casually raised his hand to catch the bartender's attention. When he took the beer stein offered by the bartender, Harold noticed that the bikers were apparently between turns in a game of darts. As the taller biker walked to the right of the bar to face a dartboard around the corner of the bar, next to the hall with the bathrooms and pay phone, Harold noticed that the girl was continuing to pay him attention. She gave Harold a long stare. But what was that he saw in her eyes – flirtation, contempt. Whatever the case, Harold sensed it was best to keep his distance. As casually as possible, he glanced her way, careful not to look her in the eyes but also careful not to look away too quickly.

At a glance, he noticed the name Morticia sewn on the patch on the front of her vest. He had no way of knowing that her name was really Brenda Meyers or that she had spent time, off and on, in juvenile homes and prisons since she was 12. He had no way of knowing that her first brush with the law came about when she used scissors to stab an unsuspecting classmate in the hand. In detention, she experienced rape at the hands of her captors. By 15, after returning to the detention center for a second tour, Brenda was on the run. She got by selling herself on the street. Her income, however, was not enough to keep up with her burgeoning drug habit. It didn't help her finances when she graduated to heroin. She had shacked up with several men by the time she hit 17. That's when she met Tex.

She was at a bar in Amarillo, Texas, with her pimp boyfriend. In a drunken rage, having rightfully concluded that Brenda had taken money from him while he was passed out at the bar, the pimp boyfriend slapped Brenda and knocked her off her feet. She came off the floor charging towards her pimp with her claws out ready to scratch. But he had an advantage of about 120 pounds and would knock her to the ground again and again before the claws had a chance to dig in. The fight had started just as Tex and a couple other bikers had walked in the bar. Their heads turned to watch, they proceeded slowly towards the bar. Then, almost as an afterthought, Tex stopped and said, "Fuck this." The next thing Brenda knew, Tex had knocked the pimp to the ground and was putting his boots to the pimp's head.

Tex had helped Brenda back to her feet. No sooner was she standing than she started kicking the pimp in the head, too. Tex pulled her away to the bar and, while laughing, asked her if she'd like a drink. Though it wasn't exactly love-at-first sight, at least not in the classical sense, the two made a connection. They were a consummated couple before the night was over. Brenda had found a protector and Tex had found someone to protect.

They moved into Tex' trailer and Brenda took a job as a stripper. She augmented the hourly wages and the tips truck drivers and oil field roughnecks tucked into her garter belt, by turning occasional tricks. In the meantime, Tex sold meth for a member of a 1% club in the area and took an occasional gig as a welder on the oil platforms out in the Gulf.

It wasn't that Tex never hit Brenda. Once in a while, during a drunken and drug-induced rage, Tex would knock Brenda around a little. But from Brenda's perspective, there was never anything vicious about it. Prior boyfriends had done much worse. When Tex lashed out in anger, the violence was short and severe, but it was administered with a purpose – to adjust her behavior. To Brenda, it also seemed cathartic. He might slap her, and slap her hard, but he seldom slapped her twice. Upon sober reflection, she saw Tex as more just when administering physical punishment. Even with a rare arbitrary beating, considering her deep-seeded sense of guilt, she believed that she somehow deserved it.

Another plus with Tex was that, though he wouldn't do so in public, privately, Tex would demonstrate a soft, caring and sympathetic side, especially after such episodes. He never apologized, but he seemed to care. He also remained fiercely protective.

Tex' protective side had developed into a little game for Brenda. If he was too preoccupied with his brothers, his bike or another woman, Brenda would find an easy mark at the bar or at a party and would come on to the guy until Tex noticed. If he didn't notice soon enough, Tex might have to go searching for Brenda. On several occasions, he'd discovered her having sex with some guy in the backseat of a car or out behind a bar. On a couple occasions, he even found her doing generally the same thing with another girl. It seemed almost a coin toss whether Tex would get jealous or just go back to the bar. If the prior, there was a good chance he would beat the crap out of some guy.

Had Harold reacted differently, Brenda might have started working her charms on the new biker who'd recently entered the bar in Bristol. Tex and Samurai were not only playing one-on-one darts, they were also engaged in a serious discussion without her. Brenda was feeling neglected. But the biker had ignored her and, while telling herself that this new biker was obviously an asshole, the only possible explanation when a guy refused her natural enticements, apparently, she would have to find another distraction.

Harold was only in the bar about five minutes when a younger trio came through the door. Two young men and a girl, probably no more than 19 or 20, sidled up to the bar unconsciously between Harold and the bikers and ordered a round of drinks.

Brian and Keith had played on the local high school football, basketball and baseball teams as members of the class that graduated the previous year. Cindy had graduated in the same class. However, rather than an emphasis on sports, she brought home reasonably good grades and was involved in various clubs and organizations. After graduating, she had surprised folks when she decided to take classes at the local junior college for a couple years. Bets had her going off to college somewhere. But she had dated Brian for several years and didn't want to leave him. If she knew that he was less committed to a long-term relationship – to marriage, she probably would have gone straight to a four-year school. But he liked having her around and the subject hadn't really come up until recently, and now the school year she'd missed was ending. Besides, she argued that she was saving a lot of money by taking her core classes at the local college.

Brains weren't Cindy's only major asset. Soft-spoken and thoughtful of others, she had a sweet disposition that made her popular in school. But Cindy also exuded a girl-next-door kind of beauty – fresh, vibrant and sincere. In a strapless white dress, with prints of red lilies, she had a spring-time aura that could bring a dead man's hormones back to life.

While Brian was a talented athlete, Keith was a star in all three sports they'd both lettered in. He had accepted a scholarship to play football at State and hadn't been in town since Christmas. When Cindy ran into him that morning, she suggested they go see Brian at the hardware store his family owned and where he was working. There, Cindy further suggested they take the happy reunion across the street to the bar for a few drinks. She had just turned legal drinking age and it seemed a very adult idea.

They came in the bar laughing and talking about their days in high school and exciting plans for the future. Cindy hardly noticed the leather-clad bikers at the far end of the bar. On the other hand, though the bikers continued their discussion about the finer points of barroom brawling, as though their hot-chick radars had announced her arrival, Tex and Samurai briefly glanced Cindy's way, just long enough for brief flashes of lustful appreciation to dance in their eyes. Though brief, the looks didn't go unnoticed by Morticia as she intently listened to Tex and Samurai's discussion. She hung on their words as though they were leading experts in the field, and she didn't want to miss a word. And they were approaching the topic from a technical perspective – the best tactics and weapons, how to quickly gain the upper hand and other refinements of the art.

Morticia had experienced more than her fair share of altercations in and out of drinking establishments – the beatings from boyfriends and pimps, the scratching fights with other women. But she'd never considered studying on the subject. It never occurred to her that she could improve on her techniques in the field. Her approach to barroom brawling was to explode with anger and wild energy. The idea of approaching it with a more refined and thoughtful approach somehow intrigued her. So, though she had little to add to the discussion, she soaked in every word of their lecture. The only distraction allowed was the follow-up glance she gave the 'citizens' (non-motorcycle club folk) and, in particular, the attractive young girl. Morticia wasn't one to wait for a good reason to feel resentment or jealousy. The instant resentment she felt for Cindy was backed up by several years of envy and spite for 'those prissy little things' from the refined category where Cindy obviously belonged.

Had Cindy paid Morticia any attention, she might have seen the sneer on the biker girl's lip. Cindy might have felt a cold sensation running down her spine when she saw the craziness in Morticia's eyes. She might have realized that there was a black-leather leopard preparing to pounce. But Cindy didn't have that streetwise common sense that considered and gauged every situation. She was engrossed in her friends and never contemplated that an attack could come unprovoked and suddenly – without any warning.

For the moment, Cindy was safe. Morticia had turned back to her male companions as well. The lecture had just turned into a fierce debate. Tex had taken issue with something Samurai had said.

"I'm telling ya," Samurai stated flatly, "I could seriously fuck you up with this." While speaking, the shorter biker palmed the bottom of a beer glass. "This is the most dangerous weapon in the place," he continued.

Tex frowned and said, "What are you talking about?"

"It's a beer glass," said Samurai. "No one expects anything when they see you've got a beer glass in your hand." Then Samurai jabbed the open end of the glass towards Tex' face, splashing a little of the contents on his beard. Stopping just short, Samurai said, "A glass will slice someone's face open like a razor, only worse. They'll be picking glass outta their face. And while they're realizing how messed up they are, you knock 'em down and kick the crap out of 'em."

Tex snorted condescendingly, "Just like you fuckin' Japs, always sneaking up on bastards."

"Fuck you," Samurai said without any real indignation. In fact, the debate ended as abruptly as it started as they laughed and slammed their beer glasses together, so hard it was a wonder the glass didn't shatter in the toast.

As the two bikers took swigs from their glasses and moved on to some other topic of discussion, Morticia was holding her near-ly empty beer glass in the palm of her hand the way Samurai had demonstrated. She moved her head from side to side so as to examine the way it fit in her hand, as though there might be a difference from a different angle. It was as though she were ex-amining a new kind of rock she had found in an archeological dig. Then she glanced back at the pretty girl a couple feet away at the bar. A moment later, Morticia's hand was holding the bottom of a jagged and broken glass that dripped with blood. On the floor at her feet was Cindy, her hand on her face and blood squirting between her fingers. Cindy's companions were standing, beer glasses in hands, with their mouths hanging open as their brains tried to make sense of what had just happened. As clarity set in, they glanced up from Cindy to the biker chick with the bloodied glass in her hand. Instinct took their minds from shock to out-rage. One yelled, "Get the glass." But before they moved, before the thought went from their brains to their bodies, their eyes shifted slightly to the left where they took in a pair of outlaw bikers who had just turned in their direction.

As quickly as the younger men started to step forward, they stopped in their tracks. In a defensive gesture, Brian barked out, "We were just standing here." And as he pointed at Morticia, he added, "She did it."

The incident had happened so suddenly that the only person who really saw what happened was Morticia. Harold, sitting just to the left of the trio was as startled as Samurai and Tex. Harold turned when he heard the scream. He saw Morticia with the glass and then turned his attention immediately to the bikers. This was the universal reaction of everyone in the bar, everyone except Tex, Samurai, and Morticia. Then Harold looked back at Morticia and the girl on the floor. He looked back at the boys as Brian was pointing at the biker chick and yelling, "She just stabbed her in the face, for no reason."

It was as Harold was looking at the younger men that he and everyone else in the place heard a loud and threatening voice growl, "You stupid bitch?"

It was as though the bar, and everyone in it, were suspended, for the merest of moments, in a freeze frame. Even Brian had ceased his protests. Then the moment was shattered into fast action as Tex stepped forward and grabbed Morticia by the wrist above the bloodied glass. He yanked her hand up and squeezed hard enough that Morticia dropped the glass and hollered in pain as tears sprang from her eyes.

Tex yelled again, "You stupid fucking bitch." Then he grabbed her by the hair and dragged her out the door kicking and screaming.

Samurai was as startled as anyone. However, he reacted as though this wasn't uncharted territory – as someone who knew that violence always could erupt suddenly. Samurai surveyed the surroundings in search of any threats. The two young men were now crouching on the floor beside Cindy. Samurai's gaze finally settled on Harold, as though he were the most likely to cause a problem. Harold thought he read a warning in the biker's eyes. He merely shrugged as though to say, "I have no idea what's going on." Still, Harold wasn't sure what to expect. So, he was caught off guard when the biker said, "Grab a bar towel or something to stop the bleeding."

Just as Harold accepted a bar towel from the bartender, a bike roared to life outside. For a moment, all eyes turned towards the door. They couldn't see Tex and Morticia from inside the bar, but everyone starred at the door as though expecting to see right through it. They collectively looked that way and heard the bike roll onto the road before the throttle opened wide and the sound wound into the distance.

The remaining biker seemed to recognize that he was suddenly outnumbered. He also noticed the bartender was on the phone. Looking back at Harold, he nodded and glanced at the girl on the floor as though to say, "Look after her," and then headed for the door himself. No one tried to stop him, and he was soon headed out of town as well.

As Harold handed the bar towel to one of the boys on the floor, he looked around and saw that all the faces had turned to him. It dawned on him that they might not know he wasn't with the three who had just left. He considered leaving but wasn't sure that was a good idea either. No one was making a move towards him and he thought it might look guilty if he ran out the door, too. By this time, there was blood all down the front of Cindy's dress, darker red but blending with the red prints of lilies. The towel had also quickly changed from white to crimson. Harold asked the bartender for another towel and, as he handed it to the one boy again, he said, "Put some pressure on it."

With his participation in her first aid, Harold noticed that the others in the bar were no longer staring at him as though he were guilty as an accessory to the assault. One of the other patrons even asked Harold what happened as a small crowd began to form around Cindy and the boys. Harold shrugged his shoulders and said, "I have no idea," and glanced at the door again when he heard a siren's wail.

The girl, still quietly in shock, was on her third bar towel when the police and paramedics arrived. Harold was watching when the paramedics lifted the blood-soaked towel from Cindy's face. For an instance, which was all the time it took for the blood to flow out and conceal the wound, Harold saw a wide, circular red line that started just below the right eye, extended down across the nose and curved back and up again on her left cheek. It was nearly a perfect circle and the same diameter as a beer glass.

Hearing that the damage had been done by bikers, the police instinctively turned from the bartender to Harold as paramedics came in the door.

"I never saw them before," Harold said as one officer copied Harold's personal information from his driver's license. Hearing from one of the boys that Harold wasn't with the other bikers, the policeman turned back to Harold and asked if he'd seen what happened.

Harold shrugged his shoulders and started to answer when one of the victim's young companions, his emotions boiling over, interrupted as he stammered in tears, "This crazy -- fucking bitch -- jammed a glass in her face -- for no reason. She didn't even say anything. We're standing here talking -- and this biker bitch just cuts her."

The cop, who had turned to Brian when he interrupted, now turned back to Harold, the cop's face asking if that was what Harold saw, too.

But Harold just shook his head, "Like I said, I didn't see a thing. I was just standing here and I heard their friend scream. I turned around and saw her laying on the floor," he said as he pointed at Cindy.

"He didn't have anything to do with it," Brian bellowed as he continued to cry. "It was that fucking biker chick."

The other officer, sensing he had his hands full with the young, emotional friend of the victim, handed Harold his driver's license. The cops turned their attention to calming the victim's friends, questioning others in the bar, and completing their reports on the incident.

Harold wasn't sure what to do for a minute. The cop hadn't exactly excused him. Harold considered walking around the cops and the boys to finish his beer but then decided that might not be the best idea either. He also considered simply walking out the door, but he really didn't want to hear one of the cops yell, "We're not done with you yet." So, Harold stood there for a couple minutes. When no one asked him any more questions, Harold nudged the one cop on the arm and asked, "Can I leave?'

Only half paying attention to Harold, the cop nodded his consent and Harold climbed on his bike. Somehow, continuing his ride didn't make as much sense anymore and Harold turned the bike back to Chester's farm. He also rode a lot slower going back then he did coming out.

Chapter 8 — The Invitation

Though Chester never asked, Harold made a point of volunteering to help out around the farm. Chester seemed pleased to take Harold up on several of the offers. When Harold would offer to help, Chester was likely to rub his chin and stare at Harold a bit, as though sizing him up for a particular task, then suggest, "Well, you could run some wire (barbed wire) on the fencing out front" or "I got a tree stump in the field out back. Wanna have a go at that?"

It was more physical labor than he'd done in a while and Harold was feeling a bit sore as a result. What was really funny, however, is that Harold was willingly offering to do chores for Chester when he used to complain and stall every time his mother had asked him to complete a task as simple as cutting the grass back in Poplar Grove. Considering that Chester was allowing him to stay in the attic at no charge, Harold felt it only made sense that he would pitch in and do his share around the farm. Since Chester was also sharing his food, it was clear to Harold that he couldn't take Chester's charity for granted indefinitely. Chester must have been of the same mind. A few days after Harold's arrival, Chester pointed out, "Suppose you'll be needing to find some work, less you got another uncle who left you a fortune or somethin'."

Between gas for the bike, a couple more beers in town and a couple hotdogs, Harold was nearly broke.

On the first Saturday since his arrived in Biesenthal, he spent the entire morning digging holes for fence posts. About noon, he saw Chester riding the tractor out across the eastern field to where Harold was working. "You gotta be gettin' hungry about now," Chester said. "Hop on back." Harold hung onto Chester's shoulders and stood precariously on the trailer hitch as Chester drove the tractor back to the farmhouse.

Chester had made some soup and sandwiches, along with a large jar of iced tea. As he poured a glass of tea for Harold, Chester brought up the subject of Harold's finances again: "I sure appreciate you helpin' out around here. I suppose I could give you a little cash ..."

"With you letting me stay here, and feeding me half the time, I don't suppose I've got much right to go asking you to pay me, too."

"Well, all the same, I figure you could probably use a little scratch now and then," Chester said.

Harold nodded, wincing at this far-too-familiar subject. Back home with his mother, food was always in the fridge and, though she wasn't an endless resource, Harold could always hit her up for cash from time to time. She would grumble and complain but would usually come through with a twenty or something. Harold had no delusions that he could expect the same here with Chester - he had not traded one meal ticket for another. He knew he had to do something about his financial plight and realized it was time to consider the unthinkable – getting a job.

"You wouldn't have heard of any jobs around here? Harold asked.

Chester pondered on the question a few seconds and then said, "If you're interested in that kind of work, I think I saw a "Help Wanted" sign in front of the tool-and-die manufacturer on the south side of town. Got any experience with that?"

When Harold shook his head "Not much" Chester said, "Well, sometimes they hire folks for shipping and receiving." Then, almost as an afterthought, he added, "I think I saw a sign at the Sinclair station this morning, too."

"Where's that?" Harold asked.

"Best bet is you head east on Willow to Timber Trail. Turn right until you hit Highway 36. Turn right and follow that into town," Chester said. "You'll see Speedy's filling station on your left as you come into town."

That afternoon, Harold rode out to Route 36 and followed that into town. Speedy's was a small Sinclair station with a two-bay garage for service and repairs. Sid, who was known to some as Speedy, a nickname he'd earned through his hobby of dirt-track racing, hadn't had a lot of interest shown in the position.

"I'm getting tired of dropping what I'm doing every time a customer comes in for gas," said Sid, a short, wiry character who smelled of cigar and had grease stains on his hands and arms that seemed almost permanent. "The job doesn't pay a whole lot."

At the moment, Harold found that a subject statement. It was his first paying gig in quite a while. He figured he'd make enough to cover his food, gas, and beer and laughingly told himself, "Mom would have a heart attack if she knew I was working."

Sid described how to care for customers who came in for gas. "Clean their windows and offer to check under the hood. But while you're checking the oil, look at the hoses and belts – anything else we might be able to sell them.

"Other than that, when you're not busy with customers, you can clean up around here. I might have you run to the parts store once in a while, too. And there's opening and closing, whichever you're here for. If you work out, maybe you can do some oil changes and such."

Harold was on the job about a week when, as he changed the oil on a Ford station wagon, he heard the pneumatic bell ring as motorcycles rumbled up to the pumps outside. Sid had run to the parts store to for a starter for Ford. Harold made sure the oil was draining into the rolling drain, placed the wrench and drain-pan bolt on the lift below the chassis and headed outside to take care of the customers.

About seven bikes were sitting on both sides of the outer pumps and the leather-clad bikers were already filling the bikes, using one pump for one side of the island and the other for the other side. The one closest to the station had his back to Harold and Harold saw they were "Banshee Riders," like the bikers he'd seen in the bar the day the girl was attacked. Harold hesitated for a second but then figured he had nothing to worry about and continued out to the pumps. It was then that he saw Samurai on the far side of the island. Realizing Samurai had also seen him, Harold nodded in recognition.

"Hey man, how you doing?" asked Samurai as though he and Harold were old friends, while passing the hose to another biker who began filling his tank.

Hearing the friendly tone of Samurai's greeting to the gas jockey, several of the other bikers turned to check Harold out, some craning their necks from the other side of the pumps. Samurai gestured to Harold and said, "This is the guy who was at the bar when that crazy bitch cut the girl." Then he turned to Harold and said, "That was some crazy shit, eh?"

"Yeah," Harold agreed. "I guess so."

"I heard you were pretty cool with the cops," Samurai said. When Harold appeared surprised, Samurai added, "I know a couple other people who were there. They kinda filled me in. Said the cops kept trying to get you to talk but you didn't tell 'em nothin'."

Of course, Harold hadn't told the cops anything because he didn't really know anything. The cops received descriptions of Tex, Samurai, and Morticia from other people in the bar and, apparently, the attack had come so suddenly – so unexpectedly – no one had actually seen what happened. But all the same, Harold liked that he had, inadvertently, gained a reputation as someone who could be trusted not to go blabbing to the cops. He particularly liked that, in this case, it was a member of a motorcycle 'gang' who was expressing his trust in Harold.

Samurai engaged Harold in what some might have mistaken for small talk. Harold had the feeling, however, that the biker was conducting a quick interview: "You new in town?" "Was that your scooter I saw outside the bar the other day?"

"I just moved up from Poplar Grove," Harold explained. "Yeah, that's my bike" and he gestured with his head out back by the retaining wall to the one side of the station where Magdelina was parked.

"Nice scooter," Samurai said. "How long you had it?"

"Not long," Harold admitted, but intentionally neglected to fill in any more of the blanks. He sensed it might be better not to let on how green he was as a rider. It didn't fit an image that was beginning to fit as comfortably as his uncle's weathered leather jacket.

He casually asked Samurai, "Did they catch her?"

"No way man," Samurai said. "She and Tex are probably halfway to California or Mexico 'bout now."

Harold looked a little puzzled again. "Aren't you worried?"

Samurai laughed. "I've got nothing to worry about, bro. I stopped by the police station later in the day."

"How did that go?" Harold asked with an expression of surprise on his face.

"They hassled me a little. Not too bad," Samurai said. Then, with a grin, he added, "I told the cops I tried to catch up to them, you know, so I could convince them to turn themselves in. Yeah, the cops didn't believe it either. But then, what could they do?"

"Do you have any idea why she did that," Harold asked.

"Sure," said Samurai, "She's fuckin' nuts"

"Chicks don't come any squirrelier than Morticia," one of the other bikers added as several others nodded and grunted in agreement.

"Nothing against Tex," Samurai said. "I mean, he's as righteous as they come. But that bitch always was a train wreck just waitin' to happen. Best thing Tex could do is to ditch the bitch, and the sooner the better. When she goes down, she'll probably take him with her."

From the way Samurai was describing the relationship, Harold had a sense Tex wasn't likely to dump her. He may have dragged her out of the bar by the hair, but it sounded as though Tex was primarily interested in helping Morticia get away from the law.

Samurai seemed to read Harold's mind. "Yeah, he'll never do it," Samurai said. "He loves the crazy bitch."

With all the tanks topped off on their bikes, one of Samurai's brothers, a gangly biker with a badly pock-marked face and a name patch that read 'Kilroy,' asked, "My brother here seems to think you're cool. If you're so cool, maybe you'll let us slide on the gas, right?"

Harold looked at the man trying to hide a mounting sense of panic. It wasn't just that Harold was new to the job and was reluctant to jeopardize his position. It was also that, though Harold was a considerable drunk, he had never been much of a thief. Once, while in junior high, he tried to shoplift some Sea-Saw shrimp cocktail from a convenience store. His only motivation was to prove himself to his friends. The owner of the store, a Middle Eastern man Harold had seen in the store since Harold was seven or eight, had caught Harold in the act. Instead of calling the police, however, the man had sat Harold down and asked him why he was doing that. In the course of a short conversation, Harold went from the horror of being caught, to shame over his actions to a sense that he'd sort of made a friend. From that time forward, when Harold went to the store and saw the owner, they would chat for a while. It was Harold's only real attempt at thievery, and it had fairly well cured him of any compulsion for stealing he might otherwise have had. Now, this biker was asking Harold to steal from his new boss.

Harold was about to tell the bikers to go on, deciding that the solution to the dilemma was to pay for their gas out of his own pocket, even though this would compound his own financial difficulties. But just as Harold opened his mouth to speak, Samurai interjected, "What are you fuckin' with him for? You wanna get him fired?"

Kilroy shrugged and grinned, as though it was all a big joke as a stocky biker with a shaved head stepped up to Harold and pulled a wad of cash out of his pocket. The biker slapped a $20 into Harold's palm. "This should cover it," the biker said and, before Harold could add the totals from each side of the pump, the biker turned and climbed onto his bike. The pump facing Harold read $9.53. Assuming the other side was about the same, Harold figured he was OK. And if it ran over a little, well, Harold was prepared to pay the whole thing a minute earlier, anyhow.

"Yeah, that's cool," Harold said to the bald biker.

The bald biker nodded slowly as though pondering what Harold's response implied. Then, apparently having made up his mind, he asked, "Why don't you come by Hildie's Hideout when you're done here?"

There was something different about this biker. He was more circumspect, somehow. Harold wasn't sure what it was but, felt he'd found a clue when he noticed the patch on the man's leather vest that read, "Tank." The name fit. He was stocky as though his body was overpacked with muscles. That and his quiet demeanor gave Harold a sense he was not someone to trifle with.

Though he wasn't sure what to expect, which was cause for some hesitation, Harold was flattered that he was asked. There was something else, too. Though Morticia's actions hadn't cast the club in the best of possible lights, Harold was impressed with the way Samurai and Tex had stuck together during the incident. Even though he obviously didn't condone the girl's insane behavior, it was also obvious Samurai wouldn't give the girl up to the authorities even if he did know where she was. That unquestioning loyalty had a remarkable appeal to Harold. Maybe it had something to do with the way he had lost more than a friend or two to his drunken behavior. He intuitively knew there was still the potential for harsh repercussions if he screwed up with these bikers, but he sensed he'd at least have a fair shake before they turned their backs on him completely. Maybe it wasn't true. Maybe that's just what Harold wanted to believe. For the moment, however, it was comforting to consider. He felt as though he might have found a place where he 'fit,' where people wouldn't look down on him and where he wouldn't feel any condemnation for the way he drank.

At the same time, Harold realized, maybe, he wasn't being completely honest with himself. Was the persona he was adapting so casually concealing a real Harold they might not find so acceptable? But he did like the bad-ass allure of the bikers. Back in Poplar Grove, people were more likely to laugh at Harold than to take him seriously. With a set of those colors on his own back, Harold was certain they wouldn't laugh. They might even fear him.

As he contemplated his answer, Harold pictured himself walking into Freddie's Place with the club's patches on his vest. He imagined Mindy's reaction. He imagined her slipping onto the back seat, squeezing Harold's chest with her arms and his waist with her thighs. The vision was cut short when Tank asked, "So, what-d-ya think?"

"Sure," Harold said, adding, "I'm not sure how to get there, though."

Tank gave Harold directions to Hildie's as patiently as Chester had given directions to Speedy's.

Harold was so caught up in the idea of meeting the club that evening, he forgot to check the prices on the far side of the pump. That evening, as Sid checked out the cash drawer, the owner looked a little puzzled: "You're $2.27 over."

"Oh," Harold said, thinking quickly. "a customer was in a big hurry and told me not to worry about the change."

"Really?" said Sid. "I've been here 15 years and I never got a tip. You're here one week and you've got customers tipping you?"

Then Sid reached into the drawer and took out $2.27. He handed it to Harold and said, "Well, it's your tip."

With that, Harold had about $4.50 in his pocket, including what was left over from the money his mother had given him. Sid seemed to sense Harold's financial predicament. He looked at Harold and asked, "I'm guessing you could use a little advance on your paycheck?"

Harold was thrilled with the offer and readily accepted the $20 bill Speedy extended across the counter. However, the owner also offered some advice. "Don't make too much of a habit of this," Sid said. "You could find yourself spending your money as fast as you make it."

Eager to meet the Banshee Riders, Harold was fast for the door.

Before he stepped out, however, Sid offered one more piece of advice. "By the way, I'm not as easy going when the drawer comes up short," Sid said. "That comes out of your paycheck. And if it happens too often, you could be down the road or worse."

It dawned on Harold that, had he let the bikers ride off without paying, he might not have had enough cash to cover the cost of the gas. In that case, Sid would have been far less pleasant about the variance in the cash drawer. And it's probably unlikely he would have offered an advance on Harold's pay.

Harold also realized that Sid had established a payment process that included advances, not just the advance Harold had just received, but other advances in the future. In a way, it felt a little like having access to his mother's handouts. However, he was pretty sure Sid would track what Harold owed; he couldn't count on coming back for more and more, as though from a well that never went dry. This was money he had to work for. Strangely enough, he felt a greater sense of respect for the money in his pocket now than the money his mother would give him.

The sun was just dropping over the horizon as Harold pulled out of Speedy's and headed east out of town. Following the directions Tank had given, Harold drove east on Route 36 through a wooded area that was strikingly different than the farm fields he was used to around Biesenthal. He turned right about three miles down and began watching for a sign that read, "Boat Rentals." When he saw the badly weathered sign, he took another right. Cedar Lane went about half a mile and then dropped suddenly about 30 feet. At the bottom of the hill, Harold spotted a little shack. At the top of the shack was a weathered sign painted, "Hildie's Hideout."

There were dirty stains on the light-yellow outer walls of the bar, stains at about the same height were also visible on trees around the bar. The undergrowth at the bottom of the hill was matted and coated with the gray residue of a recent flood. Harold could almost imagine the floodwater creeping up over the peninsula until the bar sat like a box in the water. When the waters receded, the bar owner must have done just enough clean up to open for business again, but not too much.

There were several cars in the parking lot and close to a dozen Harleys. A couple bikers Harold hadn't seen before were talking just outside the front door. From the back, he could see that one wore Banshee Riders colors, and he suspected the other did, too. As they spoke, Harold felt that the one facing him was checking him out. As Harold pulled his bike into the lot and parked at the far end of a row of bikes to the left of the front door, the other biker glanced back his way, too. Harold shut the bike off and leaned the bike onto the kickstand and swatted a mosquito buzzing close by his left ear as he got off. With the bikers eyeing him suspiciously, Harold felt the warmth of a spotlight on his face. He was thankful that the setting sun was beginning to drain the colors from the day and providing a hiding place for his nerves. He couldn't just stand there by his bike, so he hiked up his courage and headed in, nodding a quiet greeting as he walked past the two sentries by the door. The bikers simply followed Harold with their eyes and looks that implied a kind of 'prove-it' scorn reserved for new faces. The temperature on the surface of Harold's face increased as he imagined that the two could see right through his façade of coolness.

As he stepped into the bar, a wave of cigarette smoke gave the shadowed interior that typical gin-mill ambiance Harold expected. What he didn't expect was the unfamiliar sound of a country and western crooner gently mingling with the smoke from jukebox along the wall to the right of the door. Harold wouldn't have been any more surprised if the bikers were listening to opera music. He had simply assumed they would listen to rock the same as he always did. But then, as he looked around the room at the worn and tattered cutoff Levi jackets, many on top of leather jackets, the blue jeans and engineer boots, it suddenly dawned on him that this music fit, too.

As the door closed behind him, all heads turned his way. The citizens – the non-bikers – were the first to look away. However, though they took a little longer to check him out, within a few seconds the bikers had looked away as well, all accept Samurai. Harold's new friend was standing in among a group of bikers and their old ladies on the left side of the U-shaped bar. Other bikers and women were seated or standing by a table in the corner. While the others gave him looks that were tepid, if not downright unfriendly, Samurai met Harold with a greeting that was even warmer than earlier in the day.

"Hey man, glad you could make it," Samurai said.

When Harold went to shake Samurai's hand, Samurai held his thumb back further and gave Harold his first biker handshake. Harold met Samurai's shake awkwardly, but the biker didn't seem to notice or care. After asking if Harold had any trouble finding the place, Samurai ordered a beer for the newcomer and then said, "Hey, come over here. I want you to meet some of my brothers."

As Samurai led Harold over to the group standing by the bar, he pointed at the bald biker who had invited Harold in the first place. "You remember Tank," Samurai said.

Harold nodded and they both lifted their beer steins as a greeting.

"Welcome brother," Tank said in his gruff tone.

The other bikers in the group were eyeing Harold with continued suspicion. Tank's greeting, however, seemed to break the spell. Most of them simply returned to their conversations as though Harold's arrival was no more significant than a sudden noise that was easily explained.

Samurai announced to the group, "This is Harold, the brother I was tellin' you about from Cal's the other day." Then Samurai motioned to a tall, sinewy biker standing at the bar next to Tank. "This whore-dog is Snake," said Samurai with a smile. "He's cool, but you might not want to leave your old lady alone with him too long."

Rather than take offense at the comment, a slight smile creased Snake's face as he extended his right hand for another biker handshake. "So, what's your name?" he asked, as though he hadn't heard Samurai moments before.

"Harold," said Harold.

"HAROLD?!" said Snake shaking his head. "I don't know if I can go around calling you Hair-old. We're gonna have to do somethin' about that, bro," he added, looking at Samurai.

Harold wasn't sure what to say. However, it dawned on him he would have to get a biker name, too, if he was going to continue hanging out with the Banshee Riders. While Harold tried to think of something to say, Samurai interjected, "Haven't had a chance yet. You want him to have a name that fits, don't you?"

Snake smiled again and then continued as though Samurai hadn't said anything at all, "And don't go listenin' to nothin' this kamikaze pilot tries to tell yeah. I don't fuck my brothers' old ladies." With a sly grin, Snake tipped his head forward and added, "Of course, the rest of 'em are fair game."

Harold could see by Snake's dark, wavy hair and rugged but handsome features, that this biker probably had substantial cause for confidence when it came to women. There was something about him that reminded Harold of the Marlboro man from cigarette ads – a thin mustache and rugged good looks that would appeal to women.

While Samurai had apparently intended to introduce Harold all around, now that Samurai had somewhat lost the attention of most of his brothers and sisters, he gave up on the broader idea and concentrated on introducing Harold to those who were at hand. Tank and Snake had their backs to the bar. Standing on the opposite side of the small circle of bikers was an older and heftier couple. Samurai introduced a short, round woman as Bitters. Like Harold's mother, she was about 60 and had thinning gray hair. But that's where the similarities ended.

While Harold seldom saw his mother in makeup, except for serious events like weddings, funerals and the reading of wills, Bitters wore enough of the facial camouflage for both women. She also wore a pair of super-tight jeans Marge wouldn't be caught dead in. Bitters might have taken a fashion tip from Harold's mother in this area as the jeans were so tight that they seemed to accentuate every, single pound that had gathered on the woman's hips and thighs. A looser wardrobe would have mercifully left more to the imagination.

Bitters wore a leather biker jacket and a cutoff Levi. A pair of enormous breasts protruded through the vest and rested snuggly on the woman's extended belly. On the front of a tight, pink shirt were rows of blacked-out pictures of stick-drawn rabbits in various sexual positions.

Bitters greeted Harold with a big smile and handshake that were a little too warm for comfort, and a "Hello" that seemed a bit suggestive. Harold had the sense that, though she was apparently standing right next to her old man, Bitters was coming on to him. He was somewhat relieved when Samurai introduced Harold to the short-but-stocky biker standing next to Bitters.

"This is Grunt," Samurai said.

Grunt also appeared around 60, probably stood about 5-3 and had a shape that was strikingly similar to his old lady's. He wore a massive crown of salt-n-pepper hair and a like-colored beard that extended to the middle of his chest. His hair and beard conspired to hide most of his face. What Harold could see were rosy cheeks and a pair of beady, black eyes. There was only a hint of a mouth under a thick comb of mustache.

Grunt shook Harold's hand in a friendly manner though he seemed a little preoccupied. Then he turned to Harold, as though Harold were an impartial judge, and asked, "Who would kick whose ass, Chuck Norris or David Carradine?"

"Would you let it go already," Samurai said with annoyance. "Nobody cares. They're just actors anyway."

If someone had asked Harold to guess what the bikers were talking about as he came in the door, he might have said something about bikes, girls or fights. That he had interrupted a debate about something as trivial as the toughest Hollywood characters came as something of a surprise. Trying to fit in, Harold answered anyhow, "What about Rambo?"

"Rambo," Grunt said. "He's a fucking pussy."

As Grunt went on about how Sylvester Stallone was wearing padded shoulders to make him look strong, Harold noticed that Bitters was rubbing one of her enormous breasts against his arm. He looked over at her and she gave another inviting smile. Grunt also seemed to notice. For a second, as Grunt began to growl at his old lady, Harold thought he was in trouble. His fears were quickly allayed, however, when Grunt barked at her, "Would you quit rubbing your tits up against him long enough that we can talk?"

Bitters pouted for a second and then gave Harold another lascivious smile.

Snake asked Harold some of the customary questions – "Where are you from?" "What do you do?" and, most importantly, "What do you ride?"

Harold described his "1957 Pan," which was received with nods of approval. Distracted by Bitters, who continued to press her breast against his arm, Harold let it slip that he'd just inherited the bike from his uncle. While Bitters offered her condolences and seemed to use the news to snuggle up even closer to Harold, as though offering sympathy and comfort, Harold thought he read looks of disappointment in the others' eyes. To recover, he coughed up a story about owning a Sportster, the smaller brother to the full-sized Harley.

"You've got a Sportster, too," Samurai said, enthusiastically playing up his apparent protégé.

"No," Harold said, continuing the lie. "It was ripped off last summer."

"Around these parts, we hang horse thieves," Tank said with a manufactured western accent.

Playing along, Harold bitterly claimed a hanging would be too dignified for the assholes who took his other bike.

"Was it insured," Bitters asked.

"No, I was out of work for a while," Harold said. "I couldn't keep up the premiums."

"Insurance don't bring back the bike," Snake said.

"Yeah, they could kidnap this horny old bitch here," Grunt said as he grabbed a big chunk of Bitter's ass, "but they better not steal my bike."

When Bitters looked hurt Samurai offered some comforting words. "Don't worry," he said. "You'd wear 'em out and they'd bring you back anyhow."

Harold was surprised when Samurai's strategy seemed to work, and Bitters gave Harold another lascivious glance.

Snake changed the subject asking, "How long you worked at Speedy's."

"To tell the truth, I only just started there."

As though he felt obliged to offer a warning, Snake turned to Tank and said, "Remember my cousin got that DUI last summer? The cops called that asshole to come get his shovel. By the time he got done dragging the bike to the pound, it was totaled."

Harold felt a little uncomfortable hearing someone speak negatively about someone who had done Harold a good turn only an hour earlier. But Harold wasn't about to start a confrontation over it. He nodded as though to thank Snake for the advice.

Offering Harold an escape from the clutches of Speedy, someone who didn't treat Harleys with proper respect and care, Tank interjected that the company he worked for was hiring. "It's just working on the dock and cleaning up," Tank warned. "But it pays better than pumping gas. Interested?"

"Sure," said Harold, forgetting about any debt he might feel towards Sid. More money had a nice ring to it.

"It's over in Earlsville," Tank said. "Come fill out an application Monday morning and I'll tell the foreman you're coming."

Harold hesitated. He knew that he was scheduled to work the day shift at Speedy's Monday and, though he didn't feel obligated enough to continue working there for any length of time, Harold didn't like the idea of ditching out on his shift. When he pointed out the problem to Tank, the biker frowned as though he might rescind the offer. But it turned out Tank appreciated Harold's sense of loyalty and was merely frowning because of the problem scheduling the job interview. "I'll tell him you're coming in Tuesday then, OK?"

"Sounds great," Harold said with a little extra enthusiasm to let Tank know he appreciated the effort. Then, after Tank drew directions and a phone number on a napkin, Harold accepted the piece of paper and shoved it into a pocket on the front of his pants while offering another "Thanks."

As the evening faded into night, the beer flowed liberally. Harold was introduced to several other members of the club. But as he continued to drink, he wasn't sure how many of the introductions he'd remember. With the help of the beer and the cigarette smoke, the night was turning into a blur. Amazingly, however, as drunk as Harold became, he continued to show more restraint than was customary. At that state of intoxication back at Freddie's Place Harold would most likely have engaged in some kind of embarrassing behavior. It occurred to him, as he drank down stein after stein of Old Style, that, were he to lose control, he might end up outside in the parking lot getting his ass kicked. He concluded that fear of a beating was a helpful incentive for restraint. He also reasoned that, if they did kick his ass, they'd probably take his bike, too, and that wasn't very appealing either.

Eventually, Harold followed Samurai back to his place, where they had a couple more beers before Harold crashed on the brother's couch. Harold removed his shirt and shoes before falling face first into the couch. Within seconds, he was out like a light, a smile on his face as he savored his successful first night hangin' with the Banshee Riders.

Chapter 9 — The Plunge

The room was shrouded in a deep grey as a heavy overcast kept the morning sun at bay as Harold, laying on the sofa with his back to the room, heard the pitter-patter of little feet and the giggling voices of toddlers. As the grogginess began to loosen its grip, he rolled back and peered through red-puffy eyes. A pair of blue eyes were reflecting back at him only inches away. For a second, it didn't register. Harold just laid there looking into the sapphire orbs uncomprehendingly. Then Harold pulled back suddenly. The owner of the other eyes also jumped, surprised by Harold's reaction. But while Harold began to utter a curse — "What the ..." — the other eyes danced with joy accompanied by the sounds of laughter. As full consciousness returned, Harold realized he was face to face with a small, red-haired boy of about 2 wearing light-green pajamas covered with prints of cowboys, 6-guns, and horses.

Harold surveyed the room in search of clues that would answer the question "Where am I?" The walls were off-white, or in need of cleaning, with twisting-and-random Crayola renderings on the wall between a television console and a cushioned chair covered with a white sheet. As he looked from left to right, he discovered two more chairs covered with white sheets. Unlike the chairs, the sofa where he laid had a flowered-print sheet that he had, apparently, pulled down from the back to expose green fabric underneath. Even an ottoman had a sheet doubled up over it. The floor was covered with dark-brown, shag carpet that was badly matted as though trampled by herds of cattle. There was a retracted-expandable table against the wall by the door to the next room — apparently, the kitchen, judging by the Harvest-Gold refrigerator Harold could see from where he lay. There were also a couple of light-weight metal folding tables, with scarred tops and thin, pitted brass crisscross legs. The one closest to him had two Old Style cans on top, one upright, the other on its side. Spread across the entire landscape of the room were toys, dropped where they were by short-attention spans.

As Harold lay there, the television suddenly blared to life at high volume causing Harold to jump upright. Seated, a threadbare-flowered bed cover he was laying under fell to his waist. As the television began to flip rapidly through the channels it gave Harold the sensation of rapidly passing rooms, with open doors, where conversation and noise was at the highest volume. Through the mayhem, he heard a clicking and glanced to his left where a girl of 3 or 4, in a pink nighty with hundreds of Dalmatian prints, was adjusting the channel as though the goal was to create a mad visual and aural electronic kaleidoscope rather than to find any particular program to watch.

The little girl, with a long, tangled head of red hair, glanced fleetingly at Harold with a smile before looking back at the television. Before Harold could look back from the young girl, a young voice said, "Djouatch innieblu?"

As though trying to determine what language the boy was speaking, Harold stared his way again, this time taking in the blenderized red hair, a shining cherub face, with the orange powder of Goldfish crackers around the mouth, and small hands with dimpled knuckles tightly wrapped around several crumbling Goldfish.

As the boy shoved another handful of cracker bits into his mouth, he simultaneously muttered something that sounded remotely similar to "Djouatch innieblu?" accompanied by blowing fish parts that landed on the sofa cover and Harold's chest. This seemed to have caught the girl's attention and, leaving the television so that Harold heard 'Justice League … Superman, Wonder Woman' and other cartoon heroes between repetitions of "Djouatch innieblu?" The sound of the television, and the young boy's "Djouatch innieblu?" were suddenly joined by giggling shouts of 'You're naked' from the girl who had noticed Harold's shirtless chest and, apparently, had assumed the rest of him was naked, too. Or, maybe, having his shirt off was enough for her to classify Harold as naked. Whatever the case, a new cacophony of noise had erupted around Harold with the effect that his already spinning head was picking up speed and felt as though it might twist off his neck.

Harold shifted back on the sofa, as though a few inches of distance would muffle the sound a little. For a second, Harold felt his pulse increasing the way it did when he got angry. Then, as though that thought was short-circuited, a smile spread across his face. He was about to laugh when he heard a woman's voice say, "He wants to watch Winnie the Pooh."

Harold looked to his left where a tall, red-haired woman, her hair tossed in a way that matched her children's, was walking into the room wearing a threadbare, white nightgown and bare feet. Her fingernails and toenails were painted red to match her hair. In spite of her just-woken appearance, Harold found her stunningly attractive, though an angled scar across the bridge of her nose gave the impression of a fine painting that had suffered at the hands of a vandal. As she walked past, the limited light through the sheer curtains on the other side of the room was just enough to filter through the thin fabric of her nightshirt illuminating a voluptuous body, with full, firm breasts. The impression was as though she was naked behind a thin screen. Though she had walked past quickly, the image of her body continued to glow in Harold's eyes the way looking into a bright light will leave a blue shadow even if you close your eyes. Reaching the other side of the sofa, and no longer exposed by the morning light, she turned the sound down to a reasonable level, as she told the girl to 'Stop that.' The girl seemed to understand that meant to stop shouting. Instead, she stood pointing at Harold and said, "He's naked, mommy" with a big grin on her face.

Glancing at Harold, as though they had known each other for years, as though it was perfectly normal to find some stranger sleeping on the sofa in the morning, the woman said, in an accent Harold figured placed her as originally from Tennessee or Kentucky, "You don't mind if I put a movie in for them?"

"Uhm … no. That's cool," said Harold.

As she walked back in front of him, without even thinking about it, Harold's eyes seemed to seek out the outline of her naked shadow again. But just as quickly, it dawned on him that he was at Samurai's house and that he was probably checking out Samurai's wife or girlfriend. Feeling a touch of guilt, he looked away and back at the young boy who was now simply staring at him with a big grin as he continued to chew on the crumbling, orange fish, pieces periodically falling from his open mouth.

After shoving a tape into the VCR, and starting the movie "Dumbo," the woman strode past the folding table and picked up the beer cans on her way out to the kitchen. He saw her open the refrigerator door as she yelled back to him, "How do you like your eggs?"

Harold said, "However," as he watched her take a carton of

eggs and a gallon of milk out of the fridge, along with some other stuff he couldn't make out, before disappearing from sight into the area of the kitchen Harold couldn't see. A minute later, she came back into the living room and put a bowl of cereal and a spoon on each of the folding tables. One was next to Harold in front of the sofa. The woman then moved the other folding table over by a sheet-covered recliner and set the other bowl of cereal down for the girl. Then, throwing a quick smile at Harold, and without a word, she walked back into the kitchen.

Harold's eyes followed her to the kitchen, as though he couldn't look away. Then, when she stepped out of sight, he looked back from the kitchen and found that the little girl was standing right in front of him smiling and watching as though waiting for something to happen – as though he might suddenly turn into a large bird and fly through the picture window. He stared back at her for a bit before realizing that he couldn't win a staring contest with a 3-year old – realizing that a 3-year-old girl simply hasn't adopted the kind of inhibitions that make that game more difficult for adults. He intentionally blinked, as though to signal that the game was over, cleared his throat and said, "What?"

The little girl glanced into the kitchen where she could hear, but not see her mother, making breakfast. Then, with her hands tight to her side, she leaned forward so her face was only inches from Harold's and whispered, "You're naked."

Harold said, "Yeah?" Then, he grabbed the blanket over his legs and, holding it a moment for effect, flipped it off exposing his blue-jeaned legs underneath.

Giggling, the girl ran back to her cereal on the television table. But as she went, she whispered again, just loud enough for Harold to hear, "You're naked."

Still, in a haze, Harold fell into watching the cartoon without really watching. His mind was in that early-morning state between sleep and full consciousness. He sat that way until he was snapped out of the trance by the woman's voice from the kitchen again: "Breakfast is ready."

Harold picked his T-shirt up off the floor and slipped it over his head as he walked into the kitchen. He stopped at the doorway and looked at the woman. Even without the help of the sun, he could see dark circles protruding, straining at the front of her gown. She looked up at him and he had a feeling that she might have seen him looking. She smiled at him – an innocent smile or a willing acceptance of his probing eyes, he wasn't sure. Still smiling, still looking into Harold's eyes, she hollered, "SAM! BREAK-FAST." Then, as she turned back to the stove, she said to Harold, "Have a seat."

Harold took the seat opposite the sink figuring it was better not to sit where he would have little choice but to continue checking her out. He had just pulled his seat in when she slipped a plate of biscuits and gravy, with three over-easy eggs on top, in front of him. She slipped a similar plate in front of the seat across from Harold and returned from the stove with another, which she put down at the seat that backed up to the stove. There, she sat down and quickly took a mouthful of eggs. Then, looking at Harold as the thought had suddenly crossed her mind, and with her mouth half full, she said, "Mmm, Sue."

As Harold picked up his fork, he said, "Harold."

"I know," she said. Then she looked up and, as though to explain, added, "Sam told me."

Just then, Samurai walked in the kitchen buckling his belt and fully dressed. He nodded to Harold and then leaned into the living room and said, "Hey, you little rugrats."

Instantly, two young voices yelled, "DADDY." Their voices set off a small stampede as they rushed to their father. Samurai hugged the children against his legs and then asked, "Are you eating your breakfast?"

No one answered. Instead, it seemed the two young ones were trying to find something else, anything else to look at, other than into his eyes. "Get in there and start eating," he ordered. When they stood there, their heads hanging, he said, "Just got my belt on don't mean I can't take it off again." As though a gun had fired signaling the start of a race, both children charged into the living room. But Harold noticed they were both laughing as they went.

Samurai continued into the kitchen where he threw a leg over his chair and sat down. "So, you met my old lady," he said.

Having seen her virtually naked already, Harold felt a little awkward as he said, "Yeah. We were just talking."

Samurai gave no indication that he had noticed Harold was

feeling a little uncomfortable. "She makes about the best biscuits and gravy this side of the Pecos."

Harold realized he hadn't tried them yet and now made a point of raising the forkful to his mouth. Actually, he had never tried biscuits and gravy before. He recalled seeing a sign outside of a tavern once years ago, when he was out in the sticks, that advertised biscuits and gravy. He remembered wondering why they would advertise that as though it were a meal and not just something that went with a meal. Now, as he tasted biscuits and gravy for the first time, he was surprised that it did strike him as an actual meal. He was also surprised that it was a bit spicy. But mostly, he was surprised that it was really, really good.

He had planned to compliment her regardless but found that he really was savoring the flavor as he looked at Sue and nodded, "Bowiedatsgoot."

Sue seemed to see the surprise on his face and smiled proudly as she said, "Thanks." Then, she got up and returned to the table with cups of coffee she had poured from a Mr. Coffee maker on the counter. Without asking, she put a cup in front of Harold and another in front of Samurai. "If you want cream or sugar, there's milk in the fridge and the sugar's there," she said nodding toward a plate with salt and pepper shakers, napkins, and sugar in the center of the table.

"Did the monsters in the other room bother you this morning?" Samurai asked. Before Harold could answer, Samurai continued, "That's Ringo and Montana. Oh, and that's not Ringo as in some drummer – it's Ringo as in 'The Ringo Kid' – John Wayne in Stagecoach."

Harold smiled. He knew the movie well. "That's a great movie," he said.

"You bet yer ass it is," said Samurai, swelling with pride as though he had starred in the film.

Harold finished his breakfast first and asked where the bathroom was. Samurai pointed down the hall and said, "Take a shower, if you want. But don't fuck around. I've got some stuff I gotta do today."

The bathroom was a mess and, while there were several towels crumpled on the floor, only one was draped casually from the rod. He felt at it and decided it was just dry enough.

The shower felt good and seemed to wash the cobwebs out of his head as well as the dirt from his body. Harold dried himself and hung the towel neatly over the rod. He then went back into the living room and put his belt back on, his wallet and keys back in his pocket and his boots back on his feet. Then he returned to the kitchen where he found Samurai pouring coffee in a pair of plastic travel mugs with snap-on lids and levers to open and close the opening where you drank the coffee.

"I've got a little proposition for you," Samurai said as they headed out the door. "I've got a little job to take care of this morning. I'll give you $8 an hour if you want to come along and give me a hand." That was about $4.50 more than Harold's hourly wage at Speedy's and he didn't hesitate to accept the offer.

The two walked out to the garage together. When Samurai swung open the large doors on the front of the building, Harold was surprised to see a white van inside. Painted on the side of the van were the words "ACTION ELECTRIC" painted with a lightning bolt arching through the last letter. Below that was some verbiage about 24-hour emergency service and a phone number. As they climbed into the front seats and Samurai pulled out of the garage, Harold said, "You know, I don't really know much about electrical work."

"That's OK," said Samurai. "I'll find somethin' you can do."

Samurai drove about 20 minutes before pulling into a new cul de sac where the road and two partially completed homes, one further along than the other, surrounded by black dirt, were carved into what, a short time before, was an empty field. After having Harold help carry some conduit, connectors and wire into the home further completed, Samurai took a shovel out of the truck and led Harold out back where there was a foundation for a garage behind each house. He showed Harold where to start at each house and where to end up at each garage then handed him the shovel. "When you get done with that, I've got some more diggin' for you."

With the exception of a burger and a couple of beers at a local bar for lunch, Harold dug trench from morning to early afternoon. He then helped the biker electrician pull wire through conduit inside one of the houses. Then he helped lay pipe in the trenches he'd dug earlier. Finally, they completed the workday by backfilling the trenches together. Though it was still Springtime, Harold had stripped off his shirt and, by the end of the day, when he climbed into the truck, he could tell that his back was burned by the sun.

On the way back to the house, Samurai said, "So, how do you like electrical work? Up to doin' some more I can use you?"

"Absolutely," Harold replied quickly. Harold had used muscles that ached after sitting dormant most of a year. But now that he was, apparently, out on his own, the opportunity to make some better money was quite an incentive. It also felt good to relax after a full day's work. It was as though he had earned the rest and had a greater right to enjoy it.

"I'll keep you in mind then," Samurai said, "When I need the help."

They drove a couple more miles listening to the radio when Samurai turned and popped the question Harold had wondered if he'd hear earlier, though he'd forgotten all about while working all day. "How'd you like to be a Banshee Rider?" Samurai said rather suddenly." Before Harold could answer, Samurai continued, "Of course, you'd have to prospect. And there's a little matter of a vote, both to prospect and, if you ain't some kind of loser, to make probate and full patch."

Harold opened his mouth to answer again but Samurai wasn't done. "I'd be your sponsor. That means I'll vouch for you with the club. I'm your voice with the club until you make patch. In return, I expect you to make me proud. Don't do anything stupid. If you discredit yourself, you discredit me. Be smart. Watch your brothers' backs. Above all, don't do anything to disgrace the Banshee Riders."

It was clear from the way Samurai was talking that he didn't consider the possibility that Harold would say 'No.'

Harold waited a few seconds to make sure Samurai was done. Then he said, "I'll make you proud."

Samurai took his eyes off the road long enough to glance at Harold and extend a hand for a biker handshake. Harold returned the gesture as though he was giving up a last chance to back out. Samurai said, "Don't fuck up."

Harold nodded and said, "I won't." But he felt less confidence than his words conveyed. He had considered the idea before Samurai ever brought it up. And though he considered it, he hadn't really thought about what that meant. He had rather jumped over the part where he prospected as a means of proving himself worthy. He had simply pictured himself as a member with all the honors and privileges that entailed. Now, the reality dawned on him that he would have to prove himself. That's where the doubts came in. He had realized he'd have to prove himself but kind of the way a child imagines the things he'll do when they grow up. Now, facing a moment of truth, he wondered if he could keep it together. He thought about the other day where, drunk, he'd wound up on the floor of 'Freddie's.' He didn't think members of the club would appreciate that; he was sure Samurai wouldn't appreciate that. But at the same time, the idea of joining the Banshee Riders appealed to Harold. It was a goal that sprang up unexpectedly as though a flower was blooming in the middle of a barren asphalt parking lot.

He had thought he had given up on the idea of proving himself to anyone anymore. Passed out on a bar, or sprawled on a barroom floor, Harold didn't have far to fall. He didn't have to worry about failure. He certainly didn't have to worry about setting his sights too high. And yet, this idea somehow gave him hope. Maybe this was something that did offer him an opportunity for success – where he could gain the unfamiliar respect of others. And it didn't require him to stop drinking. In fact, he sensed that heavy drinking was almost a prerequisite for membership. If he could only keep it together, he could have it all – the club, the respect of his brothers, citizens who were intimidated at the sight of him, and he would have the brotherhood of people who truly cared about him. This was the sales pitch that went through Harold's head. Samurai was right – there was never any chance that Harold would say no. He had found a place where he had a shot at acceptance. And as long as he didn't screw up, people would come to respect him in a way he had always wanted, even though he had worked hard to hide that desire, above all, from himself. Harold told himself he wouldn't screw up. If he did, they'd kick the shit out of him. They might even kill him and dump his body somewhere. And that was a good thing – it gave him all the incentive he needed to make sure he didn't fail. How could he fail when failure meant destruction? The prize danced in his imagination – the club riding in a pack and Harold there, on Magdelina, a Banshee Rider patch on his back, folks on the sidewalk watching in awe and a touch of fear.

Chapter 10 — A Mongrel on the Rug

The driveway in front of the bi-level house in the relatively new subdivision was full of motorcycles. Two more were coming down the street as several Banshee Riders stood by the front door with beers in their hands chatting and waiting for the meeting to begin. Pastor Dan's wife and kids had gone to a movie leaving the house to the bikers, grown men in leather with as much of a penchant for chrome and painted steel as for a good fight or a tall, thin blonde with the body and face of Christie Brinkley.

Pastor Dan was more than merely a club name stitched into the rectangular piece of cloth on the front of the homeowner's vest. He was an ordained minister, a distinction he earned, much as a young boy would send in for a pair of X-ray glasses advertised in a comic book. Dan Kramer had completed a short questionnaire he sent away for after seeing an ad in the back of a biker magazine. A short time later, a certificate arrived in the mail and Dan was qualified to perform marriages, preside over funerals, and conduct religious services. He had never bothered with the latter. However, he had conducted the services for one brother's wedding and had read the eulogy for another brother's funeral. Hulk died early the previous year when he was hit by a car while riding his bike through an intersection. The driver of the car had a blood-alcohol level double the legal limit. Of course, Hulk was also well over the legal limit, too, though that fact was buried under the club's resentment that gave the driver of the car good reason to keep a watchful eye in the days following, right up to this day.

Pastor Dan spent considerable time looking for just the right Biblical passage to share at the service. He found it in 10 words from Colossians 3:6, plus his own words of embellishment, "... and so, to the thoughtless sin of one man, we sacrifice our brother while carrying forgiveness in our hearts but the power of righteous judgement in our souls. As the word of God tells us, 'On account of these the wrath of God is coming.'"

As the Banshee Riders were pulling up in front of Pastor Dan's, Harold was waiting back at The Cimarron saloon on the outskirts of Earlsville. As Samurai had explained, "We hold the meeting at a different brother's place each Friday. When we have a clubhouse, we hold the meetings there but we're kinda between clubhouses right now.

"You're not allowed at the meeting until we vote you in as a prospect. After that, you wait outside until you make probate."

At the Cimarron, Harold waited with several of the brothers' old ladies as they were also not welcome at the meetings and were dropped off there until the meeting was over.

When Harold met Samurai for the ride out to Earlsville, he saw Sue in her biker rag for the first time and saw that, by the name patch on the front, her nickname was 'Hot Stuff.' As Harold and Sue entered The Cimarron, he nodded hello to Bitters, the only other familiar face. He also saw several other women wearing rags and Banshee Riders property patches. Harold wasn't sure if Sue would introduce him to the other women so, rather than force the issue, he slid up to the bar close to the door a couple yards away. He was going to offer to buy a beer for Sue, but she continued into the bar and exchanged hugs and greetings with the four other old ladies there. Then she turned and motioned Harold to come over.

The idea that these weren't just women at the bar but old ladies with property patches belonging to members of the club wasn't lost on Harold as Sue said, "Ladies, this is Harold."

"Great, another wannabe," said a tall, shrewish old lady in a tone Harold found difficult to peg – was it ridiculing or patronizing. Without the biker attire, she could have passed for a strict disciplinarian at a private school: tall, thin, her dark hair pulled back in a ponytail, and her patches sewn to a black-leather vest over a motorcycle jacket obviously tailored for a woman.

"This is Viper," said Sue as though the old lady's comment had moved her to the front of the line for introductions. "And this is ..." But before Sue could finish, Bitters reached out a limp hand, the way a courtesan would offer her hand for a gentleman to kiss in French royal society of the late 1700s.

"We've already met," said Bitters in a sultry voice.

Harold gently took the hand but stopped short of the kiss. He smiled warmly, but not too warmly, suspecting that accepting her flirtations could lead to trouble.

Sue smiled in a way that suggested she wasn't surprised by Bitters' promiscuous tendencies. "This is Catnip," said Sue, gesturing to a heavy-set old lady, about 50 with thinning gray hair. Catnip gave the slightest hint of a nod while it appeared she was trying to hold back a sneer of disapproval from curling her lips. Harold had the distinct impression she didn't like him. Or, maybe she just didn't want to be bothered with him until he proved he was more than a 'wannabe.'

Then Sue turned to the last old lady in the group, a short, blonde with straight hair that hung down her back as though intended to frustrate those who wanted to check out her ass. At just over 5 feet, Harold would have guessed that "Tinker Bell" wouldn't even tip the scales into triple digits. "She's Tank's old lady," said Sue.

Harold could see, by the property patch on her back, that Catnip was "Property of Pastor Dan." He still didn't know who Viper's old man was and either Sue forgot to let him know or was somehow reluctant to do so. Since she didn't turn around so Harold could see the patch on her back, Harold was left in the dark and he wasn't inclined to ask.

She seemed to read his mind as Harold glanced her way. But rather than clear the matter up, she gave Harold a seductive smile and said, "So, wannabe, wannabuy a round for the old ladies?"

This ran counter to Harold's plans on how to stretch his limited resources, but he felt it would be awkward to refuse. Then, as he was about to offer to buy a round of beers, he noticed that Viper was holding a mixed drink in her hand. Caught with his mouth open about to speak, Sue came to the rescue. "I believe it's my turn to buy." Turning to the bar, she motioned to the bartender and said, "A round for my friends."

She turned back to Harold and asked, "What are you drinking?"

"Budweiser," said Harold.

The bartender heard and asked, "Tap OK?"

"That's fine," said Harold.

When he had filled the glass, the bartender handed it to Sue, who turned and handed it to Harold. Harold said, "Thanks" but he meant more than just thanks for the beer. Sue seemed to understand, and he thought he saw a little sparkle in her eye as though to say as much.

"So, you got a motorcycle, wannabe?" asked Viper. "Or you a sidewalk commando?"

Harold was getting tired of her attitude but wasn't ready to declare open war yet. However, his tone wasn't entirely neutral when he answered, "I don't think I'd be here if I didn't have a bike."

Sue smiled but seemed Harold sensed she took a quick swig of her beer to hide it from the others. Viper gave an exaggerated smile of her own that, at the least, acknowledged that Harold wasn't going to play doormat for her scorn. Then, she turned her back on Harold. He overheard her say something to Catnip but the only words he heard were "... bet ..." and "... ass kicked ..." Harold ignored her and took the opportunity to slide onto a barstool next to Sue and out of the center of attention.

A while later, Viper leaned over the bar so she could see around Sue and barked, "Hey wannabe, got any change for the jukebox?"

Harold pulled a couple quarters out of his pocket and slid them down the bar.

"Thanks, wannabe," Viper said as though surprised he'd come through.

When she walked past him, arm-in-arm with Catnip to go over by the jukebox, Harold looked back lone enough to see that Viper was wearing the property patch of a brother named "Falstaff."

Sue saw him look and, when he looked back, she leaned over and whispered "Falstaff's VP. Makes Viper think she's hot shit or something. Might want to watch your back for a while."

Harold nodded but didn't say anything.

When Viper and Catnip had made their choices on the jukebox, it apparently came on automatically while cutting in on the stereo that was otherwise filling the bar with Country & Western music. Suddenly, the pounding rhythm of the Bee Gees and other disco numbers took over. Harold was pretty sure he heard a construction-worker type mutter, "What the fuck?" as the musical genre changed.

When they came back, Viper stopped by Harold and said, "Come on, wannabe, dance with me."

"I don't dance," said Harold wary that she had asked in the first place.

"That's OK," she said, "I'll show you how."

"I didn't say I don't know how," said Harold expecting that this might be the line in the sand where trouble began. Instead, Viper merely pouted a little as Catnip came back from the bar with their drinks, handing Viper her Fuzzy Navel.

Viper took a sip of her drink and, when she lowered the glass, it was as though the drink had wiped away her sour demeanor. Suddenly, she had a smile and was taking a completely different tact with Harold. It even seemed Catnip had a more friendly attitude about Harold. The change was so sudden that Harold was convinced they had discussed it while playing the jukebox, as if it was part of a strategy they'd agreed on. Viper even sidled up to Harold and slipped her right arm into his left so that they were intertwined. She stood there smiling as Harold waited to see what would happen next.

Finally, she said, "Harold. You said your name is Harold, right?" as if she was trying to remember.

"That's right," Harold said cautiously.

"Ever ride with a club before?" she purred while squeezing his arm so that he could feel a firm breast against it.

"No," said Harold.

"There's a lot to learn," said Viper, "I mean, if you don't want to get your ass kicked and have the brothers dump your body in a dumpster somewhere."

"You think you got what it takes, H-A-R-O-L-D," said Catnip, some of the new tact slipping away.

"Nobody's asked me yet," said Harold, his eyes narrowing as though to watch them closely so he'd know when they were about to strike.

"Catnip just asked you," Viper said. "You heard her, didn'tcha?" Viper even looked over at Sue as though for her confirmation that Catnip had, in fact, asked.

"I'm pretty sure it doesn't count until the brothers ask me," said Harold.

"Brothers! Listen to him," said Catnip.

Viper leaned in close and cooed into Harold's ear, "Just to be straight about this, you ain't no fucking brother yet. You might want to watch that."

"I'll do that," said Harold.

Viper began to disentangle her arm from Harold's as though ready to move back to her seat when she seemed to notice that a couple of the citizens at the front of the bar were looking her way. She barked at them, "What the fuck you lookin' at, assholes."

She did it so suddenly that Harold almost jumped. He looked

down where she was pointing her anger and saw a pair of muscular construction-worker types. It occurred to Harold that Viper was putting him on the spot. If these guys took Viper's bait, should Harold defend the honor of a Banshee Riders old lady – the vice president's old lady? Should he try to distance himself from Viper if the men came over? Or should he play the peacemaker and try to smooth the waters? If he did the latter, would Viper spoil his efforts and land him in a fight he was unlikely to win? Somehow, he thought that likely.

Harold was pleased when he saw that the two didn't take the bait. They turned back to their conversation and beers as though the biker chick hadn't said a word to them. Viper seemed to notice Harold's relief and sneered as she mouthed a single word Harold was sure was 'Pussy.'

Now it was Harold's turn and he also refused the bait. Viper laughed and returned to her barstool between Sue and Catnip. Harold noticed Bitters and Tinker Bell looking down as though they were used to this game.

As the time dripped by, Harold was beginning to think that he had dodged whatever bullet Viper and Catnip were trying to shoot his way. Suddenly, he heard Viper shout out in alarm, "Aren't they done yet? They don't usually take this long, do they?"

She and Catnip engaged in an animated discussion about the possibility that something might be wrong – that the brothers were gone longer than the meeting would reasonably take them. Finally, Viper said, "Someone should call and check. You wanna call, Sue? Catnip? Bitters?"

None of them answered.

Almost on what Harold would have called 'cue,' Viper turned to face him. "Can you give them a call?"

"I don't think that's a good idea," said Harold, noticing that Sue didn't seem to want to look at him.

Viper got out off her barstool again and came down by Harold. "Really, the meetings never go this long. Something could be wrong," she said with all the sincerity in her voice of a mother worried why her children aren't home from school yet. When Harold didn't reply, she continued, "Just call and, if everything's OK, you can ask them how much longer it will be. I can give you Pastor Dan's number."

Harold took a long swig of his beer, as though for effect. He could almost picture the reaction if he called. Somebody named Pastor Dan would answer the phone and would respond, "Who the fuck is this" in a way that suggested he intended to find out later. After a long pause, Harold said, "I suspect they'll be along when they're good and ready." After another sip of his beer, he added, "If you're really worried, maybe you should call them yourself."

Viper opened her mouth as though to try another approach. Then, giving up on the effort, she walked back to her seat laughing, "This wannabe ain't no fun at all."

Harold noticed that Sue and the others were smiling, too. He realized, they were going to let him sink or swim on his own. And he was pretty sure he'd have sunk fast if he had fallen into Viper's trap and called the brothers at the meeting.

Back at Pastor Dan's, in the shadowy basement den, when the 7 p.m. meeting finally started closer to 8 p.m., the brothers were initially preoccupied in a heated debate. Not for the first time, a couple of brothers complained because the president was missing another meeting.

"This is three-weeks in a row he hasn't been here," Kilroy griped.

Grunt quickly jumped in defending his president, "The man drives over-the-road. We all knew that when we voted him in."

When a brother pointed out that, by club rules, three meetings in a row was cause for removal from office, Grunt said, "What, are we going to take money out of his pocket when his work is busy? Who's going to take care of him when his work is slow? Do you wanna tell him to give up the extra cash now? Or, maybe you'd like to be the one to tell him he's out as president?"

By turning the discussion to a question of supporting a brother, Grunt had cut the attack off at the pass. When one of the brothers persisted, Falstaff, the club's vice president, who was chairing the meeting in the president's absence, yelled threateningly, "If you've got a problem with the man, bring it up with him. Otherwise, shut the fuck up about it."

Kilroy grumbled, "I would if he was here," but the way he spoke it under his breath, it was clear he was done pressing the matter.

His brothers also knew it was equally unlikely he would bring the subject up the next time the president was in attendance. Then the VP turned the discussion to the most important matter on the agenda – Road Day.

Road Day is the ceremonial first ride of the year. It's mandatory for all members, not just that they show up, but that they show up riding their scooters. Anyone who falls short of those simple requirements is unceremoniously struck down to probate. If any of the brothers needed reminding of what that meant, there were two probates in the room during the discussion.

A probate is one step up from a prospect and one step short of a full-patch member. Of the two in the room, one, Red, had recently worked his way up from prospect. The other, Drago, had slipped down after some infraction and was eagerly anticipating his return to the status of full-fledged member. They wore all the same patches as the full-patched brothers except for the center patch. In the case of Drago, a ring of cut-threads stood out on his back where the center patch sat before he was busted down.

The discussion of Road Day resulted in another heated debate. In this case, however, the outrage was unanimous and considerably angrier. The two brothers responsible for reserving the campground at the club's destination were not at the meeting. The rumor had it, and most brothers suspected, their absence was the result of failing to follow through on their responsibilities. Snake spoke up and said, "Mongrel admitted to me the other week that they hadn't done a damn thing about it all winter."

The job actually entailed more than merely reserving a spot for the club to set up tents and such. The pair were responsible for planning the route, arranging for a backup vehicle, and ensuring that the club would have unlimited access to its fill of firewood and beer. Club members looked forward to Road Day the way children anxiously anticipate Christmas morning. It was the first big ride of the year and an event that washed cabin fever away for the summer. A brother who failed to handle their duties, in general, could face harsh repercussions. A failure related to Road Day was a sure way to universal ire from their brothers; being busted to prospect might be the least of their worries. Road Day was only around the corner and, if the arrangements weren't handled yet, the club would be hard-pressed to get the job done in time now.

The VP cut this discussion off short as well. "They're not here," he said, "so there's no point in speculating. After the meeting, I'll assign a couple brothers to look into it." Then the VP asked if there was any other business.

Samurai immediately stepped to his feet, "I don't know how many of you have met Harold. He's back at The Cimarron right now."

Everyone in the room knew what was coming but, for now, they let Samurai continue.

"He's a standup dude," Samurai continued. "He was at the bar, in Biesenthal, when that crazy bitch Morticia flipped out and cut up that citizen. The guy kept his mouth shut when the cops were questioning him and I'd say that was pretty righteous of him. I'd like to bring him up for prospect."

"You ever seen him ride," came a voice from a younger biker standing in the shadows behind several seated brothers in one corner of the room.

"Yeah," Samurai said in a slightly indignant tone. "The man's got a kick-ass scooter, too. And he rode up to Earlsville with me tonight. He ..."

The younger biker cut Samurai off as the brother was about to point out that the younger member had also seen Harold ride. But that's exactly where the younger brother was going. "I've seen him ride, too," the brother said. "He looks a little shaky to me."

Samurai started to defend Harold's riding ability when T-Rex, with a massive frame built to fit his name, spoke up in a deep, gravelly voice. "Just keep him in the back of the pack and feel him out for a while."

"Fuck that," the younger biker, a brother named 6 Pack, said with his voice growing angry. "Suppose the asshole doesn't know his throttle from my old lady's tampon. Next thing we know, he puts the entire pack in a trick-bag. We already buried one brother last year."

"That's why I said keep him in the back ..." T-Rex responded before 6 Pack cut him off too.

"If we make him a prospect, he has to ride in the back anyway," 6 Pack said.

As several other brothers began to weigh in on both sides of the issue, Falstaff raised his voice again. Though the VP only stood about 5-5, he was as solid as a rock and there were few in the room who would want to mix it up with the man unless it was absolutely necessary. Therefore, when Falstaff yelled, "Enough! shut the fuck up," the room fell completely silent. Having gained the floor, Falstaff continued, "Samurai, you're sponsoring him, it's your job to take him out and make sure he can ride, not just by himself but also with a pack."

"I already know he can ride," Samurai said defensively.

"Well, know it some more," Falstaff said. "You make sure he's up to riding with the pack by Road Day. Oh, and he'll still be riding in the back."

Then Falstaff told the secretary to call the vote by a show of hands. Harold was made a prospect by a vote of 11 to four. Expecting a unanimous approval, Samurai took the "No" votes as personal insults. The grudge he had against 6 Pack, however, was nothing new as bad blood had passed between them before. In fact, Samurai was pretty sure 6 Pack's objections had nothing to do with Harold and everything to do with 6 Pack's and Samurai's past history.

Back at The Cimarron, Samurai walked up to Harold and stopped short. After a long pause for effect, and a dour face that might have suggested otherwise, Samurai said, "Congrats. You're now a prospect for the Banshee Riders."

The two shook hands briefly and Samurai turned to Hot Stuff and said, "Let's have it."

Sue reached inside her coat and pulled out a grungy and tattered Levi vest. Samurai took it and spread it out on the bar in front of Harold so the backside was up. On the bottom was a small patch with the initials for the state. Higher and to the right was a patch with the initials "MC" for "Motorcycle Club." And that was it. There was not another patch on the vest. Compared to the vests worn by all the other brothers and old ladies this one looked strangely naked in comparison.

"It's generally the prospect's job to sew the patches on. But when Sue heard you were going for prospect, she insisted on sewing your patches on for you," Samurai said.

While Harold appreciated her efforts n his behalf, he was caught completely off guard when Sue stepped forward and put her arms around the new prospect. As she did so, she offered her own congratulations. Harold was about to say "Thank you," but, before he could get the words out, Sue anticipated his response and said, "Your welcome."

"All right, unhand my old lady," Samurai said with a grin, though his joke elicited a frown from Sue.

"Here," Samurai continued, handing a roll of white, cloth tape to Harold. "Make a big, white 'P' on the center of the back. And hurry up, we've got a job to do."

Harold wasted no time applying the tape to the jacket. While he was occupied with that, Samurai made arrangements for Sue to ride back to Hildie's Hideout on the back of a brother's bike. "I'll meet you in a while," he told her and then gave her a quick kiss on the lips.

As Harold slipped his arms into the vest, Samurai motioned for Harold to follow and headed for the door. Harold followed while noticing that Kilroy had fallen into step with the two of them. It suddenly occurred to Harold that they might be planning some kind of surprise initiation for the new prospect. At the same time, Harold sensed initiations were saved for the times when a brother earned his full patch. All the same, the thought that something might be up, and the way Kilroy, like a mobster's henchman, silently followed along with a blank forward stare every time Harold nervously looked back over his shoulder, made Harold feel a little apprehensive as they walked out the door.

As they stepped outside, as though he didn't want anyone else to see it, Kilroy, grabbed Harold's shoulder and used it to turn the new prospect around. Face to face, his face transformed by a grin, Kilroy, extended his hand for a biker handshake and said, "Congrats, man." Relieved, Harold enthusiastically shook Kilroy's hand. As he did so, Kilroy's demeanor became a little more serious. "Just make sure you don't do anything to embarrass your sponsor or the club."

Harold nodded as they mounted their bikes and pulled onto the road. He wanted to ask where they were going but Samurai and Kilroy were riding side by side up front and, following along behind, Harold could have yelled at the top of his lungs and they probably wouldn't have heard him.

Several miles and a few turns later, the trio rode up an entrance ramp to the interstate and headed west towards Biesenthal. The bikes roared in unison as Samurai and Kilroy cracked their throttles wide open and Harold followed suit. When the exit to Biesenthal came along on their right, Harold expected they would turn off the expressway. Instead, they continued west. About 20 miles northwest of Biesenthal was the city of Millbrook. Where Biesenthal was a village of about 5,000, and Earlsville on the upper side of 10,000, Millbrook was home to more than 40,000 and considered the 'big city' in the area.

The bikers took the second exit for Millbrook and were soon headed north on a broad boulevard with small trees planted approximately every 50 feet down the center of a curbed meridian. At the top of a tall hill, they turned right onto a four-lane street with frequent stoplights stretching out ahead of them. About three blocks along, they spotted a bar with a row of Harleys parked out front. Samurai and Kilroy slowed and checked out the bikes as they went by as though they were looking for one bike in particular. Not seeing what they wanted, they continued down the four-lane road about a mile and turned right into an older industrial subdivision. Factories lined both sides of the street for the first two blocks and continued interrupted only by a fenced parking lot on the left. A little further, there was a break in the bricked factory walls. Set back from the street was a small bar. The gravel lot in front was relatively full of an assortment of cars that consisted primarily of station wagons and sedans – the kinds of cars driven by blue-collar family men. However, near the front door was a metallic-green Sportster with a long, chrome front-end.

Harold noticed that, when they saw the bike, Samurai and Kilroy looked at each other and nodded before turning into the lot. Harold followed them in as they parked in the same space as the green bike. Samurai parked next to the Sportster. When Harold and Kilroy parked behind it, they effectively sealed it in. Harold wasn't sure if this was intentional.

Heavy cigarette smoke hung in a fog at the ceiling of the bar thinning as it drew closer to the floor but never completely dissipating. Harold recognized the song "Greensleeves" playing on the jukebox and remembered that it was one of his mother's favorites. Looking somewhat out of place, the three bikers waded through a crowd of factory workers, most with an etched-in-dirt coating on their hands and faces that soap wouldn't completely remove. By comparison, for most of them, their clothes were reasonably clean indicating that they had either changed into street clothes at the end of the workday or wore coveralls over their street clothes as they worked. As Harold looked around the bar, he saw that it was just like the bar his father used to stop at after a day at 'the plant.' The men were just like the men his father worked and drank with all those years. This, in fact, was the life his father had expected for Harold. Most of the men were smiling, but the wear and tear of hard work in hot, dirty places, was clearly apparent on their faces. Harold appreciated the camaraderie that was evident among the men, but it wasn't enough to fill Harold with a sense of longing. Spending 40 hours or more a week selling most of his life and health to 'the man' was not Harold's idea of how to live. "If I'm going to abuse my body, it will be on my own terms," he always told himself. "And besides, it's not the only place to find good friends" Harold now added thinking of his newfound brothers.

As they reached the bar, there was a worker leaning against it with one foot up on the brass rail. Judging from the soot on his face and hands, Harold doubted this worker had spent much time or soap trying to clean away the remnants of the workday. Unlike the others, in a room where most haircuts were short and beards were only a day or two's stubble, this man's hair was long and tangled and his beard extended down to the middle of his chest. Also, unlike the others, he was still wearing dark-green coveralls. The color of the garment only partially hid the dirt and grime that was ground into the fabric. On top of the coveralls, the worker wore a leather biker's jacket. On his feet, he wore a brown-leather pair of steel-toed work shoes with a leather flap over the laces. These, too, were covered in dirt, grease, and soot. By his overall appearance, Harold astutely concluded this man was both a factory worker and a biker and, just as likely, the reason for their trip to Millbrook.

When Samurai, Kilroy, and Harold were about six feet away from him, the blue-collar biker glanced in their direction. For a split second, Harold was sure he saw an "Oh-shit" expression flash across the man's face. However, that look was immediately replaced by a large grin as he hollered a booming greeting of, "Que Pasa, brothers? What brings you to this sorry side of town?"

Samurai and Kilroy flashed a look between them, and Samurai said, "We were in the neighborhood. Thought we'd drop in and say, 'Hi.'"

"Cool, bro," the man replied. He then turned to the bartender and ordered three more beers "for my brothers and their friend."

Then the man stuck out a dirty left hand and grabbed Harold by his right shoulder as if to fix Harold in place while the biker extended his right hand for a biker handshake. But then he pulled the shoulder to turn Harold sideways so that he could see Harold's back. Harold might have resisted, but he noticed that Samurai and Kilroy were still looking on calmly.

"What do we have here," the biker said laughing, "a new prospect?"

Ignoring the comment about Harold, Kilroy said, "Late shift tonight, eh?"

"Yeah, we went to 12-hour days Monday," Mongrel said. "We got some big push on building parts for a company in Germany or some fucking place."

"Well, can't blame yeah for taking the money," Kilroy said.

The statement seemed to imply there was something they could blame the biker for. From the quick look he gave Kilroy, Harold was sure the biker had caught the insinuation.

"Hey, you gotta take the OT when it comes along," the biker said. "By next fall, they could be cutting us back to four-day weeks again."

Over a Hank Williams tune that had just come up on the juke-box, Harold heard the biker mumble something to the effect of "You know I would have been there …" Then, in what might have been a deceptively soft tone, Samurai asked if they could talk outside.

As Samurai and the biker headed for the door, Kilroy looked at Harold and said, "Go watch from the window over there. If anything goes down, holler."

Standing by the window with his beer, Harold watched as Samurai and the biker stopped in front of the bikes to talk. At first, everything seemed fine. The biker with the flaps on his dirty shoes was laughing and even slapped Samurai on the arm a couple times. Samurai, however, wasn't laughing.

To Harold, Samurai was a soft-spoken and fairly gregarious sort of fellow. Now, however, as he watched out the window, Harold was reminded of the first time he'd met Samurai. Harold recalled that, when Morticia jammed the glass into the girl's face, Samurai had exhibited a quiet and calm reaction but with forceful demeanor. Without a word, Samurai had communicated to the victim's friends that an aggressive reaction on their part was not wise. This was the same Samurai Harold saw outside with Mongrel now.

At first, the other biker had done all of the talking. Then, however, Harold saw that Samurai was taking over. The biker was looking down at his shoes the way a kid does when his parents are lecturing over bad behavior. Then the biker looked up and said something in protest. At that, the veins bulged on the sides of Samurai's neck, his face suddenly turned a shade of purple and red, and he stepped up close to the other biker. He wasn't exactly yelling, but the way Samurai spoke seemed to have the same effect. There was something surprisingly intimidating about Samurai when he spoke this way, something Harold hadn't seen before. What was even more startling was that, even though he was furious, Samurai remained completely in control of himself. It was a measured response and, looking at the other biker, who was several inches taller than Samurai, Harold sensed it was having the desired effect.

Through the window and over the music, Harold barely caught bits and pieces of what Samurai was saying. "… your fucking responsibility …" "… you let us down …" "… when the fuck were you planning …"

Samurai's tirade only lasted maybe 30 seconds, though it probably seemed longer to the other biker. When Samurai was done, Harold had a sense the other biker was profusely promising something amid a stream of apologies and excuses. Then the biker threw his arms around Samurai and gave him a big hug. He even planted a wet kiss on Samurai's lips.

For his part, Samurai remained placidly restrained. He hugged back with one arm and his face was passively stern. As they came back through the door, Harold fell in behind them on the way back to the bar. When the biker glanced back over his shoulder, Harold had a sense the biker was annoyed to discover the exchange outside had a witness, but the biker didn't say anything.

Back at the bar, the biker ordered another round of beers. When he turned to pass one on to Harold, Harold caught a clear glimpse of the man's face. Harold recognized the trail of tears down the man's face. Aware Harold saw that he'd been crying, the biker turned away quickly and wiped his eyes and nose with the sleeve of his leather jacket. The tears seemed strangely out of place on the face of someone who impressed Harold as probably a pretty tough biker. But somehow, Harold didn't think less of him for it. The tears did, however, seem to increase Samurai's stature in Harold's eyes.

The business of the evening apparently behind them, Samurai turned to Harold and said, "This is Mongrel." Then Samurai gestured to the biker and said, "He's a good brother but, you gotta watch him. He screws up sometimes."

Mongrel looked up at Harold from the floor, sniffled a little and extended his hand, thumb up, to shake. As they shook, Samurai introduced Harold and explained that he, Samurai, was Harold's sponsor.

"Well, if Samurai's sponsoring you, I'm sure you'll turn out to be a solid brother," Mongrel said.

Harold wondered if Mongrel's comment was intended to patronize Samurai a little in consideration of their conversation outside. On the other hand, Harold sensed a sincere feeling of respect. Harold decided that, whatever trouble this biker had gotten himself into, he truly liked and respected Samurai.

On the way out half-an-hour later, Samurai explained that Mongrel and another brother, named Capsize, had all winter to set up an event called Road Day. "They didn't do a fucking thing and that's why we had to ride out here and look into matters tonight," Samurai continued.

When Harold asked about Road Day, Kilroy stepped in with an enthusiastic response. "For bikers, it's like Christmas, New Years and the 4th of July all wrapped into one," Kilroy said. "And it's mandatory. Be up and ridin' or yer ass is grass."

Then Harold asked if they were going to find Capsize now. "No," said Samurai. "He hides better."

"Yeah, and Mongrel will give him the message anyhow," Kilroy said.

From the way Samurai and Kilroy smiled knowingly at the last statement, Harold had a sense that Mongrel would probably pass along Samurai's sentiments on the matter to Capsize in no un-certain terms. Harold made a mental note that he really, really didn't want to get into trouble with the club. He felt that way from the moment Samurai had told him he had made prospect, but witnessing Mongrel's experience outside the bar, the deter-mination to stay on the good side of things with his sponsor and the Banshee Riders was reinforced.

Chapter 11 — A 6 Pack of Trouble

Over the course of the next couple weeks, Harold came over to Samurai's each day after work as instructed. Harold had taken the job with Tank in Earlsville and his workday ended at 4 p.m., Monday through Friday. Occasionally, Harold was told he would have to work until noon or 4 p.m. on a Saturday but, so far, that hadn't happened. Somehow, rain or shine, Samurai had places for them to go. And rain or shine, they always went by bike. Harold found that he was putting close to 100 miles on Magdelina every day, including the ride to and from Earlsville for work. He was feeling increasingly comfortable on the bike.

Most nights he slept at Chester's but, occasionally, he crashed on the couch at Samurai's. When he asked Chester how he felt about his coming and going, Chester shrugged and replied, more poignantly than he probably realized, "Well, I ain't yer mother."

Friday night was meeting night and, now that he was a prospect, Harold waited outside by the bikes rather than back at the bar with the old ladies. At his first meeting outside with the bikes, Harold met the club's two probates, Red and Drago. After the meeting, the probates and prospect often stood at the far end of the bar at Hildie's drinking a few beers together while waiting until they were needed.

"A probate is a step up from a prospect," Red explained. "A probate has prospected long enough and taken enough crap while demonstrating that he's a standup guy -- trustworthy – dependable. He's shown that he's almost ready for the brothers to vote him up to the next level." Red turned to show Harold that, as a probate, the biker wore the top rocker with the club's name, a detail Harold had already noticed. The only missing patch from the back of a probate's vest, or rag, was the center patch. The probate was allowed into the meetings, where he lit cigarettes and fetched beers, or anything else that was requested but wasn't allowed to talk. "As a probate, they're willing to admit that I'm with the Banshee Riders. As a prospect, they're not even willing to admit that much yet.

"Most of the time, all I gotta do is light an occasional cigarette and fetch beers for the brothers, that and guarding the bikes when we're out in less-familiar territory," Red explained. "I do get the odd job once in a while. Like once, Falstaff sent me out for a dozen jalapenos. No idea what they did with 'em."

"I'm guessing they ate 'em," Drago laughed.

"I'm good, too," said Red, ignoring Drago. "A brother hardly has a cigarette in their mouth and my lighter is there, lit and ready."

"Yeah, you're good, alright," said Drago, with a smile. Then, turning to Harold, he said, "He's so good that he almost lit Tex's beard on fire one night. Tex had a cigarette in his hand but he only raised his hand to make a point. Red flips out his Zippo and scares the shit out of the brother."

Laughing along with Drago, Red said, "I thought he was gonna kick my ass."

As though both of them suddenly remembered about Tex leaving town to keep his old lady out of jail, their laughs died off and they looked down at their beers the way they might if someone had died.

"I hope that crazy bitch hasn't gotten Tex into ..." started Red.

"He's fine," said Drago, confidently, as though saying so made it so. After another pause, he added, "Tex ain't no fool."

Red nodded and took a swig of his beer as Harold thought back to the day at the bar when he had briefly seen Tex and his old lady, Morticia. Harold was trying to divine clues, from that chance encounter, to support the qualities Red and Drago were assigning to Tex, but the event was too brief, and he decided that the loyalty to his old lady, in spite of her crazy and unprovoked attack on a citizen, was an indication of what Red and Drago meant. Harold's thoughts then turned to sizing up the probates he was standing with at the end of the bar.

Harold felt a little ambivalent about Drago, who was low key and more reserved – quiet but with a serious side that suggested a willingness to mix it up if called upon. Already having earned his patch once, and now in the process of earning it back, Harold sensed that Drago saw himself more as a brother in the penalty box than as a true probate. But Harold immediately took a liking to Red. The name, rather obviously, came from the crop of long-red locks on the man's 20-something head. He had a pubescent crop of red hairs on his chin, too. Standing about nose to nose with Harold, Red was of a similar build though his beer belly was less developed.

"The better you prospect, the faster you move up to probate," Red explained, "and then to full-patch."

Red pulled a small, tin box out of the upper pocket of his relatively new, and clean cut-off Levi. He showed Harold how the box, which once contained throat lozenges, now held an assortment of items: aspirin, antacid, needle and thread. Drago removed a similar box from his pocket, though Drago's was badly battered, so much so that the hinge was gone, and the top only loosely sat on top.

"You gotta carry a needle and some thread in case one of the brothers needs something sewn or has to stitch up a cut or something," Red explained. "Antacid, aspirin, Bandaids – any other medicine you can think of: you never know when it will come in handy." Red also produced a small packet with a rubber. "This, of course, goes without saying," he said with a smile.

Then Red glanced around to make sure no one else was watching. He picked up one of several small white pills that were floating loose in the bottom of the box. Holding it out to Harold between the forefinger and thumb, Red said, "Speed. The brothers can't make you get this for them. Used to be they could. But the club voted that it isn't right for brothers to make prospects and probates fetch drugs – you know, drugs fer fun. This is white cross. They're cheap as hell. Truckers use 'em all the time to stay up while they're driving over the road."

Red handed the pill to Harold. As Harold examined the pill in the palm of his hand, Red said, "Go ahead, bro. I've got more."

When Harold seemed to hesitate while looking at the pill in the palm of his hand, Red added, "It'll just help you stay awake longer, maybe make your heart race a bit, too. It's a good idea for us – the brothers will expect us to stay up to the wee hours and they ain't exactly gentle if the body snatchers get yeah."

As Harold swallowed the pill down with his beer, Red said, "It's a pretty cool thing for the club to take a vote like that – watching out for their future brothers and all. Of course, a couple brothers are kind of partial to these," Red added while holding up another white cross. "They can't ask for 'em anymore, but I make sure they're, well, supplied. Like I said, 'If you want to move up the ladder faster, it's best to keep the brothers happy.'"

Drago had walked to the other side of the bar by that time. The two stood quietly for a minute sipping at the beers. Then Red broke the silence, "Samurai fuck with you much?"

"What do you mean?" Harold asked.

"You know, always having you do stupid shit, like cleaning the toilet in his house or picking up dog shit in his backyard?" Red said.

Harold laughed, "No, nothing like that. Why, does your sponsor have you doing that kind of crap?"

"No," Red said. "Wide Glide's my sponsor. He's cool." Then, leaning forward and speaking in a softer tone, Red continued, "There was another prospect when I first started prospecting. His sponsor was a real jerk. He was always making this dude do embarrassing stuff in public – even in front of other clubs.

"He'd pull that shit on me, too," Red said. "But if Wide Glide sees him doing it, he'll usually find something else for me to do, like having me take his bike out for a ride or something," and with a devilish smile, Red added, "anything to get me away from the asshole."

Harold had a sense that Red didn't want to say the name of the other prospect's sponsor, and he didn't push it. However, this was the first time that the concept of other clubs had really crossed Harold's mind since he started prospecting for the Banshee Riders. Suddenly, Harold recalled the two bikers and the nasty old lady who had pounded on the rubber salesman Harold's first night in town. Harold hadn't looked closely at the patches on the back of their rags. All Harold knew for sure was that they weren't Banshee Riders.

"Other clubs?" Harold asked out of curiosity.

"Sure man," said Red. "There are five clubs in this neck of the woods – small clubs like us – the Saxons, High Riders, Satan's Undertakers, Cherry Poppers and Swamp Rats.

"You've heard of the Monks?" Red asked.

"Sure," Harold said. The Monks were a national club – one of the largest motorcycle 'gangs' in the world. Occasionally, they made the news when someone was shot or something, or if there was a big bust. "I met one once, at a bar back home."

"How was he?" Red asked.

"OK, I guess," Harold said. "I don't remember him sayin' much." Harold didn't mention he was lucky to remember anything at all about the experience, as Harold was extremely drunk at the time.

"Well," said Red, "the Monks are strong to the south of here.

But if you go about 50 miles north, it's Bloody Bastards territory."

Harold had also heard of the Bloody Bastards, though he was aware they were more of a regional club with several chapters across several states.

"Yeah, I've heard of them, too," Harold said.

"The thing you've got to understand is the Bloody Bastards don't like the Monks and the Monks don't like the Bloody Bastards," Red explained. "About 10 years ago, they had kind of a turf war in this area. A couple Monks were shot off their bikes and a few Bloody Bastards blew up in a van or something." Then, speaking with the conviction of someone who'd been there at the time, though Red was only 11 back in 1973, he added, "Eventually, they had a truce. They held a big pow-wow, or somethin', and declared this area open territory. It's kind of like a buffer zone between the two clubs. What this means to you and me is that, as long as the truce holds, we don't have to worry too much. Keep in mind it's only a truce. It's kind of like were in the DMZ between North and South Korea. As long as no one's shooting, it's a good day."

Harold's impression of prospecting for the club had amounted to fetching some beers, lighting some cigarettes, and riding with Samurai. He'd met a few people and was beginning to feel a sense of belonging. Now, with the background provided by Red, it dawned on Harold that there was another side to all this, a side where the club might expect him to do more than merely act tough. At some point, he might have to prove himself.

Harold didn't have a long string of fights in his past to base how he might fare in a serious situation. He'd had a few playground tussles, the kind where someone gets a bloody nose or something minor like that. As he kept score, he figured he'd won a few, and lost a few more than he'd won. This record didn't include the time he wound up on the floor at Freddie's recently; he couldn't remember how he actually got there so he couldn't say if he was in a fight or not. Of those that clearly qualified as fights, the most recent, the loss, however, was still several years ago. As he was extremely drunk at the time, drunk enough that he only had the vaguest recollection of what happened, all Harold really knew was that he was beaten up by two or three guys in the alley behind a bar in a rough neighborhood down in the city.

But for the most part, he had avoided physical confrontations. He was more inclined to eat crow and back down than to stand up to someone, especially if the odds weren't heavily in his favor. Harold knew, when he started prospecting for the Banshee Riders, that he would have to develop a different attitude about physical confrontations – it wasn't all for show. The discussion with Red drove the point home. Harold began to steel himself to the violent possibilities ahead. "It's a matter of setting your mind to a certain path," he told himself, "and staying on it."

The next day Saturday, Samurai had some more electrical work for Harold. During the day, Samurai informed Harold that they were going to a party that night. "The Cherry Poppers are having a little shindig," Samurai said. Then he looked up from the wires he was pulling and added, "Make sure you keep your shit together."

"No problem," Harold said with more conviction than he necessarily felt.

"Yeah," Samurai said in a tone that suggested he wasn't entirely convinced. "Just make sure you do. Oh, and don't take any shit from the other clubs. Don't give 'em any crap, but don't take any, either.

"You're a prospect for the Banshee Riders so, if one of your brothers says, 'Jump,' you jump. But if a brother from another club tells you to do something, just ignore him – or tell him to talk to me. Another thing, the other day Sue told you to get some potatoes up from the basement for dinner. Old ladies don't tell you shit. It goes president, vice president, other officers, brothers, probates, prospects, and then old ladies. The other brothers see you running for an old lady, even mine, and we'll both catch some shit."

After they packed up the tools at the end of the day, they headed back to Samurai's, dropped off the van and picked up their rags and bikes. The party was just over the border in the next state to the north. Harold realized that, according to what Red had said, the party was in the Bloody Bastards' territory. But Samurai didn't seem concerned, so Harold didn't say anything about it.

At the previous night's meeting, Falstaff had barked at the brothers that it was mandatory that they show up for this party in force. "I expect to see every swinging dick there," he said. But as was customary, that's not how it worked out. Even Falstaff was among the missing.

"Everybody gets hammered on Friday night," said Samurai, a note of derision in his voice. "Then they're too sick to drag their asses up for Saturday night, whatever's going on. Happens all the time. Most of the brothers are home stretched out on their sofas watching TV and nursing hangovers."

As it was, when the time came, only Samurai, Mongrel, Red, and Harold rode out, a minority representation of the Banshee Riders, to the Cherry Poppers party.

Harold figured he'd see other brothers at the party when they got there. Samurai, however, told him, "Don't count on it." Samurai was almost right.

Samurai, who, of all the brothers, had the best track record of showing up for events as promised, had once considered quitting the club over the issue. When he brought his feelings up at a recent meeting, he was talked out of the decision by a flurry of promises, all given with the greatest sincerity. Overall attendance improved for a couple weeks. But it quickly fell back into the previous pattern. The effort, poor though it was, was enough that, when added to a sense of loyalty and brotherhood, Samurai stayed in the club and somewhat accepted the situation with a degree of resignation. He probably never intended to quit but was merely speaking out in frustration.

This party was at a one-story brick home probably built for a son or daughter of the farming family that owned an old farmhouse down a darkened gravel road they passed just before reaching the party. There were no lights on in front of the house and Harold was somewhat surprised at how easily Samurai picked out the drive as they came down the road. In the darkness, parking the bikes among 40 or 50 other motorcycles was a harrowing experience, all the more so because of the irregular terrain. Regardless, without hitting any other bikes parked on the front yard, they eventually found a level piece of grass among the shadows where they could lean the bikes onto their kickstands.

As they dismounted and headed out back where they could

hear the music playing, Mongrel, who had narrowly avoided being knocked down to probate over the Road Day fiasco, amazingly recognized the silhouette of someone he knew leaning on the railing of the front porch and went over to talk. "I'll meet you out back," Mongrel said over his shoulder.

As the others rounded the corner to the right side of the house, Harold saw a flickering light dancing through the branches of several tall Evergreen trees that formed a picket line extending out back from the side of the house. To get there, the Banshee Rider, the probate, and the prospect had to push branches out of their way and walk through the tree line.

A bonfire was burning about 40-feet beyond the back porch of the house. Several additional bikes were parked to the side of the porch, all under the amber glow of a bug light in the fixture next to the sliding-glass backdoor. Looking beyond the porch, Harold realized they could have avoided the Evergreens if they had chosen to come around back from the other side of the house.

A few bikers and old ladies were on the porch, drinks in hand, talking and laughing as "Wild Horses" by the Rolling Stones blared from speakers temporarily hung on the wall. Considerably larger groups were at random intervals around the bonfire. However, judging from the number of people he could see in the back unless others were in the garage on the other side of the house, Harold assumed the party must extend into the house.

As Harold took in his surroundings, Samurai and Red both saw people they knew on opposite sides of the fire. Red headed right, yelling a greeting of, "Hey VD, what's cookin' you asshole?" Samurai headed the other way gesturing for Harold to follow.

Several bikers were standing in a semi-circle near the fire. As Samurai and Harold approached, most of the bikers nodded a casual greeting. Samurai returned the gesture and then turned his attention to a large, hulking biker at the far side of the group. The biker, who was as big a man as Harold had ever seen, was the last to notice Samurai and Harold approaching. As he did, however, in the flickering yellow and orange light of the fire, Harold saw a grin spread across his face as the biker yelled, in a deep, deep baritone, "Samurai, you little Kamikaze bastard, what the fuck?!" Samurai merely smiled and said, "Sasquatch."

The biker had long, stringy hair that hung down from an almost perfectly round bald dome at the top of his head. While he lacked a mustache, his long, thin hair continued down his sideburns and hung like tinsel about eight inches onto his chest following, from ear to ear, the bottom edge of his jawbone.

Instead of stopping for handshakes, as Harold had expected, the two strode towards each other and met in the middle of the circle where they gave each other a warm embrace before kissing fully on the lips. This looked a little silly as the taller biker had to bend over considerably to bring his face down to Samurai's level. Harold was still finding this kissing thing between brothers a little uncomfortable. But he could see that it was more of a cultural peculiarity than some kind of an indication of anything sexual.

Samurai and the huge biker spoke quietly for a moment, too quietly for Harold to hear over the music, the fire and other conversations in the area. But then Samurai turned to Harold as Samurai and his big friend stepped out of the middle of the group's circle. With his right arm resting on the large biker's back, Samurai said, "I want you to meet someone.

"This man mountain is Sasquatch," said Samurai. "He's Enforcer for the Saxons and a righteous mother fucker."

As the big man's eyes looked down on Harold, Samurai continued, "And this is Harold."

"Harold?" the large biker said in a surprised tone. "What the fuck kind of name is 'Hair-old?'" he said, accentuating the name as though it left a bad taste in his mouth.

"Well, I've been saving his club name for just the right occasion," Samurai said with a mischievous grin.

"Prospects," the large biker said with a note of disdain the way a parent expresses a need for tolerance when speaking of their children.

"Do you mind if I finish the introductions," Samurai said, sounding a bit sarcastic.

"By all means," said the large biker with sarcasm as he waved a bear-like massive paw in Harold's direction while stepping off to the side. In doing so, his titanic shadow fell over Harold and Samurai. Samurai turned on his heels to face Sasquatch again. The look of exacerbation on Samurai's face was even evident through the darkness. The large biker stood still for a second and then, recognizing Samurai's annoyance, stepped quickly to the side as he said, "Oh."

As the light of the bonfire washed over Harold and Samurai again, Samurai said in a softer tone, "With a shadow that frickin' big, you gotta be careful where you cast it." Then he stood looking at Sasquatch as if to say, "Well?!"

Sasquatch finally caught on and stepped forward and extended a hand to Harold. As the giant's shadow fell over him again, Harold's hand disappeared into Sasquatch's palm. "Glad to meet you," Sasquatch said with sincerity. Then he continued in towards Harold until he had the prospect in a bear hug. Harold was caught off guard. As he belatedly returned the hug, he was secretly thankful that Sasquatch hadn't planted a kiss on his lips as well.

Stepping back, Sasquatch said to Samurai, "So what are you going to do about this name business? You can't go around calling him Harold all the time." The effect when he said 'Harold,' with a nasal whine that was so comical that even Harold couldn't help smiling as Samurai laughed.

Samurai argued jokingly, "You don't give a stray dog a name until you think you might keep it."

With a sincere tone of annoyance, Sasquatch stuck up for Harold saying, "That shit ain't right, bro. The probate of today is the brother of tomorrow."

Samurai laughed and said, "Alright, alright. Like I said, 'I've been saving this for the right time.'" Then, with that mischievous grin again, he added, "But what the fuck, I might as well do it now."

Harold and Sasquatch were staring at Samurai as he paused for effect. Then, instead of delivering the name, Samurai gave Harold a short lecture on how club names worked. "Most of the time, not always, but most of the time, a sponsor picks his prospect's name. Your name says who you are."

Jokingly, Harold said, "I heard Red call some guy VD earlier does that mean ..."

"Exactly," Samurai said. "VD's has such a dirty dick it's a wonder the thing hasn't shriveled up and fallen off."

"Kinda hard for him to get laid anymore among certain circles, if you know what I mean," said Sasquatch.

Samurai paused for effect again, drawing the process out as long as he could, apparently relishing the opportunity to give his prospect a hard time. "Before you started prospecting for the Banshee Riders, your name was Harold," Samurai explained. "From now on, you'll be known as ..."

Samurai paused again, eliciting an earth-shaking rumble of "Come on already" from Sasquatch.

Seeing that Sasquatch was visibly aggravated seemed to add to the pleasure Samurai derived by dragging it out. Instead of speaking the name, Samurai downshifted again and said, "When you get your club name ..."

"SAMURAI!" Sasquatch bellowed.

Samurai stopped and looked at his large friend whose voice had attracted the attention of several others in the vicinity. "You want me to do this right, don't you?" Samurai asked.

Sasquatch nodded as though he were a child taking his medicine.

"Well then, let me do it my way, OK?" Samurai said.

When Sasquatch nodded again, Samurai continued, "Like I was saying, we don't just pick your name out of a hat or because it sounds cool. You heard about the Indian chief who named all the babies in the tribe when they were born? First thing the chief saw after the birth, that was the baby's name. That's why one Indian brave was called Two Dogs Fucking."

Several people nearby laughed. Harold, however, was becoming increasingly anxious and Sasquatch merely smirked.

"Well, you can thank Montana for your name," Samurai said, referring to his 2-year-old daughter. "Seems she's taken a shining to you. She keeps calling you 'that Naked Boy.' Who am I to argue?"

Remembering the first morning he'd woken on Samurai's couch, Harold just shook his head in disbelief. Somehow, he'd expected something tougher, more intimidating: like Wolfman or Spike. He thought to himself as he looked at his sponsor, "You get to be called Samurai, a warrior name, and you're telling me I have to go through life being called Naked Boy because your daughter didn't know I had pants on?"

Sasquatch couldn't believe it either. "Naked Boy?" he said. "What kind of name is that?"

"It's his kind," Samurai said.

"Oh, come on," Sasquatch said, sounding more annoyed than

Harold felt looking on with a crestfallen expression. "You can't call him that. Naked Boy?"

The grin disappeared from Samurai's face as he said in a serious tone, "The brother makes the name, not the other way around." Then, looking at Harold, Samurai said with finality, "Montana has spoken, deal with it."

For the first time since they'd met, Harold was pissed off at Samurai. He thought to himself, "I'd rather my sponsor had me pick up dog shit." Instead, he only muttered something about getting arrested if people went around calling him that.

"Don't worry," Samurai said. "We'll bail you out." Then, Samurai held his hands out and looked from one to the other as though puzzled about something. Harold, or Naked Boy, didn't catch on fast enough.

"Do I look like I have a beer in either of my hands? And get one for my brother, Sasquatch, too." Then, Samurai turned his back on Harold and started talking with the large biker from the Saxons as though Harold wasn't even there. It was more of a sponsor-like attitude than Harold was used to from Samurai. He sensed that his sponsor was less than pleased with Naked Boy's reaction to the name.

As Harold filled a couple plastic cups from one of two tappers in a large, oval, ice-filled horse trough, a prospect from another club grabbed a couple plastic cups that he filled from the other tapper. Standing side by side, the prospect introduced himself to Harold. "How ya doin?"

Harold glanced to his right to find a 20ish biker, had a messy flop of black hair, peach-fuzz on his chin, and probably weighed 120 pounds soaking wet, including his leathers and rag. Standing about 5-6, he was almost anemically thin.

"Name's Skunk," the other prospect said.

As the other prospect nodded hello, while making an upward gesture with the plastic cups in his hand to indicate he would offer to shake hands if their hands weren't so full, Harold almost laughed. "Just think," he said to himself, "I guess it's not so bad after all. Samurai could have named me Skunk."

"Those for your brothers," the prospect asked, gesturing towards the plastic cups of beer Harold had pinched together at the top so he could hold them in one hand while operating the tapper.

"When you're done, why don't you come on back and I'll pour you a cold one," Skunk said.

Harold wasn't entirely impressed with this biker and wasn't sure he wanted to come back. All the same, he said, "Sure," and turned to deliver the beers to his sponsor and his sponsor's enormous friend. Samurai and Sasquatch were engrossed in conversation and hardly noticed Harold other than to take the beers when Harold offered them. Then Harold returned to the tapper where Skunk was filling a couple beers presumably for the two of them.

"Who ya prospecting for?" Skunk asked. Then, before Harold could answer, he said, "I'm prospecting with the Swamp Rats, since about February."

Harold took the beer Skunk offered and paused a moment to make sure he was done speaking for a moment. "I just started prospecting for the Banshee Riders."

"Big club?" Skunk asked.

To Harold, this sounded like a silly question. What was he going to say, 'No, we're a tiny, little club?' "Big enough, I guess," said Harold with what he thought an appropriate answer.

"Us, too," said Skunk.

Just as Skunk asked, "So, what do you ride?" Harold's ears picked up a derisive comment from the porch a few feet away: "Isn't that cute? Hey, check out the prospects."

Harold glanced up at the porch where two bikers were standing, one leaning on the rail, looking at the two prospects by the horse trough. The one had a distasteful look on his face. The other, when he saw Harold looking over, tipped his head slightly and gave a distinctly unfriendly smile.

Neither of them looked particularly intimidating. Both were in about their mid-20s and stood about 5-10. They were both slim but solid. And both had long blonde hair. The one had a full beard while the one leaning on the railing had a neatly trimmed goatee and mustache. The name patch above the one's pocket, which Harold was learning to look for, read "Angler" and the other's, leaning on the rail, read "6 Pack." But since Harold couldn't see their backs, he couldn't say what clubs they belonged to.

"Cute?" said the biker with the full beard. "They look like a couple of dumb-fucking prospects to me."

Not knowing what club, or clubs, they belonged to, Harold wasn't sure that he had to pay them any attention. If either of them was a Banshee Rider, he would probably want to acknowledge them. It occurred to Harold that, if he didn't know, no one could blame him, so he just looked back at Skunk as though nothing was said. He found Skunk looking at him waiting for an answer, completely unaware of the potential problem from the porch.

"What was that?" Harold asked.

"I was saying I've got a '79 Sportster," said Skunk. "It's a sweet ride, man. What about you?" When Harold didn't answer immediately, Skunk explained, "What do you ride?"

Half paying attention to the threat from the porch, Harold answered, "I've got a '57 Pan."

"No shit?" said Skunk sounding really excited as though it was amazing for a prospect to have moved up to a larger Harley already.

Harold shrugged as if to say, 'It's nothing.'

"Hear that," the biker named Angler said. "The prospects are comparing their bikes. My old lady rides more bike than you, Skunk."

Finally, aware of the derision from the porch, Skunk was turning red with embarrassment. But Harold was getting pissed. Still, he didn't know who he was dealing with and continued trying to ignore the problem.

"Did you buy it new?" Harold asked Skunk hoping the bikers on the porch would grow tired of the game.

"That scrawny fucker one of your prospects?" the biker with the goatee asked the other.

"Yeah, but we're just keeping him around to clean toilets and shit," said Angler. "When we get tired of him, we'll probably just kick his ass and dump him in a culvert somewhere. Why, is that other lowlife one of yours?"

"Shit, I sure hope not," said 6 Pack. "I missed a meeting a couple weeks back. I hope our standards didn't slip that bad while I was gone. But then, if one of my brothers got really drunk, maybe they wouldn't have noticed what a loser he is."

Now, Skunk tried to draw back to the private conversation with Harold: "Hey, you ready for another beer?"

Harold was looking hard up at the biker named 6 Pack, as though considering whether to confront him. It seemed that 6 Pack appreciated the hesitation on Harold's face. 6 Pack grinned down at Harold almost daring him to say something. But Harold decided it was best just to let it pass. He looked down at his cup of beer, which was about half full yet, drained it and handed it back to Skunk saying, "Yeah, I could use some more. Thanks."

"No problem, bro," said Skunk as he took the cup to fill it.

"What the fuck are you doing, prospect," Angler barked from the porch, causing Skunk to freeze like a deer in the headlights.

The look on Skunk's face said that he knew he was in trouble but couldn't guess why. He looked up at the porch hoping for direction. But when no explanation was offered, he finished filling the cups and handed one to Harold.

Harold had hardly taken the cup, and was about to thank him again, when Angler charged up to the top of the stairs to the porch and hollered, "What the fuck is your problem, prospect? Didn't you hear me?"

Harold could see that Skunk was completely confused.

"Knock that beer out of that prospect's hand before I knock you upside the head, dipshit," Angler yelled.

Skunk seemed as though he was frozen in indecision. Harold noticed that 6 Pack seemed to be enjoying the show with increased pleasure.

"I said, knock that beer out of that dumb fucker's hand, prospect," Angler yelled again.

"This is moronic," Harold muttered under his breath. But he didn't say it quietly enough. Or, maybe, 6 Pack simply saw his lips move and that was enough.

The smile was gone from his face as 6 Pack stood up straight and growled at Harold, "What did you say, asshole?"

Harold ignored him, turned to Skunk, and said, "Just knock the cup out of my hand."

6 Pack stepped aggressively to stand next to Angler. "You mother fucker, what did you just say to him?" yelled 6 Pack.

"I told him to go ahead and knock the beer out of my hand," said Harold, a touch of challenge clear in his tone.

"You talking back to me, prospect?" 6 Pack said in a threatening tone that carried him to the bottom step.

Harold ignored him and turned back to Skunk, "Just knock it out of my hand already."

Skunk reached out and barely touched the cup with the back of his hand. Harold let it fall to the ground where the beer splashed over his boots.

"Why, you stupid fucking asshole," 6 Pack said calmly, as though this had settled the matter. "You let some punk-ass prospect knock your beer out of your hand? You don't take that shit from him. Kick his ass."

Harold stood looking at 6 Pack.

"I told you, kick his ass," 6 Pack repeated. "Now, dumb fuck."

"Who the fuck are you?" Harold asked.

That seemed to have pushed 6 Pack over the edge. He charged down the stairs and, with both hands, shoved Harold. But Harold saw him coming and moved one foot back to brace himself. Harold hardly moved as 6 Pack stumbled to the left. As he regained his balance, he threw a hard-left upper cut. Harold saw this coming, too, and stepped aside while he pushed off against the back of 6 Pack's left arm.

Finally, as 6 Pack was falling away again, Harold saw the back of his rag with the Banshee Riders name and center patch. A felt a sense of dread as his suspicion was confirmed. Would it matter that he didn't know 6 Pack was a member of the Banshee Riders? And what should he do now as 6 Pack appeared ready to continue the confrontation to a physical conclusion?

When Harold had pushed off against the back of his arm, 6 Pack's own momentum had carried him to the point where he almost fell on his face. He was coming off badly against the prospect and he knew it. His anger was turning to rage as he turned to rush Harold again, this time leading with his fists and clearly prepared. Harold doubted that he would be able to easily sidestep the next assault.

A flicker of a smile crossed 6 Pack's face as he saw the look of recognition on Harold's face. "Fucked up, haven't you, prospect?" he said. "Or, should I say, ex-prospect?"

In that moment when he paused, a shadow came over the fire. A booming voice hollered, "What the fuck is this?"

Harold suddenly realized Sasquatch was stepping between him and 6 Pack.

"This has nothing to do with you," 6 Pack hollered.

"Then take it somewhere else," said Sasquatch.

Another voice, asked, "What's the fucking problem here?" and Harold realized Samurai, followed by a number of others who had been by the fire, was standing off to the side.

"Your fucking prospect needs his ass kicked. That's the problem," barked 6 Pack.

"So, kick his ass already," said Samurai.

Harold prepared himself for a fresh attack. Instead, 6 Pack seemed as though he was having second thoughts. "That's alright," he said. "We'll deal with this later."

"Maybe that's what you should have done in the first place," said Samurai.

6 Pack's eyes shot darts at Harold again, for a moment. Then, he gave Harold the same unfriendly smile as before, though this time it seemed, somehow, to portend of trouble ahead. Then, getting in the last word, 6 Pack said, "Get me a beer, prospect."

Harold filled a cup and carefully brought it over to 6 Pack who hesitated a moment, as though Harold might throw it in his face, before taking the beer. "Thanks, prospect. Now, get one for my friend Angler here."

"That's OK," said Angler. "I've got my own prospect for that."

When Skunk had brought the beer over to Angler, he and 6 Pack returned to their prior spot on the porch. 6 Pack leaned on the railing, as though nothing had happened, and gave Harold another snarky smile. While he would have liked giving 6 Pack the finger, Harold realized that was probably not a good idea, especially since there was little doubt that he was in trouble with the club already. Still, Harold couldn't help but glare back at 6 Pack as if to agree, "You're right, this ain't over." But these thoughts were jolted from his mind as a hand grabbed the front of his rag and yanked him hard away from the porch. Harold turned to find Samurai, anger quietly simmering on his face, dragging Harold off away from the crowd.

Harold suddenly realized he had said "Oh shit" out loud.

Samurai actually laughed a little. But it didn't last: "'Oh shit' is right."

As they stepped back to the outside of the hedge, Samurai turned, grabbed Harold's shirt with both hands and nearly pulled him up off his feet. "What did I tell you about fucking up? Your first fucking party. Shit, I didn't leave you alone for 15 minutes and you're already in trouble."

"I didn't do anything," Harold protested.

"I saw you shove my brother," said Samurai. "I'd say that's a little more than not doing nothing."

"It was stupid," said Harold trying to explain what was happening by the horse trough.

"Damn right, it was stupid," said Samurai. "It sure as hell wasn't smart."

"I mean the whole thing was stupid," said Harold. "I wasn't doing anything, and they just started fucking with Skunk and me."

"Skunk?"

"The prospect from the Swamp Rats."

"What the fuck are you talking about," said Samurai. "Brothers fuck with prospects. If you can't take it, get the fuck out."

It suddenly occurred to Harold that this might be it; the motorcycle club experience was going to end as quickly as it started. Then, clutching at straws, he said, "You said not to take any shit from guys with other clubs."

"Well, if you haven't noticed, the colors on 6 Pack's back are the same as mine," said Samurai, while yanking Harold forward and finally letting go of his shirt.

"I didn't know that," said Harold.

"What do you mean, you 'didn't know that?'"

"I didn't get a look at his colors until he was already attacking me," said Harold.

"Then you should have played it cool until you knew."

"I was trying to, sort of," said Harold.

"What do you mean, 'Sort of?'"

"He told me to kick Skunk's ..., you know, the other prospect's ass."

"Why?"

"I don't know. It was stupid. The other dude was fucking with Skunk, I mean the other prospect, because he was pouring me a beer."

"What the fuck?" raged Samurai. The way Samurai suddenly

turned; a moment passed where Harold thought his sponsor was rearing back to deliver a serious blow. But Samurai just stopped facing the other way and shaking his head.

Just then, the bushes started shaking and Harold had the feeling that a Sherman tank was driving through the hedgerow. A moment later, he realized Sasquatch was emerging to join them.

"Hey, they're in here," Sasquatch hollered back through the hedge as he pulled a leg past a stubborn lower branch. "Sorry to interrupt, bro. Mongrel and I were looking for you."

Almost on que, a smaller vehicle – Mongrel – came through between the next break in the hedges.

"What the fuck?" asked Samurai.

"I'm sorry, brother," said Mongrel, "but I thought you should know what happened before you tee-off on the prospect."

"Know what?"

"I saw the whole thing," Mongrel continued. "It was typical 6 Pack bullshit."

"And how does that excuse the prospect?"

"I heard your prospect handled himself like a man," said Sasquatch. "6 Pack and Angler were fuckin' with 'em …"

An annoyed glance from Samurai seemed to have cut Sasquatch off. Turning to Mongrel, he asked, "So, what did you see?"

"Well, like we was sayin', they were fucking with the prospects," said Mongrel, quickly adding when he saw the look from Samurai. "I know. I know. But like I said, the prospect handled himself just fine. The worst he said was to ask 6 Pack, 'Who the fuck are you.' Ain't his fault he didn't know 6 Pack yet."

"You know how those assholes are," said Sasquatch.

Even in the shadows, Harold distinctly saw Samurai flash Sasquatch a look that said, 'Not in front of the prospect,' as though Samurai didn't want Harold to know he was getting off the hook that easy. But then, as though the cat was out of the bag, Samurai seemed to sigh, and Harold had a sense that his anger was deflating.

Finally, Samurai looked back at Harold and said, "Yes, 6 Pack is a jerk. In fact, this probably doesn't have anything to do with you."

Harold had a confused look on his face and Samurai said, "Well, 6 Pack and I have a little, well, history."

Seeing this hadn't cleared things up for Harold, Samurai reluctantly went on: "He had a prospect who fucked up a couple years ago – who was a fuck up. I was the one who called him out. 6 Pack's held it against me ever since."

There was a long silence broken when Samurai added, "Of course, you can bet the asshole will bring it up with the club next Friday."

"Well, let's deal with it then," said Mongrel. "No need to waste the night."

"That's right," said Sasquatch. "PARTY ON, MOTHER FUCKERS," he hollered while holding his beer cup in the air."

When he put the cup to his mouth and found it empty, he said, "What the hell" as though someone had played a dirty joke.

Harold looked at Samurai for a second as though to make sure the balling out was over, then reached out and took the cup from Sasquatch. "I'll get a round for all of ya," he said as he started to head back through the hedgerow.

He had hardly taken the first step when Samurai said, "Fuck that. Let's get out of here – go somewhere with a better class of asshole," and added, while looking at Sasquatch, "if you know what I mean."

As a group, they started towards the front and the bikes. But Harold stopped and turned to Samurai, "I'm gonna check and see if Skunk wants to come along with us."

"You got out front," said Mongrel. "I'll look for the prospect – see if he can come along." He looked at Sasquatch as though anticipating the question: "I'll ask someone other than Angler."

Harold, Samurai and Sasquatch waited out front long enough that Samurai was beginning to wonder if Mongrel had run into some trouble with 6 Pack or Angler too. Sasquatch, in the meantime, was checking out Magdelina and was clearly impressed.

"That's one sweet scooter, bro," he said while sitting on it and rocking it as though to get a feel for the bike.

Seeing that Samurai seemed concerned, Sasquatch said, "He's fine, bro. Probably stopped for a beer or to say goodbye to someone."

Samurai looked over and said, "Yeah, well, I'm gonna check it out" but had hardly gotten the words out when Mongrel, along with Red, who he'd collected along the way, came around from the other side of the house.

"Angler's still screwing with him," said Mongrel. "We could wait, but I don't see any sign of him letting up on him soon."

"Fuck it. Let's go," said Samurai. He paused, however, when he saw a concerned look on Harold's face. "Don't worry. I'm sure he'll be alright … and I'll try-n check up on him later."

Harold nodded reluctantly, and they got on and started their bikes.

As they were about to pull onto the road, Harold paused for a second and said, "By the way, thanks," to his sponsor.

"Thanks for what," Samurai asked.

"Well," Harold said, "thanks for believing me."

Samurai looked at Harold and said, "That's what brothers are for."

Sasquatch was straddling a dark-colored bagger and, as Samurai pulled out, Sasquatch peddled over where Harold was waiting so he'd ride in back. There was an awkward moment of silence where Harold appreciated the cloak of darkness that hid his discomfort. Then, in his gruff voice, though only above a whisper above the decibels of the bikes, Sasquatch said, "That Samurai's a righteous dude."

"Sure is," said Harold.

Chapter 12 — An Enemy and a Reaper

After another pregnant pause, and in a more conversational voice, Sasquatch said, "So, what's that yer ridin' there?"

Harold roughly described what the dark concealed about the bike.

"Sounds nice," said Sasquatch. He then described a hardtail he had at home. "Don't ride it too much, though. Messed up my back a while ago and that hardtail is murder, specially with the fucked-up roads in these parts."

Harold grunted in agreement though he was really puzzling over how, just when he was getting used to the idea of having brothers he could trust, he was discovering that, just because they were his brothers or his future brothers, didn't necessarily mean he could trust all of them. And at the same time, he was discovering that, in some cases, he could trust someone from another club, like Sasquatch, even more than some from his own club.

Several minutes later, as Samurai returned with Red, Harold could hear Red say, "What's his fuckin' problem?" apparently discussing 6 Pack.

When they reached an out-of-the-way bar Samurai knew, as they got off the bikes, Sasquatch picked up the conversation where they'd left off. "I know he's your brother but, I'm sorry, somebody needs to do something about that asshole, 6 Pack," Sasquatch said.

"Well, I'm about ready to tie his ass to a couple sewer covers and drop him in the lake, myself," Samurai said.

At that, Mongrel cleared his throat as though to remind Samurai that 6 Pack was still a brother. However, they felt about 6 Pack, Sasquatch was a Saxon. It surprised Harold to hear his brothers criticizing another Banshee Rider while speaking with someone from another club. Maybe loyalties did stop where Harold had expected.

Samurai looked at Mongrel and said, "Yeah, I know. Fucker just pisses me off sometimes."

Mongrel, who must have agreed, chuckled, "Well, he does have a way about him."

About the same time, Red leaned closer to Harold, "What did 6 Pack do?"

Harold said, "I'll tell you later."

But Samurai interrupted curtly, "You don't say anything about this unless I tell you to. That goes for both of you. Understand?"

They both nodded in the dark, Samurai led the group into the bar.

Inside were men, mostly older, in plaid shirts and the occasional baseball cap with a fish or an Evinrude Outboard Motors logo on the front. Built of darkened log timbers, the floor was made of wide, rough-surfaced slats of wood. The outer edge of the bar was a halved timber, and the top of the bar was a pine surface covered in heavy, deeply-yellowed shellac. The smell inside was a mix of beer, cigarettes, cigars and pipe tobacco from a pipe-smoking fisherman in the corner.

The bartender, a woman in her late 50s or early 60s was, beyond a doubt, the toughest and ugliest woman Harold had ever seen. Red was thinking the same thing as he leaned in and whispered to Harold, "Careful – get her pissed and she'll sick her pretty sister on you – the Wicked Witch of the West."

The way she looked at the group of bikers, Harold thought she might have heard Red and, either way, was liable to refuse to serve them. He was surprised, therefore, when she came over and, in a gruff but pleasant voice, asked, "What can I get you boys?"

In spite of Samurai's warning not to talk about what had happened at the party, or Mongrel's efforts to divert the conversation, when the bikers had drained a few more beers, tongues were loosened and, inevitably, the topic came up again.

Samurai was more intoxicated than Harold could recall seeing before. The more Samurai drank, the more candid he became about 6 Pack. In turn, Harold heard the whole story about the bad blood between 6 Pack and Mongrel. Before long, Samurai was calling 6 Pack a lair, a thief and "a low-life piece of shit."

Harold knew that, in different company, such talk could cause trouble for his sponsor with the Banshee Riders. But it was also apparent that they all shared roughly the same opinion of 6 Pack while universally holding Samurai in high esteem. Listening to Samurai talk, Harold wouldn't have been surprised if his sponsor suggested plotting a hit on 6 Pack and, yet Harold doubted anyone would object. Through his growing buzz, Harold worried about Samurai talking that way – that somehow it would get back to the club. Still, as Harold's blood/alcohol level struggled to keep pace with Samurai's, his concerns decreased proportionally.

By the next day, when Harold, Red, and Samurai woke, scattered on the floor and across the meager furnishings in Mongrel's place, nothing was said of their candid comments about 6 Pack the night before. Whether lost in the fog of a heavy night of drinking, it was as though they had all made an unspoken pact to avoid the subject. Or, more likely, without the buoyancy of alcohol, they were simply more circumspect about what they said.

Mongrel lived in a trailer-home behind a farmhouse and, the following Friday, it was his turn to host the club meeting. It was an old trailer, and, in the winter, the wind would howl through inadequately sealed pores carrying much of the already-inadequate heat out the other side. Though on colder days, Mongrel was lucky if the temperature got up to 50 inside, when the brothers showed up for a meeting, with summer on the horizon, the collective body heat made it almost unbearably warm inside. That being the case, in warmer parts of the year, brothers came to dread meetings in the cramped confines of Mongrel's home. Mongrel would have taken the meeting outside except he couldn't guarantee that the citizens he rented the trailer from wouldn't have work to do in the farmyard. It created an awkward situation trying to discuss club business while maintaining a little security. If brothers were aggravated before going into the trailer at the start of the meeting, and there was almost always something going on to cause some degree of frustration, the cramped environment inside the trailer did nothing to calm frayed nerves or rising tempers. As a result, attendance was always a little lower when Mongrel hosted the meeting. That wasn't the case on this particular Friday night.

Whether it had something to do with Road Day, which was drawing even closer, or news of the confrontation at the Cherry Poppers party, almost every member of the club was present. Harold was pretty sure it was the latter and had nursed a case of nerves all week wondering what would happen on Friday.

As the brothers filed inside to start the meeting, Harold, as the lone prospect, took up sentry duty outside by the bikes. 6 Pack was running late. Pulling up on a black Sportster a couple minutes after the door had closed, which, apparently, signified that the meeting had started, 6 Pack flashed Harold a nasty smile, as if to say, "Your time has come, prospect," and headed for the door. Then he paused and looked back at Harold and sneered, "Anything happen to my bike and I'll cut your balls off, prospect."

About half an hour after the door closed behind 6 Pack, shouting erupted from inside. Harold was certain he heard 6 Pack's voice. He also thought he heard Samurai and Mongrel, though not as loudly. Several other voices were raised, as well.

Inside, the topic of poor attendance at another party never even came up. A mix of rumors, facts, and fiction about what happened by the horse trough had circulated throughout the club. Most had heard 6 Pack's version of the incident as he was busy campaigning in the days before the meeting to make sure things went his way when the brothers gathered at Mongrel's. For his part, though Harold could only guess that this was the case, and other than the indiscretion at the bar after the party, Samurai had only discussed the matter with the president. A couple of days after the party, Samurai again admonished Harold to hold his tongue about the confrontation.

The shouting lasted about 20 minutes and then it stopped. Several seconds later the trailer door opened, and Drago stuck his head outside. "Get yer ass in here," he barked at Harold in a tone that did nothing to ease Harold's nerves.

The first thing Harold noticed upon entering, other than the mixed odor of beer, cigarettes, and sweat, along with the stifling heat, was that Mongrel had made no apparent effort to clean house before the meeting. Brothers who were smoking, which was most of them, were dropping ashes and stubbing out butts on top of overflowing ashtrays and in empty beer cans. Half a dozen such ashtrays were spread around the trailer. The kitchen sink was still full of dirty dishes, as were the counters on both sides. Newspapers, beer cans, pizza boxes, dirty laundry and more were spread about the trailer as though Godzilla had picked the trailer up and given it a good shake.

Several brothers had merely pushed the debris aside and taken seats in chairs, on counters, on tables and wherever else they found a place to sit. If they couldn't find a place to sit, they found a spot to stand somewhere on the edges of the kitchen or living room. Some sat on the floor and several accepted spots to stand in the hallway that led to the bathroom and bedroom.

All eyes turned to Harold as he stepped inside. Glancing around at the brothers, Harold was happy to see some familiar and, apparently, sympathetic faces – Mongrel, T-Rex, Tank, and Samurai among them. Red also looked sympathetic but Harold realized Red's opinion had little or no standing in the matter. As Harold continued to take a visual measure of the jurors, another face appeared sympathetic. This biker was tall and had a broad face. By the name patch on his vest, Harold knew that this was Wide Glide, Red's sponsor. Harold had counted the bikes outside and, after subtracting Red's, Drago's and his own scooters, Harold knew there were 22 brothers inside, which was an incredible number for the space allowed. He concluded there were 17 votes he couldn't count on. Of those, there were two, 6 Pack's and Capsize's, he was sure would go against him. That left 15 undecided. Harold figured he needed six or, preferably, seven, beyond those he was reasonably sure of, to be safe. As he looked around at the less familiar faces, Harold really wasn't sure how it would turn out. In fact, once the discussion began, could he even be sure that T-Rex, Tank or Wide Glide would remain in his corner?

Whatever confidence Harold might have felt, it was drained somewhat when Falstaff, sitting in one of two armchairs at the far side of the room, broke the silence and said in a harsh voice, "Get over here. In the middle of the floor, prospect."

When Harold stopped in the middle of the living room, Falstaff continued, "You have no voice in here unless you're told to speak. Do you understand?"

Harold nodded and Falstaff barked, "Speak up prospect. Do you understand?"

"Yes, I understand," Harold said in a barely audible tone.

Then the brother in the other armchair said, "You've been accused of attacking a full-patch brother. You've also been accused of acting disrespectfully to that brother in front of citizens and members of other clubs. What have you got to say for yourself?"

Harold looked at the unfamiliar brother who was apparently presiding over the meeting. This was a big man, though not quite as big as T-Rex. He wore a black T-shirt with the sleeves cut off. His arms were like tree trunks with tattoos carved up and down.

A tattoo at the top of his right arm was a smaller replica of the patches on the back of a club member's rag – the top rocker, lower patches, and center patch of the Banshee Riders. On the front-left of the shirt was a silk-screened rectangular duplicate of the name patch found on the front of a brother's cutoff with the red letters "Reaper." A leather jacket inside a cutoff Levi was hanging over one upper arm of the armchair. On the front left of the rag, Harold saw another patch that read "Reaper" and, just above it, a similar patch the read "President."

Harold had heard the name often enough that he knew, even before he saw the "President" patch, that this was the elusive leader of the club. Harold noticed that, and fittingly so, there was something more serious and intimidating about this biker than anyone else he'd met in the club so far. Harold instinctively knew this was not someone to trifle with.

"So, prospect," Reaper said, "let's hear your side of the story."

While not discussing the incident with Harold during the week, Samurai had coached him that, if he was asked to talk about the matter with the club, Harold should be straightforward, honest and brief. "Above all," Samurai had said, "don't call 6 Pack a liar or say anything else negative about him. Remember, 6 Pack is a full-patch member. In the eyes of the club, you ain't shit yet."

Harold looked at the president and explained how he had met a prospect from the Swamp Rats at the party and when the prospect offered Harold a beer, a brother from the prospect's club must have misunderstood what was happening.

"That doesn't explain why you attacked one of my brothers," the president said.

"He shoved me twice," Harold said, putting a little twist on the story. "I never hit him. When he went to shove me the third time, I just put my hands up like a reflex or something."

"Bullshit," 6 Pack said, jumping to his feet from an arm of the couch. "The fucking prospect took a swing at me and challenged me to a fight."

Then Reaper looked at 6 Pack and said, "Did he hit you or did he challenge you to a fight?"

"Both," 6 Pack said.

"Hitting you is a bit more than just a challenge, don't you think?" Samurai chimed in.

Samurai hardly had the words out when the president snapped, "Shut up."

The room fell stone quiet as Reaper turned his attention back to Harold. "Did 6 Pack give you an order that you refused to carry out?"

"He wanted me to beat the shit out of this other prospect," Harold said.

"That's not what I asked you," the president said calmly.

Harold paused for a second and remembered what Samurai had told him, "Just be honest."

"Yes," Harold admitted. "But I didn't know who he was and figured, if I had a chance to explain, 6 Pack would realize there wasn't a problem and there was no need to start trouble with another club."

"Clubs don't have problems over prospects," the president said.

Harold didn't like the way the questioning was going. He sensed that, if a vote were held at that moment, it wouldn't turn out well for the Banshee Riders prospect. However, he also sensed that, whichever way the president leaned, would carry a lot of weight.

"Don't forget, you're just a prospect," the president said, "assuming we don't decide to kick your ass and throw you in a ditch by the highway tonight." As he made the less-than-subtle threat, the president seemed as though he were watching for Harold's reaction.

Harold calmly nodded that he understood, and the president continued, "It's not your job to question brothers when they give you something to do. Now, go back outside and wait." With that, the president took a swig from his beer while turning his attention away from Harold, as though officially dismissing him.

Hardly out the door, Harold heard the yelling begin again. He clearly heard 6 Pack's voice, though the brother sounded louder and more agitated than before. The shouting lasted another 15 minutes or so when Harold clearly heard Falstaff's voice yelling, "All right, that's enough."

A couple minutes later, the door flew open and 6 Pack came out in a huff. As he walked past Harold, 6 Pack muttered, "From now on, I suggest you watch your back, prospect."

Harold didn't respond. 6 Pack started his bike and tore out of the driveway with gravel flying behind him. When he hit the road, 6 Pack did a power run, full throttle, banging gears, westward on the highway. Harold watched in that direction as the sound faded into the distance. Harold wasn't sure what had happened inside. But he knew that, if 6 Pack wasn't happy, that was a good sign. He also noticed that 6 Pack had still referred to him as "Prospect."

The meeting lasted another 45 minutes as Harold was sweating out his fate. But there was nothing he could do about it, so he sat on his bike a bit, paced a bit, sat on his bike some more, and waited.

When the door finally opened, Samurai was the first one out. He walked over to Harold and said, "Come on, let's take a ride."

They rode well out into the countryside, so far in fact that Harold laughingly wondered if Samurai was assigned to pop a cap in the prospect's head and was bringing Harold out to the middle of nowhere to dump the body. Still, Harold trusted Samurai enough that he followed along unquestioningly.

No sooner had that crazy thought crossed Harold's mind than they pulled into a parking lot of what Harold was coming to recognize as another in Samurai's database of out-of-the-way watering holes. Harold followed Samurai into the bar and stood behind him as he ordered a couple of beers. When Samurai turned to hand Harold a beer, there was a big grin on Samurai's face.

"You did good, bro," Samurai said. "Of course, it didn't hurt that 6 Pack is a fucking idiot and went out of the way to prove it again tonight."

"What happened," said Harold, uttering the question he'd wanted to ask since Samurai came out of the meeting. "Or is it OK for me to ask?"

"Probably not," Samurai said with the same smile on his face. Then he proceeded to describe the entire discussion.

"When you left, I suspect 6 Pack was sensing that Reaper wasn't entirely convinced," Samurai said. "He was pissed and started yelling. Reaper let him yell for a couple minutes – gave him just enough rope to hang himself, I'd say. Then Reaper cut him off at the knees. It was a beautiful thing. 6 Pack couldn't even convince the club to take a vote. It was treated like a non-issue.

"I think that was worse than having the vote go against him," Samurai said.

"What finally did it," Samurai said, "is when Reaper asked why, whether you had punched him, challenged him or both, why 6 Pack hadn't kicked your ass. The asshole didn't have an answer for that one. He stood there blubbering."

With that, the two held up their beers for a toast.

Then Harold asked, "So they didn't kick 6 Pack out either?"

"No," said Samurai. "Mongrel said he thought he heard him muttering about quitting though. Wouldn't surprise me a bit. He lost a lot of face tonight."

"Yeah," Harold said with a smile. But then his smile turned to a frown as he added, "But I've certainly made us both an enemy."

"Don't kid yourself," Samurai said. "6 Pack's had a hard-on for me for a long time. This doesn't really change anything."

"Maybe," Harold said, "but I'm sure this didn't help."

Samurai took a deep breath and told Harold about 6 Pack's prospect. "It was appropriate. Mustang was as big a snake as 6 Pack," Samurai said. "If we didn't catch him fucking with a brother's old lady, we'd have caught him doing something else."

"What happened to him?" Harold asked, partially because he was interested and partially because he wanted to know what he could expect if he fucked up.

"He got his hair mussed up a bit," Samurai said. "That's all."

Samurai was leaning over the bar looking forward as he spoke. Now he turned to face Harold. "I'm sorry, bro," Samurai said. "In a way, I'm the one who screwed up. I should have warned you about 6 Pack."

Harold digested the apology for a minute. Then he said to Samurai, "No problem. Everything turned out alright in the end."

As almost an afterthought, Harold added, "I'm a little worried about Skunk, though."

"Skunk?" Samurai asked. "Oh, the other prospect. Like I said, I can ask around. I'll let you know if I hear anything."

"Thanks," said Harold.

Chapter 13 — Who Seduced Whom?

"Well," Samurai said, as he lifted his glass for a toast, "tonight it's FTW, we're getting' good and drunk."

Harold returned the toast and, after taking a hit off his beer, asked, "FTW?"

"Yeah," Samurai said, "FTW – Fuck The World."

By the time they reached their third round of beers, the two were virtually rolling on the floor in laughter as Samurai described how 6 Pack had stormed out the door in a huff during the meeting and Harold completed the picture by describing how the biker had tossed a threat Harold's way before tearing off down the road on his Harley.

"You should have seen the look on his face," Harold said. "That was not a happy camper. Nice power run on his Sporty though."

As they laughed, the front door of the bar opened. Instinctively, the way wolves react to a sudden sound – positioned for defense or advantage – Harold and Samurai simultaneously glanced that way. From out of the darkness, where a couple of fisherman who had stayed late on the lake were most likely, two dark-haired, sensual beauties strutted in the door on spiked heels, the sway of their hips seeming, with each step, to spread puffs of pheromones into the bar's thick and hazy atmosphere. It occurred to Harold that the odds of these gorgeous women walking into this bar, at this time, were as likely as fish waddling in on their tail fins and ordering drinks.

The seductive parade arrived at the bar slightly to the right of a direct path from the front door, as though the ladies were drawn that way by some invisible and magnetic force. If one followed the dark-stained pine counter, and its thick and battered coat of epoxy resin, the ladies were at least 15 feet away from Samurai and Harold. But as the bar took a hard turn between them, physically, they stood only about six feet away from the pair of bikers, and virtually face to face. Seeing a pair of bikers, many would have drifted toward the other end of the bar, gaining a safe distance without obvious avoidance. But not these girls. More than that, for a fleeting moment, Harold distinctly caught, what he took to be, an interested glance in his and Samurai's direction. As he and Samurai continued to check out the ladies, a remarkable thing happened; the ladies looked back again. And then, they smiled. It was an inviting smile, the kind of smile that thawed the skepticism around Harold's most desirable fantasies of willing women. Instead of repelling from the hungry look in Harold's eyes, these girls appeared as though they were drawn to it, as though that was the very look they were seeking when they came into the bar. When Harold's tight-lipped mouth showed the trace of a smile, as he nodded lightly in acknowledgment of the non-verbal communication, this was the moment of truth – the moment when he was accustomed to rejection. The trick was to make the nod look casual, almost accidental, as though he merely had something in his eye. In this way, he could scurry back on the limb unharmed if the nod was unfavorably received.

The last time Harold was this ... fortunate with the ladies, it turned out he was merely an instrument from a woman's toolkit of revenge against an unfaithful boyfriend. Leslie poured half-a-dozen Martinis down her throat, bit her lip and took Harold to bed. Harold was captivated by her long legs and flawless body. Furthermore, even intoxicated, she was, by far, the hottest girl Harold had ever slept with though he could see the opportunity of a new high-water mark this night. Following the event with Leslie, and with all-too-predictable results, Harold was the love-struck drunk draped uncomfortably around her shoulders, literally and figuratively. But Leslie wouldn't bear her albatross for long. Soon after their encounter, when Harold slid onto a barstool beside her, Leslie tried a subtle brush-off. She gently pulled away from his embrace with a slightly pained smile. As Harold failed to take the hint or wishfully chose to ignore it, sounding almost apologetic, she said, "The other night was a mistake. I have a boyfriend."

When Harold still didn't seem to take the hint, Leslie went from subtle to jack-hammer blunt. She turned her meandering boyfriend, the one she had sought to make jealous, on Harold. Later that evening, in a scene Harold would rather forget, he had gone to the bathroom at Freddie's, a one-seat affair where the lack of a urinal was compensated for by a pernicious, and skin-soaking urine-based odor that was consistent with the cracked mirror over the sink and the layer of filth that covered everything in the cramped little room. As he stepped from the bathroom, Harold stumbled into the bulging biceps of a muscle-bound monster who, as it turned out, was the boyfriend who had temporarily strayed from Leslie. Before his booze-clouded mind could comprehend what had blocked his way, Harold was pinned by the neck to the wall beyond the bathroom door. There, it was explained to him that he would, henceforth, leave Leslie alone. With an iron grip on Harold's throat, and eyes burning into Harold's, the boyfriend gave a short dissertation on what Harold could expect if he didn't leave Leslie alone. Heartbroken and dispirited, Harold grudgingly took the hint knowing that his promise to himself that, he was only biding his time for revenge, was a ploy to save a shred of personal dignity.

Harold's other experiences with the opposite sex were relatively spotty. He seldom fared better than the experience with Leslie. While in high school, at a time when he hadn't really developed any tolerance for alcohol, if you could call it that, he had briefly dated a couple of girls. But when they witnessed his undignified drunken stupors, though they liked to party, too, they moved on to others who could better hold their booze. What alcohol took away with one hand it offered back up with another, or so Harold philosophized. It wasn't long after high school that Harold discovered a new species of women – not as charming or attractive, but with their own particular appeal. The girls who would give Harold more than the time of day, tended to share his transient, yet needy, perspective on relationships. These girls didn't hold out for the niceties of wining and dining. Courtship generally occurred at a bar, drinks in hand, where both would later have trouble remembering how they actually hooked up. The mating ritual was a relatively simple and straightforward affair where the occasional taste of vomit in a partner's mouth was easily washed away with another drink.

He'd 'scored' more than a few times with barflies he met at Freddie's Place. But most of his success came at the expense of women whose physical appeal benefited somewhat when the observer had consumed liberal amounts of alcohol. Once, they were probably all relatively attractive, but years of hard drinking have a way of casting a shadow on beauty. For instance, Harold had several encounters with a girl named Monica. At 5-3 and about 180 pounds, and with a slight mustache, Monica might have sought romance in other venues. She might have looked for someone who would have loved her for some intangibles hidden below the flesh if those intangibles weren't also submerged under rounds of tequila sunrises, her drink of choice. But Monica's alcoholism had developed hand-in-hand with a rather dour and nasty attitude. And so, it was that, when Harold and Monica hooked up, not only was love on a holiday, mere like was absent as well. Their mutual distaste for each other was an open secret even as they used each other to satisfy their animalistic desires.

When Monica's insecurity and depression led to a failed suicide attempt, Harold only volunteered to go up to the psych ward to see her after Mindy shamed him into the gesture. Without the benefit of alcohol, their meeting in the dayroom of the facility was particularly awkward at best. Harold asked Monica "How are you doing" and, without looking up from the floor, she grumbled something to the effect of "Fine." Harold made a quick exit after a minimum of long pregnant pauses accentuated by nominal small talk, escaping the dreaded hospital floor as though, had he stayed any longer, the staff might have discovered he was a candidate for a room of his own.

For Monica, Harold's visit had a profound after effect. Considering he was the only person who came to see her, she fell for Harold the way a female patient often falls for a rescuing physician. Upon her release, she sought out Harold at every turn, and would have done so at his home had she known where he lived. Harold became the prey in a misguided hunt for affection. Due to Monica's persistency, Harold had to seek out another establishment for his liquid relief. When he did venture back to Freddie's Place, he did so stealing peaks through the front window first to make sure Monica wasn't at the bar. When he saw it was all clear, only then did Harold step inside.

Mindy observed the ballet of duck and hide Harold was playing and took him to task again. Mindy's words cut deep: "You're such a fucking coward. If you're not interested, why don't you just tell the poor girl already?"

Mindy's words created a mental turmoil for Harold. On the one hand, he resented Monica for breaking the unspoken pact that had once maintained their relationship on a purely physical level. On the other hand, he realized he'd broken the pact first by going to visit her in the hospital. But as Harold saw it, though he had committed only the slightest act of compassion, he was, apparently, paying where no good deed went unpunished with a love-struck psychotic who wouldn't leave him alone. And there, he realized, in a sense, it was Mindy's fault. If she hadn't stuck her nose into the affair, to begin with, Harold never would have gone up there. Monica would have understood, and everything would have been fine. But how was Harold to say no when the guilt that drove him across the line was administered by his heartthrob? If Mindy had asked Harold to walk with a blindfold in traffic, Harold would have asked her what color of blindfold. And now, Mindy was sticking her nose into the situation again.

When Harold tried claiming that rejection might drive Monica to try suicide again, Mindy could have pointed out that avoiding Monica was a far crueler form of rejection. Instead, Mindy laughed, "Trust me, Harold, no girl is going to kill herself over you."

Sitting in the bar with Samurai, it dawned on Harold that, though these girls didn't have all those hard miles showing on their faces and bodies yet, in a way, they were quite similar to the barflies he usually scored with. At a glance, he intrinsically knew that they weren't looking for a commitment: there was no need for the customary niceties of courtship. Essentially, if the course continued, they were saying yes without the price of admission – yes to Harold's wildest desires. But it also occurred to him that, considering his history, he could still blow it. And yet, he could see that the bad-boy allure of bikers was surely in play. Harold realized it was vital that he maintains the biker image, though without overplaying his hand. As he thought about how to do this another thought occurred to Harold: he didn't have to 'maintain the image.'

"I am a biker," he told himself. "I'm the real thing. Or I'd better be. If I'm faking it, losing out with these girls will be the least of my troubles. If I'm not real, I could lose a lot more than a chance to score with one of these fine ladies. And besides, if they don't like me, fuck 'em." Though Harold didn't see it at the time, this was the definitive change. Instead of seeking the girls with a desperation they couldn't help but smell, his take-it-or-leave-it attitude was precisely how the ladies expected a biker, like a male peacock, to subtly display its plumage.

Having worked out his posture in his own mind, Harold glanced at Samurai wondering how his happily attached brother would fit into this equation. Instead of faithfulness, Harold saw the same hunger reflected in Samurai's eyes. In a way, Harold was glad of Samurai's obvious interest in the girls. It made things easier if it was two on two and no one was left out. But on the other hand, Harold felt a small, nagging voice of disappointment, too. Somehow, Harold had come to rely on the relationship between Samurai and Sue. At every turn, they seemed to treat each other with respect and with the loyalty that implied. It had never occurred to Harold that either Samurai or Sue would consider wandering. He also realized that, if Samurai cheated on Sue, it was a secret the prospect would have to keep as well. Harold found the thought a tad uncomfortable. But with the scent of the hunt deep in his nostrils, other concerns were washed away in the heat of the moment. Deceptively, he told himself that he would worry about that later. For the moment, opportunity was at hand and Harold had no intention of wasting it, not with girls as hot as this.

There was no mistaking them for twins. However, there were startling similarities about them. To start with, they probably had their Phoebe-Cates-styled hair done at the same salon, though the taller girl's hair was slightly fuller and wavier. Both girls had their 'war paint' on and were wearing tight, black, lace-fringed shirts that exposed ample cleavage between the zippers of similar black leather jackets with shoulder pads. Their spiked high heels added several inches to their slender frames. Standing on a scale together, combined, they would have struggled to top Harold's 210 pounds. If they were trying to dress the same, the only place they failed, was in that one wore tight blue jeans, rolled up neatly at the cuffs, and the other wore equally tight red jeans.

The bartender who was perched on a stool, one elbow on the bar, was invisibly checking the girls out as they came in, a look on his face that suggested he wasn't sure if this was real. As he came to take the girls' drink orders, Samurai's hand flashed out and gently grabbed the bartender's arm. The bartender stopped and looked at Samurai with startled apprehension. He relaxed, however, when Samurai said, "We'd like to buy a round for the ladies."

The bartender nodded and walked over to the girls announcing, "These gentlemen would like to buy you ladies a drink."

The girls looked their way and the Phoebe Cates with wavier hair said, in a richly, sexy voice, her head suggestively tipped to one side, "Really?"

"You girls look thirsty," Samurai said with a smile. Then he added, with more bravado than Harold would have reached so quickly, "Would you like to join us?"

Without a word, the girls glanced at each other, shrugged ever so slightly, and then walked around the bar to join the bikers. The one with wavier hair took a seat next to Samurai. The other, accepting her drink from the bartender as she arrived, stood out from the bar facing the others. In a way, it was as though they had already chosen partners – the wavier-haired girl with Samurai and the other with Harold.

Now that they were up close, Harold made out that they were probably in their mid-20s. The girl by Samurai had hazel eyes and the one by Harold brown. But regardless of the color, unlike many of the barflies Harold knew, there wasn't that vacant expression alcohol can induce. These were girls who hadn't accepted hopeless futures. They still had ambitions. Would they reach them some day or was this where all the other barflies started, before their dreams were drowned in booze and left to die like dried vomit in an alley somewhere?

"I'm Debbie," said the girl seated by Samurai, "And this is Tawny."

Tawny softly extended her hand and smiled seductively as Harold said, "Hello."

Before either of the bikers could complete the introductions, Debbie said, "I'm guessing your name is Samurai," as she read the name patch on the front of Harold's sponsor's rag.

"Wow," Samurai joked. "You must be psychic."

"That, or I know how to read," she laughed. Then Tawny said to Harold, "Why don't you have a name?"

Harold opened his mouth to answer but suddenly realized he didn't know what to say. Should he tell her, "My name is Harold?" He'd already seen how Samurai reacted to a perceived lack of enthusiasm for Harold's new club name. But if Harold up and told the girls his name was Naked Boy, how would they react? Then, remembering, "Hey, I'm a biker – fuck it," he opened his mouth to answer.

He was interrupted by Samurai who, with a big grin, said, "Of course he's got a name. Go ahead bro, tell Tawny your name."

A smile spread across Harold's face as he said, "You can call me 'Naked Boy.'"

As expected, the girls broke into laughter. Tawny snuggled up to Harold's left arm, pressing a firm pair of breasts on either side of his bicep and squealed, "Oooh, I like that name."

Debbie was laughing as she asked, "Why do they call you 'Naked Boy,' do you live in a nudist colony or something?"

Harold was about to explain – explain about the little girl who thought he was naked in the morning on a sofa – but, before he could, Samurai cut in again.

"Story goes that beautiful young ladies, such as yourselves, can't look at him without thinking of him that way."

Tawny looked Harold up and down and said, "Mmmmm, I see what you mean."

Harold fought back a blush and looked into her big brown eyes, eyes that seemed to wrap themselves around him. Out of the corner of his own eye, he saw Samurai raise his glass slightly in a toast to his brother. It was as if Samurai was saying, "I told you. Your name is just fine. It even comes with fringe benefits, and one of those benefits is hanging on your arm right now."

Harold smiled and raised his glass to Samurai, returning the salute, as he said to Tawny, "You can think of me any way you want – with or without clothes." He and Tawny then clanked their glasses together lightly as though consummating a deal.

Just as Harold began to relax and settle into the idea of his good fortune, Tawny brought up another potential problem: "Why is there a big, white 'P' on your back?"

It occurred to Harold that discovering he was only a prospect for the club might dampen her enthusiasm. When he offered a condensed version of the process of joining a club, he was pleased when she laughed and said, "Cool. I was afraid you'd escaped from a chain gang or something."

Samurai seemed to back off and allow Harold to answer their questions as the girls proved inquisitive about the biker lifestyle.

"So what does a biker gang do, I mean, for fun and stuff?" Debbie asked.

"Normal stuff," Harold answered, "You know, terrorize small towns and steal candy from babies."

The girls laughed and Samurai grinned.

"No, really?" Debbie pressed for an answer.

"Mostly, for fun, we ride. That's why we call it a motorcycle club," said Harold.

"All you do for fun is ride," Tawny asked, as though something obvious was left out.

"Sure. We ride," then, looking Tawny up and down with a lascivious look that spoke louder than words. "We ride our bikes, but we also ride ... you know ..."

"No, what else do you ride?" Tawny asked, clearly not letting him off the hook with a merely suggestive statement.

A not-so-familiar grin spread across Harold's face before he took a plunge he wouldn't have previously dared without a mutually greater state of intoxication. "We ride hot little things like you, too, from time to time."

Both girls laughed, though Debbie's laugh was caught in the middle of taking a big sip of beer that now came out her nose. As she grabbed a bar napkin to wipe her face, she asked, "Is that what you two are figuring to ride tonight?"

"That's up to you," Samurai said with a tone that, if the girls didn't want the ride, it would be their loss.

There was a long and pregnant pause. But it suddenly dawned on Harold it wasn't because the girls were uncomfortable. Rather, it was as though they were looking for a comfortable way to accept the offers.

Samurai seemed to pick up on the same feeling and he was the one who finally broke the ice: "Well, why don't we finish these drinks, order some beers to go, and find a more suitable environment where we can get to know each other better?"

Debbie smiled approvingly as she turned to her friend, "Whaddya think?"

"Sure," Tawny answered, without looking, as she planted her lips against Harold's in a first, deep kiss.

Several minutes later, the girls were on the back of the bikes, each holding a six-pack under one arm.

Harold liked the feel of a girl on the bike behind him. He especially liked the way Tawny squeezed him with her legs and rubbed his chest as she held on. The faster the bikes went, the harder she held on and Harold found himself going faster and faster just to increase the effect. Samurai sensed that Harold was either eager to get to the motel or was trying to impress his date and they were soon, side by side, doing close to 90 mph.

Just as he knew all sorts of backwoods watering holes in the area, Samurai also knew of an out-of-the-way motel by a lake a few miles to the north. They were soon pulling into the parking lot of the Shade Tree Inn Motel, nestled into a cove of tall pines that layered the sandy drive with a carpet of pine needles. Harold and Samurai went into the front office to register while the girls stayed by the bikes.

The door to the front office was locked and the lights were off inside. As the two discussed their good fortune and the party ahead, Samurai knocked lightly on the storm door. Just when Harold was beginning to think no one was attending to the front desk that night, a light from an inner room fell across the office floor as a door to a small apartment behind the front desk opened. A large shadow of a man filled the center of the rectangular pattern of light. But as the originator of the shadow stepped forward and pulled the chain on the side of a light fixture on the front counter, Harold discovered the shadow had actually inflated the image of a small woman, probably in her late 60s or early 70s, who had her hair wrapped in netting over tightly bound curlers. She wore a paisley robe that reached to the top of her knees. The robe was open in the front revealing a light-blue nightgown. With her fuzzy slippers, Harold thought the woman had a remarkable resemblance to Harold's mother.

Coming around the counter, the woman unlocked the door and gave it a small shove, just enough to prove it was unlocked. Harold and Samurai stepped inside and walked to the front counter as the woman walked around behind it. Harold noticed a strong smell of cigarette smoke and could see an overflowing ashtray next to a recliner not far inside the door of the apartment.

Samurai asked for a double and the woman said, in gruff smoker's voice, "That'll be $23," without once looking up at her customers.

Harold started to reach into his pocket for his share when Samurai said, "Don't worry bro, I've got it."

As the bikers turned to leave, the woman said, "Checkout is at 10 a.m., if you're still here in the morning."

As they walked outside and back towards the girls, Harold repeated what the woman had said but as a question, "If you're still here in the morning?"

Samurai laughed and, as they went out the door, he said to Harold, "They service a particular kind of clientele here."

Samurai and Debbie led the way to the door as Tawny draped herself over Harold's side again so that walking was actually a little awkward. In the room, Samurai turned on the 20-watt lamp on the laminated 'oak' nightstand by the curtained front window, cracked open a beer, wrapped an arm around Debbie's thin waist and fell into an old armchair beside the nightstand pulling her down on his lap in the process. From there, Debbie opened another beer, put the remaining four from the 6 Pack on the table, and leaned back comfortably across Samurai's lap. Harold took a beer that Tawny offered as she then opened one for herself. Seeing that Samurai and Debbie had claimed the only chair in the room, Harold propped up a couple pillows against the headboard of the bed farthest from the window and sat with his boots on the bedspread.

Harold wasn't exactly in the dark about what was ahead. However, he wasn't entirely sure how, with two couples and one room, things would build up to the climax he eagerly anticipated. He slapped his hand down on the bed next to where he sat indicating Tawny should have a seat, too. But Tawny had set her beer on the nightstand and was standing beside Harold. In a soft and sexy voice, she said, "You can't wear your boots in bed." With that, she pulled off the battered cowboy boots once worn by Harold's uncle. She also pulled off Harold's socks before kicking off her own spiked heels.

Instead of taking a seat beside Harold, Tawny threw one leg over him and sat on his lap facing him. She slid her arms around behind his back and leaned forward to press her lips against his. Harold sat with his arms at his side, a beer in one hand, as he returned another long, deep kiss.

They hadn't kissed long when Tawny took Harold's free hand

and pulled it up to her breast. Harold noticed how incredibly firm she felt. He even felt a stiff nipple against his palm. But while he was extremely aroused, he felt a little uncomfortable sensing that Samurai and Debbie were watching the performance. Harold unlocked his lips from Tawny's and glanced to his left. He discovered that Samurai and Debbie were in a similar embrace. He watched as Debbie aimed her arms towards the ceiling and Samurai slipped her top up and off before throwing it down on the floor on top of the jacket she had already removed. Samurai then went to work on the snap on the back of Debbie's bra. For a moment, Harold was frozen by the breath-taking sight of the other girl naked from the waist up on Samurai's lap. Before he turned back to the girl on his own lap, he felt Tawny's fingers gently on his chin, turning his head back to her.

"Do you want to watch or do you want to play?" she asked, though not in a sarcastic way – more as though it were a serious question and she wouldn't mind whichever way he answered.

There was no question in Harold's mind about his preference as he pulled Tawny close and kissed her again.

Still kissing, Tawny removed her coat and then her shirt. Soon, only a green, silk bra stood between Harold's hands and Tawny's breasts. While adjusting for a new position to kiss, Tawny whispered, "We can watch them later."

But she didn't whisper quietly enough, and they heard a muffled laugh from Debbie, who responded, "Or we'll watch you."

All hesitation was gone as Harold frantically worked on the hooks holding the back of Tawny's bra together. When he'd finally released them, Tawny stepped from the bed and let the bra fall to the floor at her feet. As Harold gazed at her perfect breasts, Tawny then undid the belt, button and zipper on her tight, red pants before shifting her hips back and forth to work the pants, like a snake shedding its skin, down and onto the floor. Finally, she hooked her fingers in her shear silk panties and slid them off while staring into Harold's eyes. Then, she stood there, naked, allowing Harold to drink it all in. She even spun around so he could see her from all angles.

"Do you want this?" she asked in a voice Harold remembered hearing when Lauren Bacall asked Humphrey Bogart if he knew how to whistle.

Before he could answer, Debbie spoke up again, "If he doesn't, I do."

Harold looked over to the chair where he saw Samurai admiring Tawny's naked body. Debbie, who was now naked on Samurai's lap, was also looking at Tawny and biting her lip in a way that suggested she wasn't kidding.

Harold reached out his hand to Tawny. She took his hand and allowed him to pull her onto the bed beside him. As he kissed her, and rubbed his hand down her left side, over her hip and back onto the cheek of her ass, Harold said, "I think she's serious."

Tawny glanced over at Debbie and said, "Of course, she's serious."

It suddenly dawned on Harold, as he heard Samurai laughing, that, though he should have noticed already, this gorgeous specimen in bed with him was hardly innocent.

Tawny smiled as though she could read his mind. "Maybe you'd like to see that sometime, too?" When Harold's eyes seemed to say, 'Yes,' she added, "But not now."

As Harold glanced back at the other two, Debbie reached out and shut the light off. "Maybe this will help you keep your mind on what's at hand."

It worked.

Tawny and Harold had explored and experienced each other's warm bodies to mutual climaxes when they heard soft footsteps and saw Debbie's naked shadow as she carefully felt her way to the bathroom. Tawny seemed to take that as a signal and rolled over to give Harold a kiss before she whispered, "Be right back."

Harold could hear the girls whispering in the other room, though he couldn't really make out what they were saying. He found it slightly disconcerting when he heard them giggle, worrying that, somehow, the joke was on him.

The light of the bathroom flashed across the floor in front of the beds for a moment when the bathroom door opened but was as quickly distinguished. Then the shadows of the girls re-emerged shuffling off to their appointed partners. However, as Tawny snuggled in next to Harold, he realized that it wasn't Tawny at all. The girls had, apparently, decided to switch partners while they were in the bathroom.

As they embraced and kissed, Debbie seemed to notice that Naked Boy had caught onto the change. "You don't mind, do you?" she asked.

For a moment, Harold thought about it. In the past, he had a tendency to think in terms of love following naturally in the footsteps of sex and, in his mind, had started down that path with Tawny already. But as he thought about it, he realized he was following a different path today. A momentary wave of jealousy dissipated instantly and, instead of answering, he merely pressed his lips to hers.

Debbie seemed to appreciate his reaction. Harold thought it might be an act of gratitude when Debbie broke off the kiss and began sliding down under the covers as her hand found his equipment and was soon replaced by her mouth.

Harold laid back and watched her head, under the covers, rise, and fall until the action compelled him to lean his own head back in moment of blissful ecstasy.

When Debbie came up for air, she leaned over the edge of the bed and dug around in Tawny's clothes until she found a pack of cigarettes and a lighter in a pocket somewhere. About that time, the light on the table came back on as though it were intermission.

Debbie took a long drag of her cigarette and laid her head on Harold's chest as she slowly and deliberately blew out the smoke. When her lungs were clear, she asked, "Did you like that?"

Harold laughed, "I think you can do that again if you'd like. Or, anytime you like."

She gave his soft joint a tug and said, "Doesn't seem like you're ready now, though."

Harold cracked open a beer, took a drink and handed the beer to Debbie. Then he said, "Only a temporary condition."

As Harold took the beer back from Debbie, he noticed Tawny leaning over the nightstand as though she was assembling something. He was admiring her tight naked ass when she looked back at him and said, "Want some?"

174

Debbie immediately slid out from under the covers and onto her feet. She took Harold by the hand and pulled so he would follow. He did, and, at the table, he found a small, unfolded piece of paper next to three white lines of powder and a single-edge razor flat on the table beside them.

Harold could see the powdery residue of a fourth line around Tawny's one nostril. She extended a rolled dollar to Harold but, playing the gentleman, he handed it off to Debbie who smiled appreciatively as she took the dollar and bent to vacuum up another of the lines. Harold then took his turn and Samurai finished off the last.

As they chatted and drank their beer, Harold began to feel that he was ready for another round with Debbie. But when he reached out to take her hand, Tawny intercepted and led Harold back to the bed.

When the light of morning began gradually illuminating the curtain at the front window, as though controlled by a natural dimmer switch turning the lights back on, no one had slept. With short breaks, the sex had continued all night. Harold wasn't sure whether to credit the coke or the thrill of his good fortune. Whatever the case, he didn't feel tired. He felt a little lethargic, as though his body was stuffed with cotton, but otherwise, he felt great. He even privately complimented himself on his 'performance' and was pleased when Tawny seemed to agree saying, "You are a tiger, aren't you?"

"So says the 'Eveready Bunny,'" laughed Debbie from the other side of the room.

At some point during the night, Harold and Samurai had discovered that the girls weren't mere amateurs; they were actually strippers from a club about 50 miles north of the state line. They had traveled that distance for a good time where they felt they were less likely to run into regular customers, and off the radar of their boss who owned the club.

About 9 a.m., Samurai suggested that they should grab a bite to eat and, one by one, they began to dress. After breakfast at the diner several miles down the road by the highway, they rode the girls back to their car and went in for an early drink. Before Harold and Samurai walked the girls out to their car, the girls wrote down their phone numbers for them. Harold put the piece of paper in his pocket and then put his arms around Tawny's waist as she wrapped hers around his shoulders and they had one-last deep kiss before parting ways. Debbie then gave him the same treatment.

As Tawny followed up Debbie's kiss with Samurai, Harold couldn't help but notice that Tawny didn't seem entirely happy with the arrangement. He had the distinct impression she was jealous of Debbie kissing him. He was telling himself he had imagined it when Tawny came back to give him another kiss, as though determined to give him the last kiss before they parted.

Harold suggested she come down to Hildie's Hideout some-time. However, as he did so, out of the corner of his eye, he saw Samurai giving him a 'don't-do-that' look. Tawny didn't respond and Harold was happy to allow the idea to slip away. Tawny did say, "Don't forget to call me." Then the girls left as Harold and Samurai went back in for one more beer.

Harold and Samurai rolled back into Biesenthal a little past noon and came to a stop light. While waiting for the light to change, Samurai leaned over and said to Harold, "It was late, so we crashed at your place, right?"

Harold realized Samurai was getting their story straight and nodded in acknowledgment. He suddenly had a desire to turn and go back to Chester's, to go anywhere other than to Samu-rai's. He realized this was the part where they had to face Sue, and, for some reason, Harold was dreading it. But he also realized there was nothing he could do but play along. There was no way he could tell Sue what had transpired, nor was there any good reason to do so. He just felt a bit uncomfortable carrying the se-cret around with someone he was coming to like and appreci-ate. Sue didn't make a big fuss about things but, in her own little ways, she let Harold know that he was accepted. He appreciated her acceptance and didn't take it lightly. Now, he wondered how he was repaying her.

Chapter 14 — Dancer and the Mousetrap

Harold showered in the locker room at work most days. Then, more often than not, he would ride straight to Samurai and Sue's house. He usually arrived there before Samurai returned from work. Harold would pick up some beer on the way. When Samurai arrived home, while they waited for Sue to finish making dinner, they would stand in the driveway watching the kids play in the backyard while the two men knocked down a few beers together.

Harold would wait outside with the beer while Samurai went in to give Sue a kiss and drop his lunch box off on the sink. When he returned outside, Harold would flip him a beer from the bag on the picnic table in the backyard. Then, Harold would wait to toast his brother. He waited while Samurai performed a short ritual. In a time when flip tops from beer and pop cans came off entirely, instead of merely pressing the flap down from the pre-punched hole, Samurai would remove the flip top then walk over by the house and stick the flip top into the dirt. Harold noticed this peculiar behavior on the part of his sponsor but dismissed it as a simple quirk, the way everyone has some funny but harmless habit.

One day, as he watched Samurai dig a flip top into the dirt, Harold asked, "So, what's that all about?"

Samurai looked up while bent down working to twist the flip top into the dry soil."

"What?"

"What?" That. Why are you always sticking the flip tops into the dirt over there?"

"I'm planting a beer garden," Samurai said with all the earnestness of a farmer discussing his plans to plant corn seed in one of his fields.

Harold laughed, "That soil doesn't look real good for crops."

"Nah," said Samurai smiling. "The aluminum requires a dryer, more stable soil. This is just right for a beer garden."

Having watched Samurai plant the flip tops day after day, Harold had an idea. On the Wednesday following the weekend of their romp with the girls across the border, Harold put his plan into action. Instead of the usual six-pack, Harold purchased a 12 pack from the liquor store next to the gas station where he used to work. Back at Samurai's, he found a shovel in the shed and went to work digging two rows of small holes in the ground in the area where Samurai planted his flip tops. In each hole, Harold planted a beer in the ground and backfilled so that about an inch of the can was exposed above the ground.

He was busy in his agricultural endeavor when Sue came out of the house and watched him unnoticed as Harold was obviously engrossed in his at work. Finally, she interrupted to ask, "What the heck are you doing?" The tone of her voice, and the look on her face, suggested she was concerned Harold had lost his grasp on sanity.

Harold cast a mischievous smile at Sue without answering and continued with his hops-and-lager gardening.

A short time later, Samurai arrived and pulled the work van into the garage. When he walked out towards the house, he saw Harold by the back of the house. However, he noticed the absence of the customary paper bag with beer. As Samurai walked over, he razzed his prospect, "What, no beer? I thought you were serious about earning your patch?"

"Oh shit," Harold said jokingly. "I knew I forgot something." Harold then turned to face the spot where he had recently tilled the soil. "Not to worry, bro. I think your beer garden is ready for harvest."

Samurai looked down at the prospect's feet and started laughing as he saw the tops of beer cans protruding from the ground in two shiny rows of six. Sue, who was watching for when Samurai arrived, had come outside to see his reaction. Harold was about to pull a can up by its roots when Sue said, "You two idiots wait right there one minute." As she turned to go back in the house, she added, "And don't touch anything."

She was back a minute later and then went straight out to the shed before returning with a metal garden rake that she handed to Samurai. It was at that point that Harold noticed the camera in Sue's other hand.

"OK, you two idiots, stand there together," she said. Harold didn't know the name of the artist or the name of the piece, but he was well familiar with the painting by Grant Wood called "American Gothic," and he realized Sue was posing them as the couple in the painting. He and Samurai laughed as they stood side by side, Samurai holding the rake upright in his left hand.

Sue raised the camera to her face then lowered it and barked, "Wipe those grins off your faces. You're farmers, act like it."

"What, you think farmers don't smile?" asked Samurai.

"These farmers don't," Sue barked back at him.

With some effort, they managed to control their laughter long enough for Sue to snap a couple shots. With the photos taken, Sue told them that she would have dinner ready in about 20 minutes. Harold got the shovel again and dug up a couple of the beers.

Samurai took the first swig and promptly spit it out on the ground. "Ugh," he said, "I got dirt in my mouth."

Harold smiled and raised his beer as though to toast his sponsor, "Salt of the earth, bro."

After a few swigs, and as their laughter subsided, Samurai became serious. "As long as we've got a few minutes, there's a few things we should talk about," he said.

"What, are you going to tell me about the birds and the bees, dad?" Harold said, laughing again.

"Sort of," Samurai said with a slight smile. Then he continued, "There are a few things you need to know about the club.

"Motorcycle clubs aren't like street gangs or any of that shit. The club holds elections once a year for president, VP, secretary, treasurer, sergeant at arms, and road captain. Seniority runs in that order – from president to road captain except in specific situations.

"For instance, T-Rex is the Banshee Riders' sergeant at arms. He keeps order at the meetings. He also keeps brothers in line if someone screws up in public and administers discipline if it's called for ..."

"That's a strong incentive to not screw up," said Harold.

"Yeeessss, but I can name another one, if you ever need it," Samurai replied with a voice of warning before continuing.

"If a problem develops between the Banshees and another club, the sergeant at arms is one of the president's generals.

"As for the road captain, that's Trailer Trash. When the club is on the road, the president and vice president generally ride up front. But the real boss of the pack is the road captain. He rides in back and makes sure no one is fucking up. He has the power to tell you you're too fucked up to ride and to have your bike loaded in the backup vehicle. He watches for loose stuff hanging off bikes and, if you break down, he helps you get going or decides if we need to load the bike. When he says 'Load 'er up,' there's no fucking debate.

"Prospects and tag-a-longs ride in back with the road captain so he can keep an eye on them. That includes you on Road Day," Samurai said with a little hesitancy, as though he expected Harold might object.

Instead, Harold said, "That makes sense."

"Cool," said Samurai, indicating his appreciation that Harold wasn't going to have a problem with it.

"You should also know about the road guards. Before the club pulls out, the road captain picks two brothers to serve as road guards. Road guards ride behind the president and vice president. They pull out and block traffic so the club can get through intersections as a pack. It's dangerous to have a cage (car) pull into the middle of the pack. Next thing, you've got brothers fightin' to pass cars to get back in a pack. That's why we keep the pack tight.

"You don't need to worry about it too much this weekend," Samurai continued. "Like I said, you'll be riding in back with the road captain. Just follow Trailer Trash's lead and you'll be fine."

Just then, Sue called out the window that dinner was ready. Before Samurai led him inside, he told Harold, "When the brothers are a little fucked up, things can get a little sloppy. You've got to watch for that, too. But" he added with a twinge of awe in his voice, "when everybody is reasonably sober, the pack is a thing of beauty. It's like a single organism."

Over dinner, Samurai bought up another important issue about the weekend. "What kind of maintenance have you done with your ride lately?" Judging by the blank stare on Harold's face, Samurai said, "Prospect, prospect, prospect. What are we going to do with you?"

Then Samurai said, "Well, don't worry, we'll have a look after dinner."

After dinner, they grabbed a couple beers and headed out by the garage where Harold's bike was leaning on its kickstand just inside the overhead door. Samurai looked it over and pointed out that the chain was loose and needed grease. The front end and mousetrap, which had several grease fittings, also needed some grease. Related to the latter, the clutch was out of adjustment.

"When did you last change the oil," Samurai said.

Harold shrugged like a kid in trouble and admitted he hadn't.

"You know, being a biker isn't just about ridin' – it's also about knowing what goes into ridin' and that starts with maintaining your ride.

"Well, you better take care of this stuff before we leave this weekend," Samurai said. "It might pay to put in a new set of plugs and points, while you're at it. We'll take a ride to the bike shop tomorrow. You can pick up what you need there."

It turned out the bike shop was more than just a business. Mack's Cycle Repair was a hangout for members of various bike clubs and serious independent riders in the area. If a customer was on good terms with Joe, the owner who had purchased the business from Mack several years earlier, Joe might even let the customer put the bike up on the rack or borrow some tools to do some personal maintenance. A larger draw, however, was the old refrigerator in the shop. Next to the fridge was a one-gallon pickle jar half full of coins and cash. Customers and friends could help themselves to a cold one and drop 50 cents into the jar for every can they took. As a result, Joe built up a surplus of cash beyond the cost of replenishing the beer. He used the surplus for periodic pig-roast parties in the gravel, weed-lined parking lot. In some cases, he even hired a band, though this usually meant folks could expect a small cover charge to attend the shindig.

First thing when they arrived, Samurai took Naked Boy over to meet Joe and his mechanic, known as Ink Spots, apparently because most of his body was covered in tattoos, including sleeves of tattoos on his skeletal-like arms. Where the mechanic was anemically thin, Joe had a middle-aged beer gut but was otherwise reasonably muscular. Owner and mechanic remained citizens (non-club members) by choice, Samurai explained, because "it might hurt business if they seemed partial to one club over the others. The bike shop is considered neutral territory.

"These are two people you're going to want to know," Samurai explained while referring to Joe and Ink Spots. "And you're gonna want to stay on their good sides. If they like you, they'll jump through hoops for you when your ride is down. If they decide you're an asshole or somethin', they won't give you the time of day, I don't care how much money you have."

After introductions, Harold gave Joe a scrap of paper Samurai had written up that listed the parts and materials needed to do the maintenance Samurai had pointed out for Harold's bike. Seeing Harold's bike through the window, Joe asked in a surprised and suspicious voice, "When did you buy that?"

Harold correctly suspected Joe was familiar with the bike from Harold's uncle. "I inherited it from my uncle."

"I'm sorry," he said. "I hadn't heard he died. He kept to himself most of the time, so I guess a lot of folks probably didn't notice."

Joe seemed to wince as though his words might sound a bit harsh to Harold's nephew, but all Harold saw was an opportunity to learn more about his uncle.

"How did you know my uncle," Harold asked, though realizing the bike and the bike shop was the logical connection.

"To tell you the truth, I didn't know him all that well," Joe said. "He'd come in once in a while for an occasional part. In fact, he bought a tire and had me re-lace the rear wheel late last fall. Like I said, he kept to himself most of the time. Still, I never heard anyone say anything against him.

"I'll tell you a funny story, though."

"Sure," Harold said eagerly.

"Your uncle came in one day last summer to pick up a new carburetor," Joe continued as he pointed out at Harold's bike to indicate that the new carb was on Harold's bike outside now. "While I'm trying to take care of your uncle, some citizen on a new bagger comes in and interrupts us as though your uncle wasn't even here.

"Well, this guy is all agitated and stuff. He tells me he wants a set of these newfangled intake clamps – the kind with the wide rubber band instead of the rubber O rings. When I started to say something, he cuts me off and says, 'And I won't pay a penny more than $28.' Every time I tried to talk, he cuts me off again. 'I'm telling you, I've looked up the price in the catalog and I can get 'em for $28 so I don't want any shit about it.'

"Well, the guy finally shuts up long enough for me to talk. By this time, however, I'm a bit annoyed, so, without saying anything, I walk over and take a set of 'em off the hook where they're marked $19.99 and bring them to the guy. 'Here you go,' I said. 'That'll be $28.'

"I think that was the only time I was able to convince your uncle to stick around for a beer," Joe said. "We laughed our asses off after the guy left."

"Did the guy buy them?" Harold asked.

"You bet," Joe said, "and he paid $28 plus tax."

Whether out of respect for Harold's uncle, for Samurai or simply because the conversation seemed to be going well, Joe invited Harold and Samurai into the back office where the owner pulled a bottle of Jack Daniels out of the top drawer of the file cabinet in the corner. Harold watched as he scrounged around among stacks of papers and parts on top of a four-drawer file cabinet until he'd found several shot glasses. He pulled them out of the debris with three fingers clenching them like the arm of a mechanical claw machine that would retrieve stuffed toys for kids. He used a bottom corner of his grease-stained front shirt-tail to wipe the glasses though it didn't look as though he did much more than smear the semi-dried residue of booze and dust around a bit. Setting the glasses edge to edge, he ran the bottle back and forth over the top until all three were filled.

"Here's to Gizzard," said Joe as they lifted their glasses in unison. When they had drained the glasses, Joe poured three more shots. But before Harold and Samurai could drain their glasses again, Joe pulled a folded piece of paper out of his pants pocket. Just like the paper Tawny had taken from her purse. He unfolded the paper to display some white powder inside. There was considerably more powder in Joe's paper, and he lined up six lines on the glass plate that covered the desktop.

When Naked Boy, who now had his name patch on the front of his rag, finished his two lines, Joe said, with a grin, "I can get that for you whenever you want. We're a full-service bike shop here," he laughed. "Today, we're offering special introductory samples. I can get you dimes and more but, of course, I'd rather you didn't go blabbing about this."

"I'll keep that in mind," said Harold. "And of course, it will be our little secret."

"You want any to take with you?"

"Not today," said Harold. "But I think you can count on seeing me again."

It occurred to Harold it might be nice if he could return the favor next time he saw Tawny. Then again, Harold hadn't paid for his parts yet and cash was running a bit low.

A quick stop at the bike shop turned into a couple hours of partying. When they finally left, fully planning to return to Samurai's for the maintenance on Harold's bike, they came across Kilroy and Red at a red light. Naked Boy and Samurai turned left and pulled up behind their brothers as the latter nodded greetings and went by in the intersection. The next thing Harold knew, the four of them were sitting at a table in Cal's Drift Inn. As customary with a bar, the clock on the wall behind the bar was set 15 minutes fast to ensure that the place was empty when the witching hour for liquor licenses rolled around. Harold noticed the clock when they arrived. The next time he looked up at it, the hands read a little past midnight.

He looked at Samurai and said, "Bro, I don't think we're going to get any work done on my bike tonight.

Samurai looked up at the clock on the wall. "Yeah, and Sue's gonna kill me when we get home. To tell you the truth, you might want to head back to your own crib tonight, bro," Samurai said. "It could get a little ugly considering she's still a little pissed that I didn't make it home last Saturday night. I'll bring your parts home with me and you can come by tomorrow after work."

After Harold put the bike away back at Chester's farmhouse, he went inside looking for Chester. After dropping his jacket and colors off on the back of a chair in the kitchen, he finally found Chester sitting on the front porch with a large bottle looking up into the night sky. As Harold reached the door, with his eyes still up in the sky, Chester said, "There's some beer in the fridge."

Before retracing his steps, Harold asked, "You need one?"

"Nah, I got my Boone's Farm," Chester said. "I'm fine."

Returning to the porch with a beer, Harold noticed that Chester had fixed the screen door. He plopped into the other chair on the porch and commented on the recent repair job.

"Well, things get done around here by and by," said Chester, who was still looking off into the star-sprinkled sky. "Speaking of that, thanks for cutting the grass the other day."

"No problem," Harold said. "If you've got any other projects for me, just let me know."

Harold opened his beer, took a swig and glanced over at Chester whose eyes were still fixed on the heavens.

After about a minute, Chester said, "You ever sit and just look up at the stars?"

"Not much lately," Harold said.

"You really should," Chester said. "It's really amazing, especially away from the city like this. You get out in the country and, without the glare of city lights, there are more stars than ... well, there's a whole shit-load of stars up there."

Harold looked up and realized Chester was right. It was as though a painter was shaking the excess paint out of his brush and was determined to shake out every last drop. The sky was spattered from end to end with stars of various sizes and brightness.

After another long silence, Chester said, "You know, people in the city really should drive out to the country to see this at least once in their lives. It kind of gives you a whole different perspective on things.

"Did you know some of those stars aren't even there anymore?" Chester asked.

"What do you mean?" Harold asked.

"Well, some of those stars are so far away that, even at the speed of light, it takes so long for the light to get here that, by the time the light gets here, the stars have burned out," Chester said. "I guess they're just cold cinders floating in space by now."

Harold starred up and pondered Chester's comments. Harold had obviously failed to pay attention to the corresponding lesson in high school science class. After a long pause, Harold said, "Really?"

"That's right," Chester said. "Some of the stars we see right now, when the light started its journey there were dinosaurs roaming the planet."

Harold looked over at Chester and said, "Wild."

After another long pause, Chester said, "Who you prospecting for?"

The question caught Harold a little off guard. Then again, he'd been coming and going with a big, white 'P' on his back for a while and it would have been silly to think Chester wouldn't notice.

"The Banshee Riders," Harold said.

That seemed to surprise Chester, who looked away from the sky and over at Harold for the first time that night. "Really?" Chester asked.

Harold looked at Chester and nodded affirmatively.

"Hmmm," said Chester. "Well, if you're gonna prospect for a club you could do worse."

The two sat looking into the sky a couple more minutes, while Harold pondered how his uncle's best friend would know one club from another before Chester spoke again. "It's not my business to tell you what to do," he said. "You're a grown man and you'll make your own way." Chester paused again before continuing, "I'd do anything for your uncle and you strike me as a stand-up guy, too. I like ya, Harold. You don't mind if I still call you Harold?"

"No, that's cool," Harold said smiling as Chester chuckled.

There was another longer pause before Chester went on. "Look, just be careful," Chester said. "It can be a lot of fun riding with a club. It can also get you in a lot of trouble – or worse."

"I can see that," Harold said, sensing that Chester might have more first-hand experience with the club culture than Harold would have assumed. "I'll be careful."

Chester nodded his head in a way that indicated he was somewhat reassured. "I am glad to hear you're with the Banshees though. They've got a little more class than one or two of the other clubs in this area. There are some real punks riding with some of these clubs around here. Of course, that little incident with the young girl at the bar in town, that wasn't very cool."

Harold winced as he admitted he was there when it happened.

"I know," Chester said and, as he got up to go inside. Seeing the surprise on Harold's face, he added, "I got my own sources.

"Like I said, 'just be careful.'"

Work seemed to drag on and on that Friday. With all the trucks that Harold had to load, and a couple he unloaded as well, he was busy enough that the day should have flown by. But Harold was eager to get off work and head over to Samurai's to work on the bike. He kept glancing up at the clock, a surefire way to slow the hands on any clock's face.

Harold knew that the soonest he could get to Samurai's was about 4:30 p.m. The meeting was at 7 p.m. and it was halfway to Earlsville. That meant, with the meeting that night, he and Samurai would only have a couple hours, at the most, to work on Harold's bike. He wasn't sure how long it would take but, somehow, even with the experienced help of his sponsor, Harold felt he'd need more time. Actually, he didn't know the half of it.

Harold was virtually dumbfounded when Samurai pointed to a toolbox and stood back to offer some advice instead of jumping into the project with Harold. He then handed Harold what Samurai called "the cookbook," which was actually a Harley Davidson repair manual, and said, "Well, good luck bro. I've got some things to take care of inside. When he saw the look of despair on Harold's face, he said, "Hey, you need to get familiar with working on your own scooter. If you break down someday and you're alone, you'll be completely fucked if you don't know your pecker from a spark plug."

"That makes sense, but ..."

"But?" Samurai cut in.

"What if I'm not ready in time for the meeting," Harold completed his question.

"Don't worry. I'll smooth things over with the brothers," Samurai said. "Besides, the day before Road Day it really isn't much of a meeting anyhow. Some of the brothers will stay home getting ready like you are. Others will just go to Hildie's and skip the meeting."

While Samurai headed out to the meeting, or to Hildie's – Harold wasn't sure which – Sue stayed home cleaning and straightening things in the house. Her parents, who were staying with the kids while Sue and Samurai were away, would arrive in the morning. She was as frantic to get the house ready before her folks arrived as Harold was to get his bike ready.

Harold had no problem changing the oil and spark plugs. Following the directions in the book and using the back of a book of matches, he did a relatively good job of changing and adjusting the points, as well. Following the directions, he managed to adjust the chain, too, while checking that the rear wheel was tracking evenly. Adjusting a mousetrap, however, is a more complicated process, especially for the uninitiated, which described Harold to a T.

For those who like chrome on their motorcycles, a mousetrap is a mechanical device rich in potential. But the chrome comes at a cost. Officially known as a hand-clutch booster, the mousetrap is U-clamped to the left-front downtube of the frame, right behind the front wheel, and built on a cast-iron base. Another narrow plate in the shape of an obtuse triangle has a pin that fits into the base piece so that the prior can pivot. A heavy-duty spring extends about six inches from another pin at the top of the triangular plate to a threaded- adjustable hook at the bottom of the base piece. The top of the base piece has a slotted arm where the clutch cable slips in and the cable housing end threads in while the cable extends down to another pin on the back of the plate. At the bottom of the triangular plate is a hole where a mushroom-headed chrome rod extends back about 20 inches to the clutch arm that extends across the top of the transmission. Here, the rod, threads into the clutch arm offering another adjustment. Glittering in its chrome finish, the mousetrap is an attractive accessory on the side of a motorcycle. Some might say that, with its spring, it's named after the trap that is designed to catch mice. Harold quickly came to the conclusion that it was named after the 'Mousetrap' game because of its complexity, as well as the way he smashed his finger when the spring-loaded monstrosity flipped back unexpectedly while he was making one of at least 11 steps in the process of adjusting the mousetrap, as spelled out in the 1957 Harley Davidson Panhead Model 74 OHV Owner's Manual" Samurai had given Samurai. Frustratingly, he found that making one adjustment was liable to change other adjustments he had already made. Though Harold followed the steps in the book sequentially, somehow, the final product wasn't what he was hoping for. At first, the cable was far too loose. When he pulled the clutch, the lever that rode back and forth over the transmission didn't have enough travel. Even to Harold's inexperienced eye, it was obviously wrong. Harold started over with little more success. The cable was still far too loose.

On his fourth try, however, he discovered the situation had reversed itself. The cable was far too tight.

Harold tried to squeeze the handgrip, but it barely moved. In frustration, Harold muttered, "God damn it," and squeezed hard. He was rewarded with a pinging noise and suddenly the handgrip was completely loose as if it wasn't attached at all. Harold looked down and saw that the cable had broken at the point where it mounted to the mousetrap. The clutch grip didn't just feel unconnected. It was unconnected.

"GOD DAMN IT," he hollered, his foot back as though he was going to kick the bike just as Sue stepped into the garage. Harold's first thought was that she heard him yelling and came out to investigate. Instead, with a slightly amused look on her face, having caught Harold in an awkward pose, she said, "If you can take a little time out from beating on your motorcycle, you have a phone call inside."

Harold looked at Sue in amazement, his frustration boiling up inside. He thought to himself, "It's not bad enough I just broke my clutch cable, now I have to stop what I'm doing to take a phone call." But Harold knew it wasn't Sue's fault and followed her inside while cussing under his breath.

Halfway to the door, it occurred to Harold, "It's probably a brother on the phone calling for something." Harold realized he might have trouble properly responding to their request, considering that his bike was now inoperable. He stepped up the pace and walked through the door almost on Sue's heels.

The portable phone was resting on the counter when Harold came into the kitchen. As he reached for the phone, Montana, the little girl who was responsible for Harold's embarrassing club name, came over and stuck her tongue out at Harold. Then the little girl turned and ran away laughing. Harold managed to force a small smile through his frustration and put the phone up to his ear.

Expecting to hear one of his brothers on the other end of the line, Harold was surprised when a familiar feminine voice came through the receiver with David Allan Coe's "You Never Even Call Me By My Name" blasting from the jukebox in the background. "Naked Boy, where are you," the voice said.

It took Harold a couple of seconds to realize it was "Tawny?! What ... where are you?"

"I'm at Hildie's," the voice purred barely audible over the mix of loud conversations and the jukebox. "When are you coming?"

Having Tawny waiting for him at the bar was certainly an enticing thought, but it was quickly washed away as Harold remembered the mechanical conundrum he was wrestling with. "No, no, I can't," Harold stammered. "I'm working on the bike. Hey, in fact, are any of my brothers there?"

"What?" Tawny asked, and Harold repeated himself loudly.

"Well, why don't you stop working on the bike and come up here," Tawny said in a pouting voice.

"I can't," Harold said, a note of annoyance entering his tone. "I can't ride until I fix the bike. Like I said, 'Are any of my brothers there?'"

"Well, how do you think I got this number," Tawny said laughing.

The way she laughed, Harold immediately ascertained that she was probably fairly well looped already. He put on his most sympathetic voice and asked Tawny, "Is Samurai there?"

"They said you're at Samurai's," Tawny said, annoyance and confusion now edging into her voice as well.

"I am," Harold said, continuing to maintain his temper. "But he's not here."

"Oh," Tawny said drunkenly. "So, why don't you come up here? I want to see you."

"Look, babe," Harold continued with the same soft tone, "I really gotta talk to one of my brothers, OK? Just give the phone to one of my brothers, whoever's closest to the phone, will ya?"

"Okay," Tawny said. "Just hurry over baby. I miss you."

With that, Harold heard a click, and the phone went dead. He started to say, "What the ..." but he noticed that both of the kids were sitting at the table watching him. He stopped himself and asked Sue, "Do you have the number for Hildie's."

Sue, who was doing some dishes, took a wet-and-soapy hand out of the sink, grabbed the phone book off the top of the refrigerator, and flipped it on the table while saying, "The number's on the back."

There, in barely discernable pencil, Harold made out where someone had scribbled "Hildie's" and the phone number.

He quickly dialed the bar to have an unfamiliar male voice

come over the line and say, "Hello," while Joan Jett and the Black-hearts belted out "I Love Rock 'N Roll' from the jukebox in the background. At least the voice sounded relatively sober. Harold asked, "Are any of the Banshees there?"

"Sure," the voice said. "Who do you want?"

"Any of 'em," Harold said. Then, as an afterthought, he asked, "Are Kilroy or Samurai there?"

Harold heard the male voice holler, "Kilroy, it's for you."

A moment later, Kilroy was on the line. When Harold explained his predicament, Kilroy asked, "How long is the cable?" When Harold said he didn't know, Kilroy said, "Well, go out and measure it. I'll wait."

Harold set the phone down and asked Sue if she had a tape measure. Sue shrugged and promised to look as she walked out of the room drying her hands in a dish towel. Harold wasn't sure if she meant that she would look immediately or if she didn't understand his predicament and was planning to look later. However, a minute later she returned with a cloth seamstress tape.

"Will this work?" she asked. "I'm sure Sam has a tape in the truck, but he always locks it."

Harold took the cloth and said, "This will work fine."

Harold returned to the house pinching the seamstress tape at the appropriate measurement. As he entered the kitchen, he looked at the table and saw that the phone's receiver was back in the cradle. He looked up at Sue who, with an apologetic look, said, "Montana hung up for you."

Harold looked over at Montana who was smiling proudly. Whatever annoyance Harold felt was washed away by the 2-year-olds smile. He smiled back at her and said, "Thank you, honey."

Montana said, "Your welcome," and skipped off to the living room.

Harold found the number for Hildie's again and was about to call when the phone rang in his hand. Harold was so surprised he actually dropped the phone. When he picked it up, he heard an unfamiliar and angry woman's voice. "Is this Naked Boy?" the voice barked.

"Yeah," he answered. "Who's this?"

Ignoring his question, the voice said, "You need to get yer ass down here now."

"Who is this," Harold asked again, quickly becoming angry himself.

"This is Dancer," she said in a huff.

"So, who is Dancer," Harold said with barely controlled rage.

"I'm Capsize's old lady, PROSPECT," she snarled back, emphasizing the last word as though to remind Harold of his place in the club's pecking order.

But Harold didn't respond as she expected. He remembered that Capsize was the other brother who failed to follow through on setting up Road Day before Samurai, Kilroy, and Harold rode out to meet with Mongrel. Harold also remembered what Samurai said about taking orders from old ladies.

"Nothing personal, but I don't care who your old man is," Harold said, barely controlling the venom in his voice as he enunciated the words slowly and carefully. "I need to speak to Kilroy, NOW."

Dancer immediately flew into a rage. "No, prospect, you need to get down here and do something about your old lady, NOW."

Harold gathered his wits and calmed himself long enough to say, "Look, I'm sorry, but I can't come down there now. I'm working on my bike and I need to speak to Kilroy. Will you please put him on the line?"

As though Harold hadn't said a word, Dancer continued, "If you don't get down here, I'm going to wring your stupid bitch's neck – do you hear me, prospect?"

With his voice beginning to ring with anger again, Harold barked, "Do what you gotta do, but put Kilroy back on the line." Before he finished the sentence, however, the phone clicked dead again. In a way, Harold figured it was OK he didn't finish the comment. He didn't really mean it when he suggested he didn't care what she did to Tawny, though Harold was hardly pleased that Tawny was apparently causing trouble at the bar, trouble that Harold might have to deal with in some way later. He had a mental image of a nondescript girl named Dancer hanging up the phone and turning to pound on Tawny. Then again, he also hadn't met Capsize yet and wasn't sure how things would play out when he did, considering the words he'd just had with Capsize's old lady.

Calming himself again, Harold picked up the phone and gave

Hildie's another try. The same male voice that had answered the last time answered again. When, as before, Harold asked for Kilroy, the man gave Harold a short lecture about how "this is a public phone and I'm not your personal secretary."

"I'm sorry," Harold said. Kilroy and I were disconnected before. It is important."

There was a long pause on the other end and then he heard the voice yell, with more than a little exasperation, "Kilroy, it's for you again."

When Kilroy got back on the line and asked what had happened, Harold blew the question off with, "I don't know. We were disconnected." Then Harold gave Kilroy the cable length.

Even over the music and through the fluctuating hum of conversation, Kilroy could hear the strain in Harold's voice. "Don't worry about it, NB. Just sit tight. The cavalry is on the way."

Before Kilroy could hang up, Harold asked, "What the fuck is going on with Tawny?"

"Your girlfriend? Well, she's a little drunk and a little stupid," Kilroy said. Then, laughing, he asked, "Where'd you find this one?"

"I don't know," Harold said, trying to answer the rhetorical question. "Nowhere really."

"Well, I'll try to get her out of the line of fire," Kilroy said. "But if she keeps opening her mouth like that, one of the old ladies is gonna pop her for sure."

"Pop her?" Harold asked in alarm.

"Yeah, hit her," Kilroy said. "Although, I think a couple of the old ladies are almost mad enough to put a bullet through her head. You should see the old ladies," he said, laughing again. "I don't think I've ever seen them this pissed.

"Hey, don't sweat it, bro," Kilroy said, realizing his comments might not be assuaging Harold's concerns. "Chances are they won't do anything. I'll see you in a little bit. Just keep your panties on."

When Harold had finished all his other maintenance projects, about 45 minutes had passed since he spoke with Kilroy. With no immediate work to do, he went inside and grabbed a beer and began watching the clock. As time continued to roll by, Harold began to pace.

He was pacing back and forth and repeatedly pulling the window curtain back to see if the Cavalry was arriving yet. Sue came in from tucking her brood into bed and pointed out, "You don't need to look out the window. Trust me, you'll hear them coming. Why don't you sit down and relax? I'll get you another beer."

As she handed Harold a beer, Sue asked, "Kind of a hectic night, eh?"

"I'll say. If I don't get this thing running tonight, I'm in deep shit."

Sue snorted as though to say she didn't exactly agree. "Don't worry too much," she said. "I've heard on the grapevine that the brothers like the way you've been handling yourself."

Harold looked at Sue in surprise. "I hope you're right," he said. "But I'll still be in trouble if I don't get my bike running."

"You'll get it running," Sue said confidently. "You might not get any sleep tonight, but you'll get your bike running, I'm sure of it."

Harold's respect for Sue seemed to grow every time he saw her. She didn't talk too much, didn't nag, not, at least, as far as Harold had seen. But when Sue said something, it was usually worth taking the time to listen. Thinking about Sue as he sat at the table, Harold felt another twinge of guilt about his part in the adventure with Tawny and her friend the other night. He wasn't guilty enough, or stupid enough, to say anything, but, in some ways, he was sorry it had happened.

Harold was almost done with the beer Sue gave him when he heard not one, but several bikes pulling into the driveway. When Harold stepped out the door, he found Kilroy, Samurai, Tank, Red and a brother Harold hadn't met yet outside.

"Prospect," Tank said, while spouting a phony pout, "what's this I hear you're having a rough night?"

Everyone started laughing. But Kilroy said, "Layoff him." For a second, Harold thought Kilroy was accepting a role as Harold's protector or something. But then, Kilroy continued, "Can't you see he's busy drinking a beer."

Harold looked puzzled as he tried to figure out what Kilroy meant. Samurai solved the riddle for Harold. "I think, in his own subtle way, Kilroy is suggesting you should grab some beers for your brothers, Prospect."

"That's right, bro," Kilroy said in a taunting but friendly manner.

"Of course, you could stand there and finish that beer first. Don't worry, we'll go back to the bar and get some for ourselves."

It was a mild threat; Kilroy's way of suggesting that they would leave Harold struggling to fix his clutch problem on his own.

Harold raised an index finger and waved it lightly in the air as he said with a smile, "You know what, you guys look thirsty. I'll be right back."

As he turned to go back into the house, he heard Kilroy laugh, "And who said you have to beat the prospect over the head with a stick before he gets a clue."

As Harold reached the door, he heard Tank say, "And prospect, make sure they're cold."

By the time Harold came back outside, all the brothers were in the garage by his bike. As Harold passed out the beers he realized that Kilroy and Samurai were installing a new clutch cable they'd found somewhere, somehow. With the cable installed, an argument ensued over the appropriate adjustment procedures.

"That's not how you adjust a mousetrap," Tank said several times until Kilroy yelled at him, "All right, smart guy, how do you adjust a mousetrap? I mean, I have no idea. I've never even seen a frickin' motorcycle before. Can you help me, please? I can see the mousetrap, but I'm not sure where the mouse goes."

"The mouse goes up yer fuckin' ass. Now, get the fuck out of my way," Tank said, shoving Kilroy aside.

Kilroy stepped back laughing. Just then, however, Sue burst into the garage yelling in a muted voice, "Are you assholes going to tuck the kids back into bed again after you wake them up?"

There was an awkward silence, as though the teacher had walked into the classroom and caught the students goofing off. Kilroy broke the silence when he said, "If they didn't hear the bikes pulling in the driveway, well sure. Let me at the little buggers."

He actually took a couple steps towards the door as though intent on going into the house, up the stairs and into the bedroom where Montana and Ringo were presumably sleeping. But Sue, who was smiling at Kilroy's apparent fondness for her children, and the fact that he probably would go up to the room, quickly stepped in front of the door to block Kilroy's path.

"No, you don't," Sue said. "You'll start tickling them and I'll never get them back to sleep." Then, with her face turning serious again, she looked at the assembled throng of grubby bikers and said, "I'm serious, you assholes, keep it down out here." Then she looked at Samurai as if to say, "You should know better." But Sue was done with her speech making and quickly turned to return to the house. She merely muttered a sarcastic "Thank you" as she walked out the door.

Harold was looking out the door at Sue as she walked away shaking her head when Tank barked at him, "Hey, prospect, do you wanna watch this so you'll know how to do it next time, or are you expecting me to come over any time you need to adjust your clutch?"

As Harold was busy learning how to adjust his mousetrap, Samurai told Red to go inside on another beer run. Harold looked up and said, "These were the last of them."

"Well, it sounds like someone needs to make a beer run," Samurai said. He tossed the keys to Sue's Pinto wagon to Harold and said, "Tank will give you a lesson in mousetraps some other time." Samurai then pulled a roll of bills out of his pocket and peeled off a couple twenties. "Be sure to get a receipt," he added.

Red went along with Harold and, by the time they got back to the house, Tank had finished the lesson without Harold. The garage was closed and there were no bikes visible in the yard. They found Samurai inside.

"Where is everyone?" Red asked. "With the run tomorrow, they kind of petered out early," Samurai said. "I locked your bike up in the garage. Figured you could crash here tonight," he added, looking at Red."

Then Samurai looked at Harold. "Tank took your bike out for a short ride. We adjusted the points a little but, otherwise, everything is fine."

Just then, Kilroy came out of the bathroom and Harold figured Kilroy was crashing at Samurai's as well. Samurai said, "Why don't you two grab a beer and then grab some sleep."

Harold had a sense he and Red were being dismissed from the room, so he grabbed a couple beers from the 12 pack under his arm and tossed them to Samurai and Kilroy. Then Harold took two more beers, gave one to Red and put the rest in the fridge. As they walked out of the kitchen, the prospect and probate said good night, but their brothers were already involved in a discussion and didn't seem to notice.

In the living room, Harold took a seat on the couch where he usually slept when staying at Samurai's. As he did, he realized that Red was headed that way, too. Seeing Harold sitting on the couch, Red frowned and turned to pull the ottoman over in front of the armchair. Then he went to the hall closet and took a couple blankets down from above where several coats were hanging. His familiarity made it apparent Red had crashed here before, too.

With the lights off, the two sat sipping their beers and talking about Road Day. They also talked about the ruckus Tawny had kicked up at Hildie's. Harold found out that Capsize's old lady did, in fact, pop Tawny in the face. Red seemed to think that someone had driven Tawny home, but he really wasn't sure. Noticing a little anguish on Harold's face, Red said, "I think she's OK. She'll probably have a black eye for a few days, but she's alright." Then he quickly changed the subject back to Road Day. It was the first such event for both of them. Therefore, their discussion consisted of hearsay remembrances and speculation about the fun they would have that weekend.

Feeling like a kid on Christmas Eve, Harold finally said goodnight and laid back to get some sleep. Red finished his beer and then stretched out on the armchair with his legs hanging over the edge of the ottoman.

They weren't in those positions long when Harold was brought upright by a sharp jolt. He opened his eyes just in time to see Samurai kicking the couch for a second time. Harold also heard the toilet flushing as Kilroy walked into the room.

"Isn't this great," Samurai said angrily. "I guess you figure my brother Kilroy should sleep on the floor while you stretch out on the couch?"

Harold mumbled something about not knowing Kilroy was staying, though Harold knew it was just an excuse. He'd noticed that Kilroy's bike was not outside the garage and had assumed earlier that Kilroy would crash there. He just hadn't thought about it when he hit the sack.

"Well he is, so get your fat ass off his bed," Samurai said in an un-customarily harsh tone.

As Kilroy got comfortable on the couch, Harold went to the

closet and picked out several blankets in an effort to soften the effect of sleeping on the floor. Harold tossed and turned for several minutes trying to find a comfortable position. As he did so, he felt an uncommon sense of frustration with his sponsor, even though he knew it made sense that he slept on the floor rather than a full-patch brother.

As he tussled with the blankets, Samurai headed for the stairs. He stopped short, however, and told Harold, "By the way, prospect, next week you've got to get over to Mack's and pay for that cable. I'd try to think of a little bonus to kick in as well. Joe made a special trip in and opened the shop for us."

There was a pause as Harold was worried his anger would seep through into his voice. Then Samurai barked, "Did you hear me?"

"Yeah, I heard ya," Harold said, doing a poor job of hiding his frustration.

"Good," Samurai said in a similar tone. His voice softened a little when he said, "I'll see you in the morning."

Samurai took one step up the stairs before Harold said, "I guess I forgot to say thanks earlier. I appreciated the help."

"Yeah, well, we figured you were kind of stressed," Kilroy said from the couch.

"That's no excuse," Harold said. "I'd have been fucked if you guys hadn't picked up that cable."

"No problem," Kilroy said as Samurai disappeared upstairs. "Now shut the fuck up and let me sleep."

Harold was quiet for about two minutes. Then he said, "Kilroy?"

"What?" came a sincerely annoyed response.

There was another pause and Harold said, "Thanks for calling me NB tonight. It sounds a lot better than Naked Boy."

"No problem," Kilroy said as they both laughed. "Now, keep your clothes on and get some sleep."

Chapter 15 — Grandma, Grandpa and the Poacher

NB, as he was happy to call himself now, woke to another sudden jolt discovering it was daylight and that, this time, Samurai was kicking him directly in the bottom of his foot. "Time to get up, sleeping beauty," his sponsor said with a grin.

As Harold sat up, he noticed that Kilroy was no longer on the couch and he could hear the other full-patch brother talking with Sue in the kitchen. Red was folding his blanket with what could loosely be called help from Ringo as Montana stood off to the side in her teddy-bear nightie. She held her battered 'blanky' in one arm, which hung down to the floor at her left side, and a stuffed tiger she called Stripie with her other arm. Montana was teasing Red that his feet smelled bad. As though he and Red were engineers trying to build an emergency support for a dam before a rising river broke through, Ringo admonished his little sister that she was interrupting them in what was obviously an important job.

While laughing at the kids, Red turned his head towards Harold and said three magic words – "Road Day, brother." Only Red didn't just say the words. They rolled off his tongue as he savored the flavor. It was the way a starving man describes a thick, juicy steak.

Harold smiled as he began folding his own blankets. At that point, Montana came over and stood in front of Harold as though her presence there would somehow be helpful. Harold looked at her and laughed, "Did you want to help?" She shook her head 'No' and smiled as she continued to watch him. Then Harold looked at Red and returned the greeting – "Road Day" as though raising a toast.

Montana then shared her thoughts on the morning by informing Harold, "Your feet smell, too."

Harold laughed and said, "Thank you, sweetie. Your feet stink, too."

Montana took the compliment well, running off to the kitchen giggling so she could tell her mother that the naked boy had told her that her feet stink.

No sooner had Naked Boy finished folding the blankets than the doorbell rang. Harold, standing closest to the door, looked around to see if anyone else was going to see who was there. Just then, Sue looked into the living room from the kitchen and said, "Harold, can you get the door?"

Harold nodded, said, "Sure," and walked over and opened the door. Standing at the door, with broad smiles was a 60ish couple. The man, about 5-8 and with a typical middle-aged expansion around his waist, wore a plaid shirt with narrow pink and two-shades of wide green lines. Below the shirt was what Harold considered the most ridiculous choice of attire he'd ever seen — pink short pants exposing knobby knees and a pair of black socks stretched up to the bottom of the knees from a pair of brown loafers.

The woman was close to 6-feet tall and looked even more ridiculous than the man. She wore a pink fishnet over her roller-filled hair. Even through the netting, Harold could see a slight red tint to the grayish-blue locks curled around tubes tightly wound to her scalp. Her over-sized, flowered dress hung loosely on her boney frame. Her sandals were white with one-and-a-half-inch heels. Lacking socks, her red-painted toenails were just visible under the flowered tent. She also wore considerably more makeup than was necessary — makeup that didn't make a lot of sense considering the curlers in her hair and the casual attire.

Looking at the couple Harold caught a whiff of cigar smoke mixing with perfume. In spite of their appearance, and deducing that these were almost assuredly Sue's parents, Harold suddenly felt a bit self-conscious about his lack of shoes and socks and his generally disheveled appearance. The couple, however, didn't seem bothered.

"We're the grandparents," the man said with a booming laugh as Harold stepped aside so they could enter the house. "And who might you be?"

"I'm Harold," he replied.

"Harold?" the woman asked in surprise, clearly expecting something a little more colorful. "Didn't they give you one of those special names, like Hound Dog or something?"

"Well, yes," Harold said. "They call me Nak ..., they call me NB."

"NB?" the man said. "That's a peculiar name even by the standards we're used to over here."

Harold shrugged as Samurai came into the room. "Mom, dad, how are you?" he asked. Before they could answer, he said, "I see you've met Naked Boy."

"Naked Boy?" the older man said while giving Harold a puzzled look. "Oh, I get it – NB – Naked Boy."

Samurai gave Harold a funny look as he shook the older man's hand. "How's your lumbago, Burt?" Samurai asked.

"Not so bad I couldn't teach you a couple things out on the links," the man replied laughing.

"Doris," Samurai said, gesturing slightly with his head towards the woman, "could teach me about golfing. What I want to know is when I can whip your butt at canasta again?"

Sue interrupted the conversation as she came in and gave each parent a hug and a kiss. Then, as Samurai gave her mother a hug, she turned and yelled, "Kids, guess who's here?"

Judging by the thunder of little hooves that erupted from the kitchen, Ringo and Montana knew who was expected and burst into the living room hollering, "Grannana, Grampy" as they ran into open arms.

"Look at how you two have grown," the grandparents commented in unison. "I'll have to put bricks on their heads to keep them from getting too tall," added Burt.

Harold was surprised how easily the older couple each hoisted a child into their arms and carried the wiggling bundles into the kitchen behind Sue. He heard Sue say something about not giving the children too much candy as Samurai turned to Harold and suggested he hurry up and get dressed. "We're leaving soon," Samurai warned.

Harold said he was hoping to take a shower, but Samurai said there wouldn't be time. "You're just gonna get stinky anyhow," Samurai said.

"Montana said he already is," Red added with a grin.

"Only my feet," said Harold as he put on his boots and was soon slipping his jacket and rag over his shoulders. He met Samurai and Sue at the door as they were going outside. Sue gave the kids hugs and kisses. She thanked her parents for helping out. Other than their general appearance, there was no discernable difference between the way Sue and Samurai said goodbye and thank you than when any other 'normal' parents went away for a weekend leaving the kids with their grandparents. And the grandparents took everything comfortably in stride as well.

"Oh my gosh, you sure owe us a lot making us spend the weekend with this lot," Sue's mother said while holding Montana with one arm and tickling her armpit with the other.

They were about to walk out the door when Burt blocked their path to take Samurai's hand. "Sam," he said. "You guys be careful out there."

"Not to worry, Burt," Samurai said. "And like Sue said, thanks for helping out."

When they pulled into Hildie's, there were half-a-dozen bikes in the parking lot already. Tank was leaning against the wall by the door smoking a cigarette and drinking a beer. "Mornin'," he said, lifting his beer mug as if in a salute.

As the group dismounted and headed inside, Kilroy stopped to talk with Tank, sending Red inside to fetch a beer as he went by. Inside they found Grunt, Bitters, T-Rex, and a petite and attractive blonde Harold took to be the big man's old lady even before reading the "Property of T-Rex" patch on her back. A couple other brothers were over at a table, including a stocky, yet muscular, balding brother with short hair and a neatly groomed mustache, Harold hadn't seen before.

If there was one other thing Harold noticed about him it was how extremely clean he was. His rag was fringed at the missing sleeves, but even the fringe seemed as though it was trimmed off at an even length. The only aspect of the brother's appearance that seemed to make sense, other than the patch on his back, was the stubble on his face as though he was due for a shave or had just decided to start a beard.

Harold tried calling Tawny to see how she was, but the phone rang and rang without anyone picking up. Giving up, he ordered a beer and, from the way their faces were stuck together at the mouths, quickly surmised that Grunt and Bitters were fairly well intoxicated already. Red suspected the same thing and raised his eyebrows to Harold before taking a couple of beer outside. Red paused in front of Harold and held the two beers out in front of him. For a second, Harold thought Red was offering one to him but, when Harold reached out as though to take one, Red pulled it back and barked, "No, dick head. This is a teaching moment. Tank's outside, too, and he'll probably want one soon. Brothers generally appreciate initiative."

Samurai had stopped at the front of the bar to speak with the owner/bartender for a minute or two. As Samurai came around the corner of the bar to join the others he spotted the brother Harold hadn't met yet.

"Pot Roast," Samurai hollered in obvious surprise. Seeing Samurai, the biker jumped up from his seat and the two threw their arms around each other for a short bearhug. "What, did you talk them into a weekend pass for Road Day?" Samurai asked.

"No man," Pot Roast answered. "I busted out."

"What?" Samurai said with a concerned tone and, apparently, willing to believe his brother had broken out of jail.

"Naah, just kiddin', bro," Pot Roast said.

"But you weren't supposed to get out for, what, … until the second week of July, right?" Samurai asked.

"Yeah," Pot Roast said with a large grin. "But they started taking in inmates from other counties that are overcrowded – found themselves with an overcrowding problem of their own."

"So, they let the petty criminals out?" Samurai said with a grin of his own.

"Who you calling petty," responded Pot Roast with a mix of indignation and pride. "I broke that asshole's jaw and nearly bit his ear off. You ask him and he'll tell you, there was nothing petty about it."

"Yeah, that's true," Samurai said with a mischievous grin that was becoming increasingly familiar to Harold, "but I heard he wants a rematch once he graduates from second grade?"

"You fucker," Pot Roast said looking a little flustered – too flustered to think of a better comeback.

"While I've got you relatively speechless, let me introduce you to someone," Samurai said as he gestured for Harold to come over. "Pot Roast, this is Naked Boy. He may be a prospect but he's a righteous brother, so don't give him any of yer typical fuck-with-the-prospect shit." Then Samurai turned to Harold and said, "Naked Boy, this is Pot Roast. He's the brother most likely to get yer ass in a sling, so watch yerself around him."

Pot Roast ignored the editorial comments about his character and threw his arms around Harold. Harold was caught completely off guard by the gesture. He was even more surprised when Pot Roast stepped back suddenly.

"Wait a minute," Pot Roast hollered. "Is Samurai your sponsor?"

When Harold nodded yes, Pot Roast threw his arms around Samurai again. "You've popped yer cherry, bro." Turning to face Harold with an arm around Samurai's shoulders, Pot Roast said, "My brother here has been a Banshee for three years now and, until today, he's been a virgin the whole time. You, brother, are his first prospect. I hope you know what an honor that is."

While Harold was digesting this information, Samurai spoke up. "Now, Pot Roast, on the other hand, has sponsored half the brothers in the club. He's even tried to sponsor prospects for other clubs. In fact, didn't you try sponsoring a little girl for a Campfire group?"

Samurai's comments brought a round of laughter from all the brothers and old ladies within earshot. It also elicited another feigned outrage of "You fucker!" from Pot Roast.

As Pot Roast was protesting, Samurai turned to Harold, "Now that you've been introduced, are you gonna stand here with that shit-eatin' look on yer face? Yer makin' me look bad."

For a moment, Harold was completely caught off guard. As it dawned on him, Samurai said, "Do yer job, prospect."

Before the words were completely out of Samurai's mouth, Harold was striding over to the bar and flagging down the owner. As Harold waited for the beers, he glanced back at his brothers by the table. Samurai had his back to the bar but Pot Roast was watching Harold with an approving smile. It suddenly dawned on Harold that Road Day wasn't just a party. For him and Red, it was a test – a chance to show their stuff and make some points towards earning their patches. Or, if they screwed up, a chance for the club to weed them out before they got any closer to making full patch. Harold wasn't sure how painful it would be if he was 'weeded out.'

Returning with the beers, Harold saw Mongrel coming in the door and walking over to the others while pulling a pack of cigarettes out from under his cutoff shirt sleeve. Before the cigarette reached Mongrel's mouth, Harold had his Bic lighter out with a flame waiting in front of Mongrel's face. Harold moved so fast, in fact, that Mongrel stepped back a moment in surprise. Mongrel's cigarette lit, Harold returned to the bar for a couple more beers, one for Mongrel and a couple others in anticipation that other brothers would want them.

As he returned to the group with the next round, Pot Roast threw an arm over Harold's shoulder and pulled him aside. "You're doing great, prospect. Keep in mind, though, you don't have to buy the beers …" As he said it, Pot Roast reached out as though to take one of the beers, "Unless you want to buy one for me, of course."

Harold smiled and said, "This one's for you," and reached out to put one in Pot Roast's hand.

Pot Roast took the beer. He tipped the beer to Harold in thanks, but he did so in a rapid and carefree manner that was obviously designed to create the splash of beer that slapped against Harold's hands and the T-shirt on his chest. Harold looked down in surprise and then looked up into a toothy grin and mischievously sparkling eyes of the brother he had only just met. If Harold hadn't decided he liked Pot Roast already, this cemented the deal and he smiled back, which earned him another approving slap on the back.

The bar had rapidly filled with brothers and was as full as if it were a Friday night. But it was not Friday night. Rather, it was Saturday morning – 9 a.m. Saturday morning, in particular. The word had come down to the prospects that any brothers who weren't there at 9 a.m. sharp, and ready to go, would be busted down to prospect. In anticipation of this deadline, Harold had periodically glanced at the clock behind the bar. The big hand was only three minutes away from straight up at the hour. Harold glanced expectantly at Samurai standing beside him. Samurai might have seen Harold looking at the clock. In any case, he seemed to recognize the unspoken question in Harold's eyes.

"That's bar time," he told Harold. "Besides," he added with some disgust in his voice, "the club is always late getting on the road. And Reaper isn't here yet either.

"Just keep busy. Mingle. See if any of the brothers need anything. This is your time to shine, bro."

Harold set about lighting cigarettes and grabbing beers for the brothers. When he brought beers to Snake and Grunt, the beer slipped through the latter inebriated brother's fingers and crashed to the floor. Though Grunt was obviously drunk, which could have been the cause of the mishap, Harold almost had a feeling the stubby biker had dropped the beer on purpose.

As Harold retrieved the empty cup from the floor, the usually affable brother growled. "What the fuck, prospect?"

"No problem. I'll get you another one," Harold said with a smile. But as he began to walk away, Grunt said, "What about this one?

Harold noticed that Snake and Grunt were giving him a look that suggested he might be in trouble somehow. Several other brothers were also watching intently. From the grins on a few of their faces, he suspected there was more to this than he might have expected.

Harold turned back to the bar intending to ask for a rag when Grunt barked again, "Where the fuck are you going, asshole?"

Harold was caught off guard. It wasn't just the way he was barking at Harold; it was also that it was so out of character for Grunt. Harold stopped and looked back at Grunt. He sensed that those around him were enjoying his confusion. Then Snake said, "Why don't you use your rag, prospect?"

Harold began taking his rag off eliciting a mass sigh of exasperation followed by Grunt's question: "What the fuck are you doing?"

Harold stopped, one arm half out of a sleeve. He looked at Grunt, who looked back with a glare. Harold glanced around the room and saw some contrived glares, but some knowing grins cracking a couple faces, too. Clearly, this was a ritual they were used to. And then, the answer struck him. Harold nearly launched himself to the floor, twisting on the way to land with a thud on his back. Harold slid his back across the floor and back where the beer had splattered as cheers erupted from the group around him.

"And who said you're just a stupid fucking prospect?" said Grunt.

As he got up, several of the brothers still laughing, Grunt, who had a beer in each hand, handed one to Harold. "Thanks, bro," Grunt said with a smile that suggested, maybe, just maybe, Grunt wasn't quite as drunk as Naked Boy had thought.

Samurai was standing behind several of the brothers who were looking at Harold. When Harold glanced over at his sponsor, Samurai lifted his beer glass slightly as if to say, "Well done." Then Samurai looked up at the clock with a frown. Harold stepped over by his sponsor and asked, "What's wrong?"

The clock read 9:43. Samurai looked at Harold and said, "Reaper's still not here yet," and shook his head.

Several of the brothers were also eyeing the clock anxiously. The majority, however, seemed entirely content to continue sitting at the bar drinking. Harold and Samurai walked outside together where they heard a commotion as they neared the door. Outside, they found that T-Rex had booted a half-full, 55-gallon, topless, green barrel that was kept off to the side of the door for people who drank outside to drop any empty beer cups. The barrel was on its side in the gravel lot and plastic cups, and some paper refuse were strewn around in front of it, as though it had vomited its contents.

"This is just great," the towering biker yelled. "Who knows what time we'll actually get to the campground? And when we finally hit the road half the brothers will be half in the bag." He looked over at Harold and Samurai and said, "You know what the pack will be like by the time we get going, don't you?"

"I know, bro," Samurai said in a soothing voice as Sue came out to join them. But with his brother looking like he might boil over, Samurai told Sue bluntly to go back inside. Looking somewhat hurt, she returned to the bar. Shortly after she went in, Tank, Kilroy and Pot Roast came out. Harold suspected that Sue had suggested they come outside.

In the meantime, Tank had reached up to put his arm around T-Rex and was leading him off about 25 feet away from the others. They spoke there for about three minutes before Harold could see that they were both laughing. He and the group by the door breathed a sigh of relief, having considered the implications of trying to rein in an out-of-control T-Rex.

Kilroy and Pot Roast were about to go back inside when the sound of un-muffled motorcycles was heard coming down the hill towards the bar. Pulling into the lot was Reaper on a stretched out black Harley, with major ape-hanger handlebars and white skulls looking forward painted on the outside of each tank. The skulls had hair that, as it flowed backward as though in the wind, changed to orange, red and yellow flames. Sitting behind Reaper was his old lady whom Harold had heard referred to as Peyote. She was probably taller than Reaper, very thin and had extremely sharp facial features, her jet-black hair tied back in a ponytail.

Riding next to Reaper and Peyote was another biker on another stretched chopper. Harold hadn't seen him before and assumed it was another brother he had yet to meet. Like Reaper, this biker had a powerful and intimidating appearance. He had a long, full beard with touches of grey that matched other touches of grey in a long head of hair that flowed behind him in a tangled mess, Harold assumed, as a result of the ride to the bar. The biker had a large scar that started at his jaw just in front of his right ear, ran across his cheek and across his nose. With a pair of wrap-around black sunglasses, Harold could barely make out a set of dark eyes through the lenses.

Behind the new biker was a familiar female face. At first, Harold didn't realize who it was. As she stepped off the bike, Harold felt a surge of jealousy realizing that Tawny had arrived on this other guy's bike. Then he saw a large, raspberry bruise below her right eye. The area around the eye had a yellow and blue appearance and Harold imagined it was probably preparing to turn black and blue. Harold also noticed that the girl's jaw was set in a way that suggested surging anger.

When the Harleys came to a stop, she stepped quickly off the bike and Harold stepped towards her. But Tawny's mind was set on leaving and leaving now. She looked away and sidestepped his approach. Without a word, she proceeded to an older white Camaro parked by the front door of the bar, unlocked the car door, slipped inside and was tearing out of the parking lot a moment later.

Though Peyote hadn't met Harold before, she seemed to understand that he was involved with the girl and walked over to offer some kind of explanation. "Tank dropped her off at our house last night after Dancer beat the crap out of her," Peyote said. "She's kind of pissed off now but she'll probably calm down later."

Harold didn't know what else to say so he simply nodded. Then, he looked down the road after the disappearing Camaro with disappointment etched on his face. He had been too busy to think about it but, once Tawny showed up, he had begun to contemplate how nice it would be to have her with, on the back of his bike, for the ride.

Peyote added, "We were talking this morning and I kinda told her she brought it on herself. She didn't like that too much."

"I guess not," Harold said.

With that, Peyote nodded and went inside.

As Reaper and the other biker approached the brothers outside the bar, Harold noticed that the biker with Reaper had a "President" patch above his left, vest pocket, just like Reaper's, and just above a patch that read "Poacher." Harold knew enough to realize the Banshee Riders couldn't have two presidents. When the biker walked a little further, Harold saw a familiar patch on the biker's back. It was a rat on a Harley riding right at the viewer. The Rat was wearing an old, spiked German helmet, was holding the right handgrip on a set of ape-hangers and was flipping its middle finger straight ahead. The last time Harold had seen these colors they were worn by Chainsaw, the biker who had messed with Skunk at the party.

The thought of meeting a president from another club made Harold a little uncomfortable, especially considering the episode with Chainsaw and Skunk. However, it didn't seem to bother his brothers at all. Instead, they all seemed genuinely happy to see the biker. Poacher shook hands all around. It gave Harold the impression he was some kind of celebrity. Though some of the brothers razzed him a little, Harold noticed that they seemed a little more restrained, even reverent.

Harold began to follow when Samurai caught him by the arm and held him up until the others had gone inside. "It appears Tawny was doing some talking last night," Samurai said. "I don't think she exactly said what we were doing, but she said enough that Sue's getting a little curious. Just be on your toes if Sue starts asking you questions, got that? I mean, she won't expect you to roll over on me, but she still might do a little digging."

Harold nodded then asked, "What will Sue do if she finds out?"

"I'm sure she'll figure it out," Samurai said. After a pause he added, "It'll blow over ... eventually."

Harold could tell by the answer that Samurai apparently had some prior experience in this regard.

As they reached the door and Harold reached for the door-knob, the door flew open from the other side and the brothers and old ladies began filing out past them. As Sue came out, she pulled Samurai aside and said something Harold couldn't hear. Though Sue had spoken quietly, Samurai responded in full voice, "Whatever you want to do." He then turned and walked over to his bike as Sue proceeded over to a van parked by the street.

As Samurai went past Harold, he said, "She's pissed. She's gonna ride in the backup truck."

"Well, that sucks," Harold said.

"Are you kidding?" Samurai replied. "You think I want the ice woman clinging to my back all the way to the campground?"

Harold frowned as it was the first time he'd seen Sue and his sponsor at odds. But there wasn't anything he could do about it now, or even later, so Harold walked over to his bike with the rest of the club. At that moment, Peyote was about to hop in the driver's seat of the backup truck when Sue walked over and said, "I'll drive."

Harold was already told he'd ride in the back of the pack. All the same, Trailer Trash came over and told Harold, "You'll be riding in back with me."

In ones, twos, and threes, the bikes roared to life. Before long, the ground was shaking from the combined power of close to 2,500 horses. Harold glanced down from where he was sitting on his idling bike and saw pebbles bouncing on the ground. One bike, Red's Sportster, wasn't quite as cooperative. He was working up a substantial sweat trying to kick-start the scooter. After about a dozen kicks, some of the brothers began turning their bikes off. Leaving his bagger idling, Trailer Trash flipped out the kickstand and leaned the bike against it. He then walked over to Red and said, "Step aside."

Samurai had also left his bike idling. He walked over by Harold as Trailer Trash prepared to kick the bike himself. "If it doesn't start in a couple kicks, Trailer Trash will have it loaded into the backup vehicle. Be ready to help."

But there was no need. On his second kick, Trailer Trash brought the Harley to life. He smiled at Red, slapped him on the back and said, "you must be using the wrong leg."

A little embarrassed, Red climbed on and, as Samurai and Trailer Trash returned to their rides, the brothers who had shut down to wait restarted.

In front of the pack, Reaper, with Poacher to his right, was looking back waiting to see when everyone was ready. Trailer Trash leaned his bike back up off the kickstand, stomped it into gear and looked up through the pack. After a quick check to see that everyone was ready, he gave Reaper thumbs up and the president led the pack, like links of a chain, onto the road. Just in front of the backup vehicle, Harold and Trailer Trash were the last bikes to move. The front of the pack was disappearing over the top of the hill to his right as Harold was just pulling out of the parking lot. He glanced to his right at Trailer Trash who smiled back. The smile Harold returned was more of a grin, a big, "I'm really here," expression of joy that broke out uncontrollably across his face. As they headed over the hill, the backup truck pulled in behind them.

Chapter 16 — The Leg

As the pack proceeded onto the main road, the joy in Harold's heart seemed to swell to the brink of bursting. As he looked ahead through the pack, the one thing that surprised him was how close together the brothers actually rode. Samurai had warned him but hearing about it and seeing it were two different things. Doing about 60 mph on the county highway leading into Biesenthal, the bikes were spaced a few feet apart from the rear fender of the bike in front to the front tire of the bike behind it.

As they rolled through town, strictly obeying the 30-mph speed zone, lest they give the law any opportunity, Harold noticed that all the heads turned to look from sidewalks, through shop windows and in cars as the club rumbled by. Some people even came out of the stores to stand on the sidewalk and stare as though an iron, leather and chrome parade was rumbling by, which is exactly how the experience made Harold feel – as though he was in a parade. Some of the older folks had looks of contempt, but the fantasy-laden stares of young girls and the envious eyes of boys more than made up for the less favorable attention. Even the contempt held a certain reward. It was, after all, attention. And though Harold was familiar with contemptuous looks from his drunken days stumbling out of Freddie's Place into the bright sunlight of an afternoon after drinking all night, this contempt was different. As a drunken sod, the contempt was far more open and direct; it was justified. Harold could remember flashes of people laughing in his face, openly ridiculing him as he stumbled and fell. As he rode through Biesenthal, Harold realized that none of the people lining the sidewalk would dare to laugh at him or the club in public. "Some," he told himself, "wouldn't even dare laugh in the privacy of their own homes."

Harold felt a sense of power that seemed to magnify the joy of the experience as he soaked up the respect from the faces of the citizens on the sidewalks and in passing cars. Whether it was respect born of a longing to hop on a bike and ride with the pack, or respect born of intimidation, Harold welcomed the sensation either way. He felt the power of the V-twin engine between his legs. Unconsciously, he sat up straighter. As the club passed a Biesenthal squad car watching from a side street, Harold even imagined a hint of fear in the face of the officer. Maybe it wasn't there. Harold wasn't sure, but he loved it all the same.

Hardly out of town, Reaper led the pack onto the interstate. A few miles onto the road, as he drank in the sound of nearly 30 Harleys pounding the pavement, Harold glanced at his speedometer and saw that the pack was doing better than 80 mph. Inexplicably, the pack pulled even tighter together. Some of the bikes were little more than two or three feet apart.

Harold noticed that Trailer Trash was constantly surveying the pack, looking for anything loose hanging off from a bike or somebody riding erratically as a result of too much beer at Hildie's. Harold started doing the same thing, but Trailer Trash yelled over the sound of the motors, "That's OK bro. You just worry about yourself for now."

There was no animosity in the statement. Harold nodded and left the road captain duties to the full-patch brother.

The club was about 25 minutes from Hildie's when a brother riding a Sportster looked back over his shoulder and waved to Trailer Trash. When he had the road captain's attention, the biker pointed at his gas tank indicating that he needed to fill up. Trailer Trash shook his head and Harold vaguely heard him grumble, "What the fuck is he telling me for?" Harold realized that, though Trailer Trash was road captain, he could hardly pull the pack over from the back.

After thinking about it for a minute or two, and seeing the brother look back over his shoulder again, Trailer Trash suddenly fell back behind Harold pulled around him onto the white line between the right lane, where the club was riding, and the left lane. Then he hit the gas and began passing to the front of the pack. Reaper must have seen Trailer Trash coming in the rearview mirror. The president slowed the pack to about 60 mph and glanced over at his road captain as the biker on his bagger pulled alongside.

"What?" Reaper yelled over the noise.

Trailer Trash merely pointed at his gas tank. Reaper looked puzzled. Most of the brothers had enough sense to fill up before they left. Certainly, Trailer Trash would know that. Trailer Trash seemed to understand the president was thinking. Trailer Trash shook his head side to side and yelled, "Sportster."

Harold saw Reaper shoot an angry glance back over his shoulder, as though the president was trying to figure out who was to blame for the interruption.

The bike behind Reaper slipped back to make room so Trailer Trash could slide in behind the president, causing a chain reaction of bikes slipping back on the left side. The pack continued a several miles before the president spotted a Shell sign high on a post near an exit ramp. The pack followed Reaper and Poacher off the interstate and around a long curve to a stop sign and then to the right and into the filling station. As soon as the pack pulled in, Trailer Trash got off his bike and walked through the pack barking at everyone to fill up. When Grunt said he had enough gas, Trailer Trash yelled, "Bullshit. I said fill up. That means everyone." Looking around, he added, using the derogatory slang for the smaller bikes, "Especially all of you Shortster riders." Then, for final measure, Trailer Trash hollered for general consumption, "And next time, make sure you assholes fill up before we head out."

Though he had a larger, split-tank setup, Harold was so excited about the trip, and so preoccupied the night before, that he had also neglected to fill up. It wasn't until Trailer Trash chastised the club that Harold realized he was probably almost bone dry. Trailer Trash was standing by the pumps as each bike filled up and Harold was certain the road captain would notice when Harold put close to three gallons in his tank. After each bike filled up, its owner rolled the bike off to the side away from the pumps and those waiting in turn rolled their bikes forward. Harold had decided Trailer Trash seemed like a good guy and he wasn't happy that he would see that Harold was as guilty as the brother who had initiated the stop. Just as Harold rolled his bike up to take his turn, however, Trailer Trash walked back to his bike and rolled it over on the other side of the pumps. As a result, Trailer Trash was on the other side of the pumps filling his tanks as Harold filled the tanks on Magdelina.

When all the bikes were filled up, Trailer Trash went into the station and paid the bill. On the way out, before getting back on his bike, he handed the receipt to the treasurer, who was positioned on the right a few bikes back from the president.

As the front of the pack approached the road, Harold saw Mongrel pull out from behind Reaper and into the road blocking traffic from the right. Wide Glide pulled out from behind Poacher and into the far lane to block traffic from the left. The hefty, bearded biker put his feet down, crossed his arms and glared menacingly at the cars that were approaching from the north. The way he looked at the cars it was as if he would melt them down into molten globs with his eyes if they drew too close. As the pack passed and the backup vehicle entered the road, Mongrel grabbed his handlebars, kicked his bike into first and rolled into the pack in front of Harold. Wide Glide did the same thing in front of Trailer Trash. When the pack was back on the highway, the road guards pulled out of the pack into the left lane, gunned their bikes and raced up front to pull in behind the presidents again.

Several bikes back from Mongrel, a lanky brother of about 6-2, was holding tight behind the bike in front of him. Derelict had hair and beard so scraggly, cloths so dirty and tattered, that he was exceptional that way even in comparison to the rest of the club. Harold had seen Derelict several times but had yet to really meet him. Harold did know that Derelict was a Vietnam vet and Samurai had suggested that the war had taken a toll on the man. "He's certifiable," Samurai said. "Once in a while, he goes out to the VA hospital and turns himself into the psych ward, just to get his shit back together." But there was one price Derelict had paid in the service that Samurai had neglected to mention.

To Harold, Derelict was a quiet, introspective sort. He didn't say much and never asked a prospect or probate for anything that Harold had seen, certainly none of the nonsense that some brothers required just to mess with a prospect or probate. The man was grubby and heavily tattooed. His arms were thin but sinewy and, considering his general demeanor, Harold suspected Derelict was not someone to cross in a dark alley. He didn't smile much. In fact, Harold couldn't remember seeing Derelict smile at all, until he saw the brother looking around as the pack blasted down the interstate.

Derelict was periodically looking left and right, casting a smile to his brothers around him. Harold appreciated seeing the pleasure clearly written across the previously stone-like face.

What Samurai hadn't told Harold about Derelict yet was that he had come home from the war a little early thanks to a landmine dug into the ground somewhere in Southeast Asia. Along with some shrapnel, he brought home addictions to pot and heroin, as well as to several prescription drugs. The latter addictions were developed from painkillers he took during and after spending several months in an Army hospital. The one thing Derelict didn't bring home was his left leg from just above the knee. By the time he was discharged from the Valley Forge Army General Hospital, near Philadelphia, he was learning to walk again on his first prosthetic limb. It wasn't a limb as nice as a civilian might receive but it was the best the U.S. Army could afford to requisition in quantity at the time.

Unable to find much work, or to keep a job for long when he did, Derelict lived at his sister's house and got by on money he received from the government, which wasn't much, and which he called "my leg money."

His bike, a 1966 Sportster, originally belonged to Derelict's brother. Derelict took possession of the bike after his brother died drunk in a car wreck. Derelict didn't have the money to do much more than maintain the bike. The only changes he made were to add a softer seat and have someone paint a R.I.P. Carl tombstone on the top of the gas tank in honor of his brother. In the 13 years since that explosion tossed Derelict in the air like a rag doll, and left his left leg in shreds, doctors had given the veteran new prosthetic legs. The latest was the best yet, though it still chafed a little at the bottom of the stub where a doctor in the jungles of Vietnam had chopped off the remnants of the leg God had given him. His new prosthetic leg was more-or-less held on by suction. It was shaped like a leg, had a reasonable rubber skin tone, and was sturdier and more flexible than the others. Derelict was only on the new leg a couple weeks before Road Day and was extremely pleased that it was ready in time.

That morning, he put his new prosthetic leg on and then his jeans. With his pants and boots on, unless the casual observer guessed by way of Derelict's slight limp, no one would know that he was missing a limb. Harold was among those who didn't know.

Derelict was in a hurry that morning, excited about the day ahead. The leg was new, and he wasn't quite familiar with it. As the pack formed, he pulled up to the left of Snake.

Whatever the reason – the rush to get ready or lack of familiarity – about 20 miles after the club left the filling station, the suction failed, and the leg began to slip down his pantleg. Derelict didn't notice. He just continued to ride, occasionally glancing, with a grin, at the brother beside him. In the back of the pack, Wide Glide was feeling confident that, if anything was loose on one of his brothers' bikes, he would have noticed by now. Still, every few minutes, he glanced up through the pack and slipped behind the prospect for a look along the left side of the pack.

Richard and Clarise Wooten motored down the highway, on their way to a picnic at a relative's farm, as they enjoyed the sunny day from the inside their air-conditioned Ford station wagon. Two-year-old Teddy was sleeping in his carseat behind his father. From the older carseat to his right, his 3-year-old sister, Elizabeth, was resting her head against the red upholstery on the inside of the door, her eyes seeing but not really watching the road roll by outside the window. Her parents assumed she was sleeping, too. Richard had passed a truck a while back and was still in the left passing several slower cars on the right.

Clarise was cherishing the occasion. She had snuggled into her seat for the drive the way a bird feathers and shapes its nest to fit. It was her way of saying, 'This is mine – my husband, my family and my day to relax and enjoy the rewards of it all.' Richard worked too long and too hard. Occasions such as this were too rare. While she looked forward to the picnic at her cousin's farm, the time alone – just the family alone in the car – this was the reward she cherished. The picnic was an interlude and interruption.

When she looked at her husband, it was with the satisfaction of someone who believes all is right in the world. Richard caught her glance and saw the joy in her smile and reflected it back to her. Words could not have shared their feelings with any greater clarity. A plant manager, he struggled with the guilt of working long hours though he understood the financial necessities. If he had communicated with Clarise just a little more, she would have found that he would have happily skipped the picnic, too, and simply spent the day, the four of them, driving in the country. But that message was never transmitted. Both, seeking to make the other happy, agreed to accept the invitation, not that they wouldn't have a good time. But when they reached Clarise's cousin's house, they would separate, as was the custom. The children would wake and would require supervision as they tested their early social skills with others their age. Clarise and the other women would gather where they could keep an eye on the kids while helping to put the finishing touches on the backyard event – creating individual place settings, bringing food to the serving table and having an occasional sip of beer or wine. Richard would gather with the men as they talked sports, shared not-too-crude jokes and drank a beer or two. Gathered around the grill, they would watch the char spread across the hotdogs and hamburgers with Clarise's cousin's husband administering an occasional flip to the sacrifices on the blackened grates. Then, when the grilling was done, they would load the offerings on a plate and all would meet at the red-and-white-check-covered tables, lined up three long across the grass, to eat while enjoying more PG-rated topics. Pleasant conversation would carry the afternoon into the evening as, having cleared the tables, the women would rejoin the men to revel in the comfort of a Spring day casually transforming into night. Richard and Clarise would enjoy the serenity of the evening while catching up with family and friends. But they would eagerly await that time when the party wound down and they could leave: when they would return to the car, just the family, and the drive home through the twilight as the children, exhausted by running and playing for hours, would sleep even more soundly until Mom and Dad carried them into the house at the end of the trip. Clarise knew this with all the clarity of a screenwriter setting the scene.

When she looked at Richard, she did so, not just with appreciation for the time together, but with wonder at her good fortune, all the sweeter since she could see a reciprocal thought in his eyes. But there was a difference. Tall and handsome, Richard was dedicated to his family. He worked hard but the driving force wasn't his career as much as his sense of responsibility to his wife and children. The family was the fuel that fired his ambition. It's not that he didn't enjoy his job; he did. But money wasn't the top priority. He saw money's value in what it meant for his family.

For Richard, Clarise had a girl-next-door beauty that fit her grounded approach to life. Theirs was more than a marriage, not that they never disagreed. It was a partnership with its foundation set in love. He cared about her and she cared about him. She wasn't one of those wives who was always demanding more. She wasn't caught up in appearances – what the neighbors or some social set thought. What's more, 13 years earlier, when he made a foxhole prayer in a jungle in Vietnam, all he asked God for was survival. Clarise was a gift he felt he never deserved, that was far beyond what he had asked for. It wasn't in his nature to take her for granted.

Even the rumble of motorcycles failed to rouse Elizabeth from her happy daze in the backseat. She hardly noticed as the back of the pack of motorcycles began to appear on the pavement beside the station wagon. The bikes drifted by as her father slowly passed the club. Her mind elsewhere, Elizabeth's eyes seemed to settle sightlessly at the point where the tires of the bikes met the asphalt. Without a frame of reference to judge the biker lifestyle, for Elizabeth, this was simply something colorful passing her secure world beyond the safety of the car window. Then, Elizabeth lifted her head off the faux-leather Naugahyde of the door as her mind sought to make sense of something even more peculiar than a pack of bikers would appear to a 3-year-old girl. As she realized what she saw, she did what comes naturally to a young girl in such circumstances; she screamed, "Daddy! Daddy! Daddy!"

The scream was so sudden, so unexpected, that Richard involuntarily cut the wheel to the right while craning to look into the backseat to see what was wrong. Fortunately, he corrected the maneuver before the car piled into the motorcycles beside them, but not before several of the bikers beside him noticed the car moving their way and cast threatening glances his way while squeezing to their right.

"WHAT'S WRONG?!" Richard hollered.

Clarise spun around in her seat to look back at her daughter then followed her Elizabeth's shocked stare out the window. "Oh my God! Richard ..."

"WHAT?! WHAT IS IT?!"

"HIS LEG!" Clarise cried out while pointing at the pavement beside the car but below Richard's line of sight.

Richard's head whipped back and forth, as though on a rising threaded spindle, trying to keep track of the road ahead while rising in his seat to look down and to his right. Unsure of the problem, he pressed the brake lightly and his speed fell off so the trend of the bikes reversed and began passing the car. As a biker second-from-the-back pulled ahead of the station wagon, Richard finally saw what had alarmed his daughter. As incredible as it seemed, the biker's leg, having slipped down into the pants until the wide top of the leg was caught in the narrow bottom of his pants, was bounding wildly into the air. Each time it fell, it would hit the pavement at a different angle and bound back up again, the booted foot pointing in random directions.

The bikers were now staring at the Wootens with consternation as they tried to figure out what these citizens were up to. Only the biker just behind the one with the bounding leg seemed to have caught on. He was trying to get the rider's attention but to no avail as all the other bikers had their attention on the car full of citizens beside them. Having their attention, Richard raised his hand and, pointing with one finger, gestured repeatedly down at the bouncing leg.

Derelict frowned as he wondered what was wrong with this crazy citizen. Through his growing annoyance, however, he couldn't help noticing that the citizen was pointing at the ground next to his bike. But when he glanced down, since the leg was stretching his pants out behind him, all he saw was pavement. He looked back at the driver as his annoyance began to turn to threatening anger. But the citizen shook his head side to side emphatically while continuing to frantically point down beside the bike, now seeming to point back a little, too. When Derelict looked down again, even before he looked back, he noticed the absence of his leg resting beside the gas tank where he should find it. He looked back up and, for the first time, saw the shocked look on the woman's face in the passenger seat, and the child screaming in the seat behind her. Clarity came like a thunderbolt. The citizen realized that the biker understood and began slowly drifting back again, apparently using his station wagon to block other drivers who might try to pass at this critical moment.

Now, as, one-by-one, the brothers around him caught on to what was happening, the problem for Derelict was stopping. With his leg bouncing on the highway behind him, there was no way to downshift. There was also no way to pull out the kickstand or lean the bike to the left when he stopped. Derelict looked around him to make sure his brothers were aware of his predicament and would act appropriately. He saw understanding in their eyes and began applying the brakes, front and rear. The pack, from the presidents up front, to the back-up vehicle behind, slowed in unison as though Derelict was operating all the brake pedals from the seat of his Sportster. At the same time, the pack began pulling onto the shoulder with the riders on the right leading the way and leaving room for those on the left. Seeing that they were working together, Derelict braked faster and was soon coasting to a stop as his tires crossed onto the shoulder. At the same time, he tried to lean to the right so he could catch the bike with his right foot – his real foot. The station wagon had fallen behind the pack and was now blocking the right lane next to where the back-up truck was on the shoulder. Cars and trucks were blasting by to the left, some honking in blind anger at the delay.

In spite of Derelict's efforts, when the bike came to a complete stop, it did so with a jolt that threw him over to the left. Unable to stop the momentum, he and the bike were soon sprawled on the pavement about 15 feet in front of the Wootens.

Richard caught a break in the traffic and jumped out before any of the bikers were able to reach their brother. He had the biker's left arm over his shoulder and was trying to lift him up. But the biker was still holding onto the bike and they were un-able to lift both. Richard saw gasoline leaking around the gas cap and felt a sense of urgency as he tried again. For a moment, the best he could do was hold equilibrium with the bike about six inches off the ground. Suddenly, as he felt other hands grabbing hold around him, the one-legged biker and the bike, the lifting came easily. One of biker's brothers pulled out the kickstand and rested the bike against it. Others relieved Richard of the weight of the one-legged biker and Richard stepped back while glancing back at Clarise. He could see her concerned expression, as well as a now-curious Elizabeth peering over the backseat. He smiled and nodded to Clarise to let her know that everything was OK. Then, he leaned down and picked up the leg that was still resting, extending out from the bottom of the pants, on the blacktop. As an enormous biker lifted the one-legged biker over his bike, and deposited him on his right leg on the road, the one-legged biker reached out to take the leg and began struggling to pull it back up the pantleg. By this time, however, the leg was firmly stuck in the bottom of the pants. With considerable effort, and some help from Richard and others, he finally managed to pull it up enough that it was relatively loose. But all efforts to slide it back up to the stump of his leg failed as the pants bunched up getting in the way.

Richard noticed that most of the bikers were laughing at their brother's predicament, which elicited angry glances from their one-legged brother. Two exceptionally scary looking bikers from up front were standing nearby watching with smirks on their faces, as though they saw the humor but were just a little-too dignified to join in the laughter. About the time Richard noticed that they both had 'President' patches on their vests, the one seemed to lose patience and barked, "Just take the fucking pants off already."

"I ain't wearin' no undies," the one-legged biker responded angrily.

"As if anyone cares," one of the other bikers said.

With that, the one-legged biker yelled, "Fine. Fuck you all," and, with a flurry, undid the buckle of his belt. His pants immediately fell to his knee.

For a second, Richard stood looking without really seeing or understanding. It was as if the biker had suddenly grown a stunted leg. Then, as it dawned on him, he looked quickly back at his car in time to see a shocked Clarise turning to cover Elizabeth's eyes. Richard stepped over so that he was between the biker and the car, blocking the view. He was surprised when he realized that the enormous biker, who had lifted the one-legged biker over the bike, had also stepped over to block the view from the station wagon.

"Thank you," Richard said softly.

"No, thank you, bro," said the biker with a tone so deep that, even considering his immense size, Richard was surprised. He was even more surprised when the biker threw a bear-like arm around Richard's shoulder and slapped him on the back.

As the one-legged biker finally pulled his leg into place, and his pants on behind it, he stepped toward Richard extending a hand, thumb up, for a biker handshake. His grip was firm suggesting strength that resulted from compensating for a missing limb. When he stepped away, the 'President' who had barked for the one-legged biker to drop his pants, stepped up and shook Richard's hand, too, as he said, "You're a righteous mother fucker, bro." He then glanced at the station wagon, smiled and nodded a thanks to the woman in the front seat.

"It's OK," said Richard feeling a little overwhelmed by the kind of comradery he used to know in the Army.

The 'President' seemed to sense his emotion and smiled as though to repeat the prior assessment with even greater enthusiasm. Then, the 'President' said, "Gotta go."

Cars were backing up behind Richard's car, occasionally honking horns while waiting for a chance to move into the flow of traffic in the left lane. Richard glanced back that way and then said to the 'President,' "I'll wait until you're all out on the road again."

The 'President' looked back behind the station wagon, smiled at Richard, and said, "Thanks," before turning to go back to his bike.

As Richard climbed into the driver's seat next to Clarise, he noticed that she was looking at him again. But this was different. She was looking at him as though seeing some part of him for the first time. Then she asked, "Is he OK?"

"Yeah. No problem," said Richard as he glanced into the rearview mirror at someone behind who was laying on the horn for him to go.

Clarise saw Richard looking back and glanced back out the rear window, too. She smiled as she looked at the impatient driver. Then she looked back at Richard for a moment before saying, "Oh my God!" while chuckling about the experience while admiring Richard's willingness to get out and help a pack of bikers that most of the people they knew would find too scary to talk to.

Chapter 17 — Ever Seen a Potroast Puke

About 30 miles after Derelict got his leg back on, the pack rolled through a long, downward curve to the left that led into a small-town main street, stick-built bungalows peeking out from behind the business district. The town of Creighton, nestled into the rolling hills of Lucas County, was a farm town. It held the usual small businesses — a locksmith, a hardware store, a couple clothing stores, a small grocer, Ben Franklin, a diner, an ice-cream shop that had opened from winter hibernation about a month prior to the Banshees' arrival, and, of course, a couple of gin mills. Other than a few newer cars, Creighton looked as though frozen it in time from a few decades earlier. Coming out of the curve and the hills to the South, the old-fashioned main street ran north about four blocks before it turned to the left, continued several blocks and then took a sharp S-curve before running back into the hills to the west. Parking spaces on Main Street were designated by diagonal white stripes angled out from the sidewalk. Just before the 90-degree turn to the left, was a small tavern on the inside of the bend. Harold wasn't sure if the club was naturally drawn to this establishment, as though by a magnet, or if it was a planned stop, possibly a place they had stopped on previous trips to the town.

As the club pulled up in front of the bar, the bikers came to a stop in the road while Reaper appeared to orient himself with the available parking options. The bikes sat idling, balanced from both sides by leather engineer or cowboy boots on the pavement as the locals, alerted by the approaching throaty rumble, began to gather on the sidewalks to gape. Most of the citizens pulled together into small groups where they spoke about the spectacle in hushed tones while keeping their distance. At the same time, the straddling bikers looked back at the citizens with looks of indifference. It was as if spectators were watching animals in a zoo though it wasn't clear which was which.

Finally, after high-level discussion at the front of the pack, Reaper turned his bike to the left and back peddled into a parking stall. Poacher and several other bikes followed suit. Since there wasn't one continuous row of parking spaces, the rest of the brothers were left to their own devices. They scanned the street for open parking spots, and, in fours, fives and sixes, the pack melted off the street amid the parked cars and pickups. Peyote, who was driving by that time, found a place to park early on. She and Sue headed into the tavern without waiting for the others.

As the brothers shut off their bikes, the little hamlet of Creighton was suddenly wrapped in deafening silence. When the last bike was shut off, it was as if someone threw a switch and, with a last glance at the bikers, the people of Creighton went back to whatever they were doing before the unexpected interruption.

The brothers were emptying into the tavern as a black squad car, with a single red light on the roof, and gold stars emblazoned on white front doors, rolled slowly around the bend from the west. The officer peered inquisitively at the brothers, not just watching but intent on letting them know he was watching. Then he continued past and backed into a parking stall several stores to the south. There, with the motor still running, he monitored the club's activity, prepared for any trouble that his presence was likely to prevent.

Tank commented to Reaper, "I think we're making the local constable nervous."

Reaper laughed, "Fuck him." The president smiled and waved to the policeman as he muttered, "Afternoon, officer Fife."

Then Reaper turned to Harold, "Go tell Mongrel and Capsize to get their asses out here."

Mongrel was probably the first, following Peyote and Sue, to order a drink. He was standing by the door and heard what Reaper said. As Harold walked up, Mongrel merely nodded and walked outside. Capsize, on the other hand, was over at the bar waiting for a drink he'd ordered and laughing with a pair of the club's old ladies Harold hadn't met yet.

Standing off to the side of Capsize, Harold waited a second for a chance to deliver the message. He tried once but Capsize, who seemed to notice the effort, simply continued the conversation only louder while turning his back on the prospect. The second time Harold tried to gain Capsize's attention, after shifting to the right and out from behind him, the brother turned on Harold and exploded. "Have you got a problem, prospect?"

"He probably believes all that crap his little whore's been feeding him," the one girl with Capsize said in a voice that sounded familiar. "Isn't that right? Your little slut tells you your something special and you actually believed her, didn't you?"

Rather than respond to the verbal assaults, Harold focused on accomplishing his assignment. But as he opened his mouth to talk, Capsize spoke up again, enunciating the last word, "You're a PROSPECT. As far as I'm concerned, that's all you'll ever be."

Harold looked at the brother passively and waited until he was finished. Then, as calmly as can be, Harold said, "Reaper wants to see you outside."

"You go tell him I'll be out there in a minute," Capsize said.

Harold was pretty sure, considering how Reaper had given the order, that the president wanted to see the brother outside immediately. But Harold reasoned it was only his job to deliver the message. He turned to go outside just as Mongrel came back in.

Mongrel walked past Harold and up to Capsize. "We've got to go check on the campground," Mongrel said.

"I'm waiting for a beer here," Capsize said, a trace of his annoyance with Harold still in his voice.

Mongrel, who hadn't caught the way Capsize had reamed the prospect, took Capsize's retort personally. "You know what," Mongrel barked back, "the president said to ride ahead to the campground. He said to do it now. You don't want to go, take it up with Reaper."

Mongrel was just turning to go when Reaper came in the door behind them. Reaper had apparently worked himself up again over the way the two brothers had failed to take care of setting up the event until the last minute. In a way, Reaper's current attitude was like that of a parent trying to teach an errant child a lesson. Seeing Capsize standing at the bar, a leg up on the foot rail and leaning back casually with no indication that he was preparing to leave, Reaper took a turn raising his own voice.

"Did I fucking stutter?" he barked at Mongrel. "Or do you assholes want the prospect and probate to handle things for you. You just give 'em your patches and they can run out there for you, OK?"

Mongrel said, "On my way, bro."

For a second, Harold thought Capsize was going to protest or argue. Just as Reaper opened his mouth as though to yell something else, Capsize started towards the door, kicking a chair out of his way, like a spoiled child. As he passed Harold, Capsize said, "If you ever tell my old lady to go fuck herself again, I'll cut your balls off, prospect."

Harold knew he'd never said anything like that but figured she had either lied about it or Capsize was just getting in the last word.

"Shut up and get going," Reaper said, glaring at Capsize as he left.

Samurai had come inside with Reaper. He laughed a little as Capsize left, which drew an angry glance from the departing brother. Samurai was explaining to Harold that the president was fucking with Mongrel and Capsize because of the way they handled things with Road Day when Reaper, who hadn't quite worked off his foul mood, turned on Harold and growled, "Are you planning to stand there looking stupid?" At first, Harold wasn't sure what Reaper was getting at. Then Reaper held his hands out, empty palms up and added, "How long do I have to stand here empty-handed before you find the time to bring your president a beer?"

As Harold stepped up to the bar to order a beer for the president, Reaper continued, "Maybe you thought I was serious about giving you their colors?"

Harold took the abuse quietly and noticed that Red and Drago were suddenly very busy lighting cigarettes and checking to see if anyone else needed a drink or anything. Harold returned to the president with two beers. One he handed to Reaper, the other to Samurai.

Samurai took the beer and handed Harold a couple dollars to cover the costs of the drinks. Then Samurai said, "Make yourself useful. Go outside and keep an eye on the bikes."

The way Samurai said it, Harold thought he might have gained his sponsor's disfavor, as well. About five minutes after Harold went outside, however, Samurai came out with a beer for Harold and said, "Here. Just thought I'd get you out of the line of fire until Reaper cools down a little."

After they both took swigs off their beers, Samurai asked, "So, Naked Boy, how'd you like the ride out?"

Harold smiled and said, "Eventful. Derelict's leg fall off often?"

Samurai almost chocked on another sip of beer: "No, that was a first. Scared the shit out of those citizens, I'd say."

"Yeah," said Harold. After a pause, he added, "But that citizen was pretty cool, getting out to help like that."

Samurai snorted in agreement. Then, when he'd swallowed the beer in his mouth, he said, "You don't run into righteous citizens like that all the time. Most of 'em would shit their pants before they got out to help like that."

After another short, pregnant pause, as though the actions of the citizen were so unusual that they defied further discussion, or maybe because the statements reflected uncomfortably, Samurai turned to go back in. As he did, he added, "Kind of keep that beer down. I'm not sure how the local police will react if they see you drinking on the sidewalk."

Harold nodded and set the beer on the concrete window ledge behind where he was leaning.

Harold assumed they'd leave for the campground soon or, at least, they'd leave after Mongrel and Capsize came back. However, the two brothers returned and went inside, with Capsize ignoring Harold as they passed. Samurai came out with another beer a little later and then Red, probably wanting to escape the demands of the brothers inside, came out and joined Harold.

Harold watched the shadows of the buildings behind him grow out across the street as the sun dipped from the sky. Dusk began to shift to darkness and the soft glow of mercury vapor streetlights, accompanied by the buzzing of electrical transformers, flickered on up and down the street.

In the course of conversation, Red asked Harold about the confrontation with Capsize. "I don't know," Harold said. "His old lady went off on me last night."

"You might want to watch that bitch," Red said. "When I first started prospecting, she pulled some crap on me, too."

"What kind of crap," Harold asked.

"Oh, you know, the usual," Red said. "She tried to tell her old man that I was hitting on her. As if."

"Yeah," Harold laughed, "Capsize might be an asshole, but you have to have a little sympathy for him when you think about him screwing that pig."

Red shook himself as if the thought had caused an involuntary shiver to run up his spine, and the two broke out laughing. When their laughter died out, the two took swigs off their beers and otherwise stood in silence for a couple minutes. Finally, Red looked at his watch and said, "I wonder when we're going?"

"What does it matter?" Harold asked.

Red gave Harold a look that suggested he was missing the point. "Have you ever tried setting up tents in the dark? And guess who sets up the tents?"

"I'm guessing that would be us," Harold said.

"Bingo," Red said before taking another swig from his beer.

The bottle was still at Red's lips when the brothers and old ladies began spilling out of the bar. As Mongrel came out the door, he saw Harold and Red standing off to the side. "Mount up, boys, we're heading for the campground."

Red and Harold downed their beers and left the bottles standing on the windowsill. Again, the club pierced the silence of Creighton with the earth-shattering rumble of internal-combustion V-twins. There weren't as many pedestrians in the area as earlier, but several faces still peered from lighted upstairs window curtains as the pack formed up in the street. A couple citizens from inside the bar even came out to watch.

Harold found himself in about the middle of the pack and, since no one complained, he just stayed there. Red was at his side. Suddenly, Samurai came up from behind Harold in the opposite lane of traffic. Samurai stopped next to Harold and said, "When we get to the campground, Red, you help Drago look for firewood. Naked Boy, you help with the tents."

The ride out to the campsite only lasted about 15 minutes. As the pack pulled into the park, Harold noticed a sign across the street, "Firewood, $2 Bundle." When the bikes parked at the sites Capsize indicated, Harold considered asking Samurai if it wasn't a good idea to go back and buy some wood. But then, Harold figured, Samurai probably saw the sign, too. He hadn't told Red and Drago to "buy some wood."

Red and Drago parked their bikes and tramped through the woods looking for stuff to burn. The problem was that, though the two certainly found some wood, since almost every camper who visited the state park did the same thing, the pickings were slim. After 20 minutes, and as Harold was helping with the last two tents, Drago and Red had assembled a pathetically small pile of sticks and branches. They knew the club was looking for a real fire, a big fire, the kind of fire that would last all night. They had enough wood for a small fire that would be lucky to last an hour. Further complicating their situation, the sky was growing darker and, with it, the ability to find suitable material for burning was diminishing proportionately.

Since some of the brothers insisted on setting up their own tents, when Red dropped a few more branches into the pile he noticed that Harold's job was nearly complete. He came over and asked Trailer Trash, who was helping Harold setup up the prior's tent at that moment, "Do you mind if I steal NB to help look for firewood?"

"Yeah, we're almost done here anyhow." Then, looking at Harold as though he were cutting a child loose from doing chores, throwing the words at him in a high-pitched, nasal twang, "Be free, little prospect. Be free."

Red started back towards the woods fully expecting Harold to follow. However, Harold had seen the fruits of Red and Drago's labor. He had a better idea. Grabbing Red's arm, he said, "Who has the keys to the van?"

"I don't know," Red said with a puzzled expression. "Probably Peyote or Hot Stuff."

Harold looked around and saw Sue moving stuff into her and Samurai's tent. "Come on," Harold said to Red.

When he reached Sue and asked for the keys, she reached into her pocket, pulled the keys out and tossed them to Harold.

"Thanks," Harold said and headed to the van with Red at his side.

"What are you doing?" Red asked.

Harold looked at his friend and smiled without a word. The short ride back through the park to the entrance took less than two minutes. Harold waited for a single car to pass on the highway outside the entrance and then drove into the driveway that was directly across from the park entrance. Seeing the sign Harold had spotted earlier, Red began to chuckle.

Harold and Red went to the front door and knocked. A short time and $14 later, including the $4 Red contributed, they headed back into the park with a substantial load of wood in the back of the van.

Backing into the parking space at the campsite, they climbed out of the van in time to hear Capsize yelling again. As he and

Mongrel were charged with organizing the event, Capsize was extending his authority to the oversight of preparations for the fire. Drago, who was several inches taller than Capsize, was glowering down at the brother as Capsize yelled about the paltry effort to find firewood. "And where the fuck are those useless prospects?" they heard Capsize ask Drago.

Drago was just responding, "Like I told you, I don't know," when Red and Harold walked back from the front of the van. Seeing them, Capsize turned his full fury on Harold, in a way Harold suspected was intended to draw the attention of the brothers around them. "Where the fuck did you two assholes go? You were told to get firewood, weren't you?"

The prospect and probate stood quietly with drawn faces stripped of any emotion. Capsize continued, while pointing back to the pile of twigs. "You expect us to make a fire out of that?" A brother over by the picnic tables hollered, "We can always burn their bikes," which elicited scattered laughter from brothers and old ladies who were relaxing with their beers watching the show.

"Well, are you planning to just stand there?" Capsize continued. "Or should I roll your bikes up into the fire?"

With that, Harold looked over at Red, who nodded in return. Red unlatched the doors and pulled the right backdoor open as Harold pulled open the left. In the process, they revealed a truckload of firewood.

Looking back at Capsize, Harold asked, "Think this will be enough?"

Capsize was knocked temporarily speechless. But once he got over the surprise, he started in, "I don't remember anyone telling you to buy firewood."

From the picnic tables near the small pile of twigs, Wide Glide and Samurai were quietly watching Capsize's verbal assault. Simultaneously, the sponsors of the probate and prospect on the receiving end of Capsize's tirade, stood and walked over. As they reached their brother, Wide Glide put his arm out blocking Samurai's path.

"I've got this one," Wide Glide said. Then he walked over, looked in the back of the van and started laughing.

"There's nothing funny about that," Capsize complained.

But Wide Glide, a former US Navy chief, had dealt with this

kind of nonsense before. He turned on Capsize and said, "Bull-shit. The prospect and probate used their heads. They showed initiative."

Capsize huffed and puffed for a minute as though struggling to think of a response. When he couldn't he mumbled something half to himself and then told Red and Harold to unload the van, as though buying the wood was his idea to begin with. As Harold went by with his first armload, Capsize said, "And since no one told you to buy firewood, you can pay for it yourself, prospect."

Harold didn't like the way Capsize said "prospect" as though the brother had something undesirable on his tongue. But in terms of the firewood, Harold had already assumed he and Red would pay for the wood. He figured it was a small price to pay, especially considering how it had worked out with Capsize. But hearing Capsize's comment, Wide Glide asked, "Did you get a receipt?"

When Harold said, "Yes," Wide Glide told Harold to make sure he turned it into the treasurer.

Harold couldn't help stealing a glance at Capsize to see how he reacted to Wide Glide's recommendation. Harold wasn't disappointed as he saw that Capsize was fuming. He looked over at Red and they both looked away fast to hide their grins.

Then Wide Glide said, "Good job. You two assholes might make Banshee Riders someday after all." Laughing loudly, Wide Glide and Samurai walked back to the picnic table and sat down again as Capsize stormed off to his tent. As he retreated, Harold saw Dancer over by the tent glaring back in Harold's direction.

By the time Red, Drago and Harold had unloaded the firewood, the sun had long since settled beyond the trees to the west. The transition from dusk to the dancing light of a campfire went smoothly as Grunt, a self-proclaimed master in the art of starting fires, took charge of transforming a bundle of twigs into the foundation of a small fire. As he piled logs onto the nubile flames, sparkling ambers, as though a flock of fireflies, floated up and over the tree line.

Most of the brothers and old ladies began drifting over by the fire and congealing into groups. Red, Drago, and Harold were kept busy at first making sure everyone had a beer and that all other essential needs were met. Then, Drago went over to the tapper and poured three plastic cups of the amber lager. He walked back over by Red and Harold and passed out two of the cups. The trio made their way over by Samurai, Wide Glide, Kilroy, Pot Roast, Reaper and the president of the Swamp Rats.

The primary topic of discussion was still the incident with Derelict's leg. Derelict, who overheard the conversation from the other side of the fire, came over and joined in, describing the looks on the family's face in the car next to him as they watched his leg bouncing on the highway. He had obviously gotten over any anger with his brothers about the incident and had discovered the humor of the event. "Did you see the look on his wife's face, I'll bet she wet herself," Derelict said happily.

Harold couldn't remember Derelict ever being as talkative or relaxed before. It was as if having his leg fall off had untied a knot in his tongue. Or was it the innate joy experienced by brothers on Road Day. Where Derelict seemed a bit embarrassed by the attention earlier, he seemed to relish it by the campfire, even making jokes at his own expense.

While Harold was thinking about Derelict's reaction, Harold noticed that Reaper was looking Harold's way. He also noticed that the president had a peculiar smile on his face. Reaper nodded with his head towards the shadows away from the fire and headed in that direction. Catching the silent message, Harold followed. When they were about 10 yards away from the others, Reaper stopped and turned to look at Harold. Even in the dark, Harold could see a large, toothy grin on the president's face.

"Prospect," Reaper began, "I've got a little job for you. You might even call it a test."

"Name it," Harold said.

"You know Pot Roast, right?" the president continued. Harold nodded and glanced over at Pot Roast who was laughing at something over by the fire. Reaper continued, "Pot Roast has, what you might call, a peculiar tendency that we, uhm ... enjoy, from time to time."

With a puzzled expression, Harold asked, "What's that?"

"Well, it seems our rough and tumble brother was born with a little-girl's stomach. All you gotta do is say somethin' disgusting and ole' Pot Roast is liable to start barfing."

"You're kidding?" Harold said, looking back over his shoulder at Pot Roast again, as though he might recognize some symptom of the condition.

"No, I'm not kidding. Just shut up and listen," Reaper said in a slightly sharper tone.

"That was pretty creative the way you and the probate handled the wood today. Now, I want to see if you can show your creative side again."

"I'll try," Harold said.

"I don't want you to try. I want you to do it," Reaper said, the smile gone from his face. "Or I could call Red over and give him the opportunity."

He paused a moment to make sure Harold was on board. "I'll start bringing the conversation around. Then, I want you to figure out a way to push Pot Roast over the edge. You got that? You pass the test when he empties his guts."

As Harold nodded, Reaper smiled again and said, "We'll call this Operation Barf Bag. Your job, prospect, is to make a Pot Roast puke."

As a smile formed on Harold's face, he said, as though addressing a military officer, "Yes, sir." He was half tempted to salute the president.

Then Reaper headed back to the fire. Harold stood where he was and contemplated his strategy. It occurred to him that he might find some kind of a useful prop. In the meantime, he heard Reaper launch into a discussion about a dead raccoon he'd seen on the road that day. Reaper was describing the entrails that were hanging out of the animal's midsection when Harold got an idea.

Harold walked past the group noticing a puzzled look on Poacher's face. Obviously, the Swamp Rats president was unfamiliar with Pot Roast's condition and wasn't sure why Reaper was carrying on about a dead animal. Everyone else, however, immediately glanced in Pot Roast's direction. Peyote, Sue and a couple other old ladies who were standing nearby, also seemed to know what was happening. They shook their heads, smiled and backed away a little. But there was something sympathetic about the way they smiled, as though they didn't entirely share the president's sense of humor or enjoyed the game as much.

Pot Roast, who was smiling broadly a moment before, was all

too familiar with this party game. He started growling, "You fuck-ers," and turned as though to go somewhere else. But before Pot Roast could leave, Reaper said, "Pot Roast, where are you going?"

When Pot Roast stopped and looked back, Reaper said, in a voice that dripped of feigned sympathy, "Don't go bro. Stay here with us a while."

Pot Roast turned and came back by the others, as though the president had given an order, as he repeated his previous two-word commentary – "You fuckers."

Other brothers were joining in on the discussion, sharing dis-gusting tidbits about bodily fluids and other such queasy materi-al. Harold thought Pot Roast was looking a little pale already and Harold hurried on his way.

Harold had earlier noticed that Bitters and Dixie, Wide Glide's old lady, had some cold, fried chicken. He found Bitters on a picnic table set back about 15 feet from the others. Grunt was just tell-ing Bitters, and several others, "We're lucky to have a Road Day at all the way those assholes fucked everything up." As he saw Har-old approaching, he stopped speaking as though he didn't want Harold to hear him complaining. Since Harold had already caught the drift of the discussion, the effort came a bit too late. As far divulging the contents of the conversation, Harold wasn't likely to do so. He had come to think rather highly of Mongrel. Capsize, on the other hand, was a different story. But Harold really didn't care about that now. He had something else on his mind.

Harold turned to Bitters and asked, "Do you have any of that fried chicken left from earlier?"

"Sure," Bitters said. "It's in the cooler by our tent. Help your-self."

"One piece is fine," Harold said with a smile.

As he walked away, encouraged by Harold's apparent lack of in-terest, the others continued their conversation where they'd left off. Harold found the cooler and dug a chicken leg out of a large plastic bag that was about half full of fried chicken pieces. He closed the bag and returned it to the cooler. Then, as he walked back by Reaper and the others, Harold pealed the skin off the chicken and ate the meat. He tossed the bone into the fire and then, with his back to Pot Roast, he carefully, shoved the skin into his left nostril. When the skin was completely buried in his nose,

Harold returned to the others holding his head slightly to the left to hide his bulging nostril.

The disgusting aspects of the conversation seemed as though they had about petered out by the time Harold returned. Reaper, however, saw Harold coming and gave Harold an inquisitive look to see if Harold was ready. Harold nodded ever-so slightly, and Reaper started in again. "Did you see the outhouse down at the end of the trail?" he asked, gesturing off to the left with his head. "Looks like someone smeared shit all over the walls. There's even handprints in it."

As Reaper added that one of the old ladies must have missed the hole inside the outhouse, Pot Roast angrily pleaded that Reaper change the subject.

"Please, change the fucking subject," Pot Roast said just as Harold forced himself to sneeze loudly.

Reaper turned to Harold and asked, "You gonna live there prospect?" In the process, Reaper drew everyone's attention to Harold.

"Yeah, I think so," Harold said. As he answered, Harold let out another sneeze. This time, as he sneezed, he leaned his face way over into his hands. While covering his face, he grabbed a corner of the chicken skin and, as he stood back up, in plain view, he pulled the chicken skin out of his nose about half an inch. Then he stood there with the chicken skin hanging out of the nostril.

Reaper played along saying, "Ohhh, prospect. You've got a great, big booger hanging out of your nose. What the fuck?"

Then, the president reached out with one hand as though to examine the offending substance. He gave the chicken skin a tug, as he said, "Here, let me help you with that," and yanked it the rest of the way out of Harold's nose. Out of the corner of his eye, Harold could see that Pot Roast was already in trouble. His cheeks were puffed out, his lips closed tightly, and he was beginning to look around frantically for a place to expel the contents of his stomach.

Holding the skin between his right forefinger and middle finger, Reaper said, "Wow, that's quite a booger. Hey, Pot Roast, check this out." Then, he looked at Harold and said, "You want it?" as though it were the last appetizer on a party tray.

Pot Roast hollered at Harold, "Don't you fucking do it, prospect."

Harold took it from Reaper and extended it towards Pot Roast as though offering a present and said, "You mean this?"

Pot Roast turned as though to leave. Harold quickly assured him, "I'm sorry, man. I'll get rid of it right now." Pot Roast looked back just in time to see Harold tip his head back, dangle the skin over his open mouth and drop it in. As Harold chewed and swallowed the skin, Pot Roast whipped around the other way and began heaving onto the ground. The brothers around the circle broke into uncontrollable laughter. The old ladies merely smiled.

Between spitting to clear out the last remnants of puke from his mouth, Pot Roast hollered, "You fuckers," and "You fucking assholes," again and again.

Making Pot Roast vomit once wasn't too difficult. Making him vomit again, once he'd already vomited the first time, was a piece of cake. Reaper told Harold that, if the brothers played the game long enough, Pot Roast would reach the point of dry heaves. He was also aware of this and, the president asking him to stick around or not, he was no longer going to stand and take it.

As Pot Roast walked away cursing, Harold felt a twinge of regret. Harold even considered the possibility that he might have created an obstacle when the time came for the brothers to vote on making Harold a probate or, later, a full-patch member. Harold looked over at Samurai who was laughing along with the others. When Samurai saw Harold's concerned look, the sponsor seemed to understand what was going through Harold's mind. Samurai smiled reassuringly and walked over.

"Don't worry," Samurai said. "Pot Roast never stays mad for long. Besides, if he likes you he likes you. After that, you've got to fuckup real bad to make an enemy out of him. He's got a heart as big as they come."

Someone with the club had brought along a selection of David Allan Coe tapes and these were piped through the stereo mounted in the dashboard of the van. When one tape ended it was replaced by another. With songs like, "Pussy Eating Pamela," the tapes were hardly appropriate listening for a family outing. At a biker campout, however, they fit just fine.

The fun with Pot Roast subsided and the party settled into a quieter phase, though occasional outbursts of laughter still pierced the night. Some of the brothers and old ladies drifted off to their tents until the majority of those still standing were those brothers who didn't have an old lady wearing their property patch. Harold took the unnecessary step of apologizing to Pot Roast and found himself sharing a bottle of wine with the brother who had completely gotten over any anger. Samurai also came over and shared the bottle as, in Samurai's words, "The temperature in our tent is a little chilly. I'd say Sue could freeze rocket fuel tonight." Harold laughed along with the others, but he really would have preferred for Samurai and Sue to work things out already. Samurai didn't seem worried about it, so Harold decided it was pointless for him to worry either.

In the flickering yellow light of the fire, the Banshee Riders settled in for the night, sleeping or playing in their tents, or drinking, drugging and cavorting by the fire. For most of them, this was enough of a reward for having endured a long, cold, heartless winter, but not sufficient reward for all of them.

Chapter 18 — Toast to the Cardinal

The Banshee Riders ranged in age from their mid-20s to mid-60s. After a day spent riding and consuming quantities of drugs and alcohol, many of "the geriatrics," as Pot Roast called his older brothers, had drifted off to their tents with their old ladies to catch some sleep or to knock off the celebratory Road Day piece of ass. When the last cassette tape in the van's stereo ran out, and no one bothered to replace it, the night was enveloped in relative stillness. Voices were hushed, and the dominant sound was the sporadic crackle of the fire that accompanied the dancing yellow light it cast around the campsite.

While the booze, drugs, conversation, and relaxation were all that some had counted on, for what the 'geriatrics' called 'the kids,' the night was still young. As Pot Roast put it, "Yawns by the campfire don't cut it." He had something else in mind. As he searched for 'a partner in crime,' his eyes fell upon Mongrel. It was a little before midnight when Pot Roast gestured with his head for his brother to follow him over by the bikes.

"You know what this party needs?" Pot Roast asked, and then answered without waiting for a reply. "Chicks."

"And we'll find those ...?" Mongrel asked, leaving the question pessimistically hanging.

"Oh, ye of little faith," replied Pot Roast with a grin. "When has my nose for the female persuasion failed? Just follow me, my brother, and I will lead you to the promised land."

"Think we'll be missed?" Mongrel asked, glancing back at the campsite.

It wasn't that there was a rule against going into town. However, this was relatively unfamiliar territory, well away from the Banshee Riders' home turf. The theory went that there was strength in numbers, and, in Creighton, it was fairly easy for a couple Banshees to find themselves outnumbered.

Mongrel was fairly sure some of the brothers wouldn't share their enthusiasm for a late-night ride into town. Additionally, with straight-piped Harleys, trying sneak off was like trying to pulling a rug out from under a pit bull unnoticed. The risk of a little trouble, however, was not likely to dissuade Pot Roast who frequently led Mongrel astray. As Pot Roast put it, "We don't need to ask mommy and daddy for permission?"

The only place that argument fell on barren ground was in consideration that, should the two run into trouble, they could drag the club into it with them. At the least, the club would probably feel obligated to back them up. And had they put the idea up for a vote, several brothers would have pointed out that Pot Roast, a former Golden Gloves boxer and with a pugnacious nature in general, had a reputation for starting trouble or, if not failing to avoid it. It was a concern but not enough of a concern to convince the pair to take a pass on adventure and they were soon starting their bikes and idling slowly out of the campground as though no one would notice.

One or two heads may have turned at the sound but those who heard were too engrossed in other activities to worry much about a couple brothers taking a ride.

When they turned out of the park onto the main road, they cranked up their engines for a power run that was hard to miss. Back at the campfire, Harold and Samurai heard the sound of winding engines and merely appreciated the sound, the way seasoned bikers do, allowing the sound to roll around their aural taste buds the way a wine connoisseur relishes a fine Bordeaux, rather than worrying that the sound might represent the fore bringer of trouble. Busy discussing the situation with Capsize back in the shadows away from the fire, they hadn't noticed when their brothers first left. Samurai's only comment was, "Boy, I love that sound," and then, after tipping their heads a moment to better capture the rapture of Harley Davidson twins in full bloom, they went back to their discussion.

A surprisingly warm day had cooled significantly as the evening turned to night. As the two brothers rode, they found that the cold air had settled into gullies and depressions. It had a refreshing effect on the two, even sobering them a little.

Riding hard and fast, the two were back in town in half the time it took the club to ride from town to the campground. As they pulled up in front of the same saloon the club had stopped at earlier, they noticed there were quite a few cars parked in the street outside. They also saw several bikes.

A steady hum of conversation mixed with the music of "Purple Haze" wafting out from the jukebox to the street through a front door propped open to allow for some fresh air. As Pot Roast and Mongrel approached, they tilted their heads down as though to duck under the layer of cigarette smoke that defied the open door. They worked their way through the crowd and found some room at one end of the bar. Mongrel ordered a couple beers as Pot Roast scanned their surroundings. It was a two-fold reconnaissance effort. It was intended to identify likely female targets as well as to scope out anyone who might cause trouble for the unfamiliar bikers.

Pot Roast didn't notice any immediate threat of the latter but also quickly identified a couple girls about six feet down the bar and, impulsively, which pretty much described his approach to life in general, grabbed the arm of the bartender who had just set two beers down in front of Mongrel.

"Hey," Pot Roast yelled over the noise, "I want to buy a couple drinks for the ladies over there."

As Pot Roast pointed in that direction, the bartender, clearly put off that the unfamiliar biker had invaded his personal space, yanked his arm away and, after giving Pot Roast a warning glance, went down the bar and took the order from the girls. He pointed back at the two bikers and the girls looked over and smiled. When they did, Pot Roast turned to Mongrel and said, "We're in bro." Then he nodded to Mongrel to follow and they drifted down by where the girls were standing.

The girls whispered to each other, as though deciding whether to accept or reject the ovation, then shrugged and said 'Hello' in warm and inviting tones. After introductions, in which the two Banshee Riders discovered the girls' names were Linda and Jade, the girls started asking questions about the motorcycle club. The questions, posed with the wide-eyed innocence of fawns caught in the headlights of Pot Roast's and Mongrel's brilliance, ranged from "What's it like?" to "Do you have to beat people up and stuff?"

The bikers were familiar with the curiosity their lifestyle engendered in citizens. But it was the physical attributes of their inquisitors, attributes accentuated by tight, short dresses and high heels, that put the two bikers at ease. Focused entirely on the potential conquest, Pot Roast affably provided answers, such as "only if they ask for it," before turning the discussion back to the girls — "Do you live out here? Do you have boyfriends? What do people do for fun around here?" The answers were "Yes," vague shrugs and "About the same thing people do most places – drink and party."

Pot Roast found the vague shrug intriguing. He surmised that the girls probably did have boyfriends but were somewhat receptive anyhow. That they might have boyfriends was inviting as it suggested the girls were as likely to forgo any interest in romantic entanglements when the fun was done.

Pot Roast assumed Mongrel was catching all of this with equal enthusiasm. Mongrel, however, wasn't paying attention. Instead, he was looking through the crowd at a couple of bikers over by the jukebox. The bikers were looking back at Mongrel and Pot Roast. When the bikers started towards the bar, Mongrel nudged Pot Roast in the ribs just as Pot Roast was in mid-sentence commenting on how hot the girls were. Pot Roast didn't take the hint and continued with his compliments the way a fisherman works a lure across the surface of a lake. Mongrel gave Pot Roast a sharp elbow in the ribs and this time gained his brother's attention.

As Pot Roast turned and said, "What?" he finally noticed the two bikers stepping up in front of him.

"I see you've met our women," the taller of the two said.

The biker was about 6-3 with moderately long hair slicked back with the help of some foreign substance, though it was likely he hadn't applied the substance intentionally. He was thin and, rather than a beard, he had a mustache and a couple days' worth of stubble on his face. The other biker was about 5-10 and a bit stockier. His dark-brown hair was shorter than the others and, though he also had a mustache, his face otherwise looked as though it was recently shaved.

The bikers were dressed in the customary blue jeans, engineer boots, black T-shirts and leather jackets. Wallet chains hung between long, leather wallets protruding from back pockets to leather loops that were fastened to their belts. The only real difference between these bikers and the Banshee Riders was that the other bikers were a little cleaner and didn't wear rags. This, in the eyes of Pot Roast, suggested they didn't belong to a club and automatically lowered them a notch in his perspective of the social pecking order. Owning bikes, in particular, American-made V-twins, meant they were several steps above sidewalk commandos or even someone on a foreign bike, but there was nothing about them to suggest they deserved the kind of respect brothers reserved for members of the universal brotherhood of motorcycle clubs. As such was the case, the way Pot Roast looked at it, shouting rights for the two girls remained open for discussion.

Pot Roast looked at the girls, tipped his head one way, then the other, as though inspecting them in search of some distinguishing feature. "Funny," Pot Roast said, "I don't see your brand on them."

"What my brother means," Mongrel interjected, "is that we're just talking to the ladies."

"We know what he meant," the shorter of the two said with a slightly threatening tone.

Mongrel might have found that sufficient instigation and chosen 'a dance partner' right there. He was half prepared for the in-your-face, step, step, kick routine he'd used before. Not surprisingly, Pot Roast was obviously chafing at the bit. But considering the unfamiliar surroundings, and the possibility that these two had friends in the crowd, Mongrel opted for a little more caution. He stepped slightly to his right just in time to cut Pot Roast off at the pass.

"Cool," Mongrel replied to the shorter biker, though he knew the biker meant anything but that it was cool. Then Mongrel offered to buy another round of drinks.

With a saccharine smile, the shorter biker accepted.

Pot Roast wasn't pleased with the arrangement, clearly preferring an opportunity to pound on a couple of citizen bikers, and simply take their girls. He also felt that these two citizens were showing inadequate respect. But Pot Roast went along with his brother's lead for the time being.

As Mongrel passed out a round of beers, he initiated introductions. The taller biker said his name was John and the other said his name was Percy. Then Mongrel asked, "Those must be your bikes out front?" When the taller biker nodded, Mongrel said, "Nice bikes," though, on the way in, he had only bothered to glance at the bikes for any sign of club affiliation, such as a decal of a club's patch on the tank or frame.

"Thanks," the shorter biker said. He then asked what Mongrel and Pot Roast were riding. The citizen bikers seemed duly impressed as the discussion of motorcycles continued for a couple minutes.

As they hadn't come to blows yet, the shorter biker suggested they move to a table that was recently vacated. The taller biker ordered a round for all six in the party and the group took seats around the table.

The ensuing conversation touched on topics as varied as the quality of roads in the area, the attitudes of the local police and the annual motorcycle rallies in Sturgis, S.D. and Daytona, FL. Nerves seemed to settle a bit and the tension appeared to pass. One of the girls even said it was a shame they didn't have a deck of cards so they could play some poker. The other girl was so pleased with the idea that she went to the bartender and asked if there was a deck behind the bar. She returned a moment later with a frown and announced, "No such luck."

"Well," Mongrel said, "we can always play Cardinal Puff."

Cardinal Puff is a game of repetitive variation. After determining that "there is a Cardinal in the house," someone who has previously completed the game and is qualified to judge performances, the first player begins the ritual with a fresh can of beer. The Cardinal, who is thoroughly familiar with the rules of the game, watches intently for any error as the player proceeds through a strict regimen of choreographed steps. In the first of three phases, the player does everything once. Holding the beer with a thumb and one finger, the player announces, "Here's a toast to the Cardinal Puff for the first time tonight." Then the player takes one swig, taps the beer onto the table once, wipes each side of his or her upper lip once with one finger, taps the top and bottom of the table once with one finger of each hand, then taps each knee with one finger, stands and sits once and nods his or her head once. Now ready for stage two, the player uses a thumb and two fingers to hold the can, announces, "Here's a toast to the Cardinal Puff Puff for the second time tonight," takes two swigs, taps the beer down twice, wipes each side of his or her upper lip twice with two fingers and so on. Step three is the same except everything is in threes. Phase three is completed as the player drains the last of their beer and, when all other machinations are finished, tips the can over and announces, "Once a Cardinal, always a Cardinal," as the player slaps the empty can off the table.

For someone who has learned the game and memorized all

the steps, it's fairly easy to play. For the uninitiated, however, the learning process is often brutal. Every time the player commits an infraction, he or she has to guzzle their beer and start over. After each successive try, as the contestant becomes more and more intoxicated, the player's capacity for rote memorization diminishes as the difficulty increases proportionately. Most Cardinals have tied on several good drunks in the process of learning the game.

Mongrel was hoping that the citizen bikers were unfamiliar with the game. If so, they might fall victim to its subtle power. In other words, they might become thoroughly intoxicated and, thereby, give Pot Roast and him a distinct advantage in the quest for the girls' affections.

The shorter biker said he'd seen it played a couple times. That suggested limited experience with the game and Mongrel proceeded to show them how to play, though he had to do so using a beer stein instead of a can. He breezed right through, only skipping the part where he would have slapped the beer off the table. When Mongrel was finished, Percy announced, "That's easy."

Right off, Mongrel had to stop the shorter biker to point out that his glass wasn't full. Percy went to the bar and had the mug filled. He returned and launched into the game as though he had already won. He had hardly started when he failed to wipe his lip and had to drain his beer.

"Bullshit," the biker said. "This is a piece of cake. He went back to the bar and filled his stein again, returned to the table and started again. On his second try, Percy only barely made it into phase two before he used the wrong number of fingers on the glass.

In the meantime, Pot Roast had purchased a pitcher of beer. When Percy drained his mug, Pot Roast immediately filled it again. Before Percy made his third attempt, Mongrel demonstrated again. Percy's third attempt was worse than his second. As he downed his beer, one of the girls said she wanted to try. But John, the taller biker, said, "It's my turn," and promptly failed as well. Before long, the two bikers were trying it simultaneously and mixing each other up in the process.

Clearly becoming frustrated, the shorter biker made it deep into phase three before skipping the part where he needed to stand three times. As Pot Roast reported the violation, the biker continued and drained his glass. He tipped it over and back again and pronounced, "Once a Cardinal, always a Cardinal."

As Percy finished, Pot Roast was hollering at him, "You blew it, man. You blew it."

"Bull," the biker said. "I did it perfectly."

"You didn't stand up," Pot Roast said laughing. "You blew it."

"Bullshit. I did it perfectly, start to finish," Percy bellowed before turning to one of the girls and asking, "You saw, right?"

When Jade nodded, siding with Percy, it was Pot Roast's turn to become angry. "It's bad enough that this jerk is arguing," Pot Roast thought to himself. "Now he has one of the girls lying for him." What really hurt was the jealousy he felt that she had sided with the other guy at all. Pot Roast had assumed he was getting along on Jade better than that. He was so sure of himself that he was already contemplating which of his brothers to bother for a tent he and Jade could use when they returned to the campsite. Taking Percy's side suggested Jade was just leading him on.

Pot Roast didn't lose face easily. Losing face to a citizen biker was a blow he wouldn't take lightly. With that, he turned to Percy and said, "You're a liar." Then, before Percy could respond, Pot Roast turned to Jade and said, "And you're a lying whore."

Mongrel was busy watching John, the taller biker, in another attempt to become a Cardinal when he heard Percy holler, "What the fuck did you call her?"

But Percy made a mistake. Instead of yelling, he should have punched. That's precisely what Pot Roast had in mind, and he didn't waste any time announcing his intention. He caught Percy with a blow square to the biker's nose. Percy went sprawling to the floor as a mist of blood hung in the air for a moment in the space the biker's face had previously occupied.

Seeing his friend go down, the taller biker stood quickly and started towards Pot Roast but just as quickly found himself on the floor under a shower of blows from Mongrel. Percy was about to get up when Pot Roast pounced on him. Percy was saved, somewhat, when Jade jumped on Pot Roast's back and started scratching at his face, searching with her fingers for the Banshee Rider's eyes. Pot Roast was trying to get the girl off his back while, at the same time, making sure Percy stayed on the ground. While slamming a right fist into Percy's jaw, Pot Roast grabbed Jade's left hand and pulled it around and away from his face. In the process, Jade left a nasty scratch across Pot Roast's cheek. It was enough to convince Pot Roast that he needed to eliminate the threat she posed, too. As Mongrel continued to pound on John, Pot Roast rose slightly from where he was crouched over Percy. Pot Roast turned slightly to his left and grabbed Jade by the hair. His other hand was balled in a triggered fist when there was a loud crack that cut across the sound of the fight with a veil of silence that "Rocky Mountain Way" on the jukebox was unable to conceal.

Those near the action, as though the fight created ripples that washed them aside, had formed in an impromptu circle of spectators. With the sudden cracking sound, the fighters all looked up from the floor. Hovering over them, just inside the ring, they found the bartender, a cut-off bat in hand. It was apparent the bartender had brought the bat down flatly on the nearest upright table. Now, he was glaring at Pot Roast. Looking back at the bartender, Pot Roast realized that the man looked bigger than Pot Roast had noticed earlier. In fact, he looked considerably bigger, with thick arms and the solid chest of a bouncer.

"That's it," the bartender said, pointing the bat with one hand at Pot Roast and then Mongrel. "You and you, outta here, now. And there's no need for you to come back."

As he released his grip on Jade's hair, Pot Roast, with blood dripping from the scratch administered by the girl, smiled broadly. As Mongrel stepped up next to him, they backed towards the door watching the bartender closely and scanning the room to make sure John, Percy or any of the bystanders didn't decide to follow them outside for a retaliatory assault.

Passing the bartender, Mongrel grinned and said, "No problem, pal. We've been kicked out of worse dives than this before."

"Just keep walking, tough guy," the bartender said as the crowd parted and the two-continued outside.

Laughing, they hopped on their bikes and headed back to camp as though it was all just part of a wonderful adventure, even if it didn't end with a woman's warm embrace.

Chapter 19 — Fishin' for Knickers and the Clansmen

Covered with dew, the grass glistened in the morning sun. About daybreak, a pesky bird somewhere in the adjoining woods had begun to caw, much to the distraction of several brothers and sisters who were still trying to sleep. Grunt had led a small contingent of brothers and sisters in a night-long vigil of booze and acid – his drug of choice. Grunt was drinking his fifth or sixth bottle of Boone's Farm Apple Blossom wine. He jokingly said it made a nice chaser for the purple microdot that he'd taken during the night. "I bought it just for the occasion," he told his brothers. However, popping acid was not a rarity for the biker. His sweet tooth was for hallucinogenic candy. He took the drug on an almost weekly basis.

Grunt began a career of abusing his body almost 48 years earlier. Considering, it was amazing how well he had held up. Of course, two stays in state pens had limited his access to his favorite mind-altering chemicals for a while, though he had access to plenty of jailhouse hooch.

While Grunt looked relatively good for his years and rough experiences, the toll was beginning to tell. His two heart attacks would have convinced most men to taper back a little, drink a little less, maybe lay off the drugs. But Grunt was set in his ways. As he was prone to say, "You can't teach an old dog new tricks."

Grunt also liked to joke that archeologists would discover his body centuries in the future and bring him back to life. He reasoned that he'd drank so much alcohol that he was not just figuratively pickled but that he had literally preserved his organs in the process. "My body is so completely soaked in alcohol that it will never decompose," Grunt argued.

While the effects of drugs and alcohol did not provide the kind of permanence that Grunt liked to joke about, the effects on his body, though he tried to mentally reject them, were probably irreversible. The most notable symptom of these effects, other than the heart attacks, was in relation to Grunt's digestive system. He battled with frequent heartburn and upset stomach. Further along his digestive tract, Grunt jokingly described his condition when he said, "I find irregularity entirely regular." As a result of this condition, the aging biker made increasingly frequent pit stops as the years went by.

About a quarter mile down the road from the club's campsite

was the outhouse Reaper had referred to the previous night when trying to gross Pot Roast out — a woman's door on the left and a man's door on the right. Grunt made his last trip to the outhouse during the waning daylight hours of the night. As the darkness grew and since the years had also taken their toll on Grunt's eyesight, trips to the outhouse were precarious and he was less and less inclined to risk the journey. Besides, he was preoccupied – the acid took his mind off his bowels. As the night went on he fought a growing pressure on his bowels. He considered stepping into the tree line among the bushes to relieve himself but lacked a reasonable substitute for toilet paper. Grunt resolved to hold it until morning when he could walk to the outhouse without worrying that he would stumble over some unseen obstacle along the way.

Along with his comment about his irregularity, Grunt had also commented, "I haven't had a solid bowel movement in years." Therefore, it was unlikely that what was building pressure in his bowels would present itself to the world in a solid form, a reality he took for granted. What he didn't account for was the suddenness with which his bowels would scream for release.

It was about 6 a.m. Grunt was taking a big swig of wine when he felt an urgent need to pass gas. He knew there was a possibility that he would pass something a little more substantial than gas. It had happened before. It was a little uncomfortable to walk around with a small amount of loose poop in the seat of his pants, especially since he never wore underwear, but it wasn't the end of the world. Even in his drunken state, Grunt made a slight effort to pass the gas without the others around him noticing. With his head back and the bottle to his lips, he cautiously, and ever so slightly, eased his rectal muscles.

A rancher once held a small herd of panicky horses at bay by placing his foot at the bottom of the barn door. Though the horses pushed and kicked, they couldn't open the door. When it quieted inside the barn, the rancher moved his foot and peaked inside. It was the moment the horses were waiting for. As the barn door opened slightly, the horses nearest the door lunged forward. The rancher tried to slam the door shut again, but without his foot at its base, there was no way he could restrain several half-ton animals that desperately wanted out. The door burst open knocking the rancher back and to the ground. Any hope of closing the door again was lost as the herd burst into the open and was gone down the road as the rancher was yet contemplating the hopelessness of the situation.

As Grunt released his grip on his rectum, he was much like the rancher. A tight grip could hold substantial pressure at bay. But after releasing even a little pressure, there was no turning back. Almost instantly Grunt's pants were filled with a foul-smelling load of diarrhea.

The sound of the accident caused T-Rex, who was standing closest to Grunt, to jump back suddenly and yell, "What the hell was that?" As quickly as T-Rex asked the question, the odor caught up with the sound. "Oh my God," the towering biker hollered. "What, did you shit your pants?"

If the others in the group hadn't heard the expulsion of waste from Grunt's bowels, they certainly heard T-Rex. All eyes were on Grunt. Standing with his legs spread, Grunt looked at everyone and then he looked down. He could feel the sticky substance dripping down his legs and realized it would soon drip in and over his boots if he didn't do something.

As the others starred at Grunt, T-Rex answered his own question. "You did shit your pants, didn't you?"

When Grunt looked up, the look on his face said it all.

"Oh, you sick fuck," T-Rex bellowed. "I don't believe it. What, do we have to bring diapers for you now?"

By the time T-Rex finished his tirade, all the others were bent over laughing. The laughter continued, and T-Rex joined in, as Grunt contemplated his immediate dilemma. It was bad enough to have soaked the back of his pants with wet feces. What he really didn't want was for the crap to reach his boots. Without hesitation, Grunt sat on the ground and began removing his boots and socks. He set the boots on the ground beside him and undid his belt and zipper. Then he stood up and removed his pants. As he did so, the others began howling again. Grunt tossed the pants aside on the ground, sat down and put his boots and socks back on and started drinking his wine again as if nothing had happened.

The others forgot all about the conversations they were having before Grunt had his accident. A series of jokes rolled out one after another, all at Grunt's expense and his inability to control his bowels. One brother asked while laughing, "Hey Grunt, what are you going to do? Are you going to ride home like that?"

T-Rex interjected, "Have you ever considered doing commercials for adult diapers."

"Yeah, and what about commercials for diarrhea relief?" someone else added.

As the smell was still with him, the others moved away from Grunt a little. When Grunt started to follow, T-Rex bellowed, "Oh no. You keep your distance, Mr. Stinky."

Not long after Grunt crapped his pants, Reaper, who had just climbed out of his tent, and Mongrel, who was drinking on the other side of the fire, noticed that Grunt was virtually naked. Out of curiosity, they walked over to find out why. "Haven't you ever seen anyone crap his pants before?"

"Just babies and people in old folks' homes," said Mongrel as he and Reaper backed away in fits of laughter.

Just then, Harold woke and climbed out of Samurai and Sue's tent, where they had let him catch a few winks. Grunt was standing about 10 feet away from the front of the tent. As Harold rubbed his eyes, he noticed his brother's partial nudity. Grunt also saw Harold.

Cleaning out his pants was not a task Grunt eagerly anticipated. Since Harold was a prospect, however, Grunt reasoned that a solution had presented itself.

"Hey prospect, get yer ass over here," Grunt said. "I got a little job for you."

Harold stepped that way cautiously, a curious look on his face as he eyed his hefty older brother and his peculiar condition — wearing nothing but his boots and his rag. Walking over slowly, Harold asked, "Uhm, brother, have you noticed that you're naked?"

In the same tone he had used answering Mongrel, Grunt said, "I crapped myself," as though that should have been obvious and nothing out of the ordinary.

As he was just a prospect, Harold wasn't as confident as the others and restrained himself from the urge to burst into laughter though he couldn't help grinning.

As Harold stood there smiling, Grunt picked up his pants by two fingers and removed the belt, wallet, keys and some money he had in one pocket. He then tossed the pants to the ground in front of Harold. "Here prospect," Grunt said. "Clean these."

The smile was instantly erased from Harold's face. Glancing at the inside of the pants, Harold saw the extent of the damage and reflexively yelled, "Oh my God."

Tears rolled down Reaper's and Mongrel's faces, as they burst back into laughter. If it was funny that Grunt had crapped himself, it was even funnier that the prospect now had to deal with the results of Grunt's accident.

Harold had tried to consider all the possible things the brothers might expect him to do as a prospect, but he had never considered anything like this. Daintily, Harold picked the pants up with two fingers by one of the snaps at the front. Holding the pants in the air he caught a good whiff of the shit inside and, for a second, he thought he might join Pot Roast as the second brother to barf during Road Day. Resisting the urge, Harold contemplated his next move. He knew that the river was back through the clearing about 75 yards north of where they were standing. Harold figured that was the best place to start. He was about to walk in that direction when he remembered something he'd seen in the backup van when he and Red were making room for the firewood.

Harold dropped the pants back to the ground and, with a smile back on his face, he said, "I'll be right back."

As Harold walked to the van, Grunt turned and walked down a path through the trees beyond the campsite towards the river, his backside glistening with the semi-transparent wetness of his bowel movement. Not wanting to miss any of the action, Reaper and Mongrel opted for following Grunt. By the river, their older brother kicked off his boots again, followed by his socks, and then he walked out into the river.

Reaper and Mongrel were sitting on a large boulder by the edge of the water when Harold approached, holding the offending article of clothing with two fingers at arm's length. Harold had turned his head away and back so as to avoid smelling their contents any more than necessary. In his other hand, Harold held something that, when Reaper and Mongrel saw it, caused them to burst into laughter again.

As Grunt rubbed at his backside in the water, sick-green water that would replace one foul odor with another, Harold dug a hook through the backside of Grunt's pants along the belt line. Grunt looked up just in time as Harold swung the pants back behind him on a fishing line. With a Popeil Pocket Fisherman in his hand, Harold cast the pants out into the river. As Reaper and Mongrel were rolling in laughter and holding their guts, which were beginning to hurt, with a crestfallen look on his face, Grunt watched Harold reel the pants in. To see his pants handled in this manner was a blow to Grunt's dignity.

As Harold reeled the pants in, they flowed through the water opening at the top so that the water ran through the legs. Harold pulled his catch up on the shore and, using a sidearm casting method to ensure that the pants didn't drip onto him, he cast them back out again.

Reaper and Mongrel had just caught their breath after gaining control from the uncontrollable laughter that had overcome them when they first saw Harold with the fishing pole. They were thinking that the show was about over when they saw Pot Roast walking through the clearing towards the river. It immediately occurred to Mongrel that this situation was something that was sure to make Pot Roast gag. He was about to say something about it to Pot Roast when Reaper grabbed his arm. He looked over at Reaper and saw a big grin as the president nodded his head indicating Mongrel should hold his tongue. Then Reaper motioned towards Pot Roast and said quietly, "Look at what our brother is carrying?"

When Mongrel looked back at Pot Roast, he almost gagged himself. In Pot Roast's left-hand he held a toothbrush and a tube of toothpaste. The most amazing thing about it was that Pot Roast, a man with a stomach as fragile as the shell of a robin's egg, was actually about to use the filthy river water to brush his teeth. The absence of logic was clearly apparent to Reaper and Mongrel but, for some reason, Pot Roast was oblivious.

Growing up, Pot Roast had developed several nasty habits, including the scrappy attitude that had exhibited itself the night before at the bar in town. He had also developed some habits that were more socially acceptable. Surprisingly for a biker, Pot Roast was a neat nick. His level of attention to hygiene was greater than any of his brothers. Part of this was a carved-in-stone routine of brushing his teeth morning and night. He had snuck off to brush his teeth after the barfing episode by the fireplace but that was earlier than usual. He was doubly determined to brush this morning. When back home, Pot Roast brushed his teeth in his bathroom sink or used the bathroom at a bar or a clubhouse. Few realized that he would sneak away to brush his teeth. Only a few had ever noticed the toothbrush tucked into a purposefully narrow pocket inside his rag. Now, without considering the full implications of what he was about to do, he approached the river's edge.

If the color, the sheen of oil on top and the smell wasn't enough to dissuade Pot Roast from his hygienic crusade, reading the local newspaper might have. Weekly stories in the paper discussed how an association of residents along the river were suing a manufacturing company upstream for polluting the river. The lawsuit stated that the company was dumping toxic waste into the water. On top of that, the motorboats and barges left regular trails of gasoline and fuel oil in the river. If Grunt should have thought twice before walking into the river, Pot Roast should have had serious reservations about introducing the river water into his mouth. Additionally, Pot Roast had no idea that, only 15 feet upstream, Harold was responsible for filtering a different and psychologically more toxic substance into the river.

As Pot Roast removed the cap from the tube of toothpaste, he swished the brush in the river. He saw Reaper and Mongrel smiling in his direction but didn't put two-and-two together yet. Pot Roast merely smiled and nodded "Good morning." Reaper and Mongrel nodded back and smiled a little broader. Pot Roast looked at Grunt who was splashing in the water, having forgotten all about his injured pride. Then Pot Roast looked to his left and saw Harold reeling something into the riverbank. Just before sticking the brush into his mouth, Pot Roast said, "Looks like you got one."

Of course, Pot Roast was referring to a fish as he saw the tension on the short, little pole. Harold did, in fact, have 'one,' but it was hardly the kind of catch Pot Roast had imagined. When Harold pulled the pants out of the water and prepared for another side-arm cast, Pot Roast took the brush out of his mouth and asked, "What are you doing?"

Harold hadn't seen Pot Roast approach and hadn't heard first comment. He did hear the question. When Harold looked over at Pot Roast, Harold saw white foam bubbling from his brother's mouth as the biker rapidly brushed his gums. For a second, the absurdity of what Harold saw clogged the gears in his brain. Harold stood looking at Pot Roast with a puzzled expression as it sank in that Pot Roast was apparently using river water to brush his teeth. The mental confusion only lasted a moment. Though Samurai had told Harold not to worry about it, Harold liked Pot Roast and was still a little concerned that the brother might feel somewhat disenchanted with Harold when the prospect was brought up for a vote.

With the pants dripping and dangling off the end of the short fishing pole, Harold leaped towards Pot Roast with one hand out as he hollered, "Awe man, don't do that."

Harold's sudden reaction caught Pot Roast completely off guard. Startled, he stepped back as he reflexively removed the brush from his mouth. He mumbled through a mouthful of foamy toothpaste, "Whadda fuck's a madder?"

For a second, Harold tried to think of something else to say. "Do I really want to tell him he's brushing downstream from where I'm washing the shit out of Grunt's pants?" Harold asked himself. But Harold really couldn't see any way around it and he resigned himself to the situation.

Gesturing to Grunt, who was still splashing about in the murky water, Harold said, "Grunt crapped his pants."

It was then Pot Roast's turn to pause and allow reality to sink in. Pot Roast looked at Grunt, looked at the pants and looked back out at Grunt. He then looked over at the boulder where Reaper and Mongrel were laughing so hard that Reaper was rolling on his back and Mongrel had just fallen off the rock and was doubled over on the ground. Pot Roast looked down at the toothbrush in his hand. A moment later, his back arched like a frightened cat's, and he leaned way forward and heaved into the river.

Harold stood watching his brother spill his guts and, when Pot Roast was done, Harold said, "I'm sorry bro. I didn't see you."

Pot Roast looked at Harold for a moment, looked back at Reaper and Mongrel and growled, "You mother fuckers. This ain't funny." As Pot Roast retreated back to the campsite, he continued to grumble a constant string of insults and obscenities along the way. His reaction only served to increase the hilarity of the situation for Reaper and Mongrel. Their laughter and Pot Roast's outburst had finally caught Grunt's attention. He stood up naked in the river, the water just higher than his knees.

Grunt hollered, "What's wrong with Pot Roast?"

Harold, Reaper, and Mongrel all looked out into the river. Seeing Grunt standing there unashamed of his nudity, his genitals shriveled and small in response to the cold water, droplets of water glistening in his beard, Reaper and Mongrel broke into a fresh round of laughter. Harold even allowed himself a small smile.

Harold unhooked Grunt's pants from the fishing pole and draped them flat on the boulder next to Reaper. He yelled out to Grunt, "Here you go, bro. Clean as a whistle."

Harold knew the pants weren't as clean as advertised, but Grunt smiled with satisfaction and headed out of the water to get dressed. Harold didn't wait for his brother. He headed back towards the campsite to put the fishing pole away with thoughts, as his distasteful and unexpected chore was completed, of starting the morning fresh with a cold beer. Pot Roast had returned to the campsite with a similar intention, though his primary motivation was to use the beer to clean several tastes, some mental, out of his mouth.

Harold arrived at the campsite just in time to hear Pot Roast yelling again. This time, Pot Roast was yelling because the beer was gone. Both keggers were empty and Pot Roast was so angry he had tears rolling down his face. Seeing Harold approach, Pot Roast came over and demanded that Harold take up a collection to go buy more beer. Pot Roast then approached Red with the same demand.

Harold and Red, hats in their hands, were soon circulating through the brothers and sisters taking contributions. In accordance with Pot Roast's directions, they even went to tents and woke people up to request funds. As a result, Harold and Red were on the receiving end of several obscenity-laden responses. Harold stood silently as Capsize blasted off with a string of predictable insults, referring to the prospect as everything from an "ignoramus" to "a scum-sucking, piece of shit."

When Capsize appeared to have run out of taunts, Harold

calmly asked, "So, does that mean you don't have anything to contribute?"

Pot Roast was close enough to overhear both sides of the conversation. He bellowed, "Tell him if he doesn't contribute, he doesn't drink."

Harold started to relay the information, but Dancer cut Harold off, "We heard him!" A moment later, the zipper on the front of the tent opened slightly and Dancer stuck her hand out just far enough to present a five-dollar bill.

A couple other brothers and sisters also complained that the club was supposed to cover the cost of beer for the weekend. This time Reaper interjected. "If you want to drink pony up some cash," Reaper said. "The club bought two kegs. That's enough."

Before long, Harold and Red had collected a sizeable sum. When Grunt complained that the prospects hadn't contributed anything to the till Reaper cut Grunt off. "They're going on the run (to the liquor store)," Reaper said. "That's their contribution."

Grunt didn't seem pleased with the arrangement, but he wasn't willing to push the issue any further. From Harold's perspective, considering that he had recently cleaned crap out of Grunt's pants that morning, the brother's attitude showed a distinct lack of appreciation. Harold wanted to say, "You know bro, diaper duty goes above and beyond the call to duty. So why don't you shut the fuck up?" With a full patch on his back, Harold would have said just that. Of course, with a full patch on his back, Harold would have told Grunt to wash the shit out of his own pants.

Mongrel seemed to be thinking along the same line. "Hey, asshole," Mongrel said. "The prospect just cleaned the shit out of your knickers. And now you got the nerve to complain about him drinking some beer?"

Harold appreciated that Mongrel recognized the value of Harold's efforts. At the same time, Harold wasn't looking for a confrontation about the situation. Personally, he would prefer to let the whole thing blow over. Harold was about to suggest that Mongrel let it go when, in a very humbled voice, Grunt said, "You're right bro." Then Grunt turned to Harold and said, "I'm sorry man."

When Grunt tried to give Harold some more cash, Harold said, "It's OK. I think we've got enough."

Harold walked away leaving Grunt standing with his hand and a five-dollar bill extended. As Grunt put the five away, he hollered after Harold, "I owe you, brother."

It took some looking to find a place to purchase alcohol on a Sunday morning in the area. With Harold behind the wheel of the backup vehicle, they drove past two bars and a liquor store that were closed and were beginning to contemplate the reaction if they returned to the campsite empty-handed. Heading out of Creighton to the south with the expectation of swinging around to come up to the campground from the other direction, they found a gas station by the expressway that carried booze – actually just over the border in the next county as, in Lucas County, there was a Blue Law banning the sale of liquor on Sundays.

Harold parked the van off to the side and they walked across the lot to the front door. As they stepped inside, goosebumps quickly formed on their arms in response to an overactive air-conditioning system. Reaper had specified that they should buy Old Style and, based on the amount of money they had raised, Harold said they could buy six cases. Red suggested that was more than was needed, especially considering that the club would make the ride back later in the day.

The brothers grabbed two cases each and carried them up to the front. "What should we do with the extra cash?" Harold asked.

Red suggested they grab some food of some kind, but even he wasn't sure how that would go over. When Harold said they should just bring the change back and give it to the treasurer, Red nodded in agreement and they stepped into the line leading up to the cash register.

Just as they reached the front of the line, Harold's face broke into a broad smile and he said, "I've got an idea." Harold dropped the two cases of Old Style onto the counter and rushed back down the aisle closest to the front window. A minute later he returned with a pine-tree air freshener in a plastic sleeve.

"What's that for?" Red asked.

With a big grin, Harold said, "Grunt. He can wipe it on his ass and maybe people won't avoid him all day."

Red's face started breaking into a smile. But just as quickly, the smile slid into a frown as Harold realized that the probate was looking past Harold at the front door. When Harold started to turn to see what Red was looking at, Red said, "Don't turn around."

"What is it," Harold said in a hushed tone.

"Let's just pay for this and get out of here," Red said. Then he added in a whisper, "Stay on your toes."

On the far end of the counter, the store had a glass-cased hot-dog machine. Hotdogs in a circular rack ran end over end as the rack turned under a heat lamp. Through the glass and between the stainless-steel frame of the machine, Harold could see three long-haired, bearded bikers wearing leather jackets under blue-jean vests. He could see that the bikers were looking intently at Harold and Red.

As Harold accepted the change from the clerk, he picked up the two cases of beer he'd left on the counter, along with the air freshener, and turned towards the door. As they stepped out of the store, they found one of the bikers was leaning back against the window. The others were standing a few feet in front of him on the sidewalk along the front window. Three Harleys were parked off to the left. Something about the way they kept glancing over gave Harold the distinct impression the bikers were waiting for Red and him to come outside.

On the back of the vest of the biker leaning against the window, Harold could see a center patch with a picture of someone wearing a black hood with only a pair of red eyes glaring out from the center. Above the center patch was a top rocker with the name "The Clansmen" in black letters fringed with red. The state patch and the "MC" patch were also black with red outlines.

As Harold and Red walked out the door, their path back to the van took them right between the three bikers Harold had seen in the reflection of the hot dog machine. With their arms full of beer, he realized that they weren't just outnumbered; they also had the disadvantage that their arms were full. Of course, he couldn't imagine why they would attack as Harold and Red hadn't done anything to them. All the same, the looks on the bikers' faces were anything but friendly and Harold wondered if it was a simple matter of territoriality.

As they walked by, Red nodded to the bikers as a way of saying hello and simultaneously indicating that, while he wasn't afraid, he had no aggressive intentions. Harold didn't look right at them or look away. He just kept walking, a step behind Red, sizing the bikers up as he went. The one leaning against the window stood about 5-8, had long, blonde hair hanging to his shoulders and sported a goatee. At about 140, the biker was reasonably lean and yet solid enough that Harold couldn't discount him as a threat. Of the two standing by the curb, one was probably 6-0 or 6-1 and at least 200 pounds. His hair was a little darker than the one against the window and was twisted and knotted as though it had never been combed. With a nose that was clearly broken at some time in the past, he had the look of a heavyweight boxer. The third biker reminded Harold of T-Rex. He stood at least 6-7, with long legs protruding up from square-toed cowboy boots. His disheveled mop of hair was even darker and ran down to the middle of his back and around his chin into a long beard.

The two larger bikers by the curb starred right at Harold and Red with bold, blunt expressions that conveyed simple messages of confidence and power. On the other hand, the biker by the window rapidly scanned his eyes over Harold and Red as if measuring them for caskets. When he looked into their eyes, Harold felt as though the biker were gauging the outsiders for their reactions. Harold turned his head towards the biker by the window and smiled slightly. It wasn't a friendly smile though. It was more as though Harold was saying, "What the fuck do you want?"

Of course, the reality was that, if Harold wasn't afraid, he wouldn't have felt the need to respond at all. He wouldn't have given the other bikers more than a passing thought and he would still be thinking about how much fun they'd have when he gave Grunt the pine-tree air freshener. But then, when considering the intentions of the three members of The Clansmen, the possibilities, and their general demeanor more than justified caution. Therefore, Harold presented a strong front as a means of dissuading the other bikers from thinking Harold and Red were unprepared or easy pickings. His simple, cold smile informed The Clansmen that Harold was on his toes and conscious. If the bikers intended to jump the prospect and probate, force would be met with force. That wasn't to say Harold thought he and Red could take the three bikers. It just meant that Harold wasn't going to go quietly, and he suspected Red felt the same.

Red had made it past The Clansmen, and Harold was right between them when the one against the window stood away from the glass and asked, "Where you boys from?"

It wasn't the military, but Harold still had an idea that all he was required to give was essentially his name, rank, and serial number. Since he didn't have a serial number, and since his rank was already obvious by the large, white 'P' on his back, the only information Harold intended to divulge was his name. And the biker hadn't asked for that.

Motioning to Red's back with his head, Harold said, "It says who we are right there."

The bikers by the curb seemed to stiffen a little at Harold's blunt response. The taller of the bikers said, "We can see that except we have no idea who the fuck The Banshee Riders are."

Though not exactly sure why he did it, Harold got a little cute with his response. "Well, we have brothers from all over. Maybe you should get out more," Harold said.

"Prospects in our club show a little more respect to full-patch brothers," the biker by the window said.

Harold almost said, "I'll remember that if I ever prospect for your club," but he decided he was skating on thin ice already. Instead, he ignored the question and kept walking.

As Harold and Red had only slowed a little in response to the conversation, Harold had by this time passed the other bikers. As he and Red continued to the van, the other bikers fell in step behind them. Red opened the side door and he and Harold put the beer behind the front seats as The Clansmen three stood a few feet away watching. Red slammed the side door shut, and as Harold walked around to the driver's door, the shorter biker with the goatee asked, "So, where are you boys staying?"

"Out of town," Red offered as an intentionally vague response.

Then the biker with the busted nose spoke up for the first time, answering his brother's question on Harold and Red's behalf. "They're camping at the state park," he said. "Isn't that right, boys?"

When Harold and Red didn't answer, the boxer went on, "Oh

yeah, they're at the state park alright, just camping out in the open like sitting ducks."

As Harold reached the far side of the van, the tallest of the three bikers blocked Harold's path. For a second, Harold thought the biker was going to take a swing. Instead, the biker said, "You tell your president and your brothers that this is Clansmen country. You got that prospect?"

Harold nodded, "I'll tell them."

With that, Harold stepped around the biker and climbed into the driver's seat. When Harold started the van and put it in gear, the other bikers finally stepped out of the way so the van could leave. As they drove by, the large biker reiterated his demand, "Don't forget." Harold nodded slightly and kept on driving.

As he waited for several cars to pass, he saw that The Clansmen had hopped on their bikes and were pulling up behind the van.

"I think they're following us," Red said. "Maybe we should take them the other way."

"They already know where we're camping," said Harold. "Maybe we should just get back and warn the club first thing."

That idea seemed to make sense to Red. However, he watched intently in the passenger-side mirror to see if The Clansmen were following. Harold drove the speed limit not wanting to let on to the bikers behind them that he and Red were eager to get back to the club. Several miles down the road, after Harold took a left turn, they saw The Clansmen pause before turning the other way.

Once out of sight, Harold hit the gas so that they were soon doing close to 90 mph. As he sped up, he commented, "The brothers will be wondering what the fuck happened to us."

Red nodded and, after a short pause, and referring to The Clansmen, asked, "What do you think their problem was?"

"I don't know," Harold said. "Guess they don't like other clubs coming into their territory or something."

As Harold and Red rolled up to the campsite, Pot Roast walked towards the van with a pissed-off expression on his face. "Where have you assholes been? You left almost an hour ago."

"We ran into a little trouble," Red answered.

Reaper, who also appeared curious about the prospect and probate's delay in returning, asked, "What kind of trouble."

After hearing Harold's explanation of the events with The

Clansmen, Pot Roast became agitated. He suggested that the club hop on their bikes and go find "these fuckers."

"Nobody's going anywhere," Reaper said. Then he turned to T-Rex, Wide Glide, Mongrel and several other brothers who were standing close by and asked, "Any of you know anything about these assholes?"

All the brothers shook their heads or said, "No."

Poacher, however, was a little more familiar with the club. "I saw several of them at a swap meet maybe 10 years back. About five or six of 'em came in together on their bikes in the middle of winter acting like they were hard asses because they rode in the cold."

"So, they are assholes?" Reaper asked.

Poacher shrugged, "I can't characterize the whole club based on a few idiots."

"So, what do you think," Reaper asked T-Rex.

The big man studied on the question a minute and said, "Well, everyone should be on their toes." Turning to his side he looked at Mongrel and said, "Pick someone and go stand watch down the road a bit. Don't go so far that we can't see you from here though."

When Mongrel protested that the prospect or probate should have the assignment, T-Rex said, "Then take one of them with you."

Mongrel picked Harold as T-Rex turned back to face Reaper, who offered his own contribution: "And nobody goes into town or leaves the campsite until we leave as a group."

Grunt hadn't told anyone, but he was considering a ride into town to buy a new pair of pants. Though Harold had done a reasonably good job of cleaning most of Grunt's mess out of the jeans, as the pants dried, they became a little hard and crusty in the seat. Grunt was finding them uncomfortable. They were even chafing on his balls. The president's decree spoiled his plan to quietly slip away for a little while.

"If they were going to do something don't you think they would have done something to the prospects already?" Grunt said, hoping to build an argument that would resurrect his idea of going into town.

"Nobody goes into town. That's final," Reaper said.

When Grunt began to complain, Reaper gestured to Grunt and told T-Rex, "If he goes near his bike, take his keys."

"My bike doesn't take a key," Grunt said in an annoyed tone.

"Okay," Reaper said as he quickly turned and stepped aggressively close to Grunt's face. "Then how about we just load up your bike right now?"

Grunt did not accept defeat gracefully. He walked away bitching half to himself but loud enough that Reaper could clearly hear.

Watching Grunt go, Reaper turned to T-Rex and said, "Maybe we should let the grumpy old bastard go, just to see what happens?" But the president wasn't serious. Instead, he suggested T-Rex send out a second shift to spell Mongrel and Harold in a while.

T-Rex nodded and then told Samurai and Red they should take over in about an hour.

Chapter 20 — Roadblock

The way the brothers and sisters dove into the beer, when Red and Harold returned, it was as if they'd spent the time while the two were gone licking salt blocks in a farmer's field somewhere. Instead of words of appreciation, the probate and prospect were accosted with occasional frowns meant to administer a touch of guilt for their dalliance on the beer run. However, news of the confrontation with The Clansmen swept through the club and changed the tempo of the party. With the music playing again, Grunt finally seemed to have accepted the condition of his wardrobe. His anger passed and he went back to work building the fire with wood left over from the night before.

Harold and Mongrel grabbed a couple beers and walked about 150 yards down the road to a grove of trees and shrubs by the entrance to the park, where they could see people coming into the campground while they remained relatively hidden. Standing among the trees, Harold asked, "We ever have this kind of trouble before."

"We've mixed it up with a couple clubs before," Mongrel said. "Several of us got into it with a club out of the city once. 'What the fuck were their names again?'" Mongrel asked himself. "But it was just fists in a bar one night. Nobody really won or lost and, after a powwow between Reaper, T-Rex and their president, the situation kind of blew over."

"So what kind of bug do you think The Clansmen have up their ass?" Harold asked.

"Couldn't say. Small club probably has this territory all to itself most of the time — they're probably just not used to having other clubs around.

"You know, the situation out by us is a little unique," Mongrel continued. "You don't find a lot of counties where as many as five clubs peacefully coexist – well, peacefully most of the time. Hell, did you know that, at the beginning of the year, the officers from all the clubs get together and compare schedules so we don't throw parties on the same weekends and stuff? It's not like we always like each other, but we cooperate. It makes life easier for everyone."

Samurai and Red joined Harold and Mongrel about half an hour after they had gone on guard duty. "T-Rex told us to spell you guys in an hour," Samurai said. "We figured, 'Why wait?'"

They passed out a couple extra beers they'd brought along. Samurai and Mongrel sat on a fallen tree while Red and Harold kept a closer eye out through the trees.

"Do you think we'll have any more trouble with these assholes?" Red asked.

"Probably not," Samurai answered. "Grunt was mostly right. If they were going to do anything they probably would have pounded on the two of you a bit and the message would have been that you came back all bloody.

"Of course," Samurai went on with a little grin as he slapped Mongrel across the back, "if the brothers who set up Road Day had done their homework, we'd have scouted out The Clansmen before we got here."

"Oh great," Mongrel said in an immediate and sincere expression of exasperation. "Now it's my fault."

"I'm just fucking with yeah," Samurai said. "It would have been nice to know, but what were you supposed to do, come out here and go driving around looking for other clubs?"

Mongrel calmed himself a little, but still griped, "Yeah know, I'll catch shit about this until hell freezes over."

"Don't sweat it, bro," Samurai said. "Like I was saying, we probably won't have any more trouble with these punks."

Then Samurai looked up at Harold and Red. "All the same, you two keep your eyes peeled," he said, nodding in both directions beyond the front entrance to the campground.

Several hours ticked by as the foursome remained on guard duty, occasionally sending Red or Harold running back to the campsite for more beer.

Even from 150 yards away, when the club began breaking down tents and dousing the fire, the four brothers by the grove of trees heard Capsize complain, "Why aren't the prospects here to break down the tents?"

Mongrel, Samurai, Harold, and Red laughed together when they heard Falstaff bark back at Capsize, "They're busy watching so no one comes along and fucks you in yer fat ass. So, you can either shut up and take your tent down or you can just leave it here when we leave."

The next sound Mongrel, Samurai, Harold and Red heard was Capsize hollering, "Drago, get yer ass over here."

"What a fucking asshole," Samurai said to no one in general. "Why can't he just shut up and take down his own tent without making it a statement about who's a prospect or probate?"

"He can't help himself because you're right, he's an asshole," Mongrel said.

Harold and Red glanced at each other with appreciative glances. Even though they were alone with Samurai and Mongrel, the prospect and probate didn't feel comfortable enough to chime in on the subject, though they clearly agreed. For Harold and Red, it was just rather nice to hear someone else say what they were thinking.

About the time that the last tent was packed away in the van or strapped onto its owner's seat or handlebars, Trailer Trash walked over by the grove of trees. He held up a pine-tree air-freshener and asked Harold and Red if they knew anything about it. When Harold said they were planning to give it to Grunt, "You know, for deodorant." Trailer Trash laughed, "Peyote's all upset. Seems she found it on the dashboard of the van, and she thinks someone's making a commentary about her choice of perfume."

"Well, she does put it on kinda heavy," Mongrel laughed. "She must carry a jug of it in that big-ass purse of hers."

"You might want to keep that thought to yourself," Trailer Trash warned Mongrel. Then he tossed the air-freshener to Harold and said, "Here, you give this to Grunt."

Samurai quickly took the air-freshener away from Harold. "Since when do prospects get to have all the fun?"

Harold, however, wondered if his sponsor wasn't running interference, making sure Harold didn't give Grunt a hard time once too often.

"Well, it's about time to go," Trailer Trash said. He looked at Harold and said, "You can ride in back with me again." Then Trailer Trash laughed, "Reaper made Derelict tape his leg on."

They all laughed as they turned to head back to the campsite. Trailer Trash took a moment to look beyond the trees to make sure everything was OK. Then he followed along as well.

The brothers formed up in two columns as the sound of

un-muffled Harleys reverberated through the woods and set birds to flight. Peyote was driving the backup vehicle with Dancer in the passenger seat. Harold looked around for Sue and saw that she was talking to Samurai. When Samurai angrily gestured back towards the van, Harold saw that Sue was arguing in response. By the way Samurai then gestured towards the front of the campground, Harold deduced that Samurai was probably telling her to ride in the van because of the potential for trouble with The Clansmen. The two argued a little longer before, to Harold's surprise, Samurai submitted, and Sue climbed on behind him.

Everyone seemed ready to go when Falstaff walked back through the pack reminding everyone to keep their eyes open in case The Clansmen decided to pull something. Harold watched Falstaff walk back to his bike with a sense that Grunt was probably right. "Besides," Harold told himself, "if The Clansmen wanted them to leave the area, why would the Clansmen fuck with them on the way out?"

At last, Reaper looked back through the pack. Trailer Trash scanned the pack one final time and nodded to Reaper who pulled ahead with Poacher at his side.

A beautiful morning had developed into an even nicer day. Harold enjoyed the wind in his face again, though it seemed that Reaper was a little more restrained heading home than on the way out. The club actually did the speed limit as it headed back to town.

As they rode through town, Harold kept scanning along their route half expecting to see The Clansmen watching as the Banshees went by. Instead, he didn't see as much as a single Harley. The only people out and about were citizens, many in their Sunday bests apparently coming home from church. They watched the bikes go by with the same non-threatening curiosity that they had watched with as the club arrived in town the day before. At the edge of town, Reaper pulled into a gas station so the brothers could fill up before hitting the open road. Though he hadn't seen anything, Harold found himself thinking it would have been better to put some miles on and then stop. Gassing up in town almost seemed like they were tempting fate.

While they took turns at the pump, Harold continued to scan the street and surrounding area for any sign of trouble. The only thing he saw was yesterday's squad car rolling slowly by. As Harold filled the tanks on Magdelina through the left-side filler, it occurred to him that the officer was even more interested than the day before, as though he expected something to happen at any moment.

"It must be time for shift change," laughed Tank, who was filling up on the other side of the pump from Harold. "Barney has to go back to the station and give his bullet back to Andy."

Harold smiled at the joke but continued to scan the area for any sign of The Clansmen while wondering if the officer was somehow aware of the potential trouble between the clubs. He was so intent on watching for potential signs of trouble that he didn't notice when the gas overflowed a little onto his tank. Tank yelled, "Bro," to get Harold's attention.

"Son of a bitch," Harold growled mostly to himself as he put the cap on the tank. Before he could do anything else about it, though, Red came over with a handful of the blue-towels the station kept by the pump. Red had quickly soaked the towels in the jug of window cleaner tied to the pole between the pumps. He handed them to Harold so Harold could wipe the majority of the gasoline off the side of his tank. Harold said, "Thanks," and, when he was done, tossed the towels into the garbage barrel between the pumps.

At last, after Trailer Trash paid the bill, the brothers fired up their bikes again and soon, the club was back on the road. As they pulled out of town, Harold saw the squad car parked on a side street as the officer watched them depart. Harold leaned over and spoke to Trailer Trash in the only kind of whisper that works when someone is shouting over a pack of Harleys, "Do you get the feeling he's watching to make sure we leave."

Trailer Trash looked in the police officer's direction and nodded in agreement. Then, he leaned back towards Harold and said, "Fuck him."

With every mile they put between themselves and Creighton, Harold felt as though a vice was loosening on his guts. When the pack pulled onto the four-lane, divided highway about 10 miles out of Creighton, Harold noticed several other brothers glance around with smiles. It was as though the interstate was the boundary between East and West Germany. Harold hadn't noticed the tightness in the faces of his brothers around him but he did notice when it was gone. The pack was free to focus again on the joy of riding.

Reaper cranked up to a comfortable 75 mph as they rode along with the sun beginning its decline that would end in a few hours below the horizon in front of them. Traffic was extremely light, and the recently paved road beckoned the club on as though a carpet was rolled out just for them.

Over the sound of the bikes, Trailer Trash hollered, "It's days like this that make winters tolerable."

Harold nodded and smiled. Camping and partying were nice, but the ride was the best part of the trip. Harold savored the feeling as though he were filing away a memory for later reference. He leaned the bike one way and the other as the pack negotiated gentle turns created by a highway engineer who, Harold almost would have believed, had designed the road with the thought of providing winding roads to enhance the experience for those on two wheels. The turns rolled through a series of hills and gullies, with little farms occasionally tucked into the crevices, suggesting to Harold that the designer had contemplated the scenery for this road, as well.

As he rode, Harold thought about how, though he'd gotten drunk the night before, and a little bit that day too, he hadn't passed out or done anything embarrassing. No one of consequence was mad at him, except maybe The Clansmen. Somehow it seemed strange that he didn't have to deal with wreckage of the intoxicated night just past, facing the people he had drunkenly insulted, discovering he had done something obscene or socially unacceptable while his brain and behavior were soaked in alcohol. In fact, as he thought about it, Harold realized that he had shown remarkable restraint since he started prospecting for the Banshees. In the back of his mind, he worried a little that his restraint might wane once he achieved the goal of earning his patch. With the pressure off, he wondered if he might revert to form.

As the club began a relatively steep climbing turn to the left, Harold resolved to continue demonstrating the control he'd exhibited since he arrived in Biesenthal. He told himself, "I'm not going to screw this up." But in the back of his mind, the question lingered – "Could he maintain that kind of control?" He realized the booze was like a sightless monster. Calm at times, if he rattled its cage, it could erupt in any direction – rage, idiocy, self-pity. He had learned to live with the random nature of the beast. Now for the first time in a long time, he had an urge to keep it in its cage. This struck him as odd. After all, the Banshee Riders were hardly teetotalers. Sex, drugs and, ... well, country music, were universally embraced by the brothers and the brothers of every other club Harold was familiar with. But Harold realized that, no matter how drunk or drugged up a brother might become, there were lines of behavior he should never cross. These weren't necessarily the same lines observed by citizens but, he suspected, they were enforced with greater prejudice.

Was it the red lights or the sound of squealing tires that woke Harold from that place where he was lost in thought? Suddenly he saw the red light on Drago's bike rushing towards him, though this was an illusion since Drago was coming to a sudden stop and it was Harold who was fast approaching. Harold's reaction outraced conscious thought. Before he knew he was doing it, Harold's right foot had slammed down on the brake pedal at the same moment that his right hand squeezed the brake lever. Almost as quickly, his left hand pulled in the clutch lever, his left toe yanked the shifter pedal all the way up to first gear and he released the clutch lever so that the engine added to his braking power. As he was locking up the brakes, the back tire cut side to side as it fought to grab the pavement. In his peripheral vision, he could see that Trailer Trash was making the same desperate effort to stop. He could see that the pack was progressively coming to a stop. Like train cars held together by string, the rest of the pack was collapsing as brothers struggled to avoid slamming into the bikes in front of them.

But for Harold, as well as many others, braking wasn't enough. To avoid hitting Drago, Harold maneuvered Magdelina slightly to the left so that he came careening to a stop with his front time alongside Drago's rear tire. Replays of Harold's near accident had occurred up and down the pack until it looked as though the pack was mushed together and its 2-by-2 form was lost.

Coming to a stop, Harold felt his heart pounding as though it would burst from his chest. He had narrowly avoided an accident and a sense of relief, a soothingly cool-wet sensation starting at his extremities, seemed to wash the panic away. But the relief was short-lived as he heard tires screeching behind him. His first reaction was to look over at Trailer Trash. He saw that the Road Captain, who had stopped with his front tire on the other side of Drago's rear tire, was looking in the rearview mirror extending up from his left handlebar. Harold looked into his own mirror expecting to see the van roaring up behind him. His body was tensed and prepared to jump off in whatever direction offered the best path of escape. Instead, he saw nothing but the empty road behind them.

There is a mathematical formula, modified by the effectiveness of a braking system, and other factors, that will otherwise determine how far a vehicle will travel once the brakes are applied. One of those factors is the speed the vehicle is traveling. Another key factor in this formula is the weight of the vehicle. To put it simply, when everything else is equal, a heavier vehicle generally travels farther while braking. The backup van was several times heavier than Magdelina, Trailer Trash's bagger or any of the other bikes. It was reasonable to assume that, at the back of the pack, Harold and Trailer Trash were about to catch the front bumper of the van in their backsides. Harold felt as though he were caught in a state of limbo, where an accident plays out almost in slow motion. He could hear the van's tires squealing but it had somehow evaporated from view.

Harold's confusion lasted only an instant as the van came screeching to a stop on the shoulder next to Trailer Trash. Peyote had adeptly maneuvered the van to the side to avoid the pack and had merged with the pack so that she neatly avoided running down Harold and Trailer Trash. Once again, relief washed over Harold and, once again, it was short lived.

At the back of the pack, Harold and Trailer Trash were at the crest of a rise in the road and did not initially see what had caused the sudden chain-reaction of panic stops. Assuming the worst – that one or more of his brothers had had an accident – Trailer Trash stood up straddling his bike. This provided him with just enough height to see the front of the pack. As quickly as he stood up, Trailer Trash sat back down.

Seeing Trailer Trash's reaction, Harold began standing but, before Harold was fully upright, Trailer Trash grabbed Harold's arm and said, "Don't." There was alarm in Trailer Trash's voice and Harold immediately froze in place.

As he slowly sat back down, he asked, "What is it." Harold's first thought was that there was a terrible accident up ahead and Trailer Trash was protecting Harold from witnessing the blood and gore of one or more of his dead brothers. In fact, assuming that Reaper and Poacher were out in front, Harold was already assuming the worst for the two presidents.

As Harold's mind wrestled with the potential tragedy up ahead, Trailer Trash said, "Get off your bike and follow me. But stay low."

Harold put the bike in neutral, put the kickstand down and, like Trailer Trash, walked towards the side of the road and around the back of the van with his head crunched down. Puzzled, Harold watched Trailer Trash open the back of the van and begin rummaging through the bags and tents. As Peyote and Dancer looked back from the front seats, Trailer Trash found a blue-vinyl bag. He undid the zipper and pulled out a semi-automatic handgun. At the same time, Trailer Trash reached inside his open leather jacket and pulled out a revolver. Handing the revolver to Harold and checking to see that the semi-automatic was loaded, he again told Harold, "Follow me."

Harold looked down at the gun in his hand. The blue-metaled weapon felt heavy in his hand as he watched the Road Captain peeking out from behind the van into the woods. Apparently convinced no one was watching, Trailer Trash continued quickly in a crouched position to the tree line about 15 feet away with Harold following. Quickly, they moved through the trees paralleling the road and moved closer to the front of the pack. After going about 30 feet, Trailer Trash came to a stop and extended his left arm to catch Harold across the chest. He then took Harold by the front of his T-shirt and pulled him down, so they were both squatting at the edge of a large tree. While holding the automatic loosely in his right hand, Trailer Trash extended his right index finger and held it to his lips indicating that Harold shouldn't make any noise. At the same time, he motioned ahead with the gun for Harold to look.

Harold glanced down through the trees where he could see the front of the pack. There, across the road in front of the pack, Harold saw a white van and a rusty, blue pickup truck stopped, bumper to bumper, blocking the road in front of Reaper and Poacher. From the passenger window of the van, Harold could see the barrel of a rifle pointed out at the pack. The rear door of the van was open, and Harold could see that someone was standing behind it aiming what looked like a double-barreled shotgun at the Banshee Riders. Two bikers were crouched in the back of the pickup with rifles drawn, another was in the passenger seat of the pickup and another, who had apparently left the driver's door open, was leaning across the hood with what Harold recognized as an M-16 or its semi-automatic equivalent. Another gunman was leaning against the front of the van between it and the pickup truck with a revolver balancing his aim against the windshield. Harold recognized the latter biker as the taller one from that morning when he and Red ran into The Clansmen. He also recognized the shorter biker, who had stood by the window of the store that morning, as one of the bikers in the back of the pickup truck.

Immediately in front of Reaper and Poacher were two bikers, one tall and the other short and stocky. From the way the shorter biker was acting, Harold deduced he was probably the president of The Clansmen. The taller biker had his arms folded in front of him cradling a rifle. The shorter biker had a pistol stuck in the front of his pants, but his hands were empty. Harold could see that the shorter biker was talking to Reaper and Poacher. It didn't seem as though he were yelling. Instead, from a distance, the biker seemed surprisingly calm, everything considered.

As Harold followed the Road Captain, it occurred to him that his response to the three Clansmen that morning might have something to do with the current predicament. It began to occur to Harold that, if they got out of this, he might have more to fear from his own club than the Clansmen.

They had continued another 15 or 20 feet when, out of the corner of his eye, Harold saw something move. He stopped suddenly while grabbing Trailer Trash by the arm and pulling him back behind another tree. Now, Trailer Trash was looking to Harold for guidance, which struck Harold as an unexpected turn of events.

Harold motioned down the hill with the revolver towards some bushes by some trees right beside the road. There, among the trees, he could see two more bikers crouched down with rifles leveled on the Banshee Riders from the side.

Trailer Trash whispered, "If anything happens, you take the one on the left. I'll take the one on the right. But don't start anything unless they do," he said while dipping his head and raising an eyebrow as if asking Harold if he understood.

Harold nodded. He realized that having the two of them in the woods gave the club an unexpected edge in a confrontation where the brothers held few of the cards. But Harold also realized it wasn't enough. There was no mistake; The Clansmen had the drop on the Banshee Riders. If the shooting started, Harold was sure some of the brothers would shoot back. With any luck, he and Trailer Trash would take out the two bikers in the woods and, if there weren't any more of The Clansmen in the woods, he and Trailer Trash would try to hit some of the bikers shooting at the Banshees from the vehicles in the road. It just wasn't enough. If there was any shooting, the Banshees would get the worst of it, and Reaper and Poacher would probably be the first to drop.

Now Harold could hear the stocky biker in the road, as though he were working himself into a crescendo, barking at Reaper. Harold raised the pistol and drew a bead on the biker on the left. He saw that Trailer Trash was using a tree to steady his aim with the semi-automatic. The Clansmen in the trees were a good 50 feet away from Harold and Trailer Trash yet, which made for a very difficult shot with the snub-nosed revolver. If the distance made for a difficult shot, the trees and underbrush between Harold and the other biker didn't help matters. Moving closer would improve Harold's aim but, the closer Trailer Trash and Harold moved the more likely it was that the Clansmen would hear or see them coming.

As Harold found a tree to steady his aim he felt a bead of sweat rolling down from his temple. His mouth dry, Harold suddenly remembered Chester's words of caution. It dawned on Harold that this is what Chester was talking about. "In a minute," Harold thought to himself, "I may kill a man." Then the possible repercussions filled his mind — "police, jail, court, prison." Or maybe Harold would have to take off like

Tex and Morticia. "Of course," Harold thought, "he wouldn't be in that boat by himself if the shooting starts." Then it occurred to Harold that, if it happens, and he starts shooting, there's a pretty good chance someone will start shooting back. It suddenly dawned on Harold that he could die there in the woods. All the same, Harold realized he couldn't run. He couldn't stand up, walk out of the woods and say, "I don't want to play anymore." Harold was in it for real and there was no turning back.

He glanced over at Trailer Trash who glanced back and nodded reassuringly. If his brother had any doubts, Harold couldn't tell. "Well, if I'm in I'm in," Harold thought to himself. Then he took a fresh aim at the biker and prepared himself to fire if things went bad.

Harold could still hear the biker yelling at Reaper. Now, he could hear that Reaper was talking, too. Through the trees, Harold caught a glimpse of Reaper looking back through the pack of Banshee Riders. Harold felt a cold chill run through his body as he wondered who Reaper was looking for. "Could he be looking for me?" Harold asked himself. In Harold's mind, it was almost certain that this had something to do with the confrontation in town that morning.

Harold could see that Reaper looked pissed. Poacher also looked back through the club. He didn't look a whole lot happier than Reaper.

With the chance that he might shoot the man in front of him and the chance that he would be in trouble even if nothing happened, Harold began to wonder if he was in a no-win situation. He sought to steel himself to that possibility. But then Harold thought to himself, "This can't be." He'd already told Reaper everything that had happened. Yes, Harold was a bit bold and unresponsive to the Clansmen, but why would Reaper care or blame Harold for that. Even if The Clansmen had ambushed the Banshees over Harold's reaction, it wasn't really Harold's fault.

Reaper and the stocky biker spoke some more. Then the stocky biker poked a finger in Reaper's chest, as though administering a warning, before turning and waving for his brothers to clear the road. And just like that, it was over.

The two Clansmen Harold and Trailer Trash had been covering began moving quietly back farther into the trees giving Harold the sense their bikes were out on the other side of the wooded area somewhere. Harold and Trailer Trash had to move quickly back into the trees to avoid being seen. Hesitating just a moment to make sure the situation really was over, Trailer Trash then motioned for Harold to make his way quickly back to the bikes. When they were safely away from the Clansmen in the woods, Trailer Trash said, "Hurry. The brothers may not have a chance to wait for us."

They reached the bikes just as the rest of their brothers were shifting into gear. Drago and Kilroy pulled over the hill as Harold and Trailer Trash started their bikes. Harold still had the revolver in his hand and Trailer Trash told him to shove it in his pants. The club was a good-hundred feet ahead of them when Harold and Trailer Trash slammed their bikes into gear and tore off after the pack with Peyote bringing up the van behind them.

The Clansmen had backed the white van off the road into the meridian on the left and pulled the pickup ahead on the shoulder to the right. As they rode through, Harold glanced at the pick-up and made eye contact with the Clansman who had leaned against the glass that morning. The Clansman smiled with what Harold took as a victorious grin and casually waved the barrel of his rifle in Harold's direction as if to say, "I told you."

Angered by the biker's flippant manner, Harold felt his face turning red. Before, he had convinced himself to shoot a man in defense of his brothers. For an moment, Harold contemplated how he'd like to shoot the shorter Clansman from the morning, not in defense of himself or his brothers but out of a pure and unbridled desire for revenge.

When they were about half a mile down the road, Harold said, "That fucker," to himself but, apparently, loud enough for Trailer Trash to hear.

Trailer Trash glanced over at Harold and said, "It's OK bro. Just keep riding."

Somehow, Harold sensed that Trailer Trash was glad to see that Harold was pissed, glad to see Harold was taking it personally. Harold also realized that he had handled himself well. He had backed up his brothers while following Trailer Trash's direction.

He hadn't run and, though he hadn't been called upon to shoot anyone, he was ready if things had worked out badly. As he felt the after-effects of an adrenaline rush, Harold also felt a warm sense of pride welling inside. He hadn't just proven himself to the club. He'd also proven himself to himself.

Chapter 21 — Black Pole - Black Toe

The following Friday, as usual, Harold was outside by the bikes during the meeting. About 20 minutes after the meeting started, the front door opened and Red stepped out onto the porch. For the second time since he'd started prospecting, Harold was called inside. He walked into the smoky room tentatively, not sure what was up or what awaited him. His fears were unfounded as Harold discovered he was up for a vote for probate. Falstaff administered another warning about not "fucking up" and, as Harold went over to stand by Samurai, Harold's sponsor handed Harold a top rocker to sew on the back of his rag. Looking at the rocker, Harold appreciated that, with the top rocker, the club was publicly admitting that Harold was one of them – not a full-patch brother but a potential brother. It also meant that, if Harold screwed up, he would do so with the club's name in big letters across his back. It dawned on Harold that this also increased the pressure to keep his shit together.

At the same meeting, Drago was voted back in as a full-patch brother, though a couple brothers complained that Drago hadn't done much to earn it other than showing up at meetings and functions. The criticism coming on the heels of the compliments Harold received during his vote stung Drago a bit. As a result, Harold found Drago a little cold and aloof after the meeting, though his annoyance didn't last long.

Then the discussion turned to the confrontation with The Clansmen. To Harold's surprise, though he'd already convinced himself he wasn't in trouble, Mongrel and Pot Roast were in hot water over the event. The entire story unfolded as Reaper recounted the discussion with the president of The Clansmen.

"I'll tell you," Reaper said to Mongrel and Pot Roast as it seemed they were trying to melt into the carpet. "I've got a mind to knock the crap out of both of you. It's bad enough that I had to sit there getting a lecture from the president of another club but, do you realize, they could have just opened up on us instead of talking."

"You'd have had your brothers' blood on your hands," added Falstaff.

Reaper sat glaring at the two for 15 seconds, that probably felt like 15 minutes to the pair of bikers in trouble, before he asked, "So, what the fuck happened?"

Mongrel and Pot Roast then gave accounts of the fight at the bar in Creighton.

Hearing about the confrontation at the bar, Harold discovered the club wasn't upset with Mongrel and Pot Roast for jumping what turned out to be a pair of Clansmen. Instead, as Reaper shouted, it was a question of not telling anyone. "I don't give a fuck that you two went into town and I don't give a fuck that you knocked a couple of those shitheads around. But what the fuck were you thinking keeping it a secret?" he barked at the two of them. "You two put the entire club in a trick bag."

Pot Roast and Mongrel acted like a pair of school-age boys called into the principal's office, spending much of the time looking down at their boots.

"We didn't know they rode with The Clansmen," Pot Roast protested. "We didn't see any problem beating up a couple citizens."

"We didn't think it was a problem," Mongrel added.

"You're right," Falstaff said. "You didn't think."

The room was silent for a second as Reaper rubbed his chin and glared at the brothers. While Reaper pondered, Harold thought to himself, "Well, it's not like the club wasn't warned." Harold realized that he and Red had delivered a warning, of sorts, when they came back to the campsite after picking up the beer. At the time, the club didn't know why the warning was administered, but the brothers had received sufficient warning all the same.

Finally, Reaper continued, "Why didn't you ask anyone else to go into town with you?"

"We were looking for chicks," Pot Roast half mumbled in response.

Several of the brothers laughed.

"Instead, you found a couple Clansmen and set the club up for an ambush," Reaper continued. "What are you planning for an encore?"

By this time, as Reaper's fury continued to grow, Harold half expected the president to jump across the room and start pounding on the two semi-repentant brothers. At the very least, Harold was certain he and Red would have the help of two new prospects or probates fetching beers and lighting cigarettes for a while. That didn't bother Harold much. But he also worried Mongrel and Pot Roast might be kicked out of the club. Harold liked both of them. Harold had messed with Pot Roast and, even though Harold was following the president's orders, Pot Roast might have developed a grudge towards Harold. Instead, Pot Roast treated Harold with as much respect as anyone else in the club. And Mongrel regularly seemed to run interference for Harold. Harold didn't like the idea that he would lose the two of them as brothers.

The room had gone silent again as Reaper pondered some more. Harold was literally biting his lip in anticipation of the decree he was sure the president would render. When the president spoke again, Harold was completely surprised that any trace of anger was gone from Reaper's tone. In fact, the president was smiling as if it was all a big joke.

"You know, most of your brothers like girls, too," Reaper said. "Any fucking homos here who don't like girls?"

With that, the room erupted into laughter. When the room quieted again, Mongrel spoke up for the first time. "Well, I have been a little worried about the way Grunt's been looking at me since he shit his pants."

Grunt half-jokingly protested with an obscenity-laden retort and the room broke into laughter again.

As the brothers settled down, Reaper got serious again. "You see how shit like this can get brothers killed?" Reaper asked. But the president wasn't just looking at Mongrel and Pot Roast. He was looking around at the entire club, using the situation as a broader lesson. "We can't tell you assholes to stay out of bars, and I'm not going to tell you that you can't pound on a couple of punks like those Clansmen assholes."

"Yeah, well, those punks sure got the drop on us Sunday," Tank responded.

"You don't think we could ambush them in our territory?" Reaper said. "Besides, we're not going to go to war every time one of you gets into a fight. If that was the case, we'd be going to war with someone new every time Pot Roast stepped into a bar."

The brothers laughed again, many of them glancing at their pugnacious brother. Pot Roast had the same pouting look on his face that he wore when the brothers did things to make him puke. He answered with his usual refrain of "You fuckers," but Harold had the sense he was really appreciating the reputation.

By this time, Harold was breathing a big sigh of relief. Then Reaper looked across the room at Harold and said, "Naked Boy, get me a beer."

As Harold went to the kitchen to bring an Old Style back from the refrigerator, he heard Reaper telling the club, "For those of you who don't know, Trailer Trash and our new probate had the drop on a couple Clansmen in the woods while we were shitting our pants out on the highway."

Listening to the president talk, Harold had the sense he was sent for the beer to get him out of the room while Reaper complimented Harold's actions.

"He showed that, if the shooting had started, he was backing us up," Reaper said. "I don't know how much it would have helped but it certainly wouldn't have hurt."

As Harold returned and handed Reaper the beer, Reaper said, "Thanks, probate."

Harold nodded and began walking away as Reaper continued, "But don't let it go to your head. You're still a lower-than-whale-shit fucking probate." Again, the brothers laughed.

Then Reaper looked at Trailer Trash and said, "Having you two out in the woods helped out with Poacher. Otherwise, we would have looked like a complete bunch of assholes."

It dawned on Harold that there was more to having Poacher ride along than simply sharing a campfire. For whatever reason, Reaper wanted to impress the president of the Swamp Rats. As Harold contemplated the implications of that, about the only motivation he could think of was if Reaper and Poacher were considering an alliance of some kind. Or, maybe, they were even thinking of combining the two clubs into one. Harold didn't like the sound of that. He'd already had a run-in with one of the Swamp Rats. Given his choice, Harold would rather see the Banshee Riders form an alliance with the Saxons.

As the club went on to the next order of business, Harold had a sense that the incident with The Clansmen had been resigned to folklore. The brothers would tell the story to new brothers in years to come. They might embellish a bit, Harold wasn't sure. But he liked the idea that he now had a place of honor in the history of the Banshees. Naked Boy was an important element in the burgeoning legend of the Road Day ambush. The only drawback was if Harold got drunk and screwed up his reputation at some time in the future. With that thought in mind, he again resolved to keep his shit together.

The next order of business was a welcome announcement from Falstaff. "My cousin and her husband are renting a summer home out on Lake Chinookan. Actually, it's more of an estate than a summer house. They'll only be up there weekends and two or three weeks over the course of the summer.

"The place is humongous," Falstaff continued. "I was out there yesterday. There's a great big house back from the road and then there's a cabin down by the lake.

"The people who own the property retired to Florida a couple years ago. I get the idea they weren't coming up from Florida much the last several years. When they were coming out, they would sometimes stay in the cabin by the lake and go fishing."

The brothers were silently looking at their vice president, wondering what the point of the story was. For his part, Falstaff looked back puzzled by the lack of understanding in his brothers' faces. "My cousin said they can rent with an option to buy," Falstaff said. When the point still seemed to evade his brothers, Falstaff continued with a note of exasperation, "She said we can use the place for a clubhouse."

"— the estate?" Grunt asked with an expression of glee rising in his voice, as though the club had just won the lottery.

"No, you idiot," Falstaff said, "the cabin. Neighborhood kids have kind of busted the place up a bit. My cousin's husband figures they'll leave the cabin alone if a motorcycle club moves in. I tend to think he's right."

It wasn't quite the news Grunt had jumped to, but it was good news all the same. A buzz of excitement rose among the brothers. Reaper, however, wasn't quite ready to jump up and down about the idea yet.

"What do they want for rent?" Reaper asked.

"No rent," Falstaff said. "It's enough having us keep the riff-raff away."

"Haaaa," Kilroy laughed, "It's like asking the patients to guard the asylum."

Falstaff shot Kilroy a hot glare. "While we're there, no one goes in the big house. What's more, if we see anyone messing around with the house, we knock the crap out of 'em and drop their asses in the lake."

Falstaff explained that he was only half joking about "whacking" anyone who snooped around the house. As he explained it, "Since my cousin and her husband won't be around most of the time, I've convinced them that the club is an excellent security system: better than guard dogs, an alarm system or some Barney with a plastic badge."

"The only problem is that, like I said, the kids got into the place and tore it up a bit, so it will need some work."

The next day, a dozen brothers, including Samurai and Naked Boy, met at Hildie's to take a ride out to the cabin. Leaving the bar, they headed back up to Route 36 and turned right away from Biesenthal. After going about 10 miles, they made two right-hand turns, the second taking them onto a gravel road with a sign by the entrance that read, "Dead End — No Admittance."

As they rode past the sign, Reaper joked to Falstaff, "We can replace that sign with one that says, 'Stay Out!'"

"Yeah," and a picture of a hand holding a gun," Falstaff laughed.

The road was narrow enough that, if cars approached from opposite directions, one would have to pull over and stop tight to one side while the other snuck past. The trees, bordering the road, occasionally intruding into the gravel with their roots, created a canopy over the road that was so thick that it gave the sensation of entering into a tunnel even on a bright, sunny day.

As they continued down the winding road, they passed several gated driveways. With each, the gravel road changed to asphalt as it extended out of sight to a hidden neighboring estate. About a mile down, Falstaff slowed almost to a stop by a large, black-iron gate. A blacktop driveway ran beyond the gate and back towards a large, white house. The gate was mounted in the middle of a fieldstone wall that extended along the road, in both directions, about 100 yards and continued out of sight around the bend ahead of them.

Without putting his feet down, Falstaff came to a complete stop and balanced the bagger in place. Motioning towards the house with his head, Falstaff told Reaper, "That's the estate." Before Reaper could ask, Falstaff continued, "There's a service entrance around the bend." Then Falstaff gave his bike a little gas and rumbled down the road with his brothers in tow.

Around the bend, the brothers found another break in the

fieldstone wall. This time set several feet back from the wall, a pair of 5-inch diameter pipes were buried in concrete extending up about 3-feet from the ground. The tops had rounded caps welded in place and I-bolts attached facing in towards the less-traveled utility path. The path had a mound of grass and weeds growing between two ruts, that ran off from the gravel road. The pipes and their caps were painted brown and between them hung a chain. One side of the chain was permanently attached to the I-bolt on that side of the drive. The other side of the chain was attached to the I-bolt by a large lock.

The brothers were expecting Falstaff to step off the bike and unlock the lock. Instead, he rode his bike at an angle that narrowly allowed him to pass between the pipe and the brick wall on the right side. The tree line started just past the post making it a tight fit to sneak through with the large Harley. It required a properly timed sharp turn to get back onto the path. If he didn't turn sharp enough, or at the right time, Falstaff might have scraped his bike or saddlebags against the pipe, the fieldstone wall or a tree.

Once inside, Falstaff looked back and saw the doubtful expressions on some of his brothers' faces. "If I can make it on my bagger, the rest of you can make it to," Falstaff yelled over the sound of the idling Harleys.

"Come on," Reaper said and then snuck his bike past the chain post and wall before heading down the path behind Falstaff.

One behind the other, the brothers negotiated the entrance to the drive and fell in behind Falstaff and Reaper. Beyond the chained entrance, the path was just wide enough to accommodate a car if the driver was willing to force the vehicle's paint job through the clawing fingers of overgrown branches on either side. This wasn't a problem for the motorcycles. The path was swallowed by the trees as it swung in a long sweeping arc to the left. One by one, as the brothers continued down the path raising their sunglasses so they could see in the darkness.

With startling suddenness, the path turned right and debouched into blinding sunlight and a clearing by the lake. Between the piercing sunlight and the fine particles of dust kicked up by the bikes in front of them, the brothers emerged into the clearing with tearing eyes. One by one, they came into the light and immediately pulled their sunglasses back down.

Harold was the last to exit the tunnel. Unable to see even a few feet in front of him, Harold came to an abrupt stop lest one of his brothers had stopped just ahead. Harold took his glasses back off and wiped his eyes, though it didn't seem to help much. As his eyes cleared, he saw that Tank and Red were about 10 feet ahead. They were side by side surveying the surroundings. With no possibility of a collision, Harold pulled forward and around the two.

To Harold's left, a sloping rocky wall extended up about 30 feet from the ground before rolling back onto the ground above towards the estate house a hundred yards, or so, further on. The ledge extended in about 110 feet from the lakeshore as though a giant's heel had smashed the ground down while stepping across the lake, though it was actually a carving made by an Ice Age glacier. The cliff ran ahead of Harold parallel to the lake almost 150 feet before it curved towards the water's edge. The ledge stopped just short of the lake so that there was a small path running beside the lake. That path opened into the shelf where the bikers were now sitting on their bikes. In the back corner of that shelf, someone had constructed a precipitous wooden staircase to the property above. The shelf was overgrown with grass and weeds with the exception of a narrow and weedy strip that extended into the clearing from the path the brothers had followed out of the woods. It ran back from the woods, like a balding man's thinning scalp, to about 15 feet from the front of a small cabin.

The cabin, with pealing and faded yellow paint and shutters on most of the windows, some hanging at odd angles due to the loss of a top or bottom hinge, was about one-third of the way back from the far end of the clearing. In a mote of tall grass, Harold could just make out that the cabin sat on stacks of cinderblocks. The front door of the cabin was missing, and Harold could see two unpainted vertical spaces about 1-1/2 inches by 12 inches extending down from each side of the door frame. The nails protruding out from the spaces spoke to the stringers that had once filled the spaces and supported the missing stairs into the structure.

The bikers, Harold included, pulled ahead with their bikes until they were next to where Reaper and Falstaff had parked. Almost in unison kickstands were swung out and bikes leaned onto them. The bikers tentatively rested the bikes on the kickstands long enough to make sure the ground below was solid enough to support the motorcycle's weight. Then they stepped off to the left of their scooters and began wandering about the clearing or walked over to the building and hoisted themselves up the three-feet-or-so into the cabin.

Harold found that the grass hid a bounty of empty beer cans, bottles, and other junk. Upon entering the cabin, he discovered its riches of garbage were even more abundant than the trash hidden in the grass. Garbage was strewn across the floor from wall to wall in the main room/kitchen area, as well as the two bedrooms on the cliff side of the cabin. In the center of the debris, and though there was a fieldstone chimney extending up from a fireplace three feet to the right, it appeared that someone had built a fire in the middle of the floor. Random 9-inch by 9-inch brown speckled-linoleum tiles were missing and the plywood beneath was blackened, charred and pitted by the fire.

"Christ," Harold heard Red say as he surveyed the dilapidated condition of the cabin.

Just then, Samurai walked out of the bedroom in the back corner of the cabin further from the lake, and said, "There's an old 110 fuse box in there."

"Does it have power?" Kilroy asked.

"Are you kidding?" Samurai asked. Falstaff and Reaper turned to face Kilroy with expressions that, though unspoken, said the same thing.

Kilroy shrugged as if to say, "Okay, I'm an idiot," and continued across to the far side of the cabin to check out the bathroom. Much faster than he entered the room he exited hollering, "Oh my God." When the others in the cabin looked Kilroy's way, their brother continued, "The water doesn't work either and that doesn't seem to have stopped the punks from using the toilet."

Together, all the brothers turned and looked at Harold as if to say, "Here's a job for you probate." His creativity with Grunt's pants seemed to have convinced the brothers that Harold was the one to turn to with shitty jobs. But Harold doubted that he could hook a fishing line to the toilet and cast it into the lake.

With a slight smile, Harold complained, "Why do I get all the crappy jobs?"

As the brothers laughed, Red spoke up. "I'll take care of the toilet." When everyone looked at Red as though he'd lost his senses, Red responded, "I've got an idea. It's not as good as hooking Grunt's pants to a fishing pole, but it'll work if you think we can get a new toilet."

"I think we can dig something up," Tank said. "What did you have in mind?"

"What does it matter," Red said, "as long as I clean things up in there?"

Tank shrugged and said, "Okay." Then he and the others turned and walked to the door and jumped down outside to discuss the architectural and landscaping alternatives requiring attention to return the cabin to a state reasonably acceptable for occupancy. Only Harold seemed to linger over the mystery of Red's solution. But Red gave Harold the same reply Red had given to Tank.

Red and Harold joined the others just as they were discussing alternatives for removing all the trash inside and outside the cabin. Red let a little of his idea out of the bag when he said, "I'll be digging a hole out behind the house anyway. I'll just make it a little bigger."

It was already assumed that Samurai and Harold would restore electricity to the structure. In spite of that duty, Harold was told he would also help with picking up garbage and cutting the grass.

Harold nodded when Falstaff broke the news about the chores. Reaper, however, added, "You don't have to cut all the grass. We just need a clearing out front here to park bikes and stuff."

"Do we have a mower?" Harold asked.

"I'll bring one out tomorrow morning," Falstaff said. "What other tools should I grab?" Then Falstaff partially answered his own question by looking at Red and added, "I'll bring a couple shovels."

Just when Harold was assuming that the brothers had resolved to start working on the clubhouse the next day, Reaper looked over and told Harold and Red, "You two can get started picking up the garbage right now."

"I've got some garbage bags in my saddlebags," Falstaff said and tossed Red the keys to the bags.

Harold and Red decided to start in the house but, as they approached, Reaper said, "You'll be cutting the grass tomorrow. You may want to make sure you've picked up out here first."

Feeling a little stupid for not thinking of that themselves, Harold and Red turned and began combing the grass picking up trash. Harold was surprised when he saw most of the brothers take bags and begin helping out. Only Reaper and Falstaff continued discussing the remodeling they had in mind for the cabin. Samurai was also not among those picking up garbage. Instead, he got back on his bike and left. Harold asked Kilroy where Samurai was going and was told that he was going home to get his work van.

"He said he might as well get started today," Kilroy added.

Falstaff must have changed his mind too. Most likely, seeing how busy the brothers were, Falstaff realized there was no point in waiting until Sunday. After he and Reaper spoke inside for about 15 minutes, Falstaff climbed on his bike and left. Within an hour, he and Samurai had both returned, Samurai with his work van and Reaper with his pickup truck.

When Falstaff returned with the mower, Harold was ready. However, the job wasn't as simple as running around with the mower. He discovered the grass and weeds were too tall and thick. The mower engine would die if he didn't tip the mower back and rock it into the undergrowth for controlled bites at the grass. Worse than that, he would occasionally run into something they hadn't found while combing the grass for garbage, such as an old bottle or a pipe that would nick the blade and could stop the engine if he hit it too hard. Other times, he would hit some paper and turn it into confetti. It was a long, arduous job.

When Samurai returned, Harold was hoping his sponsor would put him to work pulling wires or digging trenches. But Samurai said, "No, I'm good for now," and Harold went back to cutting the grass.

As he cut the grass, Harold thought about the incident with The Clansmen, the trouble he'd had with 6 Pack, the experience on the other side of the spectrum with Tawny, and how he felt like a member of Samurai and Sue's family. Harold didn't have to think long about what he'd be doing at that moment if he had never inherited his uncle's bike or joined the Banshee Riders. He pictured Mindy behind the bar serving another beer to Harold with a look of contempt on her face, maybe even warning Harold not to get out of hand or she'd cut him off. It seemed like a lifetime ago. No, Harold realized it seemed more like he was contemplating someone else's life. It was as if the Harold who used to haunt Freddie's Place was a different person -- shiftless, untrustworthy, wasting little thought on anyone else while concentrating on how to become as inebriated as possible, as fast as possible. Then, with the hangovers, he would have spells of remorse. Harold wondered how he could have been that person, someone he had as little respect for as everyone else who knew that Harold. What was even more puzzling was that Harold could have changed so much in such a short period of time.

Then it occurred to Harold: 'Had he changed? Was he really a different person?' He still got drunk on a regular basis. The possibility that Harold might get too drunk and find himself in trouble was not beyond the realm of possibility. It even seemed probable if he thought about it. If he had changed, and he generally felt he had, would it stick or was it just a temporary anomaly. In another six months, would Harold find himself back at Freddie's Place falling off a barstool or puking in the bathroom sink, getting his ass kicked as he was tossed out the door for incoherently pissing on a leg of the pool table?

Stripped to his bare chest, Harold was drenched in sweat as the day wore on. By the time the sun began to dip down behind the cliff, Harold had cut an area of grass about 60-feet wide by 75-feet deep and the Briggs & Stratton mower engine was smoking and shuddering under the strain. It occurred to Harold that, as a result of a tough day's work, the mower may have shot its load. When he shut it off, it sputtered on for a few seconds before sustained silence filled the clearing for the first time since late morning. The silence felt good, like a tonic for a pounding pain in his head that met a numbness extending from his arms and legs, the prickly feeling you get in your extremities when you've labored for hours with something that vibrates constantly.

Leaving the smoking mower in the center of the mowed area, Harold hauled himself up and went inside the cabin where he found the rest of the brothers standing in a rough circle drinking beer. Red handed a beer to Harold and said, "I figure you could use one of these."

Harold noticed that the floor of the cabin was completely clear of garbage and that someone had started scrapping the remaining tiles up with a spade that was leaning in the corner of the room as the brothers drank. Harold also noticed through the bathroom door that the toilet had been removed and was nowhere in sight.

Red also had his shirt off and, considering the layer of red dust that covered his skin and clothes, Harold was pretty sure Red had had an equally taxing day digging out behind the cabin.

"Where'd the beer come from?" Harold asked.

The brothers all laughed. But Harold had a sense they weren't laughing at him. Instead, it was if they were impressed with him somehow. Tank explained the brothers' attitude when he said, "Man, you were like a fucking machine out there."

"Have mower will travel," Kilroy said, mimicking the slogan from a television show that had ended a couple decades earlier.

As Reaper threw an arm around Harold's sweaty shoulders he said, "Bro, there's a career waiting for you in landscaping if you ever want it." But when Reaper's arm landed on Harold's shoulder, Harold realized he had a substantial case of sunburn. When he reacted and pulled away, Reaper laughed and said, "Don't worry about it, bro. If you go into landscaping, it will help if you start looking more Mexican anyhow."

Harold smiled to himself but not about Reaper's joke. Harold was remembering how his mother had to nag at him to cut the grass back in Poplar Grove. In fact, Harold was pretty sure he knew how his mother would react if she knew how Harold had spent the day. "What, you can cut the grass for a bunch of derelicts," Marge would scowl, "but you can't cut our grass without my begging you for a little help?"

Harold was surprised when he realized that it was the first time he'd thought about his mother in quite some time. He remembered how angry he used to get with her – how he felt as though she were a nag and a pain. Now, it occurred to him that, since he had left, she would have to hire someone or cut the grass herself. In fact, as though the thought had never crossed his mind before, he realized that she probably did need him around from time to time and that he wasn't much of a son when he was there. He felt a twinge of regret, though not enough that he rushed to his bike and went back down to Poplar Grove.

Through all this, Harold still didn't know where the beer came from. "I think what they were trying to tell you is that you didn't notice anything going on around you while you were cutting the grass," Red explained. "Brothers have been coming and going all day."

Harold shrugged, "Well, you could have fooled me."

"Yeah, I know bro," Red said as he lifted a hand to slap Harold across the back and then left his arm suspended there a moment when he remembered Harold's sunburn.

Harold stepped away, just in case Red decided to go through with the backslap, and said, "Thanks," meaning thanks for not slapping him on the sunburn.

After a while, Falstaff went outside and turned on the stereo in his pickup truck to a country and western station. Work transitioned into recreation after Kilroy, Harold and Red collected enough wood for a fire and built the blaze about 25 feet straight out from the front door of the cabin. Brothers found logs and whatever else they could use as seats around the fire, or simply sat on the ground or stood.

Harold was enjoying the rewards of a full day's work when he saw Samurai and Kilroy looking across the fire at him. Samurai smiled and waved Harold over to join them. When Harold started across by himself, Samurai pointed at Red, indicating Harold should bring the other probate along as well.

When Harold and Red arrived on the other side of the fire, Samurai smiled again and said, "I'm sorry to be the bearer of bad news, but the workday ain't quite over yet."

By this time, it was after 9:30 p.m. and, beyond the fire, the clearing had dissolved into darkness. Harold looked around wondering what kind of job the brothers could have for him and Red at this hour.

Samurai seemed to read Harold's mind. "Don't worry about it," Samurai said. "We just have to take a short ride. Hop in the back of the van."

Harold noticed that at some point during the day, Samurai had hooked up a flatbed trailer to the back of the van. The trailer had a wooden bed and a short, black angle-iron frame around the front and both sides. When Harold asked Samurai where he got the trailer, his sponsor explained that he had borrowed it but, the way Samurai said it, Harold wondered if the trailer's owner was aware they were using it.

There was really nowhere to sit in the back of the van so Red and Harold crouched down as best they could among the tools, electrical parts, and equipment. Samurai and Kilroy conversed casually up front as Harold and Red steadied themselves every time the van took a turn. With the stereo playing, Harold could only make out an occasional word from the front and concluded that, whatever they were up to, it had nothing to do with what Samurai and Kilroy were discussing. In fact, Harold was pretty sure the two brothers were talking about fishing. Harold looked at Red, who was apparently trying to listen in, as well. Red just shrugged and grabbed the angle-iron frame of the parts rack to steady himself as the van took another turn.

They had driven for about 20 minutes when Samurai pulled the van onto the shoulder of an all-but-deserted gravel road. Before shutting the van off, Samurai scanned the road in both directions. Convinced that no one of consequence was in sight, he finally shut off the van. Then he and Kilroy, who had also scanned the road, hopped out of the van and marched into the grass. Samurai looked back and told Harold, "There's some rope behind the wheel well. Grab it."

Outside of the van, Harold looked up and down the road trying to figure out what they were up to. Without hesitation, however, Samurai and Kilroy jumped across a small culvert and continued about five feet further. Samurai looked back at Harold and Red who stood at the edge of the culvert looking puzzled.

"Well, come on," Samurai said. "They won't load themselves."

"What the hell are we doing?" Red asked.

"Just get your asses over here," Kilroy barked. "You'll find out soon enough."

Harold and Red jumped the culvert and walked towards their brothers. When they reached Samurai and Kilroy, Harold virtually tripped over a large object hidden by the darkness and weeds on the ground between the two brothers.

"What the hell?" Harold said as he caught himself. And then he realized what he had stumbled into: "Telephone poles?"

"Well, we're not going to run a phone out to the clubhouse,"

293

Samurai said. "But we do need to run power lines, and I'd like to mount some lights outside."

There were several of the poles lying side by side in the grass at that spot. A little further down Harold could see more poles as his eyes adjusted to the darkness. The poles were obviously offloaded from a flatbed truck during daylight hours and were waiting on the side of the road for a utility crew to come along and erect the poles in a line along the highway prior to running power or telephone lines.

"How many are we going to take?" Harold asked.

"Well," Samurai said as though he were thinking out loud, "I'd like to take three of 'em if we can."

"So, you want to load these onto the trailer?" Red asked.

"Unless you can figure a way to convince them to load themselves," Samurai said.

Harold looked down at the pole at his feet. Even in the moonlight, he could make out a glimmering blackness on one side of the pole. Harold concluded that was the side of the pole that was down after it was treated to retard the effects of the elements. It meant two things to Harold: first, it meant that the shiny side of the pole was probably a little slippery and, second, it suggested that, considering the pole was thoroughly soaked with the retardant, it was certain to weigh substantially more than a dry pole. Slippery and heavy: Harold had clear doubts that they could lift the pole onto the trailer.

"Are you sure we can do this?" he asked.

"I didn't say it would be easy," Samurai chuckled.

"How big are they?" Harold asked.

"They're 20 footers," Samurai replied. "Probably Class 2 — that puts 'em at about 560 pounds.

"Anyhow, I figure we should all grab this end and lift it over the ditch here. Then we'll do the same thing to the other end."

With Harold and Red on the side towards the street, the four bent down and dug their hands into soft, wet earth under the pole. However, they only raised the end of the pole about six inches when, true to Harold's suspicions, the pole slipped out of their hands and thumped back down onto the ground.

"Is everyone OK?" Samurai asked quickly.

They all answered affirmatively, though Red added, "I got all this sticky shit all over my hands though."

The four were about to get a new grip when they saw headlights coming down the road. Samurai told the others, "If it's the law, just let me do the talking."

They watched as the headlights came closer and closer. Harold noticed that the headlights were slowing and muttered, "Oh shit," under his breath. Sure enough, about 50 yards behind the trailer, the lights began pulling over. It was then that the range between the lights separated enough that the four bikers on the roadside realized they were looking at a pair of motorcycles and not a car. As the bikes rolled to a stop, Harold saw that it was Tank and Wide Glide apparently come to help.

As the brothers dismounted from the bikes and walked over, Kilroy called out, "You came just in time."

Tank and Wide Glide didn't respond. Instead, they walked right up to the others. They looked down at the pole between Harold, Red, Kilroy and Samurai and Tank said, "What's the holdup?"

"Well, they're a little heavier than toothpicks," Kilroy said.

But Samurai corrected him, "They're just a little slippery — the dew mixed with the creosote."

Wide Glide laughed and, as he walked to the far end of the pole, he put his hands out on Harold's and Red's chests and gave a little shove. Then he said, "Out of the way, children." When Wide Glide reached the other side, he stood off the end of the pole and reached down with both hands as Tank did the same thing from the other side. The two larger brothers picked the pole up between them and started swinging the pole side to side.

"On three," Tank said. Then, each time when the pole was in the backward swing away from the road, he counted, "One, two, three." On the third swing, the brothers flung the pole over the culvert. It landed with a hard thud about two feet past the ditch.

For a second, the pole just sat there. Then, as if it had reconsidered the idea, it rolled back towards the culvert.

"Probates, stop that pole," Wide Glide directed.

Harold and Red leaped into action, diving across the culvert and catching pole at the edge of the trench. Standing in mud at the bottom of the ditch, they fought to hold the pole in place as Tank and Wide Glide jumped to the other side. Tank and Wide Glide picked the pole up the same way as before and walked over next to the trailer. They counted three again and tossed the pole over the framing and onto the flatbed where, not only the pole but the trailer itself bounced off its tires several times before settling down.

While Tank and Wide Glide were depositing that pole on the trailer, Kilroy quietly, but with a trace of urgency, told Harold and Red to get up out of the ditch. "Come on," Kilroy said. "The four of us ought to be able to do at least one of these things."

With Red and Kilroy on one end and Harold and Samurai on the other, they managed to pick up another pole that was four feet beyond the culvert. By that time, Tank and Wide Glide were almost back and Tank said, "Just drop it by the edge of the culvert before someone gets hurt."

Kilroy's didn't take the comment well. "What the fuck is that supposed to mean?" he asked.

"It means you ladies should get out of the fucking way so the men can do their work," Tank retorted.

Tank's response was more than Kilroy cared to tolerate and he dropped his hold on that end of the pole to the extent that Red jumped out of the way but not quite in time to fully avoid the pole coming down and nipping one of his toes.

Kilroy started towards the culvert in a beeline to meet Tank head on. Kilroy didn't take more than a step, however, when Red grabbed the full-patch brother by the arm and spun him around. When the first end of the pole had hit the ground, Harold and Samurai were forced to drop the other end. Seeing Red's arm cocking back for a punch, Samurai darted towards the other end of the pole with Harold, Tank and Wide Glide rushing up behind. There was no way that Samurai could traverse the distance between the two ends of the pole before Red landed a solid right on Kilroy's jaw. Caught off guard, Kilroy was knocked back but only for a second.

One moment, Kilroy was prepared to fight his brother Tank. The next moment he found himself going at it with a probate. Kilroy launched himself at Red and, as Red went down on his back, Kilroy drove his shoulder into Red's gut as he hit the ground. It was a tackle Kilroy had learned while playing high school football. The dual impact of Kilroy and the ground blasted the air out of Red's lungs and, for an instant, he was incapacitated.

Kilroy was prepared to take advantage of Red's condition by lifting himself into a kneeling position with his right cocked back to return the punch. Before Kilroy could land the punch, however, he was stripped off of Red by Samurai. As Samurai was pulling Kilroy away, Red recovered enough to stand in preparation for a fresh assault. Harold grabbed hold of Red from behind just as Tank and Wide Glide arrived. With Samurai and Harold holding Kilroy and Red apart, Tank and Wide Glide stepped into the center of the fracas.

"What the fuck's the problem?" Wide Glide hollered at Red and Kilroy.

At that point, Kilroy and Red ceased struggling. Red bent over to try to complete the process of getting his breath back. Kilroy put a hand up to check his jaw where Red had landed the blow.

It was occurring to Harold that Red was probably about to be busted down to prospect again. Harold assumed it was kind of like in the army; If you hit an officer you were in deep shit.

Harold heard Tank complain, "We thought we'd come out and give you assholes a hand, but if you don't need it, just let us know. We can always go back and drink beer by the campfire."

"Are you here to help us or are you here to fuck with us?" Kilroy yelled angrily.

Wide Glide interceded at that point. "We were just worried that with four of you, it's pretty hard to toss it across the ditch," Wide Glide said. "It's actually easier with two of us."

"We could just walk it through the ditch," Kilroy said, as his temper appeared to ebb a bit.

"You'd have a better chance of getting hurt that way," Tank said. "Look at Red's and Naked Boy's pants."

They all looked down and saw that Harold and Red had mud up about eight inches from the bottom of their boots and a shiny black substance above that.

"Now," Tank said, pausing for a second, "Do you want our help or not?"

Kilroy looked like he was thinking about it. Samurai only waited a moment before he answered. "Absolutely."

"Good," said Wide Glide. "If you guys can bring the poles over to the edge of the ditch, we'll toss them over. And if we hurry, maybe we can get it done before a cop comes along or some citizen decides to do his civic duty and drop a dime on us."

Harold, Red, Samurai, and Kilroy headed back to their original positions by the pole, but Tank said, "Here, why don't you let us get that one. You guys can grab the other one."

As they stepped out of the way, Harold saw Red and Kilroy shake hands. They shook for a moment and then they embraced each other in a big hug. As they separated, Harold heard Kilroy say, "You OK?"

"Sure," Red said. "You?"

"Me?" Kilroy joked. "You think I never been punched better than that?" As he said it, he took his jaw in one hand and moved it from side to side as if checking to see that nothing was broken.

As Harold, Red, Samurai, and Kilroy picked up the last of the three poles, Harold watched Wide Glide and Tank throw the second pole across the ditch. Watching, Harold was amazed at the strength of his two brothers.

This time, however, when they threw the pole, there was no one to catch the pole before it rolled back into the ditch. It picked up speed and hit the mud at the bottom with sufficient force that it splattered mud into the air and all over Tank and Wide Glide. As the brothers jumped back too late, Kilroy broke into laughter as though he'd had the last laugh. Tank gave him a harsh glare that quickly broke into a grin.

After dropping the third pole next to the culvert, Harold, Red, Samurai, and Kilroy stood with Tank and Wide Glide looking down at the second pole half buried in the mud at the bottom of the trench. When Tank and Wide Glide started down into the trench to retrieve it, Samurai stopped them and said, "I'll pull the truck up after you load this one. Then we can grab another one from further up the road."

Back at the clubhouse, after they had removed the poles from the truck, one each by the locations where Samurai intended to erect them later, Red pulled off his boot and examined his foot. Harold and Kilroy noticed that Red's toenail was completely black.

"Shit, bro," Kilroy said. "Sorry 'bout that."

Samurai walked up just then and said, "You're gonna lose the toenail, Red."

Red replied, "I'm thinking my toe is broken."

Kilroy looked devastated by this news and all the more so when

Tank walked over, saw Red's toe and said to Kilroy, "Good job."

Harold and Samurai drove Red to emergency care, though they stopped to drop the trailer off on the side of a deserted road first.

"Why are you leaving the trailer here," Red asked.

Samurai looked back and smiled, "Maybe it's best we're not caught with it." Then Samurai admitted he had intended to return the trailer where he found it. "But that's the other direction from the hospital."

Before Harold could get out to unhitch the trailer, however, Red said, "I can wait. Why don't we bring it back? We can stop for a couple beers on the way, too."

It was almost 2 a.m. by the time they returned the trailer, had a couple beers each at a bar along the highway and delivered Red to the hospital. A couple hours later, Red emerged from the back area to find Harold and Samurai watching television in the waiting area.

Red hobbled up to them holding a boot in one hand and wearing a white cloth boot with a brace on the bottom. "Is it broken?" Samurai asked.

Red nodded and said, "They told me to wear this thing and stay off of it. I'm supposed to make an appointment with my doctor Monday."

"Do you have a doctor?" Harold asked. When Red said, "No," Harold asked, "So, what are you going to do?"

"I don't know," Red said. "I'll probably wear this thing until it feels better and then forget it."

"Fuck that," Samurai said assertively. "I'll have Sue make an appointment for you at our doctor." When Red began to protest, Samurai continued, "What do you think we're going to do, wait until gangrene sets in and your toe falls off."

From the hospital, Samurai found an all-night tavern and the trio had some more beers. Finally, about 7 a.m., they ordered some beer to go and went back to the clubhouse. They found Grunt and Bitters curled up in their sleeping bags on the floor of the clubhouse and decided not to wake them. Instead, they went outside and sat by the charred timbers of the fire as if it were still lit and providing heat.

As they drank, Harold volunteered to begin digging holes for the posts. "That's OK, bro," Samurai said. "I've got it covered."

"What, are you going to steal a post-hole digger?" Harold asked with a smile.

Samurai smiled back. "No, I have a friend I use when I need to bore holes. He owes me a bit. I'll give him a call a little later."

Then he looked at Harold as though he had just realized what Harold said. Not sure whether Harold was razzing him or not, Samurai said, "What, do you think I'm a kind of kleptomaniac or something?"

"Well, you did steal a trailer to swipe some utility poles," Harold said. "I just thought you might want to be consistent."

Samurai took it as a compliment and raised his beer to Harold.

When their drinks were done, after insisting Red stay off his feet instead of joining them, Harold and Red began ripping out most of the wiring and fixtures in the house. "I don't trust this shit," Samurai said of the existing electrical system. "Besides, I figure I'll upgrade to 220 if we've got enough power coming out here."

Harold smiled to himself. He didn't know how the rest of the clubhouse would turn out, but he already knew that a new home couldn't expect any better. "Pays to know people in the trades," he said to Samurai.

"You bet," Samurai said without looking up from where he was working.

Chapter 22 — Scratch n Sniff and the Monk

The clubhouse underwent a radical change in a remarkably short period of time. Two weeks after first rolling into the clearing by the cliff, Harold was amazed by the transformation. The clubhouse still needed a paint job, but the roof was patched with new plywood and fresh shingles. Several brothers with carpentry experience heisted the necessary lumber and built a porch level with the front door that wrapped around the front of the house and the side facing the lake. Adjacent to the house and only a few feet in from the lake, Samurai's friend bore a hole for one of the posts. Another went in at the front corner of the cabin closest to the cliff. The third post was erected at the top of the cliff adjacent to the one by the cabin. Off the top of each post, Harold and Red attached large outdoor light fixtures with sensors so they would turn on automatically at dusk and off when the sun came back up in the east.

Inside, Mongrel's cousin, a plumber, installed a new toilet and replaced much of the plumbing to it and the bathroom and kitchen sinks. Also, inside, the brothers knocked down the wall between the living area and the bedroom closest to the front door. Across the opening, they installed a header at the ceiling and built a bar in place of the wall. The bar extended out from the exterior wall to about three feet from the opposite wall. Then the bar turned and headed back into the room. It only stopped a couple feet short of the exterior wall to allow access for brothers who bartended.

Reaper and Tank went under the house and added supports under the center of the floor in the living area. Then they nailed a three-quarter inch plywood sheet on the floor above. Half a dozen brothers, including Harold, then went to Tank's house where the club's pool table was long stored in anticipation of the next clubhouse. They brought the table back to the clubhouse and set it up on top of the plywood. Like the crowning jewel, Samurai hung a rectangular Budweiser light fixture over the pool table, even though most of the brothers drank Old Style.

Around the plywood and extending into the area with the bar, Wide Glide installed hardwood flooring. When Reaper asked where the flooring came from, Wide Glide smiled and said, "Don't ask."

Reaper smiled back and said, "We should throw a party for all the citizens around here when we're done, just our way thanking them for their contributions.

Along with the light over the pool table, Harold and Samurai put up track lighting and replaced all the receptacles. With 220-amp service, using an old panel he'd saved from a demolition project, Samurai installed outdoor electrical outlets on the back of the clubhouse and several inside the new porch. When Harold asked, "What are these for?" Samurai answered with one word, "Bands." Harold began to recognize the utilitarian nature of the club's remodeling of the cabin.

The club hung a solid-core wooden door in the front of the clubhouse and Grunt set about carving "GO AWAY!" at eye level on the outside of the door, along with a carving of a hand holding a revolver pointed directly at whoever came to the door.

For the finishing touch inside, some of the old ladies wiped the panel walls down with polish. They also brought an assortment of mops, brooms, rags, and cleaners. They gave the clubhouse a thorough cleaning paying special attention to the bathroom. "The brothers don't care if things grew in here," Peyote said. "But if I'm going to set my ass on this 'throne,' it has to be respectable."

Then Dancer brought in a canvas painting of an old Indian warrior sitting on a horse looking wistfully across a prairie as the horse grazed from the tall grass at its feet. She'd no sooner hung the painting than Reaper walked inside and blew a gasket.

"What the fuck is this?" Reaper demanded as he stared at the painting with a look of disgust.

Dancer was so completely caught off guard that the only words she could come up with were, "It's mine."

"Well, if it's yours, hang it in your house," Reaper growled. "You can even hang it around your neck for all I care but, if don't get it off my wall, I'll throw it in the fucking fire."

Capsize, who witnessed the confrontation, stepped up as though to defend his old lady. He never got a word out. Reaper turned on him before Capsize had a chance. "This is our fucking clubhouse. We don't need any doilies or flowers to give the place atmosphere, got that?"

Shortly thereafter, Reaper coordinated the decoration of the clubhouse. This included, among other items hung on the walls, a 3-D Hamms beer picture with a lighted sparkling stream that flowed across the front, a framed Easyrider poster, a black-light poster of a near naked woman with breast armor and a sword, several fluorescent beer signs, a large wooden plaque with the club's colors carved into its face, and a large velvet painting of dogs shooting pool.

One day, as they were running some wiring to a new ceiling light in the remaining bedroom of the clubhouse, Samurai asked Harold, "What would you think about doing electrical work full-time?"

"Seriously?" asked Harold.

Harold was finding the position on the loading dock in Earlsville increasingly boring. As he suspected, working for Samurai would include a nice pay increase.

"It would be kind of an apprenticeship," said Samurai. "You'll still be doing the shit work – digging trenches and stuff – but you'll also learn the trade."

"That sounds great!"

"Yeah, well, it is great, but only if you keep impressing me the way you have lately," said Samurai.

"I don't know how to thank you, bro," Harold said as he felt an emotional wave of appreciation.

"I'll tell you how you can thank me," Samurai shot back. "Don't make me sorry I hired you. Fuck up and I'll fire your ass as fast as I hired you."

"You won't regret it," said Harold, as though trying to close a sale that might slip away at the last moment.

Samurai smiled, "If I was really worried, I wouldn't have offered you the job in the first place."

With the steady use of the clubhouse, the available firewood was quickly consumed. Early the next Saturday morning, when Harold, Red and several brothers had crashed at the clubhouse following the meeting-night festivities, Harold was getting up from a blanket on the floor in the main room when he heard tires on the gravel outside. Bleary eyed, he walked out the door to find Snake and Wide Glide pulling up by the porch in a rusty, old, orange Chevy pickup truck. Harold's first thought was that something was wrong with the truck; the frontend was abnormally high in the air. But he then realized that the truck's cargo bed was overloaded with logs neatly cut in 16-inch sections.

As the brothers got out of the truck, Harold said, "Good morning."

They both looked back at him with wide grins as Snake leaned the driver's side of the bench seat to get something from behind it. As he came around the front of the truck, Harold saw that Snake had an axe in his hand. He thrust the axe at Harold: "Hey probate, got a little job for you."

Harold took the axe, with an 'Oh shit' look on his face. Then, he asked, "Mind if I pee first?"

"Knock yourself out," said Snake, with a sweeping gesture to the ground around them.

When Harold got up, he was planning to go to the john but was interrupted by the sound of the truck outside. He realized that he really didn't need to go inside to piss so he leaned the axe at the corner of the cabin, walked beyond the corner and pissed on the wall.

As he walked back zipping his fly, and reaching for the axe, Wide Glide said, "Better unload the truck first. We're going back for another load."

When Harold said, "Fuck!" Snake and Wide Glide laughed and headed up the stairs and into the clubhouse.

Harold spent a good portion of the weekend, and several evenings during the week, splitting logs and piling the firewood along the cliffside of the cabin. He had taken to giving Red a hard time about "missing all the fun" because of his bad toe. Red would give him a faux pout and say something to the effect of, "Sorry, bro. I only wish I could help," and then raise a toast to Harold with the beer in his hand.

By the following Saturday, the wood was piled about eight-feet high and about 16-feet along the cliff-side wall.

Harold had spent most of the day working on a house with Samurai and arrived at the clubhouse late in the afternoon hoping to finish splitting a manageable pile of logs leftover from his work the previous evening. Instead, as he pulled up to the clubhouse on Magdelina, Harold found Snake's pickup out front with another load of logs.

Anyone who has almost completed a long and arduous project only to find they have much more to do yet is likely to feel a sense of frustration. That's what Harold was feeling as he got of his bike. He expressed his frustration by staring at the load of wood and barking, "FUCK!"

Laughter erupted from the porch where Harold hadn't noticed Snake and Mongrel leaning against the railing. Harold's first thought was that, as hard as he had worked on the firewood, it was a bit meanspirited for the brothers to laugh at his efforts. He found himself fighting back words he probably would have said if he was also a full-patch brother.

Snake must have noticed Harold's frustration. He quickly said, "It's OK, bro. You don't have to split this now. Just pile it up beyond the wood you've already split."

Harold looked up at the brothers with a mixture of an appreciate smile that only partially erased the frown on his face. "Can I get the keys?" he asked. "I'll back the truck up along the side of the cabin."

Snake flipped him the keys and he was soon working up a sweat stacking logs. He was at it only a short time when Snake and Mongrel came around the side of the house and gave him a hand. Harold was surprised and impressed. Clearly, they didn't have to help. When he said, "Thanks," he meant it and his sincerity was evident in his tone.

Once the truck bed was empty, and the wood was stacked, Snake slapped Harold on the back and said, "You been doing a good job this week, Naked Boy." Standing back to admire all the wood Harold had split, Snake added, "That's about six cords of wood you've split already."

Harold hadn't really thought about it that way; his focus all week was on completing the job. Now, he looked at the wood with a sense of satisfaction and smiled.

"So, probate, why don't you let me buy you a beer," said Snake, and the three headed in, past the small pile of logs he had first planned to split that day, and into the clubhouse.

Inside, they stood at the bar drinking their beers as Mongrel asked Snake about some lady he'd seen recently on the back of Snake's bike.

Snake looked up at the ceiling for a minute as though trying to think who that could be. "Little brunette?" he asked.

"No. Blonde. She was wearing jeans and a bikini top," said Mongrel.

"Oh," said Snake. "That'd have to be Gretchen."

"Hard to keep track of 'em all, eh?" said Samurai, who had just come in the door behind them. "My heart bleeds for you, bro."

"Where'd you come from?" said Mongrel. "In your work truck?"

"Naah. Got the bike on stealth mode," he said.

"Stealth mode?"

"Yeah, I rolled in slow – sneaking up on you bastards."

"Wow," said Snake. "Good job."

As Snake gave Samurai a beer, Harold said, "I think I'll finish splitting that last pile of logs in front of the porch."

A short time later, Mongrel, Snake and Samurai came out on the porch, apparently, to watch Harold split logs as they nursed their beers. Even Red showed up on his bike and joined them.

Working up a sweat, Harold had taken his shirt off.

"Look at dose rippoling biceps," said Mongrel, in a voice imitating the actor Arnold Schwarzenegger from the 'Conan the Barbarian' movie he had recently seen.

Harold smirked, assuming Mongrel was busting his chops. But it also dawned on Harold that, with all the work he'd done helping Chester around the farm, on the loading dock in Earlsville, working for Samurai, cutting the grass at the clubhouse, and now splitting logs, he might have a little more definition and bulk in his arms. It even occurred to Harold that he'd lost a bit around the middle, too.

While Harold was considering improvements to his body, Samurai appeared to pop his bubble: "They're awful naked though, don't you think?"

"Well, his name is 'Naked Boy,'" said Red.

The brothers were laughing but Samurai interrupted: "No. I'm serious. He's hardly got a freckle on his arms. That just ain't right."

"I think you're on to something there," said Mongrel. "Could be we need to make a Scratch-n-Sniff road trip."

"Scratch-n-Sniff?" asked Harold.

"Don't you worry your pretty little mind about it, probate," said Samurai. "Just finish splitting those logs."

By that time, Harold was down to his last two logs. As he finished, Red was taking the logs and hobbling over to put them on top of the stack by the wall, to which Mongrel said, "Hop along there, Festus."

As Harold put his shirt back on, he saw that the others, except for Snake, were standing at the bottom of the stairs waiting for him. Samurai was even holding Harold's leather jacket and colors.

As they started towards the bikes, Harold noticed that Snake wasn't coming along and stopped to look back at him. Snake saw him looking and, smiling, said, "Sorry, bro. I got a date with that little brunette I mentioned."

Mongrel, Samurai, Red and Harold were soon rolling north and over the state line. About 20-miles north of the border, they pulled into a gravel parking lot in front of what looked like a faded-yellow Cape Cod house someone had converted into a tavern.

Inside, they ordered a round of beers and Mongrel asked the bartender, "Is he here?"

As the bartender refilled a glass for someone else at the bar, he said, "Yeah. Took some kid upstairs a little while ago."

"Mind if we take these upstairs?" asked Mongrel as he held his beer stein up.

"Just bring 'em back later," the bartender said.

Mongrel thanked him and then proceeded out the door followed by Samurai, Red and Harold. They turned right and went around the corner of the building where a rickety, rusted stairway was precariously hanging against the wall, one 3X3 square-iron tube buried in concrete and running up to the outside corner of the upper landing. With the mix of angle iron and different sized plumbing pipe for the railing, Harold had the sense the stairs were put together with spare parts. The way the stairs swayed and rocked as the four climbed, he also wondered whether it was a good idea for all four to go up at the same time.

They made it to the top without the stairs collapsing and, one-by-one, disappeared into a doorway cut into the wall. Harold followed his brothers into a small room with a heavy odor of sweat, tobacco and pot. The first room with a cheap L-shaped sofa in the far corner, had heavily matted, and dirty shag-red carpeting. In front of the sofa was a large, round, white-linoleum table, too-big to be reasonable for the room, with numerous cigarette burns, several Easyriders magazines, a Playboy open to the centerfold as though someone was called away while checking out the hot-naked blonde in the photo, a pack of rolling papers, a small mirror of the type a woman would carry in her purse and a single-edge razor. On the wall to the left, near a door opened enough to show a small sink and toilet, was a cheap nightstand with a 13-inch television, one of its rabbit-ear antenna broken and augmented with a clump of aluminum foil.

As they entered the room, the brothers turned to the right and edged, as though on a narrow cliff, passed the table and into the kitchen. The kitchen was too small for them all and Harold wound up on the red-carpet looking over his brothers' shoulders while he felt the rhythmic thump, more than the muffled music, from the jukebox in the bar below.

There was a small, single-well sink and stainless counter on the left. The sink and counter were filled with dirty dishes, as well as a one-burner, portable-electric heating element that was plugged into an outlet at the base of a light fixture on the wall above the sink. In the back corner of the room, behind a small kitchen table, was a battered, white refrigerator that stood about four-feet high.

Sitting at the table, his back to the sink, was what Harold would have described as a young jock. He was obviously fairly tall and muscular, with a thick neck and a blonde head of hair. Around the corner of the table, with his back to the door, was what Harold assumed was a man. On the back of his beat-up Levi vest, visible above the back of the chair, was a large Harley Davidson patch, its wings stretching from one side to the other. Below the shoulders were smaller patches. One read "Ass, Gas or Grass – no one rides for Free" and the other read, "Free Mustache Rides." Harold could barely make out the smaller patches as they were half covered up by long, stringy, greasy hair. He could tell that the hair was also hanging down, like a veil, on the sides of his face, which was bent down over the young man's right arm.

Harold could hear a vibration, similar to a dentist's drill, and could see what looked like a pen etching a black line on the young man's arm. The tattooist's left hand, in a pink-plastic glove, was under the thick of the young man's arm, close to the pit, holding

308

the arm steady the way a star football player would hold a ball while signing an autograph. When the artist rotated his arm, obviously stretching it from too-much time in the same position, Harold saw that, like a party favor you spin around to make noise, the back of the pen was attached to a pair of chrome plates on either side of a pair of copper coils, with a rubber band around the coils and a thin rod that ran out of the pen to a pin at the back.

Harold was focused on the tattoo pen, when the artist suddenly sat back straight and bellowed, "Think you could give me some air to breath here, damn it?"

Samurai was chuckling as Harold worked his way around the table making room for the others to come out of the kitchen, though Mongrel stayed there watching the artist at work. Samurai and Red moved past Harold and sat on the sofa where Samurai picked up the Playboy, admired the centerfold and began flipping through the pages.

A few minutes later, the drilling of the tattoo gun stopped, and they heard the artist say, "I have to change needles. If you gotta piss, or something, now's your chance."

A few seconds later, the young man came into the kitchen and worked his way past the table before going into the bathroom. Red looked at Harold and, grinning, said, "Looking a tiny bit pale, isn't he?"

Harold hadn't noticed and glanced that way, but it was too late as the door closed. Only a few seconds later, there was a large thud from the bathroom. Harold looked at the door and then back at the others. He found the others looking at him, including the tattooist standing at the kitchen door.

Harold was momentarily stunned the tattooist's complexion. It was as if the man had stuck his face into a beehive and allowed the bees to have their way with him. There were bumps on top of bumps. As he was staring at the man, he realized the tattooist was speaking to him: "Did you hear me?"

"What?" said Harold.

"What the fuck?" he said and moved, with the speed of familiarity, past the table and pushed Harold out of the way as he approached the bathroom door. He banged on the door a couple times while hollering, "Hey!" Then, he turned the knob but, when he began to open the door, it only moved an inch or so before it hit something solid. Unperturbed, the tattooists stepped back and launched himself into the door. The door hardly moved so he tried it again, attacking the door each time with increasing violence. About the fifth time his shoulder slammed against the door, he was rewarded with a groan from within. This inspired him further and he stepped back about four feet before launching his shoulder at the door with all his energy.

There was an angry "Owww" from the other side.

"Get the fuck up, God damn it," he said.

When he stepped back again, Harold worried that, if the young man had got up, this time, when the tattooist hit the door, he might go flying into the bathroom. But instead, there was a rustling inside the bathroom and the tattooist simply walked up and opened the door. Inside, Harold could see the young man sitting on the floor rubbing his head.

"Can you get up?" the tattooist asked. When he didn't answer, the tattooist looked at Harold and said, "Give me a hand."

As the tattooist stepped over the jock into the bathroom and turned to get under the young man's left arm, as he expected, Harold saw the patch on the front of his vest that read, "Scratch-n-Sniff." Harold got under the jock's right arm and they lifted him onto his feet and walked him into the living room. Making no effort to be gentle, the tattooist dumped him onto the sofa while muttering, "Fucking punks," and headed back to the kitchen.

As he reached the kitchen, he glanced at Mongrel and asked, "You looking for some ink?"

"Yeah. Not for me today, though," said Mongrel. As he threw his arm over Harold's shoulder, he added, "We need some art on our probate here. He's looking all naked and stuff."

Without asking, Mongrel snuck past went over to the refrigerator and took a spiral dirty, white 3-ring binder off the top. He dropped it on the table and told Harold, "Take a look."

Harold flipped the binder open and started looking at the pages. The first thing he noticed were the prices written in thin-tip black marker by each drawing. The prices were ranging from $50 to as much as $300 for a drawing that took up an entire page. Just as the prices were beginning to register, Scratch-n-Sniff said, "Your club gets a 10-percent discount. And if you got any coke, that helps, too."

The tattooist had hardly said this when, as though he was waiting for the moment, Mongrel dropped a folded, white-paper packet on the table.

"Now, that's what I'm talking about," said Scratch-n-Sniff. "Hey, Samurai, run that mirror and razor in here, will yeah?"

As Harold continued to leaf through the pages, while doing the math to figure out what 10-percent off would represent, and wondering what the 'coke discount' would represent, Samurai came in and put the mirror and single-edge razor on the table. In no time, the tattooist had cut five lines on the mirror, rolled up a dollar and inhaled the first line up his nose.

"Go ahead," said Mongrel. "Take another."

Scratch-n-Sniff gave Harold what he assumed was a smile and said, "Pick any tat $100 and under and it's $20 bucks." As he said it, however, he noticed that Harold was about to point out a naked woman intertwined with a snake that was marked at $120. "What the fuck," said Scratch-n-Sniff.

As the artist prepared his equipment for Harold's tattoo, he asked the next logical question: "Where do you want it?"

Harold immediately pointed to his right arm below the shoulder but was surprised when Scratch-n-Sniff gave him a look that suggested Harold wasn't too bright. While Harold was trying to decipher the look, Samurai said, "Put it somewhere else."

Harold looked at his sponsor, still puzzled. But Mongrel said, "Don't argue with your sponsor."

Harold shrugged his shoulders and looked down at both of his arms. Then he pointed at his left forearm. "How 'bout here?"

Scratch-n-Sniff didn't say a word but went back to work preparing for the tattoo.

The tattooist was drilling on Harold's arm for about 20 minutes when Samurai noticed that there wasn't any beer left in the fridge. He started to send Red downstairs on a beer run but Mongrel interrupted, "Hey, let's go down and get a drink – see if there's any action down there."

"What do you expect to find down there?" asked Samurai.

"Oh, you never know," Mongrel laughed.

About 45-minutes later, Harold heard the sound of people coming up the stairs and laughing. He was pretty sure he heard a girl's voice, too, suggesting that Mongrel's search had met with some success.

Stumbling in the door behind Red and Samurai, and ahead of Mongrel, was a 20-something girl with long-and-wild auburn hair. Her face and body had that slight-puffy look that sets in for many a barfly who doesn't worry about the calories while downing enough beer to keep them regularly inebriated. At least, that's what Harold suspected. She was wearing jeans that were just a little-too snug and a burnt-orange shirt with only two-of-seven buttons in holes, and these one-hole too high.

As she came in the door laughing, she fell forward several steps and, just when it appeared she would do a head-plant into the wall above the sofa, she caught herself just long enough to change her momentum in the opposite direction. If Mongrel wasn't coming in behind her, she might have continued right back out the door and, presumably, over the railing. Instead, Mongrel caught her from behind. His hands, however, came around in front of her and firmly grabbed two braless, softball-sized breasts that were straining at her shirt.

"Nice catch," said Samurai with a grin.

"Thanks," said Mongrel with an even bigger grin as his hands were kneading the girl's breasts.

As Harold watched, the girl began undoing one of the buttons, clearly intent on taking off her shirt. In her condition, this proved more difficult than she expected and, losing her patience, she pulled on both sides of the shirt so that the buttons popped off and went flying across the room.

"Woops," she said before breaking into a fresh round of giggles.

As she pulled the shirt off, Scratch-n-Sniff said, "Hey, Monica, here's someone who's never seen your tits before."

"Whealy?" she drunkenly responded and headed towards the kitchen as though determined to make sure there was no one left who had never seen her with her shirt off.

As she came into the kitchen, she stumbled and fell onto Harold, her breasts landing against the side of his face, and eliciting a growl of, "God Damn it, Monica," from Scratch-n-Sniff who had pulled the tattoo gun away in the nick of time.

She stumbled upright as Mongrel slid by behind her. He gave

Scratch-n-Sniff and Harold each a beer and put another 10 beers into the refrigerator. Just then, Monica noticed the patch on the front of Harold's rag.

"Naked Boy?" she hollered. She stepped towards him and pulled his head to her breasts, like a mother comforting a child, and asked, "Weel you get nakid fer me?"

"You never know," said Harold with a grin.

But Scratch-n-Sniff was not pleased. "Hey, Monica, why don't you go in the other room and take your clothes off for everyone." It was clear he was saying this to get rid of her so she would stop jostling Harold while the artist was working on his tattoo. But Monica, responding as though someone had told a kid there was candy in the other room, was quickly headed that way.

As Mongrel followed her out of the room, he said to Scratch-n-Sniff, "She got kicked out downstairs for taking her shirt off again."

"What's new?" said Scratch-n-Sniff.

Harold's tattoo took about three-and-a-half hours. He tried to converse with the tattooist but got the feeling he didn't like to chat when working, or maybe didn't chat much in general. The others had drifted in and out from the other room as they watched the progress. They also went downstairs for another beer run when the first 12-pack ran out. When Scratch-n-Sniff was done, however, it was just him and Harold in the kitchen.

"Whaddya think?" said Scratch-n-Sniff after giving the tattoo a final wipe and before covering it with Vaseline and wrapping it with sterile gauze and tape.

Hold held his arm in several positions so he could see the tattoo from different angles. Finally, he smiled at Scratch-n-Sniff and said, "That looks great."

Harold got up and went in the other room to show it to the others but found only Samurai and Red drinking a couple beers and using quarters on the edges of other coins to make them flip in the air and, hopefully, to fall into an empty cup in the middle of the table. Samurai had just sent a dime into the cup when Harold came in. As they were admiring the tattoo, Harold asked, "Where's Mongrel?" He hardly said that when he heard a thumping on the bathroom door. When he looked that way, he saw the door pressing, repeatedly, into the door jam as though the bathroom was breathing heavy.

"He's having another go at Monica in the other room," said Red.

Harold looked down at his feet where he noticed the pants Monica was wearing when she came in, as well as a pair of pink panties and high-heeled shoes.

"I'm sure you can have a turn when he's done," said Samurai as Scratch-n-Sniff came into the room.

"That girl's gonna burn her hole out before she's 30 at the rate she's going," said the tattooist.

That wasn't real appealing to Harold, but he was just thinking, "What the hell?" when someone barked, "Knock! Knock!" as he came in the door from behind Harold.

Startled, Harold jumped aside and turned to find a biker, about 40-years old, with a head as round and large as a basketball. His shoulders were so broad he might have been wearing football pads except that he was only wearing a cut-off Levi and his beefy-tattooed arms dispelled that theory. The only hair on his head was a neatly trimmed blonde goatee and mustache. On the upper-left portion of his vest, he had a patch of a large-black diamond with "1%er" embroidered in yellow thread inside. Below that was a name patch that read, "Ivan."

As he walked in, calling out, "Samurai, you mother fucker," as he went, Harold saw the patches on his back.

Red had told Harold about this club rather in the same sense that an Eastern European might have warned the town folks about roving hordes of Mongols in the 13th century. Of course, Harold had heard of them from occasional news stories going back years. On the back of the biker's rag was a center patch with a hooded figure balancing a broadsword, it's tip in the ground, with both hands on the hilt. The customary "MC" and origin patches were below the center patch. Above was a top rocker with one word — "Monks."

Harold wasn't sure what to expect. He wasn't sure how the biker had meant it when he called Samurai "you mother fucker" and he wasn't sure if this wasn't a tense moment that could erupt in violence at any moment. Harold was tight, like a spring, ready to react at any sign of trouble. But instead, Samurai came off the sofa with a big grin giving the Monk a handshake that folded into a hug, "What the fuck, you bald-headed asshole. Where you been keeping yourself?"

"You know me," said the Monk, "Comforting bereaved wives who can't get enough from the limp-dick husbands, as usual."

Samurai was laughing when Ivan seemed to notice the pounding on the bathroom door. He looked back and Samurai and then at Scratch-n-Sniff with an expression that asked, "What's that?"

"Monica," said Samurai.

The Monk laughed knowingly. Then he turned to Scratch-n-Sniff, "Got a beer?"

"In the fridge," said the tattooist.

Ivan looked at him as though thinking, "Are you going to make me walk for it?" when Samurai said, "Naked Boy, get the man a beer, will yeah?"

"Bring another one for me, too," said Mongrel, suddenly emerging from the bathroom. Harold could see Monica's bear ass and legs on the floor behind him before Harold turned to get the beers.

As he came back, he found everyone laughing as Mongrel was saying, "Well, yeah, she kinda passed out a little before I was done."

"Mongrel, Mongrel, Mongrel," asked Ivan. "Are you telling me that women fall asleep while you're fucking them?"

Mongrel looked a little red in the face as he protested, "Only Monica. And she passed out."

"Sure you ain't doin' something wrong?" the Monk said, continuing to give Mongrel a hard time, shaking his head side to side.

"Hey, she's right in there," said Mongrel, "if you want to show me how it's done?"

"You mean, after you put her to sleep?"

"Mother fucker," Mongrel grumbled as he took a beer from Harold and had a seat on the sofa next to Red.

Ivan took the other beer and looked at Scratch-n-Sniff: "Think I could get some ink?"

"No fucking way," said the tattooist in an angry tone that surprised Harold who thought he'd be more circumspect about using it with the Monk.

"Why the fuck not?"

"I just spent five hours on the probate here and some punk asshole before him," said Scratch-n-Sniff.

When Ivan looked at Harold, as though he'd seen him for the first time, Samurai said, "This is Naked Boy."

"NAKED BOY?! What kinda name is that?"

"It's my name," said Harold, a defensive note in his voice.

Ivan looked at Harold a minute, as though sizing him up. Then he broke into a smile and said, "That's cool," and extended a hand.

As Harold was shaking Ivan's hand, he could see Samurai beaming proudly from the sofa. His sponsor was clearly pleased that Harold had stood up for the name.

The party continued until the sun broke through the open door casting the red-shag carpet in an orange tint. By that time, Monica had woken, and Ivan had taken a turn behind the bathroom door. As he was banging her against the door, Scratch-n-Sniff said, "I'm thinking about drawing her outline on the inside of the bathroom door with instructions to 'Stand Monica Here.'"

Eventually, Scratch-n-Sniff did some work on an eagle on Ivan's upper left arm. In the meantime, instead of petering out, the party caught its second wind and moved back downstairs. There, the party continued until nearly midnight. By that time, Harold was surprised to find Ivan and himself, with their arms over each-others shoulders, drunkenly swearing they'd take a bullet for the other one.

When they left, grinning, Samurai said, "Might want to be careful about that; do you really want to take a bullet for a Monk?"

Though in the second day of a two-day binge, Harold was feeling a little embarrassed, even worried that he might be in trouble. But Samurai only grinned and slapped him across the back as though to say everything was fine.

It was almost 1 a.m. when they pulled into the backyard of Samurai's house and went in to get some sleep, knowing that they had to get to a job near Earlsville in only a few hours.

Chapter 23 — Ain't No Nip

When a proprietor of a new business opens the doors to customers it's common to kick off the event with a Grand Opening. The Banshee Riders saw no reason they shouldn't do the same thing. Like any business, the clubhouse created overhead expenses. In the case of the new clubhouse, this didn't involve rent, but it still included utilities, as well as material fees for maintenance and improvements.

The clubhouse was an 'underground' operation without need of a liquor license or a flashing light out at the street. Alcohol was a definite profit center the club relied on to meet its obligations, the foremost of which involved maintaining a ready supply of booze for member consumption. When the Banshee Riders were alone in the clubhouse, there was a jar behind the bar, much like the jar on top of the refrigerator at Mack's Cycle Repair. Brothers dropped a quarter in the jar for each beer they took. A can of beer cost 50 cents when visitors came calling as delivered by a brother serving as bartender. Other potential profit centers were admission fees and raffles. As with the sale of alcohol, these ventures were held clandestinely in as much as the club didn't exactly worry about laws and statutes designed to regulate such enterprises. And the best way to generate profits from admission fees and raffles was to hold a party. A grand opening was an excellent excuse for such a party.

As the clubhouse took shape, Falstaff broached the idea of a grand opening, though he merely beat others to the draw. Protocol called for a vote, though it was hardly necessary. For a brother to vote against the idea would almost have invited suspicions that the brother was possessed by a wayward spirit that thrived on causing mindless conflict. The response to the idea was so enthusiastic that Wide Glide had to speak up and remind the brothers that holding a party wasn't just fun and games. "There's going to be a lot of work if we don't want to come off looking like a bunch of assholes."

And as was usually the case, to speak up rationally at a meeting was a form of volunteering. Falstaff and Wide Glide were quickly saddled with the responsibility of organizing the party. The first order of business was to pick a date for the event. Falstaff insisted the club tackle that issue posthaste. If deciding to have a party was easy, choosing a date was on the opposite end of the spectrum. Falstaff consulted with his copy of the year's schedule that was worked out at the beginning of the year for parties and events held by the clubs in the county. To throw its party on the same date as another club's event was a sure invitation for hard feelings. Jumping a brother from another club, and beating the crap out of him, probably wouldn't do more to cause hard feelings than scheduling a party on the same night as another club's event. In fact, since all the clubs had gotten together to create the calendar of events at the beginning of the year, to infringe on another club, at this late date, would have undermined the process. Even clubs that weren't directly involved would have considered the idea in bad taste.

Falstaff examined the calendar for a few minutes with T-Rex and Reaper looking over his shoulders. At last, they came to a conclusion. In the meantime, the club had broken into loud conversation.

"All right, listen up," T-Rex said in a booming voice that quickly quieted the floor.

Studying the calendar as he spoke, Falstaff said, almost as though he were thinking out loud, "the only day that will work is Aug. 25."

There was silence as the brothers digested the information and did the math. Then, almost in unison, several brothers yelled, "That's only a couple of weeks away." As a debate ensued with all the full-patch brothers talking at once, Reaper erupted in anger. "Not enough time? Maybe we should ask the old ladies to throw our party."

"Not a bad idea," muttered Grunt, though not quietly enough.

Several brothers laughed but Falstaff didn't see the humor. "You got a problem, brother?"

"No," said Grunt a little sheepishly. But then, recovering, he added, "I just thought it would be nice to see Bitters get off her fat ass for a while."

Falstaff looked as though he would bark at Grunt again but then a crease of a smile broke lightly across his face.

"But even then, it's not really enough time," said Grunt.

A chorus of complaints broke out again about all there was to do.

"Look," Reaper said, interrupting again, though this time his voice was calm, "what do we need?" Then, holding his hand in the air, he folded a finger down with each item he counted. "Beer and wine, something to eat — hell, we've done most of the work already," Reaper said.

"Yeah," Grunt said, "so what do you plan to do about music? Or, maybe, you're planning to have the probates sing?"

Grunt's comment brought on another round of laughter. Pot Roast even turned to Harold and Red and insisted the probates give the club a short rendition of "When Irish Eyes are Smiling."

Mongrel pointed out that probates aren't allowed to speak at meetings, but Pot Roast retorted, "Unless they're spoken to." Laughing, he continued, "And besides, they won't be speaking, they'll be singing."

Red started into the first stanza of the song as Harold protested quietly to Samurai that he didn't know the words. Pot Roast had just reiterated his demand to Harold when Harold was saved by the resounding voice of T-Rex barking, "Shut up and quit screwing around."

"If nothing else," Reaper said, "we'll have our resident electrician run some speakers outside and put the stereo behind the bar."

"We should do that anyhow," Samurai said. "I mean, even if we can get a band, they're not going to play nonstop the entire night. And on nights when we're here alone, we won't have to run the speakers out the front door. Besides, I think I know where we can find a band."

"How much?" Falstaff asked.

"I'm not sure," Samurai said. "$300 or $400."

Falstaff rolled his eyes up at the ceiling as he did some calculations in his head. Then he announced, "That should work, if you can get them on short notice, and they're any good."

"They're not bad," Samurai said. "And I won't know until I ask 'em."

"You do that," Reaper said. "In the meantime, if anyone else knows of a band, try to find out if they're available. But don't commit to anything until we've had a chance to talk about it."

Grunt started to complain that, if someone did find a band that could play on such short notice, they should sign them up right away. But Reaper cut him off turning back to Samurai, "And if you could get on the stereo system right away?"

"Will do," Samurai said. Then he turned to Harold and said, "Got a little job for you tomorrow, probate."

As some of the major pieces of the party fell into place, Grunt, who considered himself something of a master of throwing such events, spoke up again. "Okay, so let's say we find a band, and we've got beer and food, how are we going to publicize our little shindig?"

Falstaff, who felt Grunt was too negative about the matter, stepped out of his seat and approached Grunt. "You know, you've been doing a lot of bitchin' and complaining lately. You got something on your mind?"

"I just think, if we're going to do this right, we should set a date that gives us a little more time to get things together and to let people know about it," Grunt said as he stood up from his seat. "It's like T-Rex said, do we really want to look 'like a bunch of assholes?'"

"We're not going to look like assholes," Falstaff said, "not if everyone does their job and helps out."

"Humph," Grunt snorted, "and you really think that's going to happen."

Grunt had crossed the line. Half the brothers were stepping up from their seats. Reaper, however, was leading the charge. While the others had merely stood with the intention of voicing verbal protests, Reaper was beyond that point. He grabbed Grunt by the collar and slammed him down, bending him back onto the pool table.

"And what have you been doing other than complaining?" Reaper said. As Grunt struggled to get free, Reaper was much too strong and kept his brother pinned to the table.

"ALRIGHT," Grunt hollered, almost incomprehensibly. "AL-RIGHT, let me up."

The other brothers were taken aback by Reaper's aggressive reaction and a strained silence enveloped the room for several moments. Reaper wasn't saying anything either. He simply held Grunt down for a few more seconds before stepping back and releasing him.

As Grunt unruffled his collar and tried to recompose his dignity, Reaper glared around the room. "We've got two weeks to get this party together," he snarled. Then glancing momentarily at Grunt, Reaper said, "That's plenty of time," and looking back around the room again, he added, "if we all pitch in."

Reaper looked back at Grunt, "You got any other problems?"

Grunt shook his head but, noticing that Reaper was still glaring his way, Grunt must have realized a verbal response was expected. "No," he said and sat down with the kind of look on his face that always looks ridiculous whenever an older man pouts like a child.

The job Samurai had in mind involved running wires outside for the speakers and hooking them up to the club's stereo behind the bar. Really, anyone in the club could have handled it but, as an electrician, the job just naturally fell to Samurai who handed off the task to his apprentice. Samurai, Mongrel, Pot Roast, Red and several others huddled inside, out of the sun, while Harold worked around them running wires.

By noon, Saturday, Harold had finished the job and was assigned the task of cutting the grass again. Having chopped down the worst of it his first time out, the second go at the lawn should have been a walk in the clearing. Instead, Falstaff told Harold, "Widen the parking area out front here." Doing so meant going at the high grass with Falstaff's old mower again. As it was a hotter day, by 4 p.m., when Harold finished, he'd worked up a considerable sweat and a fresh sunburn.

While Harold was cutting the grass, Wide Glide showed up with a couple five-gallon buckets of white paint. Wide Glide quickly put the others to work painting the outside of the clubhouse, one of the obvious tasks that had gone unattended when the club first moved in. A proper job would have involved chipping away the old paint. Either they didn't care or they figured they didn't have enough time and they painted right over the walls, chips and all. When Harold finished the grass, he went looking for a paintbrush to help out. To his surprise, Wide Glide told Harold to relax. "Have a beer, Naked Boy," Wide Glide said. "You've been working hard enough today."

For the first time since he started prospecting, Harold found himself sitting back watching as full-patch brothers did the work. When Pot Roast complained, Wide Glide blasted his brother, "He was busting his ass all day while you fuckers sat around jackin' off."

"So, now it's his turn to jack off?" Samurai said with a grin.

Wide Glide had expected an argument and was caught off guard by Samurai's joke. After hesitating, Wide Glide said, "He can if he wants to."

Pot Roast chimed in, "I think you should tell him he has to."

Then Harold added, "As an alternative to beatin' off, why don't I just help with the painting?"

When he stood to grab a brush, Wide Glide said, "Finish your beer, at least."

When Harold joined in there were nine brothers, using empty coffee cans filled halfway with paint, working on the house. Without scraping, the job was finished in relatively short order and the workday transitioned to another night of partying around the campfire.

The next Wednesday, Samurai assigned Harold to work on the rough in on a new house that was under construction. Dropping Harold off at the job site, Samurai headed off to put some bids in on other projects. He was gone most of the day.

About 3:30 p.m., Samurai came back to the house where Harold was working and looked over Harold's progress: "Nice job." Then he told Harold to pack up the tools. "We've got another job to take care of."

Back at the house, Samurai put the van away in the garage and told Harold, "Pull the bikes out of the garage while I go talk to the old lady for a few minutes."

Harold had no sooner brought the bikes outside than Samurai returned with his colors on and carrying Harold's colors as well. Tossing Harold's rag to him, Samurai said, "Hop on your bike, bro. We've got a little club business to take care of."

As Harold pulled out onto the road beside Samurai, he asked, "What are we doing?"

"A little PR," Samurai said. "We have to let the Saxons know about the party."

Just as the Banshee Riders had a bar they considered something of a home base, Hildie's, the Saxons had a regular bar as well. The Saxon's bar was in Millbrook.

To the casual observer, if there wasn't a large group of motorcycles parked outside, Hildie's looked like any other run-of-the-mill watering hole. The same was easily said about Pete's Place in Millbrook. A one-story shack, someone had painted the exterior block walls white some years before. As time drifted past, the paint faded and chipped, and the owner didn't seem inclined to do anything about the shoddy outward appearance.

The biggest difference between Pete's and Hildie's was their settings. Hildie's was in a rural setting at the dead-end of a back-road along the edge of a lake. The bar was built before restrictions on construction in the county took heed of the inevitable flooding that would occur so low and so close to the water. Pete's, on the other hand, was in a dead-or-dying industrial area in an older section of town. A brick, two-story factory building to the north was abandoned with several windowpanes receiving the attention of rock-throwing teenagers. Visible behind the broken glass were diagonal-mesh steel screens. To the south, partially hidden concrete and occasional cinderblocks stood sentry among the weeds and were all that remained of a foundation of another factory. Across the street to the east, the entire block was overgrown with weeds where another factory once stood. That building had once provided jobs for 300 workers. Unfortunately for the building, and for the people who used to work there, foreign labor was cheaper. Somewhere in China, or maybe Taiwan, a nine-fingered 12-year old was doing the same job for crackers.

If not for the Saxons, several of whom once held jobs in the area, Pete's would almost certainly have gone the way of the industries that once provided most of its clientele. The bikers weren't the only customers who regularly drank at Pete's but, without the Saxons, the others wouldn't have provided enough revenue to keep the doors open. Even then, Pete's was hardly a thriving enterprise.

Stan, the owner, had purchased the business from Pete when business was still good, when it appeared the factory across the street was still going strong. But Pete had overheard enough talk from across the bar to know what was coming. Those who knew the story realized that Pete had taken advantage of an old friend. In the process of gaining ownership of the establishment, Stan had sunk his last dime into the venture. Fulfilling his dream of owning a tavern had other costs for Stan as well. High among those other costs was his marriage.

Considering, it was not surprising that Stan was growing tired. He was closing in on 60 and had aged more than his years watching factory after factory close its doors around his little pub. As he came to realize how slim of a chance he had of ever selling the bar, he also came face to face with the necessity of adjusting his attitude to fit his new breed of clientele.

No longer was the street outside lined with station wagons and sedans at happy hour. With the Saxons came rows of loud motorcycles that shook the bar to its foundation when the bikers came and went as a pack. Not right away, but eventually, Stan began changing the options on the jukebox. Some of the country and western numbers still did well but, in place of Frank Sinatra, Louis Prima, Patty Page and Doris Day, some of the younger bikers were more inclined to listen to hard rock and acid rock, though Stan really couldn't make out the difference between the two.

No longer did his clientele wear matching tan, brown or green work pants, and shirts, with lace-up work shoes. Instead, they wore dirty jeans, black T-shirts, leather jackets and cutoff Levis, finished off with steel-toed engineer boots. Even Stan changed. He no longer worried about shaving on a daily basis and was most often seen with significant stubble on his face. Though he still wore tan work pants and plaid shirts, it was as if he was slowly transforming to resemble the bikers who frequented Pete's Place. In the process, he had become one of his own best customers.

Stan couldn't help but appreciate the bikers who frequented his place. He was fully aware that his livelihood depended on what he secretly referred to as "my filthy horde," — a mixed bag of drunken and/or drug addicted, criminals and rowdies.

As with any wise businessman, Stan took special care of his most valuable clients. Drinks were cheap, if there was trouble Stan was prone to side with the club and, if it became necessary to call the police, Stan always gave the Saxons a few minutes head start before picking up the phone.

The earlier members of the Saxons came to see Stan as almost an honorary member of the club. They showed Stan far more respect than mere citizens. Younger members, however, didn't immediately recognize the vital role Stan played in the club's culture.

Stan watched as the older members tried to bring newer members around to understand the unique, and mutually beneficial relationship. "Stan's cool," an older member would say to the new prospect. "He takes care of us and we take care of him." But somehow, the message didn't always sink in, at least not right away. By the time the prospect became a full-patch brother, it was a crapshoot whether he'd remember what he was taught or whether the new brother would approach Stan with newfound arrogance that relegated Stan to a category slightly higher than an insect. The new brother would look at Stan as an unworthy, stubble-faced old drunk.

Stepping inside Pete's Tavern, a minimum of lighting gave Harold the sense he was stepping into a cave. Even coming in from a dark, cloudy day, Harold and Samurai had to stand by the door a few moments waiting for their eyes to adjust.

As their retinas opened wider to compensate for the lack of light, Samurai glanced around hoping to spot Sasquatch. But Sasquatch was not an easy person to miss and Samurai had already realized that Sasquatch's bike wasn't among the four scooters parked out front. Still, there was always a chance that he had driven to the bar in one of the several cars that were also parked on the street.

Even if Sasquatch wasn't there, Samurai was on friendly terms with several members of the Saxons and he considered it likely that he would see a familiar face or two. Instead, he saw a couple factory workers sitting at a table in the corner and the four bikers, who apparently belonged to the bikes outside, sitting or leaning on the bar around the left corner of the bar from where Samurai and Harold were standing. The four bikers were as new to Samurai as they were to Harold. Three of them had rags with the Saxons' colors on the back. The colors were relatively clean, an obvious indication that the brothers were freshly minted. The fourth was either a brother who had come straight to the bar from work and had left his rag at home, a future prospect or a tag-a-long.

As hope of finding a familiar face faded, Harold and Samurai found that friendly faces were equally scarce. The Banshee Riders and the Saxons had been on good terms for years. Any trouble between a brother from one club and a brother from the other was either handled from above or the two brothers, without weapons, were allowed to settle matters themselves. Judging by the looks on the faces of the bikers found inside Pete's, Samurai was pretty sure someone had neglected to explain the shared history of the two clubs to the newer brothers at the bar.

Whether he knew them or not, there was no reason to assume difficulties and Samurai nodded "Hello" to the bikers as he and Harold stepped up to the bar. Samurai ordered a couple beers and then asked across the corner of the bar if he could buy a round for the unfamiliar Saxons as well.

"I've got a better idea," the tallest of the four said. "Put your money away. It's no good in here."

Many a friend had used that phrase to another friend as a way of insisting, "No, I'll pay for this round." By the tone used here didn't fit with a friendly offer. There was no warmth in the comment, and it wasn't a suggestion.

"I'll buy this round," the tall Saxon repeated, "and when you're done with your drinks, you can turn around and go back out that door, get on whatever the fuck brought you here and don't bother to come back."

Samurai took a deep breath to steady himself for a job that appeared more difficult than he had anticipated. Four sets of eyes burned across the bar as though the other bikers were on guard for any sign of a hostile reaction.

"Actually, we were looking for ..." Samurai began but was cut off before he could finish by a short, wiry biker, with pinched, sharp face, and slicked-back hair.

"The man just told you to drink up and get the fuck out," the wiry biker snarled. "Or are you hard of hearing?"

"I hear fine," Samurai said, his tone still controlled but a twinge more assertive.

"Then drink up and hit the road," the wiry biker snapped.

Samurai could understand that these bikers might feel a little defensive about their territory. He could even understand if they were just having a bad day. In spite of those considerations, however, Harold sensed that Samurai was becoming a tad annoyed. All they had to do was let him talk and he could clear things up quickly. Besides, even if he and Harold had just come in for a drink, bikers did that from time to time. Some courtesies were in order. But these bikers were cutting him off before he had a chance to drink, dance or spit.

Stan, who was quietly watching the situation unfold from the other side of the bar, decided to try to diffuse things a little. He slid two beers across the bar to the new bikers, one of whom looked slightly familiar, and said, "Here, these are on the house. Drink up and then maybe you'd better leave."

As far as the wiry biker was concerned, the bartender's contribution to the situation was not appreciated. In the wiry biker's eyes, Stan was just a lush who tended bar. Since the bartender's name was Stan, and the bar was named Pete's, the wiry biker hadn't even made the connection that Stan owned the place. The wiry biker's wrath flipped like a switch from Samurai to Stan. With a snarling lip, he said, "My brother said he'd pay for those, asshole."

Stan wasn't sure what to say. He really couldn't understand where he'd done anything wrong and, to top it off, he really didn't like someone calling him an asshole, especially in his own bar, even if the insult came from a member of his chief client base.

"That talk isn't necessary," Stan told the wiry biker.

As the wiry biker and the bartender were debating who would buy the drink and appropriate verbal decorum in the bar, Samurai used the interruption to work up all the patience he could muster. Then, in an obviously restrained tone, he said, "If you can give us a chance to explain ..."

But Samurai cut himself off as the third biker wearing Saxon colors in the group produced a revolver from under his rag and set it on the bar next to his beer stein.

"In a soft yet dangerously pregnant tone, the third Saxon said, "Hey, you fucking Nip, he told you to get out."

Watching the bikers intently as the patience evaporated from his voice, Samurai cut straight to the point. "First of all, I ain't no fuckin' Nip; I'm Filipino. My father and uncles were all guerrillas on Luzon. They killed more Japs during the war than all your father's put together. Secondly, I'm looking for Waldo," Samurai said, referring to the president of the Saxons.

The biker without colors and the one who had just set the gun on the bar had remained seated until Samurai's last effort at communication. As though they were devoutly religious and Samurai had just invoked the Lord's name in vain, the two seated bikers rose from their barstools and all four bikers walked around the corner of the bar. As they came, the one with the revolver picked up his pistol on the way. They came to a halt, four abreast and in a slight arc, just a few feet away from Samurai and Harold.

Harold's pulse was racing as he stood just behind Samurai's right shoulder and up against the bar. Harold's attention was focused on the Saxon with the gun when something flashed by in the corner of Harold's right eye. It wasn't something Harold planned to do. It happened without thinking the way someone's leg kicks out when a doctor hits their knee with a rubber reflex hammer. It wasn't that Harold realized the bartender had drawn a double-barreled shotgun from under the bar and was bringing it down to draw a bead on Samurai.

For his part, Stan merely wanted to get this pair of recklessly stubborn bikers — bikers without the sense to leave when a gun was drawn — the heck out of his bar. He had decided enough was enough and was taking charge before someone got hurt, or worse. What Stan didn't account for were the quick reflexes of the quiet biker standing behind the oriental biker.

As quickly as Stan drew the weapon, Harold snatched it by the barrels as though absent-mindedly swatting a mosquito buzzing by his head. Something had flashed in Harold's peripheral vision as the blue steel barrels came past his head and, reflexively he grabbed it and shoved the barrels up towards the ceiling.

Stan was no less surprised when, firmly in his grasp, Harold wrenched the muzzles upward. Stan also acted reflexively. As Harold pulled up and out, Stan pulled back. The reaction created pressure between his trigger finger and the triggers. It was more pressure than the triggers could passively bear and, just as suddenly, a flash of flame licked the air at the end of the weapon, followed a millisecond later by the loud reverberation of the two barrels blasting rock salt into the ceiling. The blasts might have caught Samurai across the top of his head except that he reacted even quicker than Harold or the bartender. Samurai had caught a glimpse of the shotgun coming up from below the bar and his natural instinct had caused him to duck forward.

When the shotgun blasted into the ceiling, the reaction of the four bikers facing Samurai and Harold, however, was to take uniform-and-startled jumps backward. Simultaneously, the turned in the direction of the gunfire. For just an instant, the focus of the biker with the gun was elsewhere. It was all Samurai, and years of martial arts training, needed. Before he knew what happened, the biker with the gun was empty handed on the floor. Looking up, he found the barrel of his pistol pointed at his face and firmly in the Asian biker's right hand. He had taken the pistol away as neatly as though the Saxon had handed the weapon to him.

Reaction replaced reflex a little slower for Harold but not so slow that he let go of the gun. In fact, having hold of the shotgun, he gave it a hard yank and pulled it right out of Stan's hands. Stan was left gapping in dual surprise that Harold had grabbed the gun and that he had fired the weapon.

As the construction workers who were sitting at the table scurried out the door, and before the dust had settled, Harold and Samurai's antagonists realized that the situation had taken a turn. The taller Saxon even verbalized his reaction, stating, "Fuck!" as an expression of pure surprise.

"That's right," Samurai replied, "Fuck. As in, what the fuck?

He motioned for the biker to get up off the floor and said, "Now, lift your colors and shirts and spin around slowly. That means all of you."

As they turned, Samurai stepped forward and removed a .22 caliber Derringer from the belt of the wiry biker.

Harold had spun the shotgun around as well though it dawned on him that the bartender had already emptied both chambers. For a second, Harold considered slamming the butt of the gun across the bartender's forehead. Instead, he gave Stan an incensed look and said, "Get yer ass over here," indicating the outside of the bar.

Still stunned by the turn of events, including that he had never intended to squeeze off a couple rounds into the ceiling of his bar, Stan wasn't sure if Harold wanted him to go around through the opening back by the wall or to climb over the bar. After moving hesitantly towards the opening, he leaned back as though to climb over and then leaned back as though to go around. Harold was losing patience with the bartender's indecision and barked, "Get over here."

With more than a little difficulty, Stan managed to lift himself up onto the bar and scrunch across it on the seat of his pants. With equal difficulty, he swung his legs around to the other side and fell from the bar to find himself sprawled across the floor on his hands and knees.

Samurai watched and waited as Stan got back to his feet. Then Samurai told the bartender to back up by the other bikers. As Stan raised his arms and backed up against the taller biker, Harold wasn't sure if the bartender had stepped on the taller biker's toes or if the taller biker was just annoyed at the bartender's role in the unexpected turn of events. Either way, the taller biker cast an angry glance at the bartender as he joined the ranks of the vanquished.

From the looks on their faces, it occurred to Harold they thought Samurai might gun them all down. Instead, with surprising patience, Samurai asked the bikers, "Do you know Waldo's number?"

The wiry biker nodded slowly.

Then Samurai glanced at Harold and said, "Take this asshole over to the phone and watch him while he calls Waldo. If he tries anything, use that gun to beat the crap out of him."

The smaller biker had started to move but not fast enough to suit Harold, whose blood was still pumping with adrenaline. Harold grabbed the biker by the collar and yanked him forward and in the direction of the phone on the wall opposite the bar.

Harold had barely taken a step in that direction behind the wiry biker when he heard a loud smack behind him. Stepping back and to the side, so the wiry biker wouldn't have an angle to jump him, Harold looked back to see if Samurai was OK. Harold turned back just in time to see the biker who had produced the gun crumble to the floor, the result of a solid blow to the solar plexus administered by the shorter and calmly smoldering Filipino biker.

Samurai stood over the biker as he wheezed on the ground trying to get oxygen back into his lungs. The bartender and the other two bikers in front of Samurai backed away lest the Banshee Rider deliver additional retribution. Looking down at the biker on the floor, Samurai said, "My brothers and friends can call me a Jap, Nip or almost anything they want. You can call me 'sir.' Got that?"

While wheezing on the floor, the biker nodded in understanding.

The wiry biker listened as the phone rang and rang. Watching, it occurred to Harold that the wiry biker was looking a little nervous, as though he might get his ass kicked if Waldo wasn't home. Finally, the biker turned to Harold and, in a voice pleading for mercy, said, "There's no answer."

Harold glanced over at Samurai, who had heard. Samurai said, "Then call Sasquatch. If he's not home, try him at work."

The look of fear on the faces of the bikers had just started to recede when it was replaced by a fresh and different look of fear as, verbatim, Samurai rattled off both of Sasquatch's numbers. Harold was fairly certain the tall biker in front of him had gone a little pale when he realized how familiar the oriental biker was with the phone numbers for a founding member of the Saxons. It was the first real inkling the group had that losing the upper hand in this confrontation wasn't their only problem.

When the wiry biker turned and hollered to Samurai, "I've got him," Samurai said, "Tell him Sam is here and ask him if he could stop by."

Though the Saxon had the phone to his ear, Harold could hear Sasquatch's enthusiastic reply: "Tell him I'll be right over." The wiry biker looked as though he might vomit as he said, "Okay" and hung up. Then he turned to Harold and Samurai and said, "He'll be here in a few minutes."

Harold walked the wiry biker back over by his companions and Samurai motioned for them all to walk around to the side of the bar where they had come from and sit down. Samurai told Harold, "Take a walk behind the bar and make sure our friend here doesn't have any other surprises back there."

Harold emerged from behind the bar a minute later with a short, wooden club. Then Samurai motioned for the bartender to go behind the bar again. Stan was almost past Samurai when the Banshee Rider stepped in front of him for a second. "You ever pull a gun on me again and they'll never find where I bury all the pieces of your ass, understand?"

Stan looked as though he could break into tears at any moment as he nodded with sincerity. Samurai held him there only for another moment then said, "Okay, then why don't you go back behind the bar and set us up with that round of drinks you promised."

Samurai glanced back at the door behind them, as though it posed a potential problem, and then motioned to Harold to follow him around the corner of the bar to the table the factory workers had vacated. Taking a seat behind the table and facing the others, Samurai accepted a beer Harold delivered and drained it from the foam to the bottom of the stein. He handed the glass back to Harold and said, "I think I could use another."

As Samurai finished his second beer, Harold noticed that Samurai was staring at the bartender. Handing the glass back to Harold for another trip to the bar, Samurai said to the bartender, "What the fuck were you thinking, Stan?"

Stan was fairly sure he'd seen this guy before. Hearing Samurai use his name cinched it for the bartender. As though he wished he could melt into the floor, Stan shook his head, looked down, and mumbled, "I don't know."

The bar was quiet and calm for about 10 minutes when the door opened and Sasquatch bent his head down to enter, blotting out the cloud-filtered light from outside. Another biker, who Harold thought had a remarkable resemblance to a body-building version of actor Bruce Dern, came in the door right behind Sasquatch. The patches on the second biker's rag confirmed that this was the aforementioned Waldo, president of the Saxons.

Sasquatch squinted his eyes and cast a look around the bar in a searching pattern. When his eyes adjusted and he spotted Samurai and Harold in the corner, Sasquatch only nodded to his own brothers, as he quickly strode over and threw his arms around Samurai for a big hug as the latter stood up to greet him. The enormous biker than gave Harold the same treatment. Waldo also nodded to his trembling quartet of brothers, the look of a question mark forming in his eyes, before walking over to give Samurai a more reserved hug.

Harold could almost see the hearts of the four bikers sinking in their chests as they sat at the bar watching the greetings. The familiarity and obvious friendship drove home the idea that the four bikers had screwed up.

Without waiting for orders, Harold walked over to the bar and, with a touch of irony in his tone, said, "Two more beers, Stan."

As Harold delivered the beers to Waldo and Sasquatch, Samurai turned in his seat and picked up the revolver from his lap, where he had covertly laid it when the door opened a minute before and placed it on the table. Holding the gun backward, his hands around the trigger guard, Samurai slid it across the table to Waldo. He then pulled the Derringer out of his pocket and handed that to Waldo as well. The look of surprise on Waldo's face, as he accepted the guns, was followed by the first traces of clarity as the solution to his question began falling into place. He examined the pistols for several seconds, put the Derringer in his pocket and, turned the revolver one way and the other in his hand. Then as he let his hand drop to his side, he turned towards the bar and said, "Dogbreath, doesn't this belong to you?"

Dogbreath didn't answer. He merely frowned and cast his eyes at the floor as Samurai invited Waldo outside for a conversation. As they left, Sasquatch slapped his arm around Harold's back and said, "So, Naked Boy, how's it hanging?"

It was then that Sasquatch noticed the shotgun and the club leaning in the corner next to Harold. "What are you doing with these?" he asked.

Harold pointed at Stan and said, "They're his."

Sasquatch looked at the weapon again, looked at Stan and looked over at his brothers who were still quiet as mice. He even sniffed a little, catching a whiff of burnt gunpowder. With amazing speed, from the looks on his brothers' faces, the shotgun and club on the bar, and Samurai handing Dogbreath's gun to Waldo, Sasquatch quietly arrived at a relatively accurate understanding of what had happened. He didn't know the details, but he was pretty sure of the basic situation.

With sarcasm intended for his brothers, while shaking his head side to side, he said, "Well, Naked Boy, I was going to introduce you to my brothers but it appears you've already met." Sasquatch followed the statement by casting an angry look over where his brothers strangely resembled four boys waiting outside the principal's office. At Sasquatch's critical glance, all four bikers looked away apparently unable to bear the shame of Sasquatch's wrath.

A couple minutes after they'd gone out, Samurai and Waldo

returned, laughing as they came. Stopping by the door, Waldo looked over at his four wayward brothers. Then, shaking his head side to side, he said in a mocking tone, "Kids, kids, kids. What are we going to do with you?"

There was no reply and Waldo walked to the bar where he set his beer stein in front of Stan indicating he wanted another. As Stan took Waldo's mug, the president cast Stan a harsh glance as well.

With a fresh beer in his hand, Waldo turned back to his brothers. The wiry biker met his president's stare and opened his mouth as though to say something. That was enough to set the Saxon's president off. "It's not enough that you pull a gun on our brothers from the Banshee Riders here, but then you assholes actually let them take your guns away from you." The roar of Waldo's voice shook the air and echoed off the walls of the room as though it were a cousin of the earlier shotgun blasts.

One of the four managed to say, "We didn't know ..." but, calmly, as he held up a hand to dissuade any further discussion on the matter, Waldo told him, "We'll deal with this later."

Samurai and Harold stayed for several rounds joking and drinking with Sasquatch and Waldo as the other four bikers sipped their beers quietly a few feet down the bar. Harold sensed that the four bikers wanted to leave but were unsure whether it was OK to do so. And if they were worried about that, they were even more concerned about the idea of asking Waldo for clarification. For his part, Waldo let them sit there and stew on the matter.

A little after 10 p.m., Samurai noticed raindrops on the window behind them. "Hey, we'd better be getting back," he said. "It's looking kind of nasty out there."

Harold and Samurai said their goodbyes to Sasquatch and Waldo. Samurai even nodded a sincere farewell to the four bikers down the bar and said goodbye to Stan. As they started for the door, Samurai called out to Stan, "No more pointing guns at us, OK?"

Stan nodded with a grimace and said, "Sorry about that," as Harold slid the shotgun and club across the bar.

Outside, as they were about to start their bikes, Samurai said to Harold, "These new boys were a little jumpy. Apparently, they've had a couple visits from the Monks. Of course, if we were Monks, they'd probably be dead right now, what with a stunt like that."

As the bikes roared to life, and just as the rain started coming down hard, Samurai said to Harold, "By the way, thanks for covering my ass. That was real smooth the way you took the gun away from him."

"Yeah, right," Harold said. "Rather smooth taking that asshole's gun away, too."

Samurai just smiled as he clicked his bike into gear and the two rode into the mounting storm.

Chapter 24 — Legend's Demise

Samurai and Harold walked into the clubhouse the next day for the Friday night meeting certain they had a pretty good story to share with their brothers. To their surprise, the way a local story is bumped from the front page of a newspaper, a bigger story had grabbed the lead.

As the founding president of one of the oldest clubs in the area, Poacher was easily the most respected member of the region's biker community. Even people like Grunt and Wide Glide, long-standing members of the Banshee Riders, couldn't remember a time when Poacher wasn't president of the Swamp Rats. Though many knew he was a long-time president of the club, few would have guessed that he'd actually held the position since 1967, with the exception of two years when the club had an interim president while Poacher did time in the state pen for the non-fatal shooting of the president of another club. That president mysteriously disappeared not long after Poacher was released from prison and the case was still open as the authorities searched for some kind of evidence of foul play, beginning with a body.

Derelict was once a member of the Swamp Rats. Though he never spoke about what happened, most of the Banshees knew their one-legged brother was not particularly fond of Poacher. He was polite around the Swamp Rats president but was more standoffish than was in general.

The Banshee Riders first started flying their colors in 1978. They were still one of the newer clubs in the area. This helped to explain why it was such a big deal when Reaper invited Poacher to go along with the club on Road Day. In the local biker community, it was a bit of a coup. Poacher's reputation was such that the mere act of paying serious attention to the newer club had the residual effect of giving that club a shot of instant credibility. In other words, hearing the news that Poacher went along with the Banshee Riders on a run, area bikers might be heard to say, "Well, if Poacher thinks the Banshees are a stand-up club, there must be something to it."

Samurai and Harold were not the only riders caught in the rain the night before. As the club got the word out about its forthcoming party, pairs of Banshees headed off in all directions in sort of a Paul Revere messaging system. It was a swift and direct approach to the club's marketing concerns. Other than the little SNAFU at Pete's, it was extremely effective and, otherwise, without drama.

But the Banshee Riders weren't the only area bikers the rain failed to drive off the roads. While the rain didn't drive Poacher off the road, with its accompanying lighting, it did drive the roofer off the roof. By late morning, the 43-year-old outlaw biker happily surrendered to the weather, came down from the roof and headed for The Roadside Tap, the pub in Earlsville he most frequently haunted.

Cindy Lorens, a slender and precocious 16-year old, with wavy blonde hair that cascaded invitingly over her shoulders, would start her sophomore year at Woodrow Wilson High School in the Fall. Once, she had presented her parents with report cards filled with high grades. Her mother and father came to take those grades for granted the way children expect to find gifts under the tree Christmas morning. The recently completed academic year, however, caught her parents off guard. The best grades in her fall semester report card were Bs. Her highest grade in the spring session was a C. Even worse, she had two Fs, one for English and one for P.E.

Mom and dad searched for an explanation. They patiently asked Cindy if anything was wrong and pondered even harder when she impatiently barked at them, "Everything is fine!" Cindy's parents were completely stumped until mom was putting Cindy's clothes away one afternoon after doing laundry. Cindy's sock drawer was hung up and wouldn't open all the way. Heather Lorens, an attractive middle-aged woman who presented a comforting vision of what Cindy could expect to look like in years to come, gave the drawer a couple hard pulls and, suddenly, whatever was catching on the drawer released its grip. Heather hadn't expected the victory over the drawer to come so easily. To her surprise, as the drawer surrendered to her effort, she pulled it completely out of the dresser and dumped the contents onto the floor.

"Oh fudge," Heather said as she stooped to pick up the assorted socks. As she bent down, however, something in the back of the hole created by the absent drawer caught Heather's eye. At first, Heather thought a sock had fallen over the top of the drawer and she assumed the sock was the culprit in her recent battle with the drawer. But Heather didn't feel the cloth of a sock when she reached inside the shadowy opening. Instead, her fingers wrapped around a plastic baggie that contained what felt like small twigs.

When she withdrew the baggie from the dresser, Heather studied it for a few seconds with a puzzled look on her face. Somewhat naïve about such matters, Heather might have jumped to the appropriate conclusion a little quicker. But in spite of Cindy's drop-in grades, and a slightly combative attitude around the house, Heather just couldn't imagine that her little girl would use marijuana. But Heather wasn't so naïve that she could indefinitely deny what was in her hand. As reality set in, tears sprang lightly to Heather's eyes in response to the loss of her daughter's innocence, as well as a sense that her daughter was choosing a dangerous road.

Heather and Jack sat their daughter down that night for a heart-to-heart talk. They spoke of all the dangers of drugs. They virtually pleaded with her to stay away from such things in the future. They also asked where she'd gotten the pot but to no avail. Jack was convinced that Cindy's new friend, Becky Thomas, was a bad influence. What Jack didn't know was that Becky's parents felt the same way about Cindy and were at least equally correct.

Jack watched as Cindy reluctantly flushed $20 of marijuana down the toilet. He then informed her that she was grounded for a month and was not to see Becky anymore.

Cindy and Becky continued their friendship when the grounding expired, albeit on a clandestine basis. On a rainy Thursday, as a construction worker sought shelter from a sudden downpour, Cindy and Becky stepped into The Roadside Tap to try out a pair fake IDs they'd recently purchased. In the gloomy environs of the bar, the IDs worked like charms, though mostly because the bartender didn't seem to care as much about the veracity of the IDs as he did about the tingle he felt at the sight of two attractive young women – teenagers who had done their best to look older than their puerile years.

The girls ordered a brace of beers and, when those were done, Cindy prepared to order another round.

"I think we should go," Becky whispered in a voice fraught with nervous tension.

"What are talking about," Cindy growled back in a whisper, instantly on edge to defend the opportunity. "We're in. And now you want to go?"

"We could get in trouble," said Becky, and my parents are already looking for any excuse to ground me again."

The bartender seemed to have noticed the two talking in urgent tones and was looking their way. Cindy shined him on with a flirtatious smile that instantly worked as intended, if not better than intended; the bartender was reacting as though the girl's flirtatious smile was an invitation he'd gladly accept.

Becky was becoming desperate and it showed in her tone as she asked Cindy, "Please, let's go. We can come back another time."

"Why should we come back someday when we're getting everything we want right now, today?" She could see that Becky wasn't giving in and, finally, said, "Well, if you want to go then go."

Hurt and a little afraid for her friend, Becky stepped outside as a brief clearing of the skies welcomed the evening.

Poacher had also watched the interaction between the two girls with curiosity inspired the moment the attractive young females walked in the door. It was unclear whether he heard what was said or if he truly understood the situation. By this time, he was well lubed from seven or eight beers and several shots of Jack Daniels. If he did know that Cindy was underage, he obviously didn't care. If he didn't know, he wasn't concerned enough to find out.

By 7:30 p.m., as Heather and Jack Lorens sat in their living room answering questions from a police officer who came to make a report about their missing daughter, Poacher had his arm around a young girl's back, his tongue in her mouth and his fingers working on the buttons of the white dress shirt Cindy had worn to "look old enough" before stepping into a bar.

The police stopped at the Thomas home where they found that the young girl who lived there had arrived late for dinner and with alcohol on her breath. Though the police officer doubted Becky's claim that she hadn't seen the Lorens girl that day, the officer couldn't crack Becky's veneer of loyalty to her friend.

By 11 p.m., Poacher virtually carried Cindy out to his bike as, to let go, the intoxicated girl would certainly have crumpled to the ground. With some difficulty, as he was extremely drunk himself, the biker managed to get the girl on the back of his bike. He then climbed on and hit the button for the electric start. The engine rumbled to life and they rode out onto the road. Almost the same moment they left the parking lot, as though the skies were waiting for this moment, they were hit with a fresh downpour. In the pouring rain, they road about three miles before arriving at the last stop sign before leaving town to the west.

When the dispatcher announced the missing girl and provided a description, the latter was unnecessary for Patrolman Ralph Windsor. He had a 14-year-old son and a 16-year-old daughter. Not only had his children attended the same school as Cindy Lorens, a couple summers before, his daughter had played softball with the Lorens girl while Ralph Windsor served as an assistant coach with the team. He knew little Cindy Lorens by sight.

Windsor, a 17-year veteran of the force, was a dedicated officer who took the words on the sides of the squad car – "To Serve & Protect" – as an oath of faith, was backed into an alley half a block shy of the stop sign at Porter Street and County Road J. He was just wondering if the Lorens girl had shown up yet and was thinking of checking in with the dispatcher to find out if there was any word of her whereabouts, when he saw a single headlight approaching on Porter Street heading out of town. His first thought, especially on a night such as this, was that a car had a headlight out. But as the light swayed a little, he was able to discern that he was looking at the headlight of a motorcycle. Windsor reached over to the handle by the door and swiveled the searchlight mounted on the front-left fender out towards the road. When the bike was about 20 feet away and braking for the stop sign, Windsor carefully aimed the light low, so he wouldn't blind the driver, and switched it on. As the bike rolled into the beam of light, the biker and female passenger were looking into the searchlight with deer-like expressions on their faces. Windsor immediately recognized Cindy Lorens on the back of the motorcycle. With more than a little alarm, he also recognized the rider in front.

Not only did Ronald Wiggens, a.k.a. Poacher, have an arrest photo top-dead-center in the file the department kept on criminal gangs in the area, Windsor was also one of the officers who went to Wiggens' house to make the arrest after the biker had shot another biker about nine years earlier. If it was broad daylight and Cindy hadn't been reported missing, Officer Windsor would have found the sight of Cindy Lorens on the back of Poacher's bike intensely alarming. Considering the hour, the weather and the APB, Windsor felt an unfamiliar sense of panic. What if Poacher ran when the squad car approached with its lights flashing, as Windsor was sure he had to do?

What went through Poacher's mind as he starred squinting into the officer's searchlight wasn't quite clear. Whatever it was, the biker's reaction was to open the throttle on his 1,200-c.c. motorcycle wideout and tear off into the glistening darkened road ahead.

As the bike sprung forward, the rear wheel slipped out from under it and the bike virtually fell over. As Poacher struggled to right the bike, Cindy Lorens did her best, considering her inebriated condition, to stay on the back. Both barely succeeded and, as Windsor started the engine of the 1982 Crown Victoria highway interceptor, Poacher turned south on County J and tore off down the road with the rear tire slipping back and forth behind him.

Windsor had no desire to initiate a chase with Wiggens, not with the Lorens girl on the bike. But Poacher didn't know that. As he steadied the rear tire, Poacher soon had the bike running through driving rain at a speed close to 100 mph. Several miles down from Porter Street, County J crossed a single set of railroad tracks. The bike was half a mile from the tracks as Windsor, who, in hopes that he could somehow convey to Wiggens that he wasn't in pursuit, was running with the emergency lights off and at a speed that was slightly lower than the motorcycle. It was Windsor's hope that Wiggens would realize the officer wasn't chasing him and would slow down to a safe speed. Windsor might have willingly chased Wiggens into the side of a tree if Wiggens were alone. But with Cindy on the back of the bike, Windsor's blood pressure was spiking even before he saw the freight train appear out of a grove of trees and approach the crossing with County J from the south.

341

Judging from the rates of travel, Windsor doubted Wiggens could beat the train to the intersection. Windsor wracked his brain in search of a solution to avert the potential disaster that was unfolding in front of him. Then the police officer locked up the brakes of his car in the hope that Wiggens would see this and stop running — stop risking everything on the chance that he could beat a locomotive to a single point in space and time. Poacher either didn't notice or didn't care that the officer had stopped.

What Windsor thought would be a very close call really wasn't close at all. In his intoxicated state, Poacher either completely misjudged the distance, never even noticed the train or had chosen a bloody end to a bloody life. At a rate of speed nearing 110 mph, without any effort to apply the brakes, the bike hurtled along the wet pavement, Cindy hanging on the back in a semi-comatose state. One second, two passengers were hurtling through the night as the bike's headlight began reflecting off the painted iron of the train ahead. The next instant, the bike, with its two riders, slammed into the midsection of the train's engine as though they were shot from a cannon.

For the train engine, the impact was nothing. It was as though someone had thrown an aluminum can of Coke against the side of the massive machine. The conductor, Claude Williams, a stocky 59-year-old, had seen the bike approaching and knew there was no way it would stop. He applied the brakes not because it would help but because he knew it was required when a train hit a pedestrian or vehicle. He stopped knowing that an accident investigation would follow. There was nothing he could do to avoid the collision. As he heard the impact, he slid the window back and was reluctantly leaning out to look back. He saw the flash of impact, sparks flying back from the wheels and a ball of flame.

As the bike collapsed into the side of the train, Poacher's and Cindy's momentum carried them over the handlebars and into the train. As his helmet-less head hit the side of the train it disintegrated the way a pumpkin would explode if thrown violently against a wall. Momentum carried his skeletal structure forward as organs and bones were ripped from their foundations and instantly crushed to unrecognizable proportions.

Cindy's head was cushioned somewhat by Poacher's back.

Bones in her legs, arms, ribs, and back were instantly shattered. Organs were ruptured — her kidneys, spleen, stomach, intestines, and heart. As the bike crumbled half under the train and with the rear wheel kicking over to the left, unlike Poacher, who died instantly, Cindy was still alive.

The bike folded in the middle and, as though someone had thrown a balloon filled with red paint, what was left of Poacher dripped off the side of the train. As the bike collapsed onto itself, Cindy was caught between the seat, gas tanks and bits of Poacher. In the collision, the front tire had plunged under the chassis of the train. As the iron wheels sparked to an emergency stop, the train pulled the bike underneath and Cindy with it. At almost 50 mph, it took the train almost two miles before coming to a complete stop. By that time, the wheels had severed Cindy at her midsection, leaving her upper torso on the tracks near the scene of the impact and dragging her lower section the entire braking distance of the train.

About 20-feet past the point of impact, the bike had burst into an orange-and-blue ball of flame that had dripped off the side of the train like molten metal at a foundry. Bits and pieces of flame continued to flicker when the train came to a stop as the last bits of flammable material burned off the side of the engine.

When he saw they weren't going to stop, saw, in fact, that they would hit the train squarely in the side of the engine, Windsor had sped forward relatively close to the scene. As the train came to a rest, he stood, one foot on the pavement, one inside the car, leaning on the doorframe with the police radio microphone in his hand. The officer, who had witnessed all sorts of gruesome accidents over the years, was sobbing as he called in asking for ambulances knowing their trained EMTs couldn't help, and a fire truck that would probably find the flames had burned themselves out by the time the firemen arrived. The dispatcher heard the emotion in the officer's voice and hesitated to respond. He wasn't sure if she had received the message and repeated himself through tears that continued to flow: "We have an injury accident between a train and a motorcycle on Highway J, two miles south of Porter Street. EMT and Fire Rescue needed."

Chapter 25 — Final 15 Minutes of Fame

The story that spread through the local biker community, in spite of what was seen and heard on the television, radio, and newspapers, was somewhat different than the reality Officer Windsor had witnessed. When a local legend dies, even if he's a legend to an outlaw subculture, the death somehow requires something more, more, at least, than a drunken biker with an under-aged girl behind him blindly slamming into the side of a train.

The authors of the unpublished biker versions of the story were able to uncover 'reliable sources' who heard the young girl say, as Poacher was about to pull over, "Don't stop, I'm only 16," though it was never made clear where that 'reliable source' got it's information. Equally 'reliable sources' had three squads in hot pursuit as the Swamp Rats president narrowly failed to clear the tracks in front of the train. One version even had a cop firing his handgun out of the window of the squad and hitting Poacher moments before he would have gotten clean away.

Bikers, by their nature, are a very skeptical lot. If the government, which they generally see as an evil cartel more heinous than an American incarnation of the Gestapo, suggested that night was followed by day and vice-versa, virtually to a man, the bikers would expect either eternal daylight or everlasting darkness. But when Poacher 'went over the high side,' the romanticized versions of his death were bought hook-line-and-sinker by even the most skeptical among the motorcycle-riding brethren in black leather.

The only ones who questioned the story were those, like Derelict, who had seen Poacher through a less-romanticized lens and knew that the story in the official media rang too true for fiction. They quietly watched, with some sad amusement, as their brothers portrayed the cops as vile assassins with personal grudges against bikers.

As thoroughly as the media had covered the accident, it was nothing compared to the coverage the media gave Poacher's funeral. The ceremony was a lavish affair worthy of a Mafia godfather. Virtually every outlaw biker for 100 miles around attended. Even the national clubs – the Monks and the Bloody Bastards – were represented at the event. Some bikers rode to the ceremony from hundreds of miles away. All the local clubs competed to send the largest, most extravagant flower arrangements. The procession of bikes following the hearse from the funeral home to the cemetery wound across the countryside for almost a mile. A county sheriff led the procession with the Mars lights on top of his squad silently flashing in cadence to the thunder of motorcycles behind, while other squad cars blocked side roads intersecting the route. Behind the bikes were the cars of family members and other non-biker folk. Tagging along in the rear were the vans of the three major networks and the local television outlet. Camera crews were set up at the entrance to capture dramatic footage as the procession passed by. One station upstaged the others by sending its weather chopper aloft for a wide-angle view of the event as the procession wound its way out of Earlsville to the interstate and down a country road to Poacher's final resting place, or at least where they buried the bits and pieces that were found.

The police escort, though performed by the perceived enemy and by those the bikers considered responsible for Poacher's death, seemed to punctuate the man's importance in the eyes of the bikers. As though they could absorb its energy, the bikers soaked up the attention of the media, as well as the curious stares of people lining the road or observing from passing vehicles. Some of the bikers may even have felt twinges of jealousy knowing it was unlikely that their funerals would garner even half as much attention as Poacher's. All-in-all, the spectacle of the situation seemed befitting of the deceased biker's stature in the outlaw-motorcycle community.

The hearse stopped on the paved road adjacent to a freshly dug grave about 40 feet in and about 150 yards from where a considerably smaller, and more somber, procession buried Cindy Lorens the day before. The bikers casually dismounted, and eight members of the Swamp Rats moved to the back of the hearse to accept the casket. As reporters, photographers and film crews jockeyed for position, the leather-clad mass of 'mourners' followed the casket to the grave site where a pastor from the parish Poacher's mother attended conducted a short reading and said some final, solemn words before the box was lowered into the ground.

Most bikers aren't big on tearful goodbyes, especially when the television cameras are running. Though the funeral director had managed to convince people not to drink during the actual funeral services, Poacher's brothers from the Swamp Rats had filled a backup vehicle with cold cans of beer and ice for the moment that the rituals were over. No sooner had the priest finished saying those few, delicate words over Poacher's grave than the beer appeared in bikers' hands as if by magic. Any solemnity that had existed beforehand was lost completely as a party ensued to the consternation of the cemetery's groundskeeper. All through the leather-clad horde, aluminum cans were slapped together in toasts to their fallen brother.

On-air personalities and their camera crews wound through the large throng of bikerdom seeking final interviews or doing their closing comments on the story. Photographers and reporters mingled among the crowd asking questions and snapping pictures.

In the middle of the circus-like atmosphere, Harold found himself watching an attractive 30-ish blonde interviewing a member of the High Riders. Harold had seen Barbara Brown on the television hundreds of times. Though she was as beautiful in person as she was on the tube at home, Harold was surprised at how much smaller the woman looked in person. Of course, he realized, the perspective created by the big and tall bikers around her might have had something to do with it.

Most 105-pound former beauty queens would have felt uncomfortable to find themselves standing in the middle of several hundred tattooed, bearded, beer-drinking, drugging and, most likely, heavily armed, bikers. But Barbie Brown, as she was called by friends and enemies alike, saw herself as a hardened professional. Furthermore, the bikers she was covering that sunny afternoon were, in her eyes, nothing but punks and not to be taken seriously. She may have felt there was no more reason to feel nervous in this setting than if she were interviewing a group of Girl Scouts. Her reputation and stature as one of the top journalists in the state probably assuaged any concerns over potential misbehavior by these barbarians. But mostly, for her modest stature, Barbie was driven to succeed in a male-dominated profession. If she had to work twice as hard to get ahead, so be it. Barbie reasoned that she asked for no quarter from her associates and gave none, though she conveniently downplayed the influence of her beauty pageant looks on her professional success. She was used to the public fawning at her presence and saw no reason why this mass of social rejects should act any differently.

Barbie thought that she sufficiently masked her contempt for the subjects of this assignment. And it was an assignment she had pushed for. It was unlikely that anything would happen to upstage this as the day's big story, the culmination of a week's big stories about the senseless death of a young girl in the hands of a criminal and detestable 43-year-old biker. However, Barbie's expectations about the reactions of the bikers to her status as a 'celebrity' fell wide of the mark. In fact, 'the rabble' seemed much more adept at reading the reporter's attitude than she was at reading the rabbles'. Some of the bikers avoided her, one large member of the Monks simply stared at her with something less than a friendly expression as Barbie fished for soundbites. Barbie asked a couple questions then, turned away from the 1%er and, as if the biker wasn't standing three feet behind her, said sarcastically, "Well, maybe we should find someone who speaks English."

The person she found had a patch on the front of his vest that read "Pot Roast." Pot Roast looked into the camera imagining the adoration his '15 minutes' would inspire. Then he tried to use the interview to put forth the bikers' side of the story. "It wasn't Poacher's fault. The girl had a fake ID. Considering, there was no reason for the cops to chase him."

Barbie Brown offered a pained, saccharin smile and cut Pot Roast off so she could work him around to the story she was actually after: "But what would you say to Cindy Lorens' parents?"

"Tell that to the cops," said Pot Roast. "They're the ones that drove them into a train."

Seeing Pot Roast as a lost cause, Barbie turned away, dismissing the biker without a word. Reverting to her true form — that of the hard-bitten and ambitious television personality that considered it a compliment when people called her a bitch – she scanned the crowd of bikers for a more pliable subject for an interview. But Pot Roast wasn't quick on the uptake. As the cameraman lowered the camera from his shoulder, Pot Roast stepped to Barbie's side and tried to strike up a conversation. The reporter cast an impatient frown at the biker and turned away again as if she hadn't heard a word, asking her crew, "See anyone here who doesn't look like they were dropped on their head when young?"

This was a hint Pot Roast couldn't miss. He strolled back among his brothers grumbling as they teased him about his failed effort hitting on a local celebrity. As he approached, Harold handed Pot Roast a fresh beer. Pot Roast took the beer turned and leaned back against the car where most of the Banshee Riders had congregated. Then, in a voice he was sure Barbie Brown would hear, he said, "Can you believe it, I used to think I might be willing to fuck that slut."

Barbie turned her head quickly, her mouth opening as though she were about to say something. However, since she found about 40 or 50 bikers in the immediate vicinity, looking her way and laughing at Pot Roast's words, even Barbie couldn't miss the obvious virtue of remaining silent on this particular occasion. Rather than add fuel to the fire, she glared at Pot Roast, which elicited a few more laughs from the crowd. Then Barbie turned away, her beauty-queen nose high in the air, and quietly told herself it didn't taste so bad chewing on this particular form of ridicule as "you have to consider the source."

If Barbie were as streetwise as she thought she was, she would have recognized this as a good time to go somewhere else. But Barbie was defiant. There was no way that she was going to let a pack of buffoons get the final word even if her retort was to stand with her back providing a silent form of scorn.

Looking at Barbie's back, her shapely hips and long, slender legs, an idea fermented in Pot Roast's mind. Suddenly, he turned to Harold and said, "Probate, give me your beer."

Harold handed his beer to Pot Roast as ordered and then listened as Pot Roast leaned forward and whispered in Harold's ear. As Pot Roast whispered, a grin formed on Harold's face. Finally, Pot Roast finished the directive asking Harold, "Got it?"

Harold nodded. Then he turned and slowly stalked up behind the indignant celebrity 20 feet away. Having resolved to ignore the group behind her, Barbie refused to turn when she heard another ripple of laughter at her back. As a result, she didn't see Harold coming. Harold sensed that Barbie wasn't about to turn around, but he was a little worried the cameraman and the cameraman's assistant might give him away to the on-air personality.

As it was, Barbie's camera crew said nothing. They stood quietly watching as Harold came up right behind the reporter and then slowly got down on his hands and knees. He lowered and extended his head until it was almost touching Barbie's ankles. Then Harold turned his head and looked up to examine the woman's undergarments.

Harold was halfway back to his brothers when the new and louder barrage of laughter finally prompted Barbie to look around. All she saw was a biker walking away from her. She wondered for a second what the biker was up to then shrugged and returned to her prior defiant pose.

As Harold reached his brothers, he a gave a three-word report, "Red and lacy." This brought on some more laughs from those close enough to hear what Harold had said. Pot Roast handed Harold his beer again and gave the probate a biker's handshake. Harold shook back and took a big swig of beer.

The 'Barbie Incident' probably would have been laid to rest at that point if not for a new character joining the cast. Matt Starks, a photographer with The Times, the area's largest newspaper, had watched the event unfold with amusement and curiosity. He watched Harold approach Barbie and, like everyone else who had watched, Matt wondered what Harold was going to do next. When Harold knelt down to look up Barbie's skirt, Matt laughed as hard as anyone, though he interrupted his laughter long enough to try to snap a picture. Unfortunately, he didn't react quickly enough.

Unlike Barbie, Matt, an award-winning photographer, had no sense that he was somehow superior to the bikers around him. He was aware that, were he to act really stupid in this setting, he could get himself hurt. But Matt also realized that, as long as he didn't act like an idiot, the bikers would probably leave him alone. It was kind of like walking through the lion's cage with enough sense not to ring the dinner bell.

Matt's request might have had some foundation in rivalry. Certainly, there was a little professional animosity between some members of the print and television media. Then again, maybe he just didn't like Barbie Brown, a well-known bitch who had a tendency to bark at other reporters and such when she thought they were getting in the way of a shot, as though she and her televised reporting were intrinsically more important. It's possible that, on some earlier story, she had barked at Matt, too. Or, maybe Matt simply recognized a good photo opportunity when he saw one. Whatever the case, Matt cautiously waded in amongst the Banshees Riders until he was face to face with Harold.

Matt stuck out his hand and introduced himself as a Times photographer. "I was watching what you did over there," Matt said, gesturing towards Barbie. As Harold and Pot Roast grinned in reply, Matt met their grin with a grin of his own and continued. "I was wondering how you would feel about doing it again?" As Matt asked the question, he held up his camera to indicate his reason for asking the question.

Harold looked at Matt for a second then extended his beer to Pot Roast again. "Mind holding this again?" Pot Roast took the beer and Harold began sneaking up behind the attractive, blonde reporter again, the celebrity's camera crew watching quietly, even hints of grins on their faces. Undetected again, Harold resumed his prior position and enjoyed another glimpse up Barbie's skirt.

This time, knowing that the photographer was trying to get a picture, Harold held the pose longer than the first time. As the brothers behind Harold broke into laughter again, Barbie turned to glare over her shoulder again. At first, the television reporter's keen observational skills failed to pick up the biker at her feet. When her peripheral vision did notice something on the pavement, she looked down to find Harold looking up at her with a grin stretching from ear to ear.

It was as if a doctor had hit Barbie above the knee with a little rubber hammer. Before Harold could react, Barbie brought the pointed tip of a high-heeled shoe into Harold's chin. Fortunately, there wasn't much behind the kick and Harold stood up laughing. By this time, encouraged by Barbie's screams of outrage, all those within eyesight of the incident, were nearly doubled over in laughter.

Barbie Brown, the upright, uptight product of an upper-crust upbringing, with a long and respected name among the most elite of the area's elite, screamed obscenities that would have made a truck driver blush as Harold returned, champion like, to his brothers. The welcome Harold received was enthusiastic. Their laughter wasn't just the product of a crude joke; it was also in response to what they saw as a victory over the establishment, as well as the hoity-toity citizens they looked down on with reciprocal scorn. His brothers and brothers from other clubs came by to offer handshakes or slaps on the back. And the whole time he was congratulated as though he'd scored the winning touchdown, Barbie continued to vent in Harold's direction. In the middle of the celebration, and making sure that Barbie saw him do it, Matt came over and shook Harold's hand as well.

In a loud voice, loud enough to ensure that his competitor heard every syllable, Matt said, "Thanks," and then offered to send Harold a copy of the photo if Harold would provide an address.

Seeing Matt Starks shake Harold's hand and offer thanks finally put an end to Barbie's tirade. As she glared at him, Matt lifted his camera towards Barbie and said, "I can send you a copy too, if you'd like." When she didn't respond, he continued, "Or, if you want, I'll just send it to the station."

"If you run that in the paper, you son of a bitch …," Barbie began to growl but quickly stopped when her reaction was met with catcalls and renewed howls of laughter. Finally, she took her bruised ego, flipped Matt the middle finger, and turned to go. When Barbie turned, she found that the two men in her camera crew also had large grins on their faces. She paused for a second looking at them in surprise and said, "And fuck both of you, too." Then she stormed off, as she probably should have done when Pot Roast first made his rather crude suggestion.

Chapter 26 — Trumped Monks

As the event drew near, preparations for the club's party kicked into high gear. Harold had just returned from the liquor store with Snake, and was unloading cases of Boones Farm wine, when T-Rex stuck his head in the front door of the clubhouse and hollered, "Probate! Get yer ass out here."

Harold was a little perplexed by the request. As sergeant at arms, T-Rex was the responsible for security during the party. It was his responsibility to schedule brothers for the gate and sentry duty by the estate above the cliff from the clubhouse. If someone was acting stupid, or if a couple brothers mixed it up, he was in charge of the brothers who would step in, when appropriate, to address the matter. In other words, security was there to keep unwanted elements out, to ensure that no one got into the estate and committed any theft or vandalism and to watch that things didn't reach some elusive point at the party where, even by the Banshee Riders' standards, things were out of hand. From his position in charge of security, T-Rex was aloof from the more mundane aspects of preparing for the party; he stood back while brothers and probates cleaned, organized, stacked and 'decorated' to get the clubhouse ready.

When Harold exited the clubhouse, he found T-Rex waiting beyond the porch and, apparently, outside of earshot from the other brothers. There was nothing menacing about his expression or demeanor. And yet, Harold approached as though trying to retrieve a ball from a yard with a resting rottweiler. He didn't say a word as he stepped up to T-Rex but merely looked at him inquisitively.

"You're on guard duty for the party," said T-Rex. When Harold seemed surprised, T-Rex continued, "I heard how you handled yourself the other day in Millbrook. Samurai figures you should know how to handle yourself. Just keep your shit together and back me, Mongrel and Snake up if anything comes down. And don't fuck up."

Harold was shaking his head and was about to promise he wouldn't when T-Rex added, "That means don't get fucked up, either. You can drink just don't drink so much that you can't handle yourself or anything that comes up."

A little later, Red came over by Harold and said, "Heard you're on security."

Harold nodded affirmatively but had an expression that suggested he wasn't quite sure how this had happened.

"Way I hear it, the brothers are pretty happy with the way you've handled yourself. I heard Mongrel say that your performance at Pete's Tavern iced it for you as soon as Samurai brings you up for a vote."

Harold found that pleasing to hear and allowed a trace of a smile to pass across his face. Then, as it occurred to him that Red might feel put out if Harold made patch first, even though Red had started prospecting and probating earlier, Harold asked, "What about you?"

"Oh, I figure I'm getting close, too," said Red with a full smile, as though he already knew. "Don't think I've screwed up too bad."

As they were talking, as though to emphasize the point, Snake came over and threw a brotherly arm across Harold's back and, while rubbing his hand in a circular motion in the center, said, "Seems like you're missing something back here."

Harold was caught off guard by the rather obvious way Snake seemed to telegraph a pending vote. He looked at Snake without really knowing what to say. But as he did so, he saw his sponsor watching with a beer in his hand from the clubhouse door. The look on Samurai's face suggested that he was less than pleased. Harold figured he'd better go over and find out what was on his sponsor's mind.

"Don't let that shit get you in a trick bag, probate," Samurai said. "You don't come up for a vote until I bring you up and you still have time to blow it."

Harold was feeling crestfallen by the harshness of Samurai's words and tone. As thought to soften the blow, Samurai handed Harold a beer from a back pocket but added as Harold took it, "Just don't fuck up."

It occurred to Harold that the party, and his role in security, was an opportunity. He suspected it was a final chance to prove himself or, as Samurai had put said, "To blow it." Once again, Harold steeled himself to keep it together.

The day of the party came as Red and the brothers rushed around taking care of final details that were somehow forgotten in the days before. As a member of security, however, Harold was standing off by the side receiving a final briefing from T-Rex, Mongrel and Snake.

"You won't have much to do for a while," said Mongrel. "You can hang back here with this old dinosaur while me and Snake cover the gate."

"You don't really have to worry about anything until about midnight," said Snake. "You might call that the witching hour. Folks will start getting fucked up and then, well, anything can happen."

"Mostly, the other clubs will police themselves," said T-Rex. "There'll be some citizens here but most of them should know how to handle themselves."

"Weeellll," said Mongrel, "except for some bimbo they bring along or something."

"That's true," said T-Rex as though acknowledging something he'd missed.

"Yeah," said Snake laughing. "Couple years ago, this dumb bitch just wouldn't take hint."

"What did you do?" asked Harold.

"Beat the crap out of her old man," said Snake while gesturing towards T-Rex.

"He old man?" Harold asked.

"He brought her to the party; it was his job to control her," said the sergeant at arms.

"I would like'd to have kicked her ass, though," said Mongrel.

"Didn't have to," said Snake. "Her old man kicked her ass later for getting his ass kicked."

"How do you know?" asked Mongrel.

Snake just smiled and took a swig of his beer.

Laughing, Mongrel said, "You slut puppy. You fucked her, didn't you?"

"A couple days after the party," said Snake with a grin. "She was complaining about how he kicked her ass."

"You fucked that idiot?" T-Rex asked.

"Sure," said Snake. "She wasn't half bad when she kept her mouth shut."

"Or when she had her mouth wrapped around your dick," said Mongrel.

"That, too," said Snake, quickly hiding a grin with a swig of his beer.

"By the way," said T-Rex, getting serious again. "When I say back us up, I mean when we're doing security stuff. Otherwise, back up your president and brothers in general."

"I figured," said Harold.

T-Rex didn't exactly smile to hear Harold say this. But there was a little twinkle in his eye as he lifted his beer in a toast to Harold with Mongrel and Snake joining in clinking all four beers together.

The party was hardly the Banshee's first. The club had other clubhouses before and prided itself on throwing well-remembered events. For this particular party, the club actually brought in two bands, two tattooists working in shifts, and held the usual titty contest and a greased-pig contest. The latter called Harold away from his security duties as chasing the greased pig was the special calling of prospects and probates. To the unmitigated pleasure of full-patch brothers, prospects and probates would chase the greased pigs for the honor and delight of their respective clubs.

The greased-pig event, using a modestly sized pig Falstaff brought to the party, was held during the daylight hours out behind the clubhouse. The crowd of spectators formed a crude fence and locked legs any time the pig sought to escape from this bizarre turn of events that followed after it was stolen from its pig pen.

Harold had never tried to catch a greased pig before and, true to its name, he found the pig extremely slippery. Encouraged on by his brothers, and the laughter of others, he made a valiant effort to catch the pig for the honor of the Banshee Riders. Instead, a prospect from the Satan's Undertakers caught the pig and the glory. But Harold apparently shared the glory for the way he dove face-first into a huge puddle of mud created by Falstaff who had soaked the ground behind the clubhouse before the party. Harold spent the rest of the party with his hair and clothes coated in dry or drying mud.

Harold's appearance was so pathetic that, when Sasquatch arrived later, he joked several times to Samurai, "Don't you Banshee Riders ever clean your prospects and probates."

Eventually, Sasquatch and Samurai agreed that they would have Harold ride his bike through a carwash later as the two brothers watched.

Harold also met two of the Saxons who had caused trouble at Pete's the other night. Along with noticing that they were going out of their way to be more than cordial to Harold and Samurai, Harold also noticed that they'd been busted down to probates. When Harold asked about the Saxon who had pulled the gun at Pete's, the two freshly demoted probates evaded the question with some obvious discomfort.

Later, while standing by the pool table in the clubhouse, Harold asked Samurai if he knew what happened to the Saxon who pulled the gun at the bar. When Harold asked the question, Samurai glanced over Harold's shoulder. Harold turned to come face to face with the Saxon's president as he came out of the bathroom.

For a second, Harold's heart raced as he feared he had crossed a line asking the question. But Waldo simply, and somewhat vaguely, answered Harold's question.

"We Saxons figure it's bad enough when one of our brothers pulls a gun on our friends for no particular reason," Waldo said. "But if someone can take his gun that easy, even if it's a frickin' Kung Fu man doin' the takin', well, we figure they ain't cut out to be Saxons."

Waldo had responded in a soft, matter-of-fact tone and Harold somehow knew enough not to press the question further at that time. Later, however, he asked Samurai if he knew what happened to the guy. Harold half expected to hear that the biker's lifeless body was found where it had been dumped in a field somewhere as a message to other brothers not to screw up.

"No, they didn't kill him," Samurai said, reading the look on Harold's face. "They just beat the crap out of him and dumped him in the dumpster out behind Pete's. Oh, and I think they took his bike for parts."

Though Harold didn't let on to Samurai, he was secretly relieved. He really wasn't that concerned about the welfare of the former Saxon, especially since he didn't like having a gun pulled on him. Rather, from Harold's perspective, it was a personal question. Things were going great with the club. In a relatively short period of time, most of the brothers had come to respect him. It was an unfamiliar sensation for Harold and a feeling he didn't relish losing. But considering his love/hate relationship with alcohol, Harold still had that nagging fear that it was only a matter of time before he screwed up royally and the brothers discovered what a lowly drunk he really was. That thought was the elephant in the room he was trying to ignore in hopes it would go away. But in light of what happened to the luckless former Saxon, Harold was at least relieved to know that, if or when he did screw up, he wouldn't automatically receive a bullet in the back of the head. When the time came, Harold might get his ass kicked, but at least he would most likely live to see another day. "Then again," Harold thought to himself, "if he screwed up that badly did it really matter if he lived?"

Harold not only paced his drinking during the party, he also accepted several hits of speed from Red as insurance that he would stay alert as long as his services were required. By Saturday evening, Harold was going on 36 hours without sleep. Thanks to the little white pills, he felt no inclination to find a bed either. He'd spent the time roaming around the party, drinking lightly and keeping his eyes open for trouble, of which none had come up so far.

About 7:30 p.m., T-Rex came up to Harold and said, "NB, you been at this since last night, haven't you?"

Harold shrugged as though to say, "Yeah. So what?"

T-Rex laughed and told Harold to go take a break. "Go catch some sleep or, at least, have some fun, for Christ's sake," T-Rex said. "Get yourself laid or something."

Harold laughed and thanked his brother. However, instead of searching for rest or romance, Harold grabbed a beer and went out to the porch, around from the side of the house where the band was taking a break and signed up on the sheet to get his second tattoo. Watching Harold sign the sheet and realizing the probate had been on duty for more than a day, the tattooists cut his own break short and moved Harold up to the front of the list.

Tit-for-Tat Tommy, or T4T, as many of his friends knew him, was a tall, bony and grizzled old biker with long gray hair pulled back tight in a ponytail and a mass of faded tattoos on his arms and upper body. On one arm, he had swirled waves around a large and badly burned section of skin. The skin was rippled as though it had once melted and then solidified in its lasting state. T4T asked Harold, "What are you looking for?"

Harold described how he wanted an Eagle with its talons drawn and ready for blood.

"Well, sit down," T4T said. "You've earned it."

A member of Satan's Undertakers began to complain about Harold moving above some of the names on the list. But T4T explained, "This guy's been working since last night. How 'bout you give him a break?"

The biker seemed to think about it for a minute and then, begrudgingly, said, "Fine. But you can start on me as soon as you're done with him."

"No problem," T4T said.

Harold quietly leafed through several sheets of pictures as the tattooist made his preparations. At last ready, T4T asked, "So, did you find anything?"

Harold had pulled out a picture of an eagle looking as though it were swooping down about to grab its prey. "How about this," Harold asked, adding that he'd like a ribbon clutched in the eagle's claws that read, "Live to Ride, Ride to Live."

"No problem," T4T said. "Where do you want it?"

Harold looked from side to side, pulling up his sleeves to look at his upper arms as though considering the color of mangos to see which was ripest. Merely looking at his right upper arm brought a reaction from the tattooist.

Giving Harold kind of a funny look, T4T said, "I don't think that's such a good idea," the tattooist said. "Why don't we put it down here?" With that, T4T pointed to the backside of Harold's lower-right arm.

Intuitively, Harold realized the tattooist was making sure Harold didn't screw up and put the tattoo where the club tat would go. "That'll work," said Harold.

T4T smiled at Harold and said, "From what I hear, you might need that spot for somethin' else soon, not that it's my place to say."

As the tattooists worked, he asked Harold, "So, how long you been prospecting for the Banshees." They also talked about Poacher. T4T proudly announced that he'd done several tattoos for the late Swamp Rats president. Motioning in several directions with his eyes, T4T said, "I've done some ink on most of the brothers and old ladies at this party."

Then T4T brought up the subject of bikes. "So, what do you ride?" the tattooist asked.

Harold nodded with his head towards Magdelina, which was back by the cliff and first in line of a long row of bikes. "That hard-tail over there," Harold said.

T4T looked at the bike for a minute and then turned back to Harold with a look of surprise on his face. "Where did you get that?" T4T had posed the question with an unmistakable note of suspicion in his voice.

Harold immediately sensed that T4T knew the bike. And if he knew the bike, he probably knew Harold's uncle. Rather than feeling concerned about T4T's suspicion, Harold saw an opportunity. "I inherited it from my uncle," Harold said.

T4T looked into Harold's face for a while and said, "Yeah, you look a little like old Gizzard."

"You knew my uncle?" Harold asked.

"Sure, who do you think designed that picture on your uncle's bike ... I mean, your bike?"

"I thought that was a picture of his old lady," Harold said.

"I don't know for sure who she was, but she was definitely someone who meant something to your uncle," the tattooist answered. "He gave me a picture of the girl and asked me to draw something up."

Harold asked, "So, what was my uncle like?" When he saw the confused look on the tattooist's face, Harold added, "I never knew the man existed until I heard I'd inherited his bike. I guess he had a fight with my dad a long time ago."

"I'm sorry to hear that," T4T said. "Your uncle was top-notch, bro. Never heard anyone say a bad word about old Gizzard."

Just as when he heard others talk about Harold Schneider, aka, Gizzard, the man's namesake felt a little bitterness toward his parents for excommunicating the man from the family – from Harold's life.

Harold would like to have talked longer about his uncle with T4T but a brother from one of the other clubs, who apparently knew the tattooist well, came over and struck up a long conversation that lasted well past the work on Harold's new tattoo.

As the evening progressed, Harold would peel back the large bandage on his arm to show the new tattoo every time he ran into one of his brothers. When he showed it to Samurai, his sponsor said, "You'd better leave that thing covered for a while. Oh, and if you decide to get any more tattoos, remember, don't go putting anything up here." As he said it, he slapped Harold on the top of his right arm.

"Yeah, I got that?" Harold said with a smile.

Samurai didn't seem to appreciate the smile. "Yes, I'm talking about the club tattoo," he said in a harsh tone. "But like I said before, you haven't earned it yet, so don't go gettin' cocky."

Once again, Harold felt deflated by Samurai's curt comment.

Seeing the almost crestfallen look on Harold's face, Samurai laughed, "Don't worry, if you don't get your patch, we'll have a big dick or somethin' tattooed on your right arm?"

Harold gave a half-hearted smile, which seemed to please his sponsor as a more appropriate attitude. Samurai threw his arm around Harold's shoulder and clinked his beer can against Harold's. "So far, at least, you're not a total fuck up. So, don't worry and keep on keepin' your head out of your ass."

As Samurai spoke, Harold looked over and noticed Samurai's club tat on his upper-right arm. Just then, Derelict walked in the room and Harold noticed that Derelict's club tat was on the back of his shoulder.

"Why is Derelict's on his back?" Harold asked.

"He used to have a Monk's tattoo on his arm," Samurai replied.

"Used to?" Harold asked.

"Yeah," Samurai said. "He had it covered up with that dragon. If you quit the Monks, you don't ride around with their club tat on your shoulder anymore. Ya cover it up if you don't want the Monks to take your arm off or something. As the Monks like to say, 'Once a Monk, always a Monk,' or some such shit."

Harold thought about that but, instead, mentioned how T4T had steered him away from putting the new eagle tattoo on his upper arm.

"T4T is a good man," Samurai said. "Don't go thinkin' he's a Banshee Rider, or something, but he's a righteous dude."

"So, if he had put this by my shoulder, the club would have let me put my club tat on the back of my shoulder, too?" Harold asked.

"If you put another tattoo where you club tat is supposed to go, assuming you earn it, we might decide you were too fucking stupid to ride with the Banshees," Samurai said, his harsher tone returning. "At the very least, if you had put your eagle up there, someone might have suggested you weren't really all that interested if I bring you up for a vote."

Harold glanced over where T4T was working on yet another tattoo. Then Harold ordered a beer and brought it out to the artist.

When Harold handed the beer to T4T, the tattooist said thanks with a puzzled look of surprise on his face. With his left hand, Harold slapped himself below the right shoulder and smiled.

When Harold went inside to the bar by Samurai, his sponsor had that more satisfied look on his face again, obviously appreciating Harold's expression of righteous gratitude.

Red had just walked over to join them at the bar when T-Rex strode briskly in the door. "Look sharp," T-Rex said with a frown on his face. "The Monks are about to arrive."

Harold hadn't really thought much about the fact that the club hadn't bothered to invite the Monks. But however T-Rex came by the knowledge of their pending arrival, Harold could see from T-Rex's reaction, from the way Samurai's back stiffened and from the look on Red's face, that the arrival of the Monks was not business as usual.

When the party first started, some of the other clubs arrived in packs. The rumble of their Harleys was heard several miles before they turned onto the gravel road to the clubhouse. Since Friday night, however, with few exceptions, bikes had come and gone in ones, twos, threes, and fours. While they were still loud, a few un-muffled Harleys didn't quite have the same mind-numbing effect of a large pack.

No sooner had T-Rex made his announcement than Harold noticed that the wine in a half-full bottle of Boone's Farm on the bar had small ripples on the surface. Then, as though thunder were growing to a crescendo, the sound grew closer while appearing to spread a freezing chill over the party. Everyone was virtually frozen in place, their heads turned towards the spot where the tree line was broken by the path to the road outside. The sound rose to ear-shattering proportions as lights began to flicker and bounce on the path, beams crossing and uncrossing before bursting into the clearing. Then the bikes erupted into the clearing in pairs. From where he sat on the barstool, Harold began counting as the bikes came in. He was nearly up to 24 pairs when T-Rex blocked his view going out the door.

As Harold was about to follow, Samurai grabbed Harold's arm and said, "Come here."

Samurai led Harold off to the side for a minute while motioning for Red to follow as well. "It's good for you to hear this, too," Samurai said to Red.

"You two need to watch your asses around these guys," Samurai said. "Don't fuck with the Monks, but don't show any fear either. The Monks can smell fear the way sharks smell blood in the water. If they smell it on you, they'll be on you like stink on shit. Oh, and if they start wrestling or fighting with each other, stay clear. They like to start something with each other and, the next thing you know, you're in the middle of it and they're not playing anymore."

With that, Samurai turned to go outside, and Harold and Red made like they would follow. But Samurai stopped and said, "You two stay in here and watch the bar." Then Samurai exited the clubhouse and stood at the top of the porch steps watching the Monks arrive. Capsize was tending bar a short time before but, as Harold looked around the room, Capsize was nowhere in sight. Harold decided to take Samurai's directive literally and stepped behind the bar.

Outside the deafening roar of Harleys quieted in steps as bikes were shutoff in twos and threes until the crankshafts in the last of the Monks' bikes spun to a halt. The silence that followed was as deafening as the pounding thunder that led to the acoustic vacuum. No bikes were running and no one was talking. Harold could almost hear everyone outside watching as the Monks dismounted. Then he heard a loud voice outside holler, "Your friendly-neighborhood Monks have arrived; let the party begin," as though everyone had waited in just that particular spot for hours for the Monks to arrive.

There was something about the voice, the volume and attitude, as though the voice was a flammable slick floating on waters that looked deceptively still, it rang with confidence and a touch of a challenge.

Harold busied himself breaking open another case of Boone's Farm wine when he heard the same voice, just outside the door, "Whaddya got to do to get a drink around this hole?" He had hardly looked that way when he heard footsteps approaching and Samurai came through the door followed by a pair of unfamiliar bikers.

The first, with ruggedly handsome features and dark hair flowing over his shoulders, looked like he could be Snake's larger twin. The other had slicked-back, greasy hair, and a goatee that was neatly trimmed to a sharp point like an extension of the biker's chin. Shirtless under his colors, his chest and arms were adorned with the customary permanent artwork that was entirely expected among bikers. What was significant about his arms and chest, however, was the way his muscles rippled as he walked as though he had just left Gold's Gym after a workout. The biker's rag and jeans were effectively impregnated with dirt and he had one crazy eye that made it difficult to tell which way he was actually looking. The biker also wore a broad but icy smile that, to Harold, completed an impression of criminal insanity.

Harold could have sworn that he'd felt a chill run over his body when the crazy-eyed biker locked one eye onto Harold. After giving Harold the once over, the biker glanced around the room for a second and mumbled something to the effect of, "Nice little shit-hole, though." Then the biker turned and stepped to the bar.

As Harold approached intending to take the biker's order, Harold saw three patches on the upper left portion of the front of the biker's rag. The rectangular patch on the bottom was embroidered with the word, "Shiv." The equal-sized patch above it held the word, "President." Above that was a diamond-shaped patch with an Arabic 1 followed by a percent symbol.

For several months, Harold had felt as though he was riding with a group of bikers that were as bad and as dangerous as any others. Suddenly, Harold felt as though he'd discovered he was on a semipro baseball team and was meeting a big-league player destined for Cooperstown, N.Y.

Just as Harold thought the 1%er was about to order, Shiv turned and looked at Samurai as though he had just noticed him there. "Samurai," Shiv said. "How the hell you doing? Makin' plans to bomb Pearl Harbor again?"

Samurai smiled with an ease that impressed Harold as Shiv threw an arm around Harold's sponsor's back and said, "Just kiddin' ya, bro. You know I love ya."

"How ya been, Shiv," Samurai said as though he were talking to any of his own brothers.

Then Samurai said, "NB ..." But Harold wasn't listening anymore. His attention was drawn to the door where the largest man Harold had ever seen had just come through the door. The biker was so big he made T-Rex look comparatively small. Under a remarkably clean rag, the biker wore a black shirt that read, "You ain't been fucked till you been fucked by a Monk!"

Reading the shirt, Harold realized the use of the word, "fucked," offered more than one possible meaning. One meaning suggested the pinnacle of sexual pleasure and the other an equal height of pain.

The enormous biker also had a 1%er patch. His name patch read, "Midget," and Harold suddenly had a picture of the Monks having a confrontation with another club and saying, "Wait here while we go get our Midget to take care of your champion."

Harold was almost in a trance as he heard Samurai say "NB" again and realized by how loud his name was spoken that it was probably the second time his sponsor had called him. Snapping out of his trance, Harold found that Samurai was introducing him to the president of the Monks. As Harold shook Shiv's hand Harold hoped the biker hadn't noticed the way Harold was staring at Midget. But it was too late. Shiv said with a big grin, and as though answering a question, "Big, little midget, ain't he?"

Harold recovered nicely asked, "Yeah, what do you feed him?"

Shiv laughed, "Hey Samurai, your prospect has some spunk."

Harold didn't like the way Shiv said the words. It was as if Shiv were implying that Harold would make a worthy recruit for the Monks. While Harold could see he could take that as a compliment, his loyalty was clearly with his brothers. It was as though Shiv were suggesting that, given a choice, anyone would prefer to join the Monks.

In reply, Harold offered Shiv a cool smile and said nothing.

"So, what brings you kids up to this neck of the woods?" Samurai asked as he gave Harold an appreciative glance that suggested he was happy with the way his probate had handled the situation.

"Hey, you know us," Shiv said. "Our territory is anywhere the road takes us." Shiv's crooked smile did little to betray the fact that he was really telling Samurai, and anyone else who was listening, that the Monks did not recognize boundaries the smaller, local clubs thought provided insulation from the larger clubs around them.

Samurai and Shiv exchanged arctic smiles, followed by a long, pregnant silence the Monk played for effect. The quiet was shattered by a deep voice that boomed, "Are you punks hoping we'll die of thirst or something?"

As large as Midget was, his voice was still several octaves lower than Harold might have expected. It was a menacing, gravelly voice that, though spoken softly, seemed to reverberate through the room causing the walls to shake.

"What can I get you?" Harold asked with a detached voice customary in almost any tavern or gin mill. Shiv held up three fingers and Harold filled three plastic cups from the tapper behind the bar. As he handed a cup to each of the Monks, Harold said, "That'll be $1.50."

Shiv looked at Harold with what Harold took as a mix of insincere puzzlement and amusement while asking, "What, are you Banshees too cheap to buy your guests a round of beers?"

Harold realized he probably should have skipped the money. He had a feeling the Monks president might try to build this into a problem of some sort. Harold had asked for the money almost as a reflex. He distinctly remembered the meeting where Falstaff had ripped into the brothers for taking beers for themselves and their friends and failing to put in for the drinks. Falstaff had slammed his hand down on the bar and said, "If you assholes can't pay for your drinks, maybe we'll have to put a padlock on the refrigerator."

Considering the battle that had raged over the issue, Harold felt he had no choice but to ensure that the drinks were paid for. However, it now occurred to him that he might have quietly put the money in himself.

"I'll get those for you," Samurai said as he dug into his pocket.

"What, your prospects can't speak for themselves?" Shiv asked.

Technically, a prospect was expected, in most formal settings, to be seen and not heard. And this was about as formal as it got in the world of motorcycle clubs. A probate had only marginally more voice than a prospect. But these technicalities had nothing to do with the situation. It was obvious that Shiv was fishing for any excuse to mess with the smaller club.

It was a game as old as motorcycle clubs. The bigger club showed up at the smaller club's event, clubhouse, or favored bar and, while feigning friendship, probed for weaknesses. At the very least, the members of the larger club were testing the mettle of the members of the smaller club. At some point in the process, the members of the larger club were hoping that a member of the smaller club would stumble, do something stupid or ill-advised and the larger club would have a chance to blow some minor faux pas into a major confrontation. In such a manner, the larger club might invent the justification for pulling the other club's colors or insisting that the smaller club disband. In harsher situations, a physical confrontation might ensue. If such were the case, the smaller club was always at a distinct disadvantage. In either scenario, the larger club might pick off a few members from the smaller club. Those members of the smaller club who seemed to have the potential to become members of the larger club were offered an opportunity to prospect in the big leagues. The problem was that the larger clubs tended to hand Ps out like sidewalk salesmen passing out fliers on street corners. A prospect was virtually a complete nothing in the world of motorcycling, and more of a nothing with a larger club. If, after a short trial period, the prospect was found unworthy, there was a good chance the disappointed and unfortunate soul would receive a thorough pounding that would augment his sense of rejection. There were even times, such as that night, when the larger club would take the somewhat unnecessary step of stopping at a couple bars and corralling a few temporary prospects to boost the club's numbers. In such cases, unless the temporary prospect really shined somehow, the post-prospecting drubbing was pre-ordained.

For the smaller club, the goal was to avoid trouble, to play it cool long enough that the larger club grew tired of the game and left empty-handed, their bloodlust un-satiated.

Samurai knew the game as well as Shiv. Harold's sponsor had played the game many times before, though Shiv's territorial comment was an unwelcome break with the past. Samurai smiled at Shiv and said, "Naaah, he was warned beforehand not to give out any free drinks."

"And he doesn't know that the Monks are exceptions to the rule?" Shiv said.

"Well, he's a probate. He's still learning," Samurai said. "I'm his sponsor and, to tell you the truth, I think he handled the situation just right."

"You think he's right?" Shiv said, probing and prodding for any weakness.

"He's a probate," Samurai said. "We'll tell him when and what to think."

"Well, don't you think you'd better straighten him out before I feel insulted?" Shiv said.

"I think he has the picture now," Samurai said, realizing Shiv could take the statement more than one way.

As if to punctuate his sponsor's statement, Harold said with a grin, "These drinks are on the house."

Working together, Harold and Samurai were closing the door on the Monk's probes for trouble. Shiv looked as though he were trying to think of another way to attack the problem. Finally, with almost a shrug of acceptance, the president sipped the foam off the top of one of the beers.

As Shiv continued to ponder a way to break through the Banshee Rider's defensive veneer, another loud rumble of bikes interrupted his meditation and announced the arrival of an additional large group of bikes. Just then, T-Rex walked into the clubhouse. As the Sergeant at Arms nodded to Shiv, Midget, and the other Monk inside, Harold could have sworn T-Rex had a slight and gloating grin on his face.

T-Rex walked around to the back of the bar and poured himself a beer before dropping two quarters into the till. He took a long drink of the beer and then, acting as though he had just thought of something that had slipped his mind, he said to Samurai, "Oh, hey, the Bloody Bastards are here?"

Harold looked over at T-Rex when his brother was speaking. When Harold looked back at Shiv, though the Monks president was still cool and collected, and was still smiling, the smile seemed a little more forced than before. It was as if he didn't

367

want anyone to know that something had spoiled his fun.

Nothing spoils a large club's power play on a smaller club faster than having an equally large competitor show up in the middle of the game. In the world of biker politics, it was as though the Bloody Bastards had set up an ambush of the Monks' ambush.

Harold had once heard Reaper say the Bloody Bastards are the big dogs around these parts. "The Monks are Number 2, so they try harder."

Shiv pushed off from where he was leaning by his elbows on the bar. "As casual as possible, though he failed to entirely hide his disappointment, he held his beer up as in a toast and said, "Thanks for the beer, bro." As he headed towards the door, he paused and spun back partially. "Maybe we can pick up this conversation again sometime soon." As he said it, Shiv's smile returned to his face for a moment before he left the clubhouse. But as Shiv stepped outside, Harold had the impression he was watching someone brace himself before stepping out into a stormy night. Shiv's brothers then followed him out the door, Midget ducking his head as he went.

When they had gone, Samurai, T-Rex, Red, and Harold all glanced from one to another for a second. Then, as though the threshold had a forcefield that wiped away smiles just in time, they stepped out onto the porch. Harold was looking over Samurai's shoulder as he noticed that the Monks seemed to have drifted off to one side of the compound as though determined to have their backs to a wall. He noticed a white 'P' on the back of one of the biker's rags. Even from behind, there was something familiar about the Monks prospect, though Harold couldn't quite put his finger on it — the flowing blonde hair and slender body. Then the biker turned just enough that Harold could see his face. Harold hadn't laid eyes on 6 Pack since the former brother had stormed out of the meeting earlier in the year. Since that time, Harold had hardly thought about 6 Pack. If Harold did think about the other biker, it was only to remind himself how happy he was that 6 Pack wasn't around. Now, here he was, in the flesh, a prospect for the Monks.

Then, in a repetition of the Monks' arrival, swaying headlights preceded a large pack of bikes emerged from the woods and rumble into the compound. Pulling their bikes over by the lake, the Bloody Bastards began shutting off their bikes until a relative quiet returned to the clearing.

When the Bloody Bastards parked their bikes, they generally congregated in the area in front of their bikes. While the Monks were eyeing the Bastards warily, the Bloody Bastards were putting on an air of indifference. A short-but-stocky, 50ish Bastard with a leather vest, a black beret cocked to one side on his head, and patches on the front of his vest that read "Tunnel Rat" and "President," under a "1%er" patch, waded fearlessly into the midst of the Monks as he hollered greetings to members of the Number 2 club that he already knew. The Monks returned the greeting but clearly didn't appreciate the way Tunnel Rat was showing them up as though the Monks were as harmless as a nursery full of diapered babies or, at least, as harmless to the Bloody Bastards as the Banshees were to the Monks.

As Harold surveyed the two clubs he concluded that, if one were to take the smaller clubs there and combine them into one group, then add about 10 or 15 pounds of muscle to most of the members, the Banshees, Swamp Rats, Saxons and the others would look just like the Bloody Bastards or the Monks. As a whole, the 1%ers were bigger and meaner looking. They vastly exceeded the mold seen in the average Hollywood biker movie.

Tunnel Rat was laughing and joking with the Monks in a manner reminiscent of the way Shiv, Midget, and their other brother had treated the Banshees in the clubhouse a few minutes before. There was a total absence of concern suggesting he hardly took the Monks seriously, though Harold doubted that was quite the case.

The band was on break and, preoccupied by the recent arrivals, no one had thought to turn the radio back on. As Samurai and T-Rex stepped down from the porch to say hello to some of the Bloody Bastards they knew, Harold and Red stayed on the porch watching the show. Without the competing sound of music, Harold could hear a little of the conversation Tunnel Rat was having with the Monks. He was asking questions that Harold realized weren't really questions at all.

By bits and pieces, Harold realized Tunnel Rat's questions were phrased to let the Monks know that the president of the Bloody Bastards knew where the Monks were most days and what they were doing. It was as if Tunnel Rat were saying, "... and I could take you out anytime I wanted."

For the Monks, the arrival of the Bloody Bastards took all the fun out of the party. As he watched for 6 Pack's reaction, Harold could see the guarded scowl on the former Banshee Riders face. But when Tunnel Rat happened to glance in 6 Pack's direction, the scowl was instantly replaced by a crocodile smile. Harold noticed that Red had seen the same thing. As Harold was about to look over at Red, 6 Pack suddenly turned to look up at the porch. It was as if he suddenly realized he had an audience. For a second, Harold was caught off guard as his eyes met 6 Pack's across the compound. And though Harold quickly recovered to cast a contemptuous smirk in 6 Pack's direction, it was too late. 6 Pack gave Harold a just-ate-the-canary grin and then turned back to his brothers.

It pissed Harold off. It was as if, without saying a word, 6 Pack had taken the upper hand again. Red also seemed to have caught the silent meaning of the exchange. He patted Harold on the shoulder and, in a comforting tone, said, "Fuck that asshole." As an afterthought, Red added, "Doesn't say much about the Monks if they'd let that dirtbag ride with their club." Harold realized that it was a double-edged statement as 6 Pack had once rode with the Banshee Riders. But Harold also realized that Red was showing support for a brother. Harold didn't say a word, but he threw his arm around his brother's shoulder and offered a toast that was quickly reciprocated.

It wasn't long before the Monks made some kind of excuse Harold didn't hear and took off for another party, a bar or some other undisclosed location.

He watched as Shiv climbed onto a radically stretched gold panhead, the Monks colors painted on each side, and led out through the woods. Though most of the Bastards still congregated together, Harold noticed that several of the Bastards mingled among the partiers. Tunnel Rat came inside the clubhouse where Harold went behind the bar and served up a beer. Learning from past experience, Harold reached into his own pocket and quietly put 50 cents into the till for Tunnel Rat's drink. As Harold did so, Tunnel Rat asked, "What are you doing?"

"I've got your beer," Harold said calmly.

"No way, bro," Tunnel Rat said. "In fact, let me buy you a drink."

Harold was about to protest when he saw Samurai nodding from behind Tunnel Rat that it was OK. As Harold hesitated, as though Tunnel Rat had eyes in the back of his head, he said, "You should listen to your sponsor. He's a wise man."

No sooner than Harold served up a beer for Tunnel Rat, and another for himself, then a pair of Bloody Bastards prospects came inside and ordered several dozen beers for their brothers outside. As Harold was busy filling plastic cup after plastic cup, Tunnel Rat put a $100 bill on the bar to cover the drinks Harold was pouring and said, "This should keep them coming for a while. Oh, and pour one for your sponsor, too."

Harold wasn't sure how Tunnel Rat knew that Samurai was Harold's sponsor. He wasn't sure why the president of the large club was so generous. But what Harold did know was that the Bloody Bastards' attitude was completely different than that of the Monks president. It felt as though he was sincerely friendly.

Actually, the Bloody Bastards weren't nearly as different as Harold thought. If the Bloody Bastards were less inclined to commit acts of recruitment or intimidation, they were still playing biker politics. They didn't need to inflate their numbers and probably felt that most of the members of the smaller clubs would tend to dilute the standards the Bloody Bastards were accustomed to. But since an actual turf war was less than a possibility than it was an eventuality with the Monks again someday, it was still in the Bloody Bastards' best interest to interfere with the Monks' plans.

For the smaller clubs, the Bloody Bastards' arrival was taken as a goodwill gesture. The smaller clubs were appreciative and had a sense that, in a pinch, they might be able to count on the Bloody Bastards to back them up against the Monks. Most, however, knew they shouldn't count on it unless it was in the Bloody Bastards interests. The Bloody Bastards simply played the game better that night. When they mounted their bikes to leave, they knew they would leave the smaller clubs with a feeling of gratitude rather than the resentment harbored for the Monks. When the conflict between the Monks and the Bloody Bastards heated up again, the Bloody Bastards would have a large reservoir of potential brothers to choose from without the need to intimidate half-hearted members into their midst. And even if members of the smaller clubs didn't prospect for the Bastards, the Bastards were quite certain they could count on the support of the smaller clubs, to some degree. They didn't need the smaller clubs as badly as the smaller clubs needed them, but they still knew that, if guns, knives and other such weapons came into play, having the smaller clubs in their corner was better than not having them there if only to keep the smaller clubs out of the Monks' corner.

Knowing when to leave was as important as knowing when to show up. On that particular night, the Bloody Bastards timed both perfectly. Tunnel Rat drank a couple of beers then excused himself and went outside where he and his brothers mounted their bikes to go.

Tunnel Rat knew that the longer his club hung around the more good will would evaporate. Familiarity breeds contempt, not to mention the possibility that some personal conflict might develop between a member of the smaller clubs and one of his brothers. A little problem like that could spoil the entire stew. As Tunnel Rat put it to his brothers before coming to the party, "You go in and knock 'em out with kindness. Then you leave 'em asking, 'Who was that masked man?'"

As the heroes of the night rode into the metaphorical sunset, the party had a short burst of energy, the kind of energy that commonly accompanies a strong sense of relief. But it didn't last long. Like a flame that burned brightest just before it goes out, the party settled into a quieter stage as the overdue need for sleep, along with other desires, overcame more than a few of the brothers and old ladies in attendance. In pairs and small groups, many of them returned to their homes or found nooks and crannies here and there that offered degrees of solitude. The party wasn't over, but it had certainly entered a new phase.

Chapter 27 — Thar She Blows!

The party seemed to shift into a slow motion as though a haze hung over everything and everyone cloaking all in a surreal state of animated suspension. From the time the Monks arrived to the time that the Bloody Bastards departed, nearly two hours had elapsed. Harold was still behind the bar wondering where Capsize had gone as the brother was scheduled to tend bar until midnight. It seemed to him that Capsize was last seen about the time that the Monks arrived, and the timing of his disappearance wasn't only raising suspicions in Harold's mind. Several other brothers seemed to have noticed and were making occasional and subtle remarks about Capsize's absence.

The net effect was that, as the party continued with the political grandstanding over, Harold found himself tending bar through the night and into the morning. Samurai was scheduled to take over at midnight, but Harold volunteered to take Samurai's shift so that Harold's sponsor could spend some time with his old lady.

It was as though the party took a collective sigh of relief. And following that sigh, the level of drinking intensified, accelerating the collapse and eventual surrender of many of the party goers. The degree of intoxication that was common among his own brothers and the Banshee Riders old ladies, as well as the brothers and old ladies from other clubs, was beyond that which Harold had previously experienced since his induction into the biker lifestyle. In a way, it felt as though Harold was back at Freddie's Place, though, in this instance, Harold was observing drunkards rather than setting the standard.

As the darkness of early morning wore on, encasing the clearing in a bubble of electronically illuminated seclusion, only the few who managed to pace themselves or simply didn't know when to fall down, remained upright. This small handful was a mere fraction of the 150-or-so bikers and old ladies who started actively participating in the revelry the night before, not counting the Monks or Bloody Bastards. The last survivors had assembled at the bar where Harold was the lone representative of the Banshee Riders still standing.

Awake more than 48 hours, with the help of some little white pills Red had supplied, Harold tended to the beverage needs of a brother from the Saxons and a brother from the High Riders, along with several old ladies wearing property patches of brothers from among the local clubs who were off somewhere else by that time. Two days and nights of drinking and mayhem had come down to this as though Harold was among the last cluster of cavalry soldiers on the Little Bighorn.

The Sunday morning conversation was raunchy like a whore advertising her wares at mass. To Harold's surprise, the old ladies added the raunchiest flavors to the mix.

"So, this hillbilly gets married and goes off on his honeymoon," the one old lady began. "The very next day, he returns home. His ma and pa are looking at him all puzzled and stuff. So, they ask him, 'What are you doing back from your honeymoon already?' And he says, 'Well, we got to the honeymoon and everything was goin' just fine when she tells me she's a virgin.' 'Well,' says ma, 'If she ain't good enough for her own family, she ain't good enough for ours.'"

That, and similar jokes caught Harold a little off guard. He didn't expect that from the old ladies. That isn't to say he didn't laugh. Rather, he was seeing a side the old ladies that he hadn't seen before.

Keeping pace with the conversation and laughter, the sun came up over the lake and lit the clearing as though setting it on fire. The golden rays of sunlight, automatically shutting off the lights Samurai and Harold had installed, spilled through the window across the room from the bar and were visible diagonally through the doorway from the porch. One of the old ladies, Snow, an apparent reference to her propensity to put white powder up her nose, was telling how she and another old lady from her club had decided to schmooze up to a middle-aged family-man type at a bar and grill one night just for "shits and grins.

"We were making this dude really uncomfortable," she said. Harold pictured a pair of female cayotes circling an injured rabbit in the middle of the road, especially when she described how the other old lady reached down and grabbed the man's crotch. "When Chantille grabbed his dick, he jumped up from his seat and spilled his beer all over himself. Then he fell back off the bar-stool.

"You should have seen the look on that poor, little dude's face," Snow said. "I think he came in his pants before he hit the floor."

In the middle of the laughter, Cajun, the brother with the High

Riders, pointed out the window behind the bar that overlooked the porch and said, "Hey, check this out."

Harold was walking out from behind the bar to look out the door when he heard Snow say, "What's wrong with this picture?"

Stepping into the clearing out of the path's shadows were a man and a woman. The pair, apparently in their mid-30s, were dressed to the hilt in their Sunday best — she in a formal dress and him in a suit.

The others laughed at Snow's comment. But Harold wasn't laughing. It occurred to him, somehow, that he shouldn't let these people reach the clubhouse. Locking the cashbox, he asked Cajun to watch the bar. Then Harold walked outside to intercept the couple before they came too far. His feet crunched on the gravel as he stepped purposely in their direction, like a gunfighter in a Spaghetti Western confronting the villains for a showdown. He met them halfway to the clubhouse. With a twinge of warning in his voice, Harold asked, "You folks lost?"

Summertime generally found Sebastian Boone in shorts, a Hawaiian shirt, and sandals. Sebastian liked to putter around the yard and was quite proud of his garden and, particularly, his roses. Now that he and Gladys had put the summer house up for sale, he dedicated himself to the garden year-round. The Boones were very hopeful that the young man who was renting the house up north would follow through with a bid to buy the home by the time autumn set in. If not, Sebastian would have to ask his son and daughter to close the house up for the winter. It was a job Sebastian used to handle himself. But the years had finally caught up with the founder of the Family Table restaurant chain. When he hit 65, he finally backed off from his schedule of 70- to 80-hour work weeks. When he hit 70, he retired altogether. He and Gladys had spent the next 15 years as snowbirds, commuting north in the spring and south in the fall. Now, as he neared his 86th birthday, Sebastian no longer had the energy for the trip, not to mention the labor of maintaining two homes (he'd given up on the fishing cabin by the lake long ago).

Considering that his children were well established operating the family business and had little use for or interest in the summer house, the only logical thing to do was to sell the place. A realtor had suggested that, since buyers of that caliber didn't grow on trees in that neck of the woods, they could rent the house out during the summer while it was on the market. That way, not only would they receive rental income, someone would be on hand to handle the upkeep of the house and property. "You never know," the realtor said over the phone, "with a home like this, if we offer an option to buy, your tenants could very well take the place off your hands." It was appearing things might work out just as the realtor had predicted.

Sebastian had spent that Saturday morning pulling some weeds outside and watering the roses. Around noon, he came inside, washed his hands and headed for the kitchen where he knew Gladys would have lunch waiting. Right on time, Gladys placed a plate with an open-faced tuna sandwich, topped with a pineapple ring and a slice of melted cheese, garnished with potato chips and a pickle, on the table in front of Sebastian's usual seat. He slid into his chair at the head of the table and sighed from the physical relief of sitting down.

Sebastian was hardly in the seat when the phone rang. Groaning lightly as he expended the additional energy to stand back up, he reluctantly rose and moved slowly across the room to the phone on the wall. Gladys was returning to the table with a plate of food that mirrored Sebastian's as she watched him for some clue of who was calling.

Sebastian answered the phone with a gruff, "Hello." His tone took on a note of surprise as he said, "Yes, how are you, Norman?"

They didn't know too many Norman's and Gladys quickly deduced that Norman Billings, who owned the home and property across the road from the summer house, was calling. Sebastian listened for a bit, nodding as though Norman could see that he was doing so, and mumbling, "Uh-huh," a couple times.

Sebastian took on a concerned look as he said, "I had no idea," and, after a long pause, "All summer you say?" Finally, Sebastian said, "Well, I'll look into it. No, no, it's OK. I'm glad you called."

When Sebastian hung up the phone, he turned to his wife and said, as though he were describing a termite infestation, "A motorcycle gang has moved into the summer house."

As soon as the biker approached from the front door of the cabin, a scowl began growing on the woman's face as she looked him over. It was as though she had found something particularly distasteful in her bowl of soup. Apparently a little older than the man, and standing slightly in front of her companion, she was the first to respond.

"I might ask you the same question," she said. Her comment caught Harold off guard. Before he could think of a response, the woman continued, "Our parents own this property. They called us this morning because a neighbor said a motorcycle gang had moved into the house."

There was a sharp edge to the woman's tone as though she were addressing a thief caught in the act. In a more conciliatory tone, the man said, "Our folks live in Florida. They asked us to stop by and make sure everything is OK."

While Harold didn't like the woman's attitude, he instinctively recognized the lay of the land. These people had the power to call on the authorities and evict the club from the property. There was a time to be tough and a time for diplomacy. This situation obviously called for a little finesse applied towards the latter.

Knowing it was a bit of a stretch, Harold shifted gears in a flash. He began selling the idea that a motorcycle club on the property was actually a good thing, though he understood the absurdity of his words as they left his mouth. "This place was all rundown before we got here," Harold said. "Neighborhood kids were vandalizing it, painting graffiti on the walls and, believe it or not, someone actually started a fire in the middle of the floor. You wouldn't believe how much work we've done here.

"Trust me, kids and vandals aren't going to mess around here anymore."

His argument might have had some merit if it wasn't for the fact that, the very reason the kids wouldn't come around was also the same reason having a motorcycle club on the premises wasn't such a good idea. The intrinsic connection between motorcycle clubs and violence was apparent even to the casual observer. Lacking any other real option, Harold continued his sales pitch. "Nobody is going to mess with your property while we're here," he said. But as he said it, Harold realized that he'd lost the couple's attention.

Standing facing Harold, their eyes were wide open as they stared over Harold's left shoulder. The woman's mouth had fallen open and her face was transitioning to a bright shade of red.

As Harold's voice trailed off, "... we cut the grass and we make sure no one goes up by ..." he turned his head, as he was speaking, to see what they were looking at.

Harold hadn't seen any of his brothers in several hours. He was pretty sure that Red, Preacher, and Preacher's old lady had crashed out in the backroom where the club had placed a pair of sofas and an armchair. He saw their bikes out front and knew others were around somewhere. For instance, he also saw Grunt's bike in the compound next to several less familiar rides. He had no idea where Grunt was but was sure his brother wouldn't go too far without his bike.

Beyond where the bikes were parked, beyond the clearing for the fire and clubhouse, where Harold had stopped short of cutting the grass, the tall grass gave the effect of a mote surrounding the clubhouse broken only by the drawbridge of a path that disappeared into the woods and led out to the road. The tall grass extended about 10 feet in from the lake. It was in this direction that Harold found the cause for the dismayed and shocked looks on the faces of the citizens.

When some of the people in attendance decided it was time to sleep, or whatever, they merely found spots in the tall grass to lie down. One couple had done so in the tall grass by the lake. As Harold addressed the unexpected visitors it was already close to 9 a.m. The couple, after sleeping out in the grass, had recently woken and were taking advantage of the apparent concealment offered by the tall grass to engage in a private moment.

The grass was just tall enough to suggest that it could effectively hide them from plain sight. Where the camouflage failed was in response to movement. As Harold and the couple watched, a large, bleached-white posterior rose from out of the grass, as though Herman Melville's great-white whale was coming up for air. Just as quickly, it crashed down under the waves of grass. Then, as though the beast were repeatedly coming up for breaths, the bleached bottom broached the tall grass as it rose into the sunlight.

Harold was suddenly speechless. Thinking things couldn't get any worse, he heard a small, familiar and squeaky voice cry out, "YES, OH YES. OOOHHHhhhh." Identifying the voice as Bitter's, Harold surmised that the great, white ass belonged to Grunt.

Harold continued to watch for a few moments as his brain raced from inadequate response to inadequate response. He realized that, once he turned around, once he looked back into their faces, he would have to offer some kind of explanation. But what? He had no idea what to say. It didn't bother Harold to see that Grunt and Bitters were grabbing a piece in the grass that morning. But Harold knew it wouldn't go over well with the piously dressed pair in front of him. Harold knew the situation had utterly torpedoed his sales pitch.

Finally, Harold forced himself to face the inevitable while hoping something would come to him. He turned to find that the couple was still watching Grunt's ass rise before plunging back down below the waves of grass. Their concentration on the bizarre scene beyond Harold's shoulder gave Harold a few more moments to consider his response, but, still, nothing came. Noticing that Harold was looking at them again, the couple finally turned their attention back to Harold.

The woman's face, now bright red, still wore a mask of stunned disbelief. The man was surprised but probably not as dismayed as his companion. Now they stared into Harold's face as though waiting for an explanation. Unable to think of anything to say, Harold simply stared back at them for a moment before shrugging his shoulders as though to say, "Well, these things happen." It wouldn't have been so bad except that a slight grin had crept onto Harold's face.

As the grin appeared at the corners of his eyes and mouth, the woman's look of shock was replaced by a mounting look of rage. For a moment, Harold thought she was going to say something. Instead, she turned sharply on her heels and stormed away. The man followed along behind her, though Harold was certain he saw a flicker of a smirk on the man's face, as well.

The news that week was not good, though it could have been worse. Falstaff's cousin's husband told the club that the owners wanted the club out of there. He had convinced the owners to give the Banshee Riders a couple weeks to vacate the premises, on the condition that they wouldn't have any more parties.

No one seemed too upset by the turn of events, or surprised, and Harold assumed this was because they'd gone through similar circumstances before. In fact, Harold's explanation of Grunt and Bitters' role in the club's pending eviction added a humorous element to the news of their eviction. Grunt, who had no idea he and his old lady had an audience that morning or that they had played a part in the eviction, and who took no offense at the description of his large white posterior, soon took primary possession of the story, sharing it with almost anyone who would listen.

Finding a place to call home is difficult for a motorcycle club. By comparison, it's easy to find an apartment that accepts dogs or cats. In reality, it's probably easier to rent an apartment with a herd of horses than it is for a motorcycle club to find a permanent house or piece of property to rent. It takes a very special kind of landlord. Some clubs eventually get around the problem by buying instead of renting. The problem, of course, is the cost. Even with a relatively cheap mortgage of $600 a month or so, with 24 members, that's $25 each per month. While that wasn't undoable, it didn't leave much for other activities. Furthermore, the social-economic demographic of most clubs included some who would have no trouble coughing up an additional $25. But some of the brothers were already struggling to meet their monthly membership dues of $10 without depriving them of the ability to pay their bar tabs. Parties, like the one the Banshee Riders had just held, could help to cover the rent if the rent was low enough, but they seldom came close enough to covering mortgage payments. And as much as the club enjoyed parties, in terms of making money, the clubs could only dip from that well so often, both in terms of expecting members of other clubs to attend and expecting the brothers to turn out to do the work involved in throwing a party. Then again, operating the clubhouse as an underground tavern, with all the amenities short of a liquor license, was a possibility. That also required a significant commitment of time and effort. The clubhouse, essentially, became a business and its operation a job. For a group of bikers whose first preference was to drink and ride, the necessary enthusiasm of operating a bar was usually short-lived the way a child convinces their parents to buy a dog with promises of, "I'll take the dog out for walks and feed it and pick up after it" only to have those promises fall by the wayside when the child becomes bored with the duties and the dog.

For the Banshee Riders, they counted themselves as lucky to have had a place for the summer and, though they certainly would rather have stayed on indefinitely, they were happy that they had a little time before they had to clear out. For the time being, things went on with the clubhouse just as they had before the party and the visit from the owner's children. They knew that the situation wouldn't last and made the most of things while they could.

Chapter 28 — Initiated

The Monks' and Bastards' visits, the 6 Pack sighting, and news of the club's pending eviction from its clubhouse were the primary topics of discussion when the meeting started the next Friday. Reaper was warning brothers that the period of détente between the two larger clubs was apparently in danger of a rupture. He then dropped another bombshell. "I hear the Swamp Rats are hanging up their colors and prospecting for the Monks," Reaper said.

"What, all of them?" Wide Glide asked with a shocked tone.

"Well, most of them anyway," Reaper said. "It's not the same club without Poacher, and Atilla always was a fucking idiot.

"Most of the Swamp Rats will come in as probates. Atilla gets a full patch right off the bat. You could say that the fucking sellout got his thirty pieces of silver," Reaper added.

"Matthew 26:14-16" ran through Harold's head. He wasn't sure if he was more surprised that he recognized the scripture or that Reaper actually referred to scripture.

"What about Boozer?" asked Samurai. "I can't believe he'd join those Monk fuckers."

A few of the brothers snickered at the turn of phrase but the look on Samurai's face indicated he didn't realize that the way he said "Monk fuckers" could be understood more than one way.

"You never know, one or two may hang up their colors and go independent," Reaper said. "Boozer's always been a stand-up brother. I wouldn't be surprised if he took a pass."

"Why don't we try swinging him over to ride with us?" asked Grunt.

"I wouldn't mind," said Reaper. "But we might want to wait a bit. It would look too much like he chose us over them. Could put him in a trick bag. And we could find ourselves in the same bag with him.

"The worst part of this is that the Swamp Rats are basically giving the Monks a foot in the door of the county. You all need to watch your backs. You can bet we haven't heard the last of the Monks."

"What about the Bastards?" Snake asked.

"I wouldn't start counting on the Bastards to show up every time we're in a pinch," Falstaff said with a tone that carried an edge of warning. "Besides, since when did the Banshee Riders hide behind another club's skirts?"

"So, what are we going to do?' Pot Roast asked directing the question back to Reaper as though Pot Roast thought the Banshee Riders might consider mounting a pre-emptive strike against the Monks.

"For now, we're going to do just what I said we'd do," Reaper said. "Watch your backs and watch each other's backs." Then, looking back at Pot Roast, Reaper added, "Unless someone wants to go out in a blaze of glory."

Reaper apparently thought twice about using such words with Pot Roast. He realized that, of all the Banshee Riders, Pot Roast was the one most likely to seriously entertain such a wild notion. Pot Roast might consider walking into the middle of the Monks with guns blazing as a romantically inspired idea. "And if you're thinking about it, don't," Reaper said. He emphasized the last word and stared into Pot Roast's eyes until the brother nodded his head to indicate that he had heard and understood.

Then Pot Roast, with a grin, said, "Why are looking at me? If any of the brothers is going to go Kamikaze on their asses, that would be Samurai, right?"

Reaper actually smiled as several of the brothers chuckled. Even Samurai was grinning.

"Screw that Kamikaze shit," he said, "I'd go all Bruce Lee on their asses."

The question of 6 Pack, their former brother, then came up. There was unanimous agreement when Reaper predicted, "I wouldn't worry - the Monks'll figure him out sooner or later. And I'm betting 6 Pack will probably find the Monks less forgiving than the Banshee Riders."

Then the discussion turned to the pending eviction. "We have a couple weeks to clear out," Falstaff said. "We can put everything back into my basement this weekend. No reason to wait until the last minute. Between now and then, try not to cause too much of a ruckus out here. I think the neighbor across the street called the owners."

When Pot Roast suggested straightening the neighbors out, Falstaff said, "Fuck that. It's an old retired couple. They had a nice, quiet neighborhood until we came along. How would you feel?"

Pot Roast wasn't convinced that the club didn't have a score to settle with the neighbor, but the subject was dropped. Then the order of business turned to Capsize.

Several of the brothers were unaware of Capsize's disappearance during the Monk's visit. As Capsize wasn't at the meeting, Falstaff was merely reporting the news to the brothers. "We won't take any action until Capsize has a chance to respond," Falstaff said.

When Grunt made a derogatory comment about Capsize Reaper stepped in. "Do you remember when we thought you ripped off the beer money a couple years ago? Maybe we just should've taken your colors and kicked your ass without giving you a chance to defend yourself?"

As Samurai explained to Harold later, the club had a different clubhouse at that time. The cash from the bar was kept in an old-battered-black-metal cash box. Grunt was the last one at the clubhouse one night and found that he couldn't get the box to lock. Rather than leave the box unlocked, he took it home with him. He was among the missing for a couple of days after that and, by the time he showed up at the next meeting, several brothers had jumped to the conclusion he had ripped it off.

In the current situation regarding Capsize, several brothers were fairly certain of guilt even if they intended to give him a fair trial. Several brothers were whispering predictions that Capsize would be lucky if all he did was lose his colors.

"Brothers are dropping like flies around here," Trailer Trash said with some disgust, "and no one has even fired a shot yet."

"I'd say we're better off finding out who will stick and who will run before the shooting start," said Samurai. "If I find myself in a ticklish situation, I want to know I can trust the brother who's supposed to be watching my back."

"No one has dropped yet," Reaper said.

"What about 6 Pack," Trailer Trash said.

"He was gone before he left," Falstaff chimed in. "And he was gone before we knew the Monks were making a play for the county. Besides, like Reaper said, he was a fucking weasel anyhow."

"Yeah, well a couple months ago, that weasel was one of your brothers," Snake added.

"Before we wised up," Grunt added.

"All right already," Reaper said. "That's enough. We wised up and so will the Monks. Fuck 6 Pack."

Several other brothers tried to contribute to the conversation, but Reaper cut them off. "We have other business to deal with," the president said. "And for the next order of business, I need the probates to go outside."

Harold was quietly standing behind Samurai observing the meeting, quiet as a Probate should be. But his mind was drifting as he thought about the look 6 Pack had given him at the party. At first, Harold didn't realize he'd been addressed. When several brothers looked his way his first thought was that he was in trouble for something. He was searching his mind trying to figure out what he might have done wrong when Samurai turned around and barked, "That means you, probate. Get the fuck out, now."

Outside, Harold looked at Red and said, "What do you think we did?"

Red started laughing but didn't answer.

"What the hell are you laughing about?"

"I just think it's funny you don't know," Red said. Then he stopped laughing and said, "I'm pretty sure our sponsors are bringing us up for a vote."

"Together?" Harold asked.

Red shook his head as though his patience were wearing thin. "Try not to be that ignorant when we get back inside, OK? They could change their minds, you know."

If Harold was nervous when he thought he was in trouble, he found that he was twice as nervous when he realized he was probably coming up for a vote. It was as though the hands of time were fighting through a sludge, hardly able to move. Even the ripples across the surface of the lake seemed to have slowed. Though it was little more than 10 minutes before Snake stuck his head out the door and yelled, "Hey, you fucking slugs, get yer asses back in here," Harold would have sworn it felt more like an hour. As though he were the bailiff holding the door to a courtroom, Snake, with one eyebrow raised, stood by to give Harold and Red the evil eye as they passed inside. "While I'm young, God damn it," he growled in a tone of forced annoyance.

Inside, they entered a shadowy, smoke-filled room where fluorescent illumination drifted back and forth with the sway of the light fixture above the pool table. Standing by the door, Harold felt as though he were sweating under the yellow glow of an inquisitor's burning lamp. No one spoke as Harold looked around the room finding the Banshee Riders stone faced and somber, bereft of any trace of emotion, even from his sponsor's face. "Of course, they've voted us in," Harold thought to himself. But at the same time, a nagging fear whispered in his head, "They've voted you down. You'll be lucky to get out of here alive."

"Front and center, shitheads," Falstaff barked as he pointed to the floor at the far side of the pool table.

The two walked around the pool table as though going to meet a firing squad. Then, they stopped in front of Reaper. Reaper never looked larger to Harold. His muscular chest strained at his T-shirt, ready to burst free, presumably as he reached out and grabbed two puny probates and slammed their heads together. Looking into Reaper's face, Harold could almost picture the president biting their heads off. Reading the doubts in their faces, Reaper allowed the silence to soak in for a few moments. In that silence, the tension grew. The sound of his heart pounding was drowning out everything else as Harold glanced around the room again in search of a friendly face or a clue.

Then, Reaper spoke and, for an instant, the universe was hung in suspension. "Do you know what it means to be a Banshee Rider?" Red and Harold stumbled over each other testifying to their commitment to the club and to their brothers. Finally, Reaper interrupted, "Do you know why we make new brothers prospect and probate before we let them wear our patch?"

Red was saying something about the club wanting to check people out before they made them brothers. Harold just said, "To weed out the fuckups."

Reaper started laughing. "We're all fuckups, probate. We make you prospect and probate so you can learn what it takes to be a Banshee Rider. We also do it so you won't embarrass your brothers, your club, and your colors." Then Reaper looked at Samurai and Wide Glide and nodded.

Wide Glide approached Red and Samurai approached Harold. Face to face with Harold, Samurai stuck out his hand as though to shake. When Harold attempted to reciprocate, Samurai pulled the hand away and, with his other hand, slapped a patch into

Harold's open palm. As Harold took the patch, Samurai grasped Harold's hand through the patch. "That patch is a statement of faith," Samurai said. "You understand that?" As Harold nodded, Wide Glide carried the conversation to Red asking, "You understand what we'll do if you fuck up, don't you?" Red nodded and Wide Glide continued, "I'll be the first one kicking yer ass if you do, got that? And I'll be kicking the hardest." Then he looked over at Harold, "And Samurai will be the first one stompin' yer ass."

With that, Samurai congratulated Harold as Wide Glide did the same with Red. Then the brothers were all around them, slapping them on the backs, shaking their hands and, at least to Harold's consternation, planting wet kisses on their lips. Several of the brothers shook beer cans and opened them so that the beer sprayed all over the former probates. It reminded Harold of a baseball team in the clubhouse after winning the World Series.

"All right," Reaper said trying to get everyone's attention. As it didn't quite work, T-Rex hollered, "Shut the fuck up, you assholes. Yer president has the floor."

Reaper turned to Harold and Red and said, "This is your last job as probates. I want you back here in an hour with those patches sewn onto your rags. If you don't make it, don't worry. We'll just give them to someone else."

Samurai walked the two out to their bikes. He slapped an arm around Harold's back and said, "Go to my place. Sue's waiting for you. She's got the sewing machine ready." Then he looked at Red and said, "You too."

They shoved the patches deep into their pockets and fired up their bikes. Together, they rode out of the clearing, through the tunnel of trees and onto the dirt road beyond the compound. When they hit the highway, they opened up their scooters and were soon anxiously doing more than 100 mph through the cool night air. Occasionally, they cast content smiles each other's way. But mostly, they just rode — eyes straight ahead and with a sense of purpose.

Counting the time it took Sue to sew the patches on, while Harold and Red drained a couple cans of beer, it was almost 55 minutes before they pulled their bikes to a stop in front of the clubhouse and put their kickstands down. Most of the brothers were waiting on the porch when they arrived. As Red and Harold stepped off their bikes, someone said something about them cutting it kind of close. Someone even raised the specter of possibility that they were late.

When Red started to protest, Mongrel threw a pair of beers at the new full-patch brothers and said, "Here, shut yer hole and drink up."

About that time, on either side of them, brothers parted to the side exposing a pair of barstools someone had brought out of the clubhouse and placed on the ground about six feet apart and equal distant from the fire that was burning in its usual place. Harold and Red were directed over to the barstools and told to sit down and take off one of each of their boots. A case of beer was placed on the ground next to each of them.

Sitting on the barstool, Harold glanced around at his brothers. They were all looking back with expectant grins. Then Samurai stepped up to Harold and Wide Glide stepped up to Red. Samurai smiled at Harold as he took a can of beer from the ground and opened it. He held out his hand and gestured toward the empty boot Harold was holding. "Here," Samurai said, and Harold handed him the boot. As Samurai began pouring the beer into Harold's boot he asked, "So, how ya feeling?"

"Okay," Harold said with limited conviction.

"Good," Samurai said. By this time, Pot Roast had opened another beer. When Samurai had finished pouring the first beer into Harold's boot, Pot Roast handed the second beer to Harold's sponsor, and then another and another until the boot was nearly filled to the brim.

When Samurai handed the beer-filled boot to Harold, he said, "Drink up, bro."

Harold took the boot and glanced over at Red in time to see that Red was receiving the same treatment a few feet away. Then Harold tipped the back lip of the boot up to his mouth and began drinking. He had guzzled about half of the beer, though much of it spilled down the front of his shirt when he thought to catch his breath. But when Harold went to lower the boot, he noticed that Samurai's hand was under the heel holding it up, so Harold was forced to continue guzzling. As soon as the boot was empty, Samurai, Pot Roast, Snake and several others opened beers and began pouring them into the boot simultaneously. As a result,

Harold only had a moment to catch his breath before he was guz-zling again. To make matters worse, Grunt pulled a large canning jar out from under his jacket. The liquid inside the jar glowed flu-orescent green. Grunt waved the jar in front of his brothers with a proud grin. Then he unscrewed the cover and poured a large amount of its contents into Harold's boot, mixing it with the beer. As Harold tipped the boot full of beer and mystery mix up to his lips, Grunt added some of the concoction to Red's boot.

When Harold finished his second boot full, while the broth-ers were filling it again, Falstaff dangled a small perch in front of Harold's face. The fish was wiggling by its tail in a vain and final attempt at freedom. Harold was none too pleased when Falstaff said, "Eat this quick." Harold was swallowing the fish whole when he started to choke. For a second, Harold thought he was going to puke but, somehow, Harold managed to hold back the urge and the vomit. An instant later he was pouring another boot full of green-tainted beer down his throat.

As Harold drained the boot full of beer, he felt Samurai tugging at his rag. Samurai slipped the rag off of Harold's shoulders and pulled his arms out of the sleeveless vest. Then Samurai walked a few feet away and threw the rag inside down onto the ground. As Harold was drinking from his boot, he noticed that Samurai and several other brothers were gathered around his rag piss-ing on it. Red's rag was on the ground next to Harold's and the brothers were running their piss back and forth giving both the same treatment. In twos and threes, all the brothers took turns draining golden streams onto the rags.

As Harold was watching the anointing of his colors, with a boot full of beer up to his lips, he suddenly felt something cold and sticky in his hair. He wasn't sure what it was until it rolled down his face and into his left eye. The smell told him that it was mo-tor oil. His eye was burning, and Pot Roast had pulled a bandana from his pocket and was wiping at Harold's eye. Harold wasn't sure if Pot Roast's efforts were helping or making matters worse. What Harold knew was that the oil was painfully burning; it was difficult to keep his eye open.

Harold heard Pot Roast bark at someone, "Will you stop al-ready? You're getting it in his eyes." But whoever Pot Roast said this to didn't respond other than to point the stream of oil further back on Harold's head. As Harold emptied the boot he was able to tip his head back further and, instead of rolling down his face, he could feel the cold sensation of oil trickling down his back and the sides of his neck.

About halfway through his third boot full, Harold realized Red was power puking from the other barstool. The brothers around him were cheering as though he'd just scored a touchdown in a football game. It suddenly occurred to Harold that he wasn't expected to hold it in. Bringing the initiates to the point of heaving was one of the objectives of the ritual. Harold tipped the boot further, so the beer plunged into his open mouth in greater volume. He was quickly rewarded with a fresh urge to heave. This time, Harold didn't fight it and was quickly rewarded as, beginning in his stomach, the flow in his esophagus was suddenly reversed.

As soon as Harold finished puking, Samurai shoved the boot back up to Harold's face and said, "Come on, keep drinking." Harold noticed that T-Rex was adding whiskey to the mix and Grunt, who had run out of his private concoction, was now adding Boone's Farm apple wine to Harold's boot. After his fourth boot full, as Harold was nearly done with the case of beer, Derelict handed Harold a recently captured cricket and said, "Here." Harold shoved it in his mouth and washed it down with a freshly filled boot-full of beer.

When all the cases of beer at their feet were finished, and all the beer was drained from their boots, Wide Glide and Trailer Trash stepped in front of them. There was a loud thunk as both brothers dropped one end of the heavy chains they were holding behind their backs. The chains were about 10-feet long.

Until that moment, Harold was thinking the worst was over. With fresh doubts, he and Red were led away from the fire over to where Samurai's and Wide Glide's bikes were parked facing away from the clubhouse. Pot Roast took the bandana he'd used to wipe oil from Harold's eyes and blindfolded the new Banshee Rider. Red was similarly blindfolded. Then Harold and Red were each made to sit down behind their sponsors' bikes as one end of a chain was wrapped around their legs. Harold could hear the chains clunking against the motorcycle in front of him and realized Trailer Trash was connecting the other end of the chain to the bike.

From the laughs Harold heard, he realized he had thought "Oh shit!" out loud.

"That's right, NB," he heard Reaper say, "if you survive this part of the initiation, we might just keep yeah."

Harold felt a tug on the chain as someone checked that it was secure. Then the bikes started. As the motors were revved repeatedly, roaring to higher and higher RPMs, Harold felt another tug on the chain as someone else felt the need to check. Trailer Trash, who was close by to Harold's left, yelled, "Are you two roadkills ready?"

Harold braced himself and nodded. The engines revved high again only, this time, the brothers held the throttles open, winding the engines at full throttle. As they released the clutches, Harold could hear the rear tires digging at the dirt and could feel rocks and particles of dirt kicking up in the faces and chests of the new Banshee Riders. Harold could hear the bikes tearing forward and gritted his teeth in preparation for the moment when the chain snapped tight and he was dragged across the yard. When the chain yanked, however, it wasn't with the intensity Harold had expected. The bikes came to a stop 10 yards away and, as Samurai and Wide Glide cut the engines, Harold could hear his brother's laughing. Through the laughter, he heard Falstaff shout, "Okay, drop your drawers. We want to see which one of you shit yourself."

As the chains, which were never actually attached to the bikes, were removed from their legs, Harold and Red removed the bandanas from their faces. They then accepted beers from their sponsors that were offered without a sense that the cans needed to be drained quickly. Harold had thought Falstaff was kidding about the "drop your drawers" comment. But when Red and he didn't do so, Falstaff made the comment again.

Harold said, "Take my word for it, I didn't shit my pants, close, but no cigar."

"I said drop your drawers," Falstaff barked again.

With some resignation, Harold and Red obeyed the directive and were soon standing with their pants around their knees. As he casually took a swig from his beer, Harold smugly smiled and said to Falstaff, "Satisfied?"

"Yeeesss," Falstaff said. Then he added, "Of course, if I cared to look any closer, I'm bettin' you'd have a hefty racing stripe in your shorts if you were wearin' any." As he spoke, Falstaff and several others pried the flip tops loose on beers they were holding. The beer inside was carefully aimed so that the cans exploded all over Harold and Red. The new brothers were soon doused with beer. Though Red jumped back in surprise, Harold acted as though nothing was happening. He simply continued to drink from his beer and smiled at his brothers.

With the initiation ritual complete, Falstaff locked up the clubhouse and the brothers mounted their bikes for a ride to Hildie's where several of the old ladies were waiting. As he stepped onto his bike, Harold found himself next to Grunt. Harold leaned towards Grunt and asked, "What was in that jar?"

Grunt and several other brothers laughed. Harold saw Red turn an ear in Grunt's direction as he was also curious about the mixture. "Nothing much. Just a mix of lake water, water from my fish tank at home and toilet water from the clubhouse," Grunt said. "Oh, and I added a little kitty litter for flavor."

As the brothers laughed, Red actually gave a dry heave again, and Pot Roast looked like he would join in. Harold just shook his head and said, "Yum," with more than a little sarcasm.

"You like it?" Grunt asked. "I can always mix some more up for ya."

"I'll let you know," Harold said with a big grin.

The ride to Hildie's felt particularly chilly for Harold and Red as their rags were soaked with urine, they were soaked with beer and their heads were doused in oil. After pulling into the parking lot outside the bar, and preparing to walk inside, the two had their path cutoff by Reaper. "You're Banshee Riders now," Reaper said. "I expect you to strut your stuff tonight. Don't take any shit from anyone, understand?"

They both looked at Reaper, then at each other, looked back at Reaper and nodded.

Inside, Darrell, a regular at the bar Harold had heard Trailer Trash call a "fucking wannabe," who had never owned a motorcycle in his life but liked to imagine himself an honorary member of the Banshee Riders, came over and threw a drunken arm around Harold's shoulder. "Congratulations, kid," he said drunkenly as though he were a father offering encouragement to his son. Harold didn't like Darrell much and, when Darrell pulled his arm away exclaiming, "Hey, your back's all wet," Harold merely smiled at Darrell and said, "Yeah, I know."

While Harold didn't mind that Darrell put his arm in piss, he did warn Sue when she offered another hug to go with the one she'd given him after sewing on the center patch. Sue said, "So what" in a way that indicated she already knew and gave him the hug anyhow.

Whatever Reaper had intended, in terms of strutting his stuff, Harold wasn't sure. There were only a few citizens, including Darrell, in the bar that night. By 1 a.m., Harold was fairly well inebriated but doing a fair job of holding it all together. All the same, he was tired and, since a number of the brothers had headed for the hills already, Harold didn't mind when Samurai suggested they head back to his place.

The trio drank at Samurai's until about 2:30 in the morning when Sue announced she was going to bed and Samurai said, "Wait up. I'll go with you."

Harold sat on the couch finishing his last beer of the night and thinking about the events of the day. He looked over at his rag, which was stretched out on the linoleum by the front door to finish drying. Looking at the center patch and realizing he was a full-fledged member of the Banshee Riders, Harold couldn't help but feel an overwhelming sense of accomplishment. His mother certainly wouldn't share his sentiments, nor, he doubted, would his father have, if his father was still alive. But for Harold, though he had stumbled into the process almost by happenchance, he realized that, once he had set his sights on this, he had stuck with it until he made the grade. For a low-life, worthless Freddie's-place drunk, the inner essence of the person he had long since accepted himself to be, he couldn't feel better if he was a young man who had worked his way up to an invitation to an Ivy League school based on nothing more than personal determination.

He sat and stared at his rag for a while and before he lay down to sleep, Harold couldn't help but walk over and kneel down next to his colors. In spite of the still-damp urine, Harold reached out and felt the center patch. He ran his fingers over the embroidered material, over the obscene picture of a skeleton pulling back hard on a screaming naked woman's hair while she held the axles for the front and rear wheels. He ran his hand over the patch as though he were absorbing a hidden message written in braille. Then he wiped his hands on his pant leg and flopped down on the couch to sleep, a towel on the pillow to protect it from the oil he hadn't even tried to wash out of his hair yet.

Chapter 29 — The Visit

It was the height of over-optimism to think the brothers would show up Saturday to start cleaning out the clubhouse considering the extent of the initiation party Friday night. But over the course of the next couple weeks, as the club progressively moved the bar, pool table and furniture out of the clubhouse, the inter-club tension in the county intensified. With the moral and fiscal support of their new brothers, the former Swamp Rats established a chapter of the Monks with a clubhouse only one-and-a-half miles down the road from Hildie's and in the direction of the clubhouse the Banshee would soon abandon. As a result of the proximity of the Monks' clubhouse, and their own eviction dragging on beyond the two-week deadline, the Banshee Riders found themselves passing the small cabin, where the newly minted Monks had set up housekeeping, on a frequent basis. It wasn't uncommon to observe Monks through the trees outside their new clubhouse or to see Monks on the road in the general vicinity.

The process of initiating former Swamp Rats into the Monks had moved quickly. However, it was soon understood that the new chapter of Monks was also stocked with several pre-existing Monks.

Once, while he was passing the Monks' clubhouse, a Monk had waved to Harold. Harold nodded back with a lack of real enthusiasm. On other occasions, Monks by the road in front of their clubhouse merely stared coldly as Harold went by. Samurai had noticed the same thing and, one day, he approached Reaper and said, "This is bullshit. We can't just pretend they're not there."

"What do you suggest," Reaper asked.

"I think we should pay them a visit," Samurai said. "Show 'em we're not intimidated – that we've got some class."

Reaper nodded quietly as he pondered the suggestion. Then, coming to a conclusion, he said, "You're right. Turn the tables on 'em a little."

That Friday, Samurai's idea was discussed at the meeting, just after Capsize, who claimed he was sick as an excuse for his sudden absence at the party, was busted to probate, a move Harold felt was a slap on the wrist considering. Several brothers were not thrilled with the idea of paying the Monks a visit. However, even those who thought it unnecessarily risky were reticent to vote against the plan. Following the meeting, calls went out to brothers who had missed the meeting. Even a couple of retired brothers Harold hadn't heard of before were called. Attendance for the visit was mandatory and Falstaff suggested that any brother who didn't show up might wish the Monks had beat the crap out of them. "I don't care if you're on your fucking deathbed," he said, glancing Capsize's way, "You WILL be there."

"And we're not going so you can get drunk and act like an idiot," Reaper added. "So, keep your shit together. And that's an order."

Harold asked Samurai what the deal was with retired brothers.

"They're brothers who rode with the club for five years and retired in good standing," said Samurai. "They get to hang onto their colors with the understanding that we might call on them if things get hairy."

"Will they show up?" Harold asked.

"They don't have to," said Samurai. "But if they don't, we'll probably show up at their house one night demanding their colors.

"Remember when I told you how the Monks would collect some citizen riders to swell their numbers before showing up at a clubhouse or a club's bar? Well, we don't do that, but we do call in some markers."

That next day, Reaper and Falstaff stopped by the Monks' clubhouse and drank a few beers with Atilla, the chapter's president. While there, Reaper managed to finagle an invitation out of the former Swamp Rat and made it sound as though it were Atilla's idea in the process. Reaper also managed to set up the visit for a weeknight. This was crucial as it made it easier to beg off for an earlier departure; the Banshee Riders wanted to make a statement but, the longer they hung out, the more drunk they got, the more likely it was that they would make a different statement.

Setting up the appointment was necessary because it would have been a faux pas to show up unannounced, especially since the Banshee Riders would have risked that a nervous Monk might think it was some kind of an assault and open fire. The flip side of providing the Monks with advance warning of the visit was that the Monks would also have a chance to inflate their numbers. As a result, when the Banshee Riders pulled up outside the Monks' clubhouse, it was no surprise that the Monks, along with a few last-minute recruits from area bars, had called in other chapters to support the new chapter. With their 27 brothers and retirees, the Banshee Riders were outnumbered about three to two.

For the Banshees Riders, the goal was to demonstrate that they had the balls to show up and, therefore, the Monks couldn't count on the smaller club to pack in their colors just because the Monks had moved into the neighborhood. Of course, if anyone scratched the surface of the motivation that brought the Banshee Riders out for a visit that evening, the observer would find that the very sense of intimidation the club was trying to disprove was actually the honest reason for the visit.

For the Monks, intimidation was the foundation of initiative and they had no intention of losing it, regardless of what the Bloody Bastards might have to say on the subject. Unlike the visit the Monks paid to the Banshee Riders' party, there was little chance the Bloody Bastards would come to the rescue this time. Still, the move impressed the Monks. As Shiv put it, "At least these Banshees have enough class to show up." A thin, blonde-haired prospect for the Monks was standing within earshot when Shiv made the comment. From the icy smile on the prospect's face, it was difficult for Shiv to say what he was thinking. The Banshee Riders, and Harold in particular, wouldn't have had any trouble understanding what that smile meant.

Reaper gathered the brothers into a group before the Banshee Riders left Hildie's for the short ride to the Monks' clubhouse. "We arrive together, and we leave together," he said. "And watch your asses. Anybody fucks up, getting your ass kicked by the Monks will be the least of your concerns. Nobody does anything stupid, got that? And keep in mind, the Monks will be more than happy to help you fuck up." Reaper stood surveying his brothers to make sure they'd all heard what he'd said and, more importantly, taken it to heart. Then he said, "Okay then, mount up."

The incident the club hoped to avoid was the potential fly in the ointment for the Banshee Riders' plan. Without an incident, that is to say, without something that gave the Monks a chance to overreact and dramatically hike the tension between the clubs, the Banshees would make their statement and retire to Hildie's or their clubhouse essentially intact. But if something occurred to give the Monks the excuse, any excuse they patiently hoped for, like a Venus Flytrap watching an insect lighting closer and closer to striking distance, the Banshee Riders could leave the Monks clubhouse battered, bruised, without their pride and, potentially, without their colors. It wasn't common for a club to have its colors pulled en masse, but it wasn't out of the realm of possibility either.

It was in this environment that the Banshee Riders were welcomed into the Monks lair. In the shadows of the heavily wooded lot, as the sun crept out of sight to the West, the Banshee Riders were awkwardly greeted by the former Swamp Rats, augmented by Monks from other chapters. The other Monks, most of them from the city, hung back watching until Shiv, taking the lead in spite of a pouting Atilla, broke the ice by inviting Reaper inside. Darkness soon chased most of the others into the small building as well.

Harold had an eye open for 6 Pack, as he sensed 6 Pack might welcome the Banshee's visit as something of an opportunity. But as Harold stepped through the door of the dimly lit clubhouse, he still hadn't seen the former Banshee Rider. Harold, Red, and Samurai stepped to the bar together and ordered a round of beers for themselves. When Samurai tried to pay, Shiv, who was talking with Reaper and Falstaff a few feet away, leaned over and said, "Your money's no good here, bro." As Samurai, Red, and Harold unanimously offered their thanks, Shiv added, with an obvious reference to the visit they had paid at the Banshee Riders' party, "The Monks know how to treat guests."

It came off as a little bit of a backhanded compliment, as though Shiv was commenting on the incident in the Banshee's clubhouse when Harold had tried to charge him for beers. But the Banshee Riders accepted it with grace and lifted their beers in a toast to the Monks.

As they lifted the beer steins to their mouths, Harold was jolted by a stiff arm to the center of his back that could have launched the contents of his mug all over Shiv. Quick reflexes paid off as Harold stumbled forward but managed to shift the glass to balance and restrain the contents until the waves calmed. Only a small amount of the hops escaped, and those splashed onto Harold's own shirt.

As he regained his composure and straightened back up, he turned to find his nemesis 6 Pack crouched down steadying himself with his right forearm on the edge of the bar. Harold knew better when 6 Pack said, "Sorry, I, uhm, ... tripped."

Harold had a sense that he was walking a thin line. On the one hand, he'd narrowly avoided presenting Shiv with a chance to react, for Harold had little doubt that, fair or not, had Harold's beer spilled all over Shiv's shirt, the Monk president would have relished the opportunity. There was still the question of how Harold should proceed going forward. A part of him wanted nothing more than to reach out and pop 6 Pack in the jaw, and then to follow that up with the liberal application of Harold's boots to 6 Packs face, body, and balls. But Harold hadn't lost sight of where he and his brothers were, and he suspected that launching into the former Banshee Rider, might prove an excuse the Monks could hardly dream for. Still, Harold knew he couldn't go too far in the other direction, either. He needed to avoid trouble without letting on that he was doing so.

Harold could almost feel Shiv's eyes on his back, waiting and watching for Harold's response. "Maybe I should verbally confront 6 Pack about being so fucking clumsy," Harold thought for a second. Of course, that would probably lead to an escalation of the situation. "Then again, maybe I should ignore the asshole altogether." Then another alternative occurred to Harold. He knew what 6 Pack was up to and either of the other reactions seemed to leave the door open for 6 Pack to continue prodding and poking for the desired opportunity. But there was one reaction that would make further intrigues more difficult.

Harold set his beer on the bar and stepped quickly towards 6 Pack. Anticipating an assault, 6 Pack was just beginning to stand up from the bar when Harold grabbed the Monk probate by the waist and the free arm. To 6 Pack's surprise and consternation, Harold gently helped the former Banshee to his feet as though 6 Pack were an elder citizen who'd tripped on a curb. As Harold did so, in the most saccharin voice he could muster, a voice that best presented the public demeanor Harold sought while leaving no question in 6 Pack's mind about Harold's real feelings, Harold said, "Are you OK? You know, you really should be more careful." Then, as 6 Pack stood with his mouth hanging open with a mix of surprise and confusion, Harold picked his beer back up off the bar and turned to face Shiv and the others.

Harold noticed a slight glint in Shiv's eyes. It was as if Shiv had read between the lines of the entire little charade and appreciated Harold's smooth handling of the problem. Then Shiv actually chuckled a little as he glanced over Harold's shoulder at 6 Pack who was still standing there, now glaring at Harold's back. Harold turned and followed the direction of Shiv's eyes until Harold was staring back into 6 Pack's red face. Harold smiled with a "got-ya" grin as he heard Shiv say, "Make yourself useless, probate. Make sure everyone has something to drink." As the Monk prospect turned to go, Shiv added, "And try not to fall down anymore."

6 Pack took a pitcher of beer in one hand and a stack of plastic cups in the other and headed off to make sure everyone had something to drink. As he did so, 6 Pack had a look on his face that suggested he was kicking himself over his clumsy effort to drag Harold and the Banshee Riders down. Harold could almost see the wheels turning in 6 Pack's mind, "I should have waited for a better opening. Hell, I should have hit him harder." But there was nothing 6 Pack could do at this juncture as he threw a resentful glance over his shoulder at Harold while hurrying off to pour some beers. And as the night went on, the Monks kept 6 Pack and several Monk prospects and probates running. The former Banshee Rider was either pouring beer inside or running drinks outside. At one point, in a scene reminiscent of one of Harold's prospecting experiences, Atilla intentionally spilled some beer and had 6 Pack and another prospect wiggle about on their backs cleaning up the floor. The best part of that was when Reaper had Capsize join the Monk prospects on the floor, wiggling around on his back while screaming, "I'm a dying Banshee Rider cockroach."

For the Monks, having their probates hustle filled two requirements. First, it helped demonstrate what gracious hosts the brothers were. Second, it showed the dedication and obedience the Monks demanded of their probates. It was as if the Monks were slave owners using their position over their slaves as a demonstration of power for the benefit of visiting slave owners. In response, the Banshee Riders also sent two newly acquired prospects scurrying around fulfilling occasional and inane tasks that were imbued with sudden and inflated importance.

The net result was that 6 Pack had little opportunity to take another crack at Harold and the Banshee Riders. His opportunities were running shorter as the time of the Banshee Riders' departure approached.

Harold was surprised to find that he was actually enjoying himself. Though he was sure the Monks would welcome a slipup by the Banshee Riders, the brothers from the larger club concentrated on acting the good hosts and, possibly in response to the Bastards' superior diplomatic response, seemed inclined to building better relations with the smaller club.

Harold had spent most of the evening speaking with Reaper, Samurai and Shiv and noticed that, though Shiv didn't come right out and say so, the Monks president seemed to imply that the Banshees would be welcomed should they decide to hang up their colors and prospect for the larger club. After all, intimidation wasn't the only way to persuade another club. Instead of intimidation, Shiv was now relying on attraction, though the Banshee Riders were never as attracted as the Monks might have hoped.

In spite of having a generally good time, Harold was no more inclined to complain than any of his other brothers when, shortly after midnight, Reaper announced that the Banshee Riders had some personal business to attend to and would have to leave.

Many of the Monks hung back on their clubhouse porch, nodding or saying, "Thanks for stopping by," as the Banshees headed out the door and out to their bikes. Shiv, Atilla, and a couple other Monks, however, followed the Banshees to the bikes. Harold noticed that 6 Pack was tailing along and his internal radar kicked on wondering what the prospect was up to.

As Harold reached his bike, 6 Pack stepped up and, in an overly gracious tone, said, "I just realized I forgot to congratulate you on making full patch." 6 Pack stood smiling at Harold, who realized that the former Banshee Rider still hadn't said, "Congratulations," but only acknowledged his failure to do so.

All the same, Harold played along and acted as though he'd just received the gesture and said, "Thanks."

As the Monks who'd followed along had struck up final conversations before the Banshee Riders actually left, even the Banshee Riders who'd straddled their bikes had yet to start them. More

Monks had drifted over from the porch when 6 Pack said to Harold, as though he'd never seen Harold's bike before, "That's one sweet ride you've got there."

Again, Harold said, "Thanks."

"How's it ride," 6 Pack continued.

"Rides great, you know, for a hardtail," Harold said, sensing that 6 Pack was up to something.

"Fast?"

"Relatively," Harold said.

"Yeah, but I'll bet that kicker is a pain in the ass?" the former Banshee Rider asked.

"Not really," Harold said. "In fact, I prefer a kick start."

"Why's that?" 6 Pack asked.

"I don't have to worry that I'll be running down the road someday trying to jump-start a bike with a dead battery."

"Sure, you don't mind," 6 Pack said, "but what about your brothers?"

"What about 'em?" Harold asked.

"Well, how do you think they feel having to wait for you to start your bike every time the club goes somewhere?"

"My bike starts fine," Harold said, as the scent of a rat increased.

"Well, maybe your bike is special," 6 Pack said smugly. "But I've never known a kicker to fire up with the electric starts." 6 Pack looked at Harold as though expecting a response. When none came, 6 Pack continued. "How many kicks does it take to start this pig?"

To Harold, the conversation was absurd. "Who the hell cared," he told himself. By this time, a couple full-patch members of the Monks had come over and were checking out Harold's bike and listening in on the conversation. Harold glanced at them then back at 6 Pack and said, "Usually, it's a one-kicker."

6 Pack shrugged his shoulders as though he didn't exactly believe Harold but wasn't going to argue the point. But then, almost as an afterthought, he said, "Care for a little wager?"

The mention of a wager seemed to perk the interest of several other Monks in the area. Suddenly, Harold found himself with an audience and a sense that he couldn't easily back away from the offer of a bet. Then again, Harold wasn't kidding. More times than not, Magdelina fired up on the first kick or, at least, when she was hot or cold. It was only in the mid-ranges when the bike had warmed up just a little or had run just long enough that she was between hot and cold, that Magdelina gave Harold any trouble. At those times, he knew that his ride tended to kick back roughly and wasn't as eager to fire. Considering how long the club had visited, Harold was certain that his bike had cooled completely. There was no reason it shouldn't fire up on the first kick.

As Harold seemed to be contemplating the idea of a bet, 6 Pack volunteered, "How about $20 bucks."

Harold tipped his head lightly to indicate that he accepted the bet, as one of the other Monks beside 6 Pack said, "You can put me in for that, too." When the other also asked Harold to cover his $20, Harold had found himself with $40 on the line when another Monk spoke up and the number jumped by $20. Harold said, "Fine," again and 6 Pack asked, "You got enough scratch to cover that?"

"I've got it," Harold said.

"Well, let's see it," 6 Pack said.

Walking up from behind Harold, Shiv interrupted, "If he says he has it, he has it. Besides, I'm sure he knows what the Monks do with Welchers."

Harold turned to see a sly grin contorting Shiv's face. Then, the Monks president asked, "You got another $50 to cover me?"

Harold definitely didn't like the way this was going. But if there wasn't much room to maneuver out of the situation before Shiv stepped in there was even less room now. Harold reached into his pocket and withdrew a wad of cash. Struggling in the moonlight, he counted $132 and told Shiv, "Yeah, I've got you covered."

Atilla, who had followed Shiv over, now asked for a $50 wager of his own. Feeling that the situation was quickly getting out of control, Harold said, "I'm sorry, I haven't got it."

From behind Atilla, another voice chimed in as Reaper said to Atilla, "I'll cover your $50." Then other voices spoke up, offering and accepting bets. All the bets fell along the same lines — the Banshee Riders bet that Harold's bike would start in one kick and the Monks bet that it wouldn't.

As he wondered how things had come so far so quickly, it dawned on Harold that 6 Pack had managed to set the stage

403

for a potential incident. It also occurred to Harold that, though Magdelina generally started on one kick, occasionally it took one or two additional kicks, even if the bike was at a preferred temperature — hot or cold. In any case, it was hardly a sure thing for Harold and his brothers and he was wishing that his brothers had resisted the urge to step up in Harold's defense, as he was sure that was the underlying motivation for many of the bets his brothers placed.

Harold glanced around and, sensing that all the bets were in, he reached under the right tank to lift and turn the tickler lever thereby unseating the needle in the carburetor that customarily blocked the boost of gasoline used when starting the bike. Then Harold turned the switch between the tanks allowing electricity to flow from the battery to the points. Now, Harold had a choice. Usually, he left the throttle alone when starting the bike cold. The drawback was that, if it didn't fully catch, the bike could stall out before Harold had a chance to give it some gas. When he did turn the throttle, if he turned it too fast or too slow, the bike could also stall out. Harold was pretty sure that, if the bike didn't start and then stay running, the Monks would claim they had won the bet. Another option was giving it a little gas. But this generally impeded the process of starting the bike and was not part of the preferred method even when he and his brothers didn't have several hundred dollars riding on the issue. Holding the throttle wide open was another option. This certainly helped when the bike was lukewarm and more troublesome to start. It also raised the risk of the kicker biting back at Harold. As leaving the throttle alone was the best immediate choice, Harold simply steeled himself to feather the throttle properly so that the bike would keep running after he kicked it over.

At last, Harold flipped the kicker pedal out and, while standing on the side of the bike, he lifted his right boot onto the pedal. Steadying himself, Harold was about to kick when he glanced over at 6 Pack. The confident smile on 6 Pack's face screamed "Rat" as though the word were spoken out loud. Harold hesitated, and 6 Pack snarled, "What, afraid?"

Harold's boot was an instant away from plunging the kicker pedal down. His muscles tensed and he prepared to lift his body by holding onto the handlebars and the bitch bar on the back of the bike. With everyone watching, Harold stopped. He slowly lowered his foot from the pedal. Then Harold reached around and opened the petcock, a step in the procedure he'd nearly forgotten. A couple of Monks snickered that he'd come so close to blowing the bet.

He was still looking at 6 Pack, whose face continued to wear that confident, sneering grin, as Harold raised his foot and placed it back on the pedal. Before it got there, however, he lowered it back to the ground. Several Monks groaned and he heard 6 Pack say, "Come on already."

Harold glanced over at Reaper who looked back inquisitively in the moonlight. It was as if the president were trying to figure out what the problem was without asking the question outright. Then Harold smiled, he reached around by the petcock again. This time, however, his hands felt along below the tank for the ignition cables that ran to the spark plugs. Sure enough, someone had disconnected the wires from the plugs, and Harold had a pretty good idea who that was.

While looking back at 6 Pack he snapped the spark plug wires into place by feeling around for the tips of the plugs sticking out from the cylinder heads. Though his effort was foiled, 6 Pack had an even bigger grin on his face as he asked disingenuously, "I wonder how that happened?"

Harold heard a few chuckles from those around them in response to 6 Pack's trick. Then the crowd grew absolutely silent as Harold lifted his foot back onto the pedal. This time, he only hesitated a moment before driving the pedal down hard. The bike instantly roared to life as Harold grabbed the throttle and gave the carburetor just enough gasoline to raise the idle slightly. He held it there for several seconds. Then, he reached under the tank again and released the tickler, allowing it to fall back into its seat. Magdelina went from purring to loping at idle as Harold took his hand off the throttle control. He hovered his hand over the throttle control only a second to make sure the engine wouldn't die before he relaxed and looked back at 6 Pack.

This time, the smile on 6 Pack's face was forced, barely masking the bitterness behind it. Harold was tempted to extend his hand for the money that was due. Instead, he just stared at 6 Pack waiting. Out of the corner of his eye, Harold saw Shiv approaching. "Nicely done," the Monks president said as he handed Harold two $20s and a $10. With a little less enthusiasm, the other Monks standing with 6 Pack also paid Harold who could see Monks settling their bets with some of his brothers. 6 Pack, however, was glued in place as if paying the debt was the final insult and more than the former Banshee Rider could handle. He only moved to pay up when Shiv turned to him and said, "Pay the man. Monks, sure the fuck, don't Welch on bets."

As Harold took the money from 6 Pack, Harold was quite certain he saw an "I'll get you" twinkle in 6 Pack's eyes.

"Be seeing you around," 6 Pack said in a tone that was very nearly an open threat.

Harold smiled and nodded. Then, just for the hell of it, Harold said, "You bet" as he waved with the cash in his hand.

In response to Harold's words, 6 Pack actually rocked forward on the balls of his feet as though he were about to strike. But then the probate regained his composure. "No problem," he said. "Of course, you'll have to give me a chance to win my money back sometime."

Harold merely smiled as bikes were starting all around him. Finally turning his back on 6 Pack, Harold followed the brother in front of him out onto the highway as the club turned towards Hildie's.

As they were cruising down the highway, Harold leaned over and yelled to Samurai, "I don't think he was going to pay until Shiv spoke up."

Samurai nodded. Then he said, "Well, don't start thinking Shiv is your new buddy or something. Some snakes smile just before they strike."

The warning made sense to Harold. But just then, Harold was thinking of a different snake. It occurred to Harold that, since he first started prospecting with the Banshee Riders, every time Harold was in a confrontation with 6 Pack, Harold came out on top. Odds alone suggested it wouldn't always work out that way. And Harold had little doubt that 6 Pack was hoping for another chance to strike.

Chapter 30 — Blood on the Floor

The club had a relatively quiet weekend following their visit to the Monks clubhouse. It was almost as if, between their own party and the visit, the brothers were feeling a little tuckered. Saturday night, Harold, Samurai and Sue knocked a few down at Hildie's and then returned to Samurai and Sue's house where they spent the rest of the night watching "The Westerner," a Gary Cooper and Walter Brennan film that Harold and Samurai liked more than Sue did.

Wednesday of the next week, Harold found himself out in the rain all day trenching for electrical piping at a jobsite for a strip mall. Drenched, filthy and tired, he went inside with the tools around quitting time and found Samurai looking at a blueprint as Harold loaded tools into the gangbox. Harold was half tempted to go straight to Chester's where he could shower and grab some clean, dry clothes. But on the other hand, a day like that filled him with a sense that he'd earned the right to stop for a few drinks, not that he would have skipped the idea if he felt less deserving.

"Wanna stop at Hildie's for a couple," he asked Samurai.

"Can't tonight," Samurai said. "Sue's going out with the girls and I promised to watch the kids. You can come over, if you'd like."

Harold considered the invitation for a minute and then decided he'd really rather sit down in the bar and not worry about children just then. He was cold, wet and tired and, though he was very fond Ringo and Montana, he wasn't in the mood for the proverbial 20 questions that always came when he arrived at Samurai's. As Samurai slid into the front seat of the van, and Harold prepared to start his bike, Harold yelled over to Samurai, "Maybe I'll stop by later.

"I'll be there," Samurai said. Then, leaning out the window after he'd closed the door, in an imitation of a character on the 'Hill Street Blues' television show, Samurai added, "Let's be careful out there."

Harold nodded and smiled as they pulled out of the job site and headed in opposite directions.

When Harold arrived at Hildie's, he found that he was the only brother at the bar. He sensed that the lethargy that had overtaken the club that weekend hadn't entirely worn off. Maybe he was reading more into it than there really was but, usually, he'd find at least two or three of his brothers in the bar after work. Grunt, for instance, was a virtual fixture in the bar. That night, however, there were only a few fishermen at the bar, apparently chased off the lake by the rain.

Harold ordered a beer and settled in for a few quiet rounds before he planned on heading back to Chester's. He was on his second drink when the phone behind the fishermen rang. Harold didn't notice how drunk the trio across the bar was until he saw the one fisherman stumble off his barstool to answer the phone. He also noticed that the fisherman answering the phone was Darrell, the same drunk who had thrown his arm around Harold the other day and congratulated him on making full patch.

"Who the fluck put this here," the fisherman growled as though someone had snuck the phone into his bed and woken him from a sound sleep. Then the drunken fisherman picked up the receiver and said, "Yeah?" The man listened into the receiver for a few seconds and then, as though he'd just realized it was a crank phone call, yelled, "Nobody's naked here, pal. Whaddya think we're a bunch of frickin' hippies or something?"

Harold was out of his seat and headed around the bar hollering, "Wait. Don't hang up." But it was too late as the fisherman returned the receiver to its hook and was stumbling back to his seat while laughing, "Dja hear dat? They wanna know if anyone's naked here, fricken homos." But then Darrell noticed Harold, who had stopped short when Darrell hung up the phone.

Through his drunken haze, Darrell wasn't sure which way to go – continue mocking the caller he'd just hung up on or take on a more concerned demeanor that this new Banshee Rider would appreciate, considering that he seemed interested in the call, almost as though the call was for him.

Drunk or not, it occurred to Darrell that his "homos" comment might not go over well and he tried to clean up the mess a little by politely asking, "That for you?"

Harold nodded and, as he turned to go back to his beer, Harold said, "That's OK." But then the phone rang again. Harold started back around the bar and, as the drunk was rising to answer the call again, Harold hollered, "I've got it."

Slightly startled by Harold's shout, Darrell forgot diplomacy and said, "Suit yourself," as though he'd been insulted and fell awkwardly back into his chair.

Harold ignored the drunk and said, "Hello," into the phone. Red's familiar voice came through from the other end sounding almost as drunken as the fisherman's. "Naked Boy," Red hollered. "Where the fuck you been?" Before Harold could answer, Red continued teasingly, "I've got a little surprise for you."

Harold listened for a few seconds and then realized Red was waiting for Harold to guess what the surprise was. "What's up?" Harold asked.

Instead of answering, Red asked Harold where he was, apparently forgetting that he had called Hildie's.

Harold laughed, "Brother, you called me. I'm at Hildie's. What's happening?"

"I've got a little surprise for you," Red said again but as though for the first time.

Harold heard another voice impatiently say, "Let me talk to him."

For a second, Harold could hear Red and the other voice arguing over the phone. Finally, the other voice came on and Harold asked, "Who's this?"

"It's me, Mongrel," the voice said.

"Where are you guys?" Harold asked. But Mongrel was apparently as drunk as Red. It took a while, but Harold finally deduced that they were at a bar a little north of Hildie's. They'd started drinking in the bar early in the day and were still at it.

Mongrel also said something about a surprise. With his curiosity adequately perked, Harold was beginning to get annoyed that he still didn't know what the surprise was.

"I've been whippin' out my best moves, bro," Mongrel said. "Red too. But she ain't having any of it. Just keeps talking about you."

"Who?" Harold asked with more than a little anticipation. But Mongrel kept rambling on about how the girl wouldn't have anything to do with them.

"She wants you, bro," Mongrel said, "Only you." Then he started ed drunkenly singing to the rhythm of The Platters hit, "Only you can make her pussy wet," and broke into laughter.

Harold was virtually yelling into the phone, "Who are you talking about?" when a female voice, as drunken as his two brothers, came onto the line. When he asked, "Who is this?" instead of answering, she started talking about how much she had missed him and drunkenly pledged her love for him.

Mustering all his patience, Harold asked, "Who is this."

The voice that came back was Red's. "We're bringing her to the clubhouse. Meet us there, bro." Then the phone went dead.

Harold laughed to himself at his brothers' conditions and the general craziness of the phone call. As he hung up, he turned and found Darrell staring back at him as the fishermen had apparently followed Harold's side of the conversation and were distracted when he was yelling. They continued to look at him as though they expected him to fill them in on the blank spots from the other side of the conversation. For a second, Harold thought to bark at them to mind their own business. Instead, he just smiled and walked around the bar to finish his beer. He was pretty sure he knew who the girl was and was more than a little eager to see her again and, therefore, he drained the beer stein quickly.

As Harold was reaching for the doorknob to leave, the door opened in at him and Grunt followed inside. As he came, Grunt greeted him: "BROTHER!" Throwing an arm around Harold's shoulder, Grunt led him reluctantly back to the bar. Harold wanted to jerk the arm free and run for the door. In a little while, a sexy and willing girl would be waiting at the clubhouse for Harold. He didn't want to hurt his brother's feelings but really wanted to go.

Harold decided to share a beer with Grunt while trying to think of ways to excuse himself so that Grunt wouldn't corral him into another when the first was gone. Harold paid for the beers and then, as the bartender filled the mugs, Harold started to explain. But Grunt plunged into a story, as though he were waiting for the opportunity to tell someone. "The manager at the plant where I work is a complete dick. He's the boss's son-in-law and doesn't know his ass from a hole in the ground. So, we got this big job to get out for Chrysler – heating vent parts for the new E Class, you know, with 'Elegance and Luxury,'" he said, rolling the last words as though imitating Ricardo Montalban from the frequent Chrysler commercials. "Only, the jerk had the blueprint upside down and we got all these parts bass-ackwards. A full day's work shot to hell. Even his father-in-law was yelling at him."

Harold smiled as Grunt laughed at his own story. At the same time, Grunt noticed Harold glancing at the clock on the wall. Harold was just estimating that 10 minutes had elapsed since he'd spoken with Red, Mongrel and, most likely, Tawny. It wasn't like it was a long time, but Harold was chomping at the bit to go.

Grunt recognized his brother's anxiety and asked, "What's up."

"Nothin', bro," said Harold.

"Bullshit," Grunt said good naturedly. "You got something going on. What's up?"

Harold then explained about the phone call and suggested Grunt come along.

"I'm all comfy here, bro," said Grunt as he smiled and slapped Harold across the back. "Besides, you're the one who's got a piece of ass waiting at the clubhouse. I trust you don't need my help with that?"

"No. I can handle it," said Harold with a big grin.

"So, who's the girl."

"Tawny, I think."

"You mean the little chick Dancer beat the crap out of?"

Harold frowned and shrugged, "Yeah, same one."

"Bro," Grunt said, "she's a fox – a little ditzy but a fox. What the fuck are you doing here?"

"Just sharing a couple beers with a brother," Harold said.

"Fuck that," Grunt said. "You can share a beer with me anytime. I'll see you later." With that, Grunt took the beer stein out of Harold's hand and was draining it as Harold headed out the door.

More than 15 minutes had passed since the phone call by the time Harold walked out to his bike and started kicking Magdelina over. Whether due to his impatience, the weather, or the limited amount of time he had spent at Hildie's, this time the bike was reluctant to start. He actually had to kick the bike seven or eight times before he was rewarded with the familiar sound of Magdelina clearing her throat. He glanced up at the sky and saw that it looked like it was ready to rain again. In fact, the clouds coming in from the west were so dark it was as though midnight was rolling up behind him as he headed east towards the clubhouse.

Harold came to a stop at the stop sign by the main road and felt a few heavy raindrops while he waited for a couple cars and a truck to pass before entering the two-lane highway. While the hard rain had held off so far, the road was excessively slick from rain that had fallen earlier. As he rolled out to the right, he gave the bike some gas and felt the rear tire break loose slightly. Harold backed off on the throttle and regained control. But even after he straightened the bike out, he found that the bike felt unsteady on the slippery blacktop every time Harold tried to eagerly push the speedometer up to 60 or 65 mph. Eventually, he eased the bike up to that range but was quite aware that, should he have to stop suddenly, he would have a hard time maintaining control.

At that speed, the occasional raindrops stung his face as he rolled down the hilly and twisting road that cut through a heavily wooded area all the way out to the clubhouse. As he gently powered through one of the turns Harold passed the Monks clubhouse and, back in the drive, saw a couple Monks out front by their bikes. With the darkening clouds, and even though he saw that they looked his way as he passed, Harold couldn't make out who they were.

Continuing on a few miles, Harold came out of a hard turn to the right, tracking along about a foot from the solid yellow lines that changed to a single dashed-white line in the center of the pavement when he saw a headlight bearing down straight at him. As he cut to the right to avoid a collision, he felt a blast of wind as a motorcycle flew past him at a high rate of speed. Right behind the first bike were two more Harleys. But Harold barely had time to think about them. On the wet pavement, when he hit the brakes, the rear tire began slipping wildly. He counter steered urgently while trying not to counter steer too much. It was all Harold could do to bring the bike back under control. Slowing nearly to a stop, he glanced back over his shoulder in time to catch a glimpse of the other riders. Harold could tell by the brake light that the last of the three had also hit the brakes and was looking back at Harold.

The boots, jeans, and leather jackets placed these bikers in a class with hundreds of thousands of other bikers. Harold couldn't see any colors on the rider's back suggesting that he didn't belong to a club or, if he did, he wasn't wearing his rag. While Harold didn't really have a chance to see the first two riders, he thought he recognized this one who had slowed to check him out. And if Harold was right, they did belong to a club. If Harold was right, they were Monks. The slight figure, with blonde hair, riding a black Sportster, looked an awful lot like Harold's nemesis. He looked an awful lot like 6 Pack.

Harold thought to himself, "The Monks' clubhouse is just down the road. I'm sure they're just on their way to the clubhouse."

It didn't surprise Harold that other bikers would race past him. Harold and his brothers were equally tempted by the open road. But there was something different about the way these bikers were riding. First, the road was too wet and slippery for the rate of speed they were traveling. And second, the way the first biker went straight through Harold's path suggested a sense of panic, like a frightened rabbit in flight. Harold wasn't sure what the three bikers were doing, but he suspected something was up. And the fact that it appeared 6 Pack was among them set the hairs on the back of Harold's neck on end. It also bothered Harold that, for a second, when 6 Pack looked back his way, it felt as though he was thinking about turning around and coming after Harold. Harold wasn't sure why he felt that way. However, the sensation persisted uncomfortably.

Whatever the bikers were doing, Harold wasn't going to figure it out idling down the highway in a developing rainstorm. He turned back to the road in front of him and gradually increased his speed back to about 60 mph. He glanced in his mirror and back over his shoulder one more time to see if 6 Pack had decided to come after him. Then Harold continued towards the clubhouse, drawn by the anticipation of connecting with Tawny again.

Harold reduced his speed to about 15 mph when he turned onto the gravel road that led to the clubhouse. When Harold arrived at the path to the clubhouse, he discovered that the chain was laying in the mud instead of strung across the path as expected. He pulled in past the chain, stopped his bike and walked back to reconnect it. When he pulled the chain up out of the mud, however, Harold discovered that the lock was missing from the one end. He glanced around for the lock and couldn't find it. "Maybe the lock broke and that's why Red and Mongrel hadn't reconnected it," Harold thought to himself. Dropping the chain back into the mud, Harold shook mud off his fingers as he re-mounted his bike and rode slowly through the tunnel of trees back to the clearing and the clubhouse. Red's and Mongrel's bikes were parked out front, and the front door of the clubhouse was wide open. The light from inside spilled out onto the porch illuminating a few falling raindrops. The light made it easy for Harold to find his way as the darkness caught up from behind him when he turned Magdelina and her headlight off. Beyond the light coming from the door, and beyond the light on the pole by the corner of the clubhouse, the area was bathed in midnight black, a satin black meeting a glistening black when he looked out over the lake.

Harold walked briskly up the steps eager to see his brothers and Tawny, and eager to tell his brothers about the bikers he'd passed on the way out to the clubhouse. But when Harold stepped into the clubhouse, the big room was empty. The cooler in the corner, which had replaced the refrigerator, was open and Harold could see a few beers floating in water, the ice long-since melted. He could see the plywood on the floor where the pool table former-ly filled the center of the room. The bathroom door was open slightly and Harold could see that the light was on in the bath-room. The door to the smaller room was also ajar, but the light in that room was off. Harold stepped forward and glanced into the bathroom. The area in front of the sink and toilet was empty. As he turned to check the small room, his nose picked up an odor lingering in the air.

Harold had smelled that odor before. Smelling it now puzzled Harold. There was no mistaking the smell of burnt gunpowder. Someone, for some reason, had fired a weapon in the clubhouse. He was sure of it. And with that knowledge, as though a finger-nail was sliding down his spine, Harold went from puzzled to con-cerned. Suddenly, he felt he knew the answer to the riddle of the bikers back on the road.

Harold rushed to the door of the small room and threw it open. In the darkness, he saw something crumpled in the corner as though someone had dumped a blanket on the floor. Flipping on the light, Harold's worst fears were realized. He stood, paralyzed, looking at his brothers. Mongrel was lying face up over Red, who was face down in a pool of red-tinted tar. On the wall, in large crimson letters, someone had used the blood from the floor, as though it were a painter's pallet, to write, "FMF." Harold had seen the acronym used before on a patch on Shiv's rag. Harold understood it to mean, "Fucking Monks Forever," or something like that. The letters on the wall immediately cleared up any doubt in Harold's mind about who was responsible. Careful not to step in the blood, Harold broke out of his trance and rushed forward. Looking at Mongrel staring blankly at the ceiling, Harold saw the entry point of a bullet in the center of Mongrel's forehead.

Harold stepped back quickly as he controlled a desire to vomit. Then he glanced around the room and realized he didn't see Tawny. Harold went back to the bathroom and pushed the door open. Tawny was looking up at him from where she lay, her shirt torn so a breast was exposed, her left arm and leg up over the edge of the tub. Her stare, frozen in a moment of terror, was otherwise as empty as Mongrel's. She had an identical bullet wound in the center of her forehead.

Harold stood and stared at her. It appeared the bullet had caught her just as she was about to scream and had permanently cast her face that way.

Harold jumped slightly when he heard a thump from outside. It was probably a walnut or a branch falling on the porch. But whatever it was, it set the hairs on Harold's head tingling. He suddenly remembered how the biker – how 6 Pack looked like he wanted to turn around and come after Harold. It occurred to Harold that, if 6 Pack was involved, and Harold was feeling quite confident that such was the case, the former Banshee Rider would probably consider Harold the primary target – a desired target so far missed.

It also occurred to Harold that he was a witness, sort of. He'd seen the three bikes in flight down the road as though trying to escape the scene before anyone could identify them. He had seen 6 Pack. After looking back at Harold, 6 Pack probably went all out to catch his brothers. Once he'd caught them, Harold was guessing that 6 Pack would convince them they had to go back and take care of Harold, too.

It was risky to come back to the scene of the crime – it increased the chance that the killers might get caught. But they couldn't allow a potential witness to ride away untouched. And

6 Pack wouldn't want Harold to escape alive if there was any chance of catching him – of sending him to the eternal reaches with his brothers and Tawny.

As his mind raced through to the logical conclusion that he might end up like the others, Harold became aware of every little sound, the rustling of the trees as the wind blew in across the lake, the prattle of raindrops that had caught up to Harold and were beginning to drum on the roof and on the porch outside. It was probably his imagination, but Harold was sure he heard the distant rumble of motorcycles.

That was enough. Harold raced out the door, spun Magdelina around and gave the pedal a solid kick. In his excitement, Harold had forgotten all the other steps in the process of starting his motorcycle. Frantically, he opened the petcock, flipped the switch between the tanks and tried again. The engine backfired loudly but didn't catch.

The rain was coming down harder and, as the drops pelted Harold's face, the sound was like the rumble of V-twins in the distance – or was that actually the sound of Harley's approaching? Harold half expected to see headlights pulling in on the gravel path at any moment. "They would probably turn the headlights off, even turn their bikes off, and come in quietly," he told himself. He took a deep breath, and let it out slowly, before giving the kicker another try. As he ran the pedal through he heard himself say, "Come on, baby," to the bike in an attempt to inspire Magdelina to start that time. He was rewarded with the familiar vibration and rumble of the engine springing to life.

"That a baby!" Harold thought to himself as he pulled out through the tunnel of trees to the gravel road. "What was I thinking?" he lectured himself as he continued on out towards the highway. "You had to be the big, bad biker, didn't you? Now, look at where it's going to get you. You'll probably get shot off your bike before you get halfway back to Hildie's."

"Hildie's! I can't go to Hildie's," Harold said. "I'd be riding right into them."

As he reached the highway, Harold glanced to his left. In the darkness he saw the pinpricks of headlights. Or was that his imagination. With panic catching in his throat, he shook his head, pulled off his shades and wiped his eyes with the sleeve of his jacket. "No, there's no one coming." But as the rain blurred his vision the longer he looked, he began to doubt himself again. Harold steadied himself and turned right, away from Hildie's and Biesenthal, away from 6 Pack and Monks who were almost certainly coming to kill him. There was a little too much urgency in his wrist when he cracked the throttle. Harold felt the rear tire pull out from behind him whipping the rear of the bike around to the left. He jammed his foot on the pavement and pivoted with the motorcycle catching it inches before it came to rest on its side.

Leaning the bike back upright, Harold straightened it out and, after glancing back to the west, eased the bike up to speed going east again. "If you wipe out, they walk up to you and shoot you in the head under the bike," he told himself, picturing a cowboy caught under his horse. "Easy. Build up some speed and keep the bike under control."

Within a mile, Harold was up to 60 mph and he felt that danger was beginning to fade away in the rearview mirror. But then he saw it — lights coming up behind him. "Were there two headlights or three?" he asked himself as he watched the lights growing closer behind him. The vibration of the bike shook through to the handlebars and from the handlebars to the rearview mirror mounted on the left side. When the vibration was mixed with the rain, the lights coming up behind him were not steady round globes in the mirror but, rather, were elongated, bright and shaking features that could represent a pair of headlights on the front of a car or a trio of headlights on the front of motorcycles.

"Should I speed up?" Harold asked himself. "If I do, they'll see and they'll know I'm running. Then again, if they're coming to kill me it really doesn't matter if they know I'm running."

Harold gave the engine a hard shot of gasoline. It responded with a sudden roar of additional power. The tire slid back and forth slightly behind him but soon tracked back into the desired path as Harold ran the bike up to nearly 100 mph. He barely held the bike on the road as he went around a sharp turn to the right, slowing only marginally while sliding the rear tire through the turn the way a flat-track racer would. Having gone around the bend, the headlights were no longer visible in the rearview mirror. But Harold was sure they were still coming. Relentlessly, he felt as though they were hunting him down, like wolves when the smell of blood is on the wind.

About a quarter mile down from the hard turn was an intersection. Harold wasn't sure where the side road would take him but, if he could get there soon enough, he could turn, shut off the lights and, if he stayed off the brake, coast along slowly for a while. With any luck, the Monks wouldn't know which way he'd gone. Even if they split up with one brother taking each of the three alternate routes, Harold would have evened the odds a little. Better yet, they might not realize he'd turned and keep going.

Turning the lights off was a little tricky. Harold would have to turn the switch back one click. But the switch didn't turn easy. Sometimes, as he applied the necessary pressure, the switch simply clicked all the way to the left. If that happened at this time, Harold would have shut the bike off entirely. Therefore, he resolved to wait until he had turned before he switched off the lights.

Glancing back over his shoulder to make sure it wasn't too late — that the Monks hadn't caught up to him in time to see him turning, Harold made the right-hand turn and throttled up to get behind a berm and some trees before switching off the lights. With his index finger bent back on the right side of the switch, and the side of his thumb pressed to the left, Harold pushed down as he cautiously turned the switch to the left. He felt the mechanism inside ride up over the first cam. Fighting to make sure it didn't pop right past the next seating, Harold slowly adjusted the switch so that the engine remained running as the lights went out.

The road went so completely dark that Harold struggled to see in front of him. To make matters worse, the rain was now pouring down. Drenched, cold and afraid, Harold idled along the road praying that the Monks didn't follow him, that someone in a car didn't come along and smack him in the dark or that Harold didn't simply run the bike off the road in the dark.

Watching the road in front of him was hard enough. Making it all the more difficult, Harold was compelled to watch for headlights coming up behind him. When, after a couple minutes of slowly rolling down the road, ready to flip the lights on and fly if necessary, Harold decided his plan had worked. The road behind him was as dark as the road in front. Just to be safe, he continued on for another mile with the lights off. When all remained clear, he took a deep breath and switched the lights back on.

With the lights on, Harold continued on the unfamiliar side road for a couple more miles before he came to another intersection. The new road was as much a back way as the road that brought him there, but Harold decided to turn to the right, back in the direction of Biesenthal, Hildie's and his brothers. It had suddenly dawned on him that he had to warn his brothers. Even if Harold had escaped, what was to say that another member of the Banshee Riders wouldn't ride into the same trap?

As Harold rolled back to the west, the fear subsided and was replaced by outrage and anger. "Those mother fuckers," Harold said out loud. "I'll kill that fucking 6 Pack myself. I swear it."

Nothing looked familiar as Harold continued to the west. He slowed and considered several crossroads, but eventually continued on the way he was going. He'd gone far enough that he was beginning to wonder if he'd gone too far. By that time, he should have hit the interstate or Biesenthal. There was no way to get through without hitting one or the other. And yet, Harold was as lost as though he was mysteriously dropped into another state. These thoughts were going through Harold's head when his back road suddenly ended. The highway it Teed into looked more like a thoroughfare and Harold decided to turn right. It was a little risky because, if this road took him back past the Monks' clubhouse again, he could still run smack into 6 Pack and the other Monks. But considering how far he'd gone, Harold was fairly sure he was closer to Biesenthal than that. Besides, this road seemed unfamiliar, though it was hard to say in the dark.

Harold rode about three miles all the time wondering where he was. Then, on his right, he saw the low-set outline of a darkened building. Then he recognized it – Mack's Cycle Repair. Harold realized that a couple miles down the road and a left-hand turn would run him into Biesenthal and right past Speedy's where Harold had worked when he first came to town.

Slowing as he approached the bike shop, Harold could see that the showroom out front was as dark as the sky. However, back beyond the counter, he could also see light peering through Joe's office door. An old, beat up, Olds 88 was out front and it occurred to Harold that Joe might be going over the books or taking care of some other clerical work after closing up a while ago. Harold turned into the parking lot. The overhead door to the shop was set back about 15 feet further than the front of the showroom. In the corner, where the shop door extended from the south wall of the showroom, the darkness that had cast a shroud over the countryside stood out in a starker, impenetrable shadow. Harold quickly pulled the bike into this nook and shut the motor and the lights off, so the bike was hidden from the road. Then, he walked around to the front and cupped his hand above his eyes and against the glass trying to see inside through the slit of an opening to the office. Unable to make out any sign of life, Harold pounded on the glass with his fist. The glass waved in and out but, otherwise, nothing happened, and he tried again. After waiting for what seemed like several minutes, Harold walked further down the glass window to the door at the far side of the building. He grabbed the handle fully expecting that the door was locked. To his surprise, the door swung open and he stepped inside.

It was great to be out of the rain. It was even more comforting to have found what he hoped was a safe haven for a little while. As Harold continued inside towards the office door, he was about to yell out, "Hello," but stopped in his tracks when he heard sounds coming from the office. There was a steady rhythm of fwump, fwump, fwump, as though someone was slapping a wet sock on the pavement. Along with the slapping sound, Harold could hear someone squealing. Then the voice yelled out, "Oh God. Ohhhh, you bastard." The sounds he heard from behind the door strongly suggested he was interrupting a private moment. But there was something else. Harold was almost certain he recognized the voice.

Private moment or not, and regardless of who was in the room, the situation dictated that Harold interrupt. Without further hesitation, Harold hollered, "Joe, you in there?"

Everything went silent in the office — the fwumping and the voice. Listening closely, Harold was fairly certain he heard heavy breathing. Then the rather angry voice of Joe yelled out, "We're closed, God damn it."

Harold ignored the response and yelled, "I have to use your phone. My brothers have been shot."

Harold heard some rustling in the room and then, after a few seconds, the door opened. Joe stepped out tucking in his shirt and buckling up his pants. "You kind of caught me at a bad time," he said.

"I'm sorry," Harold said. "My brothers were killed, and I think they're still after me."

"Who's after you?" Joe asked.

As he considered his answer, Harold glanced at the door wondering if Joe's companion was planning to join them. "I'm not sure I should say yet," Harold said.

As Joe asked, "Who was shot?" the door to the office opened wider and a red-faced, red-haired woman Harold knew too well stepped into the showroom.

It was all too much for Harold. First, his brothers and Tawny were murdered. "Now this," he said to himself. At that moment, he hated her. He wanted to punch her full in the face. "How could she ..."

Where Harold might have expected a look of embarrassment, all he saw in her face was an expression of concern, Sue repeated Joe's question. "Who was shot? Is Sam OK?"

"Red and Mongrel," Harold said. "And a girl, I don't think you know her."

This time when Sue said, "Oh God," it was with a decidedly different tone than the one she used from behind the office door.

"You're sure of this," Joe asked, apparently confusing Harold's reluctance to name the perpetrators as uncertainty that might translate to the entire story.

"I'm sure," Harold said. "They were in the clubhouse. If I'd gotten there a little earlier, I'd probably be dead on the floor with them."

For the first time since it happened, Harold found himself fighting back tears. Fear, anger and a sense of loss combined and welled up inside of him. But Harold fought back his emotions. "There's no time for that now," he told himself.

Before Joe or Sue could ask any more questions. Harold repeated his initial request. "I've got to use the phone," he said. "I need to warn people."

Joe picked up a black phone from a small table against the wall and swung it wide, so the cord would follow, around onto the counter where Harold could reach it. Having finally memorized the phone number for Hildie's, that was the first number he called. But according to whoever answered, none of the Banshee Riders were there. Harold returned the phone to its cradle as he considered his next call. He looked up at Sue and then dialed Samurai's number.

"What?" Samurai answered brusquely into the phone before Harold could say anything.

"It's Harold," he said. "I just came from the clubhouse. Red and Mongrel are dead."

Sue listened as Harold explained how he rode out to meet Red, Mongrel, and Tawny at the clubhouse. She heard Harold describe how he found his brothers on the floor of the backroom, and Tawny in the bathtub. Then Harold described the bikers he'd seen on the road and how he was fairly certain they had followed him.

"I'm not sure it was him, but it sure looked like him," Harold said when Samurai commented, "Sounds like 6 Pack."

Harold looked up to see Joe watching a couple feet away. Unsure whether Joe had heard Samurai over the phone, he said to Samurai, "We should talk about that when I see you."

"Where are you now?" Samurai asked.

When Harold said he was at Mack's, Sue fully expected Harold to say he'd found her there. Instead, after listening to Samurai for a minute, Harold said, "I'll be here," and hung up.

Harold looked up at Sue for a moment with a twinge of disappointment in his eyes. Then he looked at Joe and said, "I have to make a few more calls." He turned back to Sue and added, "You might want to make yourself scarce before Sam gets here."

"I'm staying," Sue said.

"The fuck you are," Harold barked at her. "I've got enough to deal with tonight. I don't need this, and Samurai doesn't need to worry about you when the Mo..., when someone may be trying to kill us."

Harold glanced at Joe and realized he'd caught Harold's slip. "I don't know that for sure," Harold said. "I'd rather you didn't tell anyone I said that."

"No problem," Joe said. But there was something about the tone of his voice that made Harold a little uncomfortable. Harold reminded himself that Joe liked to ride the fence. It was good for business. Then Harold asked himself, "Where was the fence in this situation?"

Harold was preparing to make the first of his additional calls when he noticed that Sue was still standing there. "What are you doing?" he asked. "Get the hell out of here."

Sue, as steady as a rock in any other situation, began crying as she said, "My car is back at Cal's Drift In."

"God damn it," Harold yelled to no one in particular. Then he looked at Joe. "You'll have to drive her."

"Samurai's kinda gonna notice I'm not here," Joe said.

"I'll tell him you went home to let your dog out or something," Harold said.

"The dogs stay outside. Sam knows that."

"Then think of something else," Harold yelled, "but get her the fuck out of here, now."

"Just tell him I had a girl here and I went to drive her home," Joe said, applying just enough truth to the equation to be sufficiently plausible.

"True enough," Harold said, giving Sue a short condemning glance. "Just go."

As Sue and Joe headed for the door, Joe turned to Harold and said, "I'll be back," as if Harold might not have assumed so.

Harold made several calls but only managed to reach Falstaff and Snake. Based on Samurai's suggestion, Harold didn't try calling Pot Roast. As Samurai put it, "He's liable to go off half-cocked when he hears the news."

Falstaff arrived before Samurai and listened patiently as Harold filled him in on the story. Over Falstaff's shoulder, as he was telling the story, Harold noticed three headlights turning into the parking lot. The hair on the back of his neck stood on end as he contemplated the possibility that 6 Pack and his brothers had found him here. Wondering, Harold gave Falstaff an anxious glance. Falstaff seemed to understand. He turned to face the glass and shoved his hand inside his rag where Harold was pretty sure the vice president's fingers gripped a handgun, his finger resting against the trigger. Harold swung the door shut with his fingers to dim the light spilling into the showroom.

Three motorcycles pulled up facing the display windows at the front of the store. For a moment, the bikes simply sat there, their headlights gazing straight ahead. Standing in the corner by the office door, Harold was out of sight. Falstaff, however, was caught squarely in the glow when the headlight of the bike furthest from the front door swung around as the bike came to rest on its kickstand. The longer they stood there, the more certain Harold was that they should duck down and prepare to defend themselves. Falstaff, however, simply stared back at the light as though it were a contest to see who would blink first, him or the electronic eyes beaming brightly from outside.

Falstaff won as the headlights of the bikes closer to the door switched off. The light on the far bike, however, continued to burn through the plate-glass window where it held Falstaff in its gaze. Then it swung back to the left and went out.

Through the rain and darkness, Harold could see the shadowy outlines of three men stepping off the bikes and coming towards the door. Harold only realized he was holding his breath when the door swung open and Samurai stepped in, followed by Pot Roast and Reaper. As he breathed a sigh of relief, Harold caught a glimpse of the look on Pot Roast's face. He could see the glistening lines where tears had rolled down his brother's face. Other than the trails of tears, Pot Roast's face was a mask of fury. There was something insanely frightening about his appearance, enough so to send a shiver down Harold's spine.

"Are you OK?" Samurai asked.

"Yeah," Harold said. After a long pause, his voice breaking, Harold said, "Those mother fuckers. They shot 'em in the heads like an execution."

"Did you call the cops?" Reaper cut in.

"No. I thought I should warn you guys first," Harold said.

Reaper nodded in understanding. Then he said. "We're gonna have to call 'em."

"Fuck the cops," Pot Roast snarled. "We'll take care of this ourselves."

"You won't take care of anything sitting in a jail cell," Samurai said.

"We have to call the cops," Reaper said. "And we have to call them now."

Without waiting any longer, Samurai strode over, picked up the phone and dialed '0.'

"Give me the police," he said to the Operator. "Yes, this is an emergency."

Listening to Samurai describe to the police how their brothers were dead in the clubhouse, Harold felt his anger swelling inside. He was close to siding with Pot Roast as he listened to Samurai explain where the clubhouse was located.

"We're at Mac's Cycle Repair," Samurai said. "There's no phone at the cabin. Besides, my brother thought they were coming back to get him." After a long pause as Samurai listened to the voice on the other side of the phone, Samurai said, "We're not going anywhere."

When he hung up, Samurai said, "I think you need to stay here, Naked Boy." Turning to Pot Roast, Samurai added, "But I think you should go."

When Pot Roast began to argue, Falstaff cut in. "You're on probation, brother. You don't need to get tied up in this."

"You go with him," Reaper said to Falstaff.

As they left, Harold had a sense that his brothers were babysitting Pot Roast to keep him out of trouble – to keep him from taking matters into his own hands. After they'd left, Reaper turned back to Harold and Samurai and smiled. "When the time comes, we can always just set him loose on the fucking Monks."

Harold interjected quickly, "I'm not absolutely sure they were Monks. I mean, I'm pretty sure, but it was dark, and I only got a quick look at the one."

"Why do you think they were Monks then?" Reaper asked accusingly.

"Well, other than that they were heading towards the Monks' clubhouse, the one who stopped looked like 6 Pack ... I think."

"He wouldn't have the balls," Samurai said.

"He had the balls to prospect for the Monks," Reaper said. "Might be out to prove himself."

"Maybe," Samurai said, as he glanced out the window where a strobe of red light was the first alert that a squad car was about to arrive.

As one and then another squad pulled up outside behind the bikes, Reaper picked up the phone again and quickly dialed another number. Harold could hear the phone ringing several times. When it stopped ringing, he heard a voice from the receiver but, the way Reaper spoke, it was quickly apparent he'd got the answering machine.

Reaper looked at Samurai and shrugged his shoulders as he hung up the phone.

"Who was that?" Harold asked.

"Swifty - club's lawyer," Samurai said.

"Why do we need a lawyer?" Harold asked. But as soon as he said it he realized the question was rather silly. The looks Reaper and Samurai gave him reinforced that idea and Harold added sheepishly, "Never mind."

As Harold said it, Reaper headed for the door and told Harold and Samurai to stay put. "Let me talk to the cops," Reaper said.

He was outside for a couple minutes before he walked back inside followed by one of the officers. Inside, Reaper introduced his brothers — "This is Samurai, and this is NB. And this is Officer Spenoza."

The cop looked them over as though sizing them up. Finally, he looked at Harold and asked, "NB stands for something?"

Harold didn't answer right away and, seeing that the others didn't seem inclined to answer either, the officer said, "Your friend here says you won't talk until your lawyer arrives. Is that right?"

Harold and Samurai nodded.

"I will need your names and addresses and such, however," Spenoza said, and then proceeded to take down that information from each of them while insisting on their legal names.

As he was finishing, the other cop stuck his head in the door and called Officer Spenoza outside. They spoke for a couple minutes and Officer Spenoza came back inside.

"Which one of you called us?" he asked.

"I did," Samurai said.

"I know you won't talk until your lawyer arrives," Spenoza said, "but we need to know if you're a witness."

"No," Samurai said. "I was home watching my kids when I heard about it."

Spenoza nodded slowly as he digested the information. Then the Biesenthal police officer said, "We'll need you to ride out there with my partner. Seems the county sheriffs can't find your cabin."

Then Spenoza looked at Harold and Reaper and said, "The two of you will have to come into the station."

The officer at the door seemed to hesitate as though waiting to see if they agreed though it was clearly not a request. Then he said gruffly, "Well?"

"We'll see you in a while," Reaper said to Samurai.

Then Harold asked, "What about our bikes?"

"If you want to wheel them inside you can lock them up here," the officer said.

Harold looked at Reaper who told Samurai, "We'll push yours in, too."

When all the bikes were inside, Harold realized the door could only be locked from the outside with a key. He was about to point that out to Reaper when a pair of headlights on the front of an Olds 88 rolled into the lot.

"Who are you?" Spenoza asked Joe as he got out of his car.

"This is my shop," Joe said.

"Where did you come from?" Spenoza asked.

"Home," Joe said. "I was catching up on some paperwork when Naked ... I mean, NB, called."

"How did you get in here?" Spenoza asked Harold.

Harold was caught off guard by the question and Joe's preceding statement. He was wondering why Joe didn't just tell the cops the truth, or at least the partial truth he and Joe had concocted before Joe took Sue back to her car. "I knocked and, when no one came, I tried the door," Harold said.

"Shit! I must have forgotten to lock it," Joe said. Then, seeing the curious look on the officer's face, he added, "It's OK. I trust these guys."

Harold could tell that the answers were raising suspicions for Spenoza as the officer said, "Well, we'd better get going." With that, Harold and Reaper slid into the back of the squad for the ride to the station.

As the squad proceeded through town, Harold heard a voice over the radio. "You can tell the boys in Biesenthal we've found the house."

"Do you have any bodies?"

"We have three bodies," the voice came back. "One female in the bathroom and two males in the bedroom. All three have gunshot wounds to the head, like assassinations. The female may have been sexually assaulted, as well."

As he felt the anger rising from his gut again, making his face feel warm and flushed, Harold glanced over at Reaper. "Why am I sitting in the back of a squad car?" Harold asked himself. "I should be out hunting down that mother-fucking 6 Pack. I should be putting a bullet through his head the same as he did to Red and Mongrel, and Tawny."

Harold sat in silence the rest of the way to the station, catching occasional snippets of information over the radio, but otherwise watching quietly out the rain-soaked window. He realized that the lawyer's recommendation wasn't the only reason he wasn't inclined to talk. Harold realized that, if and when he next told the story, he might lose it. He might lose control. He wasn't sure what that meant. He didn't know if it meant he'd break down crying or if he'd flip out in a violent rampage. But Harold could feel his emotions boiling just below the surface and wasn't sure what would happen if he allowed them to break through.

Chapter 31 — A Federal Case

The black Crown Vic sped down the highway tracking perfectly between the white line by the shoulder and the dashed yellow line in the center of the highway. It bounded over rises in the pavement so that the nearly-two-ton vehicle hung in the air, its suspension fully extended the way a child's hair will appear stretched out above their head when a rollercoaster suddenly drops. Though they were 30 mph over the speed limit, somehow there was no urgency about the way the car slashed across the wet pavement and darted around slower vehicles without even bothering with its turn signal. The car's speed was a pure statement of importance, proclaiming loudly that the driver was above the law – that the driver was the law.

The close-cut hair, the plain black suits, the narrow black ties framed by white shirts: it was as though the two occupants of the car were trying to cast themselves for a sequel of the recent hit move, 'The Blues Brothers,' only the men on the bench seat of the car would have snorted derisively that it was the movie that sought to copy their style rather than the other way around.

They had driven about five miles without a word – with silence that was only broken by the steady growl of the 351 Windsor under the hood and the occasional bottoming thud of the suspension – when Agent Michaels, the taller man in the passenger seat, said, "So?"

"So? What do you think?"

"What do I think? I think you whiffed. I think Casey took a mighty swing and missed."

"You wish," said a grinning Agent Rogers, the shorter man behind the wheel.

They might have discussed the brutal, gang-related killings in a cabin by a lake they were investigating out here "beyond the sacred elephant graveyard," but they enjoyed a detached professionalism of veteran law-enforcement officers who fancied they had seen it all before. That was what their demeanor said to all the hick Barney Fifes they had labored to tolerate at the crime scene. When they flashed their badges, with an economy of effort, they said, "ATF" as though it said everything that needed to be said, as if it also meant, "Just get out of our way."

In their casual reaction to violence, as they drove into town to see a couple of the punks the locals had brought in, they had picked up a conversation from earlier as though an hour hadn't transpired in-between – as though the sight of three young, dead bodies was of less importance than whether Officer Rogers had scored with a barmaid from the night before. Rogers hadn't whiffed and, somehow, the runs he had scored in a hotel bedroom tallied for both officers. It was as if Rogers' success proved and advanced the importance of both men – ATF agents in their own images as rock stars deserving of fawning fans.

Neither officer really understood how or why they needed the reinforcement. For all their bravado, their self-esteem hung around them like untucked shirts. For Peter Rogers, at least, it was easier to understand. He had barely made the height requirements to join the force. He was sensitive about his size and still felt an ember of resentment over how his older brother and the neighborhood kids had called him Pint-Size when he was young. He was a man with something to prove and the barmaid was more than a conquest; she was a figurative inch or two added to his stature.

Pulling into the station's parking lot, Rogers barely nodded, as though it were too much effort, to return the wave of an officer coming out to his squad car. Minutes later, after another flip of their leather-cased badges, they stood by the window watching the two bikers sitting by the plain-stainless-rectangular table in the room through a one-way mirrored window.

Rogers took a deep sigh as though preparing to search for the right words to use with someone whose intellectual deficiencies make communication a chore: "Didn't it occur to you to separate them, Officer Spenoza?"

"I would have, if I considered them suspects."

Michael's gave Rogers a rolled-eyes glance that spoke volumes starting with, "Why do we always get stuck with these bozos?"

"Well," said Rogers, making no effort to hide the strain on his patience, "what have they told you?" as he took a note pad out of his inner coat pocket, flipped it open and prepared to take notes with a pen from his shirt pocket.

"The two deceased males at the cabin were members of their club ..."

"Club?" Michaels asked, as though Spenoza's use of the word, rather than gang, was a clue that the officer lacked the essentials of a lawman's ability to critically evaluate a situation.

Spenoza smiled patiently and continued: "The biker on the far side of the table, a Harold Schneider, 24, had relations with the deceased female but hadn't seen her in a while."

"And the other dirtbag?" Rogers asked.

"The man at the head of the table, Brian Pittman, 29, is the president of their ... gang," said Spenoza.

The inflection Officer Spenoza used when saying 'gang' caused another round of raised eyebrows between the ATF agents.

"Anything else?" Rogers asked.

In a perfunctory manner, Officer Spenoza gave the agents the limited information he had, his tone indicating that the police officer felt it was all a waste of time.

Then, Agent Michaels asked, with exaggerated courtesy, "Would you be so kind as to put Mr. Pittman ... was it ... in a holding cell while we speak with Mr. Schneider for a minute or two?"

Officer Spenoza didn't qualify the request with an answer but merely stepped out of the room and appeared a moment later in the interrogation room. When he asked Reaper to come with him, the president looked at the mirror knowingly.

"The feds are here?"

Officer Spenoza shrugged in a way that said both, "Yes" and "There's nothing I can do about it."

Reaper stood and looked at Harold. "Don't sweat it. Just be cool."

When Reaper was moved beyond the hall and into a cell, Officer Spenoza apologized and then returned to follow the ATF agents into the interrogation room. Harold looked up, smiled at Spenoza and then surveyed the two men in black suits with suspicion.

Agent Michaels walked around to the backend of the 6X10 room, put one foot up on the chair that Reaper had vacated, and casually slipped a toothpick into his mouth as an obvious prop. Agent Rogers moved to the center of the room with the one-way mirror at his back and stood looking down at Harold as though trying to identify a species of insect. Officer Spenoza leaned back against the door and crossed his arms, a look of boredom on his face.

Rogers stared at Harold a while as though to melt the biker's defenses in preparation for questioning. Then Rogers pulled a note pad out of his inner-coat pocket and stared at the first page before flipping to the second page. Finally, he looked up from the notepad and started: "So, Mr. Schneider, you say you arrived at the cabin by Lake Chinookan about what time?"

"About 5:30 p.m."

"And where were you before that?"

"I was at Hildie's."

"Hildie's? Who's that, your girlfriend?"

"It's a bar out by Fish Lake. I stopped there for a drink after work."

"What kind of work do you do?" asked Agent Michaels.

"I'm an electrician ... well ..."

"Well what?" snapped Rogers.

If Harold Schneider thought he was merely being held at the station as a witness, the sharpness of the agent's tone seemed to confirm his suspicions. Harold gave the agent a long, inquiring look before he answered, "I'm an apprentice electrician."

"And you were working today – with all this rain?" asked Agent Rogers, as if the weather was a clue that the biker was lying.

Rather than answer, Harold simply turned sideways in his chair and lifted his boot up above the table to show the mud coating the bottoms of his pants.

Rogers gave him a scornful look that indicated he didn't appreciate what he considered a flippant response.

"And why did you go to the cabin?"

"Red called me at the bar and told me to meet them there."

"Red?"

Officer Spenoza broke in without moving from the door: "Robert Walsh. I believe you met him on the floor of the clubhouse."

Agent Rogers gave Officer Spenoza a long glare, no longer feigning courtesy. "Officer Spenoza, don't you have some parking tickets to write or something."

"This may be your case now, Agent Michaels ..."

"Rogers, Agent Rogers."

"In any case, even if you federal boys are handling this case now, you're still in my jurisdiction – my police station."

Rogers gave Spenoza another long glare, punctuated with a

deep Saccharin smile, and said, "Of course. Maybe you could try to be, you know, a little more cooperative."

"It's what I live for," said Spenoza, which elicited an appreciative smile from Harold.

Agent Rogers paced towards the wall by the door, now giving Officer Spenoza 'the look' as Rogers bit his lip in thought. Then he turned suddenly with the reaction of someone who had just thought of something: "How did he call you? I don't recall seeing a phone in the house by the lake."

"They called from a bar north of there," said Harold.

"Why did they ..." the agent began.

"They said they'd meet me at the clubhouse."

"And did you meet them at the clubhouse?"

"They were dead when I got there."

"And where did they call you?"

"At Hildie's."

"That would be the bar you were at, right?" As Harold nodded affirmatively, the officer leaned over the table, his face close to Harold's and asked, "And how did they know you were there?"

"They didn't," said Harold. "But they know I'm there a lot, so I guess they just thought they'd try."

"Why did they want to meet you?"

"I hadn't seen Tawny in a while. Red said she wanted to see me."

"Lucky you," said Agent Michaels.

Over his shoulder, Harold gave the other ATF agent a cold glance but didn't say anything.

"Tawny?" said Agent Rogers. "You mean the stripper."

"She was a dancer," said Harold.

Both agents laughed as Agent Rogers said, "You hear that? She was a dancer."

"She dance for you, Naked Boy?"

Harold looked down at the table, with a posture that said he was about done here.

"What can you tell us about the victims, Mr. Schneider?" Agent Rogers continued.

When Harold didn't respond, he said, "Nothing, eh? They were good friends you didn't know squat about, is that it? You want us to believe that Linda Sullivan was your girlfriend, but you only know her by her stripper name? Mr. Walsh and Mr. Lyons: you don't know where they live or what kind of work they do?"

By this time, Harold had clammed up completely and was sitting, slouched down in the metal chair, his arms crossed in front of him as he glared back at Agent Rogers.

"How about this, Mr. Schneider," Agent Rogers said as he took a seat on the table. "Ms. Sullivan, your Tawny, danced for you – a little extra income on the side. But you found out your brothers were getting a little extra on the side, you know, for free. How does that sound?"

"Sounds like you should go fuck yourself," Harold growled.

"Actually, it sounds to me like you're the one who's going to fuck himself, Mr. Schneider. You're the only person we can actually put at the scene of the crime. Unless, of course, you can name anyone else we should be looking at?"

This was the point where Harold could mention seeing 6 Pack and the other Monks on the road. Of course, he wasn't absolutely sure it was them. And even if he did, the mere thought of the word snitch stuck in Harold's throat.

"I didn't see anyone," Harold said.

"Well, that's too bad," said Agent Rogers. "Because that leaves you as our top suspect. Makes you kind of special, doesn't it?"

"Wouldn't mind letting us see the bottom of your boots, would you?" Agent Rogers asked.

Harold looked up before he caught himself, a question mark visible for an instant in his expression before he could suppress it.

"We found some bloody footprints on the floor. If they matched your boots, that wouldn't be so good, would it?"

"You know," Agent Michaels chimed in, "we might even find blood on the bottom of his boots."

"I already told you I was there," said Harold.

"Yes, you did," said Agent Rogers. "Did you walk in the blood?"

"Not that I know of," said Harold. "But I suppose it's possible."

"Anything's possible, isn't it," said Agent Rogers.

Harold simply stared at the agent trying not to show that the thought that he was a suspect – the prime suspect – in the killings of his brothers and Tawny was shaking him. The thought of prison crossed his mind. It even occurred to him how his mother would take the news.

From over his shoulder, Agent Michaels said, "Not so much fun being a big-bad biker, is it?"

Unwilling to concede that the agents were getting to him, Harold continued what was becoming a stare down with Agent Rogers. Finally, Rogers smiled and said, "You look you might want to think things over a bit. Officer Spenoza, could you lock Mr. Schneider into one of your cells and bring us Mr. Pittman. Maybe he'll have enough sense to be a little more cooperative."

"You never know," said Agent Michaels, "he might not like the idea of prison so much."

"You're not suggesting he'd turn his brother in to save his ass, are you?" Agent Rogers said with a laugh.

"He didn't look as dumb as this punk," the other agent responded.

"Well, the one who talks first usually wins," said Agent Rogers as Harold was led from the room.

As Harold and Reaper passed each other in the cell doorway, Reaper was looking closely at Harold for any clue of how things went. Harold saw the look and smiled as if to say, "No problem." Then, he stopped and, as a greater way of letting Reaper know what was in store, he said, "Watch out. The little fucker spits."

Reaper stopped. He noticed that even Officer Spenoza was smiling. Reaper smiled back and said, "Thanks for the warning." Reaper took another step and stopped so that Officer Spenoza walked into his back. Reaper looked back at Harold and said, "Maybe I'll spit back."

Reaper was gone for about 45 minutes. When Officer Spenoza brought him back, he was smiling. Reaper went into the cell and sat down on the cot while Harold stood leaning with his elbow in the windowsill. As Officer Spenoza locked the cell he asked, "You guys want some coffee or water, or something?"

"Got a beer?" asked Harold.

"Sorry, that's not on the menu."

The police officer hesitated by the door to give Harold and Reaper a chance to otherwise respond to his offer.

"We're OK," said Reaper. As Officer Spenoza turned to leave, he added, "Thanks," clearly thanking the officer for more than the offer of refreshments.

When the officer had left, Harold looked at Reaper and said, "Well?"

"What assholes," said Reaper. "And you're right – he does spit."

"How long do you think they'll hold us?" asked Harold.

"Not sure," said Reaper. "Hopefully, they've gotten hold of Swifty and he'll be here soon."

Harold was looking inquisitively at Reaper as he spoke about the attorney.

"He's on retainer. As you might imagine, we can use some legal help from time to time. Like, when Pot Roast got busted last year beatin' the crap out of some bartender. He got 90 days. And he was even charged with assaulting one of the arresting officers."

Reaper sat thinking about what he had said, nodding his head slowly as though in agreement with himself. At last, he said, "Yeah, in his own way, Swifty is one serious bad ass."

The time dragged by slowly until daylight and the rising sun brought the dull-green color of the walls back into focus. By this time, Harold had heard Reaper say, at least a dozen times, "Where the fuck is Swifty already?"

Harold wasn't sure if he should expect a phantom or a giant by the time the door to the jailhouse opened and Officer Spenoza led a disheveled midget up to their cell. Harold looked at the little man with a crumpled brown, pin-stripe suit and brown briefcase, the shadow of stubble around his chin, and dark shadows under his eyes, as he waited for the police officer to open the cell door.

As Officer Spenoza stepped back out of the way, the man with the briefcase entered the cell, pointlessly trying to smooth his hair to one side as though as an afterthought.

Reaper was on his feet approaching with an open hand extended as he asked, "Where the fuck have you been? I tried calling early last night."

"I was in the drunk tank in Millbrook," said Swifty. "My guess is your friends with the ATF had something to do with it – had me picked up for suspicion of drunk driving, held me overnight and then let me go this morning as if it was just a mistake. Assholes."

Reaper was shaking the lawyer's hand before he finished speaking. Then, Reaper pointed to Harold and said, "This is Naked Boy."

"Naked Boy?!!! You've got to be kidding." He shook Harold's hand and said, "Son, you might not want to go around with people calling you Naked Boy. People could get the wrong idea, especially judges."

"Wasn't my idea," said Harold as he shook the lawyer's clammy hand and noticed the blood-shot eyes.

"Of course not," said the lawyer. Then, he introduced himself as Tom Swift. "I'm on retainer to the Banshee Riders, which means that you don't have to worry about my fee, at this point anyhow."

"So, you gonna get us outta here?" asked Reaper.

"I'd have posted your bail already if these ATF jerks weren't playing their usual games. They're holding you on suspicion, but they know you didn't do it. They're just fucking with you."

"Why?" asked Harold.

"Because they can. Because they're feds and think the little people should pay homage. Because they figure, if they put pressure on you, you'll give them something to work with."

"But we don't have anything to give them," said Harold.

"Son, they don't care if you sing or compose. If they can charge someone, they've got something they can give the newspapers. At this point, it's a question of whether they'll charge you or not. Otherwise, they'll have to let you go soon."

"Soon?" asked Reaper.

"They can hold you for 24 hours before they have to charge you though they can ask a judge to hold you longer."

"Will they?" asked Harold.

"Nah, I doubt it," said the lawyer. "They want to screw with you but not if they have to work at it."

"Do they seem remotely interested in who actually killed Red and Mongrel?" asked Harold.

"Not particularly. I suppose they'll get around to it sooner or later. For now, they've got you two and their magnifying glass on a sunny day. They'll try to make things uncomfortable for you for a little while, that's all."

Just then, the outer door to the cells opened again and Agents Rogers and Michaels came in followed by an Officer Harold hadn't seen before. As the agents approached the cell, Agent Michaels asked, "So boys, did you have a nice sleep? Ready to communicate?"

"Communication," said Agent Rogers. "That's where we ask questions, and you provide answers. A little cooperation will go a long way towards getting you out of here."

"My clients have nothing more to say," interceded Swifty.

"Ah, Mr. Swift, I didn't notice you there," Agent Rogers lied. "I mean, I thought you were just a drunk or something locked in the cell with the rest of the riffraff."

"Yeah, that's very funny, Agent Rogers. But we both know you don't have anything on my clients. We all know they didn't do anything and …"

"And I'm sure they did something," said Agent Rogers. "If we root around a little while, I'm sure we can find something to pin on these two choirboys."

"Or maybe you could just do your job and try to find the people who killed my clients' friends."

"Oh my, are you suggesting we should have sympathy for these assholes?" Rogers laughed sarcastically. "I might but I'm still busy feeling sympathy for the parents of young Cindy Lorens. Maybe you heard about her."

He looked over at Agent Michaels and said, "Ronald Wiggins, wasn't that the scumbag's name – rides himself and 16-year-old Cindy under the wheels of a train."

"I heard the girl was cut in half," said Agent Michaels as he stared at Swift with a look that mixed loathing with contempt.

"Wiggins was a friend of yours, wasn't he?" asked Agent Rogers, looking into Reaper's eyes.

Reaper stared back with cold, dark eyes that said the words Harold expected to hear out loud.

"This has nothing to do with the tragic deaths of Ms. Lorens or Mr. Wiggins," said Swifty, "and you know it."

"Well, we know a lot of things," said Agent Rogers. "For instance, we know that these are not choirboys. If they were convicted of these killings, even if they were innocent, justice would be served since they've certainly done something else. And we know that their lawyer is as much of a dirtbag as they are."

Swifty smiled at Agent Michaels for a moment while nodding his head as if in contemplation. "Well, fortunately jurisprudence doesn't work that way in the United States, Agent Rogers. Of course, if that's how you want to operate, there are other countries where you can go and ply your wares – countries such as Communist China and the Soviet Union. But as long as you're in this country, I'm going to have to insist that you abide by our laws. And our laws say that you can't just pin crimes on people because you don't like them. How would you like it if someone in government decided they don't like the way you and Agent Michaels lick the mints in urinals? Would it be OK with you if they locked you in some gulag for a few years even though no one actually saw you with your face in a toilet?

As though Swifty hadn't said a word, Agent Rogers continued, "And someday, we're going to find some dirt on you, too, Swift. You'll whistle a different tune then."

After a long, pregnant pause, as though both sides were eyeing each other in the ring after a series of blows, looking for an opening, Rogers turned to the Biesenthal Police Officer and said, "Would you mind releasing these two, fine, upstanding citizens. Oh, and I suppose you can let their lawyer out, too."

The sound of metal slipping into metal was followed by the sound of metallic tumblers and the clink of the latch popping out of the way.

As they walked past the ATF agents, Harold and Reaper gave the same salute – grins of triumph. But not to let them have the last word, Agent Michaels said, "Don't worry, punks, we'll catch you doing something sooner or later."

"And probably sooner," added Agent Rogers.

Harold and Reaper stepped out of the police station and into blinding sunlight. They held their hands above their eyes and rotated their heads like owls looking for a position where they could see. As their eyes adjusted, they realized that the hazy splotches in front of them were Falstaff and Samurai leaning against the hood of Sue's car.

Though the sun was at his back, Samurai mockingly held his hand up to his brow and made a similar but exaggerated motion with his head. When he stopped, he said, "Who did you expect?"

Interchangeably, Falstaff and Samurai hugged and shook Reapers hand and then Harold's.

"How are things?" asked Reaper.

Falstaff, clearly understanding his president's meaning, said,

"Everything's quiet. We got the word out, and Tank is sitting on Pot Roast."

"There's nothing to worry about just now," said Samurai.

Standing to the side forgotten, Swifty cleared his throat. When the four brothers looked his way, he said, "As touching as this is, I think I'll run along home about now."

Reaper was the first to thank the attorney. When they had all shook his hand and expressed their gratitude, Reaper said, "Why don't you come with us for a little breakfast."

"I figured you'd want nothing but to sleep by now," Falstaff said to Reaper.

"Are you kidding?" said Reaper. "They didn't feed us a thing in there. I'm starving."

"I could eat, too," said Harold.

Clearing his throat again, Swifty said, "I'd barf my guts if I even looked at food right now." Pointing at Reaper, he added, "Call me this week. And keep your heads down. I think those ATF punks are serious about trying to nail you for something." Then he climbed into a white Eldorado that seemed to swallow him up behind the steering wheel. The engine roared to life and he instantly threw it into reverse so that it shot out of the diagonal parking space with one of the front tires hopping and squealing. A car approaching on that side of the street had to slam on the brakes to avoid hitting him. The driver gave the horn a hard blow and seemed to yell something out the window at Swifty. But then the driver seemed to notice the Banshee Riders on the sidewalk and made the connection between the driver of the Cadillac and the bikers. Whether the person low behind the steering wheel of the white Caddy was in a confrontation with the bikers, or was a friend of the bikers, the honking driver seemed to conclude it was better to avoid participating in something that would most likely end badly. He not only let off the horn but looked away innocently as though trying to say, "What horn?"

The bikers had glanced that way when they heard the horn, but not really with interest. And Swifty appeared more than used to having people honk at his driving. He was already speeding down the road away from the scene.

At breakfast in Lillie's, the others seemed to notice that Harold was particularly quiet. While trying not to show it, they periodically glanced his way as though looking to see if he was OK. Once, Samurai even asked, "You OK, bro?"

Harold looked up from the place where he was deep in thought – thinking about what he'd seen in the clubhouse and of 6 Pack on the road in the rain. Less than he heard the question from Samurai, he noticed the silence as the other three in the booth were looking his way. Recognition of the question caught up with him and he said, "Yeah. I'm fine." When they continued to look at him, as though not convinced, he added, "Just need a little sleep, I guess."

After breakfast, Falstaff dropped Samurai off at his place so he could go to work. He got out of the car while admonishing Harold to get his bike and get some sleep. "You can come back here, if you'd like. Or you can just crash here now and we'll pick your bike up later."

Harold nodded without answering. Then Falstaff drove Harold and Reaper out to Mack's Cycle Repair to pick up their bikes.

Joe seemed more than a little sheepish and Harold was sure he was worried about the word getting out that he was screwing Sue. But at that point Harold, didn't care about that. He and Reaper merely thanked him for watching their bikes and vaguely answered his questions about how things had gone with the police. He seemed to sense that they were reluctant to answer his questions and he quickly dropped it.

Seeing that Joe seemed a little awkward, as though he thought he'd touched a raw nerve, Reaper finally said, "The status of the is that the Feds are involved. In other words, there is no case. They're working on their own case – fuck with the brothers, as usual."

Harold stood next to Reaper nodding with a disgusted look on his face. Even though he was an outlaw biker, somehow, he expected better from those serving the public. It never occurred to Harold that his feelings might come off a tad hypocritically.

As they climbed on their bikes to leave, Reaper asked if Harold was going back to Sue and Samurai's.

"I don't think so," Harold said. "Think I'll just go back to my place and crash."

"Do you want to get a drink first?" Reaper asked.

"Nah, just wanna get some sleep."

"Your place is on my way. I'll ride with you for a bit," Reaper said

Harold wasn't sure where Reaper lived but was pretty sure it was in the other direction. In any case, sensing that the president just wanted to make sure he got home OK, that he didn't flip out and do anything stupid, Harold nodded. They started their bikes and headed out onto the road with Harold taking them towards Chester's farm.

When they reached Willow Lane, they nodded to each other before Harold turned right and Reaper continued on. Harold had a sense it was all the communication that was required and appreciated that was the case; the quicker the goodbye, the less likely he would breakdown.

Chapter 32 — Muddy Assassin

Chester Pearl was a relatively disconnected member of society. He didn't own a television, neglected his phone bill, which was as likely disconnected on any given day as not, and he only occasionally listened to the radio. By chance, he turned the radio on in the kitchen this morning as he fixed some breakfast.

As he stirred a batch of pancake batter, he heard the newscaster say, "And today's top story — Two members of an area motorcycle gang and their female companion were found shot to death in a cabin in the affluent Silver Pines subdivision east of Biesenthal sometime before midnight. Information about the killings is sketchy, though police reportedly have two suspects in custody. The names of the victims have not been released pending notification of their next of kin."

Chester glanced out the back window where he saw the barn-door locked. Following a short weather report, the DJ came back on the air and introduced the Hank Williams song "Cold, Cold Heart." But Chester wasn't listening. He had set the bowl, with the large wooden spoon in it, on the corner of the table. He walked over to the stairs and hollered, "Harold?" When there was no answer, he went up the stairs to the attic doorway and hollered again. No answer. While he was deeply respectful of Harold's privacy and hadn't gone up to the attic since Harold moved in, not that he went up often anyhow, he now walked up the stairs, opened the door and looked over at the empty bed. With a furrowed brow, he returned to the kitchen and went back to making breakfast. For all intents and purposes, nothing had changed except that he now carried a slight frown. He also seemed to turn his head so his good left ear could pick up the sound of any vehicles coming down the road. Realizing the radio would make it harder to hear, he reached to shut the radio off. His hand hung in air for a second as he considered whether he should or not – as he weighed the ability to hear Magdelina coming down the road sooner, should she come. But then, shaking his head as if to tell himself that it wouldn't make any difference; if Harold was OK, Chester would know soon enough and worrying wasn't going to make it any easier. The decision reached, he reluctantly went back to his pancakes without touching the radio as the last chords of the Hank Willliams song came out of the speaker.

A short time later, the radio picked up the same story again, this time, it included an interview with Biesenthal Chief of Police Brandon Lewis. "Is it true that you have two suspects in custody?" the reporter asked.

"Two members of the gang known as the Banshee Riders were in custody though it's too early to say whether they were ever considered suspects. We are working with federal authorities to track down the people responsible for this crime. These two individuals were brought in for questioning."

"Do you have any other leads?" one reporter asked.

"We have identified several possible suspects," the chief said. "But as I said, this is an ongoing investigation." Then he added, "We do have reason to believe the victims knew their assailants."

Another reporter asked how the victims were killed and the chief said, "All three were shot in the head at close range, like assassinations."

When another reporter tried to ask another question, the chief said, "We have no further comments at this time," and the radio switched back to the newscaster who recapped the story "for those just tuning in."

When he heard "Banshee Riders" over the radio, Chester's face drew tight. It surprised him a little. Harold was his houseguest and was only around sporadically. But Chester liked him. He also felt a degree of responsibility to Harold's uncle. He thought to himself, "You're just like an old woman, getting yourself all worked up when you don't know nothin'. Instead of sitting here on yer ass listening to the radio, why don't you get to work?" With that, he pushed himself away from the table, dropped his plate and fork in the sink, and headed out the back door and out to the barn. But try as he might, Chester couldn't quite get the news story from the radio out of his mind. Every time he heard a sound, he would stick his head out the barndoor to see if Harold was coming down the road.

A couple of hours had passed when Chester heard the rumble of a Harley coming up the driveway. Walking out the door, he found Harold riding up to the door. One look at Harold's face answered several of Chester's questions.

"Friends of yours?" Chester asked.

Harold simply nodded.

"You involved?"

"Only because the feds are more interested in fucking with us than finding the people who did this," Harold said.

Chester nodded. "You look tired."

"Yeah," Harold said. "Long night."

"I'll start in on the south field so you won't hear the tractor so much," Chester said.

"It's OK," Harold said. "Right now, I could sleep through anything."

As Harold turned to walk into the house, Chester said, "If you need anything, just let me know."

Harold was about 10 feet away but stopped and turned with purpose to look back. "Thank you, Chester. For everything." There was a deep look of appreciation in his eyes as he spoke. Chester didn't speak but nodded while an expression that demonstrated an understanding of his friend's loss and the serious nature of the situation. It was a look that said he understood without the need for words or other significant demonstrations of feelings. Additional words would only clutter the message with unnecessary and distracting noise. Harold understood, too, and nodded his understanding before continuing into the farmhouse.

Harold climbed the stairs to the attic, kicked off his boots, threw his rag on the floor and collapsed on the bed. He lay there exhausted, wanting more than anything to sleep. Sleep was the elixir to cure his exhaustion but, more than that, it held the hope of escape from the recurring visions of Tawny and his dead brothers. In the battle between exhaustion and the stress caused by reoccurring visions of blood and death, exhaustion eventually won out. Harold fell into a deep sleep and, by the time he woke again, it was pitch dark outside again.

Waking, he experienced that fleeting moment people who've been through tragedies know only too well, the moment upon waking when there's hope that what transpired was merely a bad dream. As the reality washed the fog of sleep from his mind, Harold found that he was hungry again.

When Harold came down the stairs, he spotted Chester sitting in the rocker on the front porch in the dark. Harold looked through the fridge but had trouble choosing something to eat.

Finally, for simplicity's sake, Harold settled for a bowl of cereal. He took a spoon from the drain in the sink and carried the bowl and spoon outside by Chester. Sitting in a wicker chair he hadn't seen before, Harold started eating without a word.

Chester let him eat for a while and then said, "You don't have to tell me what happened. But if I should worry about people coming out here looking for you, I expect you'd keep me informed."

It hadn't really dawned on Harold that 6 Pack and the others might still have him in their sights. Harold had simply assumed that, with the police on the case, 6 Pack and the Monks would be too busy worrying about the police to think about Harold. Now, as Harold considered the possibility that the danger may not have passed, he also realized that he may be putting Chester in peril as well.

"Oh," Harold said. "I'm sorry. It didn't really occur to me. I should ..."

"It's OK," Chester said. "I just like to know if I need to keep an extra eye out for the boogeyman."

As Chester said that, Harold noticed that the shotgun was leaning against the side of the house beside where Chester was rocking.

They sat in silence for a while again. Then Harold said, "I don't mind telling you."

"You don't have to."

"I know," Harold said. "But if you're going to know who to watch out for, I probably should tell you what I know." Then Harold laid out the entire story for Chester finishing with the confrontation between Tom Swift and the ATF agents. He wasn't sure, but he'd have sworn Chester gave him a funny look when he said he was pretty sure the Monks were behind the killings.

Chester sat quietly for a few moments. Then he said, "I'm sorry to hear about your brothers. And that girl."

"Thanks," Harold said.

Chester broke the next long pause in the conversation by asking Harold a question. "You've heard the old saying, 'Don't make a federal case out of it,' haven't you?"

"Sure," Harold said.

"They don't say that for nothing," Chester said. "Dealing with the local authorities is one thing. Dealing with the feds is another thing altogether. The feds don't care if their boss is reelected or not. They don't care what Joe public thinks out here in the sticks. And they don't care much about rules and laws that get in their way."

Harold couldn't help thinking that Chester must have some personal experience behind his comments. But if he did, Chester didn't offer up anything more than advice.

The two sat in silence on the porch for almost half an hour before Chester excused himself to head to bed. "You gonna be OK?" he asked first.

"Sure," Harold said. But deep down inside, Harold wasn't so sure. The thought of hunting 6 Pack down and exacting some revenge had passed through Harold's mind several times. But somehow, he realized it wasn't a good way to find himself in prison or living on the run like Tex and Morticia. The idea that 6 Pack was still looking for him, wanting to finish the job, did change things a bit. As a matter of self-preservation, Harold realized he might have no choice but to kill or be killed. And the more Harold thought about it, the more it dawned on him that the longer he waited, the more chance there was that 6 Pack would get to him first. He also realized that, though he was almost certainly 6 Pack's primary target, some of Harold's brothers were also potential targets – for instance, Samurai. Even Chester could wind up in 6 Pack's crosshairs.

Harold could see the shadow of a figure cast against the side of the house, flowing with the swaying shadows of branches from the trees before separating to slide stealthily over to the window. The window was open slightly. Sheer, white curtains waved lightly as the man slipped the fingers of both hands underneath the wood and, ever so slowly and quietly, raised the window until he could lean down, throw a leg through the frame and follow it through with his body. Watching as he crept through the living room, Harold recognized the pistol in the man's hand. A sense of panic was growing in Harold's chest as he tried to scream, tried to rise up and attack the intruder. But when Harold opened his mouth, nothing escaped. When he tried to rise, he found that he didn't have the energy. It was as if he were held down by the force of a giant and invisible hand pressing against his chest.

Lightly, the man swung open the bedroom door and slipped inside. Harold struggled to get free as the man raised the gun and pointed it at the bodies under the sheets. As a shot rang out, Harold burst free from under the hand and found himself standing with sweat dripping down from his forehead.

It was just a dream. Or was it? Maybe it was a premonition or a vision of something that was happening somewhere else at that very moment. But Harold realized it wasn't just somewhere else. The layout was wrong, but that was definitely Samurai's house and, it also figured, that was Samurai and Sue in bed.

Standing on the porch in front of the chair where he'd fallen asleep, Harold knew he had to do something. He knew it couldn't wait.

Back inside Chester's house, Harold opened the drawer where he knew Chester kept his revolver. Along with the revolver, Harold found a box of ammo. Harold flipped the chambers open and saw that five of the six cylinders were loaded. He flipped it closed and slid the ammo box open. From the Styrofoam casing, he removed half a dozen rounds and slipped them into his left-front pants pocket. Harold shoved the pistol into his belt and went upstairs to get his jacket.

In the attic, he retrieved the leather jacket from its hook on the coat stand. Then he bent down and picked his colors up off the floor. A little voice told him this was not the time to wear his colors. For a second, another voice yelled, "Let 'em know who you are. Don't leave 'em with any doubt about it, if they screw with the Banshee Riders, they'll come to regret it." With that fatalistic attitude still ringing in his mind, Harold thought better of it and dropped his colors on the mattress, went outside and pulled Magdelina out of the barn. So that he wouldn't wake Chester, Harold walked the bike all the way out to the road before kicking it over. As the bike fired up and he threw his leg over, Harold looked up at the farmhouse and wondered if he'd be back. Then he pulled out onto the road -- a man on a mission.

Harold road past Samurai's house and stopped in the street for a minute. As he looked at the window to Samurai's bedroom, Harold was tempted to go in and make sure they were OK, that all he had was a bad dream and his friends were still safe in their bed. But looking at the house peacefully in the stillness of a clear night Harold somehow knew that all was well inside. He sat and looked a little longer, wishing them and the children all the best. Then Harold headed off to fulfill his destiny.

Harold headed out of Biesenthal towards the Monks club-house. But a short distance before he came to the clubhouse, he turned right on Brighton Road that angled off at a 30-degree angle. Harold proceeded about half a mile. On his left was a foundation where a farmhouse had once stood. Out beyond the foundation was an old barn, its slats weathered and shrunken so that, in the daytime, the light would shine right through its meatless ribs. Harold slowed as he approached the property and looked ahead and back to make sure no one was coming down the road in front or behind. Seeing nothing but darkness, Harold pulled quickly off the road and switched off his lights.

With the lights off, Harold stood still waiting for his eyes to adjust to the darkness. Eventually, the grown-over gravel drive that ran back to the barn came into focus. Feeling his way slowly, Harold worked his way onto the overgrown grass and around behind the barn where he parked the bike so no one would see it from the road when the sky lightened. He put the bike on its kickstand and checked the gun in his belt. Then he stopped and looked across the field behind the barn, a field long past its last planting where irregular shapes, like jagged glass, stood darkly against the blueish darkness. He took a deep sigh, as though stealing himself for the job, before heading off to the north across the field. He knew that, out beyond that field, to his right or left, which he wasn't sure, was a small parcel of land with a small cabin recently purchased by a group of bikers who called themselves the Monks.

The idea was simple – just walk across the field, find a place to hide among the trees and wait for 6 Pack and his brothers to arrive, as Harold was sure they would. But Harold soon discovered that it wasn't as simple as a stroll through the park. The ground was still soaked from the rain that had fallen when he'd found Red, Mongrel, and Tawny in the clubhouse. Every time Harold took a step, his feet sunk into the marshy ground below the prairie grass as though the muck was trying to pull him under the ground. Then, as though he were pulling a suction cup off a table, when he lifted his foot, he heard a sucking sound as he lifted his boot out of the muck. As the mud built up thickly on his boots, it dawned on Harold that he was leaving a trail that would lead the police back to the assassin's starting point. But Harold assumed he'd be lucky to get out alive and didn't give the evidence he was creating another thought. Harold also discovered that it was surprisingly chilly out.

About halfway across the field, hidden in a bunch of straw-like grass, where a tree had once stood, a trap was patiently waiting for Harold. The tree had fallen so long ago that the evidence only just protruded above the ground and even then was well below the skyline of the marshy grass. While the trunk of the tree was buried by time and the elements, it was as though it had managed to keep one arm free. As Harold came by that spot, the mud now having worked its way halfway up his pants, he was cold and already feeling disheartened. It was then that the arm of the tree reached out and grabbed his toe and sent him sprawling forward. He came down with his right knee hitting a rock or another branch – something hard buried just below the surface. His hands, fingers spread, sought to break his fall but were sucked into the mud for their effort. Lying face-first in the mud, Harold felt a shooting pain in his knee and struggled to his feet. A full outline of his body was left, as though for a future archeologist to find, in the ground that filled with water as Harold stood. He rubbed his sore knee with one muddied hand while trying to shake the mud off the other before brushing mud from his face.

Harold hiked up his resolve and limped on about 15 feet, while continuing to struggle knocking the mud off his hands, before he noticed that something was missing at his waist. He felt as though the mud was soaking his tenacity out through the souls of his boots. He also realized that Chester's revolver was missing from his belt and was obviously back in the mud where he had fallen. With frustration mounting, Harold retraced his steps until he found the branch that had tripped him in the first place. He bent down and felt around fruitlessly searching for the weapon.

"God damn it," Harold said as he sunk to his hands and knees and continued the search the way he would look for the key to his door had he dropped it on a moonless night. At last, his hand hit something hard and Harold wrapped his fingers around the body of the .38 caliber Smith & Wesson. As he retrieved the gun, he found that, like his pants, boots and hands, one side of the weapon was covered in mud. When he checked to see if the mud had gotten into the barrel, he felt himself shoving the mud further up inside.

Harold gingerly brushed the mud away and determined to find a stick to clean out the barrel when the sky lightened up enough. However, he was no longer sure that the weapon would fire when he sighted his target and pulled the trigger. For a moment, he thought to try squeezing off a round but realized that, if it did fire, there was a good chance he would alert the Monks to the presence of an approaching assassin in the field behind their clubhouse. As far as he could see, there was nothing to do but take his chances and he hung onto the gun as he continued. Soon, he was leaving the field behind and entering a wooded area that extended the rest of the way out to Route 36 running by in front of the Monks clubhouse.

Harold paused at the edge of the tree line considering which way to go, looking off in both directions as though he would find a sign pointing the way. He wasn't sure but suspected that the clubhouse was further to the east. He stood listening for a few minutes in hopes that he might hear some of the Monks talking or making noise that he could follow the way an airplane would follow a radio beam to its target. When there was nothing, Harold began feeling his way east along the tree line.

He worried that he might go right past the clubhouse and tried to force his eyes to see the slightest variations among the trees to his left. Harold had only gone about 50 yards along the tree line when, between the trees he saw a blackness that suggested something solid. He stood and craned his head to the right and left and crouched lower to do the same thing until he was convinced there was definitely something there in the woods. He moved deeper into the woods for a better look until, at the leading edge of a clearing, he saw the silhouette of a cabin in the darkness. Slowly, quietly, like the man in his dream, Harold snuck further toward Route 36 until he could see the L-shaped porch on the front of the cabin and knew he had reached his destination. Sensing that, with the advent of daylight, he was too close and too visible from the clubhouse, he worked his way back in among the trees a little further. He looked around for an area with enough room between the trees so he could sit down and slid to the ground with his back against a large, course tree trunk.

As Harold waited, he shivered with cold and pangs of doubt about his plan, not just the methodology but the central idea as well. Doubts about the wisdom of his plan were nagging at him as though a voice was whispering in one ear. Slowly, the darkness turned to a blueish hue before the first streaks of sunlight cut through the trees and over the roof of the clubhouse. By that time, Harold had almost talked himself out of the idea as he rubbed his hands together in a continued effort to clean the dried mud away as it soaked the moisture out of his palms. He placed one palm on the floor of the woods and was about to rise from the ground when heard the sound of a motor and saw a rusty, battered two-door Toyota puttering loudly into the parking area in front of the clubhouse. Harold was surprised to see Ivan, the Monk he'd met up north, and another Monk climb out of the car and walk up to the door. As Ivan was unlocking the door, the other Monk was laughing about something and, to Harold's ears, he sounded more than a little intoxicated. In Biesenthal, liquor licenses allowed bars to stay open until 6 a.m. Then the bars had to close for an hour before reopening. It was Harold's guess that they had just left one of the bars in town. They went inside leaving the door wide open.

The sight of Ivan, someone Harold still felt some kind of connection to, seemed to reinforce the decision to leave. But then, just as Harold was guessing that other Monks would probably arrive soon, too, he heard the rumble of Harleys coming down the road. Harold was kicking himself. "What the hell was I thinking? What are the odds 6 Pack will pull in the driveway just in time for me to shoot him? And what am I going to do about the rest of these Monks? They probably won't like someone shooting at them from the trees, and you're a little outnumbered here, pal."

As he rose to his feet, Harold saw two bikes emerge from the darker shadows of the path back to the parking area. In the shadows of the trees, Harold couldn't make them out at first. The closer they came, however, the clearer Harold saw them. The biker on the first bike Harold only vaguely remembered seeing before. The second, as though on cue, was a young, light-haired biker on a black Sportster. 6 Pack had arrived.

The bikes pulled in closer and closer until little more than 40 feet separated Harold from his target. At that range, Harold considered taking a shot from the wooded area where he had unconsciously returned to a crouch. However, it occurred to him that if, with all the mud, the gun didn't fire, 6 Pack and the others would probably still hear the hammer fall. They would find him, an assassin in the woods, defenseless, with a weapon that wouldn't fire. Harold was fairly sure no one would ever see him again. Then again, even if the gun did fire, what were his chances of actually hitting 6 Pack from that distance and through all those trees. Harold hesitated. As the bikes turned towards the porch, they began moving further away from his firing position.

6 Pack parked his bike with his back to Harold and Harold noticed that there was no longer a 'P' on 6 Pack's back. Somehow, 6 Pack had jumped from prospect to full-fledged brother and now wore the Monks' center patch. Harold could easily imagine what 6 Pack had done to merit his sudden promotion among the ranks of the Monks. The anger and determination that had set Harold out across a muddy field in the first place rose up from deep inside, from his core as he considered that his brothers and Tawny had probably purchased 6 Pack's patch with their lives.

The other Monk parked further back from the porch and, as 6 Pack stepped off the bike, turning to face his brother he also turned in Harold's direction again. Whatever doubts Harold had about following through with his plan were washed away and replaced by a burning hatred focused like a laser on 6 Pack's face, a hatred that also washed away the cold and discomfort felt in joints that had sat on the cold, hard ground for several hours. Here was the worthless piece of garbage who had killed Red, Mongrel, and Tawny. Here was the man who would have killed Harold, had Harold arrived a little earlier at the Banshee Riders clubhouse that night. And considering their history, here was the man who was almost certainly still looking for an opportunity to kill Harold.

Harold repositioned himself and drew the gun from his belt. In the morning light, he examined the gun and quietly picked some more dried mud off the barrel. He steadied his shooting hand against the side of the tree he was hiding behind and wrapped his left hand around his right wrist for extra support. He figured, if he tried to race across the drive to get up close for a shot, they were liable to shoot him down long before he got there. Banking that the gun would fire at all, Harold planned to squeeze off several rounds until he got his man.

As Harold looked down the barrel of the gun and waited for just the right moment, he realized that he was positioned somewhat awkwardly and that his discomfort was making it difficult to hold his position. Was it this, or was it nerves that seemed to make the barrel shake? Harold forced himself to think about the sight of Red and Mongrel's bodies on the floor, Tawny in the bathtub, with holes in their heads and blood seeping out around them. He allowed the sight to fill him with hatred until he could feel it in all his extremities, including the finger firmly pressed against the trigger. He quietly repositioned himself as he heard 6 Pack talking and realized that the new member of the Monks was less than happy on this early morning. Several of 6 Pack's words carried back to Harold clearer than the others. Among those words, the ones that stood out were, "fucking assholes" and "God damn feds."

Hearing 6 Pack use the word "feds" Harold lowered the gun slightly. Could it be that the feds had come up with some evidence to implicate the former Banshee Rider? Were the feds doing their job after all? If Harold let 6 Pack live, would justice have its day in a courtroom and spare him the need to throw away his life in an act of vengeance? And was that enough? Would 6 Pack and his brothers be sufficiently occupied defending themselves in court to offer some security to Harold and his brothers in and about Biesenthal? Harold realized this was a real possibility. But it was only a possibility. If Harold pulled the trigger, he could put an end to it here and now, sort of. If Harold pulled the trigger, he could put 6 Pack out of commission and achieve a fuller sense of justice in the process.

Harold raised the gun again. Eyeing 6 Pack down the short barrel of the gun, Harold slowly and gently applied pressure to the trigger. Being careful to keep the gun steady, the moment that would send a hot piece of lead hurtling 50-feet across the area that separated him from his nemesis drew to a fraction of a second. But then Harold heard tires turning onto the gravel at the front of the driveway. He hadn't heard the motor, so he was sure it wasn't a motorcycle. Looking down the drive, Harold could see a pair of headlights approaching. When it entered the clearing, to Harold's surprise, he saw Agents Michaels and Rogers in the front seat of a black Ford sedan. Harold could also see two-or-more sets of headlights back in the shadows of the path from the road.

With no effort to restrain the annoyance in his voice, 6 Pack hollered, "Now what?"

As they stepped from both sides of the car, Agent Michaels said, "We've got an eyewitness who puts you in the vicinity of the murder scene at the time of the killings, Mr. Wainright. You're under arrest."

For a second, as he watched from the trees, Harold thought 6 Pack was contemplating resisting arrest. But then he saw 6 Pack look back down the drive at the other sets of headlights blazing forth from the shadows and into the clearing. Several county squads and a Biesenthal interceptor were backing up the Feds. Harold lowered the gun and quietly slid back farther among the trees. There he watched as agent Rogers frisked 6 Pack and applied handcuffs to 6 Pack's hands. The other three members of the Monks were also frisked and handcuffed. One of them complained, "You haven't got anything on us."

Smugly, Michaels said, "I'm sure we can come up with something."

As the Monks were placed individually in the backs of the squad cars, with 6 Pack in the back of the ATF agents' Ford, additional law enforcement vehicles arrived and Harold watched as some officers went into the house while others began looking around in the area outside. Harold was just thinking it might be a good time to sneak away when he heard agent Michaels say, "Don't forget to look around out here in the trees." As he said this, he swept his arm over in the general direction where Harold was hiding.

Harold froze for a moment as he recognized Officer Spenoza and saw that the Biesenthal policeman was looking where agent Michaels had gestured. Harold held his breath, certain that Officer Spenoza was about to walk across the driveway and begin looking through the trees and undergrowth where he would probably find an embarrassed member of the Banshee Riders.

The way Spenoza was looking, for a second, Harold thought

he'd been seen already. But then Spenoza said, "I'll get to it," and went back to looking through the ferns that were growing up around the sides and back of the cabin.

Harold knew this was his chance and quietly snuck back through the trees until he was walking along the tree line by the prairie. With the prairie grass ablaze with golden sunlight, and the chance that a law officer might drive by on the backroad where he had parked his bike, or that Officer Spenoza might see him from the tree line, Harold was reluctant to simply walk back through the prairie grass. Instead, he followed the tree line west until he found a shorter stretch of open field between the tree line and the farm where he'd left his bike. It even occurred to Harold to crawl down low through the grass to avoid being spotted. But he decided that crawling through the mud was absurd. Instead, he determined that, if an officer did see him, he would drop the gun into the grass and continue walking as though everything was normal.

Moving as quickly as the mud would allow, Harold was about halfway back to the barn when he saw a county squad car come around the corner from the west to head by to the southeast. In a moment of panic, Harold froze. From where Harold stood to where the squad was passing was a little more than a football field away. Standing out like a sore thumb in the middle of the field, he couldn't imagine how the county sheriff could possibly miss him. The squad began to slow or was it just in his mind. Harold gathered his composure and began walking casually towards the barn while holding the gun in his left hand behind his leg. He was about to let the weapon drop into the grass when the driver of the squad hit the gas hard and sped on without seeming to have noticed Harold at all.

As the squad disappeared out of sight, Harold decided he'd had enough of this nonsense. With no further ado, Harold drove himself hard across the field. He made it to his bike and the cover behind the barn out of breath and in relatively short order considering how long it had taken him heading the other way. As soon as he'd caught his breath, he tucked the gun into his belt again, kicked some mud off his boots against the barn wall, and wheeled the bike around to the side of the barn. After glancing down the highway in both directions until he was sure it was clear, Harold started the engine with one kick and proceeded out to the road. He hesitated for a second trying to decide which way to turn and decided to take his chances heading back towards Biesenthal by the shortest route.

As he came to the stop sign at the intersection where he had turned to come up behind the Monks clubhouse, Harold saw a black Ford pulling out of the clubhouse driveway. For the second time in only several minutes, Harold was certain the gig was up, and he'd have to do some fast talking. His pulse raced again, and he felt a drop of sweat forming on his brow. This time, agents Michaels and Rogers were looking straight at Harold as the car approached. There was no mistaking that they saw him. However, the car kept going and, as it went by, Harold also saw 6 Pack staring out the back window at him. Harold was almost tempted to offer a sarcastic wave or flip 6 Pack the finger but decided that caution was the better part of valor. It dawned on him that it was a little ridiculous to act so brave only a short time after he was shaking in his muddy boots.

As soon as the ATF car had gone by, Harold pulled out to the left and followed from a safe distance until he could turn off to go to Samurai's house. When he pulled into the driveway, he saw the garage door was open and the work van and Samurai's bike were both in the garage. Sue's car was in the driveway and it was fairly safe to say that they were both home.

Chapter 33 — The Monks

Samurai had heard the bike pulling up and saw Harold out the window. He came out to meet Harold in the parking lot with a concerned look on his face. Samurai was about to ask if Harold was OK when he saw the mud all over his brother. Looking into Harold's face, Samurai could see that Harold was close to tears.

Harold was caught off guard when Samurai threw his arms around his brother and held him for a minute. The tenderness of Samurai's reaction opened the floodgates and Harold began to cry. Through sobs, like a child explaining how he'd gotten hurt, Harold told Samurai about staking out the Monks' clubhouse, and how the ATF had come to arrest 6 Pack.

When he'd finished, with his left one arm over Harold's shoulder, Samurai led him inside. There, Sue met him at the doorway to the kitchen with an equally concerned look on her face. Harold wondered if Sue was worried about him or if she was worried about what Harold might say about the other night at the bike shop.

Like a nurse, Sue insisted Harold take off his pants and shirt so she could wash them. "Sam, could you bring him your bathrobe?" Sue asked.

Samurai nodded and disappeared up the stairs returning seconds later with a green, Terri-cloth bathrobe. Harold took the robe in the bathroom, since he wasn't wearing any underwear, and slipped his clothes off. He emptied the pockets and put the contents on the back of the toilet. The gun, however, he brought out with him and set on the table.

While Harold disrobed, Sue had found a wicker laundry basket that was half full of dirty clothes. She took Harold's shirt and pants from him and threw them on the top of the other laundry and headed down the stairs.

As soon as Sue left, Samurai turned to Harold and said, "Sue told me about the other night."

Wondering if this meant Sue had told Samurai the truth, Harold looked at Samurai in surprise but didn't say a word.

Recognizing the need to clarify, as he put a cup of coffee on the table in front of Harold, Samurai added, "She told me how you found her with Joe at the bike shop."

Harold welcomed the coffee and took a long sip before asking, "And you're OK with it?"

Samurai shrugged his shoulders. "Can't say I never done the same thing myself, can I?"

Looking down at the table, Harold realized he was never in a position to really condemn Sue since he was there during Samurai's indiscretion, as well.

"It's going to be OK," Samurai said, misreading that Harold was still worried. "I hate to say it but everything else considered, I mean what happened to Mongrel, Red, and Tawny, kind of put the whole thing in a different perspective."

Samurai fixed a cup of joe for himself and sat down at the table where the two sipped their coffee in silence.

After a while, Harold asked, "Who do you think turned him in?"

"I have no idea," Samurai said. "I think you can be pretty sure it was no one from the Banshees. After Reaper told us how the feds were acting, I think the brothers would rather cut the feds' throats than tell them the time of day, not that I think any of us would have talked anyhow."

There was another long silence and then Samurai asked, "Are you going to be OK?"

Harold looked up at Samurai for a few seconds and thought about it.

"Right now, I don't know," Harold said.

There was another long pause. Then Samurai laughed, "You were really gonna shoot the son of a bitch, eh?"

Harold looked up at Samurai and forced a smile as he nodded lightly. "I figured he wasn't done yet. I needed to kill him before he got to anyone else."

"Maybe," Samurai said. "But don't forget, he's a member of the Monks now. That means that, even if he's locked up, we still have to keep our eyes open. It also means that, if you shoot him, you're shooting a Monk. They're pretty unforgiving about things like that."

Harold nodded again as he took another sip of coffee, staring into the cup as though he would find some answers in the swirls on the surface.

As Sue came into the room, Samurai said, "Reaper and Falstaff are telling everybody to lie low for a while. I mean, if there's any more trouble, we'll be there for each other but, for now, it's better if we keep a low profile."

Sue was fixing some breakfast as the kids came into the room chasing each other and making a commotion. She came over to the table by Harold and casually picked up the gun and put it up on the windowsill and out of reach as though simply clearing room for breakfast. Then Sue shooed her children into the living room where she turned on cartoons to keep them occupied. When she came back in the kitchen, she said to Harold, "Why don't you stay here for a few days. It's not good for you to be all alone at the farm up in that musty old attic."

"Thanks," Harold said. "But actually, I was thinking about getting away for a couple days. I thought I might take a ride and see how my mother's doing."

Samurai looked deep into Harold's eyes as though trying to read his thoughts. "You know, you don't have to handle this all by yourself. You do have brothers."

"I know," Harold said in a puzzled tone.

"I just mean that you should talk to someone next time before you decide to go out in a blaze of glory," Samurai smiled in a way that said the idea was crazy but that he respected Harold for the thought.

"Glory?" Harold snorted. "I sure didn't look too glorious sprawled out in the mud in that field."

"Well, I just thought you might be planning another ambush or something," Samurai said. Then, after a few moments, Samurai continued, "Maybe it's not such a bad idea for you to get away from all this shit for a couple days. You've been through a lot."

As Sue set plates of scrambled eggs and biscuits and gravy in front of them, Samurai asked, "When do you think you'll leave?"

"Soon," Harold said without mentioning that his stomach was really too twisted up over the events of the last few days to think about eating. But Sue had made the effort and Harold figured the least he could do was to give the plate a few pokes with his fork.

"The wakes are tonight," Samurai said, "and the funerals are tomorrow. Can you wait that long?"

Harold would rather have gone outside and gotten straight onto his motorcycle. If he didn't have the bike, he would have been willing to go outside and start running and just keep running for a while. All he knew was that he wanted to get away, at least long enough so that he could think clearly. But Harold also realized he needed to be there for the ceremonies. He needed to say goodbye to Red, Mongrel, and Tawny.

Visitation for Red and Mongrel was held in the same room of the funeral home in Biesenthal. Tawny's services were held in Earlsville, though her parents got the word out that the biker world wasn't welcome. Harold was sorry to hear this but was pleased when Snake said the club had sent flowers anyway.

Red's and Mongrel's coffins were at the front and angling out at approximately 20-degree angles from an imaginary line drawn through the center of the room. Red and Mongrel were laid out with their feet pointing to opposite walls and their heads towards the center. Harold noticed that the mortician had done a remarkable job of masking the holes in the centers of his brothers' foreheads. All Harold could see was a little additional makeup in that area. But Harold didn't linger up front long. In fact, while other people gathered in the rear of the room to talk, Harold was preparing to clear out of the funeral home entirely within 15 minutes of arriving.

As Harold was walking out, he was surprised when he bumped into Chester walking in. Prior to that moment, Harold had never seen Chester and his brothers together at the same time. Somehow, it felt a little awkward, as though two different worlds had collided. But Harold quickly understood that Chester was there, primarily, out of respect for Harold.

Harold went back up front with Chester to view the bodies again. And then, after introducing Chester to Reaper, Samurai, and Tank, Harold asked Chester to come outside so they could talk.

Harold was worried that, by the time he was done talking, the respect that had brought Chester there might have diminished. Harold explained how he had taken Chester's pistol and snuck through the field fully intending to execute 6 Pack. Harold told how he had fallen and dropped the gun in the mud. "Samurai loaned me his gun cleaning kit," Harold said. "I think I got all the mud off."

"It's fine," Chester said, "but maybe you'd better hang onto it for a while, not that I'm encouraging you to use it. You just might want to have some protection until this all blows over."

Then Chester took a deep breath before speaking again. "I appreciate that you were willing to put yourself on the line for me and your brothers, but I really don't think you want to go where they'd send you if you did that. Trust me. I know what I'm talking about."

"You were in prison?" Harold asked in surprise.

"Just for a little while," Chester said. "Your uncle's the one who did some serious time."

"My uncle?" Harold said with equal surprise. Then he asked, "What were you in for?"

"I was charged as an accessory to murder," Chester said. "And I was lucky that's all I got."

"And my uncle?"

Chester drew a deep breath, as though preparing himself for something unpleasant, and then said, "Second-degree murder."

"What happened?" Harold asked.

Looking Harold in the face, Chester said, "It wasn't long after your uncle and I started the Monks motorcycle club."

"The Monks," Harold said in absolute shock. "But they're a national club. They're the assholes who ..."

"Even a national club has to start somewhere," Chester said. "The Monks started down by the city where Gizzard and I lived at the time. We started the club in your uncle's garage. Guess we had some pent-up energy to get rid of after what we'd experienced fighting the Japs."

Harold was flabbergasted but he had no way of preparing himself for what Chester said next. "It was Gizzard, me and Shotgun."

"Shotgun?" Harold asked.

"Yeah, Shotgun," said Chester, "your father. He was the original president of the Monks."

"MY FATHER?" Harold said loud enough to draw the attention of some of the other bikers who had stepped outside of the funeral home.

"Yes," Chester said as he took Harold by the arm and led him further from the front door, so they could continue talking in private. "It was about 10-12 years before you were born. I remember your mom bringing you out to the garage when we had parties after our meetings. Problem was, your mom really didn't fit in with the whole lifestyle. She didn't like your uncle much and she didn't like me much better.

"I don't mean to speak badly about your mother," Chester said, "but she may act like a blue blood but, trust me, she's from the same side of the tracks as your uncle and your dad. We all grew up in the same neighborhood. She was such a snooty little thing. As kids, she was always saying, 'I'm going to tell,' and getting us into trouble. We used to tease her just to get rid of her."

Hearing Chester talk about his mother as though she had once thought herself a debutante, just didn't make sense to Harold. Picturing his mother in her armchair in her bathrobe watching television with curlers in her hair, if it wasn't for the way he'd inherited the bike, Harold might have thought Chester had his mother and father mixed up with two other people.

"So, if my dad was a biker, how the hell did he wind up marrying my mom?" Harold asked realizing the story his mother had once told him couldn't possibly be true.

"I don't know," Chester said. "Your uncle and I were busy fighting Japs on Saipan about the time they got married. Your dad had joined up with your uncle but, after the Sullivans, they broke up brothers so they wouldn't all be killed at the same time and such. We were in the 2nd Marine Division. They put your old man in the 5th Marine Division. That's how he wound up at Iwo Jima."

"My dad was at Iwo Jima?" Harold asked. "He never said anything about it. I mean, I knew he was in the Marines but ... well, he didn't say anything about the Monks, either."

"He wouldn't have," Chester said. "He was never one to talk about the war, not that most of the guys who were actually there really do. And I'm sure your mom didn't want him talking to you about the club.

"Your old man always had the smarts, though. Your uncle and me, we were just dirty, low-down grunts. Your old man, he went off to communications school somewhere for additional training. We didn't need any more schooling to teach us how to stump through the mud with a backpack and shoot a rifle."

Chester stopped talking as he could see the shock was still on Harold's face. Almost to himself, Harold said, "My father started the Monks? What the hell."

"I don't think your father wanted me to tell you," Chester said. "But everything considered, I thought you should know."

"So, you don't have to worry much about the Monks, do you?" Harold asked.

"I don't know," Chester said. "Most of the punks riding with the club now have no idea who I am."

"How do you feel knowing I was out stalking them?" Harold asked.

Chester looked into Harold's eyes again. "I'm not a member of the Monks Motorcycle Club anymore," Chester said. "As far as I'm concerned, you're a member of my family, and about the only one, I have left. If the Monks have killed your brothers, I have no more use for the Monks than you do.

"And when I say I'd rather you didn't go sniper on 'em again, it's not because I'm trying to protect the Monks. You're young yet. And trust me, time spent in the pen is time lost. You can't have it back — that's assuming someone doesn't kill you before or after you get there. That's something to consider. The Monks always have people on the inside."

Harold nodded. "I can't say I wouldn't have shot him if the feds hadn't shown up," Harold said. "But I was a bit relieved that they did."

Chester nodded and Harold could see a look of relief on the man's face as he accepted the idea that Harold wasn't still plotting ways to take out 6 Pack or other members of the Monks.

"You said you were lucky to be charged with manslaughter — why?" Harold asked.

"Your uncle was convicted of murder," Chester said. "We got into it with another club. I was holding a guy while your uncle hit him. We didn't think the guy would die." Chester continued. "Had we known he would die or what it was like behind bars, I can promise you, we wouldn't have laid a finger on him."

"How long was my uncle in?" Harold asked.

"He served about seven years," Chester said. Then he looked down as though he were contemplating whether to go on.

"Is there something else?" Harold asked.

"The guy we killed," Chester said, "he ran your dad off the road and put him in the hospital. That's why we beat the crap out of the guy."

Harold felt anger welling up inside him. "And my dad turned his back on his brothers after that?"

"It wasn't that he turned his back on us," Chester said. "He was pretty badly hurt. And your mother was all shook up by what happened. While the trial was going on she was working on your father trying to convince him to get out of the club. He was there for us the whole time during the trial: helped pay our legal fees and everything. It was only after our conviction that he came and told us what your mom wanted and what he'd agreed to do.

"Your mom didn't want you growing up in the whole biker environment thing," Chester said. "With us in prison, she figured it was a good time for your dad to make a clean break. I guess you could say he did it for you — left the club, that is."

As Harold let it all sink in, suddenly he started laughing.

"What?" Chester asked.

"Well," Harold said. "She spent all that time and effort trying to keep me out of the biker lifestyle and I wound up joining a motorcycle club anyhow, it's like it was my destiny or something."

"I don't suppose she'd think it was all that funny," Chester said.

"No, I'm sure she wouldn't," Harold said.

If Harold felt inclined to get away for a while before Chester told him about his connection to the Monks, he felt even more so after hearing the story. Not only had so much happened but now he had this additional information to muddy the waters. He'd just found out his parents weren't who he really thought they were and the Monks, who he'd come to loathe, who had killed his brothers and Tawny, and who probably wanted him dead, were part of his family heritage. It was a lot to sort out and Harold wondered if a couple days away would be enough.

The funeral the next day was another lavish biker affair. By request of the funeral home, the ceremony didn't start until late in the afternoon as there were two other funerals that day. The funeral director had explained, "I just think it would be better for you if we didn't have to worry about the other funerals interfering with the ceremony for your brothers." Reading between the lines, it was clear he meant the opposite – he was trying to spare the families from the other funerals from having a raucous biker funeral while they were struggling with the grief of their own losses. Either way, Reaper and Falstaff understood. They even preferred it that way.

Mongrel and Red were buried side by side in plots the club helped finance with their families. As per another request from the funeral director, when the ceremony ended, the Banshee Riders quickly led the other clubs and attendees out of the cemetery and over to Hildie's.

Harold found a seat in a back corner of the bar where he watched the start of what was sure to be a party to remember. People were jammed shoulder to shoulder inside the bar and out. While the demeanor graveside was sufficiently respectful, it was as though the required decorum there had caused all the bikers to fill with pent-up energy waiting for an outlet. The party at Hildie's was that outlet.

It was beginning to annoy Harold that everyone seemed as though they were treating him with kid gloves, as though he was fragile. However, even as it annoyed him, he also appreciated it. Shortly after he arrived, and found his spot in the corner, Samurai, Pot Roast and Snake came by as though they'd been looking for him. Pot Roast started to say, "What are you doing back here in the corner" but was cut off short by Samurai who stepped in front of Pot Roast while offering Harold another beer. Pot Roast quickly got the hint and slid into the chair around the corner of the table from Harold.

There was a long pregnant pause noticeable even through the pounding rhythm of the song 'Bad Company' blasting from the jukebox. Finally, struggling for something to say, Snake said, "It was a nice ceremony, don't you think? Had to be 150 brothers riding in the procession from the funeral home to the cemetery."

"Yeah, but I didn't say any Bloody Bastards or those fucking Monks," said Pot Roast bitterly. "I suppose the Monks don't like attending funerals they ..."

"Shut the fuck up," snarled Samurai half under his breath as he glanced back over both his shoulders to see if anyone was listening. "Besides, they were there. Both of 'em."

"I didn't see them," Pot Roast protested.

"Well, I guess you weren't looking in the right places," said Samurai, clearly getting annoyed. "Shiv, Atilla, Ivan and a couple other former Swamp Rats were there. And Tunnel Rat and Wizard were there representing the Bastards."

"They were out in force for Poacher's funeral," said Snake,

clearly insinuating this was a bit of a slight to the Banshee Riders.

"Poacher was a fucking legend in the biker community," said Samurai. "He was on a first-name basis with more bikers than you two idiots have ever laid eyes on."

"Yeah, well what does that make our brothers," said Pot Roast, his eyes beginning to look a little moist.

"It makes them our brothers," said Harold, catching the others by surprise as it was the first time he'd spoken since they came over by him. "And that's what counts."

Samurai, Pot Roast and Snake stared at Harold for a moment. Then, Snake raised his beer stein, "Mongrel and Red."

"Mongrel and Red," the others all said before clanging their steins together and taking a long drink.

Harold hung out at the party for a few hours, drank a bit, but never really got into the mood of the occasion. He wasn't sure if the obvious revelry of the event was appropriate or not but, either way, he wasn't in to it. A little after 9 p.m., he started looking for Samurai. After searching for a while, he found Samurai and some of his other brothers out on a picnic table by the lake.

"Hey, there he is," said Samurai in a voice that made it clear he was beginning to tie one on. He threw an arm over Harold's shoulder and pulled his head down onto his shoulder. "Where you been, brother?"

"Just looking for you," Harold mumbled.

Once again, he found everyone looking at him as they expected him to start on fire or something.

Reaper came over and threw his arm over Harold, too. "You alright?" he asked.

Harold was glad he asked. Caught between his brothers, he was beginning to feel trapped as he planned to tell Samurai that he was heading out. This gave Harold an opening to leave. "I was just thinking of taking off for Poplar Grove," he said.

Reaper nodded his head slowly up and down in acknowledgment. But he and Samurai didn't let go. Finally, Reaper said, "One more drink to our brothers before you go."

From out of an inner pocket, Reaper pulled out a flat pint bottle of Jack Daniels. He took a big swig, swallowed and said, "To Red and Mongrel. If they ain't in heaven, may they ride forever in hell." He took another swig and handed the bottle to Harold.

Harold held the bottle up in front of him and said, "Mongrel, Red and Tawny." Then he took a big swig and passed the bottle to Samurai.

The bottle went around the table with Tank finishing the last drops as they all toasted their late brothers. No sooner was the bottle empty than Kilroy suggested calling the new prospect to get another round – "Beers and shots."

Harold began to protest that he had to go but, before he could, Samurai stepped up, "Naked Boy said he's taking off."

"Rubber side down," said Reaper as several of the other brothers raised their beer steins to Harold.

"See you soon," said Samurai, as he walked Harold out to his bike.

Harold had the feeling that Samurai said it as though trying to ensure that Harold would return.

"I'll be back in a couple days," he told Samurai.

After riding through Biesenthal, he turned the bike southeast, taking the same route he had followed in the passenger seat of a battered, butterscotch-colored 1977 Plymouth Volare Country Squire wagon with a rubber salesman in the Spring. As he rode, Harold reflected on how much had changed since he'd first come out to Biesenthal. One thing Harold was sure of — he wasn't the same person who had made the trip out.

Chapter 34 — 'Triumphant' Return

As he rolled down the highway to Poplar Grove, Harold wasn't even sure why he was returning to his old stomping grounds. All he knew was that, somehow, it felt as though he could get grounded there, as though going back to the starting point of a game would reset the score. And when he got there, he wasn't sure if he would stop and see his mother or not. What would he think of his mother considering his fresh insight into her and his father's past? They weren't the same people he had left behind when he rode out to Biesenthal all those months ago.

Of course, his mother might not want to see him anyhow. She'd already made it clear that the motorcycle wasn't acceptable there. And Harold hadn't made any effort to contact her in all that time. Had she spent the time worrying that he was dead? Was her reaction closer to one of good riddance? Was she able to keep up with the house, cutting the grass and fixing things that broke?

Stopping to see his mother would be awkward, at best. But he still figured he should stop by to see that she was OK. In spite of the way they had last parted, he felt pangs of guilt over his long absence. As he rolled onto the offramp from the highway and into Poplar Grove, following the main drag to the street that brought him into the neighborhood where he'd grown up and where his mother still lived. It gave him the feeling a high school student has when they go back to visit their grade school and discover that the halls have shrunk. Several blocks down, he turned right and continued a couple blocks until the white Cape Cod came into view

It was about 10:30 p.m. as Harold pulled into the driveway, the grass and weeds growing high, like a Mohawk haircut between two strips of concrete. He could see the flickering blue light of his mother's black-and-white television through the living room window. He parked the bike out back and walked through the dark to the back door. As long as he'd been gone, it occurred to him that, maybe, he should knock but decided to try the doorknob. When it turned, and the door opened, Harold stuck his head inside, took a familiar breath of stale cigarettes, and glanced around the darkened kitchen before hollering, "Hello." There was no response, so he continued inside.

Flipping on the light just inside the door, he found the kitchen looked just as it always did, a few dishes in the sink and a butt-filled ashtray on the kitchen table. He stepped inside, closing the door lightly behind him, and yelled, "Hello," again. The only response he heard was Johnny Carson starting his monologue from the other room. Harold walked into the living room to find his mother sitting in her recliner, an open can of beer, a box of Kleenex and a Reader's Digest open to a crossword puzzle on the TV tray next to where she slept, her head back, her mouth open and snoring lightly.

Harold stood in the arched doorway between the kitchen and the living room for a few minutes looking at his mother. Somehow, she looked older than he remembered. He felt as though he'd never really seen her before. He saw her now as if she were a stranger – any other elderly woman walking down a busy sidewalk. He was surprised that the sensation came with a touch of tenderness. He considered waking her but couldn't think of what to say if he did. Assuming he would speak with her a little later, he stepped into the hall and looked in his old room where it appeared his mother hadn't set foot since he'd gone North. The bed was even unmade and in the same condition he had left it. Harold also stood in the doorway for several moments but couldn't think of anything he really needed and closed the door behind him.

Shutting off the light as he left, Harold returned outside and stood on the porch for several minutes contemplating his next move as he surveyed the darkened landscape of the yard where he used to run and play when young. Somehow, even the neighborhood looked different, as if he didn't really know the area after all, as if he were a stranger in these parts. He tried to think of a friend to visit but he couldn't think of anyone who really mattered, who would listen to Harold, if he chose to share his feelings, and would respond with compassion and caring. Finally, he walked over to the bike and went to the only place he could really think to stop.

Freddie's Place was hopping that night as Harold could tell from all the cars in the parking lot. Without giving any thought to the colors on his back, Harold backpedaled Magdelina into a parking space by the front door where a Honda Goldwing was already parked. Then he shut the bike off and went inside.

Whale sightings in Iowa were a little less frequent than sightings of members of motorcycle clubs walking into Freddie's. More than a few people looked over and seemed to notice his colors as Harold by and stepped up to the bar. The crowd seemed to part before him, as though people weren't sure what would happen if they didn't get out of his way. He made his way to an open spot by the far wall. At the other end of the bar, filling a pitcher with beer while laughing and talking to patrons on the other side of the battered acrylic-covered wooden surface, was his old flame – Mindy. He looked for a couple of minutes as though trying to find the torch he had long carried for the woman. But Harold couldn't find those feelings anymore. Strangely, she didn't seem quite as hot he used to think. She looked human and it dawned on him that this is probably how Mindy always looked – no more or less attractive than hundreds of other girls he saw from day to day. Harold snorted thinking that the joke was on him and appreciating that it was. It was nothing against Mindy. She was still an attractive barfly, whichever side of the bar she stood on. But the image he had created of her was crumbling before his eyes.

There was an unfamiliar 20-something male behind the bar, as well, but Mindy was the first to look Harold's way. She even smiled in an interested sort of way.

"What will it be?" Mindy asked in a soft and inviting tone as she made her way over to the end of the bar where Harold stood. It dawned on Harold that she hadn't recognized him. He had heard her use that tone with other men before. It used to drive him crazy with jealousy. He used to wonder why she seemed so interested in other men but not in him. Now, he reasoned that the sparkle in her eyes was for one of those other men - a rugged biker who had ventured in from the road.

"Old Style in a bottle," Harold said, ordering the drink that had become his staple up north.

As Mindy returned with the beer, she said, "A little chilly out there tonight?"

"Not bad," Harold said, realizing her statement was really an invitation to a conversation.

When Mindy asked, "What kind of bike do you ride?" Harold nearly laughed out loud at her unmistakable flirtation. Could it be that all he ever had to do was throw on a pair of leathers, join a motorcycle club and grow a beard? Was that all it took to gain

Mindy's infatuation. But then he answered the question as well and the answer was, 'No.' He realized he had done more than change his general appearance. He realized that, if Mindy realized who he was, without understanding the other changes in his life and personality, she would quickly downgrade her opinion of the mysterious biker who had wandered in out of the night.

"Harley," Harold said, stating what he assumed she should find obvious.

His short answer suggested a coolness to her advances. Harold wondered if she would take the hint and back off or if she would dive in even deeper. When she asked, "So, where you from?" Harold smiled at how easily he could reel her in, if he was inclined. She had the tone of a woman on a mission and Harold considered the opportunity, just for old-time's sake – fulfilling a fantasy he once pined over endlessly. But the fantasy had faded into obscurity and, just now, he didn't feel it was worth the effort.

"North," Harold said, with another one-word answer that, from the look on her face, seemed to inspire her further.

Harold was passively enjoying the reversal of roles. He had a sense that it was justice for Mindy to dangle on a hook that he played out now. His aloofness, rather than chasing her away worked the way jiggling a worm does more to catch the attention of a fish. But then, he wasn't really trying. He had a lot on his mind and things he wanted to sort out. If things continued to develop with Mindy, he might go along for the ride a little while, but it would serve as a distraction. Besides, without the pedestal he'd once put her on, Harold realized there wasn't anything else there. It was always a physical attraction supported by familiarity and the intangible of something he couldn't have. The way she was now throwing herself at any old biker who happened in the door contributed to downgrading Harold's opinion of Mindy. In a way, he knew that wasn't really fair, but he didn't care right now. Being 'fair' didn't obligate him to accept her advances.

There was something else. Harold realized that he had always looked at Mindy as someone who had her shit together. Looking up at her from his former position as a town drunk, Mindy always seemed rich in common sense. But if she was so wise, why would she throw herself at some guy just because he obviously rode a Harley? If she was so clairvoyant, how is it she spent all her time working or otherwise spending her time in a tavern. Clearly, Harold had overrated her from the start. It wasn't fair. He wasn't in a position to throw stones. It was simply a matter of clarity.

As Harold was thinking these thoughts, Mindy extended a hand and in a soft and alluring voice said as a form of introduction, "Mindy, at your service." As she did so, Mindy leaned forward over the bar as though intending to present her cleavage while baiting her own hook. Staring directly into Harold's eyes, in a deeply sensual voice Harold had once heard in a movie with Lauren Bacall, she whispered, "I just can't resist a man on a Harley."

Harold was actually stunned by her brazenness. He wondered, 'should I tell her who I am?' He thought he might enjoy watching her reaction. Would she recoil, pull her hand back and respond with even greater contempt, as though she didn't like his little joke? On the other hand, he reminded himself that it wasn't entirely fair to continue playing the mysterious stranger. Harold looked at her hand for a second as he contemplated his response. The effect this had on Mindy was to increase her arousal. Her eyes grew larger and her tongue flicked between her lips the way a viper senses its prey. Her lips glistened invitingly. Harold half expected her to launch herself over the bar and jump him right there in front of everyone.

At last, Harold took the hand in his and said, "NB."

Mindy glanced at the patch on the front of Harold's vest where the words "Naked Boy" were embroidered and said, "But isn't that your name on your jacket – 'Naked Boy.'"

"Same difference," Harold said, his tone continuing to maintain the aloofness that was driving Mindy crazy.

Harold could almost see the wheels turning as Mindy was trying to think of another approach to warm up the biker when her partner behind the bar took a couple steps her way, leaned towards her and said, "How about a little help." On a busy night, Mindy had forgotten all about the crowded bar and the patrons with empty glasses. Harold was guessing that should he as much as crook a finger her way, she'd probably abandon the lot of 'em and join him on the bike outside. But Mindy wasn't ready to go quite that far yet – she wasn't ready to throw caution to the wind and quit her job for a roll with this biker. She excused herself, promising to stop back down at that side of the bar as soon as she took care of a few 'interruptions.'

While Mindy was gone, Harold sipped his beer and glanced around at the other patrons. The crowd was loud as conversation competed with conversation and back again. He noticed, to his surprise, that most of the patrons didn't seem particularly plastered as he had expected. Harold's recollections of Freddie's Place were foggy and drunken. Somehow, he had assumed everyone else was as drunk as he was. By 11 p.m. several months ago, Harold would have worked himself into a considerable state of intoxication.

Harold glanced down at his beer and, for the first time he could remember, he wasn't sure he even wanted it. He pushed the glass away from him on the bar and turned back to watch the revelers from the relative obscurity of their inattention.

Harold saw a number of familiar faces. But if anyone recognized Harold, they didn't show it. A few people glanced Harold's way but the looks on their faces were not the kinds of glances Harold used to receive in at Freddie's. Rather, they were looks of interest from some of the women and looks of envy from the guys, mixed with a cautious respect that a prairie dog gives a lion that is sunning itself nearby.

Then, through the crowd, Harold saw several more familiar faces. Across the bar to the right of the door and beside the jukebox, was a group of about five Freddie's Place regulars. Standing with their backs towards the front wall and facing in Harold's general direction was a couple — a familiar man and woman. The guy, about 6-1, 180 pounds and clean shaven, had his left arm extended as though he was demonstrating an airplane in flight with one wing. The other wing was occupied holding a tumbler full of a copper-colored liquid covering several cubes of ice. The man was talking and laughing. It was apparent that he was telling a joke or retelling a funny story.

The girl, standing about 5-3, 100 pounds, and working to snuggle up to the man as he gyrated in his story-telling, had dark, wavy hair that laid close to her head, but in an appealing way. She was wearing a black leather dress coat over a silky green shirt and a pair of blue jeans. She had a matching tumbler in her right hand and, with a larger smile on her face, it seemed as though she were imploring the others to listen intently to what the winged man was saying. It was as though she were afraid they would miss the profound significance of his joke.

The last time Harold had seen the girl was two nights before he'd gone to the lawyer's office and found out about the motorcycle he'd inherited from his uncle. That night, when he'd seen her last, Harold had mistaken her for another girl, had seriously embarrassed himself and had received a solid punch from her boyfriend, the one telling the story as Harold looked over from the bar.

Harold's gaze was fixed on the couple as though he couldn't break his eyes away. Char eventually noticed him staring and quickly looked away. It appeared she might have recognized Harold, based on the way her lips curled slightly as though revolted. But then, a few seconds later, after glancing up at her boyfriend and ensuring that he was well occupied relating his story, Char glanced back in Harold's direction. Ever so slightly, an inviting smile flickered across her face.

Harold might have been intrigued. Not too many months earlier this would have suggested that a red-letter night was in store, what with Mindy and Char both casting flirtatious signals in Harold's direction. But Harold found he wasn't any more interested in Char than Mindy. In fact, his fixed stare actually had nothing to do with Char, per se. Seeing Char across the bar had hit Harold like a thunderbolt, presenting him with a moment of clarity, an epiphany that extended all the way back to Biesenthal. Suddenly, Harold realized what was tugging at him, tearing at his gut. It was uncertainty of a critical nature and Char had cleared it all up.

Harold snapped out of his trance just as Derrick seemed to notice the nonverbal communication Char was sending the biker's way. There was an initial flicker of aggression across Derrick's face. He stood a little taller as he pulled his arm down over Char and drew her closer to her side in a way that said, "Mine." But then he followed her eyes over to Harold. Instead of seeing the drunk he'd once knocked to the floor, all he saw was a badass biker glaring in his direction. He wasn't even sure the biker was interested in Char. It occurred to Derrick he might have done something to piss the biker off as his grip on Char relaxed and his body language shifted to defensive and even a little submissive. He quickly looked away, hoping he hadn't looked long enough to have initiated a non-verbal conversation.

When Harold suddenly jumped out of his seat and started striding purposefully in their direction, a glimmer of excitement flashed in Char's eyes as a look of panic flashed across Derrick's. He stepped back slightly and nervously. Harold noticed their reactions but didn't care. Tension was quietly filling the space between them as Harold approached. But just as Derrick and Char thought their moments had come, Harold walked right past them and out the door. As he did so, he saw relief change to a cocky smile spreading on Derrick's face, as though he had faced down a biker. At the same time, a touch of disappointment snuck into Char's eyes and the creases at the edges of her lips. Harold still didn't care. He had something to do, something far more important than worrying about a pair of barflies who were only ever slightly more upstanding than the drunken sot Harold once was before he first went to Biesenthal.

Without looking back, Harold kicked Magdelina to life, swung his leg over and dropped the bike into first gear. As he pulled away, he'd have sworn he caught sight of a pair of faces watching him from the window. Harold roared back north at about 80 mph while tracking in the left side of the lane, riding with a purpose. He had a sense that he had to get back to Biesenthal fast – to get back home fast.

By the time Harold pulled into Biesenthal it was after 1 a.m. His first stop was at Samurai's house. He found the house darkened and no one came to the door to answer his knocks. As important as what he had to say was, Harold was still reluctant to wake the children. He knocked about five times and then went back to his bike.

From there, Harold headed for Hildie's expecting to find the party continuing in full bloom. Instead, he found several cars in the parking lot but no bikes. Though none of the cars appeared to belong to his brothers, Harold went in any way. Inside, he asked Lance, the bartender, when the Banshee Riders had left.

"Not long ago," Lance said. "I think I heard some folks talking about how they have to get up for work tomorrow."

Harold said thanks and Lance asked if he'd like a beer. Harold thought about it for a moment and then said, "No. That's OK.

"By the way, can you give me some change?" he asked as he pulled a couple singles out of his wallet.

With the change in his hand, Harold turned and picked up the pay phone on the wall. He tried calling Reaper, Falstaff, and T-Rex. He even called Samurai's house again. No one answered. He was about to try Grunt when Bitters and Peyote walked in the door.

"Are we glad to see you," Bitters said. "Pot Roast got into it with Rodeo from the Monks. Rodeo called the Banshee Riders stool pigeons. Said we ratted 6 Pack and Attila to the feds."

"Is Pot Roast OK?" Harold asked with an urgent tone in his voice.

"Yeah," Peyote said. "He pretty well beat the crap out of Rodeo though. Now, all your brothers are meeting somewhere to decide what to do."

"Where are they meeting?" Harold asked.

"They didn't tell us," Peyote said.

"Yeah," Bitters said mockingly as she swaggered in an apparent imitation of John Wayne heading to a gunfight. She continued in a voice that imitated the actor, "They're gonna to take care of business. Us girls need to stay here to roll bandages and pass the ammunition."

Harold hardly heard her commentary. His mind was racing ahead to the possibilities. Was it plausible that his brothers would charge into the Monks' clubhouse with all guns blazing? Even if a preemptive strike was successful, however, Harold knew they would still have the law to contend with. And if not the law, a large club like the Monks has chapters all over. The other chapters wouldn't appreciate that a small club out in the sticks massacred one of their chapters.

On the other hand, Pot Roast had beat up one of their brothers. Regardless of what the Monks were or were not up to before, they could very well come gunning for the Banshee Riders now. In fact, that seemed a far more realistic possibility. In that case, Harold guessed that his brothers were probably meeting to discuss how they were going to defend themselves.

Harold contemplated where he might find his brothers. He thought about the clubhouse but remembered that was probably still a crime scene and, either way, was not a likely spot where the club would meet anymore. They were probably at one of the brothers' houses. But which one? Then another idea crossed Harold's mind. Harold slipped off his barstool and headed for the door.

"Where are you going," Bitters said, startled by the suddenness of his departure. "Do you know where they are?"

"No," Harold said, pausing for a moment. "I have to pay the Monks a visit."

Peyote had an alarmed look on her face and Harold guessed that she might have heard about his assassination plot. But then she said, "Are you crazy? They'll kill you."

"Maybe," Harold said and continued out the door. As an afterthought, Harold said, "If you run into any of the brothers, tell them I said to chill – everything is going to be OK." And as an afterthought, he said, "I think."

As Harold stepped outside, Peyote and Bitters were looking at each other with their mouths hanging open, as though what they had just heard was beyond comprehension.

He noticed that it was a bit chilly. "Was it cold before?" Harold asked himself. "Or was I just too preoccupied to notice?" Before Harold started the bike, he stuck his hand into his belt to check that Chester's revolver was still there. When the bike was running, and he was assured that he was otherwise ready, he swung his leg over the seat and tapped Magdelina into first gear. Then he eased out the clutch and swung the bike up the gravel road.

Harold's heart was racing as he roared down the highway, back to the scene where he had earlier plotted an assassination. This time, however, Harold didn't sneak around to the back. He continued past Brighton Road and straight up to the Monks' driveway. He only hesitated a second before turning into the drive and proceeding into the parking area outside the clubhouse. No bikes, no cars, no lights: it was quickly apparent that no one was there.

Without getting off to check, and wondering how crazy it was to have tried, Harold swung the bike around and went back out to Route 36. When he got to the road, he turned left to head into Biesenthal. There were several watering holes he could check out that way. The first bar he came to was Cal's Drift Inn. There were several bikes out front and, among them, the bike Harold was looking for – a stretched panhead, it's gold peanut tank glimmering in the electric, yellow-glow from the light on a pole out front.

Now that he'd found him, Harold was hesitant to follow through on his crazy idea. When two mad dogs are going at each other it's best not to stick your hand between them. But he also realized that the situation, in general, was quickly unraveling.

More people were going to get hurt if he didn't do something about it. He remembered his dream of an assassin sneaking into Samurai and Sue's house. That could happen. It could happen at any of his brothers' homes. It could even happen at Chester's. "I have to try," he said out loud to himself. With that, he turned the handlebars and headed into the parking lot.

As he shut the bike off, he saw a familiar face looking out the window next to the door and realized Ivan was watching him. That could be a good thing, he thought, realizing that he had gotten along with Ivan in the past. But he also realized he couldn't expect any friendly feelings, in that area, to go too far. As the face disappeared back into the bar, Harold realized one thing for sure; they knew he was here.

As he stepped inside, over at the bar where he and the leprechaun had gone when he first arrived in Biesenthal, stood about seven Monks. As they turned to watch him come in the door, the group seemed to fold open until Shiv came into sight looking at Harold from the back of the group.

For Harold, it felt a little bit like an old western movie where a couple gunslingers have a showdown in a tavern. The difference, beyond fact that, instead of cowboys, they were outlaw bikers, was that, in the movie, everyone else would catch on to the tension. The piano player would stop playing and folks would step back to nervously watch the action. Here, none of the other patrons seemed to notice and the jukebox kept playing.

As Harold approached, fifteen feet or so between them stretching out for miles, he stopped just short of the forward edges of the circle of Monks. As he looked at Shiv across where he'd once seen a girl fall with a bloody face, he felt the hot chill of a blanket of tension as real and oppressive as if it were weaved with putty.

As Shiv glared at him across the floor, he finally said, "You got some balls coming in here now."

Harold simply nodded as he tried to choose his words carefully but also realizing he needed to speak those words soon while he still had a chance.

"Any reason we shouldn't just jack you up right now?"

Harold ignored the question and said, "I need to talk to you."

"Apparently," said Shiv. "Can't think of too many reasons you'd be stupid enough to walk in here like this, -less you're feeling suicidal today."

Still ignoring the threats, Harold said, "Things are getting out of hand …"

"You might say that," one of the other Monks laughed.

Harold looked his way and offered a pained smile. "… and there've been some mistakes made – some misunderstandings."

"That's right," said Shiv. "And it seems to me you've made them, you and that fucking asshole Pot Roast."

"I understand how you feel," said Harold. "If I could talk to you alone for a minute …"

But one of the Monks actually stepped towards Harold while saying, "Fuck this" and clearly intending to take action.

However, Shiv said, "Just a minute" as he looked at Harold as though contemplating the situation.

When Shiv didn't immediately respond, the other Monk said, "What are we waiting for" and seemed as though he were about to launch himself at Harold.

"I said, 'wait,'" Shiv barked as though losing his patience.

He tipped his head sideways as though seeing Harold for the first time. Finally, he said, "It really does take some balls to come in here like this." Then he motioned over to the side indicating they could speak over there.

When they got there, Shiv said, "As you can see, some of my brothers would just as soon tune you up right now. So, I would say that you should start talking fast."

"I think I know who turned your brothers over to the feds," said Harold. "I'd rather not say who, but I will say that I'm sure it was no one from the Banshees."

"What makes you so sure of that?"

"They questioned Reaper, Samurai and me," said Harold. "I know I didn't say anything and there's no way Reaper or Samurai would have talked."

"Then who the fuck is the snitch?"

Harold hesitated. "I'm not sure, but it's the only other person it could be. He overheard me on the phone, and over the phone, Samurai said … well, Samurai asked if I was describing 6 Pack. At the time, I thought it was 6 Pack."

"Why is that," said Shiv, seeming to get agitated as he spoke.

"I didn't tell the feds, but I saw three bikers on the road on my way to our clubhouse just before I found my brothers and

Tawny dead," said Harold. "They were flying down the road in the rain. The last of them slowed down and looked back at me as though he was thinking about turning around and coming after me."

"And you thought it was 6 Pack?"

"Well, he rode a black Sportster. He had the same build and hair as 6 Pack. It was dark and rainy. It was difficult to see."

"And you jumped to the conclusion that it was my brother?" Shiv asked the muscles seeming to flex in his neck.

"I never said it was him for sure, only that I was pretty sure. After all, it's no secret 6 Pack and the Banshee Riders aren't exactly on the best of terms."

"But now you don't think it was 6 Pack? Why?"

"I don't think it wasn't 6 Pack; I know it wasn't 6 Pack."

Shiv was shaking his head and shoulders in a way that made it seem he was mocking Harold, "And how did you come about this revelation?"

Harold muttered, "Ah fuck" out loud as he realized how difficult it would be to explain.

Shiv actually chuckled at Harold's obvious discomfort. "Well, this should be good," he said.

"Did you ever see people that look alike, sort of? You know. It's like I used to get Cary Grant and Rock Hudson mixed up. They're not twins but, if I didn't see them together, I'd forget which one was which."

"What the fuck are you talking about?" Shiv asked, clearly losing his patience.

"Last year, mistook this one girl I had met with another girl I had dated. It was, well, you know, kind of embarrassing. That was back in Poplar Grove where I used to live."

"Yeah?"

"So, I went down to Poplar Grove tonight. I saw that girl again. And I just knew."

"You 'just knew?'"

"It just hit me: that wasn't 6 Pack. It was another fucker who looks similar to 6 Pack."

"Fucker?" Shiv said as Harold realized he had called the Monks brother a fucker, too.

Harold shrugged apologetically. Then he continued, "You probably haven't heard this from the feds but the assholes who killed my brothers wanted everyone to believe it was the Monks."

"Why do you say that?"

"They painted 'FMF' – Fucking Monks Forever – on the wall in blood," said Harold.

This got Shiv's attention. In fact, the look on his face was frightening as though it radiated hatred and anger.

"And you know who these mother fuckers are?"

"Yes."

"Not maybe? Not sort of? You're not going to change your mind again later?"

"I've never been more certain of something in my life," Harold said, his tone solid with conviction.

They spoke for several more minutes. Then Harold said, "I think you should speak with Reaper."

Shiv thought for a minute and then asked, "You got a pen or pencil?"

When Harold shook his head 'No' Shiv looked over at his brothers and said, "Get me a pen or pencil and a piece of paper. One of his brothers produced a pencil from the bar and handed it to Shiv. Shiv wrote down a phone number and gave it to Harold saying, "Talk to Reaper and give me a call to setup a face-to-face."

"Will do," said Harold taking the paper.

Then he looked back and said, "What about 6 Pack and Atilla?"

"What about 'em?"

"The feds got them locked up, right?"

"Those fuckers ain't got nothing on my brothers," said Shiv. "We can prove they weren't anywhere near your clubhouse that night."

"Why don't you tell the feds?"

"We did," said Shiv. "I don't think they were listening – didn't want to hear what we had to say."

"By the way, I wasn't kidding when I said it took some balls for you to come in here like this," said Shiv. He put his hand out for a biker handshake. Harold shook his hand and left without even bothering to look over at the other Monks, completely focused on finding Reaper before the Banshee Riders did anything that would mess up the potential détente.

Chapter 35 — Parley

Unsure of where to go next, Harold headed back to Hildie's on the chance that some of his brothers might have arrived since he left the bar earlier. As he came down the hill, the sun rising at his back, he found the parking lot outside the bar absolutely packed with bikes. T-Rex and Snake were standing outside the door watching him closely as he arrived. They both wore expressions of relief as they saw who it was.

"Where the fuck have you been?" T-Rex asked as Harold dismounted.

"You wouldn't believe me if I told you," Harold said as the door opened and Reaper came out, followed by half a dozen of Harold's brothers, along with Sasquatch and Waldo, the president of the Saxons. Soon, other bikers were coming out and Harold recognized members of the High Riders and Cherry Poppers, as well.

"My old lady said you went to the Monks' clubhouse," Reaper said. "Are you OK?"

"I'm good," Harold said.

"Yeah?" Reaper asked. "Well then, are you out of your frickin' mind?"

"I think that's distinctly possible," Harold said. "And we need to talk."

Someone told Samurai that Harold had arrived, and Harold's brother rushed out the door with a look of concern on his face. Seeing that Harold was, in fact, in one piece, an expression of relief was quickly replaced by a look of anger. Samurai rushed up, grabbed, Harold by the collar and pinned Harold back over his bike.

"I thought you said you were done with that shit?" Samurai yelled as Reaper and T-Rex pulled him off of Harold.

As Harold stood up adjusting his collar, he said to Samurai, "Maybe you should hear this too."

Harold then led Samurai, Reaper, Waldo, and T-Rex off to the far side of the parking lot where they could talk alone. Harold turned and said, "It wasn't 6 Pack, and it wasn't the Monks who killed Red, Mongrel, and Tawny."

"How do you know that?" Waldo asked, and Harold went through the same explanation he'd given Shiv.

"And you're sure this time?" Reaper asked, sounding a little annoyed.

"I'm certain," said Harold.

"How can you be so sure now?" Waldo asked.

"When I realized my mistake, I also realized that I knew all along," said Harold. "It was the fucking Clansmen."

Harold hadn't noticed that Pot Roast had come over while he was talking. When Harold said, "It was The fucking Clansmen," Pot Roast erupted.

"Those mother fuckers," Pot Roast hollered. "I'll kill every one of the sons-a-bitches." With that, he actually headed towards his motorcycle as though he would intuitively know where to find The Clansmen and was planning to carry out his threat without delay.

T-Rex was the first to grab Pot Roast, picking him up off the ground by his waist. Suspended in the air, Pot Roast's legs were pumping comically above the ground as though he were a cartoon character who had walked off the edge of a cliff and was suspended momentarily in midair.

Harold had also rushed over and, as he arrived, he found that tears were pouring down Pot Roast's face. Harold's brother continued to curse The Clansmen and loudly proclaim his threat of killing "the mother fuckers."

At that point, it was Harold's turn to grab a brother by the collar. "Shut the fuck up," he ordered in a subdued scream. Pot Roast was startled by Harold's reaction and actually fell silent as his legs stopped pumping. With Pot Roast staring at him as though he had never quite seen Harold before, Harold continued, "We need to use our heads now."

The rest of the group had followed Harold over so that they were all standing around Pot Roast and T-Rex.

"That's good advice," Reaper said to Pot Roast. "We're not talking about some yahoos that you've run into at some gin mill. We're talking about a club, fuckers who ride on the same side of the tracks we do."

Harold then interrupted, turning to Reaper, and saying, "Shiv wants to meet with you."

"That could be a trap," T-Rex said.

"Maybe," Harold said. "But it was my idea."

"Your idea?" Waldo asked.

"Yeah," Harold said. "When I realized it was the Clansmen, and

I couldn't find my brothers, I figured I'd better go see the Monks. I was hoping to defuse the situation a little before someone made a big mistake."

Harold wasn't sure but thought he saw looks of awe and respect from those around him as the thought of Harold pulling up at the Monks clubhouse alone, and what that meant, sunk in.

"You mean, like getting into a fight with a Monk?" Reaper asked while giving Pot Roast a reproachful look.

Reaper had hardly said the words than they all heard the sound of motorcycles approaching — a lot of motorcycles. The headlights of the first bikes flashed among the trees and into the air as the bikes came up the hill. Then, in pairs, the lights fell as the bikes crested the ridge. As if on cue, Shiv led the Monks into the parking lot.

Harold was amazed at how quickly the Monks had managed to pull their strength together. As a power play, it was beyond impressive.

As Shiv stepped off his bike, he turned and yelled at a Monk a few bikes behind him, "Rodeo, you stand down." Harold made out an angry look on the face of the biker, along with a black eye and some other bruises. Then Shiv turned and walked towards Reaper.

Reaper turned to Pot Roast and said, "You too." He looked at T-Rex and said, "Keep an eye on him."

"We need to talk," Shiv said, nodding to Harold in greeting as he approached.

"So I hear," Reaper said.

Reaper turned to Harold and said, "Get this man a beer."

Harold hesitated only a second, wondering if he shouldn't be part of the pending conversation. But as Reaper turned to look in Harold's direction, Harold darted towards the door before Reaper had to bark the order again.

Inside, as Harold was ordering the beer, and a replacement for Reaper, Samurai stuck his head in the door and yelled, "Prospect."

A biker Harold hadn't seen before, popped up quickly from the back of the bar, and Samurai said, "Start running beers out here for the Monks."

"How many?" the prospect asked.

"How the fuck should I know?" Samurai barked back at him.

As Harold went to walk past Samurai and out the door with Shiv's beer, Samurai stopped Harold for a second. "I'm sorry, bro. I thought you went sniper on us again."

Harold smiled as he walked past and said, "Nah, not this time."

Harold took another step outside and Samurai added, "That took some serious balls, bro, going to the Monks clubhouse alone like that."

Harold paused and looked back at him and then said, "Actually, I found them at Cal's. And I thought it was more on the stupid and crazy side."

Samurai laughed and said, "That too." Then he stepped forward and gave Harold a hug. With beers in both hands, Harold gingerly put his right arm around his shorter brother's back and returned the hug. Then Harold walked out the door.

As Harold approached Reaper and Shiv, they saw him coming and stopped talking long enough to allow Harold to complete the delivery. Harold walked away and they continued talking as the Monks, on the one side, the Saxons, the High Riders, the Cherry Poppers and the Banshee Riders on the other, kept cautious eyes on each other under the soft glow of two yellow lights on top of poles in the parking lot. Every once in a while, and individually, a biker would glance over at Reaper and Shiv to see how the parlay was going. The tension eased considerably when the Banshee Rider's prospect began handing out beers to the Monks. After about 20 minutes, Reaper and Shiv turned and called Pot Roast and Rodeo over.

Harold watched as Shiv spoke to Rodeo and Reaper spoke to Pot Roast. In an agitated manner, Pot Roast said something back and Reaper exploded, "You'll shut the fuck up and listen or I'll knock the fuck out of you myself."

That seemed to do the trick and, as though dealing with pouting, young boys who had tussled in grade school, the two presidents instructed their charges to shake hands. Both were reluctant, though Pot Roast all the more so.

Harold could just about read Reaper's lips as he growled at Pot Roast, "I said shake his hand."

With the peace apparently restored between Pot Roast and Rodeo, Shiv finished the beer Harold had brought out to him.

Handing the plastic cup to Harold, Shiv said, "Thanks, bro," and offered his hand in a biker's handshake to Reaper and then to Harold.

"You've got a good brother here," Shiv said to Reaper.

Reaper put an arm around Harold's shoulder and said, "That's some straight shit, bro."

Shiv looked at Reaper for a moment, recognizing a tinge of the political in the response, smiled, turned and yelled, "Mount up." With that, the Monks climbed on their bikes and were soon gone, only the dust and the reverberation of their Harleys lingering in their wake.

When the Monks had left, a festive atmosphere took over at Hildie's. When the bar closed at the mandatory 6 a.m., the party continued unabated in the parking lot. When the bar opened again at 7 a.m., portions of the party drifted inside. A large group of Banshee Riders, as well as some members of the other clubs, gathered around Reaper expecting to get the lowdown on his conversation with Shiv. But all Reaper would say was, "Trust me, you don't need to know. Let me put it another way, you don't want to know."

The same question came up at the Banshee Riders next meeting. Instead of Reaper, T-Rex stepped up and said, "All you need to know is that it's being handled."

When Grunt complained, "What's being handled? By who?"

T-Rex barked at him, "I just said you don't need to know."

An undercurrent of grumbling continued for a few moments until Falstaff stood up and barked, "I don't want to hear anything else about it."

The idea that the subject was taboo was solidly reinforced and the brothers reluctantly let it go. Secrets were generally too juicy and fun to remain secret for long. With Reaper, Falstaff and T-Rex that tightlipped about the matter, it became apparent that they were right – this was a secret that the brothers were otherwise better off not knowing.

Whatever was done, and whoever did it, nothing was ever said. Lacking evidence, the feds released 6 Pack and his brother the next day. Harold was called in to testify again, as was Reaper.

Harold just smiled as Agent Rogers said, "Do you really want the people who did this to your friends to get away with it." Harold didn't say a word but rather doubted anyone was getting away with anything.

One night, a few weeks later, Harold and Samurai were watching the news while eating dinner in the living room of Samurai's house when the newscast ran a story that two men from Creighton, and another from neighboring Oslo, were reported missing. Upon the screen, the telecast showed, side-by-side, police mug shots of the men. "The three are believed to be members of a motorcycle gang known as The Clansmen," the anchorman read.

Harold looked up from his plate and at the screen. There, on the far right, was the photo of a familiar biker, similar in many ways to 6 Pack. At least one of the others looked like someone Harold had met outside a gas station while on Road Day.

Chapter 36 — A Slice of Humble Pie

Robert Jensen, a tall blonde 16-year old, had it all: good looks, a wealth of natural, athletic ability and intelligence consistently rewarded with high grades. As a sophomore, he was a starting running back and linebacker on the Biesenthal High School Bears football team that finished second in the state last fall. He started at those positions the previous year. A 3-Letterman, he was also a started on the basketball and baseball teams. Until he inexplicably broke up with her a few weeks earlier, he had dated the Homecoming Queen, a senior. He was one of those people for whom the clouds seemed to part to shower a golden carpet of sunlight at their feet. But there was a shadow on the horizon few who knew him could see at first.

Robert's father didn't waste his time praising his son for success that was expected. Instead, he focused on 'helping' Robert reach his full potential. He didn't want to hear it when Robert suggested that he should take a break from all the hard work and "have some fun."

As Robert's father put it, "You'll thank me someday."

But Robert wasn't feeling very thankful. In fact, whether an act of rebellion or simply as an escape from the prison of his success, Robert had recently fallen in with a crowd that was considered far below his rightful social strata. While those who knew him were perplexed trying to understand it, Robert looked at those in this group with envy. They didn't play in sports or participate in any school clubs or activities. If they did attend a school event, they wore cloak of anti-social animosity with a sense of honor. Since they were happy to skate by at school, their time wasn't encumbered with the humdrum annoyance of homework, either. For Robert, joining this new crowd felt as though he'd been set free. He happily accepted the heavy drinking and pot smoking pot that came with the territory.

Not surprisingly, his new affiliation came with trouble, at school and out. He was caught drinking at school resulting in detention and threats that he would be thrown off the teams if he was caught doing that again. Outside of school, he was caught breaking windows in the Biesenthal shopping district late one night. Both events lit fuses to his father's temper that only ebbed after a couple of hard slaps to the side of Robert's head and a clear admonishment that, "You're going to knock this shit off now." But

Robert was nowhere near inclined to 'knock it off.' Rather, he was furiously inspired to go further in the opposite direction.

Among his new social group, Robert was an automatic star. They were all aware of his athletic prowess. They knew he came from 'the popular' crowd. And yet, he had chosen them, chosen them over the 'in-crowd.' It was an unexpected victory for the headbangers, and Robert was richly rewarded for his betrayal of preppies and jocks. He was rewarded with adoration that bordered on awe. They laughed at all his jokes and waited rapturously on his every word and he ate it up. More than that, he played to it. He showed off in casual ways that lied that he didn't care.

In mid-April, on a cold, rainy day when he blew off a baseball game knowing the coach would surely kick him off the team, Robert went to the park where he and the headbangers hung out. Under the pavilion, they drank a few beers and smoked some pot. The latter, rather predictably, gave the group a case of the munchies. They might walk to the Jack in the Box on the west side of town where greasy tacos were a big hit when stoned. But that little café in town was closer and, when Robert suggested they go to Lillie's, since it was Robert, no one objected. Besides, it was raining.

They entered Lillie's as though they were an invading army, taking over and with no concern for the indigenous population – the others in the diner. They moved loudly to the booth at the very back of the eatery hardly noticing the older guys at the front of the counter, or the long-haired, bearded character bent over a bowl of soup at the far end of the counter.

When the waitress came over to take their order, they might have noticed how patient she was as they joked and bantered rather than respond to her question, "What can I get you?" But they didn't notice. They might have noticed how she good-naturedly said, "I'll give you a few minutes to look at the menu," as they threw sugar packets across the table at each other. But they didn't. She was a non-entity in the performance they were giving for their own pleasure.

When an early-middle-aged man came in with his two children and took a booth several booths up from their theirs, their arrival had little or no effect on the group at the back of the diner. If their language was course, and it was, it never occurred to them that they should adjust it for the benefit of young children. It also never occurred to them that these children had recently lost a mother to a drunk driver, just as the man had lost a wife.

The waitress knew this. She rightly suspected the father had worked late and brought the children in for meal it was too late for him to properly prepare, not that any of his cooking came close to measuring up to their mother's. Rather than not notice them coming into the diner, the waitress focused on the broken little family. She came over and tried to cheer the children up, the way she always did when they came in.

"Oh, my goodness, what do we have here?" she asked. Then, as she slid into the booth beside them, she hollered to the kitchen, "Better get the ice cream ready, Diego. They're back."

As the boy giggled, the little girl gave half a smile and put an arm over her brother's shoulders. "Teddy needs to eat something good first," she said motherly.

"Is that right?" Vivian, the waitress asked. "Ice cream is good, isn't it?"

"Goooood for him," Elizabeth said with a fresh grin.

Vivian smiled at the father sympathetically as they both realized that someone so young was trying to step up to fill her mother's shoes for the sake of her little brother. "Well, Teddy, what would you like to eat that's good for you?"

"Hockdog," the boy said instantly.

"A hotdog?" Vivian said. "Now, there's a surprise. And how about you, young lady?"

Elizabeth was studying a menu with a serious look on her face. "Hmmm," she said, as though struggling to decide.

"Just so you know," said Vivian, "we do have a special on chicken nuggets today."

"That sounds good," the young girl said in her most adult-like voice.

"Nuggets it is," Vivian said happily. "And how about you, Richard?"

Before Richard could answer, however, the group of teenagers in the back of the diner erupted loudly in laughter as the tall, blonde kid said something that must have struck them all as funny. From the booth with the children, the only words Vivian heard clearly were, "... and then that mother fucker said ..."

She leaned out from the booth and looked back that way as though hoping the sight of her paying attention might be enough to discourage further outbreaks of bad language. Nothing immediately followed so she leaned back in and looked at Richard again.

"Just a cheeseburger," he said.

"I don't know about any 'just-a-cheeseburgers'" Vivian said. "But I can get you one of our super-duper-deluxe cheeseburgers, if you'd like."

"That would be fine," he said with a weary smile, suggesting he'd had a long day.

As Vivian rose from the booth, she said to the children, "And if you two eat all your food, maybe your father will let you have some of our world-famous desert."

"Ice cream," Teddy said excitedly.

"Could be," said Vivian as she turned to bring the order to the cook through the window behind the counter.

But she had only taken one step when the tall blonde kid blurted out, "He's a fucking pussy. I'd kick his ass just for fun."

Vivian looked at Teddy and Elizabeth and then at Richard. When she turned to walk to the back of the diner, she just missed Richard mouthing, "Don't worry about it."

When she got down there by the teenagers, in her most pleasant tone, she said, "Hi" and waited a moment expecting someone to reply in kind. "I was wondering if you noticed we have a couple young children down here. If you could watch your language a little, I'd sure appreciate it."

"What?" said the blonde kid. "You want us to watch our language? No problem. We'll get right on that."

Vivian thought he sounded a bit sarcastic but thought to play along in the hopes that he'd come around. "Thank you," she said and headed back towards the kitchen.

She took only a few steps in that direction when the blonde kid hollered across the diner, "Hey, asshole, you worried about our language?"

The booth of teenagers broke out in laughter, though some of them nervously as though they weren't sure where this was going or how it would work out. But for the time being, at least, they were willing to follow their leader.

Richard did his best to ignore the situation. But this didn't please Robert.

"What, you can complain to the management about my language, but you can't say anything to my face?"

As he spoke, Robert shoved his way past a couple of admiring and willing friends so he could get out of the booth. He seemed to have recognized this as an excellent opportunity to show off for his new friends and wasn't going to let it go to waste. Casually, he strutted towards the front of the diner and the booth where Richard sat with his children.

"Did you hear me, old man," he said to Richard, as though 32 was ancient.

"I heard you fine," said Richard. But Richard felt as though he had a predicament. An altercation, even a verbal confrontation, was the last thing he wanted for his children. They were still far-too fragile from Clarise's recent death. Even if he was alone, he would go out of his way to avoid trouble. But with the children, it was critical that he avoid a problem. At the same time, however, he didn't want to say that he hadn't told Vivian to say something about their language; he didn't want to put it on her. The best he could come up with was, "It's OK. I didn't mean anything by it."

Instead of diffusing the situation, Richard's response only seemed to inspire the teenager's forced outrage.

"Didn't mean anything by it?" Robert yelled. "Then why the fuck did you say anything at all."

Richard's eyes only shifted to his children for a second as he tried not to let on that he was watching to see how this was affecting them.

But Robert did see it. "Are these your kids?" he asked, as though the answer wasn't obvious. "Do you really want you kids to see you acting like such an asshole?

"Hey, it's not your fault, kids. It's just that your dad's a dick."

"That's enough," said Vivian from behind Robert. "I think you should leave now."

"I'll leave when I'm ready," said Robert as he took a step to return to the back of the booth. Then, feigning an attack, he suddenly leaned down towards Richard with a fist back. Richard didn't flinch, but Robert stood back up laughing as though he had.

Robert had completely misjudged Richard. Though Robert was young and athletic, Richard was in good shape, too. And though he wasn't quite as tall as Robert, Richard had experience Robert hadn't even begun to imagine. A Silver Star and a Purple Heart, earned in battle in Vietnam, stood as evidence of physical prowess beyond Robert's comprehension. But where Robert also misjudged Richard is that the young man didn't understand that the older man didn't feel the youthful need to prove himself. There was something else Robert misjudged. That was the long-haired, bearded character sitting at the counter back by the booth where the teenagers sat. It never occurred to Robert that this was a member of a motorcycle club; that, with his colors on, Robert never would have dared to cause trouble.

Harold had a long day digging trenches in the rain. More than that, he had caught a cold or the flu a few days before, while doing some work around the house for his mother in Poplar Grove and was feeling miserable to begin with. He almost went straight home to Chester's after work but had convinced himself that some chicken soup at Lillie's wasn't a bad idea. Besides, if he went straight to Chester's, if the latter hadn't fixed something to eat, Harold would have to fix something himself, if he wanted to eat.

Tired and a bit grumpy, Harold didn't appreciate the teenagers who came loudly into the diner as though they owned the place. But he grudgingly tolerated it.

He had hardly noticed the children himself. But when the tall teenager strutted over by their booth, Harold's blood began to boil. Somehow, he didn't like the way this punk was treating these kids. It was out of bounds and he wished the father would do something about. Harold even felt a little disappointed when Richard didn't do anything. Still, as Robert returned to the booth with his friends, friends who were looking increasingly uncomfortable with the whole thing themselves, Harold figured it would all blow over and went back to his soup. But Robert wasn't quite done.

As he returned to the booth, and slid behind his friends at the back of the booth again, Robert had to get another 'last word' in. Standing in the booth, he extended both of his middle fingers

494

and yelled, "Hey, mister." When Richard didn't look, Robert hollered again, "Hey, mister asshole."

Feeling he needed to look just to get this over with, Richard finally glanced back over his shoulder.

"These are for you, mother fucker."

That was it. Harold had heard enough. He moved so quickly, so unexpectedly, Robert and his friends were caught completely off guard, especially since Harold attacked from their flank, where they weren't looking. It was as though Harold went right through the two friends who were sitting outside of Robert in the booth. In reality, he merely pinned them under him as he caught Robert by the throat and slammed him into the wall at the back of the booth.

With his fist cocked and ready, Harold contemplated smashing the shocked and frightened face that looked up from under his grip. In that moment where he hesitated, Richard Wooten also moved quickly.

Richard had no idea that this was one of the bikers from the previous summer when one of their brothers almost lost his artificial leg on the highway. All that Richard knew was that someone had come to his defense and he wished they hadn't. He didn't want a physical alteration that would hurt the children more than the episode was already bothering them. He didn't want some young punk to gain a lesson for maturity too painfully. And he didn't want this person coming to the rescue to get in trouble for his effort.

As quickly as Harold had moved, Richard saw it from the start as though it played out in slow motion and reacted instantly. Where Harold was only a few feet from the booth, and Richard was more than 10 feet away, the latter arrived there only a second later than Harold. While Harold was contemplating launching the punch, he suddenly felt a hand softly on his elbow. He turned and found Richard standing there.

"It's OK," said Richard. When Harold didn't immediately release the trigger, Richard repeated himself. "Really, it's OK. Just let it go."

Harold looked back at Robert as everyone in the place seemed to hold their breath. Finally, he took his hand off Robert's throat but grabbed the front of his shirt instead. "I think you and friends should leave now." He stared down at Robert clearly waiting for a response.

Gradually, Robert got the hint and nodded that he understood. Harold got up off of him and stood back watching to make sure he followed through on leaving. Richard stepped aside, too, as the teenagers hurriedly exited the booth and the diner.

When the door closed behind them, Richard looked over at Harold and said, "I do appreciate that ..." and left it hanging as if there was a big 'however' that he might have added.

Harold nodded and slid back onto his stool at the counter.

Richard returned to the booth by his children and said to Vivian, "If it's OK, we'll just take that to go."

Vivian seemed to have anticipated and handed a bag of food to Elizabeth as Richard took Teddy by the hand. As he led his children out of the diner, they, and particularly Teddy, were craning their necks looking back at Harold with their eyes as round as quarters.

As Harold watched them go, it occurred to him that the man looked familiar. He almost asked if they'd met before but let it go saying to himself, "Maybe he just looks like someone else." Then, Harold glanced around the diner where he noticed a couple more familiar faces looking his way. A familiar elderly gentleman smiled and nodded in Harold's direction in a way that left Harold wondering if it was appreciation or if the man thought something was funny about the situation. With no way to know the difference, Harold nodded and bent down over his soup.

As he sat over his soup, he realized that he was shaking from an adrenaline rush. Harold closed his eyes and leaned over his soup so that his nose was only a couple inches away from the surface. He sat that way for a minute as he felt his pulse slacken. When he looked back up, he realized that the two old timers and the waitress were all looking his way.

Seeing him look that way, as though waiting for permission, the waitress walked down Harold's way with the coffee pot in her hand. "Can I warm your coffee up for you?" When Harold nodded, she tipped the brown-handled, glass pot over his coffee mug.

While it filled, she explained, "Those kids have had a pretty tough time." When Harold looked at her inquisitively, she continued, "Their mother was killed by a drunk driver earlier this year. They're a little sensitive still."

As Vivian spoke, Harold realized that the two familiar, elderly faces were walking down to the back of the diner carrying their mugs of coffee with them. The men slid onto stools next to Harold and the one closest to him said, "That was a descent thing you did. Wasn't really necessary, but your intentions were good."

Harold opened his mouth to speak but the other elderly man spoke first. "That was Richard Wooten. He's a good man."

"And with a heavy load to bear raising those two without a mother," added Vivian.

"Well, maybe you could apply for the job," said the elderly man with the "Dekalb" hat.

"ME?!!! I don't think so," said the waitress. "He needs to find a young thing he can fall in love with. But not yet. It's too early for that – for him, and for Teddy and Elizabeth."

"Too true," said the man with the John Deere hat.

Harold felt as though his actions were taken as an invitation for the others in the diner to join him. It was as if he had unwittingly paid the admission to join their little group. He wasn't sure that he wanted to join, particularly when he was feeling sick.

As he contemplated his membership in the group, the man with the "John Deere" hat said, "You may not remember me. I'm Grant Bauman. I drove you out to the Old Schultz Farm your first night in town.

Harold looked up quickly, surprised that the man would recognize Harold with the beard he'd grown since coming out to Biesenthal. As he looked at the man, he placed Grant's face with his hazy memory of that night. Then he looked at the other man and said, "And you're ..."

"Virgil," said the man with the "Dekalb" hat as he extended his hand to shake. "Virgil Mitello."

"Right," said Harold. Then he looked back at Grant and said, "Thank you again for the ride."

"It was my pleasure, young man," said Grant.

"You bet it was his pleasure," said Vivian, "a captured audience for the entire drive out there listening to his stories and such."

Everyone chuckled, including Harold.

"By the way," said Grant. "When I said it was unnecessary, I meant that Richard Wooten can take care of himself. He earned the Silver Star in Vietnam. After everything he's been through, some teenager would have to do a lot more than that to rattle Richard."

"Still," said, Virgil, "kinda liked the way you put the fear of God into that Jensen boy."

"Jensen boy?" asked Harold

"Robert Jensen," said Grant. When Harold looked surprised that they knew who the punk was, Grant added. "It's a small town. Those kids should have thought about that before they came in here acting like that."

"Robert Jensen should have thought about what his father will do when he hears about this," said Vivian.

"Now, don't you go telling on the boy," said Virgil. "It's just part of growing up. Like it or not, that boy did some growing up today."

Harold realized Vivian was watching him eat his soup as he listened to the conversation. Then, she said, "That soup's gotta be cold by now. Let me get you a fresh bowl."

"Soup?" said Grant. "Get this man the sirloin platter — something that will put some meat on his bones."

Remembering that he was sick, Harold was about to say "Thanks anyhow" but then he realized that he was feeling a little better anyhow, as though the excitement had knocked the cold or flu out of him. "You know, that sounds pretty good," he said, "Long as I can get a piece of pie after."

"Now you're talking," said Vivian, as she yelled, "SIRLOIN SPECIAL" back over her shoulder to the short-order cook in the kitchen.

Made in the USA
Monee, IL
14 July 2021

73554365R00298